Praise for *New York Times* bestselling author Sister Souljah and her unforgettable novels

Midnight and The Meaning of Love

"Before there was a Shannon Holmes, a Vickie Stringer, or a Wahida Clark, there was a woman many consider the Queen of Urban Fiction, Sister Souljah."

—*Essence*

"The story weaves back and forth from the subways of NYC to overseas in a thrilling adventure with an incredible ending and a wrenching tale of love. . . . This one delivers on all promises. . . . Souljah has done it again."

—*Ebony*

"Sister Souljah's best storytelling yet. It is amazingly written, smart, erotic, and still street enough for her fans from Brooklyn to Compton, London to Cairo, São Paulo to Johannesburg to enjoy and devour. . . . There is no character in American literature like Midnight. There is no other novel like this one."

—BlackAmericaWeb.com

"Sister Souljah erases any doubt: She is a writer without peer."

—EURweb

"Sister Souljah weaves a story of love, redemption, revenge, and success with such force that it is nearly impossible to put the book down."

—NewsOne

"Souljah's storytelling is so compelling and vivid that you can hear the vinyl beat of Eric B. & Rakim's *Eric B. Is President* playing in your mind as you read the opening pages. . . . Simply put, *Midnight and The Meaning of Love* is a love story that will challenge what you think you know about cultures, people, and places."

—InkBlot Book Review

"Souljah knows how to keep you guessing and turning the page, and her latest offering is no exception."

—Soul Train

The Coldest Winter Ever

"*The Coldest Winter Ever* is a tour de force. . . . As finely tuned to its heroine's voice as Alice Walker's *The Color Purple.* . . . Riveting stuff, with language so frank it curls your hair."

—*Kirkus Reviews*

"Winter is nasty, spoiled, and almost unbelievably libidinous, and it's ample evidence of the author's talent that she is also deeply sympathetic."

—*The New Yorker*

"Intriguing. . . . Sister Souljah exhibits a raw and true voice in this cautionary tale. . . . A realistic coming-of-age story."

—*Publishers Weekly*

"Real and raw. . . . If a rap song could be a novel, it might resemble Sister Souljah's book. . . . The message is solid and one that we can never stop preaching to our youth—anything that comes too easy or too fast is also too risky."

—*Booklist*

"Souljah adds a new voice to the most marginalized of the marginalized."

—*Black Issues Book Review*

"Winter is . . . as tough as a hollow-point bullet. . . . Her voice is the book's greatest strength."

—Salon.com

MIDNIGHT
AND
THE MEANING
OF LOVE

SISTER
SOULJAH

WASHINGTON
SQUARE PRESS

ATRIA

New York   London   Toronto   Sydney   New Delhi

WASHINGTON SQUARE PRESS

ATRIA

A Division of Simon & Schuster, Inc.
1230 Avenue of the Americas
New York, NY 10020

First Washington Square Press/Atria Paperback edition October 2011

WASHINGTON SQUARE PRESS / **ATRIA** PAPERBACK and colophon are registered trademarks of Simon & Schuster, Inc.

For information about special discounts for bulk purchases,
please contact Simon & Schuster Special Sales at
1-866-506-1949 or business@simonandschuster.com.

The Simon & Schuster Speakers Bureau can bring authors to your live event. For more information or to book an event, contact the Simon & Schuster Speakers Bureau at 1-866-248-3049 or visit our website at www.simonspeakers.com.

Manufactured in the United States of America

20   19

The Library of Congress has cataloged the hardcover edition as follows:

Souljah, Sister.
    Midnight and the meaning of love / by Sister Souljah.—1st Atria Books hardcover ed.
        p.   cm.
1. African Americans—Fiction.   2. Urban fiction.   I. Title.
    PS3569.O7374M55   2011
    813'.54—dc22   2011005717

ISBN 978-1-4391-6535-5
ISBN 978-1-4391-6536-2 (pbk)
ISBN 978-1-4516-3742-7 (ebook)

Show Love

Love is a powerful emotion propelled by energy, thought, and action. It can change you and anyone around you who you love. Love needs no announcement, it is visible in the eyes and body and deeds of everyone who loves. If you cannot see love through action, it is not love. It's something else . . .

If an elder loves you, she and he and they will prepare you to do well in life.

If an elder abuses you, confuses you, misuses you, it's wrong and it is certainly not love.

Elders who do not love lose their authority and influence over you because they are corrupt and unable.

It is an elder's job to share wisdom and not conceal it, destroy it, deny it, or distract you from it.

Here are my jewels to you, the young all around the world in any and every place no matter the faith or politic.

You are not too young to love.

Intelligence is the ability to solve problems.

Wisdom is experience along with intelligence.

Ignorance is not knowing better.

Evil is knowing better but doing wrong anyway, while influencing others to do the same.

Vanity is uselessness.

A nigger is any person of any race who refuses to learn, grow, and change.

Arrogance is thinking and acting like you are better than others without true or good reason.

Look toward GOD, above every elder, and even your parents and all of your community. GOD is first, the MAKER of your soul in every religion and in every corner of the world. GOD is the reason for you and I to be humble and live respectfully. GOD is love.

Sister Souljah

BOOK 1

A BROOKLYN
STORY

SEVEN DAYS IN BROOKLYN

Chapter 1
WORD TO MOTHER

Warmhearted and young, armed and dangerous, I was moving my guns and weapons out of my Brooklyn apartment to one of my most reliable stash spots. As heavy as they were, my thoughts were heavier and even more deadly. I was trying to move murder off my mind.

Kidnapping is a bullshit English word. It doesn't convey the insult that the offense carries, when a man invades another man's home, fucks with his family or his wife, *la kadar Allah* (God forbid), and steals her away.

The man whose wife is gone stands there try'na push the puzzle pieces together of where his wife is exactly and what happened exactly. His blood begins to boil, thicken, curdle, and even starts to choke him. That's why for me, kidnapping and murder go hand in hand.

In my case, my young wife Akemi's kidnapper is her own father, her closest blood relation, a man who she loves and honors. For me to kill him would be to lose her even if I win her back. And I refuse to lose.

Ekhtetaf is our word for kidnapping. My Umma pushed it out from her pretty lips. She pulled it from her soul and gave it the true feeling that it carried for us—the hurt, shame, violation, and insult. For half a day it was all that she said after I relayed to her that Akemi was gone. My new wife had been taken against her will back to Japan without a chance to express herself to us, her new family, face to face.

For me to see my mother Umma's Sudanese eyes filled with tears tripled my trauma. I had dedicated my young life to keeping the water out of my mother's eyes and returning a measure of joy to her heart that life had somehow stolen. But Sunday night, when our home phone finally rang, and Umma answered only to hear the silence of Akemi's voice and the gasp in Akemi's breathing and the restraint in Akemi's crying, Umma's tears did fall.

There was a furious rainstorm that same Sunday. Everything was soaked, the afternoon sky had blackened and then bled at sunset. So did Umma's eyes switch from sunlight to sadness to rain and eventually redness.

Through the evening thunder I sat still, trying to simmer. They say there is a beast within every man, and I was taming my beast with music. My earplugs were siphoning the sounds of Art of Noise, a soothing song called "Moments of Love."

My sister Naja held her head low. She was responding to our mother Umma's feelings. Like the seven years young that she is, she did not grasp the seriousness of Akemi's disappearance and believed more than Umma and I that Akemi would be coming through the door at any moment.

* * *

Much later that same Sunday night, family day for us, my Umma placed a purple candle in a maroon dish and onto her bedroom floor. She struck a black-tipped match and it blazed up blue. The subtle scent of lavender released into her air. There in the darkness, I sat on her floor, leaning against the wall, and listened to her melodic African voice in the expressive Arabic language, as she told me for the first time ever the story, or should I say saga, of my father's fight to take *her* as his first bride, true love, and true heart. I knew then that the darkness in her room was intentional. She wanted to shield the sea of her emotions since there was no love more intense than the mutual love between her and my father. She also wanted to subdue my fury. She wanted me to concentrate instead on the red and then orange and then blue flame and listen intently for the meaning of her words and the moral of her story so that I would know why I must not fail to bring Akemi back home and why I had to seize victory, the same as my father did.

Monday, May 5th, 1986

At daybreak, when the moon became the sun, Umma's story was completed. She lay gently on the floor still dressed in her fuschia *thobe*. Her hair spread across her arm as she slipped into sleep. Our lives and even our day were both upside down now. I lifted her and placed her onto her bed. I put out the flame that danced on the plate in the middle of mostly melted wax.

Umma was supposed to be preparing for work, but her most important job, which took all night, was finally finished. She wanted to transfer my father's strength and intelligence and brave heart to me, her son. She wanted me to know that I must not be halted by my deep love for her, my mother. She had told me, "You have guarded my life and built our family business. I love you more than you could ever imagine. In my prayers, I thank Allah every day for creating your soul and giving you life. I thank Allah for choosing to send you through my body. But now, '*You must follow the trail of your seed.*'"

Chapter 2
SO IN LOVE

Naja overslept. When I went into her room to wake her for school I found her sleeping in her same clothes from yesterday and clutching a doll. The scene was strange. At night she usually wore her pajamas and her robe and woke up wearing them as well. She didn't play with dolls, wasn't the type, was more into puzzles and pets. As I approached her bed, I saw the doll had the same hair as my wife, long, black, and thick. *That hair is real,* I thought to myself, and reached for the doll. I maneuvered it out of Naja's hands and flipped it around. It was a tan-skinned doll with Japanese eyes drawn on with a heavy permanent black Sharpie marker. The material was sewn and held together with a rough and amateurish stitch.

Naja woke up and said with a sleepy slur and stutter, "I finally made something by myself." She turned sideways in her bed, propping her head up with her hand, and said now with confidence, "It's Akemi. Can't you tell?"

I smiled the way a man with troubles on his mind might smile to protect a child's innocent view of the world. I could've easily got tight with my little sister because she had gone into my room and removed the ponytail of hair that Akemi had chopped off of her own head one day in frustration with her Japanese family.

"It looks like her. You did a good job," I told Naja.

"Do you really think it looks like your wife or are you just saying that to be nice?" Naja asked.

"I'm saying it to be nice. Now get up, you're running late for school today."

* * *

Akemi's expensive collection of high heels was lined up against the wall in our bedroom. Her hand-painted Nikes and other kicks with colorful laces were spread out too. Her luggage and clothing, every dress and each skirt a memory of something sweet, were all there. Her black eyeliner pencil that outlined her already dark and beautiful eyes was left out on the desktop. The perfume elixir that Umma made for Akemi, but truly for my pleasure, was there also. The crystal bottle top was tilted to the right from the last use. Her yoga mat was rolled up and lying in the corner. She had left her diary out for all to see. She knew we could not read one word of the Japanese kanji that began on the last page and ended on the first. Yet she had colorful drawings in there as well. Just then I recalled her fingers gliding down the page with a colored pencil in one hand and a chunk of charcoal in the other.

Everywhere in our bedroom there were signs that this was a woman, a wife who lived here beside me, her husband, and definitely intended to stay. We are teenagers, Akemi and I, but we are both sure of our bond. Furthermore, we took that bold and irreversible step into marriage and our two hearts became one.

She had left her designer life and luxurious apartment behind and moved into the Brooklyn projects to be beside and beneath me. So in love, even in the chaos of this hood, and the glare of the ambulances and scream of their sirens, she could only see me. Each day her love became more sweeter, her smile even brighter.

After hearing Umma's story, I understood now that in the Sudan, my home country, the kidnapping of females is unusual but has happened, especially when two men were battling over the same woman. A Sudanese man will fight hard and by any means necessary to earn the right and advantage over the next man to marry the bride of his choice and make her his own.

Yet our men never battle over a woman after the marriage has already taken place, been witnessed, acknowledged, and agreed on. We never battle to win a woman after her husband has gone into her. And I had gone into my wife Akemi over and over and in so many ways that the thought alone made my heart begin to race and my entire body began to sweat like summer, but in the spring season.

I looked at my bedsheets that I had never thought about before. Umma had selected those sheets knowing that a man wouldn't mind but a woman would. She dressed up my bed one day while I was out. Umma wanted Akemi to feel good and welcomed. I had to admit that those Egyptian cotton sheets were soft and comfortable. Only Akemi's skin was softer.

Eateda is the word from back home that describes for us a bigger offense.

My mind switched to that thought. *Eateda* happens when a kidnapper steals a woman against her will, then rapes her. I promised myself that in my blood relation beef with my wife's father, this was not that type of problem. Yet I also knew that when a man is not beside his woman, protecting, loving, providing, and influencing her all the time, *eateda* is always possible by any man who is allowed to be in the same room with her, if that man is living low.

* * *

My sensei taught me the technique of breathing a certain way to lower the blood pressure and calm the mind and settle the heart. It was not a technique meant to prevent a murder. A man has to think but not too much. Thinking to an extreme can paralyze a man's actions and turn him into a passive coward. What Sensei taught me was a technique meant mainly to calm a warrior to prepare him to make the sharpest, wisest, most effective strike against his target. So I was using it as I stepped swiftly down the subway stairs and out of the spring air. Now it was Monday. My feet were moving rhythmically with my breathing. My game face was neutral, but my soul was scowling. Each time that I cleared my murderous thoughts, they would reappear.

Chapter 3
PRESSURE

I could easily recognize her from behind. As the packed train swerved and jerked, I caught quick glimpses of her pretty neck and shoulders. Her bare arm was extended upward, graceful like a ballerina's, her hands holding the grip lightly like fingers properly placed on piano keys. Seeing nice-looking NY girls was an all-day thing. But it became much more personal when it was a familiar female, someone whose bedroom I had been in before, whose swollen naked nipples I had already seen. A female who had begged me for a kiss and whose infant daughter I had once held in my arms. It was Bangs, and it was a one-in-a-million chance that we would end up on the same train on the same day at the same time, both coming from and going to different places, I was sure.

Immediately, I moved away from her and to my left, my knapsack hitting someone standing next to me. I pushed toward the connecting train doors to switch cars. The train car that I moved into was no better, a very tight crowd. But it was better because they were all strangers. There was no risk or emotion in it for me.

"I saw your reflection on the window glass," Bangs said sweetly, suddenly appearing before me. "I *know* you *knew* it was me. I wanted to see if you would come over by me or not," she said.

I didn't answer her. I didn't move or turn.

The train screeched to a stop. The conductor's voice boomed out something over a broken speaker, it was some ill transit equipment that never got fixed. He knew it didn't work and so did all the passengers. Only he knew what he was announcing. As for the rest of

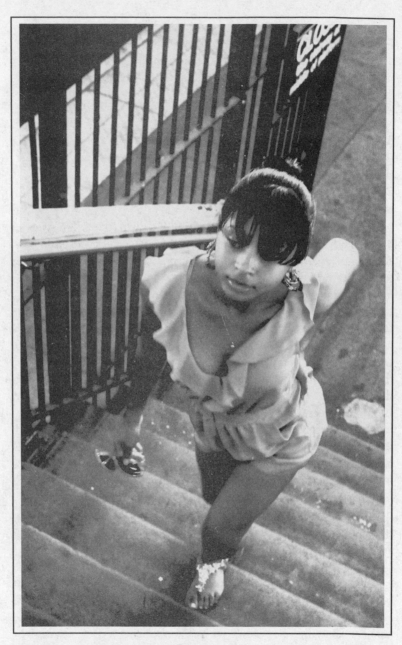

Bangs

us, you either knew where you were headed or you didn't. This is New York and if there is a problem, it's your problem, handle it.

The train doors opened and some people got off. I was facing the door and Bangs stepped into the now cleared-out space and faced me, looking into my eyes. A new crowd pushed in and now Bangs was pressed close up on me.

It was a warm day and warmer underground. Only the thin silk of her clothes separated me from her. Ever since I met her, it was like this, me not expecting to see her, her suddenly appearing, full of life, skin so pretty, baby oil glistening, and hair cleaned and pulled up into a bun, with bangs framing her eyes. Fourteen years young and already breeded, her body was full of obvious curves and power. I tried to step back, but it wasn't happening. There was nowhere to move.

"At least if you see me, you could speak, right, Supastar?" A name she had always called me, a women's way of weakening a man with her nonstop admiration. Her pretty lips were thick and natural, wearing no gloss today. Her eyes were still searching me for answers— that I had already given her a thousand times. It didn't matter to her that I am in love and married to someone else. She would keep pushing like the marathon runner she is. No matter what kind of setbacks occurred, she would slow her pace, catch her breath, reestablish her rhythm and stride, and speed up once again, completely convinced that she could win.

My mind was clear and straight, but even without looking into her eyes, my body was committing mutiny, heating up at the proximity. The train pulled left and then right. She grabbed my waist to stop herself from being tossed here and there. She kept her left hand on my body.

"You don't hafta say nuphin, Supastar. You know you still got my heart," she said softly, yet with bold style. I didn't say nothing in response to her.

"And I'm not worried about it no more because I have a secret about me and you."

I didn't know what the fuck she was talking about. There were no secrets between me and her. There was no saliva, no blood, no sperm or sweat exchanged between us. Okay, maybe some sweat—we had danced pressed together at a party once—but all her secrets were her own. I had told her everything and broke off dealing with her before anything ever really got started between us. I told her that me and her could never be. I even turned down her offers and resisted my feelings to slide my tongue into her mouth. So she had no claim on me.

"Move, please," she said to the people blocking her exit at the next stop. As she got off, I wondered exactly where she was coming from, but I shut those thoughts down by reminding myself that she wasn't my girl, wife, or responsibility. I knew she was surprised by my silence, maybe even hurt. But what was I supposed to do with her if she kept running up on me like this? I liked her, but the sexual feeling that she had swirling around her made me uneasy. It felt like whenever she came around, I had to triple my efforts to ignore and resist.

There was one good thing about knowing her, though. Whenever I was the most tensed up, she would make me smile or loosen up with her ways, and for the few minutes that we rode in the train, she paused my murderous thoughts. Yet the moment she disappeared, I forgot her and they returned.

Chapter 4
RAGE

After I buried the burners, I shot over to the dojo. I knew it might be empty. I wasn't scheduled for a private lesson and there was no class at the time either. I knew that I might be disturbing my teacher on his downtime, but I felt like fighting somebody, striking a jaw, kicking a head off, slamming a rival. So I went.

Sensei drew back the curtain and checked my face through the thick glass window before unlocking the closed dojo door. A serious and mostly silent man whose eyebrows expressed his thoughts, he stood looking at me like a mind reader before clearing the way for me to step inside unannounced.

"Rage is the opposite of thought," Sensei said suddenly. I didn't respond. "Whoever has put you into this frame of mind has more control over you right now, than you have over yourself. If he is your opponent and you will face him today, *you will be defeated.*"

I had thought that I had my game face on. I just knew I was looking neutral. Obviously, I was wrong.

"It's not the look on your face. It's your energy: all yang, no yin."

"Excuse me?" I questioned.

"It's all heat coming off of your body. Too much heat for someone so cool." He managed a slight smile with no laughter accompanying it. "Change into your *dogi*," he ordered.

After I suited up, Sensei led me into some unfamiliar movements. They were slow like a strange dance, not the swift and sharp and precise and lethal movements or kata of our caliber and mastery. The movements were so slow that it took a lot of patience for me to execute them. Sensei remained focused and performed the same movements continuously. He didn't stop, so I didn't either. Twenty or thirty minutes in, I felt myself becoming more calm and comfortable. Sixty minutes total and I was covered with a sheen of sweat and feeling so calm that I could easily ease into a deep sleep.

"*Now* we can begin class," Sensei said, tossing me a white hand towel. I tossed it back and used one of the clean white washcloths I kept in my back pocket throughout the spring and summer season. I wiped my forehead, face, and then neck. He nodded for me to take a seat on the floor and then sat across from me.

I waited for him to introduce the material for today's impromptu private lesson. But still he said nothing. I thought he might be looking for a *suki*, which is what it is called when an opponent is looking for a means of a surprise attack, when a warrior has stupidly left himself open. I leaped back onto my feet, remembering how this sensei had got the better of me in a few encounters. I had told myself that if he attempted to defeat me ever again, I would treat him as an enemy and not as my teacher of seven years and the man who had presided over my wedding, representing my wife and translating her Japanese words, thoughts, and feelings.

"*Yame*," Sensei said, meaning "at ease" or "relax." "*Suwate*," Sensei ordered, meaning "take a seat." He used the Japanese commands that I was accustomed to in our regular group training at the dojo.

"You have something to ask me. I am waiting to hear it," Sensei said with absolute certainty. For seconds I searched my mind. I thought I came to the dojo to fight, but obviously my teacher thought I needed his counsel. I was not the type to confide in any other man. My trust was in Allah, my father, myself, and my Umma. For me there was no one else. I have two best friends, Ameer and Chris, but I still kept most things from them. I'm not a liar, but I am an expert at concealing things.

So now I sat there calmly but unwilling to give up any information about my life, my wife, my war.

"*Now* you are thinking," Sensei observed. "It is so much better than rage."

I listened to Sensei's words but chose to remain silent. If anyone should understand me, it was him, a ninja, a master of ninjutsu the art of invisibility, the man who trained me to be a ninja also. We knew well that ninjutsu stands above all other Asian forms or *do*, meaning way of life. Ninjutsu is not recreation or sport. It is the supreme art of war, the science of fighting so fiercely and precisely and thoroughly that your enemies are defeated and eliminated and your survival is the only possible outcome.

We sat in silence for ten more minutes before Sensei broke it.

"There are many forms of fighting and fighting happens on many levels. You have been trained most often on a physical level. You have mastered that. You have done very well as a student of weapons also. But there is a form of fighting that happens between thinkers on the thought level." He paused, I guessed to let his words sink into my mind. And I was listening and considering what he was saying. I was even noticing how he was using his mind to maneuver around my silence and make the most accurate predictions about what exactly was going on with me.

"A warrior must know what kind of battle he is going into. If it is physical, we ninjas fight to the finish. We take our enemy down. You know that. But the same way we don't draw our weapons unless we are prepared for the finish, we must know when we are in a battle of another kind." He searched my face for reactions.

"In a thought battle, the superior fighter is the superior thinker. The superior thinker is the warrior with the best plan, someone who has stepped back and measured all the angles. A thinker who has thought about the situation from his enemy's point of view and de-termined his enemy's thoughts and moves from the beginning to the end. A thinker must have good sentinels, soldiers on his side who gather information and do reconnaissance. Or as a ninja, in an unpre-dictable situation he must know how to gather information quickly by himself."

"Sensei, let me get it right," I said, interrupting him. "A thought battle would be the type of battle that a fighter is in when he has already decided that murder is not an option, right?"

Sensei's facial expression changed. "We don't speak of murder," he said firmly yet very quietly. "Let us just say that, yes, some battles are not physical, so taking down your opponent is not your objective, but winning *still is* your objective, understand?"

"Of course." I nodded in agreement. After all, this was the kind of battle that I was entering with Akemi's father. And through this conversation with my teacher, I really understood, accepted, and confirmed that murder was not an option and that this battle was a thought battle. The only part of this battle that was physical was that at the end I had to have my wife back into my hands and living in my presence, not his.

"Then there are spiritual battles. These are the most complex. But to make it simple, let me say that if you are convinced of the truth of your cause, that what you are fighting for is right and true, *then* you will become capable of gaining the confidence you need to have the upper hand over your opponent on a spiritual level. To be certain of your rightness requires some meditation. When you came into the dojo today, you were without meditation. You were only anger. This is why I led you in a session of tai chi, to prepare you to be able to meditate and be certain that you are right in whatever your cause may be. There is always a chance *that you are wrong*. Meditation will reveal this to you."

I listened intently to what he was suggesting. I wondered for a minute if meditation was really so different from prayer. As a Muslim, I pray throughout the day and night, although I try not to pray at times when my mind is clouded and angry. Fortunately, most of the time my mind *is not* cloudy or angry, just focused.

"Do *you* meditate, Sensei?"

"Only sometimes, when necessary."

"Because most battles *are* physical?" I asked and stated with confidence. Then a natural smile came across my face. "And in a physical battle, you have no worries, no reason to meditate or hesitate, right, Sensei? And I don't either." I held up my fists to emphasize. We both laughed some.

"There, it is good to see your smile," Sensei reacted. "Your passion and your heart are your assets. The best warriors are passionate and they use the thunder in their hearts to conquer anyone and to overcome any obstacle that threatens their heart."

I thought about his words for some seconds, and really asked myself if they were true. In the streets, no one says that a man's passion is good. The streets take passion as a weakness. Niggas work overtime to prove that they are cold, colder, the coldest.

"So *who* has threatened your heart, the heart of a newlywed that should be at ease?" he asked with a half smile mixed with a true concern. Maybe he thought that he had relaxed me so successfully that he had eased me into a talkative state. But that wasn't the case.

After a momentary pause, he said with a confident and solemn face, "Allow me to guess. Your opponent, it is your wife's father, Naoko Nakamura, a man who has many enemies but even more friends."

I didn't smile or shift or acknowledge Sensei's guesses in any way. I couldn't tell him that my new wife was gone, stolen away even if it was by her own father's doing. It involved too much pain, insult, and yes, shame. In Sudanese tradition, shame is a heavy burden, like wearing a jacket and pants and a hat and even boots all filled with lead.

"Do you know him, Sensei?" I asked.

"Naoko Nakamura is neither my friend nor my enemy. We are both Japanese. That is all we have in common. He does not know or care that I exist."

"Then why did you bring his name up and speak on it as if you know him?" I asked, unable to shield my general distrust.

"Every Japanese knows him, especially in my age group. He was born on the day that the Americans dropped a two-ton bomb on the Japanese people of Hiroshima and then Nagasaki. After so much death and sorrow, most Japanese people just wanted peace at *any* cost. They welcomed the Americans in and didn't fight the occupation. Not Naoko. He lost his father the day he was born. When he became a very young man, he wanted revenge. He worked relentlessly, was not a physical fighter, but was more clever than a nine-tailed fox. He was a great organizer of men, a real team builder, Japan's extreme patriot, and a masterful businessman, so successful that he became known throughout the Asian continent as "the Man Who Never Surrendered."

I resisted bigging Akemi's father up in my mind despite what Sensei was telling me. They sounded true, Sensei's words, but in order to outmaneuver Naoko Nakamura, I had to view him as just another man, nobody's hero or nothing like that.

So I stood up. "Thank you for today, Sensei. You helped me with my yin-yang." I smiled. "I'll see you in class tomorrow night. Now I gotta go." I turned and headed toward my locker. But he paused me with his words, a final lesson of the day, I figured.

"Scholars have written books about Naoko. He is a very intelligent and accomplished man. When I saw his stamp and signature on your marriage documents, I thought, 'What are the chances of a young man from Brooklyn marrying the only daughter of this Japanese tycoon and legend?' It seemed impossible. In fact, there was more of a chance of me witnessing a solar eclipse." He smiled.

His words were a strange mixture of him giving me props while at the same time taking them away. After a quick thought, I believed that I figured out what he was really asking me. What were the chances of a talented, rich, and beautiful Japanese teenaged girl like Akemi, who doesn't speak English, marrying a black African like me, living in the Brooklyn projects in a Brooklyn hood, who doesn't speak Japanese? But his question didn't matter to me like it might have mattered to some other black American. I don't have one drop of inferiority in my blood or mind. *I did marry her* and she married me eagerly. It wasn't no mystery. It had happened right before Sensei's eyes in this dojo with his help and many witnesses. I shrugged my shoulders, shaking off the tightness that tried to creep back in.

* * *

I bounced back to my Brooklyn block with only my hands as my weapons. I had no doubt that if anybody tried to test me today, they would receive the full impact of my skill and fury. As soon as I hit my block, I could taste death in the air. There was talk of a kid in the next building who had just gotten slaughtered. First his man was killed. Instead of merking his man's murderer, he snitched to the jake. Two days later, he got to join his man in heaven or hell. I knew there would be a trail of bodies turning up any day, any minute now. Snitching always resulted in a blizzard of blood.

I had moved my guns and *kunai* because of Naja. When she went into my room without my permission and went through my things to find Akemi's ponytail, it meant two things to me. One, it meant that it wasn't her first time going through my things. She was looking for the ponytail that she already knew was there. Two, it meant that she could have easily hurt herself if she came upon one of my burners or tools. Instead of getting more strict with her, I just accepted that she was at an age of being curious. It was easier to move the danger out of her way than to rely on the fact that she wouldn't do it again if I asked her not to. Anyway, I could never forgive myself if I allowed anything bad to happen to my young sister.

Chapter 5

JEWELS FROM MY FATHER

Back in my room I pulled down the blanket that I kept folded and in the top corner of my closet. I unfolded it on my bed and then felt around the hemline. I ripped open the hem carefully and retrieved my three diamonds that Umma had sewn securely into the ragtag blanket. It had been my idea to store the diamonds this way. I thought a safety deposit box at the bank was too accessible to employees and higher-ups, and the diamonds were too valuable to me to risk it. Buying a vault for our apartment was too obvious, because the streets watch you bring it in, then plot all day every day for a way to get it out. Putting diamonds into my mattress or anywhere any criminal would look automatically was dumb.

So I kept the beautiful blankets that Umma crocheted for me on my bed and kept this cheap hospital-issued blanket that Umma had received when Naja was born in the closet. I knew this blanket would never receive a second glance or be stolen by anyone. So it made a perfect decoy. I had planned to store the diamonds there until forever. I had hoped to one day hand these three diamonds to my own son, *inshallah*, the same way that my father had gifted them to me seven years ago. That's how it works with a family heirloom. It is not the same as money a person has inherited or a piggy bank that you go in and out of, or even a savings account that you keep for a while with the intention of spending in the near future. An heirloom is something that gets passed from generation to generation. It is something cherished, the same as these diamonds were, not only because of their value, but because they were lessons from my father. In my lifetime I could work and eventually go and get more diamonds, but they would not be the same African diamonds that my father gave me in the Sudan, along with his lessons and heart and intentions and instructions. For those reasons alone, they could never be replaced.

But my father did say that the three three-karat diamonds were "three wishes."

"Use them when everything and everyone else around you fails or when you feel trapped."

I knew that Naoko Nakamura had me trapped at the moment. But I also knew that I wouldn't allow him to hold me there for long. I would use at least one of the "three wishes" to go get my wife.

It could be said that my using the diamond was the same as giving the diamond to my son. I was not too young to know that if I had a son in this world, he would be wherever my wife was, resting in the comfort of her womb.

I rode in with Umma. She had to catch the four-to-midnight shift at the Brooklyn textile factory since she'd missed her usual work time slot. We did not talk much. Umma is the kind of woman who doesn't repeat herself or nag. She knew I understood what must be done, and she would wait to hear my plan and add her thoughts later on. Besides, those midnights when I pick her up from her job are when some of our best ideas and plans are hatched.

After I was sure she was straight at her job, I headed to Manhattan to the Diamond District, to find a reasonable jeweler among thieves to buy at least one of my diamonds. Six was the magic number. I had seen six jewelers by six o clock, the time when the jewel merchants generally start feverishly packing to leave the heavily guarded area. I was not satisfied with even one of the six negotiations or offers. I knew what my father's gems were worth. I decided I would come back early the next morning and push until I found the right deal.

That same evening, moving east away from Forty-Seventh and Avenue of the Americas, where many of the jewels from around the world are stored and bought and sold wholesale and retail, I made a left onto Park Avenue. I strolled up the full length of the blocks. I looked around carefully, checking out the discreetly placed hotels that lined that expensive area. They weren't well-known like the Marriott, Hilton, Hyatt, and Ramada. I liked that. They were more exclusive. Even though their nightly price tag was more than I could afford without cashing in at least one of my diamonds, I had to find the right location to place Umma and Naja while I was away in Japan. I already knew that I would not leave them alone in the Brooklyn projects. We had only two weeks remaining before we could move into our new house in Queens, which we had bought using the money that we earned together from Umma Designs, our family business. Umma, an incredible seamstress and an expert in fabrics and textiles and designs, had created and sold enough clothing, hats, upholstery, curtains, and so on to bring in eighty thousand dollars over a five-year period. I had managed, marketed, and served as the sales, communication, and delivery person for our company.

Now, even in this crisis, the bottom line was that until I was certain that Umma was safe, I couldn't leave the city. As much as I love my wife in my heart and in my blood and even in my bones, Umma will forever be my first love, my mother, and my purpose.

After a while, I located a place called "The Inn," a small hotel in a four-story brick building on Park. The manager was polite enough to show me a suite without seeming to suspect that I was a criminal, like most small business managers and owners instinctively suspect and treat black males. A brief tour, and I became sure that this place had the right feeling, the right amount of space, and cleanliness, as well as a small kitchen for Umma's use. Immediately outside of the hotel was an upscale deli and a low-key pharmacy.

The hefty price was $350 per night. When I heard the quote, it made me lean back. Then I regained my composure by guaranteeing myself that I would only be gone for three to five days and that this place would help me feel at ease enough to do whatever I had to do to retrieve my wife.

Chapter 6
SALIM AMED AMIN GHAZZALI

Nightfall came. The New York City lights lit the way for many late-working professionals to escape. Satisfied at how my exit plan was shaping up, I shot over to the Bronx to have a meet-up with Mr. Ghazzali. He had been Umma Designs' best customer. He was Muslim and Sudanese, head of the only Sudanese family besides ourselves that we had come to know in America. The owner of a taxi business, he had enough confidence in Umma's skills to hire her to be the seamstress for his nephew's elaborate Sudanese wedding. After viewing and observing Umma's detailed understanding of Sudanese culture, Mr. Ghazzali hired her to be the wedding planner for the entire event. The ten thousand dollars that we earned from that one wedding is what put us over the top so that we could finally buy a small house in an effort to move out of the Brooklyn projects. He had hired us once, been kind to my mother and family, and paid his debts on time. Now I was gonna hire him to do some simple but important work for me.

When I arrived in the Bronx, I phoned his house from the train station. His phone rang five times, and just as I was about to hang up, I heard the voice of his daughter Sudana.

"*Asalaam alaikum.*"

"*Alaikum salaam,*" I responded. "May I speak with your father, please?"

"You sound tired," Sudana said, surprisingly recognizing my voice. But I should not have been surprised. She was a girl who had kept her eyes on me even when I was not noticing her. While I was working on her family's wedding, I stashed one of my guns at the wedding venue. She saw me when I was sure no one was looking. She laid back, waited, and removed the gun from a tall ceramic vase, where I had hidden it. She gift wrapped it in a colorful box with a bow as though it were a wedding gift. She handed it to me so politely and casually after the wedding ended. Such a beautiful Sudanese teenaged girl, who I had met after Akemi had already tiptoed into my heart and made herself at home.

"My father isn't in right now," she said regretfully.

"I'm here in the Bronx. I was trying to meet up with him," I said, thinking aloud.

"Where?"

"Down the block, train station."

"Hold on, let me call him because he really should be on his way home," she said eagerly. I heard her calling her father on what I guessed was another phone line.

"My father said you should come on over to our house. He'll meet you here."

"Are your brothers home?" I followed up.

"No," she responded. I paused. If none of the men of her house were home, it was not proper for me to enter their house. This is the Islamic Sudanese way.

"I'm only five minutes away. It sounds like your father will need some more time. So I'll wait and come by a little later," I told her.

"You are so good," she said softly. "But my father has given his permission and you can sit here in his office. Although no one else is home, my mother and sisters and brothers and father will all be here very soon. My father would not be happy if I left you standing around and waiting in the Bronx. So please come by. Is Akemi with you?" she asked softly.

I appreciated the way she always welcomed Akemi even though I could feel her attraction to me. Sudana was always more graceful than envious, unlike the American girls who fight to crush the competition with their tongues and fists and feet.

"Akemi is not with me right now," I answered.

"Oh."

"Thank you, Sudana, I'm coming through." I hung up.

It was a warm night on the hot blocks of the BX. I maneuvered around tight streets where cars were double-parked for as far as my eyes could see. Some men sat on stoops and others sat on porches. Some men repaired cars while others rushed toward their homes. The ice cream truck, Mister Softee, played his familiar jingle tune, loud enough to rattle the hood and call out the hood rats.

When I arrived at the only house on the block with a high fence, I stopped out front. I pushed the gate, but it was locked, like I knew it would be.

"It's you?" Sudana's voice asked.

"It's me." I heard the lock click twice and the fence opened only enough to let me in. I stepped inside and looked once before lowering my gaze away from Sudana's eyes.

"Come in." She smiled. I locked the fence behind me and followed her in. I didn't have to look directly at her; easily I could just be guided by her scent. Sudanese girls who know and live our traditions wear the most exotic and alluring perfumes, not the same kind that you buy from the department store. They wear handmade ones from centuries ago that merge with each woman's personal chemistry and give her an unforgettable and unique identity. A woman's smell, mixed with the perfumes that we call *kormah* in our Sudanese language, has always been unforgettable to me. I easily understood why we as Muslim men separate ourselves from the presence of women who are not ours. It is the subtle things that a woman does or wears that makes any man aroused if he is allowed to come too close. And every man in the world of any religion or no religion at all knows that he is or can be or will become attracted to many, many women if he is allowed to smell and come in close.

Inside, I removed my Nikes. She bent to remove her sandals. I stopped myself from glancing at her feet.

The inside of the house smelled like cinnamon. Sudana was cooking something, perhaps the meal for her entire family. We walked through the living room, where her school textbook was wide open on the floor, along with a few notebooks, pencils, and a pen. In a small side room with a messy desk, a telephone, and a few file cabinets, papers, and folders, a well-used soccer ball and a soiled old pair of sneakers, she invited me to sit down on a clean cloth couch. I sank in like I was a member of their family sitting in the exact same spot where any one of her brothers had sat repeatedly.

"Wait a minute, please," she said, leaving the room swiftly and leaving her sweet scent behind her.

Thoughts of the past three days of my life raced through my mind. Early Saturday morning was the last time that I had seen my wife's beautiful face and seductive eyes and felt her deep feeling emotions. By Saturday night she was gone. I had spent all day Sunday searching for her and Sunday night sitting with Umma being moved across continents by her true storytelling, which caused me to revisit powerful memories of our Sudanese estate, my phenomenal father, and our relatives, friends, and people. My heart became too heavy for my chest.

"I made this for you," Sudana said, reappearing and carrying a tray and setting it on the desktop. The aroma of the food and her scent revived me. From the corner of my eye I watched her pull out a metal tray with a stand, open it up, and set on it a dish of stew with a cup of tea and *aseeda*.

"You seem like the kind who won't stop to feed yourself unless someone reminds you." She smiled and turned to leave but then stopped and added, "And when you feel tired, you really should go to sleep."

I looked in the ceramic teacup at the unfamiliar way she had placed three tiny yellow flowers in my tea. They rested lightly on top of the hot liquid.

If I'd had the energy, I probably would have said, "No, that's okay, I'm not hungry. I'll wait till later to eat." But Sudana was right. I was hungry and had forgotten to eat so far for the whole day.

She stepped out, then walked right back in carrying a warm cloth, the steam still rising up from it. She came up to me and took my right hand, wiping each finger clean and then turned my palm over and began wiping it with the warm cloth. It felt soothing and the cloth smelled like lemon. I took the cloth from her hand and then used it to clean my other hand for obvious reasons.

"Shukran," I said to her, meaning "thank you" in Arabic.

"Enjoy" was all she said, and she turned and left as she was supposed to.

I whispered over the food, "Allah," then took some spoonfuls of the stew. It tasted good and was seasoned well. I couldn't help comparing it to my Umma's food, which is always superior. The Sudanese *aseeda* bread was hot the way I liked it. I dipped it in the stew and ate it moist. I gulped the tea, and it entered my body and began calming everything down.

"Now you look a little better." Sudana had returned as I finished. "I mean you're always so handsome, but you seemed too tired today." The fabric of her black *thobe* concealed her flesh and hid her figure. Her *hijab* covered her hair, which I had never seen. She was not wearing *niqab*, so her pretty face, flawless skin—smooth as satin, bearing one black beauty mark, which gently rested over the right side of her lip—stood out more. I avoided those hazel eyes of hers, which tended to change colors, like an African wild cat's. Unexpectedly, she walked up close, stood over me where I was seated, and then placed two fingers on the top of my head. She pressed.

It was a peaceful feeling, this sleep, like how a body rests when it feels at home and in a safe place. But I was not at home. Myself woke myself up. Now the lights in the office were dimmed. The food tray, cloth, and dishes had been removed. I leaned forward and stretched out my legs. I ran my hand over my Ceasar haircut, remembering how Sudana had touched my head. It was the last thing I felt before slipping away. I leaped up to my feet with disbelief at my own sloppiness. How could I allow myself to fall asleep in another man's home? I knew I was responsible for the mistake. But I also knew that Sudana had worked some of her Sudanese female charms and tricks on me.

How could I be mad at her when I knew she did it for my own good? I couldn't be. So I just stayed tight at myself.

Across the hall in their bathroom, I threw ice-cold water onto my face and rinsed out my mouth and washed my hands. When I stepped out into the hall, I could hear the sounds of a full house out in their living room.

When I entered the living room, all the female family members began laughing, beginning with the mother. Meanwhile, Mr. Ghazzali and both of his sons suddenly stood up from their seats. A smile forced its way across my face. I was embarrassed.

"My bad, *salaam alaikum*, Mr. Ghazzali and family."

"It's really okay," Mrs. Ghazzali said joyfully. "I tried to call Sana, I mean your *umi* Umma and let her know just how hard she must be working you, for you to have fallen asleep away from home. But *even she wasn't home.*" She smiled.

Sudana brought me a glass of water.

"Yes, Umma is at work tonight. In fact I have to meet her at . . ." I checked my watch.

"It's ten thirty, brother," Mr. Ghazzali called out.

I drank the water.

"What's happening, man?" Mr. Ghazzali's son Mustapha, asked me.

"Yeah, what's up?" The younger brother Talil greeted me.

"Mr. Ghazzali, I wanted to have a brief business meeting with you. That's why I came by tonight. I hope I haven't inconvenienced you in your home," I said, my way of apologizing.

"Don't insult me. You know that you are welcomed here anytime. I was so impressed with the way you handled your business, I was hoping we could work together again somehow."

"Thank you, Ahki," I said. It was a Sudanese way of acknowledging Mr. Ghazzali as my brother. If my father were standing right there, he would have scolded me to address Mr. Ghazzali as "Amm," or uncle, which is what a young man calls any man who is older than himself by more than a few years.

"Well, good night, gentlemen," Temirah Aunty (Mrs. Ghazzali) said, and three of her daughters followed her out of the living room area. Sudana didn't. She came over to collect the empty glass from me and looked into my eyes like she wanted to say something, but then she didn't. She turned to leave, then looked back and said, 'I mentioned to my *ub* that I saw your wife, Akemi, in the Sunday edition of the *New York Times*, the Arts & Entertainment section. I'm sure that you've seen it already. I just wanted to say that the kimono she was wearing was incredible. Did Umma make it?" she asked, her eyes filled with curiosity.

"No, Akemi brought the kimono from Japan, and then she designed the outside herself. You know she's an artist."

"Obviously a great one. They only had *her* picture in there for the entire event at the Museum of Modern Art. I guess she overwhelmed them," Sudana said.

"Yes, she overwhelms me too," I said naturally, without thinking about hurting Sudana's feelings. But her face didn't reveal any hurt. I was glad.

"It must be something having a famous wife. I mean, you know Muslim men, and we know that Sudanese men don't prefer to have their wives out in the open, right, Ub?" she asked her father. And before he could even respond, she said to me softly, "I would've worn the veil for you." It was a bold statement for a Sudanese girl, especially in the presence of her father. More than that, it was a polite offer.

"Sudana, let the men talk," Mr. Ghazzali said, dismissing his daughter. She turned and left obediently without a word of protest, as it should be.

* * *

Outside, Mr. Ghazzali sped his taxi in reverse down his driveway, stopping abruptly right before his fence. He waved me into the front seat. I got in. He got out to open the fence. His sons emerged from the dark corner of the yard to lock the fence back up.

"So what's going on?" Mr. Ghazzali asked.

"I have to make a trip to Japan," I told him, getting right into it.

"Whoa! Japan! Sounds nice, but very expensive. You know they say it's the third most expensive country to live in in the world? I had a guy in my cab once telling me a slice of fish out there is eight dollars. They'll slice one fish up ten times. They're selling one medium-sized red snapper for eighty US dollars. If I were living out there, I'd have to turn my whole family vegetarian overnight just trying to make it." He made a sound of disapproval with his teeth that most Sudanese make and understand.

"My Umma and my young sister Naja will stay here in New York. That's what I wanted to discuss. I want to set up car service for them for every morning and every evening while I'm away. I came to you because I need someone I can trust, not just a taxi driver to pick up and drop off."

"You never told me where you and your family are living," he reminded me.

"They'll be staying at a Manhattan hotel while I am away," I said, eluding him.

Mr. Ghazzali maneuvered around the double-parked cars but had to hit the brakes when he reached a triple-parked car. The Impala was in the middle of the street blocking any passage left, right, or straight. There was no driver seated in the vehicle.

"I lost a good driver from the Ivory Coast this way," he said, sitting behind the parked car without honking or cursing. "My driver leaned on his horn on one of these Bronx streets where people park like they're crazy. Some sixteen-year-old kid without a driver's license or insurance ran downstairs and shot him dead for blowing the horn too loud. The kid jumps in the car and speeds away, leaving my driver's bloody body behind. A valuable life lost for no reason. This is what I have been trying to say to you, young brother. You don't need to explain to me what you want out of life or how you want your mother and sister treated. We are Muslim. We are Sudanese. We both understand and want the exact same things. It's these animals out here," he said, pointing to the people lingering on the block. "It's them who don't understand or care. They got no God, no boundaries, no limits, no respect for life."

Just then a man dashed out of the building shirtless, jumped in the car that was blocking us, and peeled off, no acknowledgment or apology, straight New York ghetto style. Mr. Ghazzali waited five seconds and then drove on.

"So you need someone to make sure that your mother and sister are secured. You need a driver who will go inside if he doesn't see them waiting where they are supposed to be, and someone who will not pull off before they get inside safely at night."

"Yes, Ahki," I answered, appreciating not having to exchange too many words about a simple but important plan.

"And the reason they are staying in a hotel instead of with their new friends is—?" he asked, checking my face and quickly moving his eyes back to the road.

"I don't want to burden you with my family. I just wanted to hire your car service because I would feel more comfortable knowing and trusting the person who is transporting my mother and sister. I can pay for the whole thing in advance. I don't know exactly how many days I will be gone, but I'm trying to keep it under one week."

Mr. Ghazzali pulled over. "Get out," he said calmly.

His command threw me off for a second. Then I reached for the handle and opened the taxi door. With one foot in the cab and the other on the curb, I pulled out a small stack of bills and peeled off a five to pay him for taking up a brief time in his cab. He didn't move to accept it. I thought maybe it was not enough and that somehow the small amount had insulted him. So quickly I peeled off a ten and extended my arm again.

"I don't know the story of your life, young brother. But I can see that there are no friends in your world. You say you want someone who you can trust, yet you trust no one. No man can do his time alone on this earth. This is why we have the Muslim brotherhood. I invited you to our mosque, yet you haven't shown your face there at Jumma prayer. Is there anything that unites you and me other than this paper money?" he asked me with a stern stare at the measly ten dollars.

I went deep inside my own mind. My father had everything— land, an estate, money, power, family, and friends. In fact, the Muslim brotherhood met on our property, men bent in daily prayer at our mosque, whose children attended the madrassa at our estate, whose wives worked and entertained with my mother. But something did go wrong. And it went wrong enough for me to be standing in the streets of the BX and living in the projects of Brooklyn and grinding on American soil, not the rich earth of the Sudan, where I, my mother and father and father's father and father's father's father and so on were born. If my father, a brilliant and bold, degreed, rich, and successful man could not win and rely on the trust of men in the end, why should I expect it now? *My father is so much better than I am.*

"I don't know, Mr. Ghazzali. The Holy Quran says that 'Allah is sufficient.'" I answered with the only truth that came to mind right then.

"Yes, and your mother's name is Umma, a powerful name. *Ummah!* That word means 'the community of Muslim believers.' The believers have got to stand together, worship together, protect together, fight together, and eat together." He searched me for a response. I didn't have one.

"It's only a few days. Your Umma and sister are welcome to stay in our home. My wife already loves your mother and young sister. My daughter Sudana admires you, so of course she loves your mother. It is only you standing on the outside. Let me be a help to you."

"You know well that my Umma cannot sleep in your home where you have two grown and unmarried sons. And then there is also *you*, Mr. Ghazzali." I looked him in the eye.

"Of course, but there is a separate apartment downstairs. Your mother and my wife were planning to have a women's business there, remember? Umma can use that apartment. It's well furnished, with a small kitchen, a separate entrance, and a separate key," he told me calmly. I listened but questioned his eagerness in my own mind. I think my seconds of silence insulted him somehow. "Sure, you can choose to put your family in a hotel. There they will be surrounded by kaffirs (nonbelievers), unmarried or married, untrustworthy either way," he said with a stern sarcasm.

"How much do you rent it for?"

"Eh?"

"Your basement apartment."

"Six fifty. Per month," he said, exasperated, and as though he pronounced the first figure that popped up in his head and had never really rented out his basement before.

"Okay. I'll bring you six fifty tomorrow plus the transportation fees." I got out and shut his taxi door, leaned in, and handed him now a twenty-dollar bill. He took it.

"I wouldn't be surprised to see you as the prime minister of the Sudan one day. So much power, business, and intensity in such a young brother," he said.

"Good night," I told him before walking away.

Chapter 7
MY WOMEN

It was well after midnight when I carried my seven-year-old sister on my back to our Brooklyn apartment.

Umma said, "She should really walk on her own two feet."

Naja said, "But Umma, you two have been out having fun without me. Can't I at least get a ride on my brother's back?"

"Out having fun," Umma replied softly, in her way. Then she looked at me and said, "You see?"

Naja clenched me tightly with no plans of climbing down before the elevator reached our floor and she was "delivered" to her bedroom.

Umma was right, as she usually is. Naja is our protected princess who has no real idea of worry or struggle or stress. I thought that was good. I planned to protect my sister and keep her hidden away from those things that should never be revealed to little girls. In our traditions, a young girl lives under the protection of her father and brothers until she becomes a young woman. Then the father and her brothers will marry her into the protective care of her tried and tested, carefully chosen husband.

As I looked into Umma's eyes, so striking behind her *niqab* that shielded and covered everything else, I could see and feel that she was worried. I thought to myself, *Umma, don't you worry. If you are uneasy, I will not move one inch from your side. I will stay right here with you.* But Umma noticed me noticing her, and she cleared her worries and lowered her gaze.

Tuesday, May 6th, 1986

We made Fajr prayer together, my mother, sister, and me, followed by a warm and comfortable breakfast. Umma and I did not discuss the details of my Japan trip until after Naja was safely seated in the school bus to Khadijah's Islamic School for Girls. Naja waved as the bus eased off. She was so happy this morning because she had her sitter, Ms. Marcy, Umma, and me all escort her to the bus. Usually Umma and I are already on our way to Umma's job and Naja is left in the care of Ms. Marcy and walked directly into the care of the teacher who travels with the students on the bus. But today Umma would not report to work until four in the afternoon. She had switched her schedule for this week with a coworker from the night shift. She and I both agreed that there was more planning and work for us to do than time to do it. She also wanted to complete some products for me to deliver to Umma Design customers before I left for Japan.

"When you go to see the jewelers again today, you should also select a gift for your father-in-law," Umma said. She slid an old, high quality jewelry box across the table.

"Why should I? He stole my wife," I answered swiftly yet respectfully. I opened the box. It was a Rolex Datejust. The hands of the clock were paused in time. The crystal was cracked. I had never seen it before.

"Your wife is his daughter. Our family has not ever been able to meet and greet him properly. We haven't offered him anything. Yet he gave me such a lovely daughter-in-law. You just have to go there and ease his fears. Once he sees you and discovers how respectful you are toward him, and sees how much Akemi is in love with you and you with her, his heart will soften toward you. If it does not soften toward you, he will certainly soften his heart for his daughter. Remember that even though we feel sad and insulted and ashamed that Akemi is not with us, he stole her away out of love more than cruelty."

I was not focused on feeling any sympathy toward Naoko Nakamura. I was keeping him right where he needed to be in my mind just in case I had to do him something . . .

I slid the box containing the Datejust in my pocket.

"Umma, I thought I saw worry in your eyes late last night. You know I won't go anywhere if I see that." I was watching her closely.

"I was just tired and I was also thinking too much. After you told me on the train about the arrangement with Mr. Ghazzali, I wondered if he had asked his wife first, if it was okay for me to stay with them while you are away."

"I didn't give him a chance to speak with her first. I rode in his taxi with him and we talked it out right there. He was on his way back out to work for the night."

"I see," Umma said, sounding hesitant. "You know the Ghazzalis are new friends to our family. It has been good for me because Temirah Aunty doesn't ask me personal questions. It is as though our friendship began from the moment I took her and her sister's and daughters' measurements for their garments for their nephew's wedding. And she and I have moved forward from there without ever looking back or discussing the past. I appreciated her for that reason. If I go to stay over there at her house, it may all very well change."

"Then come to Japan with me," I said with a smile. I was serious and sincere. She pushed away and hit me on my shoulder as though the idea was ridiculous. "We have spent every penny of almost one hundred thousand dollars on our new house and I love it. Now we have minus three pennies left!" She laughed. "You go on and get your wife, and Naja and I will stay at Mr. Ghazzali's. Naja will be excited living in a house with such a big family, and her Arabic will improve, I'm sure." Umma brightened all the way up to reassure me that she was okay.

"You know, Umma, even though you and Mrs. Ghazzali have become friends, I handled this as straight business. It's their house, but it's a separate apartment, separate entrance, separate key, and *rent*."

"I know you have made it right for me. And I know their basement apartment is very nice. It is where Temirah Aunty and I plan to have our Sudanese women's group meetings. So I am sure it will be fine." I stood up from our kitchen table where Umma was seated. I needed to grab my things and head out to the diamond district.

In my room I stood still thinking. After twenty minutes or so, I began flipping through a short pile of papers I had concerning my wife. In a small notebook that I rock daily in my right pocket, I jotted down what little information I had on Akemi.

The first word I wrote was *Kyoto*, the place where Akemi was born. The second note to myself was Kyoto Girls' High School, the place the MOMA art exhibit event pamphlet said Akemi attended school. The third note was the address Akemi had given me for her father, Roppongi Hills, Tokyo, Japan. The fourth note was the address that her father had written down for himself on our wedding documents: Ginza, Tokyo, Japan. Those were my clues. I shoved the notebook in my pocket.

Reluctantly I pulled out the letter that Akemi had written to me and had delivered to Cho's, where I worked my weekend job, on the exact day that she went missing. She had written it all in kanji. Maybe she had explained herself in those pages, or left the name and address of where her father was about to drag her. She knew I could get the letter translated into English, the same way that I had arranged for her marriage documents to be translated into Japanese, and the same for our marriage contract. I pushed her letter into my back pocket. I wanted to know what it said. Yet I didn't want to know what it said. Either way I was gonna go get her, regardless. In a last-minute decision, I grabbed Akemi's diary off my desk, secured my diamonds, and headed out into a blue-gray cloudy day.

Chapter 8

CASH MONEY

By noon I had sold one of my three, three-carat diamonds.

"Where did you get them," the jeweler asked, eyeing the gem through his loop, which was lodged in his right eye.

"From Africa," I said, knowing the continent was so huge, that my response was the same as not answering him at all.

"How much will you give me for each of them?" I asked him, without any eagerness in my voice.

We settled on fifteen thousand dollars for one diamond. He pushed hard for a package deal on all three of the diamonds. He also tried to position his pitch as though he was somehow doing me a favor by buying the gems from me, insinuating that they were stolen and he was relieving me of my illegal goods. I smiled at the slickness of his angle, glanced around at the arrangements of counters offering hundreds of African diamonds for sale. I assured him that the three diamonds in the palm of my hand were not the stolen diamonds, and that right now, only one of these precious stones was available for him to purchase. I sold him one, watched his fingers as he counted out my payment in cash, all hundreds. I saw how each pile of bills that added up to five thousand dollars was half an inch high. When my stack reached one and a half inches high, I left the diamond district with my pockets fat and the whole day in front of me. I had the watch repaired and wore it, like my father had worn it years ago.

* * *

I walked into the first travel agency I came up on, Liberty Travel. It was a place plastered with pictures, posters, and postcards featuring discounted getaways around the world.

"Your destination, please?" the receptionist asked.

"Kyoto, Japan," I responded without any real mental picture of the country. I was good at geography, though, and could easily point out the small island on a world map. I was familiar with the country's shape and size, and even the ocean that surrounded it, but that was all.

"Please have a seat and our Japan agent will be with you in a moment."

"When would you like to travel?" the Japan expert asked.

"Right away," I answered.

She looked up from her terminal with a twisted smile. "Like this afternoon or tomorrow?" she said with sarcastic disbelief.

"How much is the ticket?" I asked, to keep it business.

"Are you in the military?" she asked me oddly.

"No."

"Can I see your passport?" she asked, like an officer of the law. But I didn't have my Sudanese passport on me. I didn't realize that I needed to present it to the travel agent. It was in Brooklyn locked in Umma's chest with papers that Umma would say if lost would make each member of our family invisible.

"You need your passport. This is a big trip, aside from the fact that by ordering the ticket at the last minute, you lose all of the discounts that you could have benefited from if you had come in two weeks to one month prior to your departure date. No one just hops on a plane to a country that's seven thousand miles away without being prepared.

If you don't have a passport, you need to go and get one. The passport office is next door to Rockefeller Center. It's open till six p.m. today. You are an American citizen, right?" she asked. Her question jarred me. I had recently gotten my American citizenship papers, but I am 100 percent Sudanese. On second thought, I would have to get an American passport now that my citizenship was official.

"How long does it take to get the passport?" I asked her.

"Six weeks," she said grimly. I sat frozen in my chair but was rapidly defrosting as the heat began to rise up from my feet, climbing and spreading into my chest.

"Well, you don't need the passport to buy the ticket from me. We ask for it because your airline ticket must show the exact same name that appears on the passport. But you will need the passport to travel outside of the United States.

"If you purchase an airline ticket from me right now, you can take the ticket plus an express fee over to the passport office and receive your passport in three days' time. But the plane ticket is gonna be expensive," she warned.

I eased back in my seat. *That's more like it,* I thought to myself. I was relieved that the conversation looped back around to cash being able to make shit move. That's what I was accustomed to.

"Let's do it," I told her and gave her my exact name as it appeared on my American citizenship papers.

"Date of departure?" she asked again.

"Friday, in three days when I'll have my passport," I answered.

"I recommend that you fly the following day, on Saturday, just in case anything goes wrong. Give yourself twenty-four hours to fix it. Once I issue this ticket, you will not be able to change your departure date or time," she said. "But you can change your return date and time for a fee."

I didn't know it then, but her recommendation would change my life.

I thought about it quickly. I had a basketball game coming up this Friday night with the black team of the Hustlers League. I had been working hard all spring for our team to win the league and for me to get that big money prize that would put me and Umma in a more secure financial space with our business, Umma Designs.

I thought about it further. Every minute and every day that I delayed, or that passed me by, put too much distance between me and my wife and too much opportunity for anyone who was trying to . . .

"Okay then, I'll leave on Saturday, May tenth, and return on the following Saturday, May seventeenth. One week, please!"

"Are you sure? It's two hundred dollars if you change the return date. One week in Japan is not a long time," she cautioned.

"One week," I confirmed.

"Would you like to fly American Airlines or Japan Airlines?"

"JAL," I answered.

Soon she was asking, "How would you like to pay for your ticket? Mastercard, Visa, or American Express?"

"Cash!" I answered. Suddenly I saw how important it was to have a credit card. Up until now Umma and I had done good business without one for seven years living in the United States. Now the agent accepted cash for my airline ticket, and for a rail pass that she recommended for the Shinkansen bullet train. She said the rail pass would allow me to pay one fare but use the bullet train all week for rapid travel back and forth between Tokyo and Kyoto.

She insisted, however, that I needed to give her my credit card for her to secure my hotel reservation. She assured me that these were peak travel months for Japan and I would be looking for trouble without "booking accommodations." The fact was, I didn't have one to give her and neither did Umma.

After one hour in the travel agency, I had my tickets in my hand and my head filled with lessons learned. I became real clear that even though I had traveled internationally before, I had been a child back then. All my arrangements had been made by my father. I had never had the challenge of considering the details. Now I had to listen carefully and absorb each piece of info completely. I had to watch more closely, read documents more carefully, and make decisions with confidence although I might not be 100 percent certain.

The travel agent had been pushy and sarcastic. She proved that even if you don't know a person or even like them one bit, you can still learn something from them to assist you in life. She booked a hostel for me and took the time to teach me the difference between a hotel and a hostel. "A hostel," she said, "can be found in almost every country in the world. It's like a hotel but it's not. It's housing reserved for traveling students. It's like a dormitory where you will stay alongside other students from all over. It's not nearly as luxurious as any three- or four-star hotel. It doesn't offer the same facility or services, but there will be a bed, in either a private room or with a roommate. The cheapest hostels give you a bed in a large room where there are several beds and other students staying there as well. If you were planning a longer stay, I could make sure that you got into a hostel that has a shared kitchen with a full stove and refrigerator and even a shared living room area. The best thing about a hostel, though, is that because it's reserved for students, it's cheap. There are some as low as five dollars for a night." I looked at her skeptically. She added, "But there might not be a television. Can you live without a television?"

I booked a private room in a hostel called Shinjuku Uchi, located in a part of Tokyo called Shinjuku. I could pay in cash once I arrived there, and all I needed to check in was my passport and any student identification card. It was twenty dollars per night and down the street from the Shinjuku station, where the agent told me there was a train going anywhere in the country.

Rushing, I dashed into the passport office to get the application and requirements. I was glad I shot by there. They were asking for all types of documentation. Now that I knew the deal, I wouldn't give them any chances to delay my passport for any reason. I planned to return there in the morning and be the first person to get my joint processed.

Precise Translations was located downstairs in the same building as the passport agency. I stood outside their door gripping Akemi's diary and debating with myself. Nine minutes later, I submitted the letter that Akemi wrote to me in Japanese for translation into English. This was a new translation company for me. The one I had used for everything else involving Akemi and me was on the third floor. I decided not to return to the same company because maybe they already had too much information on me and my young wife. Now, I wanted to believe that these translators remained neutral, minded their business, and just interpreted the words on the paper. What if they didn't? What if the battle between me and my wife's father thickened? I didn't want to be using the translator and paying for translations that might later be used as evidence against me. I held out her diary but then decided against requesting a translation of it.

Although it might contain all the information I needed, it seemed too personal. I thought about Umma and how private she was about her journal and papers and pocketbook. The same respect I would give to Umma, I should give to my wife, I decided.

At my bank where Umma's account was and the teller knew me from placing our deposits regularly, I deposited three thousand dollars of the cash I was holding into Umma's bank account. I also purchased one thousand dollars' worth of American Express Travelers Cheques for my use. The travel agent had recommended this also, and when I checked her reaction when I first tried to book a hotel room with cash, I knew that if I had a few Travelers Cheques, certain establishments would consider me more more legitimate than if I was moving around only with a pocket stuffed with dough.

At the Travelex Money Exchange, I stood on a short line checking out the long list of countries and the names of the money they used. The world was a lot bigger than the American dollar. There was the Sudanese dinar, the Chinese yuan, the German mark, the Indian rupee, the South African rand, the English pound, the Saudi Arabian riyal, and the Japanese yen. I pushed one thousand American dollars through the small curved slot at the bottom of the thick bulletproof glass. The teller turned it into Japanese yen. After being used to handling American green dollars, which were all the same color, shape, and size no matter the amounts, the Japanese yen looked like play money. There were pictures of Japanese men on each bill, some bills tan, some colored blue. The only similarity to American money was that it was all plastered with old men wearing weird hairstyles that I would never rock. They were looking real grim.

Chapter 9
"NEVER COMING BACK"

Back in Brooklyn, I bounced by and picked up Naja. We then escorted Umma to her job by 4:00 p.m. sharp.

"Where are we going now?" Naja asked, her big brown eyes exploring mine.

"You'll see," was all I offered.

Down on Fulton Street, right next to Albee Square Mall, I stopped at an outdoor photo booth. I needed to take two passport-sized photos.

"I want to get in the picture with you," Naja said. I pulled back the curtain, let her slide in first, then sat down beside her.

"It's gonna take three shots real fast, so quick get ready," I told her, and dropped in my coins. She was real excited. She pushed her little face up toward the glass that hid the camera. Then she pulled it back. The light flashed three times. I opened the curtain and then stood up. "That's it," I told her, letting her climb out.

"Well, where are the pictures?"

"Stand right there. They'll drop down in a few seconds."

"What are you doing now?" she asked.

"I gotta take some photos on my own."

"Why?"

But instead of answering her, I closed the curtain and held her little hand as she stood on the opposite side. The camera snapped three more photos, of just me alone. I opened the curtain. Naja had the first set of pictures in her hand. She stood staring at them.

"Do you think I look pretty?" Naja asked.

"Of course," I told her.

"For real? Or are you just saying that?" she questioned with a serious face.

"*No!* I'm just saying that," I teased her.

"Your pictures look better. You look real cool," Naja said to me.

"Don't put your fingerprints on the pictures. Just hold them on the sides like this."

"Why?" she asked, but then she held them the right way.

At the pizza store I brought Naja a slice and a salad.

"Do you think we're weird because we don't eat McDonald's?" she asked, before biting down on an olive.

"No."

"This girl in my class said that everybody normal eats McDonald's. She said that Muslims eat McDonald's too."

"People can do whatever they want to," I answered Naja carefully. "But in our family, we don't worry about what everyone else thinks is normal. We do what we believe is best. So follow Umma, no matter what your friends say."

"Okay." She smiled, contented.

* * *

I phoned Mr. Ghazzali from downtown Brooklyn, but his son Mustapha Salim answered the phone. After extending my greetings, I told him, "I was calling to get your father's permission to stop by your house tonight at ten. I need to hand him something."

"No problem *Wed Ammi*," he said, using a Sudanese term for *cousin*.

"I'll relay your message, but come on by. I'm sure it's okay with Father."

* * *

Feeling decent about how my day was flowing and about accomplishing shit one by one, I headed to Chinatown to do a face-to-face with Cho, the owner of the Chinatown fish market where I worked on Fridays and Saturdays. He was the Chinaman who had reluctantly broken his regular pattern of doing things and given me a job a year ago. In almost fifty-two weekends, I had never missed a workday or even ever arrived late. Whenever he needed me to do overtime, I did it, no problem. So I planned to do the honorable thing and give him a heads-up about my travel plans, which would cause me to miss three of Cho's busiest workdays.

Naja's little hand was moist in the warm spring air. I held on to it, though, not wanting her to get swept away as Chinatown got invaded by the NY after-work crowd looking for some fresh goods to prepare for dinner.

"You don't have to hold my hand. I won't get lost," she said, as her little feet had to double-step to keep up with my swift pace.

"Oh yeah?" I said still holding on to her.

"If we got separated, I could find you easily. Your sneakers are cleaner than everyone else's and your laces are so cool. How come my sneakers are dirty? How come when you walk around all day, your sneakers never get dirty?" she asked, looking up at me. I just smiled. But I did decide I would buy her a new pair of kicks. We dipped into a sneaker store. She wanted to pick. When she came back with some polka-dot skips, I chose for her instead. The DeQuan in me wouldn't let it slide. He had been the five percenter, fashion regulator, gun dealer, fight promoter, and big brother to his five blood brothers and for my whole Brooklyn block before he got knocked.

Cho and his nephew Chow were in a rhythm, satisfying the customers and knocking them off the line one by one. I waited till the small crowd cleared.

"What you do here on a weekday?" Cho questioned.

"I came to give you a heads-up. This weekend I am going to work Friday like regular, but I have to take off all day Saturday the tenth and the following weekend, the sixteenth and the seventeenth." There was a long pause between us. Cho looked like he was thinking real hard about my simple and clear request. Just then I saw Saachi, Akemi's young cousin, walk up and sit down beside Naja outside Cho's door.

"I'm letting you know now to give you enough time to get someone to fill in for me, okay?" I asked, but I was definite.

Cho folded his arms across his chest. "You chase Japanese girl to the end of the earth!"

Since I don't discuss my wife with other men, I didn't answer Cho. I knew that he knew that my letting him know was a courtesy, not a request. "I'll see you on Friday morning, Cho. Don't count me out. I'll be here for sure," I reassured him.

He mumbled something back at me, some sentences spoken in Chinese. So I figured he must be talking to himself.

"Mayonaka!" Eight-year-young Saachi jumped off the steps and put her hands right on her hips, where she liked to keep them. She was calling me by the name that Akemi called me. Mayonaka, meaning "midnight" in Japanese. Naja followed behind her. Before the little Japanese girl could start dropping her word bombs, her father, who is also my wife's uncle, appeared outside their family store door, which was four doors down from Cho's on the same side of the block.

"Ooh, you better go, you know. Here comes your father," Naja warned Saachi. But the little girl only removed one hand from her hip and said through a half smile, "He's only scary for you guys. My father's very nice to me." She turned on her toes to take off, and I slowed her down. "We'll walk over with you," I said. She and Naja began skipping slowly. Naja got her first scuff mark on her new ACGs.

"*Konbanwa*, Uncle Nakamura," I said, using the Japanese language intentionally.

"Good evening," he answered in English dryly and for his own reasons too.

"How's it going? How's business?" I asked, even though I had just seen him on Sunday when I was searching for Akemi. I suspected that he may have even called the cops on me for loitering outside of his store door, but really for loving and marrying his niece.

"Fine," he responded with one word only.

"See you next time, Saachi," Naja said.

"Good night," I said.

I purposely wanted to appear to be calm and pleasant in this "thought battle" that I was having with the Japanese men in my wife's family. There was no reason to tip him off that I was headed over to take back what was mine. Inside I was boiling once again. I could tell from this uncle's posture that they thought they had won. It was as though they believed that they lived in the first world and I was stuck in the third or fourth or fifth world, that somehow I wouldn't be able to figure out how to cross the Pacific Ocean beyond Alaska and over the Siberian mountains to get my wife. In a short time, they would discover that they were wrong.

"What did Saachi say to you?" I asked Naja.

"First she asked me what I was doing over here. Then she showed me this string that she had in her pocket and how she could twist it into a bunch of different shapes. Then she asked me if I missed Akemi and if we had heard from her."

"What did you tell her?"

"What could I tell her? I don't know anything," Naja said with her arms raised halfway and palms facing up.

"Are you sure you didn't say anything extra?" I checked.

"I just told her that I do miss Akemi and that I am sure she will come back real soon." Then Naja shifted her eyes away from me.

"And?" I pushed.

"And what?" she said softly but understanding the intensity in me. "Saachi said that Akemi is *never coming back*."

The words of my seven-years-young sister hit me in the chest like powerful kicks.

"But I told Saachi that she really doesn't know that for sure," Naja said confidently.

"And?" I continued.

"Saachi said that her father told her that Akemi's father saved Akemi from ruining her life."

My jaw tightened. I stood still on the busy block holding my sister's hand, thinking.

"That's it, that's all Saachi said. Oh, wait a minute, I left one thing out. Earlier, she told me that her real name is Sachiko but that she lets people she likes call her Saachi for short. She said Sachiko means 'happiness.' But the mean thing she told me about you ruining Akemi's life, she said that last. Then you came outside."

Chapter 10
DOJO

"Me and Chris dipped into our funds and bought you a wedding present. We *could've* got you something before, if you *would have* let us know you was getting married," Ameer said.

We were in the dojo locker room suiting up in our *dogis*—me, Ameer, and Chris, my two best friends. They were weeks late with their gift, but it was cool. Truth is, I wasn't expecting anything at all.

"So, since the money came from our car fund, that means that I paid for a third of my wedding gift?" I said, kidding them about the money that we all three had saved up over our seven-year friendship.

"True, true." Chris smiled. "But, brother, that's not the point!" Chris added.

"So where is it?" I asked, standing with my arms extended doubtfully.

"It's at Ameer's place," Chris said.

I turned toward Ameer and asked him, "Is this gift something that you used first? 'Cause if you already used it, you can keep it. Y'all know I don't like leftovers!" I slammed my locker shut, laughing.

"That's cold," Ameer answered. "Maybe I *should* use it first."

We hit the floor, taking up our positions.

Naja shrank herself into a corner beneath the large, antique gray metal fan, reading the new book I had just bought her.

During the second dojo hour, Sensei called out for sparring. Although he always chose random partners, he tried to avoid putting me, Chris, and Ameer up against one another. He put me against a muscular heavyweight instead, an old dude, about twenty-nine or so.

It wasn't a conscious choice for me to place the face of Akemi's rude-ass uncle over the face of my sparring partner. *Akemi is never coming back.* I kept hearing that one sentence. I must have heard it too much or too loud in my mind. I landed a blow to my opponent that shifted his jaw and cracked his nose. It was only his slow stream of blood running from his nose, over his lips, and onto his teeth that brought my mind back into focus and into the dojo.

"My bad, man," I said. Sensei stood staring. It didn't move me. We are warriors and some blood gotta spill sometimes. This time was not the first time someone caught a bad one in our ninjutsu dojo.

Later, outside the dojo, me, Ameer, and Chris conspired in the warm night weather.

"What's up for tonight?" I asked them.

"Nothing, man. You brought your kid sister. I wanted you to come through the East tonight," Ameer said, referring to East New York.

"Word? Chris, you headed to the East?" I asked.

"Punishment, remember? I'm still on punishment." As we all laughed, Chris's father, Reverend Broadman rolled up, pushing the Caddy, and snatched Chris up.

"How 'bout tomorrow night? I can come through after ball practice but it'll be late," I told Ameer.

"Nah, then come through in the afternoon after I get back from school, 'round four thirty. It'll be safer for you then." Ameer glanced down at my father's watch, then smiled. "You know how the East—"

"Yeah, you know me." I gave him a pound. "I'll check you tomorrow," I said as I walked away.

"I wouldn't want none of them boys around my way to steal your wedding gift from you, especially after you paid for it and I used it first!" Ameer said with a laugh. He got that one off on me.

"Later," I told him, and grabbed my sister's hand and kept moving.

"Is it wrong if I think that your friend is handsome?" Naja asked me, as we rode on the train and after being unusually silent the whole time.

"What do you mean?" I said, shocked, and having nothing else to say.

"You know like he gives a girl a special feeling when she looks at him, Ameer does," she said quietly.

"Don't look at him then! That's why the Quran teaches us to

lower our gaze. When you see boys, don't stare at them. Don't talk to them. Don't let them look into your eyes and you don't look into theirs either. Don't do anything," I scolded her, feeling off guard.

"It's only the first time I felt that," she said softly. "And I don't see boys or stare at them either. I go to an all-girls school, remember? Maybe I only noticed him because you brought me here again. Sorry," she apologized.

"I'm sorry too." I hugged my sister with one arm. "I won't bring you there no more, and you let your first time feeling be your last time feeling, until . . ."

"Until when?" she asked.

"Until it's time for you to marry."

"Who knows when that is?" she said below her breath.

Chapter 11
LOCK & KEYS

The yard light flashed on and Mustapha opened the fence at 10:00 p.m. on the dot. He greeted me first, then shifted his greeting to Naja.

"Hey, are you sleepy?" he asked her in English. But Naja wouldn't lift her head to allow her eyes to look at him or even toward him. I guess she was taking my scolding to heart and to the extreme. But I thought it was good that she knew I was serious. I thought it was even better that she was already making an effort.

"Hi. Nope, I'm not sleepy yet but I'm about to be," Naja said, still staring down at either her own two feet or the Ghazzali's grass.

"Come on in," he welcomed us.

"It's my friend the prime minister," Mr. Ghazzali said with a serious tone yet a genuine smile. I felt bad about greeting his warmth with suspicion, but somehow, suspicion had become a significant part of me. His playful tone and the name that he had dubbed me, "the prime minister," was not a compliment to me. My father had been the top adviser to the true prime minister of the Sudan. I secretly wondered if Mr. Ghazzali had known that all along or if maybe he only recently figured it out.

When my father would come home to the comfort of our Sudanese estate, El Beit Rahim, that he built, he was sometimes filled from head to toe with dilemmas. On some nights, I didn't even need the children's books that he often gifted to me. My father would sit at my side in my bedroom and tell me stories that he pulled from the depths of his mind and core of his heart. Instead of talking serious politics with me, a young boy at that time, he would give his higher-ups, and subordinates animal titles, revealing their characters and actions woven into a simple tale. He would tell me the story of one general, starring "the vulture," who invited and dined on death. One of his cabinet members he described as an elephant who no one could help but notice because of his size. An elephant who took up more than his share of space, made incredible piles of poop, ate up everything, but did nothing else. I would laugh at my father's tales and then ask him, "What animal are you, Father?" My father would think first, then break out in a broad smile, each of his sparkling white teeth set perfectly in his mouth. "I am the camel. I can go for long months without water, although I prefer to drink every day. I can store food and eat it on a day when there is nothing else and everyone else's food is gone. I can carry many men on my back through the desert to an oasis that I know for certain is there. Yet the men usually give up before we reach there, and I am left alone and saddled with their luggage."

At seven years young, I didn't know the word *metaphor*. Now, as a teenaged young man, I understood exactly what my father meant.

When I asked my father which animal our Umma is, he stood up, standing six-foot-eight, and walked a few steps in circles. "Umma," he said, "cannot be described as any animal. She is the sun. No matter where I am traveling in the world, I can feel her warmth and heat. If I look into the sky, she is there radiant and shining. She can never be mistaken for anyone else. When she walks away for even a short time, I can't wait for her return. If she were never to return, nothing else would matter."

My father silenced me with his words that night as my mind gripped their meaning. A tear did come to my childish eyes. "You must not cry," my father cautioned me. "It is our job to keep the tears from Umma's eyes. It is every man's and every son's job to bring happiness to mothers and wives and sisters."

"Good evening, Mr. Ghazzali," I greeted him.

"I know you will want to get right down to business. You and I can step into my office. Maybe your sister can sit with my oldest daughter, Basima." Mr. Ghazzali called upstairs for Basima to come down. Sudana appeared instead.

"Basima is still at Fordham U. She said she will be there studying for her final exams," Sudana told her father. Mr. Ghazzali seemed disturbed for some seconds and then pulled himself out of the mood. Sudana took Naja with her.

"My sister and I have to meet Umma at her job at midnight," I told him, so he would be mindful of my time. It was already 10:15.

In his office I paid out the $650 for rent and $500 for him to deduct his fees for his transportation services. As he dropped the keys into a small envelope and pushed the envelope across the desk to me, he said, "Here is the key for the separate entrance, and another key for the extra night lock that we place on the fence. Since Umma and Naja will be escorted each night, she probably won't have any use for the night lock."

"Let me write out the address for Umma's job and—," I began saying.

"I'll drive you there tonight so that I can be sure about the location and route. And then you will feel more comfortable also."

After a pause, I agreed. "Can I take a look at your basement apartment before we leave?" I asked.

"Sure, for the next thirty days, it's *your* basement apartment, starting"—he glanced at his modest Timex with the black leather band—"right now!" He smiled. I looked at the keys inside the small envelope, realizing that his welcoming us into his home was an act of trust even though I was paying the rent.

Downstairs I checked the place, each window and door and room. I opened every closet, cabinet, and drawer. "Sudana cleaned up very well for your Umma," he said. "Actually, the place was cleaned up all the while. I have never rented it to anyone else. I have only had a few nephews and nieces stay here—you know, family."

My eyes went to the only door leading to the outside. My mind was focused on that instead of Ghazzali's words. I knew that I would install a dead bolt slide lock. I had no way of knowing exactly how many people had copies of Mr. Ghazzali's keys, even if they were his family members. But at least when Umma and Naja were here inside the place, they could use the dead bolt to prevent anyone from outside from entering while they were home. Looking at the wall and the door molding, I knew it would take my handheld drill, either that or a locksmith. I told myself that Ghazzali would understand. I saw how he already had solid steel bars blocking all five of the tiny rectangular basement-level windows. Even if an intruder broke the glass out of those windows, there was no way to fit a body, no matter how skinny, between the steel bars.

My mind shifted again. The apartment was already furnished, decently clean but by no means spectacular. It was good enough, though, for me to begin thinking, *Why should my mother and sister ever return to the Brooklyn projects ever again?* With a whole month's rent paid out to Mr. Ghazzali, I could leave here and go get my wife. Once I returned, I'd pack up our Brooklyn apartment by myself. I'd hire a moving company to transfer the stuff from the Brooklyn apartment to our new house in Far Rockaway, then scoop up Naja and Umma from here and take them directly to our new home. Umma, Akemi, and Naja could decorate our new home however they wanted to and never again have to step their feet there, or be bothered with the Brooklyn projects.

"So deep in thought. Do you need anything else?" Mr. Ghazzali had interrupted right on time.

"We should get moving now."

Naja slept in the back of Mr. Ghazzali's taxi. When we arrived, I jumped out to get Umma and let her know we were taking the cab.

After late-night greetings given very respectfully by Mr. Ghazzali to Umma, we drove mostly in silence except for the brief interruptions of the taxi's two-way radio. I watched Mr. Ghazzali as he kept his eyes on the road and drove us to our Brooklyn block. No other legitimate taxi would take us to our address, especially at this late hour, without hiking up the price and adding a string of complaints about danger.

Chapter 12
PASSPORT

Wednesday, May 7th, 1986

Umma and I were second and third on line at the passport office. We were standing behind a panicked Pakistani American who was headed home to meet his bride-to-be, who had been carefully chosen for him by his parents. He seemed to have to tell me about it as we waited for all the workers to arrive and windows to open up. I was stuck there half listening. I'd rather him tell me than tell Umma. I think it was Umma, though, who inspired him and made him feel comfortable confiding in us. I'm certain she was something familiar wrapped in her colorful *thobe* from head to toe and delicate as a tropical flower. She had accompanied me just in case the authorities here required any sudden additional and random signatures. We were prepared. Now she stood in silent anticipation, her slim fingers wearing faded but fascinating henna designs as she clutched a manila folder containing our neatly organized official papers and identification. Umma was also completing passport forms for herself and Naja. She had decided that even though she and Naja would not receive their passports until six weeks later, it was best for our little family to all have the same official documents.

Arriving early definitely paid off. Everything was signed and stamped in less than two hours. "You can pick up your passport anytime on Friday. Bring your identification and the receipt from your payment," the tired older woman buried behind her bifocals said. I wondered how she could be so exhausted when her work day had just started.

"Alhamdulillah," Umma said thankfully. "This was much quicker than how things are done at government offices in our Sudan. I'm surprised, really." I knew that her gratefulness was genuine. It was rare to hear Umma compliment any aspect of living in America. Outside I looked up at the sky and I saw the sun lurking behind the clouds. I took it as a promise that things would improve.

It was a warm spring morning and Umma wore a cream-colored dress underneath her *thobe* that swirled gently around her ankles and revealed only her cream leather heeled sandals. "I'm going to dress victoriously," she had said early this morning after dawn prayer. "I'm going to dress as though we have already won all of our battles. I won't let one person darken our day." I felt good walking down the street with her. I believed that her presence alone caused good things to happen. Her subtle and sweet scent seemed to encourage a friendly response from strangers, who began greeting us for no apparent reason. Attendants in the shops we entered were unusually helpful.

In the Armani shop on Fifty-Second and Park Avenue, Umma watched intently as the attendant helped me into a new suit jacket that she insisted I try. "Tall, dark, and handsome," the woman assisting me said, and looked at Umma, who had no idea what she was saying because she was speaking English. My Umma only speaks Arabic. But the woman was smiling as she was suiting me up, so Umma returned her smile, confident that her colorful *thobe* was working its charm.

Finally Umma chose her favorite suit. "When you meet Akemi's father for the first time, *inshallah*, be sure to wear this exact suit. The suit does not make you into the man that you already are. But it does distinguish you for the shallow men, who will judge you this way. This suit makes you stand out!" Umma said, gesturing her approval with her talking hands. "Akemi's father needs to know and understand that you are also someone's child and that you are loved and cherished with a culture, faith, and business, and that you are not lacking in any way." She continued in passionate Arabic, caught up not just in the return of her daughter-in-law, but in pleasing and convincing Akemi's father.

"Your language sounds really nice. What is it?" the store attendant asked.

"Arabic," I answered.

"Wow, really? I would never have guessed," she said, seeming sur-prised and a little unsure.

I purchased the suit to please Umma, period. I was not interested in impressing Naoko Nakamura.

In the shoe store next door, the shoes designed by Bruno Mugliani best complemented my foot and the Armani suit. For a few hundred dollars they became mine. I was watching my money pile closely. I didn't want to see my father's diamond disappear without my holding something of true and great value in my hands in exchange. For me this would not be this suit or these shoes. It would only be my wife.

Umma read my thoughts, it seemed. She opened her leather purse and came out with ten one-hundred-dollar bills. "The suit is my gift to you. Put this away with the rest of your money." I accepted her sincerity and thought to myself, *This is how it is between my mother and I. We are both giving each other everything that we have to give so our blessings in life keep going back and forth between us.* Afterward, I led her into the hunter's and wilderness store and Paragon's for the rugged wear that I preferred to rock.

We shared a meal at a restaurant that Umma selected because of its name, the Tamarind. Umma loved the sweet taste of this tropical fruit and even used it in her cooking from time to time. When she saw the unshelled tamarind dangling in the restaurant window, she nudged me and we stepped inside. It was an elegant place, each din-ing area secluded by a beautiful curtain. The cuisine was Indian but the decor was familiar to us, the Sudanese.

Once seated, Umma closed the curtain and relaxed her *thobe* cov-ering. She and I ate comfortably yet lightly. We shared palak paneer and dahl tadka. Instead of any of the wonderful breads that come from India, we had vegetable samosa. It's something like a beef patty, but instead of beef, it's seasoned vegetables and potatoes stuffed and tucked in a fried triangular bread. Soon after the meal, an Indian ap-proached, smiling ear to ear. His name plate had only one word on it, one really long name with eighteen letters. He drew back the curtain and held it tightly in his left hand. Immediately he introduced him-self as the manager and offered two complimentary dishes of coconut ice cream. "A gift for your bride," he said, staring at Umma.

"She is my mother," I corrected him.

"Oh, Mother India!" he exclaimed happily.

"No," I said seriously, while giving him the stare of a polite warning.

He then shifted his focus onto me asking, "Oh, but she is not from India? She is wearing henna. Is she Arab, then?"

"No," I said feeling impatient.

"What, then?"

"African," I answered in an even tone.

"African?" he repeated, looking puzzled. I thanked him for his creams and told him, to please release the curtain. I was used to Umma drawing attention. Like the sun, even when fully covered, she was still radiating.

"Please come again." The manager extended his business card to me as we were preparing to leave.

I accepted it politely, then grabbed Umma's hand and carried our shopping bags in the other. We taxied directly back to Brooklyn for a few dollars over the normal price.

Chapter 13
WEDDING GIFTS

I picked up my heat and headed to East New York to meet Ameer. I wasn't expecting any beef, but I wasn't sleeping either.

Ameer was seated at the top of the bench in front of his building, a female between his legs below, his backpack still on his back when I rolled up.

"You made it." He smiled, still joking like I should be shook in his hood.

"Dana, this is my man, Midnight," Ameer introduced some girl.

"What's up?" she asked softly. I didn't answer back.

"C'mon, let's move," I told Ameer. He caught that I wanted him to lose the girl. We both knew that he never acted right when females was in the cipher. He got up and we headed into his building. When he turned the key in the lock, he pushed the door open and we stepped inside. I followed him into the living room.

"You could chill right here." He left. In the hallway he ran into his moms.

"Why you not at work?" he asked her, sounding surprised.

"I left early. I had a headache," she told him, sounding as if she could still feel the pain.

"That's 'cause you and Pops stayed up too late last night. I heard y'all in there arguing."

"We wasn't arguing. We were discussing," she corrected him. "Who's in the living room?"

"Go and see for yourself," Ameer told her. "It's someone you like."

Ameer's mom appeared. Before I could look up to see her face,

I saw her heeled house shoes and bare legs. I stopped at her hips and shifted my gaze away from her.

"Still playing shy, hmm?" she said.

"How you doing, Mrs. Nickerson," I answered without looking.

"You supposed to look at a lady when you're talking to her," she teased boldly. "Can I get you something to drink?" She asked.

"No, thank you," I answered, still not looking at her.

"Come on back here or she gonna keep messing with you," Ameer called from the back room. I got up and walked around his moms.

"What time is your practice?" he asked.

"Six o'clock for the black team. How bout y'all?"

"The red team, um, we meet at seven. I hope the coach shows up though. Last time he was talking about he got held up by his probation officer." He laughed. "But we doing good. We ain't dropped a game yet," Ameer said.

"How? We beat y'all," I reminded him.

"Yeah, but that didn't count remember? Just a scrimmage. For all the official games, we ain't been beat." He smiled.

"How long y'all think you could keep that up? You gonna have to face us in an official game eventually," I told him.

"Yeah, not this week but next week, Saturday. I got the schedule right over there," he said, pointing to his dresser. "The red team is ready for y'all, no problem." He smiled confidently.

I was just about to start talking shit, a competitive thing me and this cat, who is my best friend, had going on for about seven years now. We only rivaled each other when we were alone. When we were out there on those streets, we stuck together—me, Ameer, and Chris. I realized suddenly that there was a chance that I might miss the game next Saturday. *What if I'm still in Japan?* I thought to myself. So I cut myself short and just let Ameer brag alone.

"So you got my wedding gift or an excuse?" I asked him, joking with a serious face.

"I got it. Look, it took Chris and me a long time to figure out what to buy you. We fucked up our whole Saturday last week try'na get it right," he said, as I pictured them shopping for my gift on the same day that my wife disappeared.

"Even my pops threw something in a box for you."

"Word" was all I said, surprised and feeling moved about my two best friends.

"What you thought, we ain't got love for you?" Ameer asked.

Those words hit me hard. I been so long in America that I wasn't used to any male saying something with feeling toward another male and meaning it, no bullshit, no perversion.

"Nah, nah, not like that," I said, at a loss for words.

"I'll go get it," he said, and went into his closet and pulled down a big box.

"Hold up, let me get Chris on the line." He pushed the speakerphone button and I could hear Chris's phone ringing.

"Hello," Chris answered.

"Chris, what up, nigga?" Ameer said.

"Homework and homework and homework and punishment. What did you think was up? And, brother, why do I gotta be called 'nigga'?" Chris asked.

We all laughed.

"Oh, what's up, brother?" Chris asked, realizing I was in on the convo.

"All good," I said.

"Did you open the joints yet?" Chris asked.

"No, he 'bout to open 'em now. I knew you wanted to be in on it, so here it go," Ameer said, same as if Chris was sitting right here in the room with us.

Ameer threw a package at me. I caught it. "Open it," he ordered. I took a look at it. It was wrapped in brown paper bag. *There's a big difference between when a man wraps a gift than when a woman wraps it.* I thought to myself. When I saw the Andis brand name, the same brand that my barber uses, I said, "Clippers." I thought it was a real live gift. I smiled.

The small card taped on the clipper box had only two words written on the outside, "Stay sharp!" When I opened it, I laughed.

"Condoms, make sure you use 'em." Ameer laughed, then Chris was laughing also. I slid 'em into my front right-hand pocket and didn't say nothing else on the topic. Ameer tossed the second package at me. I suspected it was some type of gag. The box was wrapped in aluminum foil. When I took the wrapping off, I didn't know what it was. I laid it on the bed and sat there looking at it.

"What is it?" I asked.

"It's a papoose!" Chris shouted over the speakerphone.

"A what?" I asked again.

"It's for your shorty. We already know you gonna fuck up at least once and not use the condoms. So you put your son in there and use it to carry him on your back," Chris explained.

"We were gonna buy you a car seat for the baby. But then we realized you didn't have no car!" Ameer laughed.

"No car!" Chris shouted. "He ain't even got a driver's license!"

Embarrassed by these two fools, I ran my hand over my Caesar cut, a habit. I saw now that this wasn't just gonna be a few gifts but a bunch of jokes that led into a full-out ranking session. So I leaned back to get my head in the right frame of mind to fire back on these boys.

There was a moment of silence between the three of us, for no particular reason. Then Chris said, "Give him the real gift." Instead of throwing something at me, Ameer walked it over and placed it in my hand. It was kind of heavy and covered in white gift wrapping paper with gold strips and a slim gold ribbon. I could tell that they paid an extra two dollars to have the female at the store register gift wrap it right. I could see it was a serious gift. I unwrapped it, held it up, and looked at the box, then opened it. Inside was a brand-new video camera secured in styrofoam along with the battery and all of the accessories.

"Yo, this is crazy. It's nice," I said, meaning it. "It's real nice." I was genuinely shocked.

"Yeah, we figured since you got so much going on in your life, you might as well make a motherfucking movie! That's the only way the rest of us gonna be able to know what's really happening with you, ninja!" Ameer said.

"No, seriously, though. We thought you did something strange but good, getting married and all. *We* couldn't do nothing like that. Your wife, she's really pretty and different and me and Ameer spoke on it for a couple of hours about how we admire you and shit for the way you handle yourself," Chris said, bringing a true feeling to all of us without even being in the room.

"Man, what can I say? Thank you, both of y'all. I'm not sure how to use this thing," I said, flipping the heavy box around, surveying it. "But I'm sure I can figure it out."

"Well, if you need some practice, you can come shoot me on Friday night when I'm rocking the green team," Ameer joked and jumped up, faking a move.

"On Friday night the only thing I'll be shooting is the rock. I got a game, black versus blue on our home court," I told 'em.

"Alright, I'm out. You two showing off. I got to put my head back in these books or else." Chris laughed. "I'll catch up with y'all at the dojo tomorrow night." He hung up and the loud dial tone sounded.

"Here, let me get you a bag," Ameer said, leaving the room.

I sat there with my head down, thinking whether or not I should say something to them about my trip to Japan instead of just dropping out of sight for a week or so. Would I lose or risk anything by opening up and filling these cats in? The gifts they gave me were completely unexpected. They made me feel even more at ease, not because of what they were, but because of the intent behind them.

Ameer returned and handed me an ugly brown paper bag. "Here, throw it in here. Disguise it. It's better like that" was all he said.

"I gotta make a run," I announced, lifting my head and straightening my back.

"To where?" he asked.

"Japan," I answered. He looked at me real serious, paused for nine seconds, and then busted out laughing. "You see, this is what me and Chris be talking about. You just now made it sound like you was going to the corner store. Meanwhile, you going to Japan?" he asked, seeming amazed. Then we both heard the metal knocker banging on his front door.

"Hold up," he said. But as soon as he moved to step out of the room, his moms darted out of her room first and dashed to answer the door. I could tell they were both expecting something unexpected, because instead of treating it casually, Ameer stood watching the door from the back hallway. I was watching the door too, from behind him.

"Uh-uh, bitch. I know you didn't have the nerve to knock on my door," I could hear his moms saying. She was talking, not screaming. Yet her words were loud and clear and forceful. Ameer shifted and was now blocking most of my view. As soon as his mother stepped

into the hallway outside her apartment door, I stood up and followed him.

"You think I'm stupid? You think you can come to my apartment
looking for my husband?" I heard her say, her anger rising with her
volume. Ameer snatched open the front door. His presence had no
affect on his moms. His mother shoved the girl up against the neighbor's door, which was directly across the hall. The girl crashed against
it. "I'll beat your motherfucking ass!" Ameer's mom said, grabbing the
girl's clothes and keeping her from falling to the floor. The girl tried
to push back, but she was slow and got beat down.

"Cool out, ma! Come off her," Ameer ordered. But instead of
stopping, his mom now held the girl by her hair, yanking her head left
and right. The girl started swinging her hands, more slapping than
punching, trying to get Ameer's mom off of her.

The neighbor must have heard the bumping against his door and
opened it. Both Ameer's mom and the girl fell into the entrance of
the neighbor's apartment. Ameer's mom was on top, getting the best
of the girl. The neighbor who opened his door jumped back. We were
three men watching a girl get rocked by Ameer's mother and not one
of us making a move. Then Ameer stepped up and pulled his mother
off of the girl.

"Don't pull me. Pull that bitch," his mother scolded him fiercely.

"Ma, stop. Stop now. What you doing that for? She just came up
here to check me, that's all."

"Check you? She came up here looking for your father, that little
sneaky bitch."

"Ma, she came to check me. I saw her outside when I came home
from school. I told her to come up here, for real," Ameer said, trying to convince his mom as the girl pulled herself up and attempted
to straighten her clothes. A short pile of her hair was lying on the
hallway floor.

"C'mon, ma," Ameer said, calming his mother in an effort to ease
her back inside, where I stood, by using his body to lean on her. When
she was all the way in, he stepped outside of the apartment to deal
with the girl, closing the front door and leaving both me and his
mother on the other side. His mom's breasts heaved in and out as she
tried to normalize her breathing. She placed one hand on her breast
and held the other in the air, gesturing and saying to me, "I'm sorry

you had to see that." Then she began tugging at her camisole top, smoothing it out for no real reason. It was real revealing and there was no extra material there for her to use to cover anything up. She was bare-legged with short shorts on and no high-heeled slippers this time. She brushed up against me to pass me by. But then the front door opened again and she turned and looked back. It was Ameer's father standing there. She turned all the way around saying nothing and walked toward her husband. But she didn't stop where he stood. She grabbed her front door open. Ameer was still standing there talking to the girl, calming her down.

"She's here to see you, right?" Ameer's mom asked Ameer forcefully.

"Yeah, ma. I already told you that," Ameer said.

"Then bring that bitch inside," Ameer's mom demanded.

"That's alright, I'm good right here," the girl finally spoke.

"Bitch, you had the balls to knock, right? Ameer, bring her in here," the mother demanded again.

Ameer grabbed the girl's hand and walked her into the apartment, past his mother and father and me, and down the hallway into his bedroom.

"I heard you got married," Ameer's father said to me matter-of-factly, ignoring the heated scenario.

"I did" was all I answered back, mostly stunned at the situation. "Thank you for the clippers," I told him, trying to break up the tension.

His wife's glare was on her husband only. She ignited the hallway with her fury. Soon there was very little oxygen to breathe. She looked like she was in killer mode, although she was still silent.

"I'll go say peace to Ameer. I gotta get over to basketball practice. I'm running late," I said, excusing myself and heading back into Ameer's room, where the door was now closed. I knocked once and pushed it open.

"I'm out," I said, seeing the girl seated on his bed, her legs drawn in, her arms resting on her own knees. She was a pretty, smooth-skin, black girl with white teeth and a slim, curvaceous body. Her eyes didn't look innocent to me. She didn't even look like a victim of a brief but wild ass whipping. There was no fear in her eyes, remorse, or regret. Instead, she looked real determined about something. Even with her hair messed up, I could see why Ameer might have been attracted to her.

Ameer handed me the brown paper bag with my gifts. I closed his room door and left. I didn't see his parents anymore. Their bedroom door was closed now. I went back and opened Ameer's door one more time. "Come lock your front door. I'm leaving. There's nobody out here," I told him. He followed me, saying nothing. Their front door shut, and I heard the lock click.

Chapter 14

HUSTLER'S LEAGUE
The Junior Division

"I need you young motherfuckers to pay attention! I know it's spring-time and the days is getting *more* longer, and the girlies is getting *more* naked. But I need y'all to forget all that. I need y'all to forget about your mommas and your worthless-ass poppas, and your bills and books and bullshit. I only want one word branded onto your mind, just one word. Who knows what that word is?," Coach Vega asked us.

My teammate, known as Machete, lifted his head. "But Coach, why we gotta be 'motherfuckers' though?"

"Don't answer a question with a question," Vega overruled.

"How we s'pose to guess what word you got in your mind, Coach?" Braz asked.

"That's another question! Think before you talk!" Coach said, growing impatient.

"At least tell us the first letter of the word," Jaguar said smoothly.

"Okay, I'll give you the first letter. It won't help, 'cause half of you can't spell." Vega laughed.

"What's the letter, Coach Vega?" Panama pushed.

"*U*, the first letter of the word is *U*," Vega challenged, his arms folded across his chest and his face filled with doubt about our think-ing capabilities.

"That's easy," Big Mike, our starting center, said. "The word is *unity*."

"Wrong," Vega cut him down. Seated on the court, all the players fell silent.

"Undefeated," I said breaking the silence.

"You got it, *papi!"* Vega shouted excited. *"Undefeated,* we are unde-feated! That's the only thing that should be on your mind at tomorrow night's game. We don't just want to win the league. We want to sweep these cockroaches from Fort Greene to the Hook. We don't want to give them one chance to breathe. Now run me twenty-five suicides with zero complaints. I would've sent y'all outdoors to do laps around the hood, but I can't be sure that one or two of y'all might not make it back." The whole team let out a muffled laugh as we moved to carry out Vega's orders.

As the practice got more and more intense, and Vega's push and demands grew more serious, I assembled the words in my mind to tell Coach that after Friday night's game, I would be gone from a week's worth of practices. Also, that the possibility existed that I might miss next Saturday's game against the red team.

I knew if I kept my energy high and my performance strong at the two remaining practices, and played my part in the upcoming Friday night game, Coach would be less vexed about my next week's absence. But at the same time, I knew the better I played, the more dependent Coach would become on me showing up for him and the team.

I told myself, *Relax, it don't matter.* Even though winning the league could earn the top five players on the winning team ten thou-sand dollars each, and the league's most valuable player a twenty-five-thousand-dollar purse, my wife was worth way more. Vega and the team would just have to step up and adjust, the same way an NBA team had subs for even the greatest players when they got sidelined with an unexpected injury or fouled out.

Practice ended with Vega wiping his forehead down with a terry-cloth hand towel as though *he* had actually worked out alongside the rest of us. Then he laid his hand towel sideways over the top of his head and pulled out what seemed like a liquor flask.

"What's the word?" he shouted, rowdying up the team.

"Undefeated!" everybody shouted back.

"Alright, make me look good!" Vega said, tilting the bottle, which was filled with Spanish cologne, not cognac. He patted his face and neck with the cologne and ended the three-hour practice. "Alright, break out! See you tomorrow at four p.m. right here!"

I hung back to get his ear. "Coach, I'm good for practice tomorrow and Friday night's game, of course, but I'm not gonna be around next week. I gotta take care of something serious."

"Court date, trial?" he asked.

"Nah," I responded.

"Work, you gotta new job?" he questioned.

"Nah," I answered.

"Abortion, birth, or funeral?" he tried guessing.

"Nah, none of that," I said.

He grew tight. "Then what?"

"Just something I gotta take care of. Then I'll be back." I showed him a stern, straight, and serious face and a hard stare. He reached into his pocket and pulled out his money clip stacked with clean and folded fifty-dollar bills. I noticed easily. I never liked fifty-dollar bills. I preferred hundreds. I estimated he was holding much more in his stack than any intramural, community-type coach would ever earn.

"Talk to me." He stepped in too close to my face, something Latino dudes did sometimes, not because they were a funny type of men. They just had a different idea of space. Some of them used the tactic to threaten and intimidate. Others used it to relay secrets or console. I took one step back and reset my stance.

"I know you're good for it," he said, nodding his head once and holding the money hand up, gesturing that I could take a loan from him.

"Good looking out," I told him sincerely, but refused his money lending. "It's just something I gotta take care of. Then I'll be right back here for the team and the game and for you, Coach." It took Vega some seconds before my facial expression influenced him to yield. He put his money away.

"Let me know if you need some backup," he offered, as though he was a lieutenant in some vast army. Now his face switched completely, as though he never was a coach, but more like an assassin.

"Sometime you gotta let a sideline nigga pull the trigger. Ya know what I mean?" He stepped in close and grimaced after spitting his suspicious one-line rhyme. "You know you are the heart of this team. We can lose a couple of toes and maybe a finger, but we can't win without our heart." He clenched his fist and placed it on the left side of his chest where his heart rested. I felt the pressure but I had no plans to acknowledge it.

"Yeah, I'll keep that in mind," I said evenly, giving him a pound and walking off. He shut down the gym lights, whistled for the school janitor, and walked out behind me in silence. It was 9:00 p.m. and the sun was still streaking the blackening sky with strips of light. I had close to three hours to kill before picking Umma up from her job. It wasn't that I didn't have plenty of shit to do. It was just lining it up right in my head and knocking it out in the perfect order.

Marty Bookbinder's bookstore was in this same area, so I decided to shoot over there and pick up a couple of books and a map for my upcoming trip.

Chapter 15
BANGS

Just as I reached the corner, I heard the roar of the wheels on the gravel. Then she sped past me from behind and did a one-eighty in the middle of the street on her old-fashioned red roller skates. Lucky for her the light had just turned green or she could've got hit and tossed by an oncoming Toyota Celica. She saw some shock in my expression and bent over laughing and came right back up. Her head moved swiftly from right to left, calculating the remaining time to cross the street safely. But she couldn't possibly hear the cars and trucks, because she had her headphones on and her Walkman tucked at her waist. She spun on her wheels again and crossed swiftly. Now she was on one side of the street and I was still on the other, watching her with the red traffic light glaring strong. She put her hands on her waist and flagged me over. I let a few cars flash by, then dashed across still on the red. She was smiling and beaming with happiness like she didn't have one worry in this world with her long, thick red laces and short, tight denim shorts that hugged her small waist. I could see her belly button and about four inches of her naked flat belly before her tight red tee clenched onto her breasts. Her bare shoulders were covered with a sheen of perspiration, and a small wet spot leaking through revealed that she was still breast-feeding her baby. It was Bangs.

"Hey, Supastar! Do you know how to roller-skate?" she called out to me as I approached where she was steady rocking.

Vega was just easing into his car parked on the same side where Bangs was standing waiting for me. Soon as I peeped him, I got tight. I didn't want Coach to think I had some bullshit excuse why I was gonna miss practice next week, like I was out here just fucking with these girls and doing what they wanted me to do instead of what I was responsible for. Second, I didn't like Bangs showing off her banging body to any man who wanted to look. I already knew that every man would look, especially if it was Bangs. They had to. Of course I noticed Vega's eyes were riding in and out of her curves.

"Oh, yeah, that's right, you don't do nothing fun," Bangs joked, removing her headphones and wearing them now like a necklace and smiling still. Vega pulled off slowly. When I reached where she was standing and rocking back and forth on her wheels, I walked past her. She sucked her teeth and followed me.

"Supastar! Word up. I'ma start to think you straight crazy if you can't even speak to me. It's either you really are crazy or you just in love with me too and can't face up to it." She was talking to the back of my head. On the curb I turned to face her.

"Bangs, go home and—"

"Uh-uh," she interrupted. "You can't send me home tonight. It's only nine and you know I got till eleven to get home. So let me just hang out with you for a little while, okay?" She was flashing her deep dimples and still smiling while posting her attitude.

"Go back and put on some clothes. *Then* I'll talk to you," I told her.

"Walk me over?" she asked.

"Nah, Bangs. It ain't gonna be me and you up in your house. You should already know that," I told her. "I'll be at the bookstore. Put on some clothes and you can meet me over there." I started stepping.

"What bookstore?" she asked, riding over and pulling up to me from behind. Her hands were grabbing each side of my waist as though she needed to balance herself.

"You know, the one over there, by the pharmacy, where you buy your grandmother's medicine," I reminded her.

"There's a bookstore over there?" she asked.

"Later" was all I said. I left. I heard her wheels take off. All I could think was *How could she have a bookstore in her own hood and never step inside of it once?* Worse, it was as though she never even noticed that it was there. No wonder Marty Bookbinder's store was always empty. Every time I went there, I had full range of the place. I knew I could chill in there comfortably until closing at 11:00 p.m. If I was bored, I could pick up a good game of chess, although over the years I had learned to outmaneuver Marty on his own chessboard the majority of the time.

"My good friend, my main man!" Marty said. It was his version of cool. "Let me pull out the board." He was excited to have me in his empty store packed with plenty of books and magazines.

"Let me look around first," I told him after returning his greetings, and that slowed him down some.

"Look around? You know everything that's in here already!"

I maneuvered around the geography section until I found a book on Japan. I sat in the comfortable La-Z-Boy chair in the mystery section, where I normally purchased most of my books. I cracked the book open and flipped the pages until I found the map of Japan. I began examining it, looking for Kyoto, Akemi's home spot and the place where her high school was located. I was also looking for a place called Ginza. I remembered that when I wrote to her father concerning my desire to marry his daughter, Akemi, I did not address the letter to Kyoto. I wondered if it was Akemi's father's business address or if they had moved from Kyoto or if they actually had more than one or two homes. I had gotten the address from Akemi but never bothered to find out why she did not give me a Kyoto address. I could see from the map that Ginza and Roppongi were "prefectures" of Tokyo. It was like how the Bronx and Queens are boroughs of New York. When I measured the distance, I could see that Ginza was in Tokyo, and Kyoto was three hours away from Tokyo by train or six hours by car moving at sixty miles per hour. My mind drifted deep into the map as I studied every detail.

I burnt up almost an hour reviewing the atlas before I began flipping and reading through two books that I had pulled. Later as I stuck the two books back on the shelf, I saw an old lady wearing a wide hat through the small empty space where the books went. *Marty finally got a customer while I was in his store,* I thought to myself. As I stepped out into the aisle, her hat with the pile of tissue paper flowers pinned on top prevented anyone from seeing her face. She had a long flowered dress that was obviously too big for her and that dragged on the floor, like she was a homeless person wearing oversized second-hand clothing. The big white plastic pearls that were draped around her neck was the killa part of her outfit. But when my eyes dropped down to her feet, her red Reeboks didn't match nothing.

I paused for a second and looked at the red Reeboks again. The old lady purposely stepped in my way and looked right into my face, snatching away her hat and dropping her blond wig to the floor. She clapped her hands together and started cracking up. It was crazy-ass Bangs.

I was mad, but I had to laugh. I was tight, but she was funny.

"I borrowed one of my grandmother's dresses. It don't fit but I fig-ured you would like this a lot." She began smoothing the tent-sized dress out with her hands and demonstrating to me that her arms and legs and even her body were all covered. I had already noticed that without her pointing it out or exaggerating it. She smiled brightly. She was being swallowed and eaten by the dress.

"No psych! I just wanted to see you laugh, Supastar. You be way too serious," she said, dropping the huge dress to the floor. Under-neath she wore jeans and a short-sleeved blouse. She looked more decent than she had in her hot pants and roller skates, less naked. She bent over and picked up the dress that lay deflated on the floor like an old hot-air balloon. She folded it and held it in her left hand.

"What is going on?" Marty Bookbinder appeared in the back where we were standing.

"Don't ask," I told him calmly.

"Is she one of your friends?" he questioned.

"I'm Tiffany," Bangs introduced herself. Marty reached in to shake her hand. I intercepted him before he touched her and he drew it back.

"Here, Marty. I'm gonna buy this," I said, handing him the geog-raphy book while at the same time using the book to separate him from Bangs. Marty was always smart. He picked up on my senti-ments, took one last concentrated stare at Bangs, and then turned to head toward the cash register.

"Let me talk to you over there," I said to Bangs. She sat down on the chair opposite the La-Z-Boy. So I took that comfortable chair for myself.

"What's up, Bangs? Why you always chasing me?" I asked her. She just sat there staring at me with eyes brighter than searchlights, not saying anything.

"You said you wanted to talk, now talk," I pushed.

Suddenly she stopped smiling and kicking her feet even while she was sitting. Her face turned serious and she said, "I love you, Supastar."

I felt my heart melt a bit. I sat back some in my chair. I kept my face blank. I didn't want to encourage her. Yet her admiration for me, and the tone of her talk, and the sudden seriousness of her pretty face moved me some. I was searching for the words to decline her affections without being mean. The truth was I didn't hate her. I didn't even find her annoying. I thought she was real attractive and full of life and energy and jokes. But I wasn't the type to just move on impulse. I had already thought it through thoroughly. I had interacted with her some, watched her closely. I had discovered that her infant child was the result of molestation by her own blood-related uncle, and it seemed that she still had ongoing dealings with him, which turned me off and away completely. Bangs claimed she hated him. But there were signs that she allowed him to continue to violate her even after she knew it was wrong. I couldn't be sure. But for me, that was the point. When it came to my women, *I had to be sure.*

I wasn't interested in taking advantage of Bangs, although I knew it would be easy. I wouldn't take her as a wife because I knew she did not know one thing about or understand or even *have an interest* in my Muslim faith and lifestyle. I knew she would not be acceptable to my Umma, and Umma is my standard.

As a Muslim man, I knew I could have more than one wife. But this was not a game to me. My father is a great man, so he has three wives. He is a true believer, wealthy, accomplished, and proven. He deserves all that he has and chose wisely and treats his wives lovingly and fairly, from what I could see as a young man. He provides. Each wife has a separate home of her own, all on our estate, which my father built and financed and owns.

I was not foolish enough to believe that I deserved a second wife, or that I was fully prepared to protect and provide for her. Even my first wife was not part of my teenaged plan. Akemi was a great love, very much mutual, that took me by storm. I had to step up and in. I wanted to. She was a virgin. I was a virgin. She worked hard. I worked hard. She was talented. I was dedicated. We were connected solidly in every way, without a common language between us.

"You don't love me. You just think that you do. You don't really know me, Bangs. If you did, you wouldn't even want to be bothered with my way of life. *You would have to change up everything that you're doing now*, just to be considered by me. So you see, it's too much trouble for you," I said earnestly but also trying not to blame her or hurt her feelings.

"What am I doing that is so wrong?" she asked sincerely.

"It's not just one thing . . . Actually, it would take too long to explain."

"C'mon, tell me something. Run it by me. I want to know what you're talking about," she urged, flinging one of her legs across the other and easing her body forward to listen intently. After a thoughtful pause I answered her in a way that I thought she might understand, a way that might make her take a look at herself instead of only looking at me.

"How long you known me, Bangs? You never even offered me one glass of water. You see a man is out here working and even hustling on these courts a few hours every night. You never thought to offer me a cool drink. I been in your house. You never offered me a stew, sandwich, or a cookie. You think you're ready, but you wouldn't even know what to do with a man," I said, picking the smallest, easiest criticism on purpose.

"True dat," she said, regretfully.

"And how many men you been talking to since we met?" I asked, not expecting a true answer, just try'na show her something. "So if it didn't work out between you and me, would you just roll with the next cat that you had lined up?" I asked with a serious face, not angry but telling her my real thoughts. When she didn't have no quick responses like usual, I knew I was affecting her. "Didn't you say I had your heart? If I got your heart, how could there be a next man on line? Is it a game?" I asked her.

"If I don't got you *and* I don't talk to no other guys, *how* am I s'posed to get you out of my heart, Supastar?"

"Why does it have to be somebody? Why can't you just go home and take care of your daughter? Go to school and put your mind on something else?"

" 'Cause that's boring and I'm young. I need real love in my life," she answered. "And besides, when I be with other guys, that's just talking. It's *only you* who I love." She looked right at me to try and show her true intent. She didn't even blink.

"C'mon, Supastar. Let me get a do-over!" she said, smiling wildly once again. "I'll change. I'll change for you. I want you to be my man and my daughter's father, for real. I'll do anything. Just tell me."

"Nah, it ain't easy like that. It's not just something you wake up doing tomorrow. First, you got to at least have some learning and understanding."

"I'm smart! Just 'cause I'm funny and I like to have fun doesn't mean that I'm not smart, Supastar." There was a pause between us.

"What type of books do you like to read?" I asked her, not seriously expecting a reply, but trying to show her that she really wasn't serious or smart enough.

"Huh? What?" she replied, just how I expected she would.

I rephrased my question. "What is the name of the last book that you read?" I asked.

Seconds and then a full minute passed. She didn't have a title, an answer, or a clue. Not even any of the books that surrounded her here in the bookstore could trigger any thoughts in her mind or memory it seemed.

"Okay, *but I can read*! What do you *want* me to read? I'll read it. Then you can come over to my house and we can discuss it!" She said it like she might mean it, but always with her there was a strong trace of humor in everything. Always with her, she tried to ease me up into her bedroom. I knew she wanted to feel something. I knew she wanted me to go in her. I also knew that a real relationship couldn't start or be held together with just that. But at the same time, I wanted her to be a better woman, at least so she could be in a position to raise her daughter right.

"You're in the bookstore. You look around. Pick out a few books. I'll buy 'em for you. You show me that you are really going to try to improve some of your thoughts and ways. Then we'll see," I said calmly.

I really wanted to watch and wait and see what kind of books she chose. I thought it would tell me something and she would show herself something as well. She agreed, then paused. She stood up, stepped over, and then sat down beside me in my chair, squeezing her hips in close.

"But first, don't you want to know our secret?" she asked me.

"We don't have any secrets, Bangs," I said solidly.

"Ooh look at my ring," she said, holding her hand out for me to see. "It's a mood ring, and it turned all red as soon as I got close to you," she joked. "If you kissed me, the glass would probably break open. Ooh God, if you kissed me, I swear I would go crazy." She threw her shoulders and then her head onto the back of the chair. She leaned her head against my shoulder. "You really kept me waiting too long, Supastar."

She was feeling warm against me. I still shook her off. Then she stood up, still staring.

"I don't have the time to play with you, Bangs," I told her.

"You might not have the time, but I know that you want to," she said teasing. I decided then that her jeans were not much better than her red denim shorts. Even though her legs were fully covered and her belly button wasn't showing anymore, her pants seams were still squeezing and riding her curves and her blouse was thin and her figure was too powerful and alluring. Even just seeing her up close and feeling the bare skin of her forearm was too much for me. I'm not sure if it is because of where I am from that I feel and think this way. *But I like women*, and lately every little move certain ones of them make, when captured in my eye, sends a current through me that I'm forced to restrain and control. I was feeling that current right then, and immediately, I knew I had made a mistake. No matter how hard she came at me, I should have kept it moving without any words. If I had done that enough times, she would have to give up and be forced to go away, stay away.

I stood up.

"Okay, but before you leave, because I can see you're getting uptight, just let me tell you what the fortune-teller said about me and you."

"I don't believe in no fortune-teller."

Back in Sudan, this kind of thing is called *kittaba*, and even though some people involve themselves in it, most Sudanese surely try to avoid it. I had no interest in it. I thought to myself.

"Oh, but this lady is *good*. I went there with my friend Brittany, and this lady even knew that Brittany had two abortions. And it was Brittany's first time ever going there," Bangs said, fully convinced. "You see, this is how it works. You have to bring the fortune-teller something that you have that you wear on your body, like a piece of jewelry, a necklace, or a piece of clothing that you wore but haven't washed yet, or like a coin that you have in your pocket all of the time or something like that. Then the fortune-teller holds it in her hand. She closes her eyes for a minute or more, and then she can tell you about your whole life. Like she can tell you what's going on in your life now and what's happening in your future also." Bangs finally paused for air.

"No, seriously, after Brittany gave the fortune-teller her necklace, the one her mother gave her that she wears all the time, the fortune-teller told her to have a seat. Then the lady closed her eyes, and when she opened them, she said, 'It's not good for young ladies to have abortions. You have aborted two babies.' Brittany's jaw dropped open and I was shocked and a little bit scared too. Then Brittany asked the fortune-teller how could she know that about her. The fortune-teller said, 'Because your two aborted babies are here with you now. They are both seated at your side. They will follow you around for your whole life, sad at being unborn, but connected to you still!'"

Bangs jumped up out of my chair with real expression in her eyes. "Supastar, I was scared like shit! But after Brittany's half hour was up, I wanted a turn too. But I didn't have the money. It cost thirty dollars. So I asked the fortune-teller if I can come back to her. I told her I wanted to ask her about a person. The fortune-teller said if I had the money, I could return. She told me to bring something of my own and something that belonged to the person who I was asking her about. So I did."

"Oh yeah?" was all I said, feeling like this was all some bullshit and planning to pull myself out of it and leave.

But then Bangs said, "I wanted to ask the fortune-teller about you Supastar. So I took your hoodie out of my closet. Remember the hoodie that you wore that night that the police was chasing you and your friends, the first night that you climbed into my bedroom window? Well, I gave it to the fortune-teller. And I gave the fortune-teller my T-shirt that I had on that night, 'cause that night was so special to me. I was so happy that you came my way that I could just die."

Now Bangs had my complete attention. Not only had I left my hoodie at her house that night, I left one of my guns. If she took the hoodie out of the closet and gave it to some stranger, I wondered what she might have done with my gun. I had always felt grateful to her because she helped me out on a night that the police were head-hunting. In those situations they don't care who actually did what. They just want to pump bullets into black bodies and deny it later. I had picked up my hoodie and my gun from Bangs after that incident. But now that I thought back, I recalled that I waited about four days before I went and got my shit back from her. I had wanted to be sure that the commotion and the surveillance and the search on her block had died down first.

"So the fortune-teller held your hoodie and my T-shirt and she closed her eyes. When she opened them, she told me that you and I would be together for a lifetime. The fortune-teller told me that you were at my side right then, and you will always be on my side in the future." Bangs was staring into my eyes, this time to judge if her story had gotten to me.

"Did you move my gun out of your house at any time while you had it?" I asked her seriously. Maybe I even frightened her.

"Now c'mon, don't try and play me. You know I'm better than that. Not only did I not move your gun, I didn't touch it. I don't know if you had bodies on it or not. Hmph, I know that much, Supastar. I ain't dumb," she said, and it sounded true. I got calmer some.

"So what do you think about what the fortune-teller said?" she asked, looking up into my eyes as though she wished she could read my mind.

"I think it's a hustle and that lady don't know what she's talking about."

"Then how did she know about Brittany's abortions?" Bangs asked, dragging me into her soap opera.

"I don't know. She could have known already. Maybe since Brittany's mother goes to the same lady, she confided that to her. You never know. The fortune-teller's goal is just to get thirty dollars from every customer. Think about it!" I scolded her.

"Uh-uh, 'cause why we went to her in the first place was because there was this lady on our block who had a son. Her little son was born with a straight line down the middle of his palm. I mean, it was a thick brown line that went straight through and over all of the other lines in his palm. Well, this fortune-teller told the lady that her son would not live past fourteen because of that line in his palm. And that boy was named Gregory Baker. He actually died on his fourteenth birthday, shot in the head at his own party by a jealous nigga. His mother told the story of what the fortune-teller had said at his funeral. So everybody in the neighborhood got worried. It was like we were all checking the lines in our palms, then going to her to get our fortunes told."

"Bangs, you're gonna be late getting home and I gotta go. But I want to get you some books like I said. So look around and show me what you like. I'm gonna look also. Then we'll see."

That's all I could give her. I had too much on my mind to consider anything deeper, so I left it at that. I could see that she and I were worlds apart in our state of mind. We were too far to close the gap. Still, I wanted to get her started thinking differently for her sake. Muslims don't believe that it is right to hide the knowledge and turn people away from Islam or to assume that anyone in the world cannot learn the straight and narrow path to Allah. So I had a duty to at least introduce her to the right way and leave the rest to Allah.

The faith section of Marty Bookbinder's store was the smallest of all the shelves. Marty had told me once over a game of chess that he didn't believe in God. I thought it was a strange confession because I knew that he was Jewish. I wondered how he could not believe in God, or for that matter Ibrahim, Musa, Jesus, and Mohammad, all prophets sent by Allah, peace be upon them. I am Muslim and we acknowledge all of Allah's prophets. I didn't debate Marty on his beliefs, didn't even comment. But after that, I looked down on him some.

I was able to find two copies of the Torah, the sacred book used by Jewish people, two copies of the Holy Bible as followed by Christian people, and two copies of the Holy Quran as followed by Muslim people. He also had the Gita, which I learned was followed by some people from India, and some Buddhist text as followed by some people throughout the Asian continent as well as other places in the world. I picked up one of the two copies of *The Communist Manifesto*, which was also there. I had never heard of it and was running out of time, so I put it back and chose a Holy Quran. I also purchased a copy of a slim, two-hundred-page softcover book titled *The Muslim Woman*. Easily I decided that these were the books I would gift her. I didn't want to think about if they were too much information for her or too difficult for her to read and understand. I just wanted to see what she would make happen in her own life.

Thinking further, Marty Bookbinder's beliefs were different from my own, but I respected that he was comfortable providing his customers with a wide range of choices in religions and philosophies and subjects that he didn' agree with.

It was almost closing before Bangs came up with her two book

choices. For half an hour I saw her picking books up and pushing
them back onto the shelves. She walked up to me with her choices,
looking unsure of what she selected but so confident about her body
and style. Like most women, her eyes always gave her away.

"Most of these books in here is boring," she said casually, catching
Marty's immediate attention.

"What kind of books do you like?" Marty asked her, while ringing up my order on his register.

"I don't know 'cause I don't really like reading." She was answering Marty but looking at me. "Why should I read some book when I
could be out doing something?"

"Maybe if you read the right book, you'll be out doing something
better," I told her. She smiled, stepped behind me, and leaned against
the back of my body. Marty tried to act like he wasn't watching, but
he was.

"Now I see why *we* didn't get to play chess tonight," Marty said,
while accepting and counting out my payment. I smiled and grabbed
our bags and said, "Your game is better in the afternoons anyway."
Marty laughed some and followed us halfway through the door. "Nice
to meet you, Tiffany. Drop by anytime. I'll get some new books in
here that you might like. Good night, my friends."

Outside I handed Bangs her new books. She took them and
stuffed her grandmother's dress in the bag also. "It seems like you
are always giving me something, Supastar. When you gonna give me
what I really want?"

"Slow down, shorty," I told her calmly.

She jumped up once, then shook her whole body and stamped
each foot, throwing a temper tantrum. "How could it get any slower?"
she asked. "You got me waiting, waiting, waiting. It be different if
nobody wasn't getting it, *but I know somebody is getting it.* It's just not
me! Here, take this. I want to give it to you."

She pointed to her front right jeans pocket. Her jeans were so
tight, I could see from the impression that she had something in
there. I wasn't falling for what she wanted, me to put my hand in her
snug pocket. That would be too much for me and she knew it. I didn't
respond. She used her slender fingers to drag it out.

"Those are my feelings." It was the music she had been listening
to on her Walkman, I figured.

"Nah I'm good," I told her, believing that in this case accepting her music would be the same as accepting her feelings for me. She leaped up and pushed the music in my pocket and laughed and ran. Now she wanted me to chase her. When I didn't, she ran back to me.

I checked my Datejust. "You got nine minutes to get home on time, Bangs," I reminded her.

"If you give me a kiss, Supastar, you don't have to walk me back. I promise I'll run straight home and beat the motherfucking clock!" She smiled mischievously, rocking back and forth on her Reeboks and then shifting side to side. She was always bursting with energy and couldn't keep still for more than a few seconds.

"I'll walk you back," I said, a subtle way of declining her enticing kissing offer. "But I'm not going inside your house, I'm telling you now. Matter of fact, I'll take the shortcut up to the back of your house. Then I gotta break out. I got something important to do."

"You won't say hi to my grandmother? She likes you *so much*. She asks about you all the time. Since you don't come around, Grandma be asking me, 'What did you do wrong to him?' And she been feeling sick lately. If she saw us together, she would probably cheer up."

"Nah, it's late. If she's sick, she should sleep. Don't give her a hard time either. If she's sick, you should be taking care of your baby instead of leaving her in the house."

"Oh, you remember my daughter?" Bangs said sarcastically.

"Who forgets a baby?" I asked. "Besides, your milk . . . ," I said, pointing to the spot on her thin blouse.

"I know. Every time it's time for her to suck, no matter where I'm at, my milk starts leaking and shooting out." She laughed at herself, a little embarrassed. But she didn't need to be embarrassed about that in front of me. It was that kind of thing that seduced me the most. It was being up close, and seeing and feeling that, that caused me to stay away. But she kept coming back.

At the back of Bangs's house I watched as she walked slowly on purpose through the alleyway that led to the front. She knew I was watching, so she swang her hips more for me. She kept glancing back at me and smiling. Soon as she stepped to turn the corner onto her stoop, I left.

I was close to the subway about to go down the stairs when Bangs came racing back without her bag of books. "They took her," she said, stopping short and her face the opposite of how it was only seconds ago.

"My grandmother! The ambulance came and took her." Bangs was gasping, and tears were welling up in her eyes.

"Then she gotta be at the closest hospital. Take it easy. Did you lock up your house?" I asked her.

"No, I never went in the house. My neighbor, Mrs. King, was sitting right there on my stoop waiting for me. She said the ambulance came and took my grandmother, and that my uncle took the baby!" Her body began trembling. "Mrs. King said that she had offered to hold the baby till I got right back, but my uncle said no and took my daughter. Mrs. King said she didn't argue with him 'cause she could smell the liquor on him and didn't want him to start acting crazy like she knew he would. I'm gonna kill him!" Bangs spoke with a forceful tone but not a loud voice, as though she truly meant it.

"He probably went up to the hospital to see about your grandmother. She's *his* mother, right? Don't worry. He'll bring the baby right back. What's he gonna do with an infant who needs breast milk?" I said, trying to console her. But she gave me a flat stare. Without any words, she reminded me with her eyes that her uncle was her rapist. Her uncle was a man who never worried about pleasing his mother or protecting his family. In fact, he was the biggest threat to all of them. And except for her trembling, Bangs was finally standing still, face stiff with anger, spilling hot tears.

"He didn't take the baby to keep her safe. He took her to control me, to make me do whatever *he say*. That's what *he does*. He wouldn't even go and check on Grandma. That's how he do," she said, as though she was 100 percent sure that she was right.

I checked my watch but I really didn't have to. I knew for certain it was time for me to go get Umma. I peeled a twenty from the pile I had in my pocket and handed it to Bangs. "Take a taxi to the closest hospital. Go and check everything out first, before you panic."

"Are you coming with me?" she asked, as I knew she would. *Her uncle is the baby's father*, I thought to myself about the sickening truth. And even though I felt for Bangs, and hated her uncle and liked her infant daughter and grandmother, I put Umma first, *my mother* and *my purpose*.

I left.

Chapter 16
SON, FATHER, GRANDFATHER

Back at our apartment, after Umma was sleeping, I sat down on my bed thinking about my life while holding the new Sony Handycam that Ameer and Chris had bought for me. It was the latest model, an HDR-XR100. Studying the device, the buttons and attachments, I unfolded the user's manual and glanced it over. Akemi didn't like cameras too much, I believed. As an artist, her eyes and mind were her camera, and her gifted hands recreated the images that her eyes and mind saw through drawings and paintings.

How do I feel about cameras? I wondered to myself. I had never relied on them and neither had my father or grandfather. The images of my past in the Sudan were bright and colorful and powerfully clear, as though I could step right inside them and begin reliving every scene. But if I had known that there would be so many miles and meters between my father and grandfather and me, separated by continents, would I be happier if I had filmed them and could project them right onto the wall of my bedroom? Would Umma be happier if she could see my father on film when she was sitting all alone in her bedroom? Would Naja be happy if she could see a moving picture of our father instead of having to move her imaginings around in her head, full of the flaws of not really knowing or even having the pleasure of remembering?

A smile stretched across my face naturally when I thought of my Southern Sudanese grandfather. He wouldn't even give me the option of taking his photo or filming him. He was an expert at refusals. When he said no he meant it, no negotiations or backpedaling. In fact he only had one picture on the wall of his hut. It was of a European missionary man who, Southern Grandfather said, came from Europe "talking that Jesus talk with his eyes on our women and foot on our land and hands all over the place." The missionary man's photo was posted right beside a few locks of his blond hair and a rawhide strip with the missionary's teeth, fingers, and toes and his dried-out "lying tongue" dangling in the middle like a flesh jerky pendant. My grandfather, a respected elder and counsel in his village, husband of six wives and father of nineteen children, my father the youngest one, only wore his necklace featuring the missionary's demise when he needed to remind ambitious villagers or intrusive outsiders of what he was capable of and how much influence he carried and how fearless he was in the face of the British or of the presumptuous Arabs, or any pushy intruders, for that matter.

My Southern Sudanese grandfather's voice was so deep, he made the walls rattle and the snakes slide and escape deep into the ground. He never ate refrigerated or frozen foods, drank his milk straight from the udder. He never had ice cream or pizza or any modern food inventions, not because he couldn't, but strictly because he didn't want to. He was not a friend to change and believed that *change* and *progress* were two completely different words.

Although Umma's father and father's father and so on were all born and raised Muslim in the Islamic way of life, my Southern Sudanese grandfather was slightly different. He said that Allah existed from the beginning of time, before Prophet Muhammad (peace be upon him), and the revelation of the Holy Quran. He said that there was a time when man did not need a prophet to tell him and show him what to do. "That was the time of real men," Southern Grandfather claimed. Then he would hold his hands up as evidence of his claim, as though his palms contained the story of the beginning of civilization. He would show the back of his hands first and then the front. *Both* sides of his huge hands were black. Even his palms were black and the lines in his palms even blacker. "I am the original black man, not a photocopy."

According to Southern Grandfather, man was born in the image of Allah with all that he needed already. "These legs are for walking," he would say, showing his aged yet powerful legs that held him up to six feet ten inches tall. "The trouble begins when a man stops walking with these legs and begins riding around." So Southern Grandfather never rode in a car or truck. Even when his closest relatives offered him rides, he refused. And that was the natural way of Southern Grandfather—who never traveled any further than his own legs would carry him—and the difference between him and his nineteenth child, my father. My father was the only child of my grandfather who dared to race way ahead of his own father and accomplish things that his father could never imagine, not because his father was stupid, but simply because he didn't want to.

My father bowed down to Allah and acknowledged the Prophet Muhammad (peace be upon him). My father read and recited from the Quran and even led other men to do so. My father moved to Northern Sudan, married Umma, a Northern Sudanese woman not of his region or tribe.

I never repeated my grandfather's philosophies and criticisms to Umma. I just held them in my mind and weighed them out word for word. Then I followed closely, and with deep feeling and loyalty, the path of my father. It was the easiest thing to do because my father admired Southern Grandfather so incredibly and we visited the south of Sudan so often, every year, every summer for the entire season. It seemed to me that my father and his father were separated only by small talking differences. I saw both of them bow down to the same and only God, Allah.

While everyone everywhere hailed my father up as a great man—young, brilliant, and influential, a well-educated and well-traveled adviser—my grandfather would say with sincere concern and certainty that "each generation has become weaker rather than stronger. It is a son's job to be better than his father, not more dependent and more useless."

When I would watch silently and listen closely, I couldn't imagine how I could possibly ever be a better man than my father or even my grandfather, especially now that I was living in America on this foreign land of foreign ways. I was certain that it was next to impossible. Still, I was doing my best, passionately.

Chapter 17
SERIOUS-MINDED

I began packing my duffel bag for my trip. I needed the space the duffel provided because I was bringing three brand-new pairs of kicks and wanted to leave them in the boxes they came in. Also, the Timberlands always took up more than enough space, yet I couldn't see traveling without crispy beef and broccolis. I would rock my Clarks on the plane for comfort, so I didn't need to pack them. I folded my shirts exact like how they are displayed in the store. I made a separate pile for jeans and slacks and my workout clothes. My suit was hanging in my closet still in the suit bag that I purchased for travel. When I looked down, I saw Akemi's ostrich-skin stilettos standing up straight as though her pretty feet were still in them. I wrapped them in tissue paper and laid them inside my duffel bag for some reason that I didn't know yet.

Memories mushroomed to fantasies and fantasies slipped into sleep. I had one last conscious pull at resistance but I gave in, a voice from the distance reminding me that I had to rise up early on this same morning. Thursday would be my last chance to finalize all the Umma Designs deliveries. Despite all the emotion and shock that had gripped my family this week, Umma had managed to complete three more orders. So of course I would handle my business and get it to the customer and collect their final payments.

Thursday, May 8th, 1986

Some hours later I woke up. The Fajr prayer that normally came naturally like sunrise was a problem for me this morning. Even after the shower that shook me into consciousness, I couldn't concentrate. A thousand different thoughts and dilemmas raced around my head and danced through the words of my prayer and trampled the feeling in it. For some reason, I couldn't express myself spiritually at the moment. So I stopped speaking the words of the prayer and kept my head to the ground. Very slowly, the chaos of my mind began to settle. The loud thoughts and voices simmered until there was silence. I felt it would be better to be silent and still than to be halfhearted, half-true, half-false. Many minutes passed before I eased up into a straight stance.

"What's wrong with you?" Naja gave me these words as her morning greeting.

"Nothing, let's go."

I walked her to Ms. Marcy's and onto the bus. "That's three days this week," she said, smiling. "That means from now on, you have to walk me to the bus even though Ms. Marcy is here, okay?"

"We'll see," I answered.

Her little eyes followed me through each bus window until she reached her seat. She pressed her face against the window and smiled again. I nodded.

I walked Ms. Marcy back to her apartment on the ground floor. Once I heard her turn her locks, I opted to take the stairs up to avoid the morning rush and long wait for the elevator.

*   *   *

In the gray lighting of the stairwell, I came up on a nigga named Lance. He had been locked up for molesting some little girl in my building a little over a year ago. Some lawmakers somehow must've made up a reason to let him out. In the Sudan we would have cut off his hands first and then his head. Now I could see his chest and arms were swolled from the repetition of prison push-ups. He was coming down the stairs feeling like a man and casting a dark shadow that darkened an already dim space. No matter how swolled he got, to me he would remain a mouse, a conqueror of young girls, the lowest form of life. His smirk was smug. If I was sleepy before, *now* I was fully alert. My clip was empty but my mind was fully loaded. I looked him dead in his eyes to let him know I didn't need no prison to make my body hard and fists furious. I trained hard and stayed ready. Guns or no guns, I would send him back to meet his maker, easily.

I was going up. He was going down. We passed on the same step with only a centimeter separating our shoulders. As he passed I felt a cold chill in a warm stairwell where there was already very little oxygen and the stench of piss as strong as bleach, as though the pisser had never had even one cup of water in his lifetime. Lance didn't say shit, not a grunt or a groan. Words were not necessary. Some men never understand words that are being spoken. They only react to actions being done.

After opening all the locks that sealed the door of our apartment, I locked them behind me and went directly to Umma's room, knocking on her door.

"Nom," she said. Some of her latest designs were lying across her bed, others draped from hangers on her closet door. The tissue paper and boxes were out. Her incense was nearly finished burning. She was in the process of wrapping the completed and scented items for me to deliver.

"After that, pack your bag for your stay at the apartment we rented from the Ghazzalis. Then pack Naja's also," I said solemnly. Her face changed from casual and pleasant to a knowing and willing obedience. Instead of asking me a hundred questions about why she was packing two days before my plane left and before she was originally planning to move to the Ghazzalis, she simply responded, "I will."

Since it was still very early morning, I called Sudana, hoping to catch her before she left for school.

"Sudana," I said, recognizing her voice immediately and knowing by now that she liked to be the one who answered their family phone calls.

"Salaam," she answered.

"I need you to do me a favor" was all I said.

"Anything," she responded softly.

"Would you watch Naja for me today at four forty-five if I bring her by your house?"

"Surely."

"I'll see you then," I told her.

"I'll be waiting." We hung up.

I put three bullets in the clip before I hugged Umma and headed out to work with the Umma Designs delivery items. In the building lobby, I shot by Ms. Marcy's apartment.

"Ms. Marcy, I'll pick Naja up from her bus stop this afternoon. So you enjoy your day off." I handed her the pay for the week plus her money for the upcoming week, since I planned to be away.

"Why so much?" she asked, her face looking genuinely puzzled at the break in our usual routine. "Is something wrong?"

"Everything is good, Ms. Marcy. Please don't worry. Naja will be visiting some relatives of ours for about a week to ten days."

"Relatives? Naja didn't mention *none* of this to me."

"She couldn't have. It's a surprise," I told her, placing my finger over my mouth to give Ms. Marcy the impression that she was part of the secret.

"Naja will go to and from school from their home. I'm paying you because my mother loves you and we want you to continue working with our family. Now if I didn't pay you in advance and Naja just suddenly disappeared, by the time she returned, you would have found another job!" I joked and forced a smile.

"Yeah, right! Who else but your pretty momma is hiring an older lady? *And* I get to work at home! Not to mention Naja is just so smart and curious and busy. She helps me stay young. And don't you try to charm me, young man." She laughed lightly.

"Ms. Marcy, this stuff is heavy. I gotta run. Just relax until I contact you. I'll give you a heads-up when Naja comes back, okay?"

"Okay, honey," she said sweetly, her curiosity softening now with a look of trust. I left after hearing her lock on her door clicking shut.

Chapter 18
SENSEI

On point for my private lesson at the dojo, I arrived fifteen minutes early at 12:45 in the afternoon. Sensei unlocked the door and then let it drop before I could actually get inside and face him. Like normal, I went straight to the locker room and got myself prepared. It wasn't long before I heard Sensei's office door open back up and him moving around in the next room.

"*Konichiwa*, Sensei," I greeted him in Japanese, as I glanced over at the table. Whatever he had over there, rope or knives or *kunai* or ninja gear, was always a preview of the private lesson of the day. On the table was a tall bottle of alcohol and a dingy white briefcase that was plastered with a large sticker that read FIRST AID. Sensei said, "*Konichiwa, gakusei*," which means "Good afternoon, my student."

"First things first, Sensei. I showed up early for class today to let you know that I won't be here next week. I know the dojo policy, so I'm prepared to pay up front for the lessons and make them up the following week."

"Hmm, this would be the first time in several years that you have made this kind of request. May I ask the reason for your absence?" His face looked stern.

"I just have to take care of something personal. Once it's completed, I'll be back fully focused, no problem," I assured him.

"Something personal?" Sensei said with quiet anger, as though he was having an imbalance in his yin-yang. "What could be more personal than me teaching you the way of ninjutsu?" he asked quietly, yet pronouncing each syllable of each word with an extra emphasis to make himself clear.

Instead of responding, I watched him as he shifted from standing in a straight up-and-down position to having his legs spread in a more open stance as though he was about to leap. Then he moved both of his hands and held them behind him.

"Is there someone else teaching you how to defend your life? Perhaps there is another master elsewhere teaching you how to eliminate your enemies?"

I didn't have a response. I struck my stance and prepared for battle although I was unclear what went wrong and certain it couldn't be some sudden shit just because I unexpectedly rescheduled a few classes.

"Your silence is not welcomed today. Today your silence is offensive to me." He made a swift move, bringing his right hand forward. As I monitored his right hand moving slowly in front of him, he quickly used his left hand and threw his *kunai* at me. Instinctively I leaned to my right, causing his blade to miss me completely. I felt and heard it slicing the air. It didn't crash to the floor, so I was certain that it lodged on the corkboards that Sensei had mounted on the walls. But I never turned to look behind me. I dropped down to the floor instead and kicked the table over to shield myself in case Sensei had more knives. It is the way of the ninja to make his weapons invisible to his opponent, so I knew that it didn't matter that I did not see Sensei's *kunai*.

"Stand up," Sensei said, peering down on me sheltered behind the table.

But I was not a new warrior and I wasn't falling for that shit.

Resisting his command, I eased up, holding the table in both of my hands. Without hesitation or notice I suddenly rushed into Sensei, backing him up and ultimately pressing him against the wall with the weight of the table. My strength was greater than his. My arms and my wingspan were longer and more powerful.

Then Sensei dropped down to the floor and leaped through my legs with the ease of a frog. Before I could turn or release the table and clear myself from its fall, I could feel the blow to the back of my neck, and I fell forward against the falling table. I broke my fall and rolled over backward and was up on my feet in an instant. Sensei had ran toward his *kunai*, which was lodged in the opposite wall.

He seized it and threw it again. It landed in my left shoulder and the blood came quickly. Immediately I pulled it out and precisely threw it at him the way that he had taught me to wield it. He jumped midair to avoid the spinning *kunai*, but it caught him in his ankle. He dropped to the floor. Before he could raise himself, I jumped on him, tackled, and held him from behind. My forearm was around his throat. My leg was much longer than his and I used it to pin down his ankle purposely at the point of his injury. I knew that shit had to be hurting him, but he didn't make any noise, still struggling using only his body. I loosened my grip on his throat intentionally and used my left hand to undo his knot. I used his own hair to choke him instead. When it was clear that I had the best of him, I dragged and then yanked him by his hair to the wall. He twisted his dragging body, loosening himself from the hair choke by spinning. He stood up.

In his eyes I could see the impact and damage of my dominance over him in this one, fourteen-second encounter. But Sensei did not count himself out. I saw his eyes shift toward the bloodied *kunai* lying on the floor. As he dived to grab his weapon, I seized the rope that was mounted on the wall.

As Sensei attempted a *kunai* toss from the lying-down position, my swift movement landed my foot on his wrist, my big toe pressing against his ulnar artery, causing the *kunai* to be released. As he grabbed my ankle with his left hand, I moved my foot off his wrist and kicked the *kunai* across the floor in one swift motion. Now he used both hands to capture my feet, causing me to lose my balance. I went with the fall instead of breaking or resisting it, threw my weight against him and tied him up with his rope, using the method that he had once taught me and successfully and used against me also.

When you conquer a man's mind, he's finished. Sensei knew there was no reason for him to struggle further at this point. His ninjutsu rope style was so expert that the more an opponent struggled, the more the ropes trapped and confined him.

When I had him trapped and secured and in the posture of a fetus, I rolled over facing him. The pressure on my shoulder shot through my body and I was only now noticing the blood streaming from my shoulder slice.

"What the fuck?" I asked him politely.

"You learned well," he said calmly, although his chest was still pulling in and out. His rapid breathing seemed to come from his anguish more than from the difficulty of our encounter.

Sensei's face was strangely empty. I would say it was a 180-degree difference from the faces that black men make when we battle, kill, or hustle hard, like in a basketball game or fight. Our expressions are dramatic and contorted, but not Sensei's.

"You are so ungrateful. You are the reason why master teachers returned to the mountains and shut their mouths and died with their techniques unknown," Sensei stated.

"What?" I asked. I *really* didn't know what the fuck he was talking about. I wasn't even clear if this wasn't just a combat test during a private lesson. I did know that his anger felt real. Yet he obviously wasn't trying to kill me. He could have easily thrown that knife through my heart. But he was definitely trying to hurt me, shake me up some. His kick to the back of my neck came with full intent and traction. It hurt.

I stood up, ignoring his senseless accusation. I picked up the first-aid kit from the floor, where it was busted open. I closed it, sat it down, and kicked it over toward him. "You want me to put something on that ankle?" I asked him politely. "No, put it on your shoulder instead," he said with a half smile. He had put that kit out here on the table preparing for my private lesson. *So he must have planned to attack me, hurt me, and then patch me up,* I thought to myself.

The alcohol bottle had rolled into a corner. I went and got it, cracked it open, and poured it onto Sensei's sliced ankle. I know it burned but he didn't flinch. I opened the first-aid kit and grabbed the gauze and wrapped and taped his ankle nicely. I grabbed another piece for myself and stood. I left the training area and walked to the locker room.

In the locker room I took off my *dogi* and tended to my shoulder. It was still bleeding but I didn't consider it nothing severe. I just protected it from infection, splashed on some alcohol, and wrapped it. I changed into my street clothes. I fastened my watch and saw that I had a whole hour and forty-five minutes remaining for this private lesson. All that shit between me and Sensei happened in less than fifteen minutes. But I considered that Sensei wouldn't want to continue with today's lesson, being that I was sure our encounter had not gone how he had planned it. I took my heat from my dojo locker and tucked it in my waist beneath my shirt and also retrieved my cutter, then returned to the training room to see what was happening with Sensei. I picked up his bloodied knife and began cleaning it off with alcohol.

"Untie me," Sensei ordered.

"First tell me what is going on. Is this the class for today, my private lesson?" I turned up the table and laid the clean *kunai* on top.

"It's your turn to do the telling," Sensei said, still serious even though this time he was defeated instead of me. "I have been telling you everything I know. You have been telling me nothing. You are ungrateful and arrogant in the worse kind of way."

"Arrogant?" I said, surprised. I didn't see myself that way. I worked hard to be calm, restrained, and quiet. There was no conceit in me and I never show off. I wondered if men confuse confidence with arrogance. Sensei's charge seemed false, so I said nothing.

"Your distrust of your teacher is arrogance. Your acceptance of my knowledge while being completely unwilling to make any kind of exchange of your own knowledge is arrogance," he said.

"Your knowledge is in exchange for payment. This is the reason you charge student fees, right or wrong, Sensei?" I reminded him.

"Again, arrogance," Sensei repeated his accusation.

I reached in and cut his rope with my cutter. It sliced through the thick, rough rope like butter. I didn't want my weapon to be invisible. I wanted Sensei to see my blade and yield.

"Carrying a gun when your hands and heart and feet and mind are already trained in death is arrogance also!" he continued.

"You don't live where I live," I answered him calmly and with absolute confidence.

"Do you think an Asian man can set up a training camp in the middle of Brooklyn surrounded by dark bodies, clouded minds, and troubled souls and survive without knowing something about the streets?" Sensei asked in an unfamiliar melody, his voice holding even one moment and then rising suddenly before falling flat again.

"Don't you realize that every teen out here who ever saw even one Bruce Lee movie wants to test my skill?" he asked strangely.

"What does this have to do with me?" I questioned him sincerely.

"If there is a man or woman out here in this chaotic world who is willing and capable to give you the information you need to not become a forgotten statistic and victim, the least you can do is respect him," he said calmly. "Humble yourself," he commanded in a more forceful voice.

"I do respect you. I spend most of my free time here training under you, Sensei."

"So what proof is there that you trust me any degree more than any other adult who walks past you every day without a word to you or concern for your life or death?" he asked.

I thought carefully about his question. I guess I didn't come up with an answer swift enough. Now Sensei stood up from the floor and casually stated, "You owe me a new rope."

"No problem. See you at class tonight, Sensei. I hope you'll be feeling better later on tonight." I turned to exit, bored with Sensei's indirectness. I had so much mess on my mind that I could not decipher his brainteasers.

"Do you really think that you can do Japan all by yourself, without a friend or ally or even a basic understanding of the language or culture?" He was speaking to my back, but I heard him loud and clear. His question caused me to break my stride for half a second, but then I picked it back up again and continued walking across the floor to leave, believing that Sensei was trying to delve deeper into my business than I wanted to allow him.

"Miss Akemi Nakamura called me," Sensei said coyly. "She called me on Sunday and Monday and Tuesday and Wednesday. And she even phoned this morning, Thursday." Sensei knew *these* words would stop me completely, and they did.

I turned to face him, genuinely surprised at the completely unexpected news. I had no way to measure how much Sensei knew and how much he didn't know about my wife, her father, and our situation. I had wanted to move in complete silence and anonymity as usual and on purpose, but now there was a path connecting my sensei and Akemi's father, which meant that any unexpected action I took against her father, if investigated, would lead back to me. Whenever something deadly occurs not performed by one person alone and not concealed from every single other living being, the threat of its being uncovered is extremely high. I never want to strike in this situation. I was being reminded once again that the battle between me and my wife's father had to remain a battle of the mind, a thought battle, no blades or gunpowder of fists or feet even. My mind understood my situation; still it was difficult for me to fully accept.

"What did my wife say to you?" I asked solemnly.

"Oh, you trained her well. She was particularly polite yet quiet. She didn't say much, just asked if you had been to the dojo, and if you were here at that moment. I asked her to leave her telephone number. She refused, saying only that she was calling from Japan."

"What time did she normally call you?" I asked, thinking.

"She called at a different time each day. Then today when I told her you were not here yet, she became desperate. She left the telephone number for a friend of hers who she said speaks English. She asked me to pass it along to you so that she and you could arrange a way and a time to talk."

"Will you give it to me?" I asked, knowing Sensei now had the upperhand.

"Of course I will, but it would have been better if you had told me what was happening from the beginning, so that I could help. I waited every day this week for you to say it to me yourself. I wanted you to say it to me because you trust me, because you have known me, because I have trusted you, because I have trained you, but you did not. And then today you walked in here and revealed how little you think of me, by announcing that you would be out for one week. You underestimated me, as though I could and would *never* piece together what was happening."

Some seconds slipped by with silence. I figured this was the point where I was supposed to apologize to Sensei. But, for me, it didn't feel right or real. I wasn't sorry that I had learned the way of the ninja from my teacher and followed it so closely that I became offensive to the man who taught it to me.

So I said instead, "Sensei, please tell me what I need to do, how I need to train to set everything right with you and me. When I get back, I'll do it. I'll work hard at it." This was my compromise.

"I have a feeling that you're not coming back. I have a sense that this is the last time I'll see you."

"Impossible," I said with certainty. "I'll be in class tonight at eight." I smiled, then turned to leave.

"You have one hour and thirty-nine minutes remaining on today's private lesson. First follow me to my office for that phone number." I followed him, glad that he didn't require me to press or beg him for Akemi's information.

"Here." He slid a book across the table to me. I picked it up. *Never Surrender: The Unauthorized Biography of Naoko Nakamura, An American Nemesis.* I studied the book cover, then looked up at Sensei.

"Your wife's friend who speaks English is named Iwa Ikeda. She lives in Tokyo. Her telephone number is written inside on the bookmark." Immediately I opened the book and I checked for her name and number. I found it.

"In Japan, males call female acquaintances by their last name as a form of respect, unless the lady introduces herself by her first name. Then it's okay to use it. When you phone, you should address her as Ikeda-san, instead of by her first name." Sensei taught me something I did not know.

"I have one more thing for you." He stooped down a bit to open a drawer close to the floor. He handed me a second book; *Peculiar People: The Japanese Way* was the title.

"You will need to learn the Japanese way if you want to remain married to a Japanese girl and her family. Japan is a different society than America. Their way of thinking and living is completely different down to the smallest detail. If you try and reason with a Japanese person without knowing the Japanese way, you will lose." Sensei reached into his pocket and pulled out a business card. "Here is the card of a good friend of mine. He runs a dojo out in Takadanobaba. He has about one hundred fifty students. If you need to train or work out or if you need some help, just mention my name and he will open doors for you."

"Takadanobaba?" I repeated the six syllables.

"It's a prefecture in Tokyo. You *are* going to Japan, aren't you?" he asked. Now Sensei was being direct, but I needed time to figure out my strategy before just giving up all of my well-guarded information.

"I'm just gonna give this girl Ikeda-san a call and speak with my wife. Akemi's just worried because she has been calling me at home and not getting through because my whole family has been working hard, sometimes even two jobs," I explained.

"I see," Sensei said with slight suspicion. Ignoring my indirect denial, Sensei added, "Before you go, let me caution you. Japan is a magical place, completely unique. Many foreigners go there and never want to return to their homes."

"But you are here in the US, Sensei, and you have not ever mentioned returning home," I challenged him. My words were true.

"Be sure to read both of those books. In Japan there are more than thirty-five thousand suicides each year. The Japanese people look upon suicide differently than the Americans. I am mentioning this to you because your wife's voice sounded sad and it became sadder each time that she contacted me." He gave me a serious stare. For the first time in all my encounters of today, I became afraid. I turned away from the mind search he was conducting on me. Instead I flashed through the pages of one of the books in my hand. I wasn't reading. It was just a diversion.

"I didn't leave Japan because it was not magical or unique to me," Sensei said and then paused. "I didn't return to Japan because the Japanese way is hard on the Japanese. We are expected to all do the same things the same way, and when one of us is different from the majority, we pay a heavy price, sometimes with our lives. Your wife, in choosing you and coming from the background that she comes from and the place where she was born and raised, has done something extremely different, and I am sure that many of the people closest to her are making her suffer because of it. I hope that you don't take her life lightly. After meeting and listening to and watching her, it seemed that she did trade it all in for you."

I lowered my head, an unusual but honest reaction.

"My own brother is one in that huge suicide statistic. He was born mentally challenged. *He was different.* Japan did not open its heart to him. He was isolated and ignored until he decided that death was better than life. I came here to America bringing along everything that is great about Japan with me, and leaving the rest behind."

Sensei placed his hand on his chest and said solemnly, "In my heart, I have to believe that there is hope for the underdog. Every day I awaken, I want to stand beside the man who is *not* expected to win."

Without regard to either of our injuries, Sensei led me in an intense one-hour session on "resisting torture," the separation of the mind from the physical pains and desire that your body is experiencing during torture. My sensei's lessons were incredible to me. I could actually feel the warrior within myself strengthening. And despite anything that my Japanese teacher may have believed, I *was* showing him respect my way; by listening intently to *his* instruction, following *his* example, and mastering even the smallest details of *his* techniques.

Chapter 19
SUDANA SALIM AHMED AMIN

Standing still on my Brooklyn block, something I don't ordinarily do, I waited for Naja's school bus to pull up. Although lots of kids were getting back from school, Naja's bus was green, not yellow, and stood out because it had "Khadijah's Islamic School for Girls" displayed on the whole of one side.

"Where's Ms. Marcy?" Naja asked smiling.

"Your big brother is here instead," I teased her. "C'mon." I held her hand and walked her over to the cab waiting on the curb where I had been standing. Umma was inside, the meter was running, and their suitcases were in the trunk.

"Hey, where are we going? Umi Umma!" Naja crawled into the cab and threw her arms around Umma, causing her to push back against her seat. Naja kissed all over Umma's face as Umma laughed and tried to gently push her off. Naja's book bag fell onto the cab floor. I closed their door and then jumped into the front seat. The Bangladeshi driver's experienced eyes surveyed me carefully. Without words he let me observe that I was not supposed to be in his front seat. Without words I remained, pulled some cash out my pocket, and began counting it to calm him down.

I directed him to Umma's job and instructed him to wait. By then the meter read $19.50 so I peeled off a twenty and handed it to him. "Wait here, I'll be right back and pay you double. My suitcases are in your trunk, so don't pull off." I let him see me looking at his driver's identification number and photo posted on his dashboard.

"No problem, you are good customer," he said.

"Allah hafiz," I said, a small sign to him that we are all Muslims and he should simply do his job and act honorably with us.

I told Naja to get out so we would both walk Umma inside. There was no way I would leave her sitting and waiting in the cab while I escorted Umma.

"Oh man, I thought we were all going out to eat or to do something fun. This is Umma's job again!" she complained softly.

* * *

"Pop the trunk," I told the driver when Naja and I arrived at Mr. Ghazzali's house in the Bronx. "Come out, Naja."

"Suitcases? Okay, what's going on?" she asked me.

"You'll see," I told her. Then, before I could knock on the fence or ring the bell, Sudana opened it, all smiles as if she didn't have one problem in the world.

"Salaam alaikum, Sudana! You told me to come back soon and visit you. I wasn't planning on it, but I guess I am here," Naja said playfully.

"Don't you like my house? I made sure I got here early just so I could see you," Sudana said to Naja.

"Me or my brother?" Naja asked smartly.

"Both of you!" Sudana embraced it.

"Is your father home?" I asked her.

"Laysa," Sudana said, meaning no. "Everybody in my house is either at work or school."

"Aight, so I'll put these suitcases downstairs and then I'll leave. I got the key," I told Sudana.

"Leave?" Naja said, surprised.

"Sudana has agreed to watch you while I'm out and while Umma is at work," I explained.

"Then what are the suitcases for?" Naja pushed.

"When I get back tonight, I'll explain everything to you, okay?" Naja nodded yes but pouted also.

I opened the side door to the basement apartment and brought the suitcases inside. Sudana and Naja both followed me instead of going in the front door and remaining upstairs in the house, which is what I expected them to do.

"Aren't you two going upstairs?" I asked.

"Yes, I'll take Naja up. I cooked something for her. I know you're hungry after school and all, right?" Sudana asked Naja.

"Yep, long as it's good!" Naja answered.

"Tell Sudana thank you," I corrected Naja. "You already know that it's good because Sudana cooked it."

Sudana's smile lit up the dim basement. Her hazel eyes sparkled like pretty marbles or glow-in-the-dark trinkets.

"C'mon, let's go up," I told them. Sudana followed me. Naja followed Sudana.

Outside in the warm air I watched them go in the front door. Sudana turned toward me and asked, "Can you come inside for a minute?"

"Since your father is not here, I'll just leave now," I told her with certainty.

"It's important, just for three minutes," Sudana said, and then made the kind of face that older people make when they don't want to speak freely in front of a child.

So I said, "Okay, three minutes and then I gotta go."

Inside, Sudana whisked Naja away into a back room, the kitchen, I guessed. I heard the plates and cups clinking and then heard a television come on, a loud commercial blaring out before Sudana must've lowered the volume. I heard Naja's little hands clapping because she is never allowed to watch television when we are in our Brooklyn apartment.

Sudana emerged alone. "Would you take off your shirt, please?" she requested.

"What?"

"Take it off. I need to see something," she said with a straight face.

"Nah. I'm out," I told her.

"On the back of your shirt there is a small spot of blood. It seemed fresh and I want to see your wound," she said as though she were a medical professional. "I can take care of it for you. I'm going to become a doctor in the future, and my sister, Basima, is already in medical school and training to become a doctor also, so I know well how to treat a wound. Please, sit down and let me look at it."

"Not in your father's house," I denied her.

"Okay then, we'll step downstairs to your apartment. It is yours for the month, right?" she said, smiling politely, not like a come-on but as if she were already a nurse. She left the room and returned with a medical bag. I figured it had to be Basima's bag.

"It will be quick, I promise. Oh, but it does depend on how bad it is. If it is something I cannot handle, I'll send you to straight to the hospital."

"It's not that serious," I assured her. "I'm definitely not going to the hospital."

"Follow me," she said. She opened the door that led to the basement apartment and went down six steps. She turned around facing me and said, "You can sit here on the step so we can hear Naja if she calls us or comes." Sudana flipped a switch and a bright light shined down on the stairs. She was standing over me and I was seated.

"Take it off. I won't look at you as a man. I will look at you only as a patient."

I didn't believe her. *Women are all emotion*, I thought to myself, recalling my father's lessons. Yet I found myself cooperating with her anyway. I reminded myself that last time she had put me to sleep using some strange technique and pressing down on the center of my head with her two fingers.

I pulled off my shirt. She saw my gun. I moved it out from my waist and laid it down on the stairs beside me, facing the wall. When my chest and shoulder and back were bare, Sudana looked at me like a woman looks at a man. I could feel her heart softening. I could see it also in her eyes. She caught herself and redirected her energy. She began unwrapping the cut from my duel with Sensei. When she saw the whole thing, she suddenly made a sound, *ssssss*, sucking the air in through her teeth, as though the wound was worse than she expected, and as if she felt my pain also. The sound she made with her mouth made me feel something that I was trying not to feel. She opened her medical bag and used her free hand to begin searching through the items inside.

"Wait one minute," she said. "I'll be right back."

She returned with a needle and a cigarette lighter and some hefty thread. "You need stitches," she said confidently. She set herself up on the stairs.

She cleaned my wound first. The cold alcohol against my warm skin and her light touch and gentle rub with the clean cotton felt way better than when I had wrapped the wound myself. She flicked on the lighter and burned the tip of the needle until it turned black. Then she swiped the thread with alcohol and threaded her now sterilized sewing needle.

"This is going to hurt a little but help a lot," she said softly, standing so close to me that I could feel her body heat separate from the warmth of the atmosphere. She stood so close that I could see the texture of her pretty lips and smell her seductive Sudanese scent. She pierced my skin with the needle, and it pinched but wasn't nothing to me really.

"I gave you ten stitches. You really only needed eight, but just to be sure. When you leave on your trip, Akemi can take your stitches out. I can write her a note and tell her exactly how to do it. Or maybe she knows how to do it already?" Sudana said, smiling. She was a subtle and seductive teenaged female. I understood all her hidden messages even though I never acknowledged them. Looking up at her, I broke out in my first genuine smile of my day.

"So handsome," Sudana whispered. "Please don't smile at me." She packed up her medical bag quickly. The second she had it all organized, she brushed by me, climbing the six stairs and flicking off the light as she moved up.

"Put your shirt back on," she gently ordered me.

"I'm sorry," she apologized while my back was toward her.

"For what?" I asked her without turning around.

"I tried, but I ended up looking at you as a man, not as a patient," she said softly. Switching to Arabic, she added, "Now I can never take back what I've seen and what I felt, and I don't even want to." Our language, in this situation, seated in the dark staircase of her home, aroused me.

I threw my shirt on swiftly and stood right up. "Sudana," I called her back. "I'm gonna lock this door from the inside and go down here to make my prayer. I'll leave from out the side exit, okay?"

She nodded knowingly. As Muslim, we needed prayer to keep our minds right and our actions also.

"When I ring your bell, meet me outside so you can lock your fence. Oh, and thank you, for healing me," I told her. She smiled and moved her eyes away.

When I pressed her bell, she came to the door alone. She handed me a man's shirt without looking at me. "It's my older brother's shirt.

You can wear it for now since you have that blood spot on the back of your shirt still."

"Thanks, but I'm good. I'll take care of it," I said.

Outside in the sunlight she seemed embarrassed to look at me, even though now she had seen much more of me than she was ever supposed to. So I didn't stare at her either. I shifted my eyes and said, "I'll see you. I mean, I'll see your family tonight when I bring my Umma."

On my way to practice I picked up a new shirt and white tee from a random shop. I stuffed my old shirt with the blood spot in my back pocket and just rocked it like that. I wasn't about to leave my clothes at any woman's house who was not my wife from here on in. In my mind I pictured crazy-ass Bangs taking my hoodie to some zany fortune-teller and started laughing, even though I was alone.

Chapter 20
FRIENDS

"Your left shoulder is moving a little slow, my man!" Vega yelled to me. "If you got one good shoulder and one good hand, you better practice shooting with them. Like I told all you players, if you gotta fight or fuck, do it after the game, not before. I need all of you to be in top condition to make me look good!"

After basketball practice, Bangs didn't show up uninvited like she normally would. Only my eyes did a quick and thorough search. I didn't move one other muscle or limb to go looking for her. I had dojo tonight and everything in my Thursday schedule was back to back. I left the gym in a pack with the others and headed down the steps to the subway with a few of them. I jumped on the train and headed to the dojo.

* * *

On the street outside the dojo, I could see Ameer. He was coming from one direction and I was coming from the other. Other fighters walked up and pulled up one by one and entered the dojo. I stood waiting for Ameer to reach me. Meanwhile, the Caddy pulled up smoothly. I watched as Ameer seen the Caddy from a distance. Then he dropped back some, and sidestepped and waited for Chris's father, Reverend Broadman, to pull off. I wondered why.

"What's up, brother?" Chris gave me a pound.

"I see you got your chauffeur service in full effect," I kidded him.

"Yeah, I got a ride here, but I gotta get the train home. Tonight *The Cosby Show* is on and my father watches it with my mother and

little brother and sister religiously! I mean nobody can schedule anything when that show is on."

"*The Cosby Show*?" I repeated.

"C'mon now, I know you heard about it before and seen it too,"
Chris said.

"I ain't seen it," I assured him.

"Man, there's a girl on that show I'm gonna marry, Lisa Bonet!
Damn, she's fine. Let's go in," Chris said, grabbing my injured arm.

"Ameer's coming up now." I pointed.

Two black eyes and a busted lip, that's what Ameer was hiding.

"What the fuck happened to you?" Chris asked first.

"Who we gotta see?" I asked Ameer seriously. "Whoever did this
shit to you, we gotta see him. We could do that tonight. We could do
that instead of dojo." I was running on immediate reaction.

"It ain't like dat," Ameer said calmly. I was used to him being the
one who's hyped up and me being the one who's calm. Now there was
a reversal.

"You saying it's not like that. Your face is saying that it *is* like
that," I told him.

"Let's just find out what happened first," Chris said, as he threw
his rational thinking in. "If we skip the dojo, we can go get some pizza
and see what's up with all this, you know, come up with a plan."

"Aight, I'm down," I told them.

"You're gonna skip dojo!" Ameer smiled through his mangled
face.

"You look like you need to skip it also. Besides my shoulder is a
little fucked up. I need to rest it before tomorrow night's game."

"What happened to your shoulder?" Chris delved.

"Nah, it's just a little something. It's nothing," I dodged.

"Hold up, we got three minutes before class starts. Let me say
something to Sensei since we are all three skipping dojo," I told them.

"I'm gonna chill out here," Ameer said. "Me too," Chris agreed,
as though Sensei was our father, who the two of them were afraid to
confront, disagree with, or disappoint.

The usual advanced fighters were on the floor waiting for our
teacher. I gave my greetings to some of them and pushed off straight
to Sensei's office.

"*Konbonwa*, Sensei," I greeted him. I pulled the envelope with the payment that I was supposed to give him at our private lesson out of my back pocket. "You and I got distracted earlier. These are my fees." I handed him the envelope.

"No, thank you," he said politely, using his trained hand to push the envelope back toward me. "This money has somehow confused our bond as teacher and student," Sensei said. I understood what he was getting at, but I didn't want to enter into some long and deep exchange with him right before he was scheduled to teach and while my friends were outside waiting.

Slowly and clearly, without any disrespect in my tone, I said, "Sensei, I respect you and I am grateful that you have been my teacher. I want to pay as usual and continue our training when I return. I don't think that simply because I finally won one match between you and me that our bond is any different. And I know that if you wanted to throw your *kunai* this afternoon and stop my heart, you could have. Now please, *accept* my payment."

"I won't accept any more money from you. If you really do return after a week's time, we will continue." He nodded his head but still seemed doubtful. I grabbed him up and gave him a first-time hug. I knew this was not his tradition.

"Thank you, Sensei," I said sincerely. I was good to go as long as he wasn't trying to cut me off for what I thought wasn't a good-enough reason.

"Three things before you leave, one, never carry a firearm to an airport," Sensei said evenly.

"I would never," I assured him, as though that couldn't apply to me.

"Two, even though you say that you are not traveling to Japan, if you do find yourself there, never purchase a gun. It is not like New York. If you are captured with a gun, they *will* put you in their prison *forever*." He stared hard at me to push his point.

"Three, if there is any complication between you and Naoko Nakamura, and he refuses to allow his daughter to return to the United States, let her choose whether to leave or remain in the country. If she chooses to leave, let her leave the country of her own will on her own two feet."

"What do you mean?" I asked.

"Don't put yourself in a position where any authority could accuse you of kidnapping or any other kind of crime that carries a severe penalty. If you do, *you* will pay the price for *every foreigner*."

"Pay the price for every foreigner?" I asked.

"The Japanese as a people have always distrusted foreigners. Don't give them any excuse to snatch your freedom from you."

"Sensei, I understand," I told him.

"Here, take this . . ." Sensei opened his top desk drawer. Before he could hand me anything else, I put up my hand for him to stop.

"Sensei, you have given me more than enough, too much," I protested. He ignored me and pushed a ring across his desk where I was standing. The ring was not made of gold. It was shaped for a man's finger and made from pearl. On the top surface was a wicked black insignia made from onyx. It looked powerful on the white pearl. On second look and second thought, I could tell that the ring must belong to Sensei, because the size of it was definitely for him. I looked down at my own big hand.

Sensei, watching me intently, said, "Wear it on any finger. Just be certain to display it. In Japan, and in many Asian places, this ring will win you favors that otherwise would be forbidden. Possessing it may allow the impossible to happen. It may even save your life."

I listened, but I didn't believe in charms and material items that supposedly have superpowers, although the ring was nice-looking. I knew I could not refuse him, without causing further insult. I accepted it and thanked him. Sensei said, *"Sayonara."*

Sayonara. It was the word I hated most coming from my wife's lips. I paused and felt a chill. Sensei walked toward the class with a slight limp.

"Ameer and Chris are with me. They will both miss class tonight also."

"Of course," Sensei said. "They are your friends. Let them bid you farewell."

* * *

We walked away toward our regular pizza spot. At a newsstand Chris tossed a dollar for some cheap children's sunglasses. "Here, put these on," he joked Ameer.

"Fuck it. It's about to be dark. I don't need 'em," Ameer said, but then he put them on just to go along with Chris's joke. "At least you

picked the right color, red!" Ameer cheered, fucked up but still thinking about his ball team. I was silent and thinking on how both me and
Ameer would be playing tomorrow night's Hustlers League games
with injuries, a slight handicap.

With a large, hot cheese pizza pie at the center of our table and
two Cokes and one water, we each grabbed a slice and dropped it
down onto the too-thin white paper plates. Chris grabbed the salt
and I grabbed the crushed red pepper and Ameer grabbed the garlic. Instinctively, I whispered *"Allah, la ilaha illallah muhammadur
rasulullah"* over my slice before I bit into it.

"So why are you hesitating to do something about your situation?" I asked Ameer. "Or is it that you already took care of it? If
you already took care of it, you don't have to speak on it. But if you
let somebody do all that shit to you, they'll feel crazy confident
and come back and finish you off if you don't get 'em back first," I
warned him.

"Does the cat that did that to you live on your block or is he on
your team? Is he somebody you gonna come across again and again?"
Chris asked Ameer.

"It's somebody who I have to see, no doubt," Ameer confirmed,
being vague.

"Oh, shit," Chris muttered.

"Who is it?" I asked, pushing for the details.

"It was my pops," Ameer said, and then smiled, his busted lips
split and discolored.

"No way, I don't believe that. What happened?" Chris asked.

"Word up!" Ameer said. "I came back from school today and Pops
was waiting for me outside right at the bench. Soon as he saw me, he
threw the gloves at me and said, 'Let's go.'" Ameer looked as though
he was reliving it. "I wasn't scared and shit. You know a young nigga
be wanting to kick his father's ass from time to time. We just never
get a real opportunity, but we wish we could, right?"

Chris looked puzzled. Then he broke out and laughed a short,
nervous laugh. "True, I wish I could take a swipe at my father some
time, but I know it's impossible," Chris said sincerely.

"Nothing's impossible," Ameer assured him.

"So what happened?" I asked, pushing further.

"So we went down to the basement in my projects and shit and

I was thinking like, I didn't want to use the gloves. *I'm not no fucking boxer.* I wanted to use our bare hands. But my pops said, 'Keep the gloves on, raise your fists up. You not gonna use the karate I paid for, on me!' Ameer imitated his father's cool old hustler's voice. We all laughed some.

"So we start boxing. That's my pop's thing, so he's getting the better of me. Then he started feeling himself and pulled his gloves off and just laid into me. Next thing I know, he started punching me in the face, raw hands and all. I tried to block his jabs and swings, you know, and restrain him and control him, but it was like the old nigga was having flashbacks or something of some dude who had done him dirty in the past! I mean *I'm his son, right*, but he is really trying to crush me. I got some good shots off on him too, but I wasn't trying to lay him out. I wasn't trying to finish him off. I know I could've if I threw my heart into it. I *wanted* to punch him in the face a few times but not *injure* him or *kill* him. I mean we both gotta live in the same house together, right?"

Ameer might as well been performing in a play. That's how he told a story. He made anybody wish they was there. He used all of his talking skills, gestures, and energy to make you feel like you *was* there. Chris was amazed and entertained. I, on the other hand, didn't deal with it like that.

I could not imagine actually fighting my father. I definitely couldn't imagine trying with any real intent to punch my father in the face, scar him, whip him, or even to win. I mean my father taught me various fight moves when I was real young, but the way Ameer's face looked, this was no joke. It was real difficult to get my mind around the idea that his father tried to do him something extra dirty-dirty.

"So what happened?" I pushed Ameer to finish telling his story.

"Afterward we both went upstairs like it wasn't nothing. When my mother got home, she went off! My father told her, 'Stop with the drama already. You know boys fight. Your son had a fight in school and obviously he lost this one time. It happens.'"

"What did your mother say after that?" Chris asked.

"She asked me if I had a fight at school. I told her, 'Yeah, but don't worry about it. You should see the other guy!'" Chris and Ameer laughed again.

After some seconds I asked, "But what was his reason? Why did your father want to attack you like that?"

"Oh, 'cause I fucked his little girlfriend," Ameer said casually.

"The girl I saw at your apartment yesterday?"

"Not the girl Dana, who was on the bench with me when you rolled up."

"I know, the one that was sitting on your bed."

"Yeah, her," Ameer confirmed.

"I thought you said she was one of your girls," I reminded him.

"Nah, she was really looking for my father and I knew it and my pops knew it too. I just didn't want my mother to get arrested over her. You know my mother's smart. She wasn't just gonna believe right off the top that the girl was there looking for me and not my pops. She already didn't trust the girl from something before. That's why my moms told me to take the girl to my room. That way if the girl was there looking for my pops, my pops would reveal himself by the way he acted."

"Did he reveal himself in front of your moms?" Chris asked.

"Nah, you saw how cool he was when he came back home, right?" Ameer directed his question at me, since I was there with him yesterday.

"Yeah, right" was all I said.

"Well, the girl was in my room and she was tight at my father, so she was coming on to me. So I fucked her. My headboard was banging against the wall of my parents' bedroom and the whole nine. The whole time I'm fucking her, I'm covering for my father and hoping that it's convincing my mother that she was really my girl, and it did. The next morning Moms was all cooled out. I bumped into my pops in the bathroom and he didn't say nothing rude or nothing. Later when I got home though, he was just laying and waiting for me with the gloves."

"What about the girl?" Chris followed up.

"Oh, I fucked her good. At first she was just angry with my pops and fucking with fury, like a revenge fuck, yah know what I mean? Then I could feel her body loosen up and giving in. She slowed down and started moving her hips like music. We grinded some more and soon she was moaning. When she wanted some tongue, I knew I had her all the way open. When we was through, she started looking at me like she was all turned out and in love. I told her not to bring her ass up to our apartment no more. If she wanted me to keep fucking her, or even if she wanted my father, she needed to stay her ass downstairs and wait till one of us come check her."

"Did she go for it? What did she say?" Chris asked.

"What the fuck is she gonna say? She said okay!" Chris and Ameer laughed again.

I wanted to laugh also but I couldn't. I was still trying to figure out why Ameer's father had to hide his relationship with the female. From time to time, like many Americans I've met and known, Ameer and his father claimed to be Muslims, to have some knowledge of Islam, or to be some kind of Five Percenters. A Muslim man is allowed to have more than one woman. In fact, a Muslim man, according to the Holy Quran, can have up to four wives. So what was the dilemma? If I chose to take a next wife, I would be up-front with it. I would introduce her to Akemi. I would teach her to love and respect Akemi as first wife. Akemi would accept her also. Both of them would understand that they are my responsibility, women I would protect with my life and provide for. Each of them would be for my pleasure and comfort. Each of them would become mothers of my children. I would be their husband and father to all my seeds. I would treat them all well and fairly.

"Why didn't your father just take the other girl as his second wife?" I asked Ameer.

"This ain't Baghdad, motherfucker!" he snapped at me. "My moms ain't having that shit. Besides, me and my pops are Muslim, but my moms ain't Muslim no more."

"My moms wouldn't go for that shit either," Chris said. "She be watching all them ladies in the church like a hawk. She ain't playing, word to mother!" They both laughed for a good long while.

I let it go. I could see that somehow, both of them thought that it was better the way that they were living. Ameer thought it was okay to fuck his father's woman to cover for his father fucking her in the first place. His father thought it was okay to fuck a woman without marriage or any degree of honesty. His father let another woman upset his household. For me a wife is your "peace," and no one should be allowed to disturb a man's peace.

And what about my friend Chris? What if his father chose a

second or third woman from the congregation? Would it be okay for his father to go up in them without marriage or acknowledgment? Would it be cool and acceptable to the church people as long as no one discussed or exposed it? And what would happen when Reverend Broadman created life in a second or third womb? Would he abandon his children, like a fool and a coward? Would he deny that the relations he had with the women ever existed, the way Ameer's father pretended and denied the female?

I thought about Sudana, a really good and pretty and well-raised daughter, whose attraction to me I could feel so strongly. Yet I already knew that I would not go into her just for my own pleasure and without seeking her family's counsel, without thinking or planning and being ready and capable and being up-front with everyone I loved. I knew I wouldn't go into her without marriage, and this is why I worked hard to guard myself from being led solely by my own deep desires.

"Brother, what are you thinking about and where did your mind go?" Chris questioned.

"He's thinking about Japan. You know he's leaving in two days," Ameer said.

"Japan, word?" Chris looked amazed and astounded into silence.

"Listen, don't mention my trip to anyone else. Solid?" I asked them.

"Why?" Chris asked.

"Because he's a ninja!" Ameer joked. Chris laughed.

"Seriously, don't, aight?" I reinforced. "Not even to Sensei. If I want anyone to know anything about me, let me be the one doing the telling," I said.

"What could we tell anyway? You been to my apartment plenty of times. You and I both been to Chris's house, but neither of us two ever been to your house," Ameer said with a serious tone, as though he had been cheated by me for all these years.

"You want to come by my apartment?" I fired back. "C'mon."

It was nothing for me to shoot by my block to meet Ameer's challenge and resolve their curiosity and maintain our friendship. I would take them and we would get a game going on my court. I needed to work my left shoulder and arm anyway. True, I had never invited them or anyone else over to my place. This was the place where my Umma and sister were kept. Why should I allow anyone to enter? But now we were moving out. Ameer and Chris did not know this, but I planned to pack up my apartment as soon as I returned from Japan, and to never have my mother or sister or wife back on my Brooklyn block. We would all leave from Mr. Ghazzali's home to go to our new house as soon as it was available and prepared, *inshallah*.

*   *   *

Chris and Ameer were content with the fact that I invited them over. For the sake of time, we played ball at one of our usual courts down from the dojo. Chris was afraid to aggravate his father and cause him to double up his punishment. "Man, I can't be the Reverend's prisoner for two seasons. I'm trying to do what my father demands for the springtime and then be free to roam the streets for the whole summer!"

Later Chris left, saying to me, "Take it easy, man. Thanks for finally inviting me to your place, and take the movie camera with you to Japan. I'll be the first standing in line to check your movie!"

Me and Ameer remained on the court. I practiced my dribble using mostly my right arm only. I worked on one-handed layups and jumpers.

"Let's put some money on tomorrow night's game," Ameer suggested.

"Why?" I asked.

" 'Cause we both in fucked-up condition, so let's see who the best man is between us. Which one of us can persevere through our injuries and come out on top." He smiled, he was always so hyped up to make a bet.

"What if we both win and come out on top in our games? We both playing different teams anyhow." I wanted to show Ameer a different angle instead of moving it like he and I should be rivals when we are best of friends. "Besides, *your* injuries are on your face. That's not gonna interrupt your mean-ass jumper."

"Don't sleep. I use this face to get a lot of shit accomplished. It'll be hard to talk shit on the court when I look like I got Brooklyn mobbed. That's why I didn't want to go around your block tonight. Them cats around your way, seeing me for the first time and shit, would be looking at me like I'm a easy vic."

"True," I admitted. "But I would have held you down."

"I wouldn't've even came out my apartment tonight if it wasn't to go to the dojo. I knew you and Chris would show up, so I showed up," Ameer said.

"Yeah? Or is it more like you hiding from your pops?" We both laughed.

"You kind of good at catching shit. I'm definitely try'na stay out his face for a few days. Tonight I'ma crash at this female's house I know. Her mother works the night shift. She told me, 'Ameer I hate sleeping alone.'" He imitated the high-pitch voice of a stupid female. Then he laughed and even hollered. "I told her that tonight I'm gonna help *you* out."

"You could stay by me tomorrow night. Come by after your game, about 11:30 p.m." I offered.

"Good looking out," he accepted.

"Small bet, a hundred." Ameer was back focused on a wager.

"Do you even have a hundred dollars?" I fucked with him.

"You a foul nigga," he said.

"Aight, a hundred. If I win, give this hundred dollars to Sensei at your next class. Tell him I said please hold my spot till I get back. Just pay him and remember not to tell him nothing else." I handed Ameer the same envelope I tried to pay out to Sensei earlier. Ameer took the envelope, flipped it open, and checked inside. He saw the money.

"Slow down, you acting like you already won," Ameer complained.

"I don't plan on losing, not ever, you know that."

"Every man is losing something sometimes," Ameer philosophized.

"I know. I just said I never *plan on losing*. A man who plans on losing loses every time."

* * *

In the remaining hour I had open before going to pick Umma up from the late shift, I decided to give Bangs a call just to check on her situation. I had never phoned her before, but her number was embossed in my mind because when I first met her, she would say it, sing it, rhyme it to me repeatedly, hoping I'd give her a call.

Purposely, I jumped on the train and exited at a random stop that I never use. I selected a random telephone booth. When I pressed the first number, I saw one dude here and one dude there watching the booth as though it was their private house phone and they were all expecting a call. I pressed the other six digits, disregarding them.

"Hang up the phone!" I heard a male voice yell over the line before whoever picked up could even say hello.

"It might be Grandma calling from the hospital," I heard Bangs's voice say as though she was holding the receiver down against her side instead of right to her ear.

"That's why you got that speed knot on your head, 'cause you always talking slick," the male voice said.

"Hello, Grandma!" I heard Bangs's excited voice say, as though now she had the phone to her ear. Then the phone dropped and I could hear hands dragging it back and forth and then *click*. I knew who the male voice belonged to. I had heard it before and it wasn't one of the young fools from around her way.

Chapter 21
THE MEANING

"Look at the moon," Umma said to me. We were riding in the back seat of the taxicab together, both of our windows lowered halfway. Umma was turning her face toward the window to feel the night breeze. "It's hard to believe that this moon I see is the same as my Sudan moon," Umma remarked softly. "How could it be so powerful and brilliant back home and so dark and dim here?"

We were in a notorious New York traffic jam on the FDR, cars crawling from Brooklyn to Dyckman, the borderline between Manhattan and the Bronx. I thought I would rush hardworking Umma home in a taxi, but now we were in for an expensive, slow, long ride after the midnight hour.

"You know, son, your ticket to Japan is Saturday, May tenth, and our holy month of Ramadan will begin that same evening. I've been thinking about the meaning of that," she said.

I listened to my Umma, her words overpowering my thoughts which were jam-packed and colliding like bumper cars in my mind. *How could I forget Ramadan?* I asked myself. But it was not that I had forgotten it. Every Muslim knows that this is the most important time of our year. Ramadan comes annually according to the moon, so the date of the arrival of Ramadan each year is different, unlike Christmas, which for Christians and non-Christians is always December 25. Ramadan is the month in which Prophet Muhammad, peace be upon him, received the revelation of the Holy Quran, our book of guidance from Allah. Our Quran gives us guidance for life and sets limits and boundaries for what all believers should, should not, and must do.

"You know, son, when I pray, I ask Allah to make you capable and strong in the face of life's test. Your physical is solid," Umma said, turning inward and placing her palm on my chest. "But it is your faith that will pull you through every time."

"Agreed" is all I answered.

"Since you are traveling, you can be excused from the fasting and make up the days when you return," Umma said softly, her eyes widening to search my soul.

Every Muslim is required to fast the entire month of Ramadan. Our fast is from food and water. We take our last sip of water before sunrise right before we see that thin thread of light that separates the night from day. Then we don't eat or drink or make love to our wives, until we see the daylight devoured by the night at sunset. For thirty days in a row we do this, using our time to thank Allah and to read the Quran, hoping to be forgiven for our past sins. The only Muslims excused from this fast are the ill and the traveling. Even those who are excused because of illness or travel are required to do serious acts of kindness and charity throughout the observance.

"I will travel, Umma. And I will fast while traveling," I assured her.

Her approval was revealed as she smiled brighter than the New York moon. I knew it would please her most if I fasted. More important, I knew that was the best and right and truest thing to do.

"Alhamdulillah!" she said, "And for this I believe Allah will make you successful in retrieving your wife, our Akemi."

"Inshallah," we both said at the very same time. Umma laughed some.

"Umma?" I said. "I know a girl. She is unmarried and fourteen years young." Umma shifted her hips in her seat and was now facing me fully. She waited for me to continue. "She has a baby," I said. Umma kissed her teeth, a sound of shame and uttered "Zina," an Arabic term for sex between unmarried people, which is forbidden. "Her mother's brother is the baby's father," I added. Umma took some time to understand what I had just told her. So I repeated it.

"He ruined her," Umma said. We sat in silence for three minutes.

"Is she really ruined?" I asked Umma, already knowing her sentiments and our culture.

"He ruined her and ruined himself," Umma answered. The weight of Umma's words silenced us both. For minutes we rode up one extremely narrow lane as the second lane of the FDR was suddenly blocked, leaving all the drivers and riders alike only one way out.

"You're sleepy," I said, as I saw Umma's eyes become heavy. We had finally crossed Dyckman, and the lanes opened and traffic was thinning out.

"I am," she admitted. "But it's okay. I will get to sleep late tomorrow morning. Oh! And don't worry about Naja for tomorrow. I have something special planned for her."

"Something special?" I pushed for details. I wasn't used to Umma making plans on her own and then telling me about it after they were all set up.

"A mother-daughter day. I plan to take your sister out to lunch. We'll sit down together while I explain to her the sudden changes in our lives. It's a big thing to a little girl. Naja will have to adjust to getting back and forth to school from a new location, and we still haven't told her that you are going away to Japan. So I will tell all while she eats her favorite things. Then we'll go out shopping," Umma said, now sounding more excited than sleepy.

"Shopping, where? Lunch, where?" I asked calmly.

"Oh, lunch is at a place that Temirah recommended. It's called Serendipity's. She says her daughters really enjoy it. It's on—"

"I know where it is, on Sixtieth," I said. "So you'll shop in that same area?"

"Yes, and Temirah Aunty has arranged for Mr. Ghazzali to pick us up when we are all three finished. He will come anytime after Jumma prayer. All she has to do is give him a call."

"Okay, I'll speak to Mr. Ghazzali and make sure you and Naja have a cab from the Bronx apartment to Serendipity's. That's the only thing missing from the plan you made. No problem."

* * *

In the downstairs Bronx apartment late that same night but in the early morning dark, Umma fell asleep on the couch instead of in her temporary new bedroom. Naja was upstairs sleeping in Sudana's house. Slowly, I was pacing the floor. My mind felt like it weighed a ton. Not one to allow my thoughts to turn into quicksand, I began moving around the apartment quietly, searching for the telephone. After a drawn-out debate with myself about whether I should call

Akemi's friend and leave a message, I decided I would. But as I entered the last room of this apartment, I didn't see a telephone. I had been more concerned about the windows and doors, security and changing the locks. I missed out on the fact that there was no telephone down here. Quickly I decided that I could buy a telephone tomorrow and run a wire and a splitter from upstairs down to here. I would definitely do that, but it wouldn't help me for making the call right now, which would've been the perfect time because Japan is thirteen hours ahead of the United States in time, or at least ahead of New York. *It's 2:30 in the afternoon in Tokyo,* I thought to myself. *What is my wife doing right now?*

Moments later, I began thinking about Ameer and Chris. Was I messed up for not straightening them out? Was I a hypocrite for having two friends so far away from my beliefs? I must have thought so, or I wouldn't have been thinking about it. Yet I didn't want to think about it. Those two were my only American friends. Still, a voice in my head kept telling me if I didn't take responsibility for setting them right in their thoughts and actions, something would happen to cause me to have a break with them. I paced faster, questioning myself—or perhaps questioning Allah to ask if I was responsible for them. Can a young man ever be responsible for his friends' thoughts, ways, and actions?

My mind switched again and Bangs popped up, but I shut that down. I didn't want to think about anything that would lead me to a thought that might interrupt or delay my trip to my wife. I know the order of things for a man, and I know the order of things in my heart.

I looked over at Umma. Simple things, like her going out shopping with some women friends, concerned me. Every move she made concerned me as if I knew that she would forever be a foreigner here in America. She was a reminder to me and everyone else in the world who ever had the pleasure of encountering her beauty, her words, her voice, and her ways, that she was right and everything else was wrong. That made her the center of attention in my mind. Because either way, wherever she went—all covered in *thobe* or *hijab* and *niqab*—she still stood out. This made me want to shield her from the world and all the twisted people who didn't deserve to see or know her. But how could I throw a blanket over the sun? And if I was troubled that she planned to shop without me there to protect her, how would I handle being thousands of miles away? Even though I planned the details out precisely to secure Umma in every way, my emotion concerning her was deep and strong, alive and active.

On the table next to the couch where Umma slept was her Quran. I needed to quiet my mind. I especially needed to rest. I had Vega and my team standing on my back along with everyone else. I had to figure how to unload all this and fall into a healing sleep.

I rinsed my mouth, washed my hands, face, feet, and then washed my hands again. I opened the Quran to a random page, something that I did often after the first time I read it word for word from the beginning to the end. I told myself whatever page I opened to first would contain a message for me, something to guide me on my way. I landed on the *sura*,[1] called Al-Baqarah. My thumb held the page right at the forty-second *ayat*[2]:

> *"And don't mix up truth with falsehood, nor hide the*
> *truth while you know."*

Immediately, I closed the Quran. For me, the Holy Quran is like this. Every word in every line is clear and easy to understand. Yet it is the meaning of the words that is so heavy. When I read from the Quran, my spirit is aroused and my soul shakes. My responsibilities are reinforced and I become mindful.

So is this the answer to my question that I asked Allah concerning my friends, I asked myself. I could not be certain but I felt it was. Of course I needed to do a better job at helping my friends to become more steady and true. I needed to separate the truth from the falsehood and set a better example through myself and not hide my way of life. I needed to convey the meaning of Islam through my living. How else would my friends learn it? I sat still for a while before opening Umma's Quran once again.

This time the book opened to the *sura* called Al-Nisa, which

---

[1] A sura is the Arabic word for chapter.
[2] Ayat is the Arabic word for sentence.

translated into English means "The Women." My thumb sat right at the 135th *ayat*. It read,

> "*All believers be maintainers of justice, bearers of*
> *witness for Allah, even though it be against your own*
> *selves or your parents or near relatives, whether he be*
> *rich or poor. Allah has a better right over them both.*
> *So follow not your low desires, lest you deviate. And*
> *if you distort or turn away from truth, surely Allah*
> *is ever aware of what you do."*

These words reechoed in my mind in the original Arabic language in which they were written. I stood still while these words spoke meaningfully, passionately to my soul.

It was growing late and my eyes were beginning to weigh more than my heart. My thoughts were running their last lap. I then promised myself to open the Holy Quran only once more before resting. I landed on the sura called Al-Ma'idah. It was the thirty-second *ayat*. My thumb covered the first sentence or two, but the words which followed after my finger were:

> "*. . . whoever kills a soul—unless it be for manslaugh-*
> *ter or for mischief in the land, it is as if he had killed*
> *the whole of mankind. And whoever saves one life, it*
> *is as if he had saved the lives of all men."*

I knew exactly what that meant. Or, should I say, what I believed it meant.

In the past I had read the Holy Quran many times, from the beginning to the end, every single word on every single page in search of the meaning of life.

I lay on the floor fully clothed next to the couch where my Umma slept and I rested finally.

Friday, May 9th, 1986

By three thirty on Friday afternoon, I had my American passport in my hand. My heavy heart felt some relief. I did not love the eagle, but my passport was crisp and new and valid, and exactly what I now needed to become international and legitimate in the eyes of the law, as a world-class traveler, like my father.

I walked up eight blocks, from Rockefeller Center where the passport office was located, and over three blocks, to the area where Umma said she would be shopping. It took me twenty minutes to locate her.

She didn't see me. She was there with Mrs. Ghazzali, who brought along her youngest daughter and Naja, who was smiling away and seeming completely content. Like a young, young boy, I wanted to run inside and show Umma my passport. Yet I didn't. I wouldn't disturb her. I was just checking to see that she was okay and was where she wanted to be, doing what she wanted to do, safely.

A Harlem haircut, a short trip to Dr. Jay's, where I bought new shorts and sweats and kicks all black, because I was on the black team. By game time, I would be on point. Yet I needed a place to rest. The five hours of sleep that I had the night before wasn't carrying me.

I rang the bell at Chris's house. The heavy front door of his brownstone opened slowly.

"What's up, man! Come in." He was surprised. "I just got back from school. C'mon in the kitchen. You want something to eat?" He offered.

"Nah, I need a favor."

"What?"

"Let me lay down in your room. Wake me up at seven thirty for game time. It's a straight shot from here to the court. You think you could do that?" I asked him.

"That's easy. That's nothing," Chris said. "Me and my man Phil wasn't about to do nothing but crack these books open and study for a test we got on Monday morning. Phil, this is my man Midnight," Chris introduced us. I gave the schoolboy a pound. Afterward, I followed Chris to his room and put my shopping bags down. He closed the door, saying, "Seven thirty, no doubt." I felt cool at his spot, no worries just a warm family-type thing.

Facing a wall with a small poster titled THE TEN COMMANDMENTS, I began reading from the bottom up. It was something about a man not desiring his neighbor's house or woman or possessions. I agreed with that 100 percent, then fell into an instant, mindless sleep.

* * *

"Do you think this is a hotel?" Reverend Christian Broadman asked me as he pushed the door open at 7:30 p.m. "You owe twenty-five dollars to the Broadman Corporation."

"You got it, Reverend," I answered, pulling into consciousness.

"Do I look like one of your buddies?" he asked.

I corrected myself. "Yes sir, I'll pay you twenty-five dollars right now, Mr. Broadman." He laughed two controlled *ha ha*'s, accepted my twenty-five dollars, and said, "Good luck on your game. Stay out of trouble."

Chapter 22
RICKY SANTIAGA

It was like the whole Bed-Stuy territory cleared out and surrounded the outdoor court where we were scheduled to ball. It felt good to roll up to such excitement, yet it seemed like much more than a junior league game deserved. And I want to win, plan to win, but I definitely do not want to be famous. I pushed my way through the crowd and joined my team five minutes before game time. Out of habit I surveyed row by row in each direction.

"This crowd is crazy," my team member Panama pointed out with a nod of his head. I acknowledged the same way.

"You think it's us, Black, but it's not," Machete, another teammate, said. We were all leaning forward on the players' bench.

"Of course it's us, we're undefeated," Jaguar said aggressively.

"Look over there to the left. That's Ricky Santiaga, our team owner," Machete exposed.

"Who said?" Braz asked.

"He's from around my way, a big-time businessman, if ya know what I'm saying. I been peeping it. He been making a lot of smart moves lately." Machete put us up on it.

"You saying people coming out here just to see him? Can't be, he's just a local player. There's mad hustlers representing out here," Braz said.

"Catch up and pay attention," Machete said as though he was the underboss. "Look who Santiaga is standing next to, Mike Tyson, the up-and-coming heavyweight champion of the world. I heard this kid is an official Brooklyn 'killer.' His body is as wide as a building, and his fist broader than your head. And check the rapper standing next to him." All team heads shifted to search.

"Oh shit," Panama said, and then stood right up. "And check the other side, the whole uptown crew, and Calvin and Rich and them.

"Take your seats, it's about to go down." Vega screamed 'cause he could hardly hear himself talk. "Machete, Midnight, Panama, Jaguar, and Big Mike, let's go," he shouted. He motioned so hard with his hand for us to move that his cologne almost knocked me out.

We were in the middle of the court now. The air horn went off, the whistle blew, and Big Mike snatched the jump ball and sent it sailing right over to Panama. We all was running now.

* * *

Three seconds before time ran out in the fourth quarter, Machete passed the ball to me and it seemed like the whole crowd went silent and all inhaled at the same time. I was standing at the top of the key, where I have stood a thousand times. I pulled up, ignoring my sore shoulder that had been pulling on me all night. I didn't have even two points in this game. I'd just kept feeding Panama, a reversal of our normal strategy. He lapped it up and proved himself handily. He had twenty-eight points on the board for self. That's why the man who was supposed to be checking me was double-checking and double-teaming Panama and I was free and clear.

Inside of a second, although I never knew there was an inside to only one second's worth of time, I said to myself, *If I make this shot, what I been thinking has to be done, has to be done. If I miss it, it's not for me to do.* I closed my eyes. I had the feeling and the dimensions of this court embossed in my memory. My fingers pushed and then flicked the ball, and when I opened my eyes, me, the crowd, and my team were all midair cheering, swoosh. It was my only three points, but it was the most important and pivotal shot in the game and in my life for the moment. The players rushed me, crushed my left shoulder some more, and the crowd went haywire.

I pushed all the rushing girlies toward my teammates, wanting to ease out of there. Purposely, I had played low-key throughout the game but now I had brought too much attention onto myself.

"That was a mean-ass shot," Vega yelled as he pulled me out from the growing, clawing crowd. "Step to the side with me for a minute."

He pushed me forward with one hand and the crowd back with the other. I followed him and he used his authority as a coach to keep the crowd off my trail. Panama and the fellas were still entertaining the crowd, holding up the number one, their arms raised up high, index finger toward the sky. Girls gathered around them and began cheering.

"Let me ask you something, man?" Vega said. "Right before you took the winning shot, *did I see you close your eyes?*" He was leaning in toward me like I was about to reveal some unknown magic potion. "Listen, tell me what you were thinking in that split second, *please?*" He looked serious and too curious. So I lightened him up.

"I was thinking that I had to make Coach Vega look good," I told him. He smiled and hugged me up like one of my excited teammates.

"Listen, this weekend is the International Auto Show. I got tickets for you and the other four starters. I want to introduce you to somebody influential. Matter of fact, I *could* take the credit, but *he* actually asked me to introduce you to him," Vega said, speaking rapidly and emphasizing the importance of the meet-up. "Before you say no, just let me tell you we got a white Mercedes 300E Hammer being unveiled. It's the—"

"World's fastest passenger sedan, V-8 engine made by AMG, 375 horsepower, seven airbags, and it goes from one to sixty miles per hour in four seconds flat. I know, it's a beautiful machine." I finished Vega's sentences. I always kept up with the car magazines.

"Okay, the New York Coliseum, right across from Central Park. We meet up at about seven tomorrow night," he stated like it was a confirmed fact.

"Wish I could, Coach. But I won't be seeing you until game time for the next game. Remember I told you in advance I had something to take care of?" I reminded him. He gave me a stare, conveying his disappointment, then must've decided he still needed me.

"Aight, my man, I got you, my bad. You did tell me that. Hold up, let me grab the other four then, and we can do this right now." He dashed into the crowd and pulled Panama, Machete, Jaguar, Big Mike, same as he did me. That broke up the furor, and the crowd began to slowly move out and off the court. Some girls sucked their teeth. Others waited impatiently. Some of the players' peoples chilled outside the fence for them.

"Let's walk," Vega ordered the five of us.

On the dark side of the building, Ricky Santiaga sat calmly on the hood of a black Ferrari 288 GTO. Only a fool didn't know how exclusive that joint was. It cost almost $170,000. Off the top I wondered if it was his or if he rented it just to see jaws drop open, like they were dropping right now.

His men were grouped up at the corner of the building within eyesight. I figured they were there to block off any curious heads and to make their boss feel at ease. My eyes captured the car of course, the soft white leather seats and precise piping. Every detail popped out before me. His new Tod's, the black suede driving shoes he wore as he rested his feet against his front fender. A single lamppost casted a beam of light around them as if they were being displayed in the shoe store window of a Park Avenue shop. I checked my Datejust. It was 10:05 p.m. I had shit I had to handle and had to meet up with Ameer at 11:30. As I eased my eyes off the face of my watch, I saw his Cartier. Yet what really stood out was his gold band topped off by one clean princess-cut diamond, a modest one-and-three-quarter-carat diamond being rocked on his married finger.

"You got an appointment?" Ricky Santiaga asked me in a cool and even tone.

"I do," I answered calmly.

"This is the appointment," Vega intervened, giving Santiaga a pound and then introducing him to the five of us. Santiaga eased off the hood of the Ferrari and stood. He was at least as tall as me at six-one.

"My man Midnight says he has an appointment tonight and I believe him. So we're gonna make this quick. Y'all ran a good game tonight, made me feel proud. Your teamwork was crazy and that's what killed off your opponents. Y'all outsmarted them, made hood history. I like that. It made me want to meet you. So let's get to know each other real fast. I'm gonna erase everything I heard about each of you from other people up until tonight." He checked his watch. "You do the same, aight?" he asked us.

"Aight!" My four team members called out immediately.

"I'm gonna ask each of you three questions, any three questions that I choose. You get one chance to pass if you don't want to answer one of the three questions. Then each of you gets to ask me one question. I'll take one pass for myself, got it?" he said, looking each of us in the eye one by one to get his feeling across. He was talking slowly and seriously. He commanded everyone's attention with his style and method, and now Vega was unusually silent.

"Machete, where are you from, originally?" Santiaga asked.

"La República Dominicana," Machete responded without smiling, in his normal laid back, intentionally threatening style. Yet I could see clearly that he was in awe of Santiaga.

"Jaguar, where are you from originally?"

"Belize," Jaguar answered.

"Panama, from Panama right?" Santiaga asked and answered.

"No doubt," Panama confirmed, so excited you would think he had been MVP of the league already, his gold framed teeth all exposed.

"Braz, same question." Santiaga pointed.

"Las favelas de Rio de Janeiro, Brasil," Braz said proudly. It seemed everybody was suddenly rocking their accents and mother tongue.

"And you?" Santiaga asked me with a slight smile.

"I'll pass," I responded.

"No problem, that's your one," Santiaga said patiently. "So we'll start with you this time. What's the meaning of team?" Santiaga asked me.

I paused and then answered, "It's a group of people who decide to work together to accomplish one or more goals. If one person falls or fails, every team member covers for him. We all keep pushing until we get it done right, the way we agreed in the beginning."

Santiaga looked at Vega one time as though they could communicate without words. Then he refocused on the next player. "Machete, what are your plans for the future?" Santiaga questioned.

"I'm hoping to be alive in the future, that's the first thing. Come to think of it, I want to be like you, so large I can sit on a Ferrari like it's nothing and have a bunch of dudes who got my back standing around just waiting for me to give the word." My teammates all laughed, not just at his answer but at Machete's style. We were used to him, but Santiaga was just getting a taste.

And so the questions went around just like this. I said in the future I wanted the black team to win the tournament undefeated. They all cheered for that, overlooking that I never answered the question of how I see my future and what I wanted to become. For his third and final round, Santiaga got more serious, in his face and his interrogation.

"Machete, what is success?" he asked.

"Twenty-five million dollars!" Machete didn't even pause to think about it.

"Panama, what would you do to get twenty-five million dollars?" Santiaga asked.

"Any fucking thing," Panama said confidently. My teammates laughed, then confirmed.

"Braz, what is your definition of a traitor?" Santiaga asked.

"Anyone who gets in my way of what I'm try'na do," Braz responded seriously.

"Jaguar, if you had to sacrifice one thing on your body, what would it be?" Santiaga asked.

"Damn, why me? Why ask me that?" he said, disappointed.

"Answer the question." Santiaga didn't give him a way out.

Jaguar paused. "My middle toe," he said after a minute. Everyone laughed. "No, seriously," Jaguar said, "'cause I got two on each side of the middle one and I could still walk or run without it, and nobody but my girl would know it was missing." Everyone laughed.

"Midnight, my man, what is the meaning of life?" Santiaga asked me, turning everyone's attention to my reaction.

"Family." I said just that one word. No one said anything. For seconds, no one moved.

"Alright, let's speed it up. You each get one question, ask me anything," Santiaga ordered.

Braz asked, "Where are you from, originally?"

Santiaga looked at me and then answered, "I'll pass."

Machete asked, "Why are you putting money up for this league?"

Santiaga quickly said, "Because we can't let no one else get a monopoly over our young." Machete took one step back as though the answer was too deep for him.

Jaguar asked, "Why did you choose us players in the first place?"

Santiaga said swiftly, "Because I know what kind of men to surround myself with."

Panama asked, "What do you do for a living?" Everybody got quiet. He knew it was a dangerous question and so did we.

"I'm a businessman, of course," Santiaga said with a smile. "You know, an entrepreneur."

"About that pendant that you wore the last three times I saw you, the gold pendant of the baby shoe. Why did you choose that piece?" I asked him, truly wanting to know.

" 'Cause babies are innocent and men are guilty," Santiaga said. Then he touched the pendant he was rocking tonight, a 24-carat gold chess piece. It was the queen piece, surrounded by a link made up of forty 24-carat gold king crowns. "Alright, time's up. Now we know each other a little better. Great game, keep it up until the job is done."

He gave each of us a pound. I was last. Strangely, he gripped my hand when I gave him a pound and pulled me into his embrace.

We all walked past the Ferrari to view it from another angle as we left. Purposely I didn't delay. It was 10:25 p.m. now. I walked out with a few players and random youth who were still excited and involved in heated conversation, which included reenactments of small pieces of our game. I hopped on the train with a few and rode toward my Brooklyn apartment. I got off six stops later. Slowly I quieted my mind and blocked out any thoughts of basketball, money, or the game. Calmly I walked by and with anonymous passengers. I went up the stairs, crossed over, and went back down into the subway on the other side and hopped back on the train moving in the opposite direction.

There is a pathway by her house that nobody should be on unless they live there, and an alley with only one window facing a solid brick wall. I only had a half hour to give. The results would be based strictly on chance. I wouldn't want to attach this act to Allah without His permission. I crouched there, black sweats, black Nikes, my black fitted riding low. Warm weather made my face moist. I could smell the cement and the trash and traces of spilled Kool-Aid, which had attracted a bunch of busy bugs.

In only twelve minutes, he came creeping. It must have been his appointment with destiny. He was using the back entrance, because he was the type who was hardly ever welcomed willingly through her front door. This time it cost him. I leaped up from the ground, certain I was nothing but a silhouette in the dark of the night. He was startled, surprised, and unprepared, of course. My guess was that he was only used to fighting girls. Men like him think they'll have a free hand forever.

I struck him one precise and powerful blow to his throat, so swift with my right closed fist that when his head tilted forward, he never saw my right leg at a 120-degree angle. My sharp kick made his head stand back up straight and his body fall backward against the wall. I disappeared faster than the mist, before his body could even slide down to the ground.

They say that a leopard grabs its prey by the throat, drags it, and then rips it apart with his teeth. When he's done, he leaves nothing but blood and broken bones behind. As I moved swiftly yet calmly, taking forty-five seconds to walk through the back streets of Bed-Stuy and down the stairs of the subway, I thought to myself, *Bangs wanted me and her to have a secret.* Now *we have a secret.*

Chapter 23
AMEER NICKERSON

"Where is everybody?" Ameer said, as he entered my Brooklyn apartment for the first time.

"Everybody like who?" I dodged, taking a few steps over to close Umma's bedroom door.

"Your family," he emphasized, like I should've already known.

"They're away, because I'm going away tomorrow, remember?" I told him.

"Oh yeah, I knew you were going. I didn't know they were going also," he said, looking around my living room. I never corrected him on that matter.

"I hope you got some food up in here," Ameer demanded.

"If the red team would've lost tonight, I would only let you get a bowl of hot water. I would put it right there in the corner on the floor," I joked with him. "You're lucky y'all won."

"I *still* got your one hundred dollars though," Ameer said, like he had one up.

"Yo, give that money to Sensei like I asked you to. Ask him to hold my spot."

I pulled some food out of the refrigerator, which Umma had wrapped up and stored. I placed everything on the countertop. "Here, you heat it up. I'll be right back."

In my room I moved my duffel bag onto my bed and took some personal items that belonged to my wife and packed them inside. I ignored my new Armani suit hanging in my closet.

"Hey, how come this food is all crushed up?" Ameer yelled from my kitchen.

"It taste good. Just heat it on a low flame," I hollered back.

"It smells good, but damn, it's like baby food," he complained.

I didn't bother telling him the answers Umma would have given, that "Sudanese foods like eggplant and chickpeas and beans and lentils are often ground and merged with delicious spices. It's great for your digestion and Americans would eat them in this manner *if* they knew better."

"There should be some lemon chicken breasts in there. Try 'em. Heat mine too," I told him.

"Do I look like your fucking housemaid?"

"Just do it. You're doing yours anyway. I gotta make an important phone call," I told him.

"You got any Wonder Bread?" he yelled back. "I only eat Wonder Bread!"

I picked up the telephone in my room and pressed the fifteen numbers it took to contact Iwa Ikeda, Akemi's English-speaking friend Sensei had told me about. I calculated it was 12:40 in the afternoon in Tokyo, and although it was late Friday night in New York, it was already the next day, Saturday afternoon, for them.

Four rings and then an answering machine switched on. Her entire message was spoken in Japanese. All I understood was the beep.

"Peace, Ikeda-san, this is Mayonaka calling for Akemi. She left your phone number as a contact. Thank you for helping us with our communication. Please tell Akemi that I'll call her back at nine p.m. Tokyo time on Sunday night. If she can be there at your place at that time, we can talk. Please tell her everything will be okay, so take it easy," I said, and then hung up.

My plan was to arrive at Narita Airport in Japan at 8:00 p.m. Tokyo time, clear customs, give Iwa Ikeda a call at 9:00 p.m. and arrange to meet up with my wife on the spot. I already knew I couldn't stand to hear her crying over the phone while I stood uselessly, seven thousand miles away. Face to face was my true desire and only strategy.

True, I knew that I had conflicting information. I had two addresses for her father, one in Ginza and the other in Roppongi. I had the telephone number for Iwa Ikeda, who was staying somewhere in Tokyo, which led me to believe that Akemi was somewhere in Tokyo. I had the name of Akemi's birthplace, where she also said she had lived, which is called Kyoto, and the name of the high school she attended, Kyoto Girls' HS, that was listed on the literature from her show at the Museum of Modern Art. The high school was also located in Kyoto.

As I flipped through the pieces of paper with her information on it, I was beginning to feel like one of the characters in the many mystery novels that I had read over the past couple of years.

"This shit is good!" Ameer said, scooping up his crushed vegetables with a spoon. "Word up, I thought it was gonna be nasty."

"What did your coach say when he saw your face messed up like that?" I asked him.

" 'You're late! Get on the court so they can fuck up your face some more!' " Ameer imitated his crazy coach.

"Nah, that ain't right," I said with disbelief.

"True," he said matter-of-factly.

"We met our team owner tonight," I shared.

"I bet he was filthy," Ameer said, commenting on his riches.

I laughed. "He was Ferrari filthy!" I said calmly, but I guess with some passion to it.

"Oh my God!" Ameer said, truly amazed.

"I'll tell you one thing, he didn't seem like none of these hustlers from around here," I pointed out.

"Yeah, I didn't see no Ferraris parked down front of your building," Ameer laughed.

"He was asking us some questions that no man in the street ever asked me before."

"What, was he kicking the mathematics?" Ameer was talking his Five Percenter lingo.

"Nah, shit like, who are you? Where are you from originally? What's more important than your life? Like that," I told Ameer, as I thought back on it.

"Was he high?" Ameer asked.

"No, he was sober and clear. He was the type of cat that for some reason you might want to tell him a lie, but you end up telling him the truth."

"Like you." Ameer laughed once or twice and then turned quiet.

"So what do you want to do in the future?" I asked Ameer.

"Well, teacher . . ." Ameer switched his voice into a joke mode.

"Seriously."

"Um, I want Sensei to offer me private weapons lesson without me having to ask him, like how he did with you. I want to have a girl that's so bad, who makes me go so crazy, that I would do anything for her—"

"Would you marry her?" I asked him.

"That's what I mean," he said. "I want a girl who makes me lose my mind to the point that I would stand in front of a room full of my closest friends and family and say, 'I do, I'll do anything for you!'"

"You just fucking around," I told Ameer.

"If you could get it, I could get it," he said with a straight and serious stare. I didn't take no offense to it. I thought if him looking at me try'na do the right thing made him want to do better in life, then all praise is due to Allah.

"And . . . I want my father to respect me," Ameer said. "I want him to see me do good in life. And on his own, without my mom's encouragement, I want him to say, "Son, you did good. You did even better than me." Ameer looked like he was speaking to me honestly, while recalling something else. But with all jokes aside finally, it sounded like he was saying something true that he actually felt and meant.

Later that night after my bags were all packed, I threw Ameer a light blanket and a pillow. I dug my television out of my closet and set it on the table in the living room so he could watch it. I had to hear ten minutes of his jokes about my small television set, "an antique," Ameer declared. Then he called me "Fred Sanford," a name that I didn't know. Next he accused me of treating him like "Grady," another man I never heard of. Then he asked for a wire coat hanger. I handed him one. He threw it back at me and told me to stick it in the hole on top of the TV. "Move it to the left." He laughed. I moved it and then he said, "Okay, stand there just like that. Don't let it go." He cracked up. I dropped the wire hanger and left the room and prepared myself for a makeup prayer. Ameer, still laughing, fell to the floor from the couch.

I made the prayer in my room on top of a clean towel, first standing—"Allahu Akbar," which simply means "God is the greatest"— and then bending and eventually putting my head to the floor. Almost half an hour later, when I finally opened my eyes, I found Ameer standing still at my bedroom door watching me.

"What do you need?" I asked him.

"That's how you pray?" he asked.

"Don't you?" I asked.

"Never did," he said.

"Why not?" I asked.

"Don't know, just didn't," he said.

"You want to learn?" I offered.

"I do, but not now. Maybe when you get back home from Japan. It seems like if I do that, right now, if I start praying that way, something might change. Maybe after I finish, I won't recognize myself."

"Whenever, just let me know," I told him.

In my prayers, I had asked that we make it through the night without a rude banging on my front door, a gang of officers coming to take me away for assault with a deadly weapon, my feet and my hands.

I had known what had to be done since the day that Bangs's body shook with anger, the night her uncle snatched away her baby. I also knew I had to separate my Umma and my sister from anything that I might do. I knew I had to execute it swiftly and immediately afterward to be joined by one or more people whom I could use as an alibi in case there was an investigation. I knew I needed everyone to see me at that ball game last night and to also see me leave the game along with others. I also was certain that everything could go terribly wrong, but I calmed myself to accept that however it ended up going was how it was supposed to go.

If Bangs's uncle hadn't been at her house, my plan would've failed and I would've had to leave for Tokyo with the task undone. If her uncle had never come out of the house or stepped through the alley within the amount of time I had allotted myself, then nothing would've happened to him. I concluded that if he hadn't deserved it somehow or if it wasn't supposed to be me who avenged him for abusing Bangs, then he would have been *nowhere* in her vicinity. I had faced the dilemma like a complicated riddle. Admittedly, I even tried to excuse myself from doing anything about it. One voice in my mind argued, *Bangs is not my wife . . . If something goes wrong with me defending Bangs, I could miss out on rescuing my real wife, who I do love immensely, and to who I am willingly responsible.* Then the same voice argued, *Maybe Bangs is in this trouble because of something she did.* But in the end, I thought to myself that Bangs's uncle was worse than a vulture, a creature that at least waits till *after* a death to pluck and pull at the flesh. Her uncle was a man who did every fucked-up thing he could get away with, because he was confident either that every other man was doing the same thing as him, or every other man was absent, or every other man was too much of a coward to take him out. For me it became a matter that almost wasn't about Bangs. It was about men needing to check other men and make sure they respect some boundaries and limits. And I knew from the moment that I got here on American soil, in the Brooklyn borough, that some of these niggas just had to go.

Saturday, May 10th, 1986

Sunlight came uninterrupted and remained, thankfully. I woke up at 9:00 a.m. I woke Ameer up at 9:30. I saddled him with my duffel bag and a knapsack, before he could even consider washing up or showering in my apartment. I didn't have the time to give.

"You carry it. What the fuck is in here, cement?" he asked.

"I would, but it's better if you carry it. I don't want niggas around here to think I am going away. You know the streets. They might get excited and run up into my spot while I'm gone." I also carried a knapsack on my back.

"True," he said, and carried my stuff willingly all the way to the trunk of the taxi.

"Pull over on the right corner for a minute," I told the cab driver when we reached the subway entrance.

"Your meter is running," he told me in a heavy Indian accent.

"No problem," I assured him. I took my backpack off and handed it over to Ameer. "You want to hold something?" I asked him, looking him dead in his eye to convey that it was one of my burners. He paused. "Nothing on it," I guaranteed him.

"Hell yeah, word up," he said calmly.

"Hold it for me," I told him. He grabbed the backpack and climbed out of the cab.

"And be easy," I added.

"Later," we both said at the same time. He slammed the door.

I saw Ameer walk down the steps to the subway, the knapsack slung over his shoulder as my taxi sped off.

Chapter 24

WISDOM

Even though the two living spaces at the Ghazzali home were separate, the scent of Sudanese foods being prepared was not. The entire place was filled with the warmth of spring and the scents of Khartoum.[3]

I placed my duffel down and walked to the back room, looking for Umma. I found her in her new bedroom seated on her blanket, a pen in one hand and surrounded by papers. I wondered why even though I knocked, she did not answer. Gently, I pushed her door open; oddly, she did not look up at me.

"Umma!" I called.

She shook her head, used her right hand to move her hair from out of her face, wiped away a few tears, and finally held her head up to face me. Even though I had called out her name, seeing her expression, I couldn't speak. She looked me over with a slow study.

"Allah is merciful," she said. I heard these kinds of words many times, but not with the same kind of sorrow.

"I had a feeling last night," Umma said. "In the evening it was just an anxious feeling. Then about ten o'clock at night it was a feeling of great joy. Then less than an hour later, my joy turned to a feeling of vulnerability—like I was in great danger. I was upstairs, myself and Naja and all the Ghazzali women. We were cooking, preparing for today. The men were here in the house, Mr. Ghazzali and his sons. Temirah must've noticed something also. As I kneaded the bread,

[3] Khartoum—capital of Sudan

she asked me, 'Sana, are you feeling okay?' I said I was, but I wasn't. It took some seconds for me to search myself. I didn't want to worry Naja or anyone, so I stepped away. In the bathroom I made a prayer. Even as I was speaking to Allah, my moods were moving, heart racing a bit. When I opened my eyes, I knew I was not in danger. It was you."

Standing still in the entrance of her door, I could now feel Umma's intensity moving inside my chest, stirring inside me.

"*Alhamdulillah!* Allah the merciful heard my prayer. You are here!" she said with a muffled excitement.

I smiled as a look of great relief came over her face. My own tension began to diffuse.

"You must remember son about the nature of a mother's heart. Wherever you are in this world, if you are at ease, I am at ease. If you are troubled, I am troubled. This is the nature of true love. So whatever you consider, consider it first in your own mind. Then consider it again thinking only of me. Treat it as if we are one heart, one life, you and I."

"Is that the meaning of love?" I asked, finally breaking my silence.

"True love is like this," Umma said. "And since Akemi loves you and you love Akemi and she is there and you are here, you must know that true love is like this," Umma emphasized, but her words also felt like a question placed before me. I thought of Naja, Umma, and Akemi. Afterward, all I could do was agree "Yes, true love is like this."

But when I thought further, I said to myself, *I'm a man. I don't have the same emotions as a woman. Those kinds of powerful emotions would paralyze me. Yet for Umma, Akemi, and Naja—I would sacrifice my life.*

"As for the girl with the child . . . ," Umma said softly, switching topics, to my true surprise. My soul shook. How much could Umma possibly know about last night? I already knew that I would never discuss it with her or anyone else. What's done is done.

"Be careful with her. She has already entered your mind. It is a short trip for a woman to enter your heart once she is already in your thoughts."

Umma's bomb exploded inside me. I didn't react, and Umma

didn't reveal that she was aware of the intensity of her words, although we both knew their strength and impact and meaning.

"And you *already* have three women living in your heart—your mother, your wife, and your sister. It is *already* a lot, for a young, young man. Carry only what you can carry well and properly. The rest must be carried by other men. Each man should do his part."

Chapter 25

FINALLY

Back to back behind a boys' baseball team, I boarded Japan Airlines flight 322. I counted eighteen of them, all wearing the exact same jacket, sixteen of 'em teenagers. Even the two male adults had their team windbreakers on. It was warm outside and air-conditioned in the airport, but my head was hot. I had a list of things revolving in my brain while my eyes monitored everything and everyone, my heart hoping there wouldn't be one hitch before takeoff, a sudden voice calling me, "Hey, you! Step out of the line!" But it didn't happen. I had moved smoothly through the scanners, metal detectors, and airport security. So far, so good, I thought to myself.

When I booked this flight, I had imagined that I might be the only teenager flying, surrounded by two hundred fifty old heads wearing business suits. But I was wrong. It was Saturday, late afternoon and the gate had been filled with all types and ages, a number of teens in T-shirts, all of them organized, quiet, and preoccupied by some toy or technology or book. Some were having excited conversations softer than a murmur and only their faces revealed emotion. Directions were spoken in a soft, polite voice, first in Japanese, then in English.

I reached my seat, an aisle seat at the bulkhead in coach class, so there was no one seated in front of me. I had room to stretch my legs. I placed two bags in the overhead compartment before sitting down. I loosened the laces on my tan suede Clarks and unbuttoned the top two buttons of my suede Ralph Lauren shirt. I ran my hand over my fresh Caesar cut and fastened my seat belt. I glanced at my Datejust—twenty minutes till takeoff—then I took a deep breath.

As passengers filed in, searching for their seats and wheeling their carry-ons behind them, I put in my earplugs and turned on my music. I took the black case from my pocket, removed my new Gucci sunglasses, and eased them over my eyes. The darkening of the cabin and all the images that surrounded me soothed me some.

Sudana had gifted me these and insisted that I open her gift right then and there as she and everyone else watched. I never expected the royal send-off, the gifts and celebration that Umma, Naja, and the Ghazzalis had prepared for me. It was a sweet gesture and a magical meal made with great care and a deep love, from how the dishes were positioned on the table, to the look and garnishings on the food, to the aroma they created in the Ghazzali home. The taste and blend of the spices was Umma through and through. And as she stood there dressed in royal robes that she made and beaded by her hand, it was simple for me to see that this all was an expression of a mother's true love for her son.

Despite me being tired and stressed and having an endless checklist churning in my mind, I was moved.

Tilal Salim, Mr. Ghazzali's younger son, filmed it all using the camera that Ameer and Chris gifted to me. Then Naja threw the whole place into a frenzy when a frog leaped out of her pocket and onto the table where the food was still being admired. The green creature was lucky he had not leaped into the steaming soup pot.

"I'm sorry, I'll catch him. I'll catch him." Naja jumped up from her seat and chased it. Umma and Mrs. Ghazzali stood shocked. Mustapha Salim helped Naja while Tilal kept filming and the Ghazzali daughters just laughed.

"I found him in the backyard," Naja confessed, cupping the captured frog between her two palms. "Sudana—" Naja began, almost snitching.

I looked at Sudana. She gave Naja a stern look and placed one finger by her lips.

Naja understood immediately and changed the direction of her talk. "His name is Panic because every time people see him, that's how they act. But I don't know why!" Naja said, peeking in at her frog.

"Naja, put him back outside," Umma said softly. "And then wash your hands and return to the table."

"Yes, Umi Umma," Naja agreed immediately, exaggerating her

obedience. I knew she had a plan. I looked at my sister and smiled, my stress easing some. When Naja and Sudana returned all cleaned up, Mr. Ghazzali said, "Wait, let's take a photo!"

"Tilal is already filming," Basima, his eldest daughter, pointed out.

"A photo with *my* camera," Mr. Ghazzali insisted, pointing out that the movie camera would be leaving with me when I left.

As everyone stood and merged together for the photo, I looked toward Umma, who was looking toward me. A memory as swift and impossible to catch as lightning flashing through a cloud shot through my mind, and I was certain it shot through Umma's also. It was a memory of our last night living in the Sudan, though no one knew it would be our last. Our big family was gathered together. A photographer who my father had hired called out suggestions for how each of us should sit or stand to be captured in his lens. We were all dressed in our best. My father, seeming taller than a tree and more important than the sky, had his three wives and most of our family present.

Mr. Ghazzali clicked three photos. He then handed his camera to his wife, gathered all of us men, and Mrs. Ghazzali clicked a photo of Mr. Ghazzali, myself, and Mustapha and Talil. Then we all prayed and ate together.

Afterward we all resisted the power of sumptuous handmade food and spices that pushed people into relaxed postures. Umma and the other females piled gifts for me onto the table where only the desserts remained. Mr. Ghazzali leaned on me to get moving or risk missing my 6:00 p.m. flight. Mustapha and Talil loaded my luggage into the trunk of their taxi while Umma and I excused ourselves and went downstairs to speak privately.

"I went to Queens this morning to check on our new house," I told her. "Mr. Slurzberg is an interesting man."

"What happened?" Umma asked.

"Him and his wife were sitting on the porch doing nothing. The wife offered me some water. I accepted her offer because I wanted to go in and see how they were progressing with moving out."

"And?," Umma said.

"The place looked exactly how it did when you saw it, nothing packed away and a mess."

"What did they say about it?" Umma asked.

"I told Mr. Slurzberg if he didn't move out on time he would have to refund the rush fee that I paid him.

" Umma laughed. She knew the ending of my short story.

"Mr. Slurzberg said, "I have six days and six hours left. In six days, six hours and one minute this place will look like we were never here." We both laughed.

Umma slid me a final gift. "This is for Mr. Nakamura, a gift from your father."

I looked into Umma's eyes, knowing that she had gift wrapped one of my father's possessions for a man who she hoped would accept her son properly into his family. I understood my Umma's heart, but in this matter I did not share her sentiments. I accepted the gift with mixed and incomplete thoughts about how I would handle it.

"Okay, Umma, I'm about to go now. I love you." I looked around. "You have the keys, money in your purse, and a safe place. You will be driven everywhere and watched over. You have everything," I said.

"Except my son." She said tearing.

I embraced my mother strongly and kissed her cheek, whispering in her ear, "Don't worry, I will return to you, *inshallah*."

* * *

The plane began moving forward slowly. It picked up speed until it was moving so quickly that it seemed to be standing still and we lifted into Allah's sky.

Through my dark sunglasses, I surveyed the area of the cabin where I was seated. Every seat seemed occupied, and the crowd was almost completely Japanese. As the air conditioning blew out above each seat, some people wrapped themselves in blankets. A few passengers reclined their seats. Some slid black face masks over their eyes to seclude themselves. Some men read newspapers and other people read books. There was a fourteen-hour flight ahead of us, and people seemed the opposite of anxious. They appeared relaxed and well prepared.

Here was a place so different from my Brooklyn block. No matter young or old, everyone on board was going somewhere for a specific

reason and had paid a premium price. Everyone was peaceful, probably hoping for the same thing, a safe flight.

My side seat tray was down already.

"Would you like a drink?" the polite, petite flight attendant asked.
She was the only European, blonde, her blouse crisp and spotless, her
hands clasped in front of her, the same as the Japanese flight attendants working the aisles. The drink cart was behind her. I pulled one
of my earplugs out.

"No, thank you," I answered, holding down my stack of index
cards in my left hand and my marker in my right hand. My English-
to-Japanese word and phrase dictionary was laid out on the tray.

She smiled and asked, "Will you teach yourself Japanese in"—she
checked her watch—"thirteen hours?"

"No, just a few words," I replied with a smile. She smiled back
and turned to serve the passengers seated across from me, using both
English and the Japanese language with ease. There was a pattern of
requests for green tea by the elders and diet Coke by the young. Businessmen requested drinks—Asahi, which is a Japanese beer, sake, and
hard liquor as well.

I went back to thinking of the most useful words and phrases that
I needed to know while moving around in Japan. Then I'd look them
up in English and learn the Japanese translation. I'd write it down on
the index card in Japanese on the front of my cards. Then I'd write the
answer key in English on the back of the card. So far, I had completed
52 study cards and I was aiming for around 100 or 150.

"*Mido*, I'm Yuka," some girl said to me. She was walking past my seat for the second time. "Let's trade music," she offered with excited eyes. "You are listening to music, aren't you?"

"Yeah," I answered.

"So let's trade. I'm in seat 42A on the aisle right up there." She pointed to a more forward area, but I believed it was still part of the coach section.

"What kind of music are you listening to?" I asked her.

"You'll see, here." She handed me her headphones that she had been wearing around her neck like a necklace. She used her left hand to touch the wire of my earphones, so sure that I would lend them to her. So I did.

"*Arigato!*" she said softly with great excitement. She then continued forward toward her seat, her slim legs swishing in some new Levis. She wore black Adidas on her feet and rocked her small purse on her backside instead of in front of her or on her side like most American girls did.

The brief exchange with Yuka got my mind to roaming. For the past week in Brooklyn I hadn't had the ease or comfort to let my thoughts run free. Like sand spilling through the narrow passage in an hourglass, I had been in a mad race against time. I had to focus, control, and execute precisely. Now I laid my study cards down and closed my eyes.

BOOK 2

JAPAN STORY

Mayonaka

Chapter 1

DIAMONDS IN THE SKY

First darkness and then a small spotlight. Akemi's thick, natural lips appeared. They began moving, speaking to me in her foreign tongue. Her voice was a melody of whispers. Her words were not as important as their intensity—or the subtle shapes that her lips made when forming certain phrases. She had perfectly white teeth in both worlds, the real one and the one I was seeing now, and a pretty, pretty smile. Uniquely shaped eyes wide and dark, filled with both curiosity and mischief, hers were magnetic and seductive. Those eyes of hers always shined for me and reflected my image. In them were written her confessions of love.

I saw her long, pretty neck and lean and feminine shoulders where her dark hair draped. The feeling of her was all softness mixed with nothing else but sweetness. She was always warm for me, and got more warmer the closer I came to her. Even when her lips were not moving, her silence was elegant and she made it known in her every gesture and movement that everything she had was exclusively for me.

Suddenly I opened my eyes and the seductive images slipped away. *Absence is a powerful aphrodisiac,* I thought to myself. But I didn't want to go too deep, feel too much, too soon, or have a private reaction in a public place. Instead I reached into my inside right pocket and pulled out the translation of the letter Akemi had written to me a week ago on Saturday, the last day that we saw one another in New York City. It was sealed in an envelope. Even though I'd had the option, I had refused to read it while still standing on American soil and before I was coasting through beautiful blue and white swirled skies to the Land of the Rising Sun. I didn't want to know or hear anything from

her that could possibly interrupt or delay or distract or discourage my
journey to get what belonged to me—her. Now that I was suspended
midair with no possibility of anyone or anything turning me back, I
opened it and read it slowly, carefully.

MAYONAKA

We are young, but not too young to love.
We are naïve, but not too naïve to know what we are feeling.
Who put this love into the atmosphere and this craving into
      our bodies?
Who put this feeling into our hearts and these thoughts into
      our minds?
Who brought us together, if we were supposed to be apart?
We did right. So why do they say us is wrong?
If not speaking any words in common could not stop our love,
If being divided by culture or blood relations or even oceans
Could not stop our love,
What can stop our love?
No one, none, nothing . . .

OTOSAN

Please don't hate my father, because Okasan loved him so,
And I love my mother more than anyone could know.
She has returned to the Earth but lives on in my heart.
Sometimes still, we speak, even though we're worlds apart.
Daddy asks me what do you see in him?
I answer, a hot spring on top of a cold mountain.
Or my bare skin against a sizzling hot rock.
Remove him from your heart!
Could I pull my teeth out, one at a time?
Or maybe peel off all of my own skin beginning with my fingers?
I couldn't ever . . .
I need him, like a poor girl needs everyday rice.
He is the deepest feeling I have ever felt,
Like water rushing down from the steepest waterfall.
If you are asking me not to love him, kill me.
But if I should be reborn, I would love him still.
My soul loves his soul. His soul loves my soul.

No one can say they love Akemi, yet try to separate me from
   this feeling.

MAYONAKA, they could never understand us. How could they?
   They don't even want to.

MAYONAKA, I'm so nervous . . .

I read it once. Then I read it again, more slowly than the first time. I imagined my wife locked in the bathroom in the VIP section at the Museum of Modern Art on the day of the New York and American debut of her art-work. Wrapped in an awesome kimono with a multimillion-dollar hairstyle, she stood bare-footed on the cold marble floor with pretty feet

GET THE FREE APP AT
http://gettag.mobi

SNAP IT.
WATCH IT.

ATRIA AUTHORS ON
YOUR SMARTPHONE

Download the free Microsoft Tag
app at http://gettag.mobi. Then hold
your phone's camera a few inches
away from the tag image, and it will
automatically play an audio of Akemi
reading in Japanese.

and designer toenails. She was drawing kanji onto the page of her letter to me, the black ink smeared only by her tears, her heated thoughts and fears put into poetic verses. The crowd waited for her, while she worried and waited for me. I could tell from her letter that she had argued with her father, her heart being pulled to one side by the man who had sired her and pulled the other way by the man she had married.

But I didn't know, never knew. She knew I didn't know what was happening to her. So she sent a woman flying by foot to my job in Chinatown to deliver a letter to me written in a language that I couldn't understand because she felt that it was urgent and that something was about to go desperately wrong. And even still, she didn't spell her situation out clearly, or fill the pages up with rage and curses. She knew that would be *too much*. She knew me and what I was capable of. So she tried to convey the seriousness of the situation in the carefully placed words of her poem. I could feel my love for her swelling in my chest.

After the feeling subsided some, my brain took over and shifted strictly into strategy. I looked up the word *otosan*, although I believed I already knew what it meant. It means father, and *okasan* means mother.

"Would you like chicken or beef?" The fight attendant had re-turned. "For your dinner service," she added.

"I don't want anything, thank you," I told her.

"Something to drink?"

"No, nothing," I responded. She smiled and moved on to the next passenger.

All that hard memory work only ate up two more flight hours. Just as I reclined, random people in the cabin began getting up and heading for the bathroom. I glanced down the aisle and saw that there was a line building up. I decided to try out Yuka's music and slipped on the headphones. She was listening to Megadeth, *Killing Is My Business*. She must've liked heavy metal, 'cause that's what I was hearing. It was cool as long as it was instrumental. The bass player and the guitar player were killing it, but then some dude started screaming out his lyrics. His voice was so loud, rough, and scraggly that I couldn't even figure if he was singing in Japanese or in English. I fast-forwarded and the music got worse. I took it off and laid it to the side.

"The in-flight movie selections for your enjoyment tonight are *Dragon Ball: Curse of the Blood Rubies* or *The Color Purple*." The announcement was made in Japanese and then in English.

Unfastening my seat belt, I got up to head to the men's room. I needed the short walk to splash some cold water on my face. As I walked the narrow aisle, the now-familiar flight attendant approached heading in the opposite direction. I turned sideways to allow her through, yet still she brushed her body against me. And when our bodies connected, she paused right there. "When you're finished in the lavatory, stay in the back. I'll come and quiz you," she said with a lowered voice, and then smiled and flashed forward. I didn't know what the fuck she was getting at.

Coming out of the toilet, I bumped right into her. She was leaning on the opposite wall that was filled with compartments.

"Ready?" she asked. "Where are your cards? Let me see them." She held her hand out. She wore light pink-tinted polish, had clean nails, and a cheap watch. Realizing her intent, I pulled the cards out of my pocket, so she could use them to quiz me.

"*Ohayou gozaimas,*" she said in a small voice not to disturb the other passengers.

"Good morning," I answered.

"*Tasukete?*" she said smiling.

"Please help," I answered.

"*Otosan?*" she asked.

"Father," I answered.

"*Migi?*"

"To the right."

"*Hidari?*" she said.

"Um, to the left," I answered.

"*Masugu.*"

"Straight."

"*Chotto matte?*" she asked.

"Um, wait a minute," I remembered.

"You're good!" she said, smiling some more. "Are you sure you didn't know these words before you boarded our plane?"

"No." I smiled at her distrust.

"You have a great mind. At first I was expecting to find an unaccompanied minor sitting in your seat. Instead I found a handsome man"—she gestured with one hand beside her face and moved it downward, actually touching me—"well dressed and a genius!" she tried to gas me up. "Okay, one more. Here it goes," she said excitedly. "*Utsukushi!*"

I had a mental picture of the words I had printed on my cards and I didn't recall that word at all. "That's not one of my words," I told her calmly. "What does it mean?"

"It means beautiful," she said, handed me back my cards, and proceeded down the aisle before me. An elderly woman seated in the last row beside the men's room lifted her mask to reveal only one of her eyes and smiled at me. Then she put the mask back on. I guess she had overheard our exchange and had an opinion about it.

*   *   *

Four more hours into the blackened and now cloudless sky, I became restless and wanted to get my music back. I headed up to seat 42A, where I discovered three solid rows of teenaged girls sitting side by side in Yuka's section. I wondered what kind of group they were traveling in.

I didn't see any adults, but I figured there had to be a chaperone. Come to think of it, there were not any complete families traveling on this flight, it seemed, at least not in the coach section.

"Yuka," I called, but four arms went up immediately and all at once each turned on their overhead lights. Now I had eight Asian eyes focused on me. But one girl in the middle didn't turn on her light. She was asleep. She was also pretty enough to distract me from swapping back my music. She was obviously Japanese and also obviously black, her skin the color of honey. Her eyelashes were as black as could be and unusually long. She wore cornrows, precise and perfect, that looked like bolts of lightning laid tight and zigzagging across her scalp. Her hair was thick like ours but long like theirs. I predicted that when she awakened and stood up, she would stand about five feet seven inches tall. Even though she was still sitting, I could see that she had the curves of a filled-out African female but the delicate frame of a Japanese woman too. I thought to myself, *Seeing her is like looking at a blue diamond, something you would hardly ever see, but if you happened to get a glimpse of one, you'd find yourself looking at it again and again.*

"Chiasa," Yuka said. Her voice brought me back to the reason I was there.

"What does that mean?" I asked her.

"*Her* name is Chiasa," she said, concerning the sleeping girl.

"I came for my Walkman," I told her. But I glanced at the sleeping one again. She had a gold medal dangling on a red ribbon that she wore around her neck. It was rising up and down as she breathed in and out.

"Are you part of a team?" I asked Yuka. The other three girls were all watching curiously, but not speaking or joining in.

"I speak English, but my friends only speak a little," Yuka said, holding up her two fingers to gesture, "a little bit." Yuka turned her body around away from me while still seated, revealing the chenille fabric kanji letters across the back of her jacket.

Looking at them by the snatches of available light on the mostly darkened plane, I asked, "What does it say?"

"Girls' Kendo Club of Japan," she said with pride.

"Kendo Club?" I asked.

"We fight," she said, smiling.

I laughed. "What kind of fighting?"

"Sword," she answered smoothly.

I stepped back one step, impressed. "How many are you?" I asked.

"Sixteen," Yuka said. "We are returning home from the competition."

"Your team won?" I asked, while assuming.

"Our team came in third place," Yuka said. Then the girl seated next to her pointed to the sleeping girl but didn't say anything.

"She won?" I asked her.

"Chiasa won the one-on-one competition," Yuka said reluctantly. "*Now* she is just *sleeping.*"

Yuka wanted me to stay and talk to her about music and everything else. "How many pairs of sneakers do you have? Who's your favorite performing artist? Have you ever seen the movie named *Wild Style*? Is this your first trip to Japan?" She hit me with a slew of questions. Meanwhile her three friends watched intently and seemed impressed with their bilingual leader, Yuka. They were in awe of her command of the all-English conversation. None of them could put together a complete English sentence, but when they did try and make little comments, I could understand their simple meaning and gestures each time. Each one of them was different from the others in looks and ways and feeling, and believe me, they checked me out thoroughly also.

"Let's trade something we don't have to take back," Yuka invited.

"I don't think so," I told her. "Everything I have I'm planning to keep." Just then, the sleeping girl shifted in her seat.

"Later," I said, and then turned to leave.

"*Wait!*" Yuka said. "You didn't tell us your name."

I paused. "Midnight," I answered.

"Oh," Yuka said. "*Doushite?*"

"Huh?" I asked.

"Why are you called Midnight?" she asked, her head looking up to me from her seat.

"Why are you called Yuka?" I asked, standing still in the aisle.

"I'll tell you," she volunteered. "*Chotto matte!* Will you stay a little longer?" I was noticing, as I listened with the intent to learn, that Yuka was mixing a sentence half in Japanese, the other half in English. "Here, I'll write it out for you." She took out a pen and some paper. "All Japanese names have a meaning. It really depends on which kanji your parents used when they gave the name. My name is like this." She wrote on the paper. "It means 'Superior flower.' Her name is Yuki. It's like this," she said, writing. It means 'snow.' Her name is Hikari and it means 'light.' And her name is Chou. It means 'Butterfly.' I watched and listened closely. To me, the kanji writing always looked powerful, passionate, and mysterious even without me knowing its meaning.

"Chiasa, what does her name mean?" I asked casually, noticing that Yuka had skipped over her.

"I don't really know which kanji . . . ," Yuka answered hesitantly, and laid her pen down on her tray.

"One thousand mornings!" Yuki answered, proud to participate and overpronouncing and pushing out each English word separately.

"One thousand mornings," I repeated. Chiasa's name sounded soulful to me. Then I wondered about the true meaning of it. I wanted to know why she had that name, the story behind it. It sounded more powerful than the simple definitions of the other girls' names.

"What about yours? What does it mean?" Yuka asked.

"Think about it," I answered. "It was nice meeting you, Yuka, Yuki, Hikari, and Chou." They applauded because I remembered.

I wondered if they had met other foreigners who couldn't remember or pronounce their short and simple names. Then I threw the thought right out of my mind. Them girls were just bored and anxious to get off this tight flight, same as me. We were all teenagers traveling in an adult world, our bodies packed with energy but forced to sit still on a flight for hours and hours.

* * *

As I returned to my seat, I caught glimpses of one of the in-flight films playing on at least half of the screens in my area. Even without the volume I could see a full cast of black men as fools, clowns, and useless, cruel creatures. *Those are the black Americans,* I thought to myself.

With time I became more and more anxious to see my wife. So time cruelly doubled down and began to move twice as slow. We were halfway there now. I prepared to have the dinner that my family packed me, feeling some strange sense of comfort about eating as most of the other passengers slept. After washing up in the men's room and pulling down the shopping bag with the metal tiffin containers of my food I hit the call button and requested water.

"*Mizu,*" the flight attendant said, offering the Japanese word for water. "*Kappu,*" she said for cup. She looked at my food and said, "*Oishi mitai deska*! It looks delicious! *Karai?*" she asked. "Is it spicy?" she translated.

"Definitely spicy," I admitted, as I tried to write these new words that she was using down in my memory.

"Definitely better than plane food," she said, leaning in too close. She laughed lightly.

"Right" was all I said. Finally she left.

As I enjoyed the way Sudanese leftovers can taste even better and even richer than when they were first prepared and served, I thought about how Ramadan began at sunset on Saturday in America, which meant fasting would begin at sunrise on Sunday morning. I kept myself occupied trying to figure out what time it was now and what was my exact location over which country. I recalled the map I had surveyed, then purchased at Marty Bookbinder's bookstore. I was flying from the United States—New York, to be exact—out over Alaska past Canada, past the Siberian mountains past Russia . . . Then I broke out into a smile. *A man has to work hard for his woman*, I thought.

Moments later I checked my watch, still set on New York Eastern Standard time. Back in Brooklyn it was 2:00 a.m. I cleaned up my area, content, and headed to the back to rinse my containers.

Returning, I met Yuka walking up the aisle. We both stopped at my seat. As I packed the clean containers back into the shopping bag and pushed it back into the overhead compartment, Yuka made me an offer.

"Let me keep the music that you let me listen to before. You can choose one of these." I sat down, not feeling right about standing over her in such a closed-in area. She pulled up my tray from its side pocket, which made me have to straighten up my posture. She laid down a piece of paper shaped like a bird. "It's a paper crane, you know, origami. It's good luck. Yuki made it." I just looked at it. It was crafted well but I didn't feel no connection to it. She put a card down. "It's a Japanese phone card. It's mine, but *you'll need it*," she said, so sure that she had me open. My nonresponse made her put down her next item. It was a red patch with two black swords clashing in midair. I liked it. "It's from our dojo," she said, knowing it was worth more than the other choices she was offering. I figured it probably belonged to one of them girls, or was supposed to be worn on their jacket sleeve or uniform.

"You must really like my music," I said. She ignored my statement and tried to flip it on me.

"You like it. I can tell," she said, then pointed at the patch. "When you like something, it shows just a little bit on your face," she said holding up her two fingers once again, for "a little bit."

"Oh yeah? No one *ever* said that," I told her swiftly.

"Maybe they were not looking closely," she said, and held her hand out for my music. "Take this one." I slid her the cassette Bangs had given me the other night. It was Frankie Beverly and Maze, a joint called "Before I Let Go," "Sweet Thing" by Chaka Khan, and a bunch of slow cuts I didn't want or need to feel.

As she put it in her pocket, an older lady appeared and stood behind her in the aisle. Just one look, the older lady gave her, and no words. Yuka turned, bowed to the older woman, and then rushed up the aisle back to her seat. The lady turned and followed her and stood by her seat once she reached it. If she was scolding Yuka, it was a silent scolding, because I could not hear a word or see her attitude in her gestures or body language. *She must be their chaperone,* I thought. Somehow, whatever adult is assigned to chaperone teenagers always falls asleep before us, or is absent at the exact moment that something they are supposed to be preventing is going down. Or maybe she was seated up in business class or first class even, as her girls were packed like sardines in coach.

* * *

In the morning the cabin lights were on full blast and it was too bright. I thought the sunlight was forcing me to squint, but it wasn't. The stink of pork hung in the stagnant air as passengers sucked down two one-inch-cubed squares of egg and one undercooked-looking slice of ham.

I looked to my left toward the window as the passenger across the aisle at the window seat began lifting his window cover. It was actually nighttime all over again, although my watch set on American time read 6:00 a.m.

"We are one hour away from Narita Airport. The time in Tokyo is now six p.m. Your flight attendant will be coming through the cabin collecting your trays and accepting trash. We would appreciate your cooperation in keeping the aisles clear. We will be landing at seven p.m. Tokyo time. Please accept and complete your landing cards and customs documents. Your flight attendants will be distributing them throughout the cabin."

My tray was still up but my patch was gone. I smiled at the thought that I had been hustled by Yuka, played out before I even touched down on their soil. I leaned over, thinking maybe I dropped it beneath my seat. When I raised my tray and leaned forward to look, I was more than surprised to see the patch sewn onto my jeans on my left leg.

I pulled at it, thinking, *Nah, that's impossible.* But the patch didn't fall off or peel off into the palm of my hand either. It was stitched on crudely, not expertly, but attached. I sat up, put my right hand on my head instinctively and held it there. I imagined Yuka sitting in the aisle late at night next to my seat, sewing the patch on so secretly that even I could not feel or detect it. I felt a cross between being a dupe and being snagged off guard.

*   *   *

The landing form required me to write in the address where I would be staying in Japan. I was also asked to report exactly how much money I was carrying. They asked if I'd ever been convicted of a crime. I answered thankfully, *No!* The paperwork warned that I must always be in possession of my passport as I traveled throughout their country. I printed in the address for Shinjuku Uchi my hostel, located in Shinjuku, Tokyo. I filled out all the custom forms and pressed them inside my passport. I placed the items in my inside pocket and unfastened my seat belt and stepped to the bathroom. When I returned to my seat, there was a folded piece of paper on my chair. I removed the paper and read it. It was an address with Yuka's full name on top, as well as a telephone number. I pushed it in my pocket and sat down. I wondered about their whole crew, their ages and all. I was sure they were teens. A couple of them might have even been a couple of years older than me. I was also sure that they could never guess my age either. Mostly everyone thought I was older than I am. I didn't correct them either.

"Fasten your seat belts for landing." All standing passengers slowly returned to their seats, pushed their belongings back into the overheads, lifted their window covers, raised their seats, and fastened their seat belts. I can't front, my face was calm and regular but now I was hyped up like crazy and completely awake.

Narita Airport was very bright, clean, and well organized. While riding the belt that moved hundreds of passengers forward as they stood still, I took note of the colorful photography. Among the advertisements were huge pictures of cherry blossom trees, various flowers, and even animals. It was as though they wanted us to feel outdoors while being indoors. When I looked out through the huge windows and onto their tarmac, I saw several huge aircraft lined up from countries spanning the world. I watched as the luggage from arriving passengers was moved by conveyor onto luggage trucks and driven away to their terminals. The geography book I had read about Japan in the Open Mind Bookstore described it as a "small island." As several uniformed workers in jumpsuits moved around the tarmac, and the active airport extended as far as I could see in each direction, I thought to myself that this place looked huge, profitable, and powerful. On our way to customs, through wide corridors that seemed empty except for the hundreds of passengers from our flight, I reached an intersecting corridor. A whole new flood of people joined in, and that made about seven hundred of us moving toward the customs area. Signs positioned above the flow of the people, printed in every language, broke up the huge crowd and ordered us to different locations. Japanese citizens returning home to Japan went one way and all other passengers went the other according to the signs that applied to them.

When my group arrived at the designated location, we were met by about fifteen floor guides, Japanese men and women in identical, spotless, and well-pressed uniforms, men in blue pants, white business shirts, and jackets, and women in jackets, white blouses, and skirts, with silk scarves around their necks. Most of the women had their hair pulled back and expertly wrapped, folded, and pinned into an array of styles without a strand escaping. I noticed how they all held their hands interlocked in front of themselves, instead of casually at their sides. Their stance seemed trained and uniform.

Red ropes directed all our movements, and from time to time the guides used their hands to gesture without words, which I found interesting. They were all wearing white, sparkling clean gloves.

The line advanced quietly and slowly. I thought about pulling out my pocket dictionary and practicing vocabulary words while I waited. I took a few steps forward, stopped, and took a quick look back. To my surprise, I saw the girl they said was named Chiasa on the line a few spaces back. I was perplexed now. She held an American passport in her hand. But wasn't she part of a Japanese Girls' kendo team just returning from a competition in America? I didn't want to stare, even though I was curious. I turned back toward the front, facing the single-file line that went on around a maze of ropes and barriers.

Five minutes later I looked back again. Immediately I saw she was looking my way. We both shifted our eyes away from one another. One of the floor guides appeared on the opposite side of the rope where I was standing. I thought he was going to say something to me. Instead he went to the man standing behind me, apparently a father with his wife and their two children. The floor guide held up the landing card as if to ask, Where is it? The husband turned to his wife and she turned to her son. The floor guide pointed the four of them off the line and over to the desks where there were more cards available for completion. Now Chiasa was standing directly behind me. I thought to myself, *She feels like a gift from Allah*, although I didn't really know the reason.

Then I imagined if Akemi and I had a daughter, she would look like Chiasa. And what would our son look like? I wanted him to be black-skinned like me, although it would be okay if he weren't. But as I pictured my great-grandfather, grandfather, father, myself, and then my son, I wanted us all to be similar in complexion, size, thought, and action.

"*Sumimasen*, move up," someone said softly. I stepped forward and looked back. When we were facing each other, we both asked one another at the same time, "Are you American?" Then we both smiled at the coincidence and we both answered simultaneously, "No!" Then we both looked at each other's hand—her left, my right—and we were both holding blue American passports with the eagle emblazoned in gold. Neither of us bothered to explain.

"Nice patch," she said, staring down at my pant leg. "Is it just fashion or did you fight for it?" Her arms were now folded in front of her, and she was still holding on to her documents.

"I didn't fight for it. But I can fight," I answered her with a serious look.

"What's your weapon?"

"I don't advertise it," I told her. "But I know yours is the sword," I added, to let her know that this was not my first time seeing her. Her eyes widened a bit. I could see how her long lashes could shield anyone from seeing directly into her silver-gray eyes.

"I saw you sleeping on the plane," I revealed.

"I wasn't sleeping," she said with a completely straight face. "I was practicing."

"Practicing what?" I asked.

"I was practicing making people feel sure that I was sleeping," she said.

I paused. I thought our conversation was feeling strange. She was a young female traveling alone and I was a young man doing the same. I just turned my attention back to the front of the line, moved a few steps up, and waited.

"When people think that someone is asleep, they say things that they wouldn't say when the person is awake." She broke our silence, leaning in a bit to speak to me from behind.

"I get it" was all I said.

"Are you in the military?" she asked.

"No," I responded, thinking to myself, *Maybe she is*. She started this conversation asking me if I could fight and about my choice of weapons and now if I was in an army.

"That's good." She smiled. I wanted to know what her smile was about.

"Are you in the military?" I asked her, but I wasn't serious.

"No, but my father is," she said.

That straightened me. I knew the difference between a girl who has a father and a girl who does not. And I was sure now that since she mentioned her father, he would be standing somewhere near the luggage arrival waiting for his beautiful daughter to arrive back into his care.

"He is a decorated marksman. He could kill you from a long distance," she said calmly, as though this were casual, everyday information. I figured she wanted me to know that she is protected the way daughters who have fathers are protected. I got it.

"He has perfect vision and so do I," she added.

The feel to her was different than anything I ever felt coming off a girl. She didn't speak with arrogance or conceit or eagerness in her tone. Yet she was softly saying some powerful and proud statements that lay on top of a hidden threat. And she was exotic and pretty as a puma.

I turned forward and didn't say nothing back to her. Soon she stepped to my side, glanced at the landing card I was holding, and asked, "Are you staying in a hostel?"

"Why? Do you have a recommendation for me?" I asked her, dodging.

"It depends on what you are here to do and see." She said it like it was a question. She wanted to know what I was in Japan for. I wasn't about to start spilling my guts on the line, when I was about to meet up with a customs officer. So I didn't say.

"You're staying in Shinjuku. That's one five-second train stop away from me. I stay in Yoyogi with my grandfather."

She was reading the documents as I held them in my hand. "I told you I have perfect vision. I saw it written on your cards," she said, answering a question that I never asked her! *"Nihongo ga hanase masen?"* she asked sweetly, staring at me while one of her eyebrows raised up a bit, anticipating I would fail her test.

But I was already searching my mind. I knew I had a phrase like that written in my study cards. I had a six-second delay before I answered her, *"Iie! Nihongo ga hanase masen."* Which means "No, I don't speak Japanese." It was the answer to her question. She laughed quietly but still lifted her hand to cover her mouth and muffle her sound. With her hand lifted, I could see her landing card where she had entered her birth date. Now I knew that she was sixteen years old with a birthday coming up in two months, on July 25th.

"You will need a tour guide!" she said. "And you will need a translator." She raised both eyebrows this time.

"I'll get one," I told her. "I'll take care of it."

"How many days are you staying here?" she asked, while reaching into her pocketbook, placing her passport and landing cards inside, and then pulling out a small yellow calendar. She opened it up. The pages were worn. She ran her finger across the days of this month of May. She had something written in most of the boxes that represented the thirty-one days.

"A short stay," I said. "I'm good though. I'm meeting someone in Tokyo."

With her calendar raised and covering her nose and mouth, only her eyes could be seen. "We should meet for just one afternoon, you and I," she said.

I was looking right back at her. Before I responded to her bold approach, she said, "Let's meet up and fight. You said you *can* fight, right?" She was straight-faced and feminine and soft, but her words were the opposite. Now she was holding one hand behind her back. My natural smile broke out. I was considering how each woman is a different combination of traits, and what a combination this one had. Her voice was soft and slightly raspy, like a girl on the third day of a cold. But the words coming out of her mouth didn't match her feminine appearance or sultry voice.

"I don't fight women, not ever," I told her truthfully. "When I'm next to a woman, the last thing that I'm thinking is that she and I should fight." She stared for a few seconds and then smiled. But then she became suddenly shy. "Besides, why would I fight a girl who just told me her father is a marksman?" I reminded her.

"My father's stationed overseas right now. He won't be back to Japan until the Autumn Festival. That's . . ." She counted on her long, slim fingers. She had clean nails, clipped short, and wore no jewelry. "That's five months from now, but even though he's not here, if he thought someone had done something bad to me, he'd find him and kill him."

"If I had a daughter, I would do the same," I assured her.

"It wouldn't matter if they hid. My father can find anyone in the world no matter where they run." I didn't comment any further. She had a strong love and a spoken loyalty and pride about her father and I thought it was fly.

"You know, you've arrived during Golden Week, but you've already missed a lot of the events," she said, switching topics.

"Golden Week, what's that?" I asked, completely blank about it.

"Golden Week," she repeated. "It's the second-largest Japanese holiday. All schools are closed, and many companies are also. It's called Golden Week, but sometimes it goes on for about ten days to two weeks. Most Japanese spend this holiday with their families. A lot of us travel during this time, as you can see."

I guess that's why there were so many sports teams on our flight. Immediately my mind jumped to my wife. Maybe that's why she had been calling me from Iwa's house in Tokyo instead of from her own house in Kyoto.

"So, have I arrived at the beginning or the end of Golden Week?" I asked her.

"The end," she responded.

Umm, I thought. Chiasa had given me useful information in less than five minutes. I was grateful.

"So, the person you are meeting in Tokyo, is it Yuka?" she asked.

"Nah, I just met her on the plane," I told her.

"Good, because she's originally from Osaka. I was born in Tokyo and lived there my whole life. I used to deliver pizza on my motorcycle, so I know all the streets and cool places."

"You drive a motorcycle?"

"Yes, my father bought it for me on my sixteenth birthday. It was an apology gift because I hadn't seen him for six months. My mother hated it, but I loved it. My mother will only pay for things that she likes me to do. So she pays for my piano lessons and dance classes because she says those things are for 'good Japanese girls.' I have to work to pay for the lessons I want and the things I like. I hate playing the piano and dancing ballet, but I do it because it keeps my mother happy." She shifed her body slightly. Ballet dancing obviously kept her body right, I thought to myself.

"You said you stay with your grandfather?" I reminded her.

"Yes, my parents are divorced," she admitted in a much softer voice with traces of hurt and regret. "It was one of those nasty divorces. They don't speak to one another and I can't mention my father's name to my mother or ask any questions. They both love me, just not each other."

I felt sorry that her mother and father had somehow lost their love for one another. It sounded foreign to me, losing love for anyone you had ever loved. And the same way when I first laid eyes on this girl, I could see traces of her Japanese mother and her African father, without ever seeing either of them or knowing them, I wondered now how could they have this lovely daughter together, see her and not see themselves. When the father saw the mother through the daughter, didn't it make him remember loving his wife? Wouldn't it cause him to love her even more? I guess not. Man to man, I would want to ask these kinds of questions and get serious responses. When men gather, we don't talk like that, and the questions that sit on our minds, we won't ask.

Again I felt an urgency about my wife as I was being presented with the exact picture of what I never would allow to happen in my family. In the Quran, there are instructions about exactly how a divorce can be carried out. But divorce is discouraged in our way of life. The Quran gives a man not only instructions but boundaries, limits, and goals, to hold his head and his family together, and to deal with his wife in a just way that will help them to stay together.

"But my grandfather is cool. My mom is his daughter, so of course he loves her. But he loves my dad also, so I love him! So I stay with him. Anyway, I'll start school in one month and move out into the dorm. Oh yes, school in Japan begins in April. I know it starts in September in America, right, and ends in June? Well here, our school year has just begun."

"Your school year just started in April and already you are on vacation," I said thoughtfully.

"I know, it is different, but this is Japan. We do it our own way," she said, smiling. And while she smiled, I thought of how Akemi's father probably snatched her up and took her right to school to start the Japanese school year after her year of living and schooling in New York City had come to an end. He probably was acting as though nothing significant had really happened in her life. As though she never met me, fell in love, married, and gave me her oath and virginity and life.

"My school actually also began in April but not for me. Foreign students had to come in and take an intensive Japanese language course. I didn't need to, I was born here and I speak fluent Japanese and English. So you see it works out good for you because now I'm off from school, and for twenty-nine thousand yen, I can show you around Tokyo for the next five days. I'll be your translator and your tour guide. I can meet you in the morning and stay each day until the job is done." She was speaking softly but with confidence and a gentle persuasion, as though I had no choice but to go along with her plan.

I was still stuck on the figure 29,000 yen. I had not shifted my mind into their money exchange system yet, but the number she was throwing around sounded expensive, crazy, extreme, and not happening. "Where did you come up with that number?" I asked her.

"That's how much it costs for my next flight lesson. I'm studying to get my pilot's license."

She had my head spinning. Now I was picturing her in the cockpit.

The floor guide gestured for me to step up to customs. So I said later to Chiasa and moved up to the booth. I saw her move to the booth beside mine on command as well.

At customs, the kind of tension that was so thick when I arrived in America from the Sudan with Umma was not present in Japan. The male authority who faced me didn't appear to believe that I was a problem that had to be eliminated, guilty on sight. Even though he represented Japanese law, he didn't try to put in place a whole new set of rules and restrictions *just for me.* The officer, a blank-faced Japanese male, simply looked at my passport and then up at my face. He stepped to his left, pointed a camera at me, and snapped my photo. He stamped my passport, inserted a piece of paper, and waved me on. I looked at the stamp and the paper. It said I could visit Japan for ninety days before I was required to leave. It also instructed me to keep my passport in my possession at all times.

At the luggage conveyor while waiting for my duffel bag to come around, I calculated finally that 29,000 yen was about $250. The American dollar was stronger than the yen, and $85 would get me 10,000 yen. *Five days for $250,* I thought. *That's fifty dollars a day.* It was high but not too high. I knew from the jump that I would have to get someone to translate for me along the way. This girl Chiasa had offered me enough information in a short period of time for me to feel comfortable with her offer. I'd get her phone number and use her services when I needed them. For now, I was throwing my belongings on a cart and heading for the phone to call my wife.

"Midnight!" I heard a voice call. It was Yuka and her friends. They were waving wildly. I put my hand up once as my way to say *sayonara.* I did notice that the rest of their Kendo team seemed to be traveling

together, but Chiasa was left standing alone, pulling her belongings
off the belt for herself.

*   *   *

Beyond customs and baggage, when I reached the Japanese side of
the airport, everything changed. Signs were all written in kanji.

At the airport convenience store I stood silently in the aisle observing. The foods and drinks were all labeled in kanji. I recognized
some American candies like Snickers and Juicy Fruit, only because of
the identical colors of the Japanese packaging, but the names of the
candies were all written in kanji. Even the ingredient listings were all
in kanji.

As I approached the cashiers and instinctively spoke in simple
English, they looked at me curiously. I realized they spoke and understood only Japanese, even down to words like yes and no as well as
greetings. I wanted to purchase a phone card but stood staring at the
wall, unable to decipher which was what.

Unable to read properly, I thought about Umma. Her everyday
life in America was like this. As a man, it was an uncomfortable feeling to me, to not be able to read the language of the place where I was
standing, living, and breathing. Illiteracy reduced me, I thought, into
the position of a young child.

I observed the cash transactions taking place. Unlike the Americans, the Japanese cashiers received the payment from the customer
and placed it down on the register for both the customer and cashier
to see. They repeated the amount of the purchase, the amount they
received, and then counted out the change and handed it to the customer before putting away the cash the customer had paid. I figured
they wanted to eliminate any problems before they could occur. A
forgetful customer or con man would never get away with saying, "I
gave you a twenty!" When they had really only paid with a ten.

I liked the way the girls folded the bills perfectly between their
fingers and held them there. I liked the way the cashiers counted back
the cash rapidly after spreading the bills like a hand fan.

I picked up my bags, turned, and walked out, looking for a public pay phone. When I finally found it, I picked up the phone and
stood staring. All the printed directions were in Japanese. I couldn't

even figure out the cost of the call. I put the receiver to my ear. The recorded voice on the other end of the phone was speaking only in Japanese. I looked around the well-lit, immaculately clean, and well-organized airport and thought to myself, *I'm in Japan!*

I searched out the customer information desk, was told *"Chotto matte"* by a small polite man who raised his index finger up to signal wait one minute, please. *Chotto matte.* I repeated it to myself for my own memorizing.

The woman who appeared to help me spoke some English. She asked me a few questions, then told me which phone card to purchase and how to work the pay phone. She also told me how and where to purchase my ticket for the "airport limousine" to Shinjuku. I didn't need a limousine, but the ticket only cost twenty dollars. It was a two-hour ride. So I agreed. Then I called Umma.

"Alhamdulillah," she said in her early-morning relaxed Sunday voice. "We are all safe and fine. You know that you can call me anytime you want to talk. But focus on your wife now. She needs you more," Umma said graciously.

I called Iwa Ikeda at 9:00 p.m. The call went right through.

"Moshi moshi," a feminine voice said.

"Is this Ikeda-san?" I asked.

"Hai!" she responded softly yet with excitement.

"This is Mayonaka. Thank you for taking my call. Is my wife there?" I asked calmly, though I was feeling anxious.

"Nande?" she asked. I knew that meant "What?" in Japanese.

"Akemi Nakamura, is she there?" I asked, patiently and politely as well. Iwa Ikeda said something in response, but I couldn't hear it because an announcement came over the speaker system in the airport. The announcement was spoken in Japanese, so I ignored it.

"Ikeda-san?"

"Hai! Chotto matte," she answered. My heart raced some.

"Mayonaka?" I heard Iwa's voice again. "Where are you?" She was speaking English now in an even higher-pitched tone than she'd used before.

I paused. I wanted to hear Akemi's voice first, before answering any questions. Instead I heard a click. The pay phone went dead. Immediately I called back. I got the answering machine. Her message was spoken all in Japanese, but even an idiot could understand to begin leaving his message after the beep. So I did.

"Ikeda-san, we were disconnected. I'll call back again in five minutes."

Five minutes later I called and got her answering machine *again*. I hung up. I stood there thinking, *What's the meaning of this?* Five more minutes and I called once more. Her machine came on; calmly I left my second message: "I'll call back in the morning. This is Mayonaka." I was tight now, uneasy and perplexed. This was some unnecessary bullshit.

My limo was due to arrive outdoors at space number 18. I pushed my cart through the sliding doors. As I eased down the walkway, I saw Chiasa standing on a line behind her pushcart loaded down with bags and big items. She had one item that was in a case that stood seven feet tall. She also had what looked like a trombone case, and two suitcases, one big, one small. She was about five-foot-seven with a powerful body in a petite frame. I didn't know how she was gonna move around all that stuff on her own once she had to ditch the airport cart and travel back into Tokyo.

"Can I have your telephone number?" I asked her, handing her a pencil and my small pad that I kept in my pocket for important info and contacts. She wrote it down instantly, as though she had been sure that I would find her and ask.

"I'm never really home, so we should set a time," she said. "Let's meet tomorrow night. That will give you time to figure out that you won't be able to figure anything out," she added, completely assured. "Then we can meet at my dojo, fight, and get it over with. I think people respect each other faster if they fight first, experience each other's style." Then she wrote down the name of her dojo and the address and, in bold ink, 6:00 p.m.! "We'll eat dinner together afterward."

Chapter 2
FOREIGNER

I checked my watch and looked for the number 18, hoping it was written in English. When I saw my limousine, it was a bus!

"Airport limousine" hired hands took my luggage and stored it below. After receiving luggage tags, we entered the bus single file. It took only a few seconds to notice that no one six feet tall or taller had ever ridden the bus comfortably, as the ceilings were too low and the seats too close together. However, the bus was obviously brand-new and very clean. The bus windows even had curtains fit to size that were retractable. The workers and the bus driver were very polite. The seats were well upholstered in quality cloth and colorful designs. The headrests were covered with removable white lace, without a trace of dirt or grease or stains. There were twenty-two passengers besides me. Each of us spread out, trying to keep the seat directly next to ourselves free for our extra use.

Compact cars seemed to be the preferred ride out here—Toyotas and Honda's and some other unrecognizable vehicles that aren't for sale in America, different styles, makes, and models. Even the trucks were less wide and tall than the American kind. The highways were well paved and free of potholes and detours and debris. The lanes were wide and clean. The ride was smooth. The lines on the ground looked perfect, as though they had just been painted on.

Soon the scenes changed from the stretch of airport property to rural to suburban to city. The traffic was flowing steadily without any congestion. Other than vehicles, billboards, and buildings, I couldn't clock much because it was night. The dim lights in the bus made it difficult to see out unless I pressed my forehead to the window glass.

A female's clear and soft voice, a recording, offered narration over a speaker system, explaining where we were, where we were headed, and calling out the name of each stop in several languages. The bus was so organized and clean that even though I wished the seats were bigger, the trip was more comfortable than a NYC ride anywhere, by bus, train, or car.

I thought that arriving in Shinjuku late at night would put me at a disadvantage since I was unfamiliar with the place and its layout. Yet at Shinjuku station, the night was the same as day. Although it was now 11:00 p.m., the station was packed with people as though this was their peak hour. Even though New York is known as "the city that never sleeps," Tokyo was quite different. In New York there is a day crowd and a night crowd. No way can the New York night crowd match the numbers that flow through the city during work-ing hours. But here in Shinjuku, it seemed to be happening. Men and women in suits, teenagers, families, and tourists were all mov-ing about. This wasn't the club crowd or the party crowd. These just seemed like everyday normal people ignoring the time and living to the fullest or perhaps just getting off from working twelve-hour days or coming back from night schools. I wasn't sure. Everything was all lit up with high-watt fluorescent bulbs. The only crime was to stop moving, because the heavy population was constantly flowing in what seemed like a daily march routine and rhythm.

I put one strap of my duffel bag on my left shoulder and the other strap on my right. I picked up my carry-on and began walking. I had an option to jump in a cab but I decided against it. I had checked the map, knew the direction I was to move in, and was drawn in by everything I was seeing and feeling.

It was bugged out seeing hundreds and thousands of Japanese and a splash of other Asian faces and no whites. It was obvious that this was *their* country. Confidence comes in numbers, I know. They were packed in escalators and in all the corridors, the small and the wide, spinning through all the turnstiles and jamming through all the exits and entrances all at the same time. As I exited the west side of Shinjuku station along with three hundred other walkers, I ran up on a wall of vending machines. I stepped all the way in to keep out of the way of the flow. Of course I had seen vending machines before in Brooklyn back when Umma was in the hospital giving birth to Naja.

Yet these machines were different, with different designs and styles and products for sale and much more plentiful. I counted seven on the wall I was staring at and five directly across the street.

Less than sixty seconds standing on my feet in Shinjuku and all I could think about was business. One vending machine sold cigarettes, a variety of brands. I thought about how that couldn't happen in the US because you had to be a certain age to buy cigarettes and in the business district you would definitely get carded. On my block and in some local hoods, kids could cop "loosies" for a quarter each. Even though the kids were underage, some shop owners would risk their license just to keep the peace with the customers and particularly good customers who sent their ten-year-old daughters and sons to pick up cigarettes for them.

The next vending machine was selling beer and liquor. I didn't recognize some of the brands but I imagined how much money a vending machine liquor store could make on my block alone. Except if there was a vending machine offering beer or liquor on my Brooklyn block, the owner would have to bulletproof it and use Plexiglas instead of real glass. He'd have to build it sunken into the cement and still put heavy chains around it also.

The next machine sold hot coffee, iced coffee, hot tea, or iced tea. Drop a coin in that sucker and the can came out fully heated. I tried it out even though I didn't want to drink no coffee. The can was so hot, I had to throw it back and forth in my hands to cool it off.

The next machine sold hot soups of various kinds.

The one beside it sold water, juices, and sodas.

The next machine sold toothpaste and shaving cream, combs and toothbrushes, and even had a row of men's new and clean white underwear individually wrapped that could be purchased. Drop in a coin and they fell right out the bottom slot.

But the most fascinating vending machine was the last one on this row. It had a slot for bills and a separate one for coins; put in your yen and get a brand-new pair of kicks. *Get the fuck out of here*, I thought to myself, *sneakers! What about a Nike vending machine!* What a quiet and intelligent way to earn money twenty-four hours a day, three hundred and sixty-five days a year. I would be earning money on the Christians' Christmas, on New Year's Eve and New Year's Day, on all the dead presidents' birthdays and Labor Day too. It was a good legal business, but I imagined it involved about 85 percent less effort than Umma Designs. If I owned even one of these machines, I could come around at three or four in the morning, collect my stack and rack of bills and bags of coins, and no one would even know who was the mastermind behind my operation. I would switch up my schedule, keep it random so that no one could clock my movements. Unlike being a store owner, and having to sit in the same store all day and welcome any type of customer, if I owned all seven of these machines, no one would even know my name or address or personal information, ninja style.

I looked the machines over searching for a company name or phone number. I wanted to jot it down in my notebook and maybe take a serious look into the business of it. I found a metal plate with information on it, all written in kanji and completely incomprehensible to me.

I pushed off. But I knew I'd be back. I planned to hold on to the idea. As I moved, my mind kept coming up with estimates on how much each machine cost, how much it cost to stock it, and guesses about how many people flowed through this Shinjuku area day and night, night and day.

In this city of lights, every single store was lit up with bright colors that popped. It was impossible to overlook those brilliant reds blaring, some blinking, some neon. There were hot pinks and electric blues and blinding yellow-gold lights as well. On the building tops were gigantic television screens flashing advertisements, the product changing every few seconds. There were people hired to hand out cards and flyers and tissue packs with ads plastered across the backside. There were dancing girls in go-go shorts and leather boots singing jingles to draw in customers. The lights were not in just one section. They went on as far as my eyes could see in every direction.

I was passing by late-night bookstores. Imagine that, a place where readers could chill and read no matter the time of night. These bookstores were packed, not empty like Marty Bookbinder's. And in the slow walk I was on, it seemed that there were as many bookstores in Shinjuku as the hood had liquor stores and churches.

The streets were lined with vendors manning food carts. They had raised umbrellas and hung lanterns and brought in stools seated close to the ground, they also sat on upside-down crates. There were small portable tables with stacks of chopsticks and sauces in glasses placed on each one. I couldn't tell you what food they were serving. I looked but I didn't recognize it. The main thing was, businesswise, people were eating it up eagerly. Several couples were seated side by side enjoying. I wondered if these carts were considered licensed and legal, or if at a certain moment they would have to break it all down and pack it up and start hauling and running like in New York, where random vendors live a dog's life and get got for their products by crooked cops who steal their merchandise from them and still hand them a high-priced ticket for a "city code violation." But I didn't see nobody running and I didn't see no cops! Everyone was working or walking calmly, serving customers or minding their business and keeping it moving. I respected that.

I thought it was an oversized arcade, but it wasn't. It was a spot called "Pachinko." It took me about three and half minutes to figure out this was their gambling spot. *Strange hustle*, I thought. There were about three hundred fifty men sitting in front of individual machines that looked like pinball machines, with a bucket filled with tiny silver balls. They kept feeding the machines with the balls in hopes of a jackpot. But it looked like they never reached the jackpot. A lot of these men appeared to be businessmen who hadn't been home from work since they'd left probably early this morning. Still wearing their suits, they had their briefcases and one or two bags of groceries sitting beside them. There was nothing between them and that pachinko machine except tobacco clouds, as they smoked more and more with each try for fast money.

Rows and rows of restaurants were squeezed into tight spaces. I laughed at joints that were legit "eat in" spots, so small that they only had three tables and six chairs. I tried to do the math on how many guests they had to turn all day to make their money back with only a six-person capacity. Some small spots had no tables but had instead one long counter for their customers to eat on and six stools. Their customers all ate facing the wall, not too cool for families and couples, I figured.

The architecture and craftsmanship of each of these shops was dope, though. And each one has its own style. Some were made all from glass. I could stand outside and see everything that was going on inside. I could see the cooks, who were mostly males wearing either white chef jackets or long chef aprons, their pants wide and baggy but cinched by a drawstring at the waist and ankles. Most of them covered their heads with white hand towels wrapped half like a turban and half like how some Brooklyn cats rock it in the summer or after a game. I could watch them chopping vegetables, grilling fish, and boiling pots of water and stirring soups with a paddle 'cause the iron kettles were so wide and deep. Right next door would be a restaurant made only of wood, no glass. I could not read the kanji signs that identified who they were and what they were selling, but when the doors slid open, I could see the crowd seated elbow to elbow and could tell whatever it was, it was in high demand. Noodle shops were easy to recognize. They were packed with mostly men, each of them seeming not to be with the other, all their backs bent over and faces close to their bowls.

On the streets of northern Sudan, where I'm from, many men moved with men and their sons or their fathers. So a place where men and women moved in separate packs, at separate times, to separate places, was not unfamiliar to me.

It didn't take long for me to note that in many cases, I stood taller than the front door of these establishments. The seats were so close together and people so uniformly slim that I thought I might be too broad and muscular to fit into their shoulder-to-shoulder seating pattern. This made me feel bigger than life and dominant, like this character named Gulliver whose story I once read.

I was a foreigner watching each of them and all of their things and ways so closely, yet not one of them was watching me. I felt like a black leopard in the chicken coop or even out in the wetlands where the gazelles gathered, while I was camouflaged by the night. Not that I was on the prowl or the attack, but I was definitely capable of being provoked.

*   *   *

Before I rounded the bend to the side alley where the hostel was supposed to be located, I saw one half-wooden, half-glass shop on the corner, where there was a full pig's leg with the black hoof still attached, hoisted and mounted on the same counter where the customers sat eating. The cook stood on the opposite side of the counter and carved slices of the pork and placed it in boxed plates for the customer to eat. It got me more alert. I always know, as a Muslim, I have to be mindful of any eating place because of the difference between what we are forbidden to eat and what others accept. I knew the international symbol for halal restaurants and stores. Tomorrow at sunset, when my first day of fasting came to a close, and during the time leading up to sunset, I would be looking out for that symbol before sitting down to eat anything. I had already walked almost two miles and I had not seen one halal shop so far.

A narrow alley, completely different from the wide main street that I walked down, led me to my Shinjuku hostel. There were no noises in the alley. It was lit with dimmer light and colors and very peaceful. It was completely clean, no garbage anywhere, no piss in the corners or even globs of gum mashed into the ground. There were no tossed or empty bottles or cigarette butts. There was no dog shit or dogs, there were no mounds of mucous or spit on the curb.

There was a cool breeze, like there often is in the warm spring when the sun has been down for hours. I stood still for some seconds, let the breeze move over me and the silence soothe me. I took a deep breath, thinking this is how Tokyo feels after being here for less than one hour. It was an unfamiliar feeling from my seven years in America. The Japanese were conducting business or being served. There was not one menacing glare. There was not one man who exuded a threat. I had not seen one cop or even thought about my guns. Maybe when I woke up tomorrow, it would all change. But for now, I was feeling alright.

* * *

In my temporary room, the heavy and attractive door slid open from right to left. It was well built and perfectly on track. I inspected it carefully. I didn't know if it was because my Southern Sudanese grandfather was a craftsman, who worked with wood and made and built all types of things, that I always paid attention to the quality and craftsmanship of everything. I just knew that it was something I did.

As soon as I shut the door behind me, I noticed and then confirmed that it actually had no lock on it. It was not that the door was damaged or broken. It simply was not designed with a lock on either side.

A quick walk back down the hallway, I asked about the lock. The same security guard who had let me in and performed a deep bow to greet me when I first arrived, explained in a series of mostly gestures that the front door to the hostel was locked and secure. The only way for anyone to enter was with the electronic key, the same kind he had given me after I paid for a two-night stay. Or I could be buzzed in, but he assured me that he was in full control of the buzzer and that there was twenty-four hour security. Therefore, there was no reason for the individual guest room doors to be locked.

The Sudan in me observed his humanity and understood his manner and believed in the honor system. The Brooklyn in me did not, could, would not, *refused*. Back inside the room, I put my duffel bag up on my bed. I unpacked only the items I would need for one night. Even though the two-night fee I had already paid was non-refundable, I decided I would be up and out of here in the morning with my mind set on finding a better spot to chill while I carried out my plans to link back up with Akemi.

I don't exactly know what kind of impact being transported from empire to empire has on the human body. But I do know that it *does* have an impact. To snatch my energy back and regain my focus, I pushed the bed all the way into the corner. I moved the desk all the way over and slid the chair underneath. With a wide-enough space now, I did 200 push-ups, 250 sit-ups, and 150 deep knee bends. I sparred an imaginary rival and I didn't let up until I defeated him. When I did, I collapsed onto the hard floor, dragged myself to the wall, and sat with my back pressed against it, my knees bent below me and my body balanced on my toes. I would remain this way until I thought everything through.

With my injured shoulder tightening up some more and eighteen minutes into thought, I concluded that when the girl Iwa Ikeda heard the airport announcement that came over the loudspeaker in Japanese, she realized that I was somewhere in Japan. Maybe she even deciphered that I was calling from Narita Airport. For some reason, she was willing to help me and Akemi in the beginning, at least to connect over the telephone. I figured that was easy for her as long as I was seven thousand miles away, but not in person. She must've never expected me to come here. My arrival had shocked her, surprised her, or maybe disappointed her. She was like the others. She had underestimated me.

More troubling to me was that I never got to find out if my wife was actually there at Iwa Ikeda's house waiting to talk with me when I called, like I had requested her to be in my previous voice mail that I left days ago. Did this girl Iwa only need to turn around and hand Akemi the phone, but instead had smiled at her and said, "It's nobody. It was the wrong number"? If Akemi was there waiting, could the girl have pretended that I never kept my word and called?

Or maybe she never gave her my initial message in the first place. And who was this Iwa anyway and how close a friendship did she and Akemi share? How good a friend could she be if she knew Akemi's true heart and still sabotaged her?

The voice in the human mind that purposely tries to argue in the opposite direction of life and love suggested that maybe Akemi was at fault somewhere in all of this. Maybe *she* wanted my call but not my visit. But I shut that voice down. The devil is a liar.

Under a dim lamp, I pulled out those three addresses once more. One was in Ginza, which was close by and a prefecture of Tokyo, and the other in Roppongi Hills, which was also part of Tokyo, and the last one was three hours away in Kyoto. I needed to solidify my strategy. Should I attempt to meet and talk with her father first, as Umma suggested, and anticipate that he would allow me to see Akemi afterward? Or should I seek Akemi out face to face first and then confront her father soon after?

Chiasa said that all schools were closed in Japan for Golden Week. This meant that the school address that I had in Kyoto wouldn't work at this moment. I needed to check with Chiasa and find out exactly when the schools reopened. For now, the other two Tokyo addresses were my only option. I just had to be careful not to do anything that gave Akemi's father the upper hand. After all, he wanted to steal her away from me permanently, didn't he?

After dealing with my study cards, flipping, reciting, and memorizing, I wanted to go back outside to explore the Tokyo night. Easily, I could get over to Ginza and peep and feel out the place where the address was located. Was it Nakamura's house, their Tokyo apartment, or his office? But I couldn't leave my luggage in an unlocked room. I wouldn't gamble with my Tims, Clarks, Laurens, or my gear, compounded by the value of my Umma's gifts and the items that belonged to my wife.

I took out the book that Sensei had given to me concerning Akemi's father. Sensei was right, I needed real information on this guy to know what I was up against. "Know thy enemy," Sun Tzu had written in his book *The Art of War*, which Sensei required me to read when I was twelve years young. It took me some time, a lot of thought and vocabulary word checking in the *Webster's Dictionary*, but I read it.

So I cracked open the old but well-kept pages of *Never Surrender*, the softcover book, a biography written about my wife's father.

FOREWORD

Born on August 9, 1945, the same day that America dropped a two-ton bomb on Nagasaki, Japan, three days after America dropped the world's first atomic bomb on Hiroshima, Japan, Naoko Nakamura is said to have revenge embedded in his soul. He never got the chance to meet his father, an ammunitions mogul who was evaporated by the American bomb, the grand finale to an unprecedented bombing campaign that made most of Japan a heap of toxic ashes scattered around impromptu graveyards. Instantly his father's body liquefied. After it evaporated, only his teeth remained to identify him and confirm his death.

Hisashi Nakamura's teeth were discovered more than a year after the atomic blast. They were lodged in the cement of a Nagasaki sidewalk, much like the prints of dinosaurs and other ancient creatures that have been excavated from rocks. He did leave a will, however, in which Naoko Nakamura, his only son, was bequeathed several hundred acres of prime property in various locations throughout Japan. Naoko Nakamura, according to the will, was to receive deed to the properties on his twentieth birthday, at which time he would become their legal owner.

During his early years, Naoko Nakamura was an erudite student obsessed with military history, military training, political science, and strategies of amassing power. As the majority of Japanese were rebuilding and busy actively forging friendships with America, as well as social and cultural exchanges and partnerships, Naoko Nakamura was patiently plotting and planning his own financial and political wealth and quietly ensuring his influence.

Known for being inflexible, calculating, and cold in both his business and personal dealings, Naoko Nakamura parted ways and severed ties even with his own mother. Enraged that Hana Nakamura, while he was still a child, had sold off prime portions of his father's properties to the American government, which then used the properties to erect and expand American military bases in Japan, Naoko at age twenty grabbed what remained of his inheritance and discontinued his communication with her, even becoming estranged from his two stepbrothers born of her second marriage.

Within a year, Naoko Nakamura was rumored to have formed a secret and financial alliance with Yakuza boss Omote Tora, wherein Naoko laundered hundreds of millions of yen for the gangster. These illicit revenues formed the foundation of Naoko Nakamura's wealth. It also won Naoko pivotal friendships and solid connections because of his ability to access, appropriate, lend, and borrow huge sums of capital. Naoko Nakamura and Omote Tora both deny that any secret alliance existed between them, yet Naoko benefited from the rumor of being aligned with "major muscle." They have never been seen or photographed together in any public or private setting.

By 1970, when he was twenty-five, Naoko Nakamura's company, the Pan Asian Corporation, was poised to take over several key lucrative Asian markets where Americans had dominated in the past. Using a brand of "Asian solidarity" that his critics considered a false cover and a method of increasing his own wealth, Naoko grabbed the ghost of the past to forge forward and dominate.

When I finished reading the Foreword, I had circled six words: *excavated*, *bequeathed*, *erudite*, *estranged*, *laundered*, and *illicit*. Immediately I looked them up and wrote them down in my pocket notebook after committing their meaning to my memory. As I sat thinking, there was one major point in the book that stood out in my mind: "He never got the chance to meet his father." I thought to myself that this one fact could easily make any boy half a man. As I tried to imagine never having met my own father, I couldn't. I couldn't erase the deep love or powerful lessons that came to me directly from my father in person. I tried to subtract the parts of me that came from my father, but nothing was left over. As I tried to push myself to imagine it, my thoughts simply exploded and I didn't want to know. Maybe if I had not ever met my father, I'd just be crazy like those Brooklyn boys in my American hood.

"Inflexible, calculating, and cold . . ." the author had described Nakamura. I didn't need to write that down. I would remember that description for as long as he would remember that atomic bomb.

Heavy-minded, I lay down with my back purposely pressed against my luggage. If there were an intruder here at Shinjuku Uchi bent on robbery, he would have to be clever enough to get past me as I slept and behind me to remove my fifty-pound duffel bag without me waking. *Impossible*, I assured myself. When I lay down, something in my duffel was poking me. I got up and grabbed the bag and un-hooked the top. When I looked in and felt around, I could tell it was Akemi's five-inch heels that were digging into my back. I snatched them out and also removed her hardback diary. I placed the shoes on my desktop, stood them side by side. I lay her diary down at first. Then I picked it back up, flipping through the first few pages.

Even under the dim lamplight, embedded between, beside, and below her kanji handwriting, her drawings lit up, stood out, and some-how seemed to breathe life. On one page in the back of her book, I saw the kanji for my name, Mayonaka. I knew it because she had drawn it for me on a napkin at a Jamaican restaurant on our first date up in Harlem. I smiled to myself. It was a curious thing how a man born in the shadow of a bomb, with a heart hardened by history and circumstance, could bring forth such a sweet young daughter, Akemi.

I hooked the duffel bag up and threw it back up against the wall. I lay back down and eased myself into a sleep.

Chapter 3
THE ELEPHANT

The orange sun saw me first, so bright it burned through the paper-thin curtains and cast colors onto the cream-colored walls. Warm like a sauna, it woke me at 5:00 a.m. boasting that it had cheated me out of my Fajr prayer, which normally had my head pressed to the ground before dawn, especially on this first full day of the Ramadan fast. I took it as both a sign and a reminder that to win on this side of the world, I had to move faster, rise up earlier like their sun, think quicker, and adjust.

I slid my room door open with ease. I glanced down the hall. There was no one out there. I grabbed my towel, washcloth, T-shirt, boxers, and bathroom bag, a black leather case filled with everything I needed.

I walked all the way down to the only men's room servicing the first floor. Inside there were five showers, and five urinals and three toilets. Instead of the urinals being on the wall and positioned at waist height, their urinals were on the floor! Seemed like the Japanese felt closer to the floor, so they designed the urinals for shorter, smaller men. I took aim.

After showering and dressing, I returned to my room and spread out my second towel onto the floor to serve as a prayer cloth. In the Asian heat I made my prayer.

At 6:15 a.m. in Tokyo, I continued my studies. I cracked open my book on Japanese culture. Even by selecting just a few passages or pages, I believed I might stumble on something useful. The author of *Peculiar People: The Japanese Way*, even before beginning his book, provided a list: "Ten Things I Am Sure You Don't Know about the

Japanese." I liked nonfiction writers who could get to the point in a reasonable amount of time, so I decided to concentrate on the list:

1. The Japanese believe that they are superior to all other people in the world. For two thousand years, they did not even allow any foreigners to enter Japan, and they made it illegal for Japanese citizens to leave Japan and go anywhere else in the world. It doesn't matter who you are, European or African. It does not matter if you are also Asian as well, Korean, Chinese, Thai, Vietnamese, or even Indian. The only thing that matters to them is whether or not you are Japanese. Every non-Japanese is believed to be less or below them and is described as "foreign," or *gaijin*, which in Japanese means "outside people."

2. The Japanese have the most complicated writing and language system in the world. They use three different forms of writing, hiragana, katakana, and kanji. Years ago there were up to ten thousand kanji that students and citizens of Japan had to learn and perfect. Today the average Japanese student must master hiragana, katakana, and three thousand additional kanji letters. Students beginning from a young age spend ten to twelve hours a day in school and afterschool and night school programs in their highly exhausting and competitive educational system. The Japanese use the fact that most foreigners consider their language impossible to master as evidence that the Japanese are superior.

3. The Japanese are very hard on one another. They do not believe in being or doing minimum or less than the most. They believe every Japanese citizen should strive to be excellent and work for the first-place position every day and all the time. Every Japanese should be *ichiban*, meaning "number one."

4. The Japanese are obsessed with all Japanese people being the same and doing the same things. They believe that this is how harmony is maintained in a society. Therefore when you enter a Japanese business or school or government office, all the employees and students are normally dressed exactly the same way. The workers and students look down on anyone who dares to break the "harmony," or the "sameness." A person who dares to be different can suffer a lifetime of ridicule and isolation and loss. This practice is known as *kata*, or the Japanese way, and the Japanese have learned a precise uniform way of doing each and every task, including living life.

5. The Japanese do not know how to express themselves honestly. They repress their feelings intentionally because historically, the punishment they received for

self-expression or for doing anything that was not approved or prescribed by authorities was severe and often cost them and their family members their lives. Even though today the Japanese no longer live under an emperor or any type of oppressive government or authority, they still believe in speaking less, expressing less, appearing satisfied even when they are depressed and unhappy. They are suspicious of all foreigners and anyone who does the opposite, such as talk too much, grab too much attention, or burden other people with their problems.

6. The Japanese of today can only tolerate foreigners as long as you are a tourist on a short stay. They will be pleasant and polite and accommodating to this group because they will also earn money from this group through tourism and other business ventures. However, if foreigners try to remain in Japan beyond a short stay, they will experience a great and solid social and cultural isolation, and they will eventually feel the full power of the Japanese law. Japanese immigration policy is one of the most unwelcoming, exclusionary immigration policies in the world.

7. It is the responsibility of every Japanese to "save face." This means that the Japanese must work overtime to look good and be good and be successful in every way down to the most minor details. They must be successful in conversation, business, education, family, and friendship. To be embarrassed is to be shamed. To be shamed is to "lose face." To be embarrassed would be to not fit the Japanese formula, the Japanese way in all things. Each Japanese person will apply the formula to every other and pass judgment severely on anyone bringing embarrassment or shame onto their name, their family, their friends, or their business.

    If you are a foreigner and you are speaking to a Japanese, for example in English, even if the Japanese person does not speak English, he will not admit that he does not understand you. To admit this would be to say that he does not know something. Even a simple matter like this will cause him to lose face. Therefore, a Japanese may choose not to speak to a foreigner at all and ignore him instead, rather than experience embarrassment. They are more comfortable knowing that *you* cannot speak Japanese and that this is the real problem!

    Saving face is so important to the Japanese that a Japanese person would consider committing suicide as a reasonable option to cover up, prevent, or atone for a loss of status and loss of approval from his coworkers, peers, and neighbors. The Japanese historically have even had a procedure for how suicide should be carried out properly, so as not to disturb or burden anyone else any further with their miserable life or even their death.

8. If a foreigner is successful in doing business with the Japanese, no matter how long the business alliance lasts, the Japanese will never accept that foreigner as "one of us." You may take part in all business functions and business affairs, but you will never be welcomed to marry into their families, to attend their weddings, memorial services, or rituals. For a Japanese person to invite "outsiders" to such events would be considered a disruption of the "harmony" and the Japanese way. Today the Japanese are so suspicious of foreigners that they have even become suspicious of full-blooded Japanese citizens who have traveled to other countries and resided there for long periods of time. They look at them as Japanese who have compromised their Japanese-ness. Japanese persons who marry outsiders or foreigners run a high risk of losing their family, friends, and respect. They become victims of *izamae*, a collective and powerful disapproval that leads to a solid ignoring of this person's existence.

9. Despite being a small island, Japan has dominated, invaded, usurped, and degraded all its larger neighbors, including the overpopulated and massive mother of Asia, China. The Japanese had never lost a war until World War II, when they were conquered by the Americans. Even after being conquered, bombed, and occupied, the Japanese worked so hard and so harmoniously with such precision and perfection that they rebuilt their country and brought their economy back to life and dominance in a short period of time. They are the third-largest economy in the world today, and Tokyo is the third-most-expensive city for people to live in, in the entire world.

10. The Japanese do not believe in God. (Their roots are in Confucianism, Buddhism, and Shintoism.) Today there is no Japanese religion, despite the effort of many groups and organizations, including Christian missionaries, to influence their nation. The Japanese believe in themselves, their relatives and ancestors. They believe in "harmony," perfect manners at all costs and even during a crisis. They believe in discipline and controlled organization, peace and law and order. They believe in money and hard work, but even when presented with the opportunity for great profit, they will not sacrifice or exchange "the Japanese way of life." They believe that the Japanese method or process is the smartest and only method. If they lose business with outsiders who are unwilling to do it their way, they believe that they are smart enough to earn the business that was lost by some other means, while maintaining their superiority and exclusivity.

The list was mind-blowing to me. At first it made me suspicious about the author, and the author's intentions. Next I felt forced to reread the list and separate each numbered item and pause and think about it and compare it to my few experiences with Akemi's Japanese family in America. Then I had to circle the words that I didn't understand on the list and look them up.

On my second read, I picked out the things on the list that were similar to what I know about my own people, the Sudanese. There were a few cultural similarities, but there were definitely more differences. I had never thought of Akemi as an atheist. For a Muslim man to marry an atheist is *harom* (forbidden). She never felt like a nonbeliever to me. A woman with no God or faith or belief would feel cold and empty, I guessed. She would have no standards or boundaries, I figured.

On further thought, it was impossible for me to look at my wife in relation to this list. It was also not possible for me to lump her in some big category, like "the Japanese." I could only look at my wife based on what I learned of her by watching and observing and interacting and feeling. I didn't know if this list was all true. But I knew that the list felt cold and empty. My wife felt warm and full of life and love and pure sweetness and talent, like my Umma.

In my and Akemi's marriage contract, I had gifted her a beautiful blue-bound and hardcover Holy Quran translated from Arabic to her Japanese language. I had it here in my duffel. I never got the chance to present it to her properly, which I'd intended to do right after her big art show at MOMA. I looked forward to her reading it slowly and learning it, side by side with me as a help to her. I wanted her to embrace it because her soul had embraced Islam knowingly and not just because I told her to.

Another thought occurred to me. The list did match my idea of Naoko Nakamura, my wife's father. At least it matched the profile that was slowly forming in my mind. I became certain that this was the reason Sensei gave these two books to me. As I reflected, Sensei had said that my wife was under tremendous pressure here in Japan. This list certainly helped me to understand why, and what kind of isolation she might still be facing. It also created a deep curiosity in me. If these listed items had any truth, why would a girl like Akemi, raised in this way, leap over the carefully drawn bold boundaries of her culture and into my arms, heart, and life?

* * *

At 8:25 a.m. I was lying on my back on my bed with the book opened and pressed on my face, thinking. When I pulled the book off, I checked the time and jumped up to make the morning call to Iwa Ikeda, like I had promised to do.

The hostel pay phone was on the first floor like me, but on the opposite side of the building in the corner. I walked down and over and made the call, hoping.

Iwa's phone rang three times before her voice mail kicked in. Immediately, I hung up. I took a deep breath. I sat there for a moment. Six minutes later, I picked the phone up once more, prepared to leave another message. After all, this was the only telephone number for my wife that I had.

"Ikeda-san, ohayo gozaimasu. Boku-wa Mayonaka deska. I am calling to speak to Akemi. I was hoping to arrange a conversation with her. She left your number as her friend, and the person to contact. Thank you for your help. I'll call back later today. If I don't reach you, I'll keep trying. Hopefully we won't be disconnected at that time."

After I hung up, I just sat there. I was debating in my mind whether I should have left Iwa Ikeda my telephone number here at Shinjuku Uchi. I already knew that even if I were not in at the time that she might return my call, the front desk receptionist would take messages for me and place them in the tiny mailboxes up front reserved for paying guests. But maybe calling back to leave a number would backfire on me. I had already begun to distrust Iwa's motives.

I got up and walked back down the hall and over toward my room, regulating my anger. Anger was not the correct posture for Muslims fasting during the Ramadan holy holiday.

When I slid my room door open, Chiasa was sitting on my bed with her shoes off and feet propped up. Her unpolished clean, clear toes were unblemished. She pressed them into my sheet. Situated below her feet on the floor were Akemi's high heels. I saw that she had removed them from my desk where I kept them last night.

"Nice shoes," she said half smiling, noticing my eyes frozen on the floor.

"What are you doing in my room?" I asked her before getting tight.

"You called me," she said casually, without even a grin.

"No," I said, treating her statement as a question even though it wasn't.

"You did." She smiled and sat up straight. Now her feet were dangling above Akemi's shoes. I could see Akemi's diary lying beside her on my bed. She had also removed that from my desk.

"Hand me that," I told her, referring to Akemi's diary. She handed it over.

"I received a telepathic communication from you," she said, with a straight no-nonsense look.

I didn't respond, just looked at her hard. My face must have triggered something. Suddenly she seemed insulted by it.

"Honestly, if you say that you didn't say my name *once* in your mind since you said good-bye to me at the airport—if you didn't think about me *at all* or see me in your dreams—I'll leave you right now and you'll *never* see me again." Her soft voice had no humor mixed in it. She spoke sweetly but with confidence. She was challenging me now and revealing that she had a slight mean streak running through her.

"Did you?" she followed up, her gray eyes searching mine. "Did you think about Chiasa?" Her long lashes affected me.

"I did, but—" I was gonna let her know it was not how she seemed to be thinking about it. But she interrupted me.

"You see, you did. I knew it," she said, turning as though she was talking to someone standing beside her. Then she threw her hands up in a gesture that normally meant "touchdown," and fell backward, back onto my bed.

"I received your message right here," she said, with one index finger pointed at her head. "So I came."

"Chiasa," I said, "I'm only out here for a few days and I have a lot to take care of before I leave. I don't have the extra time to play games."

"This is business. Let me cut your time in half. Let me help you," she pleaded with one hand on her hip. "I speak the language, you don't. I know the train system, you don't. I can connect you with any-

thing that you need in Tokyo. And if you turn down my business offer, I'll go tell my boss that I am back home from the States and start
delivering pizzas. Honestly speaking, I'd rather work for you. Japan is
a no-tip country." Her tone softened.

"What?" I asked.

"In Japan no one expects a tip for anything they do. If you take a
taxi, or if a bellman carries your luggage, or if you receive a food delivery, no matter how hard a worker works, or how good a job someone
does, we don't require or accept one penny over the actual price. So
whether I deliver two pizzas or twenty-two pizzas, it's all the same.
If I work for you, there's no hourly rate. I name the price and you
pay it. I'll do whatever it takes to get the job you want done, completed."

She was wearing a Le Coq Sportif peach-colored sweat suit and
orange Converses with orange laces. Her sweat jacket was off and lying across my bed. The honey-colored skin of her shoulders and arms
glistened. She was wearing a thin, tight tee, yet her full breasts were
not exposed, nor was her belly button, but her curves were killer. She
shifted from lying down to lying sideways, her head was now resting
in the palm of her left hand. She seemed eager for an answer, but
at the same time, she was perched lightly like a bird that could take
flight in a quarter of a second and disappear into the endless sky.

No woman besides Umma or my wife had ever sat on my bed. Yet
I had just met this girl yesterday and not even twenty-four hours ago,
and she looked very comfortable. She was very helpful and unique
and pretty, but I was here in Japan for only one reason and that reason
definitely wasn't gonna change. I took a deep breath and thought to
myself, *Here I go again* . . . If I could remove whatever type of magnet
I had in my body that drew these women to me and kept them coming continuously, I would be faced with less of a challenge. I would
be able to focus.

"I'm checking out of here," I told her.

"Why?" she asked.

"This place has no lock on the bedroom doors. When I come and
go, my luggage isn't secure. You walked right in here, so you know
what I'm talking about."

"You don't need to leave here," she said casually. "We Japanese
don't steal."

I let off half a laugh. "Nobody Japanese steals?" I repeated, to let her hear how ridiculous she sounded to me.

"Seriously, I know. I grew up on an American military base. *All* kinds of stuff got stolen *all* the time. Eventually, they even had to install cameras in certain areas. But outside of the base, on Japanese territory, no one Japanese steals. I can leave my bicycle or motorcycle or anything, no matter the value. No one Japanese will take it. I promise you. It's the Japanese way!"

"I thought you said that you grew up in Tokyo," I checked her.

"I did. My mom lives here in Tokyo, and she and my dad had a house on the Yokota Air Base about forty-five minutes from here. Even though the American military bases are located here in Japan, inside the base is considered to be America. So I grew up both ways. That's why I can speak both languages fluently, no problem."

"So are there a lot of Americans living here?" I asked.

"Not really. The American military personnel and their families never leave the base except when traveling to the airport coming and going. They have their own little world going on in there, plus everything that they think they need. But when we lived there, I left the base every day. Besides, my *Japanese* family lives in the *real* Japan."

I reached into my pocket and pulled out a small stack of bills. I counted out thirty thousand yen and handed it over to her. She took it easily as though she had expected her pitch to work all along. Immediately she handed me one thousand back. She was giving me my change and at the same time proving both of her points—no stealing, no tips.

She bowed down completely and eased up, singing, *"Arigato, gozaimasu!"* I understood that it was her culture to do so, but I said to her, "Don't do that anymore."

She looked at me curiously.

"You can do it, just don't do it to me," I corrected myself.

"Wakarimashta," she said, meaning she understood. But I knew she didn't.

A woman bowing before me is erotic. When my wife does it, it gets me crazy. But I didn't want each female I met out here doing it to me. I needed help keeping everything in perspective.

"Get me a Tokyo phone book from the front desk. They should have one, right?"

"Business or personal?" she asked swiftly.

"Personal," I responded after a pause. She was up and out. Not even three minutes passed before she showed up with a massive book in her hand.

"Twenty-seven million people in Tokyo. Who do you want to look up?" She was ready.

"Iwa Ikeda," I told her. She sat on my bed and opened it up. She moved her fingers across the pages, swiftly scanning the extra-small-sized kanji.

"I counted about four pages of people last name Ikeda, that's about four hundred families. But there's no Iwa. Maybe she's listed under her husband or father's name. That would be normal. Do you know it?" She lifted her eyes from the pages to peer at me curiously.

"Nah, but I have her phone number," I answered.

"What?" she followed up.

"I'm looking for her address. I already have her phone number," I explained.

Chiasa stood. Staring, she said, "So why not call her, and ask her where she lives?"

I pulled Iwa's phone number from my back pocket and handed it over. Chiasa sat back down and tried to match the phone number to one of the numbers listed in the book. If it matched, she would discover the address printed beside it. I liked that she had a quick mind.

"Her number is not listed. Her family probably has money," she said nonchalantly. "Those are the types that would pay extra to keep their information out of the phone book. It's not usual though."

"Do you want to kidnap her?" she asked, too casually. "That costs extra." She smiled slightly.

"Nah, I don't kidnap. If a woman doesn't belong to me, I don't touch her," I assured.

"What next?"

"Ginza," I told her. "I gotta get to Ginza to check something out."

"You know Ginza is high-end? Whatever you are buying from there, I can take you somewhere else to get it or something close to it for much, much less."

"Nah, I'm not going shopping." I pulled the address out of my pocket and handed it to her. She held it with both hands and studied it like it was a riddle. She handed the paper back to me and said casually, "That's easy."

"I gotta move out of here first. I gotta move my luggage to a place where I can lock it up," I told her as I began repacking the few items that I had left out of my duffel.

"I see you don't trust anyone," she said. "My aunt Tasha says that a person who cannot trust anyone always ends up trusting the wrong people."

I thought about her statement. It seemed like a tricky phrase that someone who wanted to be trusted made up for their own advantage. I moved it out of my mind and finished packing.

"Do you have a camera?" Chiasa asked out of the blue.

"Why?"

"Because what type of tourist wouldn't have a camera?" she asked.

"I don't need it for now."

"Bring it. It's better to have something useful then to not have it." She smiled.

I pulled the movie camera out of my bag. I paused for a second, then looked up at Chiasa and thought, *This female is a sharp one.* She had probably searched my bag already when she was in my room uninvited and alone. She asked me if I had a camera, but I was guessing that she already knew the answer and was on to the next stage of her plan, whatever that was. But I had too much on my mind to try and figure her out. In one hour she had been more useful than anyone or anything else.

As we left the room, I noticed Chiasa's jacket lying on my bed. "You forgot your jacket," I told her, after forcing her to understand that she could *not* carry even one of my bags.

She answered, "I'm leaving my jacket here."

"Why? I'm not coming back here," I told her.

"I just want to show you something," she said, "you'll see."

We walked out, leaving her jacket behind. She returned the phone book to the front desk as we exited. Outside the hostel and into the warmth, I saw her put something small on top of the cement post beside the hostel door.

I looked up into a white sky and crimson sun.

"I know, our sun is really bright, right?" she asked. I didn't answer her, though my eyes were squinted enough for her to already know what I thought.

"Here in Tokyo, the sun rises real early, but it also sets real early. But I don't live my life by the sun. I'll move around in the daylight or in the moonlight, just the same," Chiasa said with ease.

She took some steps out into the street and flagged down a taxi. "Don't touch the door," she said suddenly, and the taxi door opened automatically. She leaned in and spoke Japanese to the driver. The trunk opened automatically. I put my luggage inside and shut it. I jumped in the back beside her. We were off.

"Enjoy the ride," she said to me, while looking out the window in the opposite direction. "This is the only time that we will take a taxi. It's too expensive. But since you had to have your luggage . . ."

Shinjuku in the early morning daylight was like a fascinating amusement park with its one million still and blinking and blaring lights turned off and its best rides shut down. Now it was just a place where hundreds of people were walking and riding through just as a means to get somewhere else.

When the wheels of the cleanest, most well-kept taxi that I had ever rode in turned off the main road, Shinjuku easily seemed like a suburb or a village. I saw a Japanese mother of three riding a bicycle with a baby seat in the front and another two seats behind her holding two happy, silent babies chilling. I saw other Japanese women dressed in business skirt suits and moderate-heeled shoes and stockings, carrying pocketbooks, purses, or briefcases in their baskets, watching and weaving through traffic while holding a compact mirror and applying lipstick at the same time.

We pulled up steep hills and coasted down the slopes of narrow streets and hugged curbs around corners. My eyes were like hungry beasts scanning it all, leery of missing one alley or alcove or outstanding piece of architecture. Everything was so completely new that I neglected using the map I had in my back pocket, not wanting to overlook the real thing while checking for printed data on the paper. I can't lie. It was a busy yet strangely peaceful place. The men in suits moved in packs, all seeming neither happy nor sad to be headed to work. Laboring men wore stylish jumpsuits—all baggy, nothing tight—and quality work boots. Teens traveled in troops, all moving slow in identical uniforms, boys separate from the girls. Motorcycle riders eased by with little effort in the continuous flow of light traffic. People pimping pamphlets and coupons were setting up their distribution and promotion schemes, offering every walker an invitation to spend money at some place of business.

Thin girls glided up hills without huffing or puffing. They remained seated and unstressed, pedaling in an unbroken rhythm on their bikes the same as if they were on flat land. Old people were energetic and agile, not swollen like sausages or withered like raisins or defeated with diabetes or crippled by arthritis. Their clothes fit and matched, were clean and pressed.

Any newcomer could tell that someone somewhere loved the seniors enough to help them maintain. I looked away once to check on Chiasa. She was facing front and sitting quietly. I liked that she was comfortable with silence. I liked that she was smart enough to let me become familiar with my surroundings uninterrupted.

* * *

We soon reached a wooded area that was blocked off by a long, heavy chain held up by two metal poles. Chiasa and the driver spoke some in their language. The driver swerved and entered what seemed to be a restricted area that led us into a paradise-like park with trees of every size and height and flowers of every color blossoming and spilling out to the service roads.

"Where are we?" I questioned her.

"Home," Chiasa said calmly. I checked the meter and paid the driver, laying the bills in a rectangular dish that he tapped lightly. There was no bulletproof glass to protect him from me or from being choked or murdered by angry passengers. No little metal slot to drop the money in that you couldn't snatch back. No divider between the civilized and the suspicious and dangerous public customers like there is in Brooklyn, New York. Wearing his spotless white gloves, he picked up the dish and laid my change back in it with my receipt.

"*Arigato gozaimasu,*" he said to me and Chiasa both. My door and the trunk opened simultaneously, automatically.

"Whose home is this?" I asked.

"My grandfather's. I mentioned him to you. Actually he's a retired park ranger. This is Yoyogi Park. Follow the stone path."

I followed her. "Why are we here?" I asked her.

"You need someplace secure to leave your luggage. That's what you said. That's why we are here."

"Hold up. You can just take me to a new hostel. I have a list of them in the area."

"But you already paid for two nights' stay at Shinjuku Uchi," she answered.

"How would you know?" I asked, a swift reaction.

"I talked to Jun-san when I arrived at your place this morning. He was working the front desk."

I'm not slow, I told myself, *but she is speeding.* I knew I had to shake off whatever kind of fog my mind was in and watch her moves closely. Like my sensei would say, "You have to make your mind light. If the mind is too heavy, you've lost your use of intuition and instinct, which every fighter needs."

She led us up to a house and then walked past it. We were entering what I assumed was their yard. But actually the whole park appeared to be their yard, because hers was the only house in the area. I thought about her grandfather, "the park ranger." Where was he? *Does a park ranger carry a gun?* I asked myself. "What about your grandfather?"

"He's not home."

"How do you know?" I followed up.

"Because his bike isn't out front. He's gone somewhere."

"How were you going to introduce me to him when you don't even know my name?" I asked her, and she stopped walking, her back to me. She turned around with a calm and blank face. "I know your name. I told you I was not asleep on the plane. But you told your name to Yuka first. I don't like her and I refuse to use anything after she has already used it." Chiasa folded her arms in front of her. "I decided to call you something different, but I have only narrowed it down to three choices so far. I'm still deciding," she said, as though she could assign me a name.

I had to smile naturally. "You think you can give me a name? You think it's that easy?"

"Since you gave Yuka your fake name, and gave a different name to the Shinjuku hostel, I figured it *was* that easy." She stared back at me. I marked the date and location down in my mind; "the first time I ever been checked by a girl." She turned back around and continued to walk toward two sheds, one made of metal, the other made of brick. She slid her hand into her left front pocket and pulled out some keys. She unlocked a heavy padlock on the brick shed and gently opened it up.

"You can put your luggage in here. This is my storage and the other is my grandfather's," she said. I paused.

"And since you don't trust anyone, I know that includes me, so after you put your things inside, I'll give you the key until you take your stuff back out." She was dangling the keys between two pretty fingers with clear, unpolished nails. I stepped into her brick shed. She reached her arm past me and flipped on the switch. Now her shed had lights. I was inside as she stood outside, so confident in what she was doing that her back was to me.

It was a fort of ammunitions. There was a large gun lying against the wall, but I wasn't familiar with the brand. Then my mind skipped ahead. *She wanted me to see all this for a reason*, I told myself. "Chiasa," I called her. She turned and faced me. I pointed out the gun with no words or hands, only my eyes.

"Just a tranquilizer gun. You know in Japan, we have some wildlife. Seriously, we have bears," she said with a half smile. "I got it from my grandfather. I borrowed it," she said casually.

"Yeah," I acknowledged. "What about that? I saw you with that at the airport." I pointed.

"It's a *kyudo* bow." She turned toward me and stepped in and blocked the only entrance to the shed.

"*Kyudo*?" I asked.

"You know, like a bows and arrows kind of thing." She positioned her arms and hands as though she were aiming and shooting one. However, the bow in her shed was the largest I had ever seen. She stepped up and unzipped the case, revealing the dynamic weapon. As quickly as she showed it, she zipped it back up.

* * *

I put my duffel bag up against the wall, right below some handcuffs that hung on a nail and across from some old nunchucks, also lodged

Chiasa and her *kyudo* bow and two arrows.

on the wall. Beside several stacked storage boxes were a few pairs of mountain boots of different styles. On a nail were some rain ponchos. On the floor was about thirty feet of coiled colorful climbing rope. In addition to a well-used industrial-sized flashlight, there was a megaphone. When I saw some walkie-talkies, I stepped closer to them. "We can use them," she said excitedly. The rest of the items Chiasa had in there were all inside cases. There were three long cases made of a thick blue cloth with wicked white kanji painted on. There was only a flap and blue string tying down the tips of the cloth cases.

"My swords," Chiasa said. "Old ones."

I looked at my watch and saw that it was 10:15 a.m. "Let's go," I told her, stepping forward so that she would step out. I pulled the door closed, noticing that it swung out and in like an American door, instead of sliding sideways. I padlocked it and dropped the key into my pocket.

"My father built that for me. My grandfather's metal shed was always here. But when I came here to stay with him, my father built this one." She was speaking softly, more like she was talking to herself or moving with a memory. I remained silent, deciding right then and there that she was the first gift of Ramadan on the first day of the fast. She was my sentinel, which Sensei said every ninja on a mission should have.

When we reached the front of her house, she said, *"Chotto matte."* She bent down and removed her kicks and placed them together on the corner of the step. She entered her house, leaving me standing outside. I liked that she didn't ask me inside while her grandfather was not home.

But I didn't like her clothing change. Chiasa emerged wearing a dark blue miniskirt, a light blue blouse, and socks, and carrying penny loafers.

"Why the change?" I asked.

"Everybody knows that a girl in a school uniform can get anything she wants in Japan. So you should just look at this as my costume. You'll see," she said, without flirtation. As she kneeled to put on her shoes, I felt uneasy. She had a book bag, the strap resting on one shoulder and pressing across her breast and down to her opposite hip, where the bag rode. She had a second strap crisscrossing the same way. She pulled it off and over her head and handed it to me. She opened her book bag and pulled out a box.

"Welcome to Japan," she said, handing me the items. The army green canteen was filled with liquid. I opened the box. It was filled with perfectly sliced and neatly arranged fruits. "You must be hungry. You didn't eat," she said, smiling.

"Thank you, Chiasa. I should've told you. While I am here visiting Japan, I'll be fasting during the day, from sunup to sunset," I confided.

"For the whole week?" she asked, incredulous.

"For the whole month," I said solemnly.

"Why?" she asked.

"I'm a Muslim. This is a holy month for us," I said. She stood silent; her gray eyes widened some and one of her eyebrows lifted. She paused, thinking.

"That's so fucking cool," she said softly to herself. "I like that. Then I won't eat or drink either. We'll both eat together at sunset."

* * *

After switching train cars and going three stops, we arrived at Ginza. We walked a while, through well-constructed, clean, and well-lit underground tunnels. The tunnels were so dope to me. It was clever to be moving underground, beneath the city. They stretched a distance and were not hot stinky, crowded holes in the earth like the subway system of New York, where the rats raced. We reached a steep sequence of stairs leading us up and out into what had to be the heart of Ginza.

From Shinjuku to Yoyogi to Ginza there was a quality leap, I swiftly noted. The other two prefectures were definitely not low-quality, but Ginza was obviously high-quality, like Fifth Avenue in New York or Fifty-Seventh Street, but better, cleaner, and more attractive and elegant. I could see that the top designers of the world had their flagship stores located here. This place was about big business and buildings and billboards, as multinational corporations squared off to see which one could post its name and logos up the highest with dominating widths. In between the corporate wars were unique Japanese boutiques and tailors and haberdashers and upscale restaurants and bakeries and art stores and timepiece workshops and retailers and acupuncture lofts and therapeutic massage spas and ice creameries and yogurt dens.

I got drawn in by an astronomy shop with impressive telescopes and powerful lenses. I had never owned one but the design of the shop and display of the unusual equipment caught my eye. It was an awesome concept and invention, a lens that brought beautiful shining stars close to the eye of the human holding the piece of equipment.

Every single car on the street seemed brand-new. The few that weren't were so well cleaned and polished and free from dents and blemishes that they blended in. In Ginza, there wasn't only a handful of hustlers riding large like back in Brooklyn. The whole prefecture of Ginza was bubbling with limousines, Crown Victorias, Benzes, Rolls-Royces, Mazeratis, and Lamborghinis.

The streets were wide and clean and free of potholes. The traffic was at a bare minimum and the flow of people was orderly but steady. Men wore suits, tweed jackets, linen, spring suedes, and comfortable cottons. Some rocked ascots, Gucci, Louis Vuitton, and Yves Saint Lauren belts and briefcases, designer ties or expensive traditional silks, robes, and slippers. Business shirts were crisp and ironed. The absence or presence of cufflinks and of course the quality of the silver, gold, and platinum ranked them, one from the other. Not one shoe was run-over or cheap, from the workers to the execs.

Women were almost unanimously dressed in expensive, well-tailored clothes of every style from both the European and Asian continents. There were fine silks and lace and cotton and linens, and even their denim was threaded better, cut better, styled better, the material a deeper blue and more durable-looking.

As we walked further, my eyes cast down only to be introduced to a high-heeled heaven. Every feminine shoe seemed an expression of personality and poise and even preference. Each lady in front of me and moving past me was petite. Here in Tokyo, "fashion model slim" was not relevant. In Ginza, every female of every age was slim and sleek and flowing with a unique style of her own that made it difficult to determine a trend.

It wasn't long before I realized that I had not seen any white people, Americans or Europeans. I'm not saying that there were none here, but I didn't see 'em. So many people, and each face clearly Japanese. Whether I glanced at the workers in the stores, the people in the streets, the executives moving about, the money earners, money spenders, the owners, buyers, or sellers, the limo drivers or limo pas-

sengers or even the window cleaners, they were all uniformly Japanese. This was Japan, and everything I saw confirmed that this was
clearly their country!

"This whole area is Nakamura Plaza," Chiasa said, as she stopped
walking and gestured. "The building with the exact address that you
are looking for is there across the street," she pointed. "And the guy
whose name you had on the paper, Naoko Nakamura, he should be
there on the top floor." She had her finger pointed toward the sky.
"Let's go," she said confidently.

"Hold up," I told her.

As I stood stiff, she said, "The paper you showed me said Naoko
Nakamura, and this is Nakamura Plaza and over there is the Nakamura building. Usually here in Japan, the most important people
have their offices located on the top floor of an office building or in
a penthouse or co-op or condo. Isn't it the same in New York?" she
asked innocently. I didn't answer, was no longer focused on her or her
voice.

Looking up toward what I counted as the thirty-third and top
floor, and then beyond into the white cloudless sky, I inhaled and
wished that I was fighting this fight using my father's mind—instead
of my own. I needed to be backed up by my father's empire and assets.
I needed my father's ingenuity and access to the world. I exhaled, my
mouth drying some from the start of the fast. What would be my
next move? What would my father do in this scenario that I was facing? What would my father advise me to do now? I felt like the black
king on the chessboard with no frontline defense—no pawns—and
no sideline defense—no bishops, no rooks, no knights. Meanwhile
Naoko was chilling, the white king piece. Although his queen was
dead—his wife, who was also Akemi's mother—his knights, bishops,
and rooks, and a billion pawns in his multimillion-dollar establish-
ment were still securing him and assuring that he appeared monu-
mental with an untouchable monopoly over my wife and his empire.

"What's the plan?" Chiasa asked cautiously.

I turned my head in the opposite direction from where she was
standing only to see a pack of teens and what I assumed was their
chaperone gathered on the same side of the Nakamura building. An
idea was forming.

"Do you know how to work the camera?" I asked her.

"I will in thirty seconds," she answered. I handed it to her. She studied it. "Okay, I got it," she said softly. "Let's go make a movie. You be the director. I'll shoot whatever you want me to shoot." She smiled.

"Follow them in," I said, using my head nod to point her eyes in the direction of the schoolgirls.

"But we are wearing different school uniforms," she protested immediately.

"I didn't say join them. Just follow them in. See if they are getting any kind of tour of the building. See if they give them any private information. If they do, you get it also. Use the camera to film the inside of the lobby—and everything that is going on."

"But what are you looking for?" she asked.

"I need a printout of the building directory. Like the staff list. I need you to get in the parking deck. You can read the signs. Act like you're lost. Find the executive parking and film the cars and plates of the executive vehicles."

"You're not going to do anything crazy, are you, or illegal?" she asked defiantly. Before I could answer, she added, "'Cause if you are, my fee has to be raised to the tenth power." She smiled, but I knew she wasn't joking. She seemed to want to let me know, in some subtle way, that she was down for whatever as long as she was dealt with fairly and paid her asking price. She didn't have to worry. I would treat her right, naturally. Besides, I would not forget about her father; I didn't need two madmen trying to destroy me at the same time.

"Nothing crazy, nothing illegal. I'm just collecting information. I'm just looking for something," I told her solemnly.

"Are we looking for the girl whose little feet fit in those hundred-thousand-yen heels?" she asked straight-faced. I didn't answer. "That gotta be it," she said coyly. "Don't worry, I'll get it done." She left with the camera in hand and the power button on and the red record light all lit up.

As I stood thinking in the midst of the moving crowds, I believed I heard my father's response to my frustrated call for guidance. The volume of the comings and goings of Ginza dropped down. I could only hear him. My father said to me, "Naoko Nakamura is an Asian elephant, known for his wisdom and intelligence. He's too large to confront or directly charge into. He is mammoth. He's someone you've got to go around. Stay out of his area or you'll set off a stam-

pede. Lay low in the tall grass. Give him the day. You take the night."
And his voice left as swiftly as it arrived.

So it was decided. I would not enter Naoko Nakamura's building
to demand to meet with him and ask, "Where is my wife?" Or enter
into any diplomatic display of etiquette and approval, as my Umma
had suggested.

My eyes followed the skyline. Having turned three hundred and
sixty degrees twice, I selected a suitable target building and began
walking.

At the astronomy boutique, I copped a powerful pair of water-
proof, fogproof, shockproof Nikon binoculars for $250. When I got
to my target, I eased on my sunglasses and entered like I belonged
there. Confident, I strode in like a paying customer. Perched on the
thirty-second floor of a building adjacent to Naoko Nakamura's, I
adjusted the button that put the powerful binocular lenses into focus.
Although the windows of the Nakamura building, the top executive floors, were covered by expensive wooden vertical blinds preventing me from seeing in, I could see through all the other windows. I
looked into his place, brought so close into my view that it cast the
illusion that I could just extend my arm and touch it.

I learned very little. The Nakamura building was just that, a well-
built tower of expensive offices and well-dressed employees. Sprinkled
in between were high-end restaurants, tearooms, and lounges. Every
now and then the lens would capture suited smokers gathered in a
specific area or workers conferencing at the watercooler. I peeped also
what seemed like a company gym stretched out over an entire floor
with all kinds of equipment and in steady use. There was one place
packed with pets and another floor with loads of lit-tle children—
and their chaperones or teachers. No one was using the staircases.
I assumed their elevators were in full rotation, but I could not see
those. The parking decks were on the lowest floor. I could view tops
of cars, but cement walls shielded the car bodies. I saw some medical
offices and thought to myself, *Here is a man who seems to have thought
of everything, a veteran of years of "thought battles."* My mind began to
race as I tried to determine what exact advantages I might have.

Akemi's father was my opposite it seemed. He was high-profile
like an elephant that stands thirteen feet tall and weighs 8,000 pounds.
I told myself, *He can't avoid being seen. His every moment shakes the*

earth. He's so high-profile, in fact, that he must be discussed and written about in Tokyo and throughout Japan all the time. Whatever business or events where he would appear *must* be reported, I figured. And further, if I could locate him at a specific place and time at a public event, perhaps my wife would be there also. I had to maneuver to use his high visibility against him, I concluded.

I left the hotel where I was posted as soon as I caught Chiasa in my lens outside the Nakamura building shooting footage of a gang of school kids, most of them holding two fingers up to form a peace sign. She looked happy and excited magnified in my lens. She was real comfortable giving them directions about how and where to stand. She even convinced a girl to climb on top of a statue.

* * *

"It's done," she assured me. "But we'll have to go to my house to watch the footage. That's the only way you can play the tape. And I got these." She handed me a short stack of flyers, papers, and newsletters, as well as a map.

"Put 'em in your bag and hold 'em for me. We gotta get to Roppongi Hills," I told her.

"Roppongi Hills," she repeated. "Expensive taste," she murmured. I pulled out the second Tokyo address I had for Naoko Nakamura. I was hoping it didn't end up being a business complex like this one. I was still hoping to discover my wife there. As we moved through the streets of Ginza, Chiasa pointed out things in English and then told me the Japanese word for those things She began with the binoculars. *Sougankyou* she said.

sky—*sora*
tree—*ki*
car—*kuruma*
bus—*basu*
man—*otoko*
woman—*jyosei*
student—*gakusei*
store—*misé*
book—*hon*
window—*mado*

building—*biru*
motorcycle—*baiku*
police—*keisatsu*

When she said a word that I had already learned from flipping through my study cards, I would call it out before she could translate it. The little word game was helping my language lessons to stick.

When we both saw a kid drinking bottled water, Chiasa smiled and we both said, *"Mizu."* Chiasa crossed both her forearms into an X to show me that she remembered that there's no drinking anything until sunset.

On the amazingly clean train with the carpeted cushions, I viewed the digital commercials and professional postings but was unable to decipher exactly what the hell was going on. I stood challenging myself to try and figure out what product was actually being promoted through the Japanese ads. Chiasa broke my focus.

"Is she looking for you? Or is it only you looking for her?" Chiasa asked, as she sat and I stood over her on the train. Her questions were spoken slowly and softly, as though she was formulating the words at the same time these thoughts occurred in her mind. I knew for sure that she was piecing things together with each speck of information I told her or she observed. I liked that better than telling her my whole story up front.

"Is she an older lady or is she a teenager like us?" she continued. "What does she look like? I mean is there anything special about her or something that stands out, like a scar or a mole or something? Do you have a photo of her?"

"It doesn't matter if she is looking for me because I'm looking for her," I answered automatically. "When she sees me, all her feelings will be revealed." I believed this and was waiting anxiously for Akemi's live expressions. "She's sixteen, same as you. She's five feet nine inches in her hundred-thousand-yen heels and five-four when she takes them off. Her skin is flawless. She has no scars. She has a beauty mark on the inside of her right thigh," I recalled and smiled. "Her soul is mysterious." "Her spirit is sweet. Her smile is like sunrise," I said aloud, but as I spoke, I was also thinking to myself, reminding myself of Akemi.

Chiasa sat silently for the remaining ride. In my silence I wondered, *Is Akemi looking for me? Of course she is. That's why she called each day for seven days, my apartment, the dojo, my sensei.*

Does she know that I'm here in Tokyo? Would she believe that I would come to her home country? Did Iwa Ikeda let her know?

Akemi, I need you to leave me some clues, little traces of yourself, I thought. *And I will leave you some clues also. Something to shake your heart and let you know, "Your man is here."*

* * *

"Roppongi is like Washington, DC," Chiasa said, as we stepped from underground. "There are a lot of embassies here, like the Chinese embassy, the American embassy, and the Dutch embassy. And as you can see when you look around, here is where you will see a lot of people from different countries. Foreigners like Roppongi because of the nightclubs, hostess bars, and the girls."

"How would you know that?" I asked her seriously.

"I had a friend who came here and got rich working at a hostess club. She needed a certain amount of money, so she said she was going to work as a hostess for two months. But then she liked the money so much, she never came back to school. She even missed her exams and her graduation."

"Sounds like it paid much more than delivering pizzas," I said without thinking.

Chiasa stopped walking. "You and I are scheduled to fight tonight. I'll get you back for that comment. You know that wasn't right," she corrected me, softly yet sternly, with no joke in it.

"You're right. My bad. I take it back. I was completely wrong," I said sincerely.

"Hostess bar work does pay more, but a girl has to dress in a nightgown or like a long, flowing, phony dress, and she has to drink liquor all night long even after she is already drunk. And she has to flirt with the customer so that he will stay in the club and keep ordering more drinks! If I would've worked with my friend, I would have earned my whole tuition for flight school in less than a month. But I don't drink liquor, I don't smoke, and I can't flirt with a guy that I don't really like. I'd rather fight him!" she said, caught up in her mounting emotion.

"Like how you want to fight me?" I asked.

She smiled, embarrassed for the first time. She paused and answered softly, "I don't want to fight you because I don't like you. That's not my reason."

I didn't follow up and ask her why she did want to fight me.

"Besides, if I were a hostess, my father would kill him."

"Kill who?"

"The customer! Any one of them or maybe even all of them. He would find him, kill him, kill the owner of the club, blow the club up, and if I did something like that, he would probably kill me too!" She said it calm and matter-of-fact.

"He made me promise to tell him before I give my virginity away. My father said the right man has to be strong enough to stand in front of him and explain why he wants permission to be with his daughter. If the one I choose can't face my father, then I'll have to walk away from him completely." She gestured with her right hand, waving it across her neck to show me that a coward had no chance of winning her.

Chiasa was becoming more than a feminine outline in my eye's view. She was like a drawing that was just beginning to be filled in with shades and colors. I respected her this minute more than five minutes ago. No smoking, no drinking, no fake flirt, sixteen and still a virgin. In her father's absence she was maintaining his rules and conditions for her living. In my father's absence, I was trying to do the same.

We walked and climbed the several steps to Roppongi Hills under the beam of the sun until we reached the top. "Need water?" I asked Chiasa. Her breasts were rising and falling faster than regular breathing.

"I don't if you don't," she said. "Once we get to the top of that winding staircase over there, we'll arrive at your address. But I think you should decide now if you want me to walk through and film the location like in Ginza or whether you want to actually go over there and inside. Or maybe you want us to go in together. I can speak in Japanese for you if you have something to say or ask."

I didn't answer right away. I was thinking.

"This girl who you are looking for, she must speak English, right? Otherwise how would you even know her?" she questioned.

"I'll wait here, you walk through the whole block. Make sure you capture everything, the address, the place to the left of it and to the right and in front and behind. Even any cars parked over there. Get it all on film," I directed her.

"Easy," she said, as we approached the stairs. "I got this now."

* * *

I made the Dhuhr prayer on the winding staircase of wide, clean cement. There was a peace and stillness in Roppongi Hills, which seemed to be the residential extension of Roppongi. Here, everything was blossoming or had already blossomed. The mansions were sturdy and well built. People here seemed to spend more money on expensive designer doors, security walls, and iron fences than on the land itself. Each property was high-quality but condensed. I couldn't see from the outside looking in any pools or huge courtyards, backyards, or play areas. They were showcasing amazing nature more than anything else, orchids and pansies and roses and exotic plants and flowers down to designer bushes and rock gardens. All of the trees were magnificent expressions of Allah. I could see that luxury vehicles were routine here, and every one of them glistened as though they were washed, polished, and buffed as many times a day as I made my prayers.

Strolling, I came up on a merchant alley modeled with miniature stores and short doorways. Quietly people walked in and out, purchasing an array of items. I imagined that these people were house servants, maids and cooks, or drivers sent here and there to make purchases for their wealthy employers. In the Sudan when I was young, our servants were sent to market daily. Umma always made sure they bought the best and freshest from the butcher, halal of course. After a few months of living in the United States, I could detect any dish prepared with old meats. The taste of the fresh kill was completely different than meats that had sat out, then been frozen, then defrosted and frozen over again, which were the way most Americans seemed to be accustomed to handling and consuming their flesh.

In a tiny market I purchased peanut butter ground from peanuts right in my presence, as I waited, also, a few bananas and oranges. I had not seen any halal restaurants yet, and these were items I could trust, just in case I had nothing for breaking the fast at sunset. I already knew that I would not allow Chiasa to prepare my meal tonight. She hadn't offered to, but I could see there was a possibility that she might. I didn't want to eat from her hand. Umma would say, "Food from a woman's hand to a man's mouth makes the two of them familiar." *I wanted my wife to serve me.* Until that was possible, and while out here in Japan, I would be fed by stangers at selected restaurants or I would shop at food markets and feed myself.

Easing around the corner, I caught sight of a lone building on a short hill that towered over all the other residences. I took the short walk up. When I arrived in front, I entered the building behind a young boy with a bike. His hand was shaking as he tried to hold on to his bicycle while opening the locked door. His bike fell, but he got the lock opened. He held the open door with his foot and leaned over to lift his bike. He then tried to balance himself and push his bike through as he walked. He looked up at me when he felt the weight of the door he was holding disappear. He bowed his head slightly to thank me and pushed his bike in smoothly down a short corridor and further down a short ramp. The elevator arrived. I got in. On the top floor I walked off, found the stairwell, and climbed a few steps to the roof. A workman was on his break up there, hiding out and smoking a cigarette. I acknowledged him with a nod and acted calm and cool like I lived here.

I looked out over Roppongi Hills first with my eyes and then through my binoculars. I pulled out my map and my compass and tried to pinpoint the location of the Nakamura address. As Chiasa had mentioned, it was difficult to decipher. I could easily locate the name of the street, but the numbers of the houses and buildings did not go in order the way they would have in New York. Instead the numbers were random, based on when the structure was built, which I thought was crazy. Or maybe it wasn't crazy. Maybe it was just the Japanese method of disguising things or making them so complicated that only they could understand. It definitely helped them to lock outsiders out. I couldn't be mad at that.

My lens was focused now on the right street. Which house, I had no idea. I was glad that it was a house and not a building or a complex. I took my time and looked at each property one by one.

The chain-smoker smoked his cigarettes slowly. I counted. He was inhaling his twelfth one. His face had the stain of sleeplessness and worry. He didn't say nothing. Neither did I. When he left, I left.

I ducked into the smallest hardware store I had ever seen. It was shaped like the letter U, one aisle only that bent once and led you down to the cashier and out the exit. "*San* bags *domo*," I said to the only visible staffer. "Three bags, please." I wrapped up my purchases securely so inquisitive Chiasa could not see through and discover some more pieces of the puzzle. She was already doing enough piecing together without my permission.

At a pay phone tucked beneath the canopy of a florist shop, I phoned Iwa Ikeda to check in. Unlike yesterday, my heart was no longer filled with anticipation that she would pick up or even convey my message to Akemi. Still I tried. My wife must've trusted her for some sensible reason. Yet after pressing the digits, I ended up with absolutely nothing. As I held the receiver, I had a stupid thought. *What was the reason to open a florist shop in the middle of a small village packed with flowers, plants, and trees growing naturally?*

"Any problems?" I asked Chiasa, when she returned to the winding stairs.

"None," she said confidently. "There were some people passing by. I asked a couple of them if they wanted to be in my movie. It's interesting how the camera makes strangers become so friendly and talkative, and it's almost like they'll do anything that the person holding the camera suggests."

"I gotta check into a different hostel," I said, pulling out my list. Chiasa stepped in and looked at the list.

"Here, this one is in Harajuku! It's very close to my house," she said with a bit of excitement.

"Okay, let's go take a look," I told her.

"I hope they have locks on everything so you'll be glad to stay there." She smiled as we walked more swiftly.

I had already told this girl Chiasa that I was only here for a week. How could she get so excited at me staying close to her house for one night? She didn't know that if nothing here in Tokyo worked out, and if I couldn't find Akemi here, I would leave for Kyoto early tomorrow. I checked my watch. It was going on 3:00 p.m.

Chapter 4
HARAJUKU

It was as though I were in another country, and it happened suddenly. Instead of calm and orderly passengers, the train was now packed with pumped-up youths. There were more teens than seats, and they sat and stood stuffed in at every angle, but somehow without touching. There were hands on every strap. Fingernails from natural to nine inches long and decorated with diamond dust, sculptured replicas of flower pots, and other objects that were strange to see on nails of every type, with color galore. When the train doors finally eased opened and the feminine voice whispered "Harajuku," the young came pouring and popping out, spilling and squeezing onto the platform and pushing without touching, down a slim tunnel.

In Harajuku the alleyways were narrow and packed with thousands of teens. The air smelled like sugar, vanilla, and cream. Every few feet an outdoor vendor was wrapping ice cream into soft, hot crepes and decorating them with fruit and confectioner's sugar. The narrow passageways were framed by small stores and signature shops, places to get nameplates and earrings, fake necklaces and rings, T-shirts and ribbons, lace gloves and panties, sneakers and jean belts and pocketbooks, lotions and perfumes, socks and stockings, hats and umbrellas, boots, shoes, and bicycles, as well as barbers and beauticians and piercing and tattoos and tans and anything else a teenager could want. The theme was "too much." A pretty girl with long black hair wore over a hundred barrettes separated by one centimeter each. Instead of one headband, girls rocked two, three, four. Eyes were painted with patterns and purples and pinks. Earmuffs in the spring, long boots with mini skirts, and real girls with fake furry cat tails!

There were no cops or controllers, no parents or babysitters and no babies. Just teens—and a few adults who owned the businesses that served teens. The crowd moved in waves, shoulder to shoulder, three across, hundreds headed north and shoulder to shoulder, three across, hundreds headed south, all down the same narrow alleyway. But the bugged-out thing was not none of that. It was the weird way the kids in the crowd were dressed.

"What's going on here?" I asked Chiasa.

"Everything, anything," she said casually.

There were teenaged girls dressed up like baby dolls with wigs and face makeup that I was sure was making them look less attractive than they knew. They wore miniskirts with layered lace beneath, making the skirts shoot out. They wore corsets and ribbons, no stockings with bare thighs and bare legs, and some slight suggestion of butt cheeks exposed. There were chicks dressed as cartoon characters, vampires, birds, mice, and cats, heroes, aliens, heroines.

"Is it Japanese Halloween?" I asked.

"Nope. This is Harajuku. This is everyday. Some of the kids dress up as their favorite characters from children's stories like Strawberry Shortcake, Alice in Wonderland, Little Bo Peep, and some from Manga books and anime films like Hantoro and Naruto. Some are just doing their own thing—like them." Chiasa pointed. There were three Japanese girls in black fishnet stockings and panties, wearing no skirt, no dress, and no pants. Around one of each of their thighs was a garter belt made of satin and lace. On the back of their panties were big red bows as though they were gifts given to the public. They had to be about thirteen, fourteen, or fifteen years young.

"I won't stay here," I told Chiasa.

"You can. The place where you'll be staying is in the nice section. It's called Omotesando. We just need to keep walking." Hundreds of dark-eyed girls in high school uniforms swarmed around us. Their skirts were hiked up to their hips and blouse buttons open. I ran my hand over my Caesar cut.

Omotesando was all upscale boutiques and shops with the same crowd. I peeped three Syrian men grilling beef and chicken kebobs serving fifty-nine nearly naked schoolgirls who lined up and waited patiently with pockets filled with money. Their dusty beige Syrian faces were covered in a sheen of sweat from the hot meat and heated grill. I knew they were fasting. I could tell. Many Muslims worship and restrain themselves quietly, while watching others run amok.

I didn't cast even an eye on these strange Japanese teenage dudes.

The hostel was on Kat Street in an old mansion with Spanish architecture. "Let me look around first," I told Chiasa as soon as we entered. She remained at the front desk while I explored.

"*Habari gani*," a guy passing by in the hallway called out to me. I stopped and turned, recognizing his Swahili greeting. My father said every black person everywhere in the world should learn Swahili. "It's our common language," he told me.

"Peace," I told him.

"Haki, from Kenya." He extended his hand to me.

"Midnight, from New York," I countered.

"You just arrived, right?" he asked knowingly.

"Yeah."

"How long will you stay?"

"One night," I responded speculating that I'd bolt out on the bullet train at sunrise.

Haki laughed a bit and said, "There are guys here who came for one night and stayed for two years!" Then he smiled and said, "Brother, if you need anything, let me be your friend."

I gave him a pound. "One minute, how are the rooms? Do the room doors have locks on them?" I asked, since that was much more important to me than the scenery.

"What kind of place doesn't have locks on the door?" Haki laughed some.

"I heard the Japanese don't steal," I said, smiling at the stupidity of my comment.

But Haki said, "They don't. But everyone else does! So of course there are locks."

"You got it," I told him.

"Wait, my room is two doors down. Take a look inside for yourself." Haki unlocked his door with a metal slide key. He slid his door open. He looked completely settled there in the room, his books stacked in piles like pancakes, his shirt flung over his chair, and worn shoes forming a line across the wall.

"A bed, a desk, a lamp, and a closet—the basics," he said. "But there is no real crime in Japan and it's clean and comfortable."

"Alright, good looking out," I told him, stepping out to leave.

"For fifteen hundred yen extra per night you can get a room with a bigger window and a terrace. Me, I'm on a budget. Most of us college students are" was the last thing he said as I left. I saw three more guys walking in the same hallway and began to wonder if this was an all-male hostel.

"Over here," Chiasa called, as she shot out of a side opening that led to the stairwell. "We're on the second floor, room 202."

"I didn't check in yet," I told her as she climbed the stairs ahead of me. I kept my gaze on the marble steps.

"I did. I have a passport and I paid the six thousand yen. Besides, you don't like to give anyone your name and information anyway," she said in a serious tone, no laughter.

I did the conversion swiftly. "Six thousand yen, that's high for a hostel."

"I signed you up for two nights, that's why it sounds high. You can add on the rest of the nights if you like it. I have a receipt, you can reimburse me for my expenses on this mission, right?" She reached the top stair and turned and looked down at me.

"Why not?" is all I said.

Chiasa got a room bigger than Haki's. There was one big window and a fire escape that Haki had called a terrace. I leaned out the window and saw plenty of people passing by—shoppers, skaters, athletes, musicians, and some of those costume dress-up types. I pulled backed inside and had to laugh at myself. *What kind of place am I in? I'm a Muslim in the middle of a brothel with no walls that's in the middle of a nuthouse during Ramadan.*

I picked up the receiver on the desk phone, listening for a dial tone. "What about this phone? Does it work?"

"It does work, but you can only receive calls if you give them a credit card at the front desk. I don't have one on me," she said. She didn't ask if I did. "But you can call from room to room in here." She handed me the room key and the small folded leaflet that came with it. I pulled it all the way open; in ten different languages were the rules and benefit listings for hostel guests. I put it in the drawer.

"This is Naoko Nakamura's current photo," she said, pulling a paper folded in fours out of her bag. She laid it on the desk and pointed.

"Where did you get it?" I asked her, as I eased in to take a close look. My eyes shot to the top of the page; it was dated today. Yet Naoko Nakamura's appearance was not much older than the way he looked in an old picture in the book Sensei had gifted to me. With a head full of black hair styled by a precise barber, he was a sharply dressed executive in a one-thousand-dollar tailored business suit. He stood taller than the two men pictured at his side. He didn't wear glasses like many Asian men. Determination in his eyes, he didn't seem like the obvious villain.

"But we're not looking for him, right?" Chiasa said, interrupting my thoughts. "This is a love story, right? So where does he fit in?" She stood up straight now. I thought to myself, *Chiasa, quick like lightning.*

"He doesn't," I said solemnly. "Who are these guys standing beside him?" I asked her. "And what's going on in the news story?"

She leaned over to read the Japanese captions. "Oh, this man is the vice president of Nakamura's Pan Asian Corporation. His name is Bishamon Ikeda." Chiasa pulled her face up and her jaw dropped open. But I was a second ahead of her.

"Iwa Ikeda," we both said aloud. I locked in my game face.

"The girl you are looking for is Iwa Ikeda and this is her father!" Chiasa pronounced.

Purposely I did not correct her. It would be better for her if she did not know. As my anger was stirring up slowly, it had nothing to do with Chiasa. I would not allow her to get caught in a deadly mess. And what if she got questioned in a situation where this became a police matter? Yes, it would be better. The less she knew, the less she could tell. But I could tell she wouldn't tell.

"Or maybe you are after Bishamon's wife and *she* is named Iwa Ikeda!"

"I never intefere with another man's wife," I told her, and her light laugh and suspicion evaporated.

Seeing that the only television here in the Harajuku hostel was in an open-area lounge, I asked Chiasa, "If your grandfather agrees, could we go by your house and view the footage? Does he have a VCR?"

"It's mine. I have to ask if I can have you over or not. But my grandfather knows that I'm a businesswoman. He wouldn't restrict a great client!" she said with her brand of calm excitement—and eagerness.

"Let's move then. I gotta pick up my luggage from over there anyway."

On the walk over to Yoyogi, which was next door to Harajuku, my curiosity intensified. I got Chiasa to translate the newspaper article and sum it up for me in English.

"It's announcing Nakamura's trip to Singapore this weekend, which is his first stop on his Asian corporate tour."

I stopped. Would he take my wife across the continent with him? Or would he leave her at home? Where is her home? Is it Tokyo, or is it Kyoto? Were Iwa and Akemi being heavily supervised right now and simply waiting for their fathers to leave on the trip, so they could contact me? Then Akemi would just pick up the phone when I called Iwa and say, "Take me back to New York. I want to go home with you. I want to see Umma."

What-ifs were choking me. The thought battle was fucking up my head. The other voice in my head said only two words, "Take action."

Chapter 5
FIGHTING

"We should stop here," Chiasa said, as we stood in front of a bicycle stop in Yoyogi. The bicycle game in Tokyo is serious, I had discovered. Although it was my first full day here, I had actually counted more bicycles than cars. I was shocked to see a parking deck for bikes only. On our way over, I saw policemen on bikes in Shinjuku, and now delivery and messengers on bikes in Yoyogi. Some women seemed to balance their whole lives on the bike, their babies and children and food and purses and other items. I saw a Ginza policeman issuing a parking violation to a bicycle. One minute later a flatbed arrived and towed the bike away. In addition to armored trucks to transport money, they had armored bikes.

As she pushed the shop door open, Chiasa shouted *"Tadaima!"* She looked up and down and then called out, *"Ojiichan."* No one answered. She flagged me in. I stepped inside, not really interested but checking out a mountain bike for 100,000 yen, which is almost one thousand American dollars. On display also were mopeds of different styles and brands. There were some cheap bikes available for a hundred or even thirty dollars, but they were stacked off to the side.

Chiasa disappeared. I walked toward the back of the shop. By a silver curtain I could hear voices. One of them was hers. They were both speaking in Japanese. I stood close to the curtain. I guess that's why Chiasa bumped into me as she emerged with an elderly man. *"Ojiichan kare wa Ryoshi,"* Chiasa introduced us. *Ojiichan* was one of my vocabulary study words. It meant "grandfather," and for some reason she told him that my name was Ryoshi.

"Ryoshi?" her slim, tall, laid-back, silver-haired grandfather responded. Chiasa nodded.

"*Hai*, Ryoshi." I went along with it, assuming she had her reasons for the cover-up. Or maybe by now she realized this job she had offered to do for me could end up with almost any type of mysterious outcome.

"*Hajime mashite Ryoshi deska,*" I greeted him. He smiled and seemed less stiff and formal than the few Japanese men I had observed so far. He fired off some Japanese sentences too advanced for me. Then he and Chiasa got into a quiet, respectful, and friendly back-and-forth. I stepped a few feet away and checked my watch. It was four o'clock.

"My grandfather says I can't have company in the house while he's away. He won't be home until nine fifteen tonight," Chiasa said.

"I can understand him," I said.

"I don't know. It's the first time he ever told me that. Usually I ask for something and he agrees."

"How many men have you invited over before?"

"None, but—"

"Well, that's it then," I said. "I'll just have to find another way to view the tapes."

"No!" she said anxiously. "My grandfather said we can use the backyard. I'll bring the TV out and run an extension. We can eat dinner back there also. It's nice and warm."

I knew in my mind there wasn't gonna be a picnic with me and her in her backyard. I didn't want her to get too comfortable.

"Sunset is at six thirty tonight," she announced. "My grandfather said so. What are we going to eat?" she asked. Then she added strangely, "I don't eat any four-legged animals."

"What?" I needed to hear that one again.

"No four-legged animals," she repeated. "No cows, no pigs, no sheep, no goats, no lambs, no anything with four legs."

She faced front as she walked. I walked beside her and looked at her profile. She was different from any woman I had ever known. I smiled.

She sensed me looking and asked, "What?"

"Nothing," I responded. "No four-legged animals. That's cool with me, *wakarimashta!*" I said. She laughed each time I used Japanese vocab.

The shade of the maple tree shielded the glare of the sun from the television screen. The red sun had simmered purple with a pink hue but had not settled yet.

The film footage that Chiasa shot in the lobby of Akemi's father's building was clear and crisp. Her hands only shook the shot once or twice. We were both watching the screen. Chiasa narrated. I was watching the details of the visual more than I was listening. "Nakamura was on the thirty-second floor, like I suspected. It was a penthouse. This is the elevator that the public uses, but here is a private elevator," she pointed out. "The regular public elevator doesn't take you up to the top floors. They are labeled executive levels. If you press an executive level number, a recording comes on explaining that it's restricted. The stairwell goes up to twenty-eight, but then it seals shut. This is me in the lobby." She pointed to the image of herself being filmed.

"I see. Who is holding the camera?" I asked her.

"One of the school kids," she said, as we watched her huddled in with eight school kids throwing up peace signs beside the company directory. Both her smile and her skin stood out on film. Standing beside those other school kids, who were probably her same age, she appeared more powerful. It was not just her body but something coming through her eyes, an energy that swirled around her and that could be seen and felt even on film.

"Hold it!" I said. She pressed pause.

"You are so smart!" she exclaimed softly to me. "There it is, what you were looking for!" Now she had her slim finger on the screen. "Bishamon Ikeda!" she said, pointing out his name on the directory. "Even if I hadn't given you the *Daily Yomiuri* news article, you would've found his name right there listed on the wall directory."

My mind shifted back onto the Iwa Ikeda problem. When Iwa heard the Narita Airport announcement, she panicked and hung up the phone. Either she told my wife that I was here in Tokyo or she didn't. Either she told her father that I had arrived here in Tokyo or she didn't. Either Bishamon Ikeda told Naoko Nakamura or he didn't.

"What is the meaning of his name, Bishamon?" I asked randomly.

"Let's see . . . ," she said, examining the kanji. "It is the name of the god of war." Chiasa pronounced each word with emphasis. There was no fear in her voice, but a hint of excitement was apparent.

"Press play," I told her. As the film continued, images of the parking deck came into view. "There was a guard there, private security," Chiasa explained. "I waited until one car pulling out stopped at the guard's booth. When the driver and the guard began speaking, I slipped in but didn't have to go far. The executive vehicles are all parked on the ground floor. You see there. It's a private elevator. So no one would ever see them entering the building through the front, side, or rear doors," Chiasa explained.

I was listening but focused on the vehicles. The first one was a Toyota Century Royal built and designed like a Bentley, but it was not British-made. It was Japanese. "Have you seen this kind of car before?" I asked Chiasa. "I might've seen it before but never really noticed it." It was a clever answer, not admitting that there were some things that she didn't know. But I knew that if she had seen the car before, she would have remembered. People who love motorcycles, cars, boats, and planes don't forget the top-of-the-line items, ever.

This vehicle on the screen was obviously customed after the Bentley but made to suit Japanese tastes or even Japanese politics. "It's pretty. The seats are wide and wool-upholstered. I couldn't get up that close to get all of the features on camera, but the inside of that car was really pretty. It's Nakamura's. Or at least the reserved sign said CEO." She pointed to the kanji and translated. *I'm sure it's his.* I thought to myself. *But he probably leaves the driving to his driver.*

"You know, two men smoking cigarettes approached me. That's why this part is so shaky," Chiasa narrated and explained why the camera image suddenly shook, then dropped and turned upside down facing only a cement pillar.

"What were they saying?"

"Not much, just asked what I was doing. I played dumb, giggled like girls do, and told them I thought the car was pretty."

So she is an actress too, I thought to myself, and then remembered this was the same girl who pretended to be asleep on the plane ride for at least an hour.

"It's not the same as New York out here. No one is expecting anything to happen. We don't steal and there's no crime."

My mind drifted. I could tell that she believed what she was tell-

ing me, but I didn't believe either of her last statements. If there was
no crime, what were all those crazy movies I saw when I was young,
Ameer and Chris and the whole movie theater of black faces cheering for gangs of Asian guys beating the life out of each other ruth-
lessly? Limbs were being broken, eyes poked out, bodies sliced up,
and whole crews left for dead. They had to be fighting over something. Only them boys on my Brooklyn block fought over nothing—
clothes, kicks, and colors, over buildings and territories they didn't
own and couldn't afford, over blocks, benches, and bullshit every
fucking day. Nah, these Japanese cats were onto something major, the
battle of billions, the war of nations, the push of politics. I just needed
to slide my girl out from under their noses and leave them to their
business.

One thing Chiasa said did stand out in my mind. It sounded true,
and I would use it to my advantage: "No one is expecting anything to
happen." It echoed in my mind. I was glad that they were not expecting anything to go wrong.

I sent Chiasa inside while I made the Maghrib prayer at sunset.
She had fasted for the first day of Ramadan and handled it easily. No
food for twelve hours is a small thing to many, but no water or drinks
of any kind is torture to those used to satisfying their thirst. So she
did well under the red sun, yet I understood that she didn't know the
meaning or reason of the holy month. In my prayers I thanked Allah for the revelations of today. And I thanked him for Chiasa, who
I believed Allah had sent as a helper. Also I asked for guidance in all
that I knew I would do in the Tokyo late night. I had already given
the elephant Nakamura the day. Now things would shift.

Raw fish and brown rice with the fruits she had offered me earlier, that's what Chiasa ate. I scooped peanut butter and ate it off the
spoon the Sudanese way—without bread. I had three rice triangles,
called *onigiri*, made of brown rice stuffed with a tablespoon of salmon
and wrapped in a sheet of seaweed. They were simple and satisfying. I
added a bag of raisins. On Ramadan many Muslims tend to eat light.
Each year, Umma and I did the same.

Chiasa's backyard was impossible to separate from the wilderness that surrounded us. The lone house made of huge stone had no
neighbors but the flowers, plants, and trees. I also worked out back

there. It felt better than working out in a small room indoors. In fact, it felt great.

"Let's go," Chiasa said. When I turned, she was wearing her dark-blue *dogi* cut from a thick cloth. She had a deep-blue skirt with a high waistband cut from a lighter-weight fabric. The skirt was quality, I could tell. It was cut long, just above her ankle. Hanging across her back was a long sword inside a wickedly crafted cloth case. In her left hand she held her gym bag.

"Let me take that from you," I said, reaching for her bag. She hesitated at first but then handed it over to me. I smiled at her ways, naturally.

She responded with four words spoken softly and seriously. "It's time to fight."

I followed her out of her yard into Yoyogi Park, curious.

* * *

In a clearing where the trees no longer gathered in an intense crowd and under the strength of the Tokyo moonlight, the dopest dojo I have ever entered was right there in Yoyogi Park, about a quarter mile away from where Chiasa's house was located. If she had wanted to impress me and capture my attention completely, in this moment she had succeeded—with the beauty of the facility itself.

The architecture appeared ancient and maybe had been constructed by fifty to a hundred workers for some imperial or samurai, I imagined. The rooftops were not flat and without texture, like I had seen in many places. The roofs were on wicked angles, swooped down and curled upwards at the end. The texture was created by baked and curved red clay tiles, each one laid near the other carefully and perfectly placed. I had seen this type of roof before in films where the scenery surpassed the story and ninjas tiptoed and glided so light and fluid like butterfly assassins to the complete shock and horror of their prey. Standing here in the night in a small clearing in the woods in the park facing this dojo, I felt like someone had dropped me into an ancient film that was already fifty minutes into the viewing.

"Come this way," Chiasa said.

The fact that it was wider than any indoor fighting/training space I had ever seen was not even its strongest point. The floor was made of bamboo laid in perfectly for the length of a football field. It was so clean, flawless, and polished, that it seemed impossible to imagine that anyone had ever placed a foot on it. The ceilings were forty-eight feet high. I pretended to myself that this was in case a fighter wanted to fly. The ceiling too was designed with great care and precision. Like a complicated math problem, a craftsman had cut the entire ceiling into even squares and surrounded more than two hundred squares with bamboo borders to outline and highlight its perfection. Some of the squares were lit up brightly, which the floors reflected, the light giving everyone the opportunity to see every movement that any fighter might make. Even in the hallways the floors were incredible, the wooden seats placed at even distances and immovable, so that no one could alter the order and the measurement and the count—or the seating arrangement.

The female fighters in Chiasa's class sat on their knees. Their silence and their form was elegant, their uniforms flowing with the contour of their bodies. Not tight, not too loose. To the left of each was a face helmet, a type that I had never seen but admired. The male fighters sat across the room, their robes as expertly tied, tidy and neat. The elder men sat at a table, which of course raised them above the heads of both their male and female students, who all sat with their swords to the side.

At first I believed a sensei would take charge and begin to lead the class. On second thought it seemed the presence of the elders signaled some kind of ceremony or ritual. Because I couldn't understand the language, I watched it like a video with the volume dropped out. This made my eyes pay even closer attention to each detail.

An elder laid out several medals on the head table. *An awards ceremony*, I guessed.

Suddenly Chiasa stood up, held her helmet at one side and sword at the other. She approached one of the elders and bowed before him. The elder man spoke softly to her and at length. Chiasa was completely subdued, silent, and humbled. At his last words he lifted a gold medal with a red ribbon on it and placed it around her lowered head. She in turn did a deep bow before him. Quietly she turned, her eyes seeming to survey the room. Then she walked over to another seated female fighter. She stood before her, then slowly put on her helmet. She tied its long strings back, her fingers moving expertly

Chiasa wearing her kendo dogi.

behind her head as though she had easily tied it a thousand times. With the helmet secured and in her full uniform, she looked completely different and more incredible to me. She raised her sword and lowered it at the head of the seated girl. Without notice, all the other seated fighters slid either to the left or the right and stilled once again on their knees, now all facing the girl who was left seated alone.

Slowly the girl stood up. She picked up her helmet. Before she covered her head, I realized that it was Yuka, the girl from the plane who had introduced herself to me univited by simply saying, "Let's trade music." I leaned forward on the wooden bleachers where I was seated and watched intently.

The tremble of Yuka's finger was so slight it could've been missed. She tied her helmet and raised her sword. It seemed to signal that she had accepted the challenge.

Chiasa crashed Yuka's head with the sword with a dizzying speed. It woke Yuka up and their battle began. The bamboo sword striking both the metal helmet and the thick *dogi* made loud crashes. Yet even louder were the warlike cries and shouts of Chiasa as she set to conquer and humiliate her opponent on the dojo floor.

The style of fighting was unusual to me. The helmet offered too much protection, I thought. The fight was waged with the upper body and not the feet. Although their feet moved in a rhythmic dance. From the strike of the sword, I could calculate that they were both aiming only at the head, the throat, the stomach, and the wrists.

The elders were transfixed and absorbed by the battle. Even I was completely drawn in. It seemed that men battle one another individually and in groups, gangs, and armies all across the globe, yet warring women mesmerized us all. No longer seated, the elders were each standing on their feet with their arms folded before them. Their eyeballs bounced and jumped at each movement the girl fighters made.

Chiasa's style was unforgiving. When her and Yuka's raised swords met, she stepped in even closer and thrust Yuka backward. Yuka was propelled by the push but caught herself from falling. She was lighter than Chiasa, although both of them were slim. Yuka danced forward again, her feet moving in a calculated rhythm. She raised her sword to strike Chiasa. Chiasa blocked her sword and moved out of the block faster than Yuka, striking both of Yuka's wrists in two sharp blows.

An elder gasped. Yuka was hurt. One sensei yelled out something in Japanese. Yuka raised her sword again. Her two hands tight on the sword grip, she charged Chiasa, but Chiasa altered her approach and didn't advance. Chiasa lowered her sword some as Yuka advanced and lunged it into Yuka's throat, and all the elders stepped in, calling out commands in Japanese. They each raised one hand, which caused the sparring to cease and acknowledged Chiasa had won.

The match was finished now. The girls still faced one another, holding their form. In a precise movement the girls raised their swords so that they touched. Then they dropped their swords at their waist and both took five steps backward. They both took a deep bow acknowledging each other, both saying, *"Arigato gozaimasu."* The politeness seemed important to the Japanese—even in the most heated and hateful exchanges. I was certain that I was not the only one who could feel that the fight between Yuka and Chiasa was more than just a practice or training exercise. It felt intense and personal. It felt deadly.

Yuka returned to her original position on the floor and Chiasa remained standing. The fellow fighters applauded her now. When the helmets were off and the quiet resumed, Chiasa spoke out some words in Japanese to Yuka. Yuka's facial expression tightened. The elder spoke some words to Yuka, and it seemed whatever they had been debating was solved. Chiasa bowed again to the elder. Their bowing seemed endless. One bow led to another.

Soon Chiasa left the room. I stood up from the top bleacher where I was positioned. Yuka's eyes connected with mine. Her face softened and filled with both surprise and delight. In the one second that it takes for a thought to occur, Yuka snatched back her warm expression and glared at me with the look of having been betrayed. I walked out to meet Chiasa wherever she had gone to. It didn't matter. I knew from the way they were swinging the swords at each other that I had to choose between them—and of course, easily, I had chosen Chiasa.

Leaning against the wall opposite the women's locker room, I waited for her. Twenty minutes passed by before I began to search around. Back in the main dojo, I stuck my head in. She wasn't there. Yet as all the fighters began to file out to the locker rooms, Yuka was on her knees, a cloth in her hand, wiping the floor. She was cleaning the cleanest and largest dojo floor I had ever seen. The elder who had spoken Japanese to her in a hardened tone was the only adult remaining. I closed the door. I had opened six doors before I located Chiasa behind the seventh. She wore now a black *dogi* and had donned a red belt, no helmet, no skirt, no sword. My entrance didn't break her concentration as she fought a girl wearing a black belt. Her sensei stood almost inside the fighting circle as though he was part of the match or maybe he was a caution sign. Their fight ended seconds after my arrival. I wish I had seen it. I sat on an empty bench.

Just as I believed that she was done for the night, I stood up. As I did, a Japanese youth stood also. He wore a black belt. As I watched, he and Chiasa bowed before one another and struck a stance.

"Chiasa," I called her out. The sensei, the fighters, and the guy she was about to fight all shifted their eyes to my direction. Chiasa did not. She kept her eyes on her opponent. Her sensei said something to her. Chiasa answered him back in Japanese. The sensei spoke again and then she spoke again. Her opponent said some words, and then Chiasa said to me, "Come on, are you ready to fight? My opponent has yielded to you." The sensei watched me intensely, his blank face no longer reading caution. Now he was a green light and behind it was curiosity, anticipation, and fear of the unknown that I could sense and see. I had only called out to Chiasa because I didn't want her fighting a male fighter. I couldn't sit by and watch it for sport. Now she wanted to fight me instead of him. No problem, at least I knew I wouldn't strike or hurt her.

My army-green Girbauds were loose-fitting enough. My shoes were already off. I approached. We were both supposed to bow. She bowed. We both struck our stances. I recognized her perfect form— yet somehow it was entertainment to me. She showed me that it was not entertainment for her. Serious-faced, she angled left and made the first strike with her right foot followed by her right hand. I blocked both. She pulled back and moved both her feet and her eyes around looking for a *suki*. I could tell she wanted me to make a move. I didn't, just watched her, moved my feet around but held my hands in a defensive position. She lunged forward striking out again with her right hand. When I moved to block she moved her left leg like lightning and kneed me in my stomach. I held her right fist and twisted it and brought it behind her body to immobilize her. Purposely, my grip was not strong or tight. She used her left elbow, a reverse move to strike me strategically against the left side of my jaw. I felt that. She had caught me off guard. I jumped back and looked at her then smiled. She took my smile as an insult, ran up on me, and leaped off the floor into a double flying kick. Instead of blocking, resisting, or striking, I sidestepped and snatched up her body from midair. I threw her over my shoulder then spun her around like a five year old to confuse her vision. I set her down on her feet. As she steadied herself, I took full advantage. Within three seconds I folded Chiasa up and carried her out of the dojo in my arms with zero protest from her sensei and the fighters who she had been intimidating all night. As I moved swiftly past the passive observers with their female champion, no sword-swinging samurais or silent ninja assassins or karate killers emerged to defend her honor.

I put her down on the ground outside the dojo. Then I sat down beside her. She smiled at me. Naturally, I smiled at her. I loved her spirit. All fire.

"See, now you respect me," she said, slowing down her breathing. "And I respect you more," she added. "Two people can spend weeks together and never develop the respect that two fighters can earn in one match. I know that guys don't respect girls too much. So I fight to let them know I am Chiasa, a whole woman, not half a person. Treat me right."

As we walked back through Yoyogi, all the lampposts switched off. As my eyes adjusted to the darkness, I was reminded of the complete blackness that enveloped my grandfather's Southern Sudanese village—when the moon and the stars went on break, as they sometimes do.

I could smell the scent of pine trees and of the cypress and zelkova and oak all intermingling.

"I do respect you, Chiasa," I admitted.

"Arigato gozaimasu," she replied softly without bowing down. I was grateful.

The cicada sang as we moved in silence. I thought about how she was training in so many different fighting styles—kendo, *kyudo*, and karate. She must have some reason pushing her.

"Chiasa, which style of fight is your favorite?" I asked.

"I'm bored with it all. I don't want the bamboo practice sword. I prefer the blade," she said softly. I don't want to aim at a stable bulls-eye, I want to fire on a live moving target."

"The real thing would kill your opponent," I cautioned her.

"As long as we both knew that before we fight, that's fair and square," she said without laughter.

* * *

I left Yoyogi and returned to the Harajuku hostel, where I secured my luggage. Then I worked out hard. As I was moving and training my muscles, my mind was formulating ideas and strategies, storing some in my memory and throwing the rest out. I drank five tall bottles of water when I finished. It's important to take in enough water during the night to keep your body working properly during the fast of the day. At 1:30 in the morning, I was showered and dressed, wearing my black nylon Nike suit and a black tee and my black uptowns, my gloves in my back pocket. I wanted my hands free, so I rocked a Black Jansport containing the few items I might need.

I stepped outside the Harajuku hostel expecting shit on the streets to be winding down, but the Harajuku party seemed at a boiling point, with all kinds of kids and kooks and characters milling around and mixing in with the young fashionable crews as well. Was it my imagination, or as I began walking, did a huge chunk of the crowd begin to move in the same direction as me? I was accompanied and followed by about a hundred and fifty youth and preceded by about eighty more, as we all walked and squeezed down the tight Harajuku alleyway to the train station. Feeling like an actor in *Thriller*, I played the corner as the freaks packed the compartment of what I discovered was the last train for the night.

As I moved through the network of underground tunnels that lies beneath Roppongi, I was not alone. There were many foreign men in motion, as well as Japanese men still suited up from work and groups of girls who I'd guess were from fourteen to twenty-five years young. The crowds were not loud or rowdy. Everyone seemed focused on getting to a specific destination uninterrupted. I was noticing now that every Tokyo prefecture had its own personality. In fact, as you climbed up the endless stacks of stairs from the train to the outdoors, you could not find anything similar to the last stop that you came from. Each location would be completely new and unique.

There were no wives, mothers, or children in Roppongi night-life. For four blocks to the north and four blocks to the south and four blocks to the east and four blocks to the west were all night-clubs, hostess bars, and restaurants. As I moved in the night breeze, I blended right in, which made me feel some ease.

"Bro-da!" an African voice called out to me. "Check it out. We have what you are looking for. You are looking for girl, yes?" he said oddly.

He was six-eight, towering over me, a more massive giant in the land of little people. Dressed in a not-too-cheap suit, he extended his hand. "Come now," he said. "Club is free, drinks cost money, girls are very friendly. What you like? Japanese girl, Russian girl, Swedish girl, American girl? You choose."

"I'm good," I told him. *"Ramadan Kareem,"* I added solemnly. *Ramadan Kareem* is a Muslim greeting offered to Muslims around the world at the start of the Ramadan fast. I could tell this man was from Nigeria. I also knew from flipping through my atlas and maps that they had almost 150 million people in their West African nation, most of them Muslim. By offering him the holiday greeting, I could move him out of my path and maybe off of his corrupt purpose.

It backfired and piqued his curiosity instead. "I am Olatunde the Nigerian," he said as he extended his hand, announcing himself as though he were his nation's representative. "But here in Japan, friends call me Ola." When I didn't move or grasp or shake his hand, he took one step forward and looked down on me.

Brooklyn don't break from no next man's menacing stare. That's hood basic 101. I stepped to his left to move beyond him and caught a glimpse of a four-foot-tall Japanese girl in eight-inch heels, the top of her head still barely above the Nigerian's Pierre Cardin belt. From behind him she handed me a party card invite advertising the club that she was standing in front of. He turned and spoke harsh Japanese to her. She stepped all the way back to the club entrance.

"Tell Ola, what is your business here? You are in Roppongi for Ramadan. Surely you did not come here to pray in the land with no God." He smiled a smile of satisfaction with himself.

"I'm good," I told him again and stepped to his right, bypassing him. Before I was six steps away, I heard his rhyme begin again. "My friend, club is free, drinks cost money, girls are very friendly." As I checked the late, late night, early morning scene, this appeared to be the formula, an array of Nigerians fishing for any men to come trick a pile of cash on some doe-eyed female wearing an evening gown, nightgown, or miniskirt. And there seemed to be no shortage of takers.

When I reached the outer boundary of Roppongi Hills, the party scenes subsided and the lights were not glaring. The residential section was separate from the chaos of the clubs. I put my gloves and wool hat on, believing that if I could move swiftly through the shadows, I would go unnoticed. There were not many people out. I mainly saw closed boutiques, craft shops, and minimarkets. The houses behind them were woven in and up and on the various hills and slopes and narrow paths. The hour of the night, the trees and gardens made my invisibility possible. I walked nonchalantly past the front of Akemi's father's house without moving my head to inspect it. To reach the backyard, I would have to walk past the front, uphill, make a right, and then another. So I did.

There were two fifteen-foot-tall walls that ran down both sides of the street behind Akemi's house. At the top of the walls were bushes, and no matter left or right, all you could see was wall and bushes. But her neighbor had a tree with a sturdy trunk and heavy branches and leaves that shielded the house from street-level onlookers. The tree extended into the sky. It was now the second day of Ramadan, and I considered that tree my second blessing.

As I climbed, gripping the bark with my gloves and my kicks, I cleared my mind of what-ifs and focused. I leaped from a branch onto the top of the wall. When I landed, my body brushed hard against the bushes, tiny little thorns sticking me enough to cause me to straighten up and balance and be mindful. I duckwalked across to Akemi's side, and when I got there, I attempted to see through the bushes into her yard, but the bushes were too dense. I considered clipping and clearing through the bushes, and crawling through the clearing, but didn't because although I might be successful in getting in that way, the next morning the gardener or any curious person would have just the evidence needed to confirm that someone had intruded on the property. Turning sideways, with my back now to the bushes and face to the wall, I pushed through the three-inch space between the wall and the bushes. The prickles scraped against my sweat jacket and pants and wool hat and socks and boots but not enough to pierce my skin or cause my blood to flow.

Her yard was darker than the streets, and all the house lights were off. No dog—had there been one, he would've begun barking minutes ago when he smelled the unfamiliar scent of my presence even as I climbed the neighbor's tree. Surveying, I counted four floors to the sturdy cement home, which resembled the best-built Brooklyn brownstones in its quality and the way it was carefully constructed. The top floors had cement terraces. With no fire escapes, there was no ladder or means of climbing up or down from them.

I began to walk in calculated steps. The grass crunched beneath my feet. Fortunately, the hum of a nearby generator should have made the sounds undetectable. I walked around the perimeter carefully, and up to the east side of the house. It was all good until I reached the eastern corner that led to the front. I heard a click and then some sort of motor started up. I saw a high beam approaching from the distance, and the heavy black iron gate that sealed off the front of their house began to open slowly. I eased back, pressing my body against the house on the dark side, so as not to be exposed by the increasing light. Adrenaline released in me, and swiftly I walked backward to the backyard and crossed over to the west side of the house, where I could escape the light and still see into the front. My jaw was tight and I began taking deep breaths to overcome my anger. I didn't appreciate Nakamura creating a circumstance where I had to creep like a thief. But fuck it, he had. The car eased onto the property but the bright headlights prevented me from seeing details. The gate remained open, so I was sure that there were at least two passengers inside, one who intended to leave. Otherwise the gate would've closed behind them.

The driver's door opened. A suited man leaped out and rushed around to the back passenger-seat door. He opened it and stood patiently like an employee. The passenger took his time, like an employer accustomed to being served would do.

When Nakamura finally emerged, the driver went into a series of bows to him and then ran around to the trunk. Nakamura followed, and now the trunk shielded my view of them both, and any possible view they could've had of me. I took a couple of steps back to a darkened ground-level window and tested it to see if it would slide open.

I was surprised when it did. I left it open by about only two centimeters, enough to stick my gloved fingers back in if I needed to.

More confident now that I had a definite way inside of the house, I walked toward the backyard again to shield my presence and wait. As I moved, I happened to look up. "Always look up," my sensei had taught me. When I did, I saw for the first time that on the fourth floor of the west side of the building was a yellow light left on in an otherwise completely darkened house. Then I knew.

I heard the front door of the house opening. The car was moving now, and I heard the sound of rocks beneath the tires. Then the ignition switched off, and the glare of the lights deaded. The car door opened and closed. I could tell by the sequence of sounds that the car had only been parked. The iron gate had not closed yet. Suddenly I heard the sound of another car starting. The sound of the engine was a dead giveaway that it was a lower-quality vehicle. It moved, the sound of the car getting further and further away. The front door of the house shut as the iron gate also began closing. Then the sound of the second car was no more.

Carefully, I walked to the front again, using the west side of the house. The Japanese Bentley was parked against the house at the front. The gleaming blackness of the exterior was glossier than the blackness of the night. I drew closer to look at it. The interior was "pretty," like Chiasa had said. The thick wool seats were piped out in thick leather, the seams solid and the inside incredible with granite fixtures, which would normally be used in a house. My stare into the car was broken only by the light switched on in the house on the ground floor on the front eastern side. I dropped down beside the car but did not touch it. I looked up. Another light came on then, on the second floor.

Believing that Nakamura was now upstairs, I duckwalked over to the front door of their house. I had observed that the Japanese normally left their shoes lined up right outside their house door before switching immediately into house slippers. Aside from Nakamura and possibly his daughter, who else could live here? A housemaid, or butler, or some security personnel? Yet if there were any security personnel on their property, they were doing a poor job.

I figured the shoes wouldn't lie to me. Using my penlight, I beamed on the first pair of shoes. It was a men's pair labeled REGAL. I believed it was a custom-made shoe. There was a second label stitched inside embossed in kanji. I assumed it was Nakamura's name in kanji letters, their version of a monogram. I'd say the soft leather shoe with the streamlined design and careful stitching was valued at about a thousand American dollars. Obviously they were the shoes that Naoko Nakamura had just eased his feet out of. A cheap pair of black, women's work shoes. A cheap pair of white, well-worn, clean women's work shoes. A pair of expensive pink pumps. I moved my light back and forth over those. They were expensive, but not expensive enough to be Akemi's. Who could these belong to? Then I focused on the black-leather spring Gucci boots, so lovely they got my blood boiling. The bottoms were designed like sandals, but the rings of thick black leather curled around all the way beyond the ankle and up the calves. Imagining my wife's pretty legs in them moved me. And I knew she had to have dropped at least two thousand American on those. Then there were the men's high-top Converses seated beside them, a crime in and of itself. *Who the fuck wore those? The gardener,* I answered my-self, trying to calm, calm all the way down.

With five pairs of shoes counted, the risk in this caper heightened. There was no way to tell where each of the people in the house who owned these shoes slept, or even if they were actually inside or not. I stood thinking quietly. I opened my Jansport, pulled out Akemi's hundred-thousand-yen heels and switched them with her Guccis. I knew that if she saw the shoes that she had worn in New York with me to a wedding Umma and I had worked at, she would be 100 per-cent sure that I was here in Tokyo. Further, once she discovered that her Guccis were gone, she would know that I switched them. The Japanese don't steal, right? So who else could've taken them? For now, alerting her that I was here, in Tokyo, would have to be enough for me. I had brought along the perfect clue.

Angry and tight, I threw my Jansport on my back and walked away along the west side of the house. On the fourth floor, the yellow light still beamed. It was the same color of light that lit up the base-ment at Cho's where Akemi and I, newlyweds, first made love. It was the only light on the fourth floor that was on. Looking at it caused me to break my stride and to pause to think for a second. Then my legs started moving again.

Inside of me, I began to feel more like an animal than a man. An angry animal, a hungry animal, and that fury worked its way through my chest. I left back out through the slot in the bushes. Like a tightrope walker I walked the wall off Naoko's property and onto his neighbor's side. I leaped up onto the same tree, the tree of the blessing, and climbed the branch like a gymnast on the parallel bars. I swung my feet up and reached a sturdier branch and used it. I kept climbing until I saw a way down. Then I dropped from the tree onto the neighbor's barren roof. I sprinted across and jumped twelve feet to land back onto Naoko's property—the rooftop. A black leopard can climb trees. In a tussel with the mighty lion, we are swift enough to snatch his meal and maneuver up to the high branches, leaving him below with no options but to watch and roar.

Blood pumping, swiftly I checked it all out. There was a strange bubble in the center of the roof, but I didn't move toward it. A tilted white tent in one corner began to worry me. Was someone inside? Would Nakamura be strategic enough to station security on the roof? Nah, not likely. If so, how could he sleep through the thump of my jump over here and be considered a real professional security man? I did not approach it, though. Instead I looked over the top and down into the backyard and dropped down onto the terrace, the one positioned next door to the window on the west side with the yellow light.

The darkened window was halfway open; I moved the glass slowly to the left and peered beyond the thin, sheer curtain. There were two girls asleep in one queen-sized bed. The one closest to the window, where I was, was not Akemi. But the one wrapped in the colorful silk robe was. My pulse picked up and began racing, even though I held my perch stiff as a statue. I didn't have to worry about anyone seeing me from the street as I squatted on the terrace. I already knew that the wall, the bushes, and the tree shielded all views. Still, I didn't want to linger long. Yet how would I get her attention without arousing the other girl? Forty-five seconds and an idea formed. I remembered how she and I slept in my single bed in my Brooklyn bedroom. She used to think that my body was warm, and she would wrap her leg around me as she slept, her face on my chest, her hand on my balls, her hair brushing against my chin. We breathed together. When I shifted, she glued herself to my back and eased her arm through my arm, her fingertips brushing lightly against my stomach. Akemi, vibing so hard on me, that when I would awaken, she awoke a second after as though she could feel and measure my breathing as she slept. As though she had one pinky finger on my eyelids as we slept to alert her about when I awakened, but she did not, she was just full of feelings—my feelings, her feelings—whether she was sleeping or awake. I guess I could call her a "light sleeper." I was hoping so. And I could hear the subtle snore of the girl closest to me.

I pulled out the bottle of Sudanese perfume that I had wrapped in a white washcloth in my backpack. It was the scent that Umma had made and blended only for Akemi and gifted to her at our *Walima*. I poured a little on my clean white washcloth and tossed it over toward Akemi's pillow. A powerful potion, the scent filled up the room. It was the same scent that had disguised the natural aroma of our love-making.

Seconds passed and she shifted her body, her robe falling open. More seconds and she lifted her head. A few more seconds and she sat up. I could hear the scent racing up her nostrils as she inhaled. But she was still.

Suddenly she pulled her legs around and slipped her feet into her slippers. Slowly she stood. She walked out of the room and into the hall. My only thought was that she went to the ladies' room. I removed my wool cap and my gloves. I stuffed them in my back pocket. I removed my Jansport and took off my jacket, turning it inside out, and laid it on the floor of the terrace. While hearing her urine trickle softly, slowly, I crouched and waited, balancing my weight on my toes. The faucet sent water gushing down, the rhythm broken only by her fingers washing her fingers, one hand to the other. Her footsteps were completely silent. She reappeared in the bedroom without notice. Her well-curved Asian artist's eyes peered through the darkness with only a dim moonlight to highlight my silhouette. She stood still, staring. Then she closed her eyes. She reopened them and concentrated. Seconds later, her eyes filled with tears. I didn't move, didn't say nothing. Her tears spilled to the floor. She walked toward me slowly, silently, and when she reached me, she punched me in the chest with two limp fists and then laid her head there. I wrapped my arms around her and held her tightly, feeling her figure, five pounds lighter than usual. Her body heated up inside mine and her silent tears soaked through my T-shirt. I knew she wanted to say that I had made her wait too long, but it had been seven thousand miles of separation and it was only with Allah's grace and my father's diamonds and advice that I was able to embrace her now.

I had missed her so much, both my heart and my body ached. Surviving that feeling was only possible by ignoring it. Picking her up into me and standing, I eased both of us outside and onto the terrace. I leaned against the terrace and she leaned against me, pressing her body against mine. Easing her hands beneath my T-shirt, she was feeling me all over, slowly causing me to feel so aroused that all thought and caution disappeared and nothing but emotion and touching remained. I moved my hands beyond the silk of her lovely robe and rested them on her butt, and went down further, feeling the skin on the back of her thighs. Her breathing picked up, and now her slim fingers were easing up my arm and her nipples were poking out through the silk and pressing against my chest. She caressed my muscles and eased to my shoulders and with her perceptive fingertips paused and felt my stitched-up shoulder wound. She inhaled in surprise and withdrew her body from mine by a few inches. Her eyes looked into mine to question what she had felt. I removed my T-shirt to show her and lowered my shoulder to her eye level. She touched it again and looked as though to ask me, Does it hurt? I shook my head no. She licked my wound and pulled the loose stitches out with her teeth. She sucked her tongue as though she enjoyed the taste of it. She touched my fingertips and pulled my hand slightly to show me she wanted us to go back inside.

She is my wife. During Ramadan, I could go into her only at night. The sun was down and had not signaled a desire to rise yet. Of course, I wanted to follow her, had a strong feeling to push inside her. After only one week of separation from her sweetness, I knew that I couldn't risk going into her now, she being balm to my heart and comfort to my soul and pure joy to my physical, perhaps the mother to my seed, daughter to my Umma, sister to my sister. If I followed her inside only to have her yanked, ripped, stolen away from me once again, then what? Or maybe she would walk away from me out of some exaggerated loyalty to her father. That would be too much. To open my heart freely without any hesitation, I needed to be sure, as sure as I am that when my head leaves a room, my body comes along with it unquestionably—willingly, automatically, because they belong together. So I asked her the question that had began as a lurking thought eight days ago. I had suppressed it at first, yet the thought kept revisiting me, so much so that I had looked it up and translated it into Japanese for this exact moment.

"*Erabete Ottosan matawa otto, Tokyo matawa New York*," I said slowly. It meant, "Choose father or husband, Tokyo or New York." Her eyes revealed great surprise at my using her language. She began to whisper to me in return in full, relaxed, fluent Japanese.

I stared at her, saying nothing and with no response. She paused, her Japanese words growing softer and softer until they were no more. She smiled a bright wide smile, knowing that she was teasing me using her native tongue so sweetly, so seductive is her smile and her use of her language. I had to restrain my own passion, remain solid and say solemnly again, "*Erabete!* Choose."

She lowered her head and then her eyes. Then she raised them back up slowly. "Mayonaka New York City *hai!*" she said warmly, with no sign of doubt or regret.

"Today, we meet today at Roppongi station at two," I told her in English and then in Japanese.

"Akemi and Mayonaka, two, *hai!*" she repeated.

"*Yakusoku*, promise?" I asked her.

"*Hai! Yakusoku*," she said, meaning, "Yes, I promise."

I picked up my knapsack from the terrace floor. I unzipped it and pulled out the book that had been weighing on my mind. It was a gift that I had promised her in our marriage contract, a Holy Quran, written entirely in the Japanese language. I wanted her to understand that I was a serious man, with a serious faith, and that as my wife she and I had to grow together in many ways. It was not okay to me for us to be in different countries growing apart instead of together. It was not okay to me for her to be surrounded by other men, even her father, in place of me. We needed to become of one similar mind and way. Our lovemaking was explosive already and fresh in my memory, in my body, and in my groin. I knew I could have her whole body tingling with powerful movement and pure pleasure. I knew I could make her cum so hard her legs collapsed. That was only seconds away . . .

Yet I had to show her that I was more than the "most powerful feeling that she has ever felt." I am a true believer who would love her forever, protect her with my own life, exchange my life for hers, and disconnect her father's head from his neck if he ever again interrupted my peace, kidnapped my wife, or threatened my seed to come. She needed to learn the meaning of Ramadan and the mercy it brought alive in the Muslim heart. Because it is this mercy which shielded me from charging down two flights and slaying him in his own home after making sweet love to his cherished daughter, my wife.

She moved her pretty fingers across the dark-blue, hardcover, engraved Holy Quran. She opened it. She read in Japanese the first page, the first few lines. The *sura* is called "The Opening" in English. I loved the sound of her speaking. Although it was new to her, she read the lines with feeling. I knew the words in Arabic by heart, so even though I didn't know them in Japanese, I could still feel their meaning.

She looked up to me and closed the cover. *"Arigato gozaimashta."* She bowed all the way down to me, head toward the floor. I lifted her up until she was standing once again. In this moment I didn't want to mix it up. She should love me intensely and treat me with great respect. We should serve one another loyally, and fight and struggle through any troubles side by side. Yet she should worship only Allah and so should I. If we both did that, our love would in turn be unbreakable.

She ducked down to enter back through the window and said only, "Please." Her robe was lying on each side of her leg, revealing the flesh inside her thighs. The moonlight shone on her pretty toes, still soft and beautiful, still pedicured light lavender with a thin line in dark purple around each border. I stuffed my T-shirt in my Jansport and threw my sweat jacket back on.

Of course I followed her in. She laid the Quran on her desk silently and walked the eight steps past her sleeping friend or relative. Then we walked down a dark corridor. She stepped into a washroom but did not turn on the light. After moving around a bit and running the water some, she came out.

I could smell the alcohol that she used to carefully wipe my shoulder where the stitches had been. Then with a hot cloth she wiped my face and then my hands lovingly. She stepped back into the washroom again and came out linking her fingers onto my fingers and walking ahead of me into a closet.

She closed the door behind us and we were in a tight, empty space facing one another. I looked up, only to see the sky. She turned around and placed her hands into the wall and began climbing upwards. Following her, I placed my hands into the indentations also, thinking what a clever design, a ladder made by pockets in the otherwise wooden wall. You place your foot in the lower pocket and your hand in the middle pockets and climb, a pattern that went all the way up until your head hit the top. At the top she pressed a button. A sound like hydraulics on a car lifted the skylight lid. She crawled through and immediately turned to check me, her face so sweet and gentle, and her hair falling onto my hand, which was gripping the last pocket.

We chilled on the rooftop, completely absorbed with one another, asses on the ground of the roof and backs leaning against the short wall. She knew me well, felt what I felt, and sensed that I would feel more at ease not lying in a bed inside her father's house, our naked bodies sprawled across the mattress deep in the deepest love. Me, lost in the sweetest pussy, first a target, then a dead man caught off guard at my most vulnerable point.

The surface of the roof was cold. It must have been sizzling when yesterday's sun was at its peak. For some few minutes we wasn't saying shit. Our silence was seduction to me. Talking is sometimes overrated. On a Coltrane cut, called "My Favorite Things," my father's choice, the instruments spoke without words or a songstress to interpret or suffocate his horns with the weight of lyrics. Our situation was like those sounds and melodies.

I pulled her bad-ass Gucci sandal boots out of my Jansport and returned them to her. She looked at me curiously and then laughed a quiet laugh. She slid her little feet into those sandals, lifted one leg to show it off to me, and stood up suddenly. She hiked up her silk robe to show me her style. I was her mesmerized viewer as she danced around slowly. Taking turns kicking each of her legs up high with great grace and ease, she struck a pose. Her body was curved, one hand holding her foot up in the air like a phenomenal flamingo. Instead of applauding, I leaped up and grabbed her around her waist, swinging her around and down gently. Her robe opened completely and her skin glowed in the softened moonlight. She licked my lips once like she was licking an ice cream cone that she really enjoyed,

then wiggled loose and began crawling away from me. So nervous
that I might not be following her, she would crawl some and look
back at me, her eyes shining like a cat's and not worried about scraping up her pretty knees or shoes or nothing. As she crept inside the
tilted tent, I caught her ankle and pulled it lightly. I released it easily,
knowing that she liked to make love in strange places.

Facedown and me right behind her, she pushed a tiny switch on
a strange little lamp inside a clear jar. As she lay on her side to face
me, I reached over and pulled one of the brushes down from her
easel. The lamp sent white polka dots swirling around the dark tent.
I smiled at her sweet craziness. She smiled, believing, I guess, that
I liked her little light. Slowly I began stroking her with the brush,
beginning with her face. Her good feeling was revealed as her lips
parted with excitement. Her eyes were filled with passion, love for
me, and mystery. As I stroked down, her skin was soon covered with
tiny goose pimples and her nipples were fully extended. As I tick-
led her silky hairs below, she inhaled and whispered only one word,
"Please." I ignored her purposely, brushing the inside of her thighs
and over her kneecaps and on to her calves. She placed her pretty
hand over her pussy and asked me again, "Please, Mayonaka."

I don't know which set of her lips was sweeter. I kissed her mouth
gently and naturally the kiss grew more powerful, me sucking her
tongue. Akemi licking my neck. Me sucking her neck and her becoming so excited that she snatched my hand and placed it on her
pussy, pressing her fingers over mine so I would press her clitoris. One
of her legs was cocked up, the weight of her little foot in her pretty
sandals resting on her toes.

I pulled my mouth away from hers and moved it down between
her thighs where she wanted it. With my tongue I stroked her clitoris softly and her body wiggled with pure pleasure. As I swirled my
tongue around, she began to moan and purr, her whole body beating,
pulsating like a heart. And as she came, so did a slight rainfall, more
like a mist. She threw her hand back over her head as her wriggling
body was calming.

As I lay on my back beside her, she wrapped her whole self
around me, curled into me, saying nothing, but I knew. She was saying
that she had never wanted to be separated from me in the first place,
and she never wanted to be separated from me again. I stroked the

hair on her head now, and even this excited her. She placed her pretty toes beneath the band of my sweats and played in my pubic hairs. She used one foot to undress me.

I entered her so powerfully I could feel her opening—opening and wrapping around my dick, like a tight elastic and strong suction.

As I thrust up and into her, there were feelings mounting on top of emotions. The inside of her felt so good to me, I kept grinding. She kept moaning. My mind was gone and my body a network of nerves experiencing a feeling too intense to place into words. As I moved her and tossed her and bent her, I could feel her nails scratching into my back and I liked that shit. I welcomed it. I passion-marked her neck and body with my mouth because she is mine. She marked me with her nails because I am hers. We mashed, moved, and pumped, and grinded like that until our own bodies could not take the pureness of it anymore.

She is my girl, my woman, my wife who cums over and over again and keeps cumming. My every touch brings down her Victoria Falls. I once even believed that she was cumming from being aroused by only my stare into her eyes. There is this look that she has at that precise moment of orgasm, when all of her energy is released. There is extra moisture in her eyes, as though she is about to cry, but she isn't. She bites her own lip and then releases it and quivers. I knew for sure that she was not a woman to be left unattended and unguarded. I was the first and only to create that feeling inside of her. And I knew that she wanted and needed me to do that, to create that powerful feeling in her constantly. I wanted it also.

She was teaching me many things about myself that I never had the opportunity to learn from any other woman. First, it was not just the fucking. It was something particular about *this girl*. She raised up a feeling in my heart and in my body so extreme, her every movement moved me. Simply her sitting or standing, and the beauty of her joyful tears, which came so rapidly and streamed so softly and fell so silently. Her smile and cleverness—her art, her body, her language, her complete admiration of me—she had me locked, naturally, locked up with no cuffs or prison or warden, simply locked into, specifically, her. I learned about myself also—that I love intensely beautiful things. It could be a finger or a neck, toes or even some mean-ass shoes or exotic eyes and skin that glows. I love pretty fingernails and pretty pussy hairs or even the way a beautiful girl rocks a beautiful handbag made of crocodile and crafted well. And my love for genuinely beautiful things, pure things, and clean things is both *extreme* and *exclusive*. Akemi is a beautiful thing, my beautiful thing.

I found my lips pressed against her left ear breathing warm breath. "Two o'clock today at Roppongi station, bring everything that you can't leave behind." She flipped off the strange lamp and the globs of polka dot patches disappeared. She crawled upwards on my body, her hair touching my neck and said "Two, Roppongi station, Akemi, Mayonaka isho-isho (forever)." She kissed me in my ear and set it off all over again.

* * *

We lay glued onto one another. Her thighs were still wrapped loosely on me. I flipped her around, laid her down, and checked my watch. It was four o'clock in the morning. There was one hour left to sunrise. I felt around in the darkness for my clothes and eased into them. I looked around the crazy tilted tent with my penlight. I was thinking to myself that I should have known that this tent belonged to Akemi. Who else would have placed a rickety hut on top of a sturdy, attractive, impressive, million-dollar Roppongi Hills home and prefer to live there? I imagined that she sat in here when she needed to feel that kind of isolation that made her create such powerful drawings and paintings. In fact she had one mounted on her little easel right then and there.

It was a drawing of various sets of eyes. The magnificence of it however was that I could recognize in the drawing her eyes, Umma's eyes, Naja's eyes, and even my own. I smiled. I was glad I hadn't seen the details of the drawing while I was loving her. It would have been real strange to see Umma's eyes watching me giving it to my wife with no restraint. And those eyes that I was seeing with the help of my penlight were definitely my mother's. Akemi's skill was that great. She filled her drawings with so much emotion that each set of eyes let off a unique energy and contained the story of its owner's life. Aside from these four sets of eyes, there were three more sets. The eyes at the center of her canvas had to be her father's. The drawing of his eyes contained different feelings—anger, control, coldness, and even concern, which she conveyed by the strokes and shadings of her pencils and brushes. Down to every detail including the eyelashes, their precise shape, length, and width, she captured it all, amazingly. Oddly, though, there were only eyes, no faces or eyebrows, no head, hair, or chin. It was a drawing that felt to me like it came from her soul and not her hands.

I caught sight of a pretty ceramic teapot and one cup, as well as a box of sesame crackers off in the tent's corner. I drank her leftover tea and crunched a couple of her sesames. Then I closed her robe over her pretty, petite body. I didn't wake her. I wanted to, but I wanted more that she not see me leaping across the rooftops and jumping onto the branches as I left the same way that I had arrived. But of course she was awake. She said softly, "Mayonaka, two, Roppongi station, *hai*," and was so smart she didn't move to watch me leave. I pinched her butt and I was out.

Chapter 6

CLOSE

Chiasa was in my bed; she looked asleep, but I wasn't so sure. Was she sleeping or pretending to sleep? She was wearing all her clothes, a new outfit from yesterday. I stood behind my now-closed door, not wanting to get too close to her revealing my private scenario and scents.

"Thirty-five minutes to sunrise," she said, shifting. "I brought you some food." Without turning and looking at me, she raised one arm and pointed toward my desk. There was a box, wrapped in a silky scarf, and a canteen.

"You found her?" she asked. I didn't reply. "No refunds," she said softly.

After my swift, thorough, hot shower, I ate one rice triangle and a few spoonfuls of peanut butter and drank water. Chiasa had green tea in the canteen. When I didn't drink it, she did. She stood now outside on the terrace at sunrise as I made the prayer.

"Wait for me," I told her. "I have important work for you to do with me today." She agreed.

Seated in the window with Chiasa seated on the fire escape, I told her, "I'm going back to New York, either tonight or tomorrow. I'll need your help at the travel agency to change my ticket and to buy another ticket as well. But the most important thing is, I need you to translate for me and my girl at two o'clock sharp today at Roppongi station."

Chiasa sat quietly for two whole minutes. "How did it happen?" she asked.

"How did what happen?"

"You and her, without understanding one another?"

I smiled. My whole body was relaxed now and my mind at peace. "We understand one another. We just don't speak the same language."

Chiasa stared at me. Her pretty eyes were searching me with a deep curiosity. I turned my eyes from hers. She inhaled and said softly, "That's so fucking cool."

"I gotta sleep some," I admitted.

"Me too," she said quietly. "I was up all night."

"How come?" I asked her. She ignored my question. This made me think she wanted me to ask her again. Or maybe I really was curious. "How come?" I asked again.

"I read through all those papers from the Nakamura building searching for clues. Finally I found out the name of Ikeda-san's hometown. I went there to his house. I walked around there, must have been twenty-two times—waited in an alley behind his house for you," she said.

I didn't say nothing. I just sat quietly thinking. A wave of feeling came over me, like it does sometimes when a female reveals her admiration for me. I was grateful toward Chiasa, deeply grateful.

"Do you want me to meet you at your house later, or would you rather us meet up at one forty-five in Roppongi at the station?" I asked her.

"No, I'll sleep on the floor right here. You sleep on the bed. When we wake up, we gotta go to Shinjuku. You have to check out of there this morning," she said.

"I don't have nothing over there and I paid them up front," I corrected her.

"Yes, but I left my jacket, remember?"

I stood up from the windowsill and invited her in. This would be me and her last day together. So I decided not to worry if her feelings would grow.

"You sleep on the bed, I'll sleep on the floor," I told her. She lay down, her back facing me. I sat down on the floor, my back against the wall. It was 6 a.m. We slept.

* * *

Harajuku's streets were jammed. In addition to the strange things that normally went on there, someone for some reason had trucked in a plastic slice of strawberry shortcake twenty feet tall and ten feet wide. The Japanese crowd of teens seemed fascinated by it. They gathered around in hordes to take pictures of it, lean into and pose up close on it, and linger around it. *Japan is weird,* I thought to myself. And for once in my life—perhaps because I had only been here for two and a half days, I could not tell by listening or watching what was going on in their minds or culture.

Chiasa's electric-blue Kawasaki Ninja 250R was mean and pretty. It was parked on a street behind the Shinjuku hostel. She swung her leg around and mounted the deep-blue leather seat. If she were in Brooklyn, Harlem, Queens, or the Bronx pushing this, she would've had all the hustlers sweatin' her hard. I was glad she was in Tokyo where the males didn't seem to notice or distinguish the beauty, elegance, and exquisiteness of one female or the other.

"See, it's perfect. No one even touched it," she said, smiling and surveying its body. She hopped off then, opened a seat compartment, and pulled out her blue leather riding gloves and her goggles. Then she put them right back. Her helmet was there on the bike unbothered. She left it there. I guess she had made her point.

When we reached the front of Shinjuku Uchi, Chiasa reached up and pulled a coin from the top of the cement gargoyle. "You see it's still here." She smiled and laid the coin in my palm. It was a Japanese coin worth five dollars. "Japanese people don't steal," she emphasized sweetly.

We collected her jacket, which was lying on my old bed the same way she had tossed it. The room with no lock seemed undisturbed, but I was still glad I had moved out. As we left, the front desk attendant, who I had not encountered before, presented me with an envelope.

"Thank you berry much." He bowed some. "Inside is your receipt and you have one message."

"Thanks," I told him, and forgot him the same second.

I pulled the papers out of the envelope until I found the message. It was written in Japanese on otherwise blank stationery. As Chiasa and I pushed out into the noon Shinjuku sun, I handed her the paper. "Read it to me," I told her.

"Meet Akemi in Shibuya at two at Hachiko on Tuesday," Chiasa translated. "Who's Akemi?" she asked.

"Who signed the message?" I questioned.

"No one. I guess it's from Akemi, right?" she asked, trying to connect the dots.

"Is there a date and time on the message?" I asked her.

"No, nothing else," she said, flipping the small square of stationery back and forth. "I can go check it out." She did a turn and went back in the hostel. She returned and said, "The front desk clerk said he wasn't the one who received the message. He just clocked in at eleven this morning. He said that since no employee signed or dated the message, it must have been hand-delivered."

The sun had erased every trace of morning mist. The streets were dry and clean as if it hadn't rained in Tokyo in months. With the noon sun massaging me, I stood thinking, my eyes squinting for protection and Chiasa's big eyes just slits as she squinted also, then placed her hand over her eyes to block or lessen the sun's significance.

It was impossible for my wife to know where I was staying when I first arrived in Tokyo. How could she? Only me . . . and Chiasa . . . and customs knew where I would be staying. My suspicions began to intensify. Scenarios of every kind were lining up in my mind.

Perhaps Iwa's phone registered the return number to the pay phone in the Shinjuku Hostel. She called the number back, some resident answered, and Iwa said, "What location is this?" The resident answered her truthfully. Afterward, Iwa told Akemi where I was staying. Akemi had hand-delivered the message yesterday. She was so excited to meet up with me that she forgot to sign it or explain anything else. That's why when I saw her early this morning in Roppongi, she seemed to have expected to see me, although not in her bedroom window.

The second scenario taking place in my mind: Iwa Ikeda told her father that I was here in Tokyo after she discovered that I was in Narita Airport. Her father told Akemi's father and Naoko had this note delivered to draw me out to a location of *his* choosing. It was a trap. Or a more deadly possibility, Naoko knew now that his daughter had allowed a man, an unexpected, unwelcomed son-in-law into his home and into her. Furious, he pressured his daughter to reveal our secret, and she sent someone to Shinjuku to change the meet-up place. Maybe it was Iwa who delivered the message. Maybe Iwa never told her father or Naoko where I was staying—if she knew. Maybe Iwa was really *for* our love and marriage and not against it.

Nine scenarios had lined up in my mind, split into two, and became eighteen. If this dilemma had involved myself and Umma, I would have known exactly what to do in less than a second. Umma and I *always do* exactly what we promise to do, exactly as we stated it to one another. And we let no one interfere or interrupt or confuse any words we say to one another, mother and son. That was our way.

But Akemi and I are newlyweds. Our first month of marriage had been interrupted, manipulated, and stolen. Now I was certain of my movements, *but not of hers*.

Chiasa's golden skin baked more brown in the sun. She was silent, patient, waiting for instructions, my sentinel and a sharp one too.

"What did you see at Iwa's house last night?" I asked her suddenly.

"It was a quiet and residential neighborhood in Kichijoji."

"Kichijoji? How far away is that from here?"

"About seventeen minutes on the Chuo line," she responded. "I mean Kichijoji has plenty of nightlife, restaurants, and stores and shops and everything. But where Ikeda-san's house was located, it was dark and quiet. Oh, yes, the pretty car drove right by me when I first got there about twelve thirty a.m. It pulled out and left way before me at about one thirty," she reported.

"The Japanese Bentley, right?" I asked.

"*Hai,* that one," she confirmed.

I stood thinking. "I need you to get to Shibuya by one forty-five," I announced.

"It's almost one. Shibuya's close, four stops from here on the Yamanote line," she said.

"Are you riding your bike?" I asked.

"No, Shibuya is crazy. There are so many people there! The train is easier. What do I do at Shibuya?" she asked.

"Go to Hachiko just like the note says. What is that anyway, Hachiko? Is it a café or a restaurant?" I asked.

Chiasa laughed. "No, it's a dog!"

"A dog?"

"It's a famous statue of a dog. Everyone in Japan knows it. Also it's a meet-up spot for lovers and people all around the world looking for new lovers." She monitored my response. My jaw tightened at her description. Yet the good thing about her words was that now I felt sure that Akemi had not left that note.

"Go there and film at that exact location. If you see a Japanese girl there waiting, sixteen years old, wearing the most expensive shoes available in Tokyo, carrying a mean-ass handbag and with a smile that is only second to her beautiful eyes, that's her. Introduce yourself and tell her you are the translator for Midnight and that she should meet me in Yoyogi Park. I'll be there at three p.m." I planned aloud as I spoke. I was fairly confident that I would be bringing Akemi to meet Chiasa in Yoyogi Park and not the other way around.

"Where in Yoyogi, at my house?" Chiasa asked.

"On the bench in the park outside your house," I told Chiasa, whose eyes were also intense and lovely, although I had the feeling that no man had ever told her so. She hesitated for some seconds and then we both walked, headed to Shinjuku station, where we separated and went in different directions.

Thoughts about the power, range, and reach of Naoko Nakamura raced through my previously calm state of mind. Still, I was at ease feeling that I had gotten the better of him. Only thirty hours after my arrival at Narita Airport, I had invaded his territory and didn't have to snatch or seize his daughter the way he had. She came eagerly, passionately to me, separating herself from his idea of me. She had chosen me over him, again. Besides, I knew his address, and now that I had seen Akemi, I could climb into her tent anytime. So I suppressed his name and face from my mind's eye.

In Roppongi early, I played with the idea of getting a haircut. I had not even powered up the clippers that Ameer's father gifted to me. My last cut was four days ago before game time. But when I leaned my face against the barber's window and saw a place packed with exclusively Japanese heads and four elderly Japanese barbers, I decided against it. Maybe tomorrow. Why experiment and fuck up my head right before meeting my wife in the brilliant Tokyo sunlight?

* * *

Pink pumps, I recognized her shoes. She was not my wife, but she was wearing the pink pumps that had been outside my wife's house last night. So I paid attention. She seemed nervous, took quick glances my way, and then dropped her head down and continued to walk in my direction as she appeared to be watching her own feet. It was five minutes after two. She passed me by. As I watched her, I caught her looking back. She tried to play it off but soon turned back toward me. Now she looked up at me and then toward the café situated behind me. She walked past me again. My eyes followed her into the café. I looked around the outside to see if Akemi was approaching from any direction. But she wasn't.

When I checked the café window, Pink Pumps was still standing there watching me. I went over. As I entered the café, she moved away from the window to a back booth. I hesitated to walk up on her. She seemed like she was fragile, might break in half or, worse, start screaming for the police. So I went to the cash register instead, ordering coffee I would not drink. When I turned back to take a look, she was speaking to a waitress softly in Japanese. She stood up and both girls began bowing to each other. I couldn't interpret what was happening. I left the café to check again for Akemi.

"Mayonaka." The name spoken in that way in the Japanese accent and a soft tone sent a rush and a current through me. I turned to check the voice with the person. It was Pink Pumps. "Follow" is all she said, not looking up at me or even acknowledging my presence. I followed her. She walked down into a side street and ducked into a photo booth and closed the curtain behind her. I stood outside the curtain.

"Akemi-san was taken away this morning," I heard her voice say in English, but I had to strain to hear and listen.

"Taken away by who?"

"Father."

"Taken where?"

"Kyoto."

"Why?"

"I don't know. Maybe for school. Maybe for keep away."

"Keep away?"

"From you. I don't know."

"Who are you?" I asked, but she was silent. "Who are you?" I asked again.

"You don't believe?" she asked me strangely. "Okay, I leave now."

"Wait," I said calmly. I stood thinking. "When was she taken?"

"Early morning surprise," she answered.

"What did Akemi tell you to tell me?"

"Akemi-san is berry sad. She say 'sorry a thousand times.' She say her father is too determined."

"What did her father do to her?" I asked.

"Father give Akemi-san eberything. But now he say no more money, no more trabel, no more credit card, no more bank account. No more freedom."

"Why?"

"You will never understand. You are foreigner. This is our way. *This is Japan*," she said. It was the strongest tone that she used through the whole conversation. Then three Japanese boys gathered and hung back behind me at the photo booth and waited as though I was on line to use it also.

"How come you find out to meet Akemi here at two o'clock?" she asked. I had to repeat her question to myself to dissect it. She was trying to figure out how Akemi and I had communicated and set up a meeting. Now I knew.

"Are you Iwa?" I asked her. But she was silent.

"Can you give me Akemi's address in Kyoto, a phone number or something?" I asked her.

"I give. You will find on the seat when I leave here. Time's up, I go," she said.

"Wait, why did you come to me?" I asked, since she was obviously nervous, uncomfortable, and didn't even want to face me.

"Akemi-san do bad thing to fall in love with you. Dishonor to her father. Dishonor to my father, our family and friends. But I think she not recover from this love. So I give in to help Akemi-san." Her little fingers emerged and she ducked from behind the curtain, keeping her face turned away from me as though I had not already seen her clearly. She left and never looked back. I didn't chase her. The important thing was the address and telephone number. I yanked back the curtain and picked up the paper that she left for me. Everything was written in kanji. No problem. I sped over to Yoyogi to meet Chiasa.

Chapter 7
CHIASA

"This is so much better than pizza, piano, and practices," Chiasa stated with her excited softness. She sat down on the bench in Yoyogi Park beside me holding my camera like a baby.

Deep in thought, I didn't speak right away.

"Let's go to my house. You have to see this," she said, standing up again. "Besides, I have to keep myself occupied to keep my mind off our fast!"

That's the opposite of the Muslim mind-set, I thought to myself. We want to keep our mind on the fast, its meaning, its reasons, and on making our prayers. Although I had been steadfast in not taking food and water from sunrise to sunset, I knew I was wrong for not being focused on Ramadan. My mind was jam-packed with winning back my wife.

Chiasa removed her shoes at her front steps. "You can leave your sneakers here," she said. "No one will steal them and I have some slippers for your feet." I paused at the bottom of the three cement steps leading to her front door.

"His bicycle is there. Grandfather is home. You can come in," she said happily. On the inside of the door was a shelf with racks of house slippers wrapped in plastic. Chiasa opened a pair and bent down to place them on my feet.

"Thank you. I got it," I told her, sliding each foot in one.

"Okay." She smiled halfway, slid into her slippers, and shouted, *"Tadaima!"* We both entered her living room.

An ebony grand piano absorbed most of the space in her humble house. It glistened as though it had just been polished moments ago and appeared to be more expensive than everything else they had, combined—furniture, floor mats, and decorations.

"*Konichiwa, Ojiichan,*" I said, afterward recalling from my study cards that I had just called him "grandfather" as though he were my own and *not* by his proper name.

He spoke "*Konichiwa . . .*"

"Grandfather welcomes you," Chiasa summed up his words.

"*Arigato gozaimashta,*" I thanked him.

Chiasa said some words to her grandfather, then turned toward me, saying, "Drop that here," referring to my luggage. I laid my duffel down and my Jansport. I was both hesitant and anxious. I felt inadequate about entering a home for the first time, empty-handed. I was a newcomer and should present a gift. I felt at the same time anxious to talk with Chiasa and get on my way to Kyoto.

"*Chotto Matte,*" I said. I bent on one knee to open my bag. I dug in and pulled out one of the gifts that Umma had prepared, "for anyone who is good to my son." I opened it and pulled out the sterling silver case of Umma's homemade cigarettes. I approached him, holding the case with both hands on either side, presenting it. I said, "*Kori wa present o Ojiichan notamani.*" (Grandfather, here is a gift for you.) Both he and Chiasa smiled with great surprise. Chiasa clapped for me. Her grandfather stood up all smiles himself, thanking me. I looked beyond the smiles, feeling that I had done the right thing but wondering if on the inside they thought my beginner's use of the Japanese language confirmed that all foreigners are fools to be tolerated as tourists only for a short period of time.

I eased up the steps uncomfortable at being invited and allowed to enter a young single female's bedroom, and also under the watch of her grandfather. His eyes followed me up, but once I reached the top, there was no way for him to survey me any further.

The second floor was sealed off by what appeared to be a paper wall. I looked up and saw that it had thick metal borders, which lined the top, sides, and bottom. Chiasa placed three fingers in a slot and slid the wall all the way from left to right. Her amazing room had been revealed. She entered first, moving past a four-foot-tall textured globe. She used one hand to set it off spinning. "I know the name of every country on every continent and even most of the major islands," she said.

I didn't comment. I thought it meant that she had a sharp mind and unusual discipline but must've also been lonely to dive into such study.

"I always wanted to know for certain where in the world my father was and exactly how much distance there was between us," she told me as she set up the television, VCR, and camera.

"You have to see this . . ." She pressed rewind.

Her bed was a thin and narrow mattress laid in the furthest corner of her room on the floor, topped off by a peculiar pillow. It didn't seem like she could sleep comfortably.

"So beautiful, who's this?" Chiasa interrupted my thoughts. Umma's face was paused on her television screen. "She looks like a film star," Chiasa remarked.

"*Umi*, my mother," I answered, using the Arabic word for mother rather than *Umma*, which is my mother's name.

"*Honto!* Really," Chiasa exclaimed and touched the screen with two fingers as though she were touching Umma's skin. Chiasa seemed to be on pause like the picture. Then she bowed down to my Umma as though she were here in the room with us. As Chiasa stood up, she pressed fast forward.

"Here it is!" She pressed stop, then play. My mind dumped every other thought and focused. The screen was bursting with hundreds of people or perhaps thousands, mostly Japanese, mostly young, but all types streaming in between them. I could see the unimpressive Hachiko statue off in the not-too-far distance. People crowded around it together, yet it seemed as though each of them was there alone, just in the same space. Also standing near the statue were groups of people talking to each other, waiting for each other, or looking for ones missing. Chiasa caught one mother's panicked expression and mission as she searched for someone, probably her child. I could see that Chiasa trailed her with the lens around the area of the Hachiko. From the film I understood now that Shibuya was an extremely overcrowded space, even more so than Shinjuku station, but what else?

"There he is, now watch him," she said, a moment later. It was easy to notice him, because she had captured him in the lens and zoomed in. He was a well-dressed Japanese man with a concentrated stare and pronounced jawline. He stood still in the swelling, swarming crowd and looked hard, moving his head and eyes in tiny measures.

"So while I was looking for the hundred-thousand-yen shoe girl, I found him," Chiasa said.

The man's shoes were quite expensive and complemented his suit. After about forty-five seconds of shooting him from every angle, the camera followed him a few feet only, where an African man was standing alone. The Japanese man spoke to him, but his words were inaudible in the rowdy crowd. He placed a hand on the African guy's shoulder. The African guy turned around and talked to him for about three seconds. The Japanese guy returned to his original spot. He searched around again. He moved in the opposite direction, to the other side of Hachiko, and approached another dark-skinned man. The same thing happened. By the fifth try, the young black guy he approached was standing with some friends. He began barking on the Japanese guy and then three more suited men appeared from the crowd to the Japanese guy's rescue.

"Keep watching, now, check out their headsets." Chiasa pointed out that all three of the newly arrived Japanese men were wearing them. They were the kind that sit in and around one ear only, instead of being strapped on both sides. She zoomed in on the four of them, and the lens scanned them from head to toe. The argument with the African teens broke up immediately after the three extra well-suited guys appeared. Then there was a break in the images and all I could see was upside-down hordes of people.

"Keep watching," Chiasa said. The lens picked back up on the original suited guy leaving Hachiko at 3:00 p.m. sharp. Chiasa obviously followed him to the corner through tens and hundreds of people to the curb. A Crown Vic rolled up at 3:06. The three extra guys were inside, one of them driving, two in the back. The original guy leaned in and talked to them and then walked away. The camera followed him.

"There he is!" Chiasa jumped up from her chair and pressed pause. On the screen was the Japanese Bentley, the back right window lowered halfway. "That's Naoko Nakamura! That's him," she said in a muted but excited tone. She pressed play again. On the screen now was the original suited man. He raised his right hand, shielding his image from Chiasa's lens. Then she dropped the camera to her side, and all I could decipher was Chiasa's voice saying *"sumimasen, sumimasen, sumimasen"* before the picture went cold. The camera was off.

We sat quietly. "I can help you," she said. "You came back alone. So I can see that *you do need some help.* I've been paying attention the whole time. So it's not Iwa. It's Akemi. Last night, I was at the wrong house. But that's only because you didn't trust me. It's Naoko Naka- mura giving you a difficult time. *He* sent the note to the Shinjuku hostel. *He* pretended to be Akemi. *His* men showed up at Hachiko and intended to snatch you. Or at least throw you in the car or have you picked up by police. If you weren't *so smart,* they would have got- ten you."

She thought some more and added, "But probably not the police. Falling in love with a girl is not a crime, even if her father and friends don't agree." She paused again. "As long as *she loves you too.* And *why wouldn't she?*" Chiasa's voice trailed off to a low murmur.

From my front pocket I pulled out my wife's address and phone number in Kyoto. *That's my next move,* I thought to myself.

"Chiasa, I need you to take care of two things for me. First I need you to call Akemi's house and ask to speak with Akemi. When she gets on, in Japanese tell her that you are a friend of Mayonaka's. 'Mayonaka says not to worry. I'll arrive in Kyoto tonight. Keep your bags packed. Mayonaka will pay for everything you need. I promise I won't take too long.'"

"That's it?" Chiasa double-checked. "Introduce myself as a friend now, not the translator?"

"That's it," I confirmed.

"Alright, let me give myself a name," she said, straightening her- self in the chair as though Akemi or whomever answered the phone could see her and pass judgment. "Okay, I'm Aya. That's the name I'll use, and if she's not home, then what?" Chiasa asked. "Should I leave any kind of message?"

"Just excuse yourself. Don't leave any information. Say you'll call back later," I told her.

"And if she picks up and asks for you?" Chiasa questioned. I liked that she was so precise.

"After you tell her what I said, I'll get on and confirm," I in- structed her.

"Okay, give me the number," she said. I slid it across her desk. Chi- asa was sitting still holding the phone number in her hand. Quickly

I pulled out my study cards and began flipping through them for the Japanese words to express myself over the phone.

Maybe Chiasa wanted to memorize it, I thought. She laid the paper down and said the same thing she said when I first met her a few days ago.

"My aunt Tasha said people who don't trust people end up trusting the wrong people. Who gave you this information?" she asked me.

"What's up?" I asked her.

"This is not an address or a phone number. Whoever gave you this message misled you."

"What does it say?" I pushed.

"It's not cool," she said.

"Just tell me," I told her. Then she began to read it to me.

Sorry I cannot give you Akemi-san's telephone number and address. She wants you to know it. She will believe that you have it, but I have already done too much. I feel great shame. Go home! It is better that you leave Akemi alone so that she can forget. You don't even speak Japanese. True, you are very handsome, but this is not enough.

Her simple words were weighted with insult. Without knowing me, she had decided that I was nothing, nothing but a handsome man. She had boiled down my existence to only the mud I was made of, as though I had no purpose, no faith, no heart, no soul, no business, no talent, no culture, and no place in the world, especially not here in Japan. I sat back in my chair, ran my hand over my Caesar. I dropped my head down, then lifted it back up. Inside of myself I shouted, *Why is this bullshit going on?* But in my posture I remained calm. Chiasa had the decency to look away from my agony. Moments later, I understood that I needed prayer, to quiet my mind. Not just a recitation of words but a consultation with Allah. So I excused myself to the men's room, washed my face and nose, hands and feet. When I returned, I was left alone in Chiasa's room. She understood me in this, I thought. In her room facing the west, the direction of the Kaaba, I made my prayer.

Very comforted and soothed after an amount of time unknown

to me, I raised my head from the floor. My eyes and ears readjusted as I turned my head left, then right, and got up from my knees. The humble house, which had been silent before, was filled now with beautiful music. The tones were crisp and clear and soft and soothing and sweet and melodious as they were seeping and pouring through her paper wall. It was not music that I was accustomed to hearing or that I played in my earphones. It was live piano playing and it was obvious even to me, who played no instruments, that it was perfect. She did not interrupt my prayer and I would not interrupt her piano. I walked around her room, seeing Chiasa for the first time, it seemed, even though I had met her days ago and been upstairs in her bedroom for almost two hours. And as I saw, her music spoke to me somehow.

On my right was a wall of photos. On the left was a warrior's wall of wicked swords, not of the bamboo, but of steel. The kind she wanted to use, the sharp and deadly type, raised up above a bookcase filled with books in both languages. As I surveyed them, I thought her choices were unusual. She wasn't reading Manga. It was mostly biographies and autobiographies.

I moved toward the right side, pulled in by a poster-size photo of Chiasa, probably around age thirteen, in a marigold ballerina tutu wearing gold toe shoes. She appeared long and slim. She was balancing herself on one leg and standing perfectly straight on only the toes of her left foot. Her other leg was raised and bent, her toe shoe pointed to the inside of her right knee. Her arms were lifted and locked into a graceful positon above her head. Her skin was smooth. But more than all that, the pull of the photo was the way she twisted up her lips and screwed up her face at what had to happen less than a second before the photographer snapped the shot. It was as though she wanted the whole world to know that she hated ballet. Her normally powerful, pretty gray eyes were saying, "I don't want to dance but I'll do it just to shut you up." I smiled.

Beside the vertical ballerina blowup was a long rectangular shot of about 180 Japanese people. On first glance I assumed it was a school photo. On a closer look it obviously wasn't. There were babies and toddlers and children and teens and mothers and fathers and elders. It was not a casual shot like a family gathered at a reunion or a barbeque. It was more like each of them struck a stiff pose, their clothes crisp and high-quality, someone older resting their hand on someone younger than themselves almost to keep them still and perfect also. It was outdoors with nature as the backdrop. I wondered what the event or purpose of their coming together was and why she had it posted on her wall. As I surveyed it more, there was one thing that was different from everything else. It was Chiasa's little black face, floating in a sea of "others." Everyone in the picture was Japanese, but only Chiasa's face was sun-kissed. If she had a smile, it wasn't anywhere to be found in this photo. As I looked at the other pictures she had posted, the feeling in her eyes remained the same.

Suddenly the piano playing softened as though she had gone from playing all the keys to playing only a few at the far end of key-board, and then just three keys and two keys and then only one. I overheard her speaking in her language. Then a man's voice began speaking in Japanese, different from the voice of her grandfather. Then her grandfather and she thanked him repeatedly. I pictured her bowing two or three times, as they seemed to do at hellos and good-byes, and overdo before teachers and elders. Her front door opened and closed, and she rushed up the stairs, excited.

"Are you okay?" she asked.

"Of course," I responded.

"Sorry about that! If I don't do my piano lesson—that's the one thing that'll make my mother show up here. So I do it." I thought her comment was strange and sad. "It's half an hour until sunset. Should I cook? You didn't even eat the breakfast I made for you." She frowned dramatically.

"What's this?" I asked her pointing at the rectangular shot.

"Family photo," she answered, turning suddenly serious.

"What about your father?" I asked cautiously, knowing that it was too personal a question, but seriously wondering how she could have a wall plastered with photos from top to bottom but no trace of the one she talked about openly, affectionately, and constantly. She walked over and stood facing the photo wall. Then she pointed to a patch of Polaroids.

"My father sent me this on my eighth birthday." It was a picture of the huge globe she had seated in the center of her room. "This was when he went to Germany." Then she moved her finger and said, "This was from ninth birthday." I moved closer in to where she was standing and looked. It was a red Schwinn bicycle. Then she pointed to another. "And this was for my tenth birthday." It was a karaoke machine with Chiasa standing in front of it holding a microphone. "That's when he was stationed in Saudi Arabia."

As Chiasa showcased her gifts of all types, she said, "My father promised to give me whatever I ask for each year on my birthday. It's like one wish a year that I always look forward to. There is only one thing I'm not allowed to ask for, and he didn't make up that rule until *after* I asked for it." She smiled a melancholy smile. I just looked at her. I knew she would tell me if she wanted to. "One month before my twelfth birthday I asked if he could come home on my twelfth birthday to celebrate with me. I told him that was all I wanted. He was in Afghanistan. He told me that I'm not allowed to ask for that because he is working and that he is helping so many people around the world. So it's selfish to ask him to stop helping them and come see me. Besides," she said, "my father says he will always come home to me at some point each year."

"Does he?" I asked.

"Yep, I wait and I wait and eventually when his work is finished, he comes." She smiled. "So aren't you wondering what gift he gave me on my twelfth birthday instead of coming home?" She turned to me, excited. I didn't look back to her Polaroids.

"Probably that big piano downstairs," I guessed. She frowned.

"*No!* I hate playing the piano. My mother brought that thing. Look!" She stepped in front of the picture she had been blocking! It was a beautiful black mare standing strong in a wide open field of glistening green grass.

"She's beautiful," I said staring, and I meant it.

"I love riding her. She's at the stables in Nagano. I go there on breaks and holidays when I'm not fighting in tournaments." I imagined her on that horse galloping through the wide open fields at a high speed. As my mind wandered further, I snatched back the image and refocused. She was up to her sixteenth birthday now. "That's my bike. You saw it today." She smiled.

"No, *that's* your bike," I said pointing to her ten-year-old gift, the red Schwinn. "This is a mean-ass racing machine for pushing the limits," I told her, while again admiring the electric-blue color.

"My mother hates my motorcycle. But when I ride it, I feel free," Chiasa said.

I knew what I was doing, collecting information on this girl who had become too close and too necessary to my life in two and a half days. I was forming a more detailed picture of Chiasa. Like usual I would take a few hours to think and feel and then I would decide to trust—or move on with my solo style.

"Seventeen is coming up. What's your wish?" I asked her.

"I'm still thinking," she said. "It might be something that is impossible for Daddy to get for me. But he'll like that. He loves a challenge and he'll say nothing is impossible once he decides on it." She paused a minute. "My grandfather says you feel like my father," she said strangely.

"I look like him?" I asked her.

"No, you feel like him," she said softly. "Anyway, he's in the military, not like a low rank. He can't be photographed, so my pictures of him are held in my heart."

Carefully, I listened. "Not a low rank," she had said. *Of course not,* I thought to myself. He had to be some secret service type. Probably he pushed himself up from the bottom, though. No, I refigured; his position was so top secret, even Chiasa didn't know the truth. Or maybe she did. I knew for a fact that regular army guys and even other military types take photos. I had seen plenty—especially in the homes of customers I delivered Umma Designs clothing to. But I didn't ask for an explanation concerning her father. How could I, when I wouldn't answer one personal question about my own father, not to anyone other than Umma and maybe Naja or my wife?

"Do you plan on working for the military?" I asked her.

"Definitely not. I'm going to have my own company. I'm gonna be a mercenary," she said solemnly. But I didn't know that word, so I didn't comment. I would look it up tonight.

"Sun's down," Chiasa announced.

"Let's drink some water and split a banana. Then we'll go out for dinner," I told her.

"Okay, if you want," she agreed.

"Have you ever seen this symbol?" I asked her, drawing the symbol for halal foods on a scrap of paper.

She looked at it curiously, paused, and answered, "No, but I have seen this one." She drew another symbol. Immediately I recognized it, same as my ring, the one Sensei had gifted to me. She walked

Chiasa unbraided.

away, opened her desk drawer, and placed the same ring on her finger. "I've seen it on you. Now you see mine on me. It is the symbol of the Secret Society of ninja trained warriors," she said softly. Then she added, "Comrade, please take me seriously." She bowed her head, but not her body.

* * *

Ebisu was where we ate dinner, a halal restaurant owned by some African Muslims from Senegal. Haki, the Kenyan who I met in Harajuku, put me up on it.

"It depends on what you are looking for in terms of atmosphere," Haki said. "You will find halal foods in Shin-Okubu prepared by the Pakistanis, in Shinjuku prepared by the Indians, and in Ikekuburo prepared by the Nigerians or Bangladeshis, or in Ebisu by the Senegalese. Which one do you prefer?" Then he added with a smile, "And I see you are still here. Your one night in Harajuku has turned into two and this is only the beginning I am sure," he joked.

The Senegalese, I knew, were similar in presentation to the Sudanese, tall, blacker than black, and regal, strong men. A delegation of Senegalese had visited my father's estate once. While I joined and sat silently watching, I heard them joke of the ways they shared and other ways they differed. One of them boasted that my father was just getting started with his "small group of only three wives." My father told them that it was his understanding that in Islam "Allah sets limits because it is best for us." He then added that "Yes, I have only three wives, but they are the best three women in the world, with more purpose and value than three hundred!" My father's words may have made them curious. However, Muslim-male-style, that delegation would for certain never get to lay eyes on my father's wives.

Chiasa had unbraided her hair while she waited for me in Harajuku. Now it was long and thick like rope. She shook it with her fingers and wore it wild. After seeing my reaction to her "school uniform" and then the thin blouse that she tried to wear out to dinner, she knew to dress modestly. She was chilling now in a sky-blue linen dress with matching pants and blue leather sandals. She was not my woman, but I believed that when a man stands side by side with a woman, he is responsible for her in that moment. And if anyone offended her, it would be the same as if they attacked me, because she was with me. So I believe that any woman walking in public or traveling anyplace outside her home puts all the men at risk if she is immodest and nearly naked. I knew from living in America that for me to think this way was unpopular. But my faith and beliefs as well as my heart were all homegrown, in the soil tilled and built on by my father, his father, and his father's father.

We ate at a restaurant named Terenga. The owner, a tall, dark Senegalese wearing natural locks, greeted me with a welcoming West African smile and embrace of brotherhood. He introduced himself as Billy, a ridiculous name, I thought. I knew however, that many Muslims and people of any and all faiths in foreign lands give themselves ridiculous English names to make it easy for others to pronounce and remember. Besides, I had not told anyone my name. Of course in the telling of my true name is the name of my father, grandfather, and great-grandfather.

So the owner was "Billy" to me, no problem.

The warmth inside and the vibrant music and scent of spices created that feeling that separated Chiasa and me from the fact that we were in Tokyo. In fact it reminded me that I hadn't heard any real music for three days! Now it was as though we had been transported to Dakar. The walls were all earth tones and the cooking station formed an aisle, which made two sections in the same restaurant. Whatever side you chose, you were unable to see the other. So all the customers gathered to one side, African-style. It was as though every customer had arrived at the restaurant in one same group and had known each other for weeks or months or even years. The owner and host, Billy, raised the topics of conversation and invited and stroked and pulled till everyone joined in comfortably, like one family.

Chiasa was hungry and didn't seem to mind that she was surrounded by about eight African men. When we arrived, they were speaking in Wolof, the main language of Senegal. They would shift into French at times. But when I ordered our food in English, Billy switched to using English, and then everyone followed.

"So, my brother, how long have you been in Tokyo?" Billy asked me loud enough for all.

"Three days," I told them.

"And already you are losing weight, welcome to Japan." All the men laughed. "You have come now to the right place. We will give you an African man's meal, and when you have finished, no matter where you go in Tokyo, you will be banging on Billy's door. And most of the time Billy will be here. But sometimes, Billy go out!" he dramatized in his deep voice, like my Southern grandfather. They all laughed. I looked around. "Take it easy, brother, we are all friends here. All of us are married men," he admitted. "But we are all missing our mommas." They laughed some more as the cooking seasonings thickened in the air and brought a fragrance that could also fill up the belly. I eased some. They were married, and for me that is a good thing.

"I figured out that if I didn't cook my food myself, I couldn't survive Japan; such stingy and tasteless little meals make a big man angry." He performed, and I saw Chiasa smile. Billy's show continued. "So I call Momma. Momma say, 'Come home, son. I cook for you everything.' Billy say, 'Momma, I sent you much money today for our family. Japan is good for making money. So I stay.' Momma say, 'My son has to eat good food. I'll send good Senegalese wife to cook for you!' But Billy say noo . . . 'Noo, Momma, don't do dat!'" Now everyone is laughing. Billy turns to me and says, "Senegalese girl is good girl! But Japanese wife no like! In Senegal woman knows how to share and behave. In Japan Billy needs Japanese wife for *immigration*!" He hollered out the word. Two African male cooks came rushing out from the kitchen, looking startled. Meanwhile the male waiter came carrying me and Chiasa's meal still sizzling on one large tray, same way we serve it in Sudan.

As the comedy continued, Chiasa and I cleaned our fingers with the steaming hot washcloths we were given. I whispered "Allah" over my food and began eating with my right hand from me and Chiasa's one tray, African style. Chiasa looked at my hand and her eyes scanned the other tables. She hesitated. She opened her handbag, pulled out a pair of chopsticks, looked at them, looked around the room, and put them back.

"Before Billy married Japanese girl, he had to creep around Tokyo like dis . . ." Billy raised his more than six-foot frame on his tiptoes and began tiptoeing across his restaurant. "One day back then I am at apartment with friends. Police come on the block, I say, 'Oh no!'"

All the African men in the restaurant stopped joking, and their laughs turned to murmurs of disapproval. It seemed all around the world African men all felt the same stab and burn when the word *police* is spoken, even more whenever cops come around. Billy continued. "First come police. Then come *immigration* police. Now I am on the fire escape crouching like a tiger. But Japanese immigration is mean and patient. They wait on the block, search on the block for six hours. When finally they leave, my legs are so painful, I cannot stand, cannot walk. I tell my Japanese girlfriend, 'Okay! We get married.'" Now everyone was laughing again.

I didn't know the particular powers of the human mind. But truthfully, my own mind was divided into at least five parts. I could hear Billy's performance and see all his dramatic actions. He was in my fifth mind. Meanwhile, I observed Chiasa closely, considering whether or not to bring her all the way into my purpose and mission here in Japan. She was in my fourth mind. Then there was my wife, who sat in the center of my visions and made my heart move and rush and race. She was not a compromise or a convenience. She was not a plaything or an immigration decoy. She was not second to any unmarried woman I know or knew or would ever come to know. Akemi was in my third mind. The method and the fight and how to make it all happen with conflicting information and conflicting interest with a foreign tongue and on foreign land—that filled up my second mind. Then there was my Umma, my heart and my purpose. She's always in my first mind. I needed to contact her to be sure that she was at ease and to put her mind at peace. But I was feeling a shame of a particular Sudanese kind, that I had held Akemi in my arms last night, and then let her slip away. But kidnapping and murder are capital crimes. Strategically, I knew, as Sensei had cautioned me, that Akemi needed to leave her father of her own free will, out her own front door, on her own two feet, not by climbing a tree, sliding down a back wall, crawling through a thick bush, and leaping into a back alley without any consideration. That would be no good.

Billy's booming voice grew extra excited. My fifth mind took over the others and I listened. "In Japan an African man needs two passports! One like this"—Billy pulled his passport from his back pocket—"and . . ." The restaurant door opened, causing Billy to pause. It was two Japanese girls, coming through all smiles, carrying groceries. Billy seemed surprised, but he pulled them into the drama. "And my Japanese wife!" He walked over and hugged her. The male customers let out muted laughs and were obviously already familiar with Billy's wife. The two Japanese girls bowed to the customers and walked over to the other side of the restaurant and disappeared. Billy continued at half the volume. "If you want to be a part of it, you need *two* passports. If you want to own land in Japan, you need *two* passports. If you want to own a business in Japan, you need *two* passports. This one here," he said, holding his passport up for all to see. "And that one there." He pointed toward the room where his wife had walked away.

I could tell Chiasa had never tasted Senegalese food. But I could also feel that she was enjoying herself. She was reserved, and aside from her light laughter, she did not say one word to any other person in the room. I thought it was a clever position she was in. No one had to know that she was Japanese or that she spoke Japanese, unless she wanted them to. She blended in well with the Africans, because she was one. She fit in with the Japanese, because she was one. It was also interesting how she knew so much about Tokyo, its customs, its streets, it prefectures and all, but here was a place minutes from her house that she had never seen with her perfect vision. True, we were three flights up on a side street in Ebisu in the Tokyo night, but sometimes even when you know a lot about a place, there is still much to learn.

Billy was easing into his finale. He asked the African men gathered, "My wife here asked me, who is more important to you, me or your 'mother'? So I put the question to you, my brothers, who is number one?"

All the African men stood. All were six feet tall or more. All the African men were as black as or blacker than me, all masculine and built sturdy and strong. In one chorus they all shouted, and then the shouts became a chant and they jumped and danced. "Momma, Momma, Momma!"

Billy said, "Of course it's Momma! When my momma say to me, 'You are a good boy, you look fresh and clean in your *jelabiyah*. You have done a good job, son,' I smile like this." Billy's smile spread brightly across his face.

"No woman nowhere can top that," Bill said and they all chanted "momma" in agreement.

The night at Terenga in Ebisu ended with a competitive game of darts. Billy had the waiters push all the tables on our side to the wall.

As new customers arrived, he had them seated on the opposite side. The dart competition heated up, and each of the eight African men became deeply serious when they took aim at the bull's-eye mounted on a far wall.

"You are winning because you have a good luck charm," Billy said to me, while nodding his head toward Chiasa.

"I don't think that's it," I told him solemnly.

Chiasa stepped up to the board, pulled loose five darts, and stepped all the way back behind the line drawn on the restaurant floor. Without talking or smiling, she fired each of the five darts into the bull's-eye. Amazed, the men cheered for her.

Throughout the night I saw and heard Billy speak six different languages: Wolof, French, English, Japanese, Italian, and German. He was a gracious host, a humorous man, and a Senegalese Baye Fall Muslim. He loved his momma and handled his business and was not anybody's fool. Although I never would allow my wife to be my "passport," I didn't look down on him. Speaking six languages and sending his money home to his village was worthy of respect, and the way he flowed in his use of the Japanese language got me hyped. I made myself a promise that night: hiragana, katakana, three thousand different kanji, whatever. I would learn to speak Japanese fluently with that kind of ease and dexterity.

I paid, and left with my "lucky charm."

*　*　*

"Chiasa," I said.

"*Hai,*" she answered with a smile.

"Do you believe in God?" I asked, to my own surprise.

"Um, I believe in right and wrong," she said softly.

"Do you believe that you were created?" I asked her. She didn't answer, and we continued walking slowly through the streets of Ebisu toward the station.

"Look at the moon," I told her. She looked. "Now look at your fingers," I told her. She looked. "Now touch your skin." She lifted her pretty hands to her face and stroked her own cheek. "I believe that Allah created all of this, and these beautiful expressions of Allah cannot be duplicated by any man." We walked silently through the crowds and into the station. On the train we took the two-seater in the corner situated right by the exit.

"I'm leaving for Kyoto in the morning," I told her. Both of our eyes were facing forward and not toward one another. "You have been helpful to me, and I thank you, for real."

"Do you believe in fate?" she suddenly asked. "Like something happened simply because it was supposed to and nothing that you do could have prevented things from going that way?"

"It sounds familiar to something that Muslims say. It goes like this: 'I plan, you plan, we plan, they plan, but Allah is the best of planners,'" I shared with her. She smiled and sat back some to think on it.

"It's funny how life goes, isn't it?" Chiasa asked, speaking to me but more like she was thinking aloud. "I met you because of my enemy Yuka. I hate that. But I saw you first. I was walking the aisle to get magazines from the flight attendant. You had your sunglasses on indoors. I thought that was funny. When you lifted your hand to adjust them, I saw the ring."

I looked down at the ring Sensei had given to me. I recalled my disappointment with the fact that I had left my gold band, the one symbolizing my marriage to Akemi, on the sink at the Ghazzalis'. While riding in Mr. Ghazzali's taxi to JFK airport, I wondered if mistakenly leaving my wedding band behind meant anything. I convinced myself, however, that it was a simple mistake, not an omen or a sign.

Walking now through the streets of Harajuku, we reached the point where we could separate. "I'll walk you home," I told her.

"You have to come and get your camera and things. Unless you just want me to have them." She smiled.

After gathering my few things from her home and saying my farewell to her grandfather, I eased out of the house slippers she had once again provided, and back into my Nikes. She followed me outside and offered, "I'll ride you back on my bicycle."

"So I walked you home. Now you'll ride me back. Then I'll walk you home again?" I asked with a laugh. "Nah, I'm cool," I told her, then left.

Two and a half minutes into my walk back to the hostel, I stopped in the middle of the Harajuku madness, stood beside some Japanese dude dressed like a pirate and two others like elves, and asked myself, *What are you doing? You have three days to find your wife before Nakamura leaves on his Asian tour. Will he take her with him? You have one location to check in Kyoto, Akemi's high school, and that's it. Would she go back to school there? You have four days before your flight back to New York. Will you return empty-handed?* All five of my minds began to merge and shook off my doubts that were occurring in my fourth mind about Chiasa. Yes, her father was high up in the American military, and if I fucked up, there would be great consequences for me. Naoko Nakamura hated Americans, so Chiasa's father and Akemi's father would be natural enemies. Besides, I wouldn't let Chiasa get hurt. I'd just buy her translation and tour guide services same as I had been doing here in Tokyo. If not Chiasa, then who? I would have to find help down in Kyoto. So why not the girl I already got to know? So what was it? What was holding me back? I questioned myself. Then myself fought myself.

In order to be completely honest with myself, I focused in on only that one question. *What is the holdup with you concerning Chiasa?* The answer came bursting from my brain. It was something that I had known from the moment I saw her. *This girl Chiasa is a pretty, bad-ass, beautiful girl ninja. More than I could have ever cooked up in my imagination. I met her three days ago and the energy is moving too fast. If I could control the energy, at least on my part, we could work together. If not, we couldn't. Under these circumstances I couldn't allow anyone to distract me from my mission. And my wife is the only one I love. So why spark something else up, while I'm trying to get my love back and settled and secured?* My mind was putting it together swiftly. Now that I had moved beyond the emotion and the thing that was holding me back, I could shoot straight to the strategy that I was trying to organize in my mind over dinner.

One, I would have Chiasa read Akemi's diary and translate only the names, addresses, and information I needed for the search. We could look up the places beforehand on the map. Maybe there were even some phone numbers in her diary. I could have Chiasa make calls for me while I was in Kyoto and I could have her sit by her phone and wait for me to call in and give her instructions on what I needed or wanted to ask.

That was it. That would work. I was certain now. I did a 180 and headed back to Chiasa's. Before reaching her house, I jumped in a phone both and called her. There was no answer. It was 10 p.m. Could she have fallen asleep that quick? Or did she go out into the night? Was she out riding her motorcycle and erasing me from her thoughts and feelings?

When I opened the door to my room in Harajuku, Chiasa was there, her eyes filled with emotion. "I had an idea," she said.

I interrupted her. "I have a couple of things for you to do for me. You're paid until Friday anyway, right?"

"Right!" she agreed.

"I'm trusting you," I told her. I walked to my duffel and pulled out the diary. "Read this for me. Write down any names of friends or family addresses and telephone numbers you find in here and give them to me. Come back in the morning and translate for me. I have to activate my rail pass for the bullet train. Afterward, I need you to stay by the phone at your room, like it's headquarters. I'll let you know who I'll need you to call and what I need you to say and do. Okay?" I asked.

She smiled. "Akemi's diary, right?"

"Hai!" I told her. She laughed some at my random and limited use of the Japanese language. She sat on my bed and hiked up her legs and laid the diary on top of her knees and began reading. I had meant for her to take it home with her, but she looked like she thought she was home already.

"I'll be back," I told her and left.

For an hour, I spoke to Umma, until my phone card burned out. Naja was excited. "Did you see Akemi?" she had asked me. "Of course," I told her confidently. "Was she trying to speak English?" Naja asked coyly. "She was speaking English the same as Umma," I answered, and me and Naja had a good laugh because we know that is not at all. "Is she coming back with you?" Naja asked. "Of course," I told her, truly believing so. "How was she acting? Was she acting right? Or was she acting funny?" Naja asked, curious as usual. "Akemi is sweet. She is my wife. Of course she was acting right," I told her.

After the call, I walked over to the Harajuku dollar store and picked up a new notebook for Chiasa to place the info in. I was hoping that there was some real info in Akemi's diary to help me locate Akemi swiftly. I was blocking my mind from showing me images of Akemi's tears, the ones I knew she would have after Iwa (or the girl in the pink pumps, probably the same person) gave her a twisted, lying message about something that I never said or did. I knew the sadness that would engulf her at the thought that I might not show up in Kyoto. At the same time, I knew that my wife was smart. Purposely, she had placed a yellow bulb in the lamp and left it on overnight at her Roppongi house, probably every night. She knew that if I saw that light I would know that, yes, Akemi is near. After all, this was the color of the bulb in the basement at Cho's where she and I, two virgins, made love. She had left me the right clues once before, and I trusted she would leave a trail once again.

I resisted imagining the real-life scenes where her father was forcing her to move from place to place to stay away from me. I would be smart also and have faith that Akemi was my fate and I was hers.

When I opened the door to my room, Chiasa's big eyes were tear-filled. When she saw me, her tears spilled. I didn't know what happened.

"What happened?" I asked her.

"You're married?" she asked.

"Yes," I responded. "Why are you crying?"

"What an incredible story," she said softly, wiping her tears.

"Any names, addresses, phone numbers? Write them down in here," I told her, tossing the notebook, which landed on the bed right at her feet. She clutched the diary and held it against her breasts as though it were her private truth.

"That notebook isn't good enough for this story. I'll meet you back here in the morning," Chiasa said.

"What time?" I asked her.

"I'll be here before sunrise so we can eat and drink together," she said softly.

"Why are you fasting, Chiasa?" I asked her seriously.

"Because it feels like the right thing to do. Because I think you are so cool walking around in Japan, doing something that no one else seems to be doing. Not eating or drinking in the Tokyo hot sun, that's amazing to me. That's how I am and I want to become, unlike anybody else, completely different." Oddly, she left out in a hurry.

There are over three billion Muslims in the world, I thought to myself. *And each of them is required to fast for Ramadan, unless they are sickly or traveling. I am not the only one, thankfully.*

Chapter 8
THE KIDNAPPER

The Shinkansen train I was booked on departed at 8:00 a.m. With the help of Chiasa translating, I handed them my rail pass and was issued an activated ticket that was good for me to travel roundtrip from Tokyo to Kyoto for an entire week. Chiasa and I parted at the point where all passengers are required to insert a small rectangular ticket into a slot that then opened the turnstile for each paying customer to enter. When I looked back to where she was standing, she was waving nonstop, something I noticed Japanese girls tend to do. First the bowing, then the waving until they couldn't see you and you could no longer see them.

She had held on to Akemi's diary and handed me a note with a few names, places, and addresses translated into English. She also handed me a new stack of index cards to study with phrases she thought would be more helpful for me to know. Some of them were funny like, "Have you seen the 100,000 yen shoe princess?" Others were words she thought I should learn and listen for, like, "Don't move, you are under arrest." Her study cards were much better than mine. She included on each of them the Japanese word written first in kanji and in romanji, and on the back she printed the English translation for me. My cards were white, hers were green. She put them in order of the topics and even included the Japanese translation for "I am fasting for Ramadan until sunset, no food or water please." I cracked up when I shuffled down to the last few cards and seen that she had written and translated out all of their Japanese curse words. It felt good knowing that she would be here in Tokyo on point for me.

And although her company for the past few days was good for me, I felt like my regular self, moving around alone, once again.

The comfort, cleanliness, speed, organization, and beauty of the bullet train was something I had grown to expect in Japan. This seemed to be their way of life and atmosphere. I thought to myself that perhaps I was being spoiled here. When I returned to New York, it would be more no good than it had ever been—hot, dirty, disorganized, disrespectful, and cold at the same time.

White gloves over feminine fingers interrupted my thoughts. Well-dressed, humble, and subdued, the train attendant offered me softly, "Coffee, green tea, chocolates, almonds, water."

"No, thank you," I said. The doe-eyed attendant pushed away with her tray full of temptations.

It was remarkable to watch the Tokyo urban turn to rural. With several shades of green grass of varying heights and incredible trees framing farms and rice fields, my eyes were in constant motion, measuring and memorizing sights, sliding up and down hills, and climbing mountains. I was exploring an Asian empire, but more than that, thinking about how versatile and all-powerful Allah is to have created such unique things—nature, people, culture, languages—and scattered them all over the world.

Pulling out my paperback book on Naoko Nakamura, I would use my time to continue reading up on him. I was convinced that he remained in Roppongi moving back and forth, to and from Ginza, in preparation for his Asian tour. The girl with the pink pumps said that he took Akemi in "an early-morning surprise." Still, Chiasa had filmed him in Shibuya at 2:00 p.m. *My wife is in Kyoto*, I thought to myself, *without her father's direct supervision or control.* So how did he intend to keep her still and separated from me without her cooperation?

As I opened up to the table of contents, my eyes moved across each offering of detailed information about Nakamura. There were chapters on his early childhood, military training, and education. Under the topic of education, there were separate chapters on his high school and his training at the University of Tokyo. In the university he must have been involved in everything, because there were separate chapters on his participation in the University of Tokyo Debate

Team, as well as "the Movement to Discontinue English as a Core Requirement." He had also created some organization called Defenders of Japan and wrestled on the U of Tokyo wrestling team. I moved beyond all these because I was not interested in politics and couldn't see how learning about his politics could help the matter that I was involved in. As far as him being a wrestler, no problem. It was not worth considering to me. Fortunately, after those chapters and the listings of chapters concerning Nakamura's Yakuza connection, businesses, travels, and influencial friends, there was an entire section on his private life. I flipped to page 306 and began reading there. The chapter was called "Mysterious Marriage." This mattered to me because Naoko's wife was Akemi's mother and Akemi was very connected to her and to her memory of her.

I was intrigued by the opening lines of the chapter.

Naoko Nakamura chose his wife without ever meeting her in person. Nor did he do any of the traditional Japanese prewedding procedures. Perhaps because his biological father was deceased and he had become estranged from his own mother, he didn't see a need to do so. However, upon further investigation, the marriage of Naoko Nakamura becomes more and more murky. None of Nakamura's closest relatives, friends, or allies participated in any part of the Nakamura marital ceremony. There were no wedding invitations, nor was any party given an opportunity to offer congratulations or gifts of good fortune. Because Naoko Nakamura by this time had become a prominent businessman and political force, as well as a high-profile agitator in Japan. This clandestine wedding was viewed with great suspicion. One source, who asked to remain anonymous, said about Naoko Nakamura's new bride, "Shiori Nakamura appeared out of nowhere like a sudden breeze."

Folding back the top of the page, I closed the book for a minute. That one paragraph got my mind racing. I knew that Akemi's cousin from New Jersey had once said to me that Akemi's mother was Korean, not Japanese. I knew that the name of Akemi's mother was printed in the program that I had gotten from Akemi's art show in Manhattan at the Museum of Modern Art. It was the same program that said that Akemi was a student at Kyoto Girls' High. I'm good at remembering both names and faces. I was sure that her mother's name began with the letter *J* and was simple, like *Joo*. I snatched my Jansport, unzipped it, rifled through my papers, and pulled out the program. "Joo Eun Lee"! That was the name. And the program also said that Joo Eun Lee was a "celebrated North Korean author." So who was Shiori Nakamura? Was she a first wife? Were there some other brothers and sisters that Akemi had that I didn't know about and that she didn't mention and that no one in her family had mentioned?

Not knowing the Japanese culture and beliefs, I was at a loss for answers about my wife's family. So I picked the book up and read on.

". . . Shiori Nakamura appeared out of nowhere like a sudden breeze."

As an investigative author, I was certain that each human life has a definite history. I was determined to uncover the truth about the cold and calculating nemesis of America and American expansion. After several attempts to interview Naoko Nakamura's relatives failed, I attempted to interview his closest friends, acquaintances, and business associates. When these avenues were also closed, with each of them refusing to meet to discuss, in person or over the phone, any aspect of Naoko Nakamura's life, I turned to pursuing the truth by way of interviewing Naoko Nakamura's enemies and disgruntled underlings. The following chapter represents the documented conclusions of seven years of tireless research and travel.

Naoko Nakamura, a die-hard nationalist, whose life efforts were toward building a self-sufficient, financially and politically independent Japan, free from American occupation and American military air bases and control, as well as a Japan with its own sovereignty protected by its own well-trained and militarily equipped army, was having difficulty convincing top Japanese business elites of his credibility and, furthermore, bankability. Existing major Japanese corporations and their CEOs and executives were already in both formal and informal financial working relationships and alliances with American corporations. Even some of the most conservative Japanese corporations were in "secretive subcontracting and consulting relationships" with American consultants, experts, managers, and companies. Japanese corporate giants and executives did not trust that Naoko's philosophy and method of "independence," along with the elimination of the American corporate presence and inroads into Japan's economy, would be fruitful.

Nakamura therefore began covertly courting business alliances and contracts with former enemies of Japan like China and North Korea. Under his new motto and banner of "Asian Solidarity," Nakamura formed the Pan Asian Corporation, rumored as having been funded in part by monies obtained through his Yakuza connection. In the process of promoting his newly formed corporation's business, he traveled throughout the Asian continent, representing himself *not* as the staunch Japanese-only, pro-Japanese military guy but with a new face of the Asian-friendly business tycoon who wanted to help all Asian countries to distance themselves from dependence on and domination by America and American businesses.

Naoko won big by brokering an exclusive car manufacturing deal with the government of Thailand, which gave Toyota the exclusive right to design cars for Thai citizens' purchase. The Thai government gave Toyota, through a deal brokered by Nakamura, unfair trade advantages and in turn taxed American-manufactured cars at the rate of 300 percent, making the American vehicles unaffordable to the people of Thailand. As the nation of Thailand moved from bicycles to motorbikes and motorcycles to "tut-tuts" to cars, Naoko Nakamura's Pan Asian Corporation won big confidence in the Asian business region, big benefits, incentives, and great wealth. It was this deal that won Naoko Nakamura acceptance by influencial CEOs, who then began to trust Nakamura at least as a broker of lucrative deals.

It was in North Korea, however, that Naoko Nakamura discovered his wife-to-be, Joo Eun Lee.

I put the book down, thankful that the author was about to get to the point. I was interested in the whole business-building thing though. I thought there was a real simple way for the author to break it down, if he really wanted the reader to understand it. Naoko wanted to make paper in his country and use his power to protect his nation and people and family. He wanted America to get the fuck out so he and his crew could be the heavyweights on the block. He wanted the old boys who had been running things to team up with him and run the enemy out. That's how I understood it. I did have to, however, look some words up in my dictionary. They were *clandestine, nationalist, conservative, sovereignty, covertly, staunch*, and *broker*. I looked them up, wrote the definitions down in my notebook, and continued reading about my wife's parents.

Joo Eun Lee was the daughter of a North Korean government official who controlled printing and the North Korean propaganda machine. His business was printing North Korean–approved books, manuals, and pamphlets for the North Korean educational system. However, his reputation was tarnished when his wife suddenly defected to South Korea, leaving behind two daughters, one of whom was fourteen-year-old Joo Eun Lee.

Joo Eun was a fan of great books and authors from all around the world. She led a sheltered life in a protected environment. Her best friends were books that her father kept hidden and locked in the basement of his home as part of a private, secret collection of world literature. It is believed that the influence of these books spurred Joo Eun to take the uncommon and bold step in a Communist country of becoming a "free thinker." She wrote her first book, which was more of a pamphlet, at age fourteen. It was titled *Omahnee,* which simply means "Mother" in the Korean language. Using her father's privtate printing equipment, she and her best friend printed out the pamphlets and had them secretly circulated and distributed. The well-written, scholarly ten-page anonymous letter printed in the pamphlet caught on like wildfire. Some say it was because of the political argument that Joo Eun raised in her writing as she spoke to her anonymous mother about freedom, family, and national loyalty all being the same concept. Others say the pamphlets became popular because they were "forbidden fruits." However, the most compelling reason for the popularity of the pamphlets among North Koreans young and old, male and female, military and civilian, was the provocative picture of a young, perhaps fourteen-year-old naked Korean girl on the cover, lying on the floor in the fetal position with her newly blossomed breasts and curves and a full flow of long, straight black hair concealing her face.

Omahnee was only the first of Joo Eun's famed underground writings. She went on to publish twelve pamphlets in total, all following the same for-mat of politically charged, passionate, and scholarly arguments enclosed in a cover displaying an attractive young teen, a long-haired girl naked and faceless, striking a highly seductive pose.

A pamphlet entitled *One Womb,* Joo Eun's twelfth publication, is rumored to have landed in Naoko Nakamura's far-reaching hands and moved him so passionately that he had to have the then fifteen-year-old anonymous girl for his own. In this, her final political pamphlet while living in North Korea, Joo Eun wrote and argued passionately that North and South Korea are born of the same womb, sisters of the same mother. She used the metaphor of two sisters, bound by blood and love and life, who got into a heated argument. One sister got married to an "outsider" (an American) and allowed the outsider to prevent the sisters from ever forgiving each other or making amends. The two sisters therefore became strangers to one another, forsaking their true blood relationship and one of them bonding only with the stranger instead. Joo Eun argued heatedly that no matter what, despite all arguments and disagreements, the depth of the sister's relationship and sister's destiny will forever be entangled and intertwined and inseparable because they share the same blood, the same language and culture, and because they emerged from the same womb. She argued convincingly that North Korea and South Korea on closer inspection also share the same enemy. Joo Eun accused the American stranger of augmenting a hatred between sisters and pursuing the complete isolation and elimination of one sister, namely North Korea.

It is the photo on the cover of *One Womb* that caused the rage, however, and led the free anonymous underground pamphlet to triple its printing. The attractive teen on the cover was photographed naked and sitting with her legs opened on the edge of a simple wooden chair. The young girl's head was down, disguising her face. In Joo Eun's signature style. Her long hair was hanging from her head and flowing down, finally intermingling and resting in her vaginal hairs.

Naoko Nakamura, according to an undisclosed source, paid 1 million yen ($100,000) to a North Korean agent to identify the girl on the cover. He then paid 1 million yen to another North Korean man to capture her.

Fifteen-year-old Joo Eun Lee arrived in Osaka, Japan, by sea on the dark waters of the dark night.

No source has confirmed or documented what happened between Naoko Nakamura and Joo Eun Lee once she arrived in Japan. However, on her sixteenth birthday, Naoko Nakamura married her at his Kyoto home. Sixteen is the legal age for females to marry in Japan.

On Joo Eun Lee's first public sitting, she was presented by Naoko Nakamura as his new wife, a sixteen-year-old Japanese bride whom he introduced as Shiori Nakamura. Months later, the couple announced the birth of the daughter who would be their only child, Akemi Nakamura, born at midnight at their Kyoto home on December 31, 1970. Perhaps her entrance into the world was clouded by the Japanese New Year celebration, which is the most important holiday of their year. It marked a new beginning for the couple as well as ushering in the financial high point of the Pan Asian Corporation.

Both of my sources of the above information were murdered in Japan on separate dates and in separate places and by different means. Both of my source's murders remain unsolved. This information, therefore, cannot be corroborated at the time of this book's publication. However, as an author, I testify to these facts, which I obtained against a wall of cultural silence, and as an outsider, a *gaijin*. My written and secretly recorded interviews with both of my sources for the above information remain secured at the time of publishing. This first publishing makes those interviews a matter of record.

Mind-blowing, that's how I felt about the unauthorized biography, *Never Surrender*. I looked up the words *nemesis* in my English dictionary and *gaijin* in my Japanese dictionary. The new words I was learning danced around in my mind.

"Captured at fifteen . . ." In what month of her fifteenth year was she captured? She was still in North Korea when she published her last pamphlet at fifteen, the book said. It had to take some time for it to be distributed, read, and discussed and for Nakamura to get hold of it as well. Then she was captured and brought to Japan but not married until sixteen. Did he go into her before their wedding? Joo Eun gave birth to my wife Akemi "months later." *How many months later?* I asked myself.

Murder, I thought to myself. *Men will murder to protect their land, women, beliefs, and profits.* However, Nakamura was not an honorable

man. He wasn't driven by any true beliefs. He believed only in himself
and what he wanted at the moment. He took by force, what should
never be taken by force, a woman's heart and a woman's body. He
was so far from the truth that he would not even allow his wife to
keep her name. Why? In the Sudan a woman will always keep her
name, the name of her father and the name of her father's father.
We are a country of fathers. We are all traced through our fathers,
and no one will think of taking that away from a woman. Even after a
Sudanese woman's marriage, she is still identified through her father.
I began considering, *What are the consequences in a nation of fathers
when a person has a father who is corrupt, without faith or boundaries or
limits?*

Then my mind returned to murder. The author's two sources were
both eliminated. Pushing the puzzle pieces around, I figured that
these were the same two guys that Nakamura paid the money to, to
get his hands on Joo Eun. He made agreements with them, signed
them, and paid out the proper sums. Then he merked them. I was
realizing this was his style. He comes in the form of business. He
makes agreements as though his word is bond, like any true man's
word is bond. Then he doubles back and betrays his own word and
signature and agreement, the same way he did when he signed the
marriage papers for Akemi and me. He gave his word, printed his
word, and then doubled back and kidnapped his daughter, the same
way that he had kidnapped his wife! *Deceitful motherfucker!* I thought
to myself. Then I breathed some to erase my anger.

Returning to the few remaining pages of the chapter titled "Mysterious Marriage," I continued to read on.

Joo Eun Lee's or Shiori Nakamura's loyalty to her husband Naoko Nakamura
was solid and impeccable. During their first year of marriage and her pregnancy, she was seen only at selected high-profile social gatherings with her
husband, where she was reportedly joyful, polite, alluring, and silent aside
from introductions, greetings, and small nicities.

Readers and fans of her anonymous free pamphlets were not given any
new writings from Joo Eun until five years later. Her new pamphlets, published as small, thin, softcover books, were not anonymous and were not free.

They were written, published, and advertised, and sold under the name Shiori Nakamura. After a careful and thorough analysis of the writing style, the word usage and placement, the passion and the philosophy driving the work, England's famed historian Robert Barringer concluded that Shiori Nakamura's books and the underground North Korean pamphlets do indeed share the same author, with an acknowledgment of an identifiable maturing as well as philosophical and intellectual growth.

Shiori Nakamura, the author, debuted as a young Japanese mother, convincing other mothers who read her letters, stories, and poems that women are the key to national security. She argued that if new mothers raised their children with an unreserved, unconventional love and emotion, a new and more compassionate generation would emerge and seize the reins of power. A more compassionate, loving, loved child will put forth a more compassionate philosophy, politics, and policy, thus saving nations from war and death and hunger and disease and chaos. She taught that only this new philosophy would save Japanese mothers from their depression. Shiori's writings elevated the abnormally conservative and servile posture of the traditional Japanese woman. She issued controversial writings that were broadly discussed and debated. She emphasized a more balanced, well-learned, and peaceful global community. She delivered a best-selling manual called *How to Raise Strong, Feminine, Knowledgeable Daughters.* When she was not writing or offering her annual reading, she was an at-home wife and mother completely dedicated to the raising of her one child, reportedly in the manner which she described in her work.

Naoko Nakamura allowed her. Extremely clever, he knew well how to make maximum use out of each piece and person in his kingdom. He believed that his wife's philosophy was not in conflict with his "Pan Asian" philosophical face, from which he benefited financially over many years.

Shiori Nakamura would read her work publicly only once a year. She appeared demure and lovely, speaking well-polished and perfect Japanese. She refused all interviews, nor would she answer questions.

Shiori Nakamura died tragically young at the age of twenty-eight from brain cancer. This author sympathetically submits that it must have been difficult and debilitating for her to live a life of secrets, particularly a secret identity, which may have complicated her health in the end. Her daughter, Akemi Nakamura, is noted throughout Japan as a young artistic genius to watch for.

Below is Joo Eun Lee's last poem, which offers subtle hints of her evolution and beliefs and secrets and sorrows and joys. The young North Korean woman having emerged from a Communist country, makes overtures to God in Sufi-like implications and pays homage to life and love. The first and only slight disagreement with her husband is hinted at here in the lines she penned. Perhaps Joo Eun saw her life's end approaching.

Hananihm

People who love are different from everybody else.
People who feel are more fortunate than all.
Rich men who buy and grab up things are just moving them around.
They have bought these things with money, which they can never
    own.
A mother with life in her womb is the one who is truly wealthy.
A newborn in the arms is beyond oil in one palm and pure gold in the
    other.
Father says that there is no God, so that I might worship him.
But something is moving in the atmosphere . . .
Not for viewing, but for sensing and being changed by.
That I can feel. I am certain.
My first love was the sky. Who created that?
My second love was my mother's eyes that revealed a reflection
    of me.
My father had a house of great beauty built for us all.
But who created the mind, the memory, and the imagination?
I'd sit in the soil surrounded with no walls just to talk to that ONE,
    even without words . . .
Diamonds are lovely, but sound is lovelier.
Roller coasters are thrilling. My clitoris clothed in my vagina is more,
    more, more.
Why turn on the lights when we can lie under the glare of the moon?
Why listen to the call for war when we can make love?
He wants revolution, but I want passion revolving in my soul.

A man invented the fan, but who created the wind and caressed it
    into a breeze
Then converted it into a storm?
A cloud holds the water, yet both clouds and water were created.
Impress me not with castles, cars, or clothes. I'd rather meet the
    Maker of rain—
But would be content with simply being showered while lying in the
    grass
Facing a darkened sky pregnant with thunder and leaking lightning.
My husband asks me, Do you love me? So gently, I answer him.
"I love the Creator of life. This is *why* I can love you."
Yet everywhere that I see and feel a trace of the Creator, the Light of
    life,
There is so much love in it for me.

By Joo Eun Lee

The poem, I read it five times over. When I read the last words for the
fifth time, I felt a new love born within myself for my wife's mother,
and an even deeper love and understanding of my wife as well.

Joo Eun Lee showed me the parts that make up the soul of
Akemi, and the reason that Akemi was capable of such deep love for
me. I could see now why and how Akemi was at ease with my faith
and so captivated by my beautiful Umma, who has a soul similar to
Joo Eun's resting in her bosom. True, their methods and manners are
extremely different, yet their intent and their meaning was beginning
to feel the same to me.

Chapter 9
INVISIBLE MAN

Three hours passed in thirty minutes, it seemed. "Next stop Kyoto," the soft voice announced in Japanese and in English.

When I looked up and through my window, the images that we were now moving past were not what I imagined they would be. As the train slowed to a halt, my first impression was that Kyoto was a place of dull metals and grayness. I was certain, however, that it would get better. It would become comparable to my wife and suitable to her artistic eyes. It had to.

When I stepped off at Kyoto station, it was almost noon. I threw my backpack and belongings into two secure lockers, dropped in the coins, and searched for a phone.

Chiasa answered with her sleepy voice. "Wake up, you're on the payroll" was my greeting.

"You sound excited," she said. "You got there safely, I see."

"What did you expect?" I told her. "You got all the info?"

"About one more hour and I'll have it all completed," she said, making her voice sound more alert. "I know you think it's just about the data, but her diary is really emotional and it pulled me into a secret world that was amazing and unfamiliar. I felt myself . . ." She paused, then never finished her sentence.

I filled the silence with my new requests. "I got a couple more things for you to look into."

"Tell me," she said sweetly, like any request was no problem for her.

"Go to the bookstore and look up an author named Shiori Naka-mura and buy all her books," I said.

"All of them?" she repeated.

"Yeah, and while you're there, check out one more author. He's an American." I flipped the softcover biography around. "His name is Seth Arrington."

"Got it," she said. "Stay out of the direct sunlight 'cause it's hotter down there in the south where you are. Call me later. I'll have everything ready."

"Aight." I hung up.

Walking through and out of Kyoto station was like a stroll through Pastry Lane. There was a glut of bakeries displaying cakes decorated with fresh fruit slices, all assembled in intricate designs. Some of the Japanese fruits I couldn't recognize. There were also shops with only fresh-baked cookies and some with fresh-baked breads. The smell of maple syrup seeped into the air and led to a couple of waffle stands. Lines were forming and customers were dipping fresh baked small waffle slices into the syrup. I kept it moving.

"Kyoto Women's College," I said to the bus attendant in the booth. He gave me the bus number using only his fingers.

The bus was not an "airport limousine" experience. It was smaller and the seats were positioned in an arrangement different than I had ever seen on public transportation. It was clean and organized. The driver was polite without words. I dropped my exact change in and tried not to stand out as the tallest, only black African man or person on board or in sight or even visible walking on the streets. The people didn't stare. Most of them didn't even look, glance, or peek. It was almost like I was invisible. The elders sat up front. The middle-aged adults sat and stood in the middle. The teens and college kids sat and stood in a raised section where the seats were up a few steps and raised up high.

The ride was completely silent. The Kyoto kids were more laid-back than the Tokyo cliques. There was no Harajuku crew sporting strange costumes. Nor were there any high-fashion types or naked females or freaks. Some passengers were reading. Others were nodding or sleeping. School kids were studying. The vibe was calm and ordinary.

The names of the upcoming bus stops were displayed on a digital screen in Japanese and then in English. After a minute, the scenery shifted, and rows of beautiful trees and flowers and plants began to emerge. The town seemed old and special. Most of the shops were small and made of wood. I stood looking through the bus windows, especially when the bus would stop and lose some passengers as well as pick others up.

My stop was coming up. As I got off, surprisingly most of the passengers unloaded with me. Now we were all facing what turned out to be a temple. Many of the elderly people entered. I was still at first. I had never seen a real temple in person before. It was wide and mysterious. The architecture was attractive and appeared ancient. I could smell incense burning. Yet the place was designed so that you really had to go inside to discover whatever they had happening. You could not tell from the outside what the experience would be like. I was definitely curious, but I let it go and turned sixty degrees instead. The street sign read "Shichijodori." It was not the easiest to remember, but I would remember. Now I was facing what seemed like a long museum situated across the street. It extended over and down a few blocks. When I turned directly to my right, I could see the sign for Kyoto's Women's College and the arrow pointed uphill. I began walking in that direction. The college was on a street named "Higashiyamaschichijo"—what the fuck?

Oddly, Akemi's high school was on the same campus with the college. I had learned that from the MOMA pamphlet and checked it on my map of Kyoto. I planned to go to her high school and sit outside until the bell rang and classes were dismissed for the day. Then I would just wait and see if she simply came walking out.

Once I crossed the street, I looked toward the sky. It was so bright, the white so intense, the blues so clear, the sun so orange that none of it could be taken on directly. The power of that sky pushed back and forced all eyes to bend and turn away.

As I began climbing the hills, which were framed by mountains piled up way off in the distance, I had to smile at this scene, a succession of hills being climbed up and down by females of varied ages, dressed mostly in miniskirts and matching school uniforms, only a handful rocking individual style and clothing. Hundreds of female students all on an incline beginning with toddlers in short pants and pressed shirts, all fifty of them with the same short hair, wearing yellow hats, being led on a walk by two female teachers in front and two female teachers in the rear, all carrying raised umbrellas where there was not even a drop of rain.

There were slightly older schoolgirls playing in an enclosed yard.

There were junior high school girls shielded behind a black iron gate, each plank crafted like a spear sharpened on top and pointing toward the sky. You could see in, they could see out, but you could not get in to where they were.

Further up hill there was the Kyoto Girls' High School with the locked entrance and elaborate intercom system with steel buttons, a steel box, and steel speakers. Immediately across from it was the Kyoto Women's College, all its entrances flung open, girls seventeen, eighteen, and nineteen pouring in and out, dressed how they wanted to do it, it seemed. I had reached the top.

So far, I had not run into any police. But now I could see the security booths situated in front of the high school but behind their gate and off to the side. The same kind of security booth was at the opened entrance of the college as well. They were little brick stations in the shape of an octagon with uniformed elderly men stationed inside. The only other men I saw moving in the midst of the girls were workmen, driving trucks, making deliveries, doing gardening and ground maintenance, as well as driving the campus shuttle. Other than that it was girls, girls, girls.

There was a sitting place made of huge black rocks right between the high school and the college. I headed over and leaned there, watching and waiting.

A few young Japanese work guys, in wide-legged pants with drawstring waists, T-shirts on top, and heads wrapped in a white towel or in a bandana, sat at the top of the rocks, some reading Manga, smoking cigarettes one after the other and watching girls go by. Lunch break at one of the twenty-five businesses that ran up on one side of the hills. On the other side was where the girls' school, buildings, fields, and gates stood. *Lucky bastards,* I thought to myself. Could I imagine five or ten Brooklyn dudes from my block working in a world of only girls with big feline eyes and hiked-up skirts and bare legs? The old sixty- and seventy-year-old uniformed security guards seemed in good shape, but standing in their brick booths, they would represent no threat at all. Brooklyn would run through snatching up everything.

Nakamura had it all figured out, he thought, raising a talented, intelligent, beautiful, and rich daughter in an almost exclusively female environment. Being a member of the college board, as it said in the MOMA pamphlet. He probably intended for Akemi to graduate from the all-girls Kyoto high school and walk twenty feet away into the all-girls Kyoto Women's College. Believe me, I understood and I understand. We sent Naja to an all girls' Islamic school for the past three years and she was only seven now. And I intend and have always intended for her to remain in an all-Islamic school of girls until she either graduated or married.

Nakamura's mistake, I reflected, was allowing his teenaged daughter to travel alone seven thousand miles to New York City. He must've felt confident because he had two or three step brothers living there. And he was even more confident because he had "raised her right." *I plan and we plan and they plan* was all I could think to say to myself, *but Allah is the best of planners.* It seemed that Allah brought Akemi and me together, perhaps for his own reasons, which no human had the means to know.

I had written to Nakamura of my intention, desire, and plan to marry his daughter. I included the documents required, since we were young and parental signatures were necessary. He signed the documents and impressed his seal confirming it. I married Akemi after she handed those documents to me. Those signed documents and the life of Akemi Nakamura went from his hand to mine. Now he wanted to dishonor me with a takeback. But marriage cannot be taken back, and my going into her and releasing my seeds could never be erased.

By three o'clock hundreds of females poured down from the hilltops and flowed in a thick and steady wave passing me by. I must've looked like a fool, my eyes searching through and into and beside and beyond what appeared now to be thousands of girls with black hair and Japanese eyes and legs made shapely from walking and climbing all these hills daily. I did not see my wife. I wasn't 100 percent sure that I had not missed her, though, perhaps looking right when she went left, or straight by the time she was already moving behind me. *But if she had been part of this massive crowd, she would've seen me, right?* I asked myself. Then there was a possibility that she was not one of the walkers. Perhaps she was in one of the private red luxury-line buses. Labeled, "Princess Line." Herds of females boarded the bright sparkling vehicles lined one after the other, seven strong, moving slowly down the hills and off the campus. My eyes scanned each window as the buses inched by, but my wife was not there either.

I had an hour and a half before I needed to head to a spot oddly named *Tamisa, New York Style Yoga.* There were two places that Akemi had identified as relaxing places that she went when she was feeling real emotional. Akemi had written that the Japanese don't like to burden one another with their emotions. To express them is considered selfish as well as a personal weakness. Akemi wrote that she found it difficult to restrain her emotions, so she separated herself when she felt them coming on strong. She would go to a special area of Kyoto named Arashiyama and walk alone there, or to yoga class, to release and soothe her soul. Chiasa had told me this after my morning prayer and during our breakfast before sunrise. In fact Chiasa wanted to give me detailed descriptions of Akemi's written thoughts and words and feelings. But over breakfast of orange slices, boiled eggs, and soup, I told Chiasa that all I wanted was the list of names and addresses of my wife's friends and family members. The truth is I didn't want to invade my wife's private thoughts, feelings, and writings. If I could use the names, addresses, and telephone numbers that Akemi mentioned in her diary to locate her, she could express all her emotions and thoughts directly to me in her own way.

Moving downhill, when I eased off the campus completely, I found myself facing what looked like an art gallery. As I walked all the way around the building to the entrance, I discovered that it was a three-story hotel. In fact it was a Hyatt Hotel, an American brand. As I looked around, I thought, *American-owned, Japanese-style.* Before approaching the uniformed women who were stationed outside the main lobby, I put on my sunglasses. The women were petite and dressed similarly to Japanese flight attendants and customs workers. They wore tight blue skirts with matching jackets and pretty silk scarves around their necks. They wore standard business pumps on their feet, not too cheap, not too stylish. They stood welcoming customers and signaling taxis.

"*Konichiwa,*" I greeted them.

"Checking in?" one of the ladies asked in English.

"Maybe," I responded.

"All inquiries at the front desk." She pointed inside.

I walked in to one of the five desk clerks. "Reservation?" the suited Japanese man asked me, getting right to it.

"Not yet. What's the nightly rate?" I asked.

"You need a reservation."

"Okay, what's the rate?" I asked again.

"We are completely booked," he said, his voice soft unlike a man's, and his manner polite, but somehow I *still* felt like he was insulting me.

"No problem," I told him. I turned and crossed the spacious lobby floor, where people sat silently on plush, fashionable furniture. The ceilings were high and decorated by intricate woodwork instead of paint. Pansy flowers were arranged in clay vases throughout the lobby. A dining room area was open and framed by a wall of windows from floor to ceiling. Diners could see the display of nature, a rock garden and flowing fountain, while enjoying a meal. I could tell that it was too expensive to stay here, not like the short list of Kyoto hostels I held in my pocket. As I approached the concierge station, I organized my inquiry so I wouldn't seem suspicious. I needed to find a way of asking, "Where is the rich area of Kyoto located?" I didn't have an address for Akemi's home, but I was sure she lived in the wealthiest neighborhood. I reminded myself that even though the Hyatt had an all-Japanese staff, it was an American hotel and everyone would be required to speak English comfortably.

"*Konichiwa*," I said, laying my American passport on the concierge's counter.

"*Konichiwa*, may I help you?" she asked softly with an eager smile.

"Yes." I removed my sunglasses to place her at ease. "I would like to visit the best neighborhoods in Kyoto. Can you help me with that?" I asked her.

"Yes, of course," she agreed rapidly. "What are you most interested in—temples, nature, architecture, museums, foods, fabrics, or would you like to visit the traditional area of the *geisha* and *maiko*?"

"Architecture," I said smoothly. "I'd like to tour the best-built homes and neighborhoods."

She walked from behind her counter to a pamphlet stand. I followed. She reached in and pulled out a map. She handed one to me and returned to her station. With a red pen she checked the most

interesting traditional and upscale neighborhoods—and even offered the exact public bus information after I declined joining the
private group tours that they had leaving from the hotel the following
morning. Then she added, "I think, however, that the most wonderful
homes are hidden in the mountains. The nature that surrounds those
places makes them the most beautiful."

"Are those areas open to the public?" I questioned.

"Of course you can travel up the mountain. We have tons of tours
of selected mountain areas. But you cannot tour the private homes
in the same way that you would tour the sacred temples. We have a
cable car that will also carry you over the mountains, and the view is
most lovely."

"What about these mountains that sit directly behind the college?" I pointed.

"Which ones?" she asked. "Each of them is different." Voluntarily
she came from around her counter and led me on a walk outside the
hotel lobby. "Those are called the Hieizan Mountains. You can tour
them. The other one next to it is privately owned."

"Privately owned?" I repeated incredulously. "Someone can own a
mountain in Japan?" I asked, genuinely shocked at the idea.

"Yes." She laughed a bit. "Not often, but it does happen. In this
case it is a very famous Japanese actor who owns that one. He is retired now and having *een-say-e*."

"What is that?" I followed up.

She smiled. "Well, in Japanese it means 'secret life.' It happens
when a powerful person retires early because of great success in his
business but continues controlling and even managing events quietly
and from afar, unknown to most." She placed a finger over her lips.
I thought to myself, *Japanese people seemed to love the words* hide, hidden, secret, invisible . . . , and apparently they also loved secret life-
styles.

"Well, you can't visit *his* mountain or the one beside it. That one
there"—she pointed—"is owned by Naoko Nakamura. He . . ." Then
her words trailed off and I could no longer hear them.

* * *

At 4:45 p.m., I sat in a small smoky café in the corner by the window,
where I could lean up and watch or lean back and be shielded by the

wall. It was next door to the Tamisa, New York Style Yoga dojo. I waited for my wife to appear, believing that if she found peace and ease and comfort here, surely she would show up.

I watched for expensive cars pulling up and for limos. I imagined that she might be driven by a driver who was instructed to deliver her to the front door of the yoga dojo and to pick her up immediately afterward. Or she might be casually accompanied by a "friend," who would report back to her father, the same way Pink Pumps or Iwa Ikeda did. Akemi had been stripped of her marriage, money, and mobility by a mogul who owned a mountain and only Allah knows what else.

Empty-handed after clocking arriving cars and all yoga student faces and waiting for an hour even after students stopped arriving, I left. I grabbed a taxi and said one word to the driver, "Arashiyama." I knew it was a long shot, but maybe not. I had no idea exactly where I was going or where I should look, yet I didn't like the idea of my wife strolling around, possibly alone in some public place, looking for peace and privacy and filled with heavy emotions.

The beautiful waterfall in Arashiyama reminded me of Akemi. As I stepped out of the taxi at the edge of a river, I understood why she would come here for peace. She was like the river, and ever since I'd met her, there had been water beneath my feet. The Arashiyama area was on the water, with wide, open spaces, nature, mountains, and sky. It was not crowded. In fact it seemed that as I arrived, many groups were leaving on tour buses. Surprisingly, they were not foreign visitors from America and Europe or Africa or Australia. They were Japanese people touring their own sights and land.

Seated at the side of the river, watching the waterfall, were local people, mothers and daughters and sons patiently playing, picnicking, and admiring. A few fathers were off strolling on the boardwalk. The mothers had the comfort of locals as their one- and two-years young wandered toward and close to the edge of the water playfully, unafraid as only people familiar with a place could be. I could see their small houses nestled at riverside. They were the kinds of houses that people blessed with awesome surroundings could be happy living in, because their real home was outdoors just like in my Southern Sudanese grandfather's village.

Some women wore *yukatas*, the summer version of the kimono.

The Japanese *yukata,* a summer kimono.

The colors were striking and the wide sleeves stylish and sensual. Their faces were natural though, which was pretty to me. There wasn't a trace of that white powder that I had seen smeared all over the faces in drawings of the traditional geisha. I thought that white geisha makeup and those drawn-on little red lips were the definition of ugly.

The sun was no longer at full power, yet it still spread light. I knew it would set a half an hour or more after the early sunset times in Tokyo, just by looking at its current position in the sky. I was cool with that. I had to race the sunset and get a look around.

I crossed over a small footbridge, which led to a series of craft shops. They were for tourists, I figured, so I kept going. I reached a small inlet where a man sat silently on a modest narrow boat. One or two pushes of his paddle and he would be thrust out into the body of the main river.

Soon I reached a wooded area, although I could still hear the water gushing and pushing and streaming. I was drawn to a series of stairs that seemed to create a path through and up into the woods, yet the stairs went on forever, as though when you reached the top, you could even touch a cloud. No one was around. I thought maybe my wife would go where no one else was going. I thought she might be in those woods with her easel and brushes and pencils and paints. So I went.

The wide cement stairs were not a straight walk up. Every twenty or so steps, the stairs would switch direction as though they were placed by someone with a wicked sense of humor. I climbed. Suddenly, the wide cement stairs narrowed and soon there were only stairs made of logs. Even though I was climbing high toward the sky, there were no protective barriers to keep a walker from falling down below. Soon the set of narrow wooden stairs turned to stairs made from mud and stones. As I advanced, I was still surrounded by beautiful trees of every color as though it were autumn, not spring. There was a breeze within the woods. As I peered between plants and branches and trees, I didn't see her or anyone else for that matter. There were directional signs, but they were all written in Japanese kanji. There were a few wooden stands lodged into the soil, pamphlet dispensers. I assumed that normally they would offer a map of this specific area for the lost, or translations for foreigners, but there were no more pamphlets left anywhere.

After climbing forty sets of stairs with twenty steps a set, on the eight-hundredth stair I reached the pavilion of a small mountain. As I looked around happy to see a clearing, there was no one up there except me, and about thirty medium-sized monkeys. Instantly I threw my hands up to guard my face, recalling how baboons would swing down suddenly and attack uninvited guests for play. But these weren't baboons and they didn't attack. In fact they glanced at me like, "What the fuck you looking at?" I smiled and withdrew my guard. They were tan long-haired monkeys with red faces and funny fingers. They had mouth pockets where they were obviously storing food for themselves and their little ones. As I checked out their details, I could distinguish the males from the females. The male ones had two long and sharp canine teeth. Some of the mothers lay flat on their backs with their little ones arranged on their bellies. Some were swinging, some picking insects out of the next one's coat, some eating, some just chilling and grabbing and pulling and playing with their groins. A group of them were dropping shit from their red-colored assholes like chestnuts. As I looked back, I could see now how there were monkeys in trees that I had already walked past. If this had been the ghetto, I would've gotten got! I just had not seen them camouflaged there, brown fur on brown branches. Still, I knew there was no excuse for my oversight. Although I felt slack for missing them, I respected them damn monkeys for being so easy that they could actually go undetected by the unpredictable predator, the human.

I walked toward the edge and looked down over Kyoto. It was amazing to see the town from the sky down, a kaleidoscope of treetops and hundreds of houses and rooftops, not situated on flat land but riddled through the hills and hidden in the valleys and surrounding the waters, all different shapes and sizes and colors. Amazed, I took a deep breath, then turned my face toward the bluing sky. *Akemi, where are you?*

It took me three-quarters less time to get down those steps than it did to climb up. I rushed across the same footbridge that brought me over and asked a vender, "Do you have a map of Arashiyama?" After answering my evening greeting, he answered one word, "Closed." Then he pulled out a worn map of Arashiyama from his own pocket. "You are here," he said in a way that let me know he didn't know many other English words to use. He circled the location where he and I were both standing, although it had been circled a few times already, and said, "Monkey Park."

I had to laugh at myself. I had been searching for my wife unknowingly in a monkey forest.

I made my prayer by the water at dusk. Before I closed my eyes, the sky was light gray. The sun was orange. The moon was white. When I opened my eyes, the sky was black. The sun had escaped. The moon was yellow.

* * *

Using my new phone card, I called Chiasa to check her. Instead of my on-point sentinel, my lucky charm, the one who had my wife's diary and all the information completed by now, I reached a recording.

"Ryoshi, wait for me. I'm coming. Meet me at the station at seven p.m. Don't eat without me!" she said in English, and then her voice mail began speaking in Japanese, I presumed for all other callers. I put the phone down. I should have known that Chiasa would follow me even though I told her to remain in Tokyo. I had thought about it, in fact. I had thought that the $300 roundtrip bullet train ticket, Tokyo to Kyoto, would separate her from her enthusiasm and determination. But it didn't.

As I moved toward the station at 7:15 p.m., already past her meet-up time, I speculated on what she had told her grandfather for him to allow her to travel here. Or if she had spoken with her own father on the phone before leaving Tokyo, and how much had she explained to him? Or had she kept every detail a secret, like I preferred her to do? Also, where would she sleep when I didn't even choose a place to stay for myself? And what was her reason for coming?

Black Birkenstocks, black cargo pants, and a tight black tee. She had her pretty silver eyes outlined in black eyeliner and something else on her was also switched, but I broke my stare.

On her back she carried a purple backpack stuffed with two weeks' worth of items, it seemed. Her sterling silver belt buckle was embossed with two clashing swords modeled after the patch I got from Yuka. She smiled as soon as she saw me. I smiled too.

"What's happening?" I asked her, my curiosity very elevated.

"Did you eat?" she asked.

"Not yet."

"Good, let's go," she said, bumping me with her elbow.

"Let me take that from you," I said, with my hand already on one of her backpack straps.

"Where's *your* backpack?" she asked.

"Here in a locker. I didn't get a room yet," I told her.

"We got a room. I have a lot to report to you," she said with serious excitement.

Everything moved ten times faster with Chiasa here. We picked up my backpack and jumped on the bus to what she said was the Kyoto downtown area. Rocking two backpacks, one on my back, the other in my hand, we pressed ourselves further into the packed bus.

The night breeze was warm, a rush of heated air massaging our faces. We walked among medium-sized continuous crowds on a main strip of shops of every imaginable kind. Some boasted 500,000 yen silk kimonos that could not have been more perfect unless designed by my Umma! There were stores exclusively selling wooden shoes of every style. There were restaurants of sushi and sashimi, yakitori and *taki yaki*, sake bars, teahouses, and even burger joints. Most canopies, awnings, and signs were written in kanji. I began to recognize and distinguish the food places by their flags, which for some reason they displayed right outside their restaurant doors.

A red flag with the crescent and the star appeared. I knew it was Turkish. We dipped down on some black-iron narrow stairs into a basement. Both of us needed a good meal. I knew we would find some spicy soups, hot bread, and well-seasoned meats on rice there. I ordered for us both.

"You know what I hate?" Chiasa asked, as she separated her bread into smaller slices. I just looked up from my water glass, acknowledging her.

"When somebody tries to stick their hand in something and change someone else's fate. You know, someone who tries to block natural things from happening. That's what Akemi's family is trying to do to you two. I'm on your side one hundred percent. I put my heart and my life on that." She dipped her bread into her spinach.

Her words kicked me in my chest and played again in my mind. *I put my heart and my life on that"* Chiasa had just said.

"You know, I used to like one boy named—"

"Don't tell me his name," I interrupted her.

"Oh, sorry. Well, I liked him—"

"Why?" I asked.

She smiled. "I was going to tell you. I liked him because he could fight better than the other boys in our dojo. So when I realized that I liked him, I told Yuka."

"Why did you tell her?" I asked.

"Because at the time we were best friends. Besides, we had both sworn to one another that we didn't like boys. We agreed that they were all stupid and slow. We promised one another we wouldn't act ridiculous over the boys the way *other* girls did. But then I began to feel something right here." She placed her hand over her left breast. "So I went to Yuka first and told her the truth and asked her, What did she think? She said it didn't matter as long as I didn't start acting dumb about the boy like the other girls do. So I was like cool."

Then Chiasa suddenly stopped telling her story. We ate in silence with only the sounds of our chewing and the fast-paced Turkish music playing in the background.

"So what did you do?" I asked her five minutes later.

"I was waiting to see if you cared. I don't want to bore you with my silly story, when I already know your story is so deep and true and important," she confessed. But there was no real reason for her to worry about boring me. Dinner is a time when I try to relax, especially my mind.

"What did you do about it?" I asked her again.

"I didn't do anything. Japanese girls wait for the guy to make the first gesture," she said.

"Oh yeah?" It didn't sound true to me. I pictured Akemi waiting for me on the side wall of my job in Chinatown, with her English-speaking cousin there to introduce us. I smiled at the memory.

"So did he make the first move?" I asked her, because it seemed like she wanted to tell me.

"Well, he chose me to be his sparring partner at one of the sessions. That was the first time he did that," she said proudly.

"Did you two fight?"

"Yes, I let him win. I could've beaten him."

I laughed, naturally. I was thinking, *How could she choose a guy because he was the best fighter in her dojo, but she could whip him?* It meant she could defeat all the boys in her dojo. None of it was a good look for young samurais. But I didn't say shit.

"Seriously, I could have," she pushed.

"If he liked you, he wouldn't have fought you," I told her. Then I thought about what I had just said.

"Japanese boys will fight girls. We spar one another often. They hit hard too. They're not the same as you," she added swiftly.

"So after he beat you, what happened?" I followed up.

"Well, in our dojo, if you lose a fight, you have mop duty. So I had to stay after everyone else except the sensei had gone, and mop the whole floor. I was on my knees drying it with a special cloth when he came back alone and actually helped me. We dried the floor together. I was so excited. Afterward, he gave me a ride on his bicycle, to my grandfather's house. I didn't invite him to come inside because my grandfather wasn't home. But I was still happy that at least he knew where I lived and it was so close to our dojo." She paused like she was seeing it all in her mind.

"On White Day, all the girls were secretly giving guys who they liked chocolates," she began again.

"White Day?" I asked.

"Yeah, it's like the American Valentine's Day, but here in Japan the girls give chocolates to the guys," she explained. I thought it sounded crazy, girls giving men sweets instead of the other way around.

"I didn't, though. I thought it was corny, all the girls giving the same thing. So I made a gift for him instead and left it in his sneaker." She paused. I just looked at her and waited. "It was a slingshot," she said. I smiled. I thought it was a dope gift.

"I left a note with it saying, 'After class, I can show you how to shoot it. Let me know if you want to.'"

The waiter arrived with our tea. He placed the small hot cups on the table. Chiasa held the tiny cup with both hands. Her nails were clipped and clean, without polish. "I waited for him on the steps after dojo. He walked right out with his friends. I thought he didn't see me. But then he looked back. We just stared at each other for some seconds. He kept going with his friends. I was disappointed. As I walked home, I heard someone behind me. I turned and it was him. He had the slingshot in his hand and was smiling at me. So I walked toward him to show him how to shoot it. He said he already knew how." Chiasa laughed as though she was laughing at him.

"I bet he didn't" was all I said.

"You're right! He was setting up targets and snatching up rocks. He would shoot and miss. I tried not to laugh, but I did laugh just a little. So he challenged me. He said that I couldn't do it any better. Well, that was it! I forgot that I liked him. You know Aunt Tasha says if you don't play dumb and let boys win at everything, they won't like you. But I wasn't thinking about that. I was just thinking about the challenge. So I told him if he didn't believe that I was better than him at it, he should run and I would shoot him and I wouldn't miss. Well, he ran. I let him get far away. I took aim and the rock sped through the air like crazy and caught him on his calf and he fell!" She laughed. "I ran over to help him. He didn't want any help. Just like Aunt Tasha taught me, he was angry. So he hopped home," Chiasa said softly, before looking up at me to check my reaction. I just started cracking up, a rare good laugh at the punk she had chosen. So she began laughing also.

"I put a note in his sneaker like three days later. "Sorry about the bruise. If you don't like me anymore, you can give me back the White Day gift and I will understand."

"What happened?" I followed up.

"Waiting for a Japanese guy is like waiting for spring to come again during the summer season. So I asked Yuka what I should say to him or do. Yuka said, 'Let's plan a *gokan* party,'" Chiasa explained.

" '*Gokan*,' I repeated. Does that have anything to do with the Japanese chess game?" I asked, thinking that couldn't be a real way to hook up.

"No, not the chess game. A *gokan* party or a *go* party is when Japanese girls and guys all meet in a restaurant or place together. And everybody talks and laughs and shares eats and drinks. You know like to take the pressure off of the real couples from being alone face to face with one another."

It sounded strange to me. Were the two people who liked each other afraid to be alone in the same public place? I could understand if they were trying to avoid being alone in a private place. Maybe they had some rule like the Muslims and wouldn't have sex before marriage, therefore they didn't trust themselves to be alone in a private space. Chiasa must have realized my confusion just by looking at my expression.

"It is very difficult for Japanese people to express their true feelings to one another. There is a shyness that is shared and expected. For a Japanese girl to just come out and boldly say to a guy what she is feeling or wanting or thinking would be taken the wrong way," she said as I listened intently.

"So every five minutes—*go* means 'five' in Japan—we just switch partners and talk and get to know the next person a bit more. The idea is that after the *go* party is over, every girl tells her best friend who she really likes, and the guys tell their male friends. Then the best friend makes the call so the two who really like one another can meet up." She was finished.

"Meet up alone?" I asked.

"Not necessarily. But maybe this time it's less of a group than before, but the girl and the guy who really like each other are definitely there and the other friends are trying to help them to get together."

"Okay" was all I said.

"Well, Yuka set up the *gokan* party. When I got there, there was only Yuka, me, and him, and that's not how a *go* party is supposed to be. Then Yuka said to him "Chiasa likes you a lot." I felt embarrassed. But truthfully, I was excited too and grateful to Yuka for saying what I had never clearly said to him. Then Yuka said, 'I told Chiasa that you and I are dating already, but she insists that you should tell her that personally.'" Chiasa frowned and leaned back, her chopsticks loosely held in her fingers.

"What did the fool say?" I asked Chiasa, referring to the guy that they both liked.

"He didn't even look at me. He turned the other way and said, 'Yuka-san is right. Yuka is my girlfriend.' So I just drank the glass of water that was in front of me and I left," Chiasa said. "Later Yuka and all her friends, who just the day before had all been my friends too, gathered around me and watched while Yuka announced, 'Chiasa is *konketsuji*.' They all laughed. Then Yuka shouted, '*Hafu*, don't you know that Japanese boys will always choose a Japanese girl?'"

"Did you fight her?" I asked.

"No. Yuka and I had promised one another that we would never fight over boys. So I just walked away. I always keep my promises," she said solemnly.

I didn't know what *konketsuji* or *hafu* meant, yet Chiasa's pronunciation of the words and her tone and expression of disgust made the insult in them clear.

" 'Half a person.' That's what *hafu* means, and *konketsuji* means, 'child of unlike things put together.' For me, Yuka was saying that the part of me that is Japanese from my mother is human. The part of me that is from my African-American father is not."

Moments later Chiasa said, "I realized I never loved that boy anyway. I just liked him and was a bit impressed. But I did love Yuka. Anytime I thought about what happened with her, I would be shocked all over again. I cried. My whole body would hurt. It was difficult for me to accept that anyone could be so close to me, talking and laughing with me, sometimes sleeping over and us going out together, then could really have felt hatred for me all along. After a long time I realized that Yuka did not even like the boy at all. She just didn't want me to like him. She was my best friend and didn't even want me to be happy."

"That boy wasn't your fate," I assured her. "If he was, he would have been with you, even now, *still*. He was a coward. It sounds like he allowed Yuka to control him, instead of being true to himself as a man."

I paid for our meal, thanked the waiter, and tipped him. Chiasa opened the billfold, subtracted the tip, and laid it on my side of the table.

"Japan is a no-tip country," she said. "Even in a Turkish restaurant, Japanese laws are the same."

*   *   *

The completely booked Hyatt Hotel welcomed Chiasa and me as she checked in. We were escorted to her reserved room. I carried our belongings. She opened the door. There were two well-dressed beds with crisp white goose-down quilts and a wide window that led to a lighted garden. The lamps were shaded with rice paper and the drawings on the wall were beautiful displays of kanji as Asian art. The curtains were made of white linen. The floors were made of tatami. The bathroom was two steps up and enclosed by thick glass. The faucet and sink and toilet and shower stall were all glistening clean. The air smelled like a very subtle perfume, a clean scent but not antiseptic.

I wanted and needed to hear the important information that led Chiasa to travel all the way down here to help me locate my wife. But I already knew that right after I heard it and discussed it, I would be up and out of her hotel room for my own sake, for Chiasa's sake, and to keep true.

Chiasa opened her backpack and pulled out a stack of books tied in size order. "These are the books written by Shiori Naka-mura," she said. "While I was in the bookstore, I read one of her poems. So powerful!" Then she pointed out that each book had been wrapped in a beautiful evergreen book cover, with a gold seal that read "Kinokuniya," the name of the store.

"Thank you," I said, moving the stack over to my right and pulling out my pocketknife to cut the string. Just as I picked up one of the books, Chiasa said, "They are all written in Japanese and unavailable in English. I checked."

"What about the author Seth Arrington, did you check him out?" I asked her.

"Looking him up almost made me miss my train. I checked on the shelves first before asking customer service in the Japanese section on the first floor. They could not find anything or even pull up his name as an author. I thought maybe you or I had the name wrong. Then I went upstairs to the seventh floor, the English section. I checked the shelves again and nothing! When I went to the English customer service desk, they actually found his name and told me that the author had only written one book and that the one book he wrote, *Never Surrender*, was out of print and unavailable in Japan. She said that author had a really short career."

"Out of print?" I repeated.

"She said that means that the book company is not printing any more copies of it. You would have to go to a used book store or something and see if you could find it," she advised. "Oh, and the lady was like, 'What do you need this book for? Is it a school assignment? Is it for you or someone else?' Can you believe her?" Chiasa stared into me for answers.

"Was she Japanese?" I asked.

"Of course, everyone at the English section is Japanese! It's just called the English section because you can buy books written in English on that floor, and all of the other floors are books written strictly in Japanese.

"Oh and about Akemi's diary."

"I have completed the list for you," Chiasa said, and handed it to me. "In most cases, Akemi wrote about her friends and family, but she didn't list their addresses or even refer to their location. It's a diary, like a daily account of what was happening in her life from right before she left Japan to go and study in New York up until her art show in Manhattan. I believe she probably has a bunch of diaries stashed somewhere else that leads up to this one here." She held up the diary.

"It's not an address book. So I had to read carefully a couple of times and figure out who was who from where. Then I went to the library, right after you caught the train earlier today, and got the directory for Kyoto from the reference desk. I looked up each name that she mentioned in her writing, in the Tokyo directory and then in the Kyoto directory. I know you only wanted the names and addresses and phone numbers of the people Akemi mentioned in her diary as well as the names of the places she went to often in Kyoto. But I think you *should listen* to what her relationship is to certain people. She writes about all of them, and that will make it faster for us to locate her," Chiasa said sincerely, and she had my full attention.

"For example, she writes very affectionately about a woman named Mayu. I put her name on your list. Well later on in her diary when Akemi and her father had a conflict, Mayu took Akemi's side, although she pretended to support Mr. Nakamura because he is her employer. Anyway, at one point in the diary I found Mayu's last name—it's Morita. Then I looked up Mayu Morita's phone number and her address here in Kyoto. Now, Mayu works at Akemi's home seven days a week from seven a.m. until seven p.m. as the house manager. Since I now know Mayu-san's home address, I can go there at say five a.m. and follow her to work. I'll end up at Akemi's house, simple!" Chiasa's stare was intense and she waited for my reply to her detailed detective work.

I smiled and said, "Sounds good, but you could've just given me Mayu's address over the telephone and let me check it out."

"I could have, but you couldn't follow Mayu-san at five in the morning and go unnoticed. Mr. Nakamura and his men are already on the lookout for anyone fitting your description. 'Young, African, male.' Probably Mr. Nakamura has no idea that you are even here in Kyoto. We should keep it that way," she argued. It didn't take too many seconds for me to see her strategy emerging.

Chiasa was right. I was already imagining that the Kyoto home would be different from the Roppongi house, where security was lax. I expected this location to be Nakamura's estate, an expensive spread, completely secured and alarmed.

Chiasa opened Akemi's diary to further express her point of view. "From the way Akemi tells her story in her diary, she has got about four different sets of friends. She doesn't mix them together because she said each set has their own mind and ideas and none of them want to be any different than they already are."

"Are those her words?" I asked Chiasa.

"Exactly," she answered. "So powerful, right? You know, near the end of her diary, on the corner of one page, she had scribbled,

> *They were flesh without nerves, veins without blood,*
> *bodies without heart, these Japanese men.*

* * *

"It made my body shake, her words, so true," Chiasa said. I didn't say nothing, so Chiasa continued reporting.

"There is one girl that Akemi is really extremely close with. She isn't part of any of the four sets, and when Akemi spends time with her, it's usually just the two of them. This girl is from Nepal. She's two years older than Akemi and she attends Kyoto Seika University. I put her name on your list also. It's Josna, but Akemi calls her Jo. If everything else fails, based on the story Akemi writes about her life, if you find Jo, she'll lead you directly to Akemi. This girl named Josna knows all Akemi's secrets."

"Secrets," I repeated, but not for an explanation or response. I had catalogued the two names in my mind permanently, Mayu Morita and Josna, aka Jo.

"Any last name for Josna?" I asked, while searching the list in my hand.

"No, sorry. She didn't write it."

"What about this person named Himawari?" I asked, noticing that she was the third person listed after Mayu and Josna.

"She's Japanese and Akemi's friend. They have some kind of girls-only club that meets at a location nearby their high school, but there's no exact address. From the way Akemi describes it I don't know if it's a house or apartment or what. Akemi mentioned Himawari six or seven times, and the rest of the girls only briefly.

Now, if we divide up the lists, we should definitely be able to locate Akemi tomorrow," Chiasa said confidently. "I'll follow Mayu in the early morning. That might be it. But if not, I'll check the first three places and you can check the last three places," she said taking charge during the silence of my thoughts.

"*Inshallah*," I said, still trapped in my thoughts and measuring out my next moves.

"What?" Chiasa asked.

"What?" I responded.

"*Insha* what?" she asked.

"It means 'God willing.' If Allah wants us to be successful, we will be," I explained.

"First you said God, then you said Allah. Which one is it?" Chiasa asked.

"Allah is God. *Allah* is Arabic for God in English," I explained. "Sometimes English-speaking people get tight or scared or crazy when they hear Muslims say *Allah*."

"Allah or God, hmm? The two words sound so different from one another," Chiasa said. "*Allah* sounds softer and nicer," she continued. "I'll say *Allah* because it sounds better to me." She turned away from me, then turned around and looked back. "And you're right. My aunt Tasha would probably faint if she heard me say *'Allah'*! She goes to church every Sunday, and when I visit her in New York, I have to go too." Chiasa smiled.

"There's only one God. So Aunt Tasha could chill," I told her. Then I got up to leave.

"Are you leaving?" Chiasa asked.

"I have to," I said.

"There are two beds," Chiasa pointed out.

"Yeah, two beds and one room," I told her.

"They have breakfast downstairs beginning at sunrise. We are on the same block as Akemi's high school. I checked it all out on the map. This is a strategic location," she said.

"I'll meet you downstairs for breakfast at five a.m.," I responded. "Then we'll head out. I'll take the high school and the first three places on the list. You take Mayu's house and the last three places on the list. Let's meet back here afterward and compare notes. Hopefully Akemi will be with me when I get back here." I meant it.

"Here, you need to show this key at breakfast." Chiasa handed it to me.

"Do you have one for yourself?" I asked.

"Hai!" She smiled.

I left. I had seen the small Holy Quran in Chiasa's backpack pocket. I'm sure she had just bought it from the bookstore today. I liked that she didn't pull it out and show it to me, like it was some kind of prop to win points. I believed that she bought it out of a real curiosity and with a true intention.

Outside the Hyatt, as I descended the hill, the thought dropped into my mind: *I know now what Chiasa switched.* She had straightened out her hair. It appeared much thinner and longer now. It gave her a different look. Her new look was nice. Her old look was very nice too.

*   *   *

After breakfast in the Hyatt dining area, a light meal and eight glasses of water (I wouldn't let her drink any fruit juice. "The natural sugar will just make you more thirsty and hungry," I explained to her.) Chiasa left and moved into action.

I used my hotel key to access her room alone. Stripped down to my boxers and T-shirt, which I still wore from the night before, I unpacked my clippers from their heavy packaging. The bathroom mirror, which was divided into thirds, was perfect. I pulled up the left and right sides of the mirror so I could see the sides and back of my own head. I mapped out my plan in my mind. I switched the clippers on. When I heard them buzzing, I got busy, slowly. Without anyone or anything to disturb me, and the Do Not Disturb sign on the door, my hands were steady for my first real attempt at barbering my own head.

When I felt good about the job I had done and had checked my head out thoroughly, I switched them off and used the edger to make my cut look professional. I eased out of my T-shirt with the coils of hair clinging everywhere. I balled it up and tossed it in the miniature garbage can. I checked out my shoulder. Ever since Akemi licked my wound, it had healed and disappeared. It was easy for me to believe that her saliva was salve, maybe because I wanted to. Thinking about her got me distracted. When I refocused, it sped me up. I wanted to get to the schoolyard before the students arrived so I could search each one as they climbed up, my eyes looking for only *my wife*.

After a high-powered, soothing shower, I cracked open a new pair of Fruit of the Looms, a new pair of kicks, some blue Girbaud cargos, and a deep-blue Polo shirt. I changed my mind and put all that shit away and chose something better, also all fresh and crispy. I picked up my mess and then reached for my camera to use as a prop. Within seconds I realized that Chiasa had already taken it. In fact, it seemed like it had been hers since I first arrived in Tokyo. My binoculars would have to do. I dropped them around my neck and checked to make sure I had my shades. I turned off the digital Do Not Disturb sign and turned on the Make Up the Room sign.

In the hotel lobby I grabbed a free newspaper, folded it over, and wore it in my back pocket.

Outside the parade of felines was about to jump off. I hurried up the three or four hills and posted at the top. On purpose, I behaved like a tourist. Through my binoculars I scanned faces, focusing on this one and that one and refocusing on all the rest. After a while I flipped my aim down toward arriving shoes. It might sound crazy, but it would be faster and easier to identify her by her footwear. However, I kept coming up with penny loafers, mediocre pumps, flat and high-heeled sandals, as well as Converses and New Balances. My wife wasn't in the mix. Soon the gates of the high school were drawn open to allow the students to enter. I posted on the side of the wall and watched the females who were streaming in from the Princess Line buses. An hour later, when the guards closed the iron gates, I moved. I walked around the perimeter of the high school toward the sides and the back, where I had not gone before. There were sports fields of every kind behind the black iron fence of spears. On the back side there was a basketball court. On my left, there was another full basketball court. This one was not locked behind an iron fence. It was wide open. So in my mind, it had to be part of the Kyoto Women's

College, where everything was unlocked and accessible and females flowed in and out. I stood still, thinking.

It was hard to believe how expertly the Japanese mind their business. In Brooklyn I spent many hours considering how to move around uninterrupted by unwelcome assholes who jocked and harassed. Here it was the opposite. Each person is ignored so well, it's bordering on insult. As I searched for my wife in the early morning sun that had just begun its slow boil, no one greeted me. No cop asked me, "What are you doing around here?" No teacher or professor said, "May I help you?" No student questioned, "Are you looking for someone here at the all-girls school?" No one offered to give me directions or show me around. I didn't run up on anyone African, American, Latino, Indian, or even European. They were uniformly Japanese.

As I descended the hills, when I entered any of the small places of business, no one trembled or jerked. No attendant followed me up and down the isles. It was as though I was free and safe and invisible. It felt extremely peculiar to me.

I began thinking, how could I break the ice and get even one of these Japanese worker dudes to loosen up and look me in the eye and start spilling his guts so I could collect some clues, figure how they run shit out here in Kyoto? Even though I was a foreigner to them and they were all foreigners to me, I figured there had to be something common among men, besides women—a more neutral thing that could get the conversation started and keep the tempers of men from flaring. A plan was formulating in my mind.

At noon I returned to the schoolyard right between the high school and the college in my sweats and my Brooklyn T-shirt with a basketball in hand. I walked up on the guys who posted up on the rocks during their lunch break. I pushed my ball into one of them, right in his chest, and said, "*Konichiwa*, play ball!" He looked startled at first. Then a smile came through. He turned to his friends, who were slow to pick up. I walked away and he began to follow me. They began to follow him. I didn't look back, but I knew they were still behind me because two of the five of them were smoking.

On the court I went right to it, getting the feel of the court and the nonregulation basket. Intentionally, I showed them my skills. They stood on the sideline watching like girls. I walked up to the original one and pushed the ball to him. Then I picked two of his

guys for my team, and gestured two of his guys to go to his side. I
flagged the extra kid who was smoking a next cigarette, letting him
know to move off the court and out the way. Using all hand motions,
I checked the ball and we began to play. We were off to a slow start.
Once the adrenaline started pumping, they would become more comfortable and the pace would pick up.

In three minutes a couple of females got drawn to us and stood
watching. The guy I had tapped originally got pumped up at their arrival. Two minutes later he was out of his shirt. I went easy on them,
letting them showcase their rudimentary performance. They played
ball like they were keeping count of each step and move they made. It
seemed like someone had taught them specific plays and moves and
they thought they needed to stick to them like dance steps.

More girls collected. They weren't rowdy though. They whispered to each other and watched with intense gazes. Two girls sat
and opened their bento boxes and ate with their wooden chopsticks.
Twenty minutes in, one of the players on the other team threw up the
time-out signal and ran to the side, lifting the water bottle out of a
girl's hand and drinking some. Now I knew that he knew her, good.

By the time game one finished, there were twelve girls gathered
around the six of us men and the seventh one seated on the sideline
chain-smoking. I threw up two fingers so we could run the second
game. A player from the other side threw up the X symbol, so I knew
he had to leave. I motioned to the smoker, and he jumped up and
replaced him. Six dudes in a circle organizing a game, but now the
girls had formed a circle outside our circle like they were part of it.
The original Japanese guy I chose to get the game started said to me
in English, "name?"

I answered, "Mayonaka." A girl from the outside circle repeated,
"Mayonaka?" It was in the form of a question.

"*Hai,* Mayonaka!" I said confidently. I asked her, "*Namae?*" The
two circles became one as they all gasped at my use of one short
Japanese sentence.

"Reiko," she answered, telling me her name. That set it off, and
each person in our male/female circle announced their name. As I
watched them become a bit more easy with each other, I'm thinking,
That's right, I got my own gokan *party going on.* The Japanese dudes
seemed grateful. I figured they might have sat on those rocks reading

Manga and checking out comic-strip chicks with abnormally large tits and smoking for years without getting up the heart to approach one of these females before she graduated! In fifteen minutes that had all changed.

"Brooklyn?" One girl mispronounced it as she read my T-shirt in the form of a question.

"New York," I responded, knowing that they would be more familiar.

"New York!" three of the girls gasped. One clapped and said, "I like New York." They all giggled. Then the original Japanese guy, who I now knew was named Udo, pointed to my kicks. "I like," he said.

"Yeah," I acknowledged, not used to any male talking about how he liked something I was wearing.

"Michael Jordan?" Udo added.

"*Hai*, you know it," I said. He was admiring my Nikes, Jordan's black 1s. I understood. These joints were famous. Young Michael Jordan had come into the league last year and switched up the game with the all-black sneaker. The league was charging him a five-thousand-dollars violation fee per night just to rock these joints, and he was rocking 'em anyway. That's why I called these my 5,000s.

Udo was now placing his foot beside my foot and saying "big," referring to mine. I didn't correct him. His feet were tiny, but why point it out? I was wearing an American size 10 men's, not big for my six-foot-one height. I stepped back and bounced the ball to get the second game started. The girls dropped back into the background.

My team won the second game also. It was easy, since all six of the Japanese guys were basically watching me hoop. When we finished, I gave Udo the extra Brooklyn T-Shirt I had stuck in the fence for bargaining. I gave Yoshi my fitted and asked him to call the girl who gave him the water over here. When he came back with her, I asked her, "*Himawari-san wa doko ni imasuka?*" which means "Where is Himawari?" Yoshi and the girl both looked at one another first. Then the girl repeated, "*Himawari-san?*"

"*Hai!*" I confirmed. "*Tomodachi*," I said, meaning friend.

"*Wakarimashta*," she said meaning that she understood. Yoshi, the guy, and Reiko, the girl, began speaking Japanese to one another, for what seemed like a long time. Yoshi then turned to me and said, "*San ji ni*," which means at three o'clock.

"Doko ni?" I asked, meaning "Where?" He flagged me to follow. We all walked back to the rocks that divided the high school from the college.

"Koko ni," Yoshi said, meaning "Right here."

"Arigato gozaimasu!" I said coolly. Inside I was excited. After the girls left, I walked down the hill with Yoshi and Udo. Udo worked at a nearby noodle shop. Surprisingly, Yoshi worked at the laundry station on the back lot of the Hyatt Hotel! Both of them asked before going back into their work, *"Ashita?"* They wanted to play ball tomorrow. All I could say was "Maybe."

I didn't know if "maybe" was one of the few English words that they would understand or not.

I stepped inside the Hyatt lobby to cool down. I was thirsty. My non-Ramadan behavior was delivering my punishment rapidly. But I would not break.

After chilling in the plush seating in the lobby and lowering my body temperature, I checked for Chiasa. Her hotel room was cleaned now and as good as new. On hotel stationery on her desk she'd left a note, "Ryoshi, I have all the info. I'll meet you back here at sunset, wait for me. We'll eat and drink together, okay?"

On the top of my list of places where my wife might be wandering was the Bamboo Forest. It was back in Arashiyama. I didn't think I could get over there and through the forest in time to get back to the three-o'clock meet-up with Himawari. So I shifted my strategy and bet on my three-o'clock appointment instead. Besides, I knew that word was traveling now that I was on campus. I needed that to happen to counteract the girl with the pink pumps or Iwa Ikeda, telling my wife that I flew home to New York defeated, so that she could help Akemi to "forget" me. My objective was to let enough students notice me so that if my wife was actually here in Kyoto, it would be impossible for her not to catch word. Further, after thinking about it real hard, I had decided that even though the Japanese wore a game face of uninvolved, unemotional disinterest, they had to be like most human beings, both nosy and curious.

I showered and cleaned up again to cool down some more. After the Asr prayer, I left. I was out of wearing all black for now. Chilling in Calvin Klein, the white linen fabrics were repelling the sun, instead of swallowing it the way my black clothes did. My white-on-white kicks were moving me smoothly uphill.

I felt only a piece of regret about dropping Himawari's name at the basketball game when I did not actually know her. The fact was I would never drop my wife's name out there in a mixed crowd of males and females in public. I knew that wasn't cool and I knew that there was a chance that Himawari might not show up because of the curiosity or damage it might create around her reputation as a young woman. I had already prepared myself for the possibility that at three o'clock I might end up standing by myself.

Chapter 10

FELINES, FRIENDS, AND WOLVES

As I waited, standing up straight, not wanting to lean against the rocks and fuck up my wears, I saw a real pretty female climbing up the hill with musical grace and rhythm. Her hips swung left, then right, her legs crossed one over the other. Her shoulders were high and and arched back for leverage. Her full and firm breasts bounced up and down, very slightly but impossible for any man in range not to notice. Through my binoculars, her pretty beige skin was shining as though it had a coat of olive oil over it. Her skin tone was even, light brown all over, unlike a white-skinned woman with a suntan, which sometimes causes blotches of brown but not everywhere. My high-powered lens took me between those two tight titties and in there was brown too. Her thighs were well oiled and glistening exquisitely, yet it was her 500,000 yen alligator sandals with the shapely carved short heel and alligator straps that crisscrossed her pretty toes and wrapped around her slim ankles and wound up around her toned calves and all the way up above her knees and tied on the sides of each thigh that killed me. My jaw dropped. Even my binoculars fogged up. I knew it wasn't Himawari, who I knew was Japanese. Then I realized that my binoculars fogged because she had arrived and was too close to me to be caught and focused in my lenses.

"She said you would look. 'It's impossible for him not to look,'" the beige girl said, spoken in perfect English with a soft and peaceful manner.

"Who said?" I asked her, trying to control my eyes from traveling off on their own.

"Your wife."

Off guard, I paused. Then my smile came through naturally. "Josna?" I asked.

"Ha!" she said.

"You mean *hai*?" I asked.

"In Hindi 'yes' is *ha*. Japanese 'yes' is *hai*. I'll just say 'yes' in English, okay?" She settled and smiled. A point-two diamond was set in her gums. It appeared sparkling, right between two of her pretty, perfectly white teeth. When the sun angled on the diamond, my eyes cast down from the light it tossed. That's when I saw her diamond belly ring set in her navel so sweetly, it seemed she might have been born with it. She wore a tight turquoise half tee and a turquoise mini-skirt made of soft, paper-thin cotton. The loose-fitting thin cloth was decorated with miniature gold-colored bells hanging all around the hem. I was 100 percent guilty in the glare of the Ramadan sun of admiring such a beautiful girl.

"These are Akemi's sandals," Josna admitted. It made sense now. That's why her clothing could not compare to the extravagance of her footwear.

"She made me wear them for you, although I didn't mind at all." Again, she smiled, revealing unflawed, brilliantly white teeth. "You want to meet Akemi, yes?" she asked me.

"Definitely" was all I said.

"She will meet us at my studio. So you should come, if you please." She turned and was more than confident that I would follow her. As her hips swung, the bells jingled and there was nothing I could do to keep myself from being turned on. She rocked a short, short haircut, the bare minimum. Her hair was an artistic design of jet-black swirls, shorter even than finger waves, but glistening and mesmerizing, a style only taken on by a female who is a thousand percent certain of the complete elegance and design of her face. I had to laugh at myself struggling to remain focused. Allah was not only above comprehension, but Allah also had a dimension of humor, I felt. As I eased up to walk beside her, I could see that instead of earrings she wore beautiful printed Hindi letters around the perimeter of her ears. Even around her wrist were drawn-on jewelries consisting of Sanskrit designs. I wanted to know what it all said and meant. I had no idea. Oddly, she smelled like saffron, a precious and expensive seasoning Umma used and I tasted and enjoyed.

Turquoise toes with a thin gold line on each nail. She was a motherfucking work of art. A woman so beautiful, a man loses his religion and thoughts and there's nothing left but curses on his tied tongue. Perhaps she was one of my wife's unique drawings, come to life. When we reached the last hill remaining to descend before reaching the bus stop, and three blocks before reaching the first train station in walking distance, Josna's musical hips stopped moving, breasts stopped vibrating. Her bells came to a slow jingle and then ceased.

Seated before her was a wolf on a leash. Its wild eyes flashed a serious warning. It didn't belong on a leash, I thought to myself. Yet the leash lowered and then canceled out the threat. As I looked up at the girl walking the wolf, I saw that her eyes were the same as the wolf's, wild, dangerous, filled with energy, and completely unpredictable. She was backed up by three girls, who seemed invisible standing behind the ice princess with the peculiar pet. The princess didn't move out of Josna's way or crack a smile. She looked me over thoroughly from head to foot first and then from foot to head. She was surely pretty, but she was exuding coldness and Josna was an exquisite pure blue flame. I could have snapped out of my trance, the one Josna had cast over me, and moved the cold princess out of her way, but for some unknown reason, the ice princess was wearing my Umma's two gold bangles, one of four bangles, two gold, two diamond, that I had gifted to my wife on our marriage day.

"Himawari?" I said suddenly, having put the pieces together. Her eyes turned away from Josna and onto me again.

"Hai?" she answered, and with the sound of her voice, her wolf stood up on all fours from his previous seated position.

"She doesn't speak English," Josna said, in a tone which let me know that these two already knew each other and also suggested that Josna felt that she was superior to Himawari. I ignored the bad energy between them since I was the one who had invited Himarawi to meet with me. I checked my Datejust and saw it was now 2:55 p.m. Uninterrupted, Himarawi would have arrived right on time.

"*Konichiwa,*" I greeted Himawari. "*Boku wa Mayonaka des.*"

"*Watashi wa Himawari des,*" she responded. The three with her bowed to me but she did not. Josna intervened in Japanese, fluent, rapid-fire—soft but powerful Japanese spoken with passion and emphasis. Himawari's glare at Josna was filled with a definite expertly controlled anger, but she removed the two bangles and handed them to me. She extended her hand toward me. Her nails were unusually long, five inches, and lovely and colorful and curved. I reached out my hand. She flipped my palm. Her wolf growled. She spoke softly in Japanese to the wolf as though he was a close and beloved friend. He stopped growling and sat still. She reached out with her other hand, and without her saying anything, one of the invisible girls handed her a pen. She wrote down her telephone number on the inside of my palm, or at least that's what I believed it was. She did print the numbers in English with no extra words or kanji.

"*Arigato gozaimasu,*" I said to her. "Thank you for coming," I added in English. Maybe one of the invisible girls would translate my few words. Then I turned my attention toward Josna. Her little bells had begun jingling again. "*Ja mata,*" I said to Himawari, and turned to follow Josna's bells. After all, she was the one giving me what I wanted, my wife.

We rode the train in silence, like all the other passengers. I wrote Himawari's phone number down in my notebook.

I found myself asking myself stupid questions, like, *How come Josna has no polish on her fingernails?* Then I answered myself, *Because like my wife, she is an artist who works with her hands.* Staring at her sideways, I thought to myself she was prettier than a peacock or a cobra or a lynx. Although if she were a wild cat, she would definitely be an exotic cheetah. As I mulled it over in my mind, my thoughts changed directions, separating the beauty of Josna from the feeling of Josna. She had the feeling of a mongoose, the swift and beautiful snake killer. Unlike Iwa Ikeda the hyena, or even Himawari the wolf, who was better than Iwa yet just as unpredictable, Josna felt like a true friend to Akemi. Furthermore, how clever was Akemi to send them both there to meet me at virtually the same time, both wearing items that would reassure me that their messages had come from her. If one failed, the other surely would not. I wondered how Akemi knew I had arrived in Kyoto. I doubted that it was the basketball plan.

Could Akemi have organized both of her friends that quickly? And
why hadn't she appeared in person to meet me instead?

* * *

"Akemi should be here, um . . . soon," Josna said, as we approached an
odd-shaped house. The front of it was like an igloo I had once seen in
a *National Geographic* magazine. Instead of blocks of ice, it was made
from blocks of cement and was semi-oval with no windows.

The middle of the house was one story higher than the semi-igloo
and rectangular with a chimney on top. The rear of the house was only
one story high, just like the igloo portion, but was triangular like a directional arrow. Both the left and right side of the triangle had beautiful stained-glass windows. The architecture of the three different yet
simple shapes each connected to the other was unlike anything I had
ever seen anywhere.

Now both Josna's door keys and skirt bells were jingling as she
pushed the key in and then pressed her body against the metal door.

"Please come in, it's okay," Josna said, sliding her door open. I
looked around outside, thinking only that this was not the type of
block I thought girls or women should be traveling down alone.
On the left side there were only woods. On the right side there was
one six-story factory, the first three floors of windows clouded so
no one could see in. Next to the factory was what appeared to be a
huge warehouse surrounded by a large parking lot. And then there
was this odd-shaped templelike place where Josna lived. Forty feet
down from Josna's place was a row of six one-story wooden houses
that looked more like they were for play or for pets than for families
or full-grown adults. I'd have to bend over or squat low to enter into
any of those front doors. Once I entered, their size would've prevented me from standing up straight.

"I'll wait out here for Akemi," I said solemnly. But when I looked
back toward her door, she was gone.

"Akemi left these for you." She reappeared holding a pair of black
and gold embroidered men's house shoes. By now I was accustomed
to removing my shoes, a habit that I had previously fallen out of while
living in New York, when entering friends' or customers' houses or
anyone's apartment beside my own.

I removed my shoes and put on the ones Akemi left for me, I entered the igloo and surprisingly had to take five steps down into her sunken home. The inside curved walls of her igloo were covered with colorful, expertly cut and placed and decorated ceramic tiles. There was a dull lime light on the ceiling that cast a glow on two indentations in the wall where small potted plants in ceramic flowerpots posed. I felt like a leopard, trapped in a small but exquisite, exotic cave. The stairs that led down to the igloo were made of expensive, high-quality marble.

As soon as I entered the rectangular portion of the house, the marble floors gave way to floors of simple gray cement. The climate of spring warmth outside switched to complete coolness inside the rectangle, which appeared to be a wide-open gallery. Instead of a living room with a soft feeling and comfortable furniture, there was a workshop with a huge metal tabletop work station. On the table were three fifty-pound mounds of earth-colored clay loosely wrapped in a thick, soiled plastic. Besides the mounds of clay there were soiled tools made from metal and wood, as well as a two-foot-long sturdy piece of wire cable. Off to the side and behind the work station was an incomplete, moist clay, loosely wrapped sculpture of a female. On the side wall were shelves sectioned into cubes. Every other cube held a pot or vase of various designs. The cubes between were shelves of oversized books on art, art history, culture, and religion.

Josna excused herself and then tiptoed into the triangle situated at the back of the house behind a dark purple velvet curtain.

I stood motionless, yet my eyes were surveying all the handmade creations with wonder. The curious layout of this place, where unlike things were all merged together, was bizarre but exciting.

When the girl that my wife called Jo returned, she was not jingling anymore. She had switched into blue denim shorts with the threads shredded around each of her thighs. Both breasts, full like mangoes, pressed against a tight blue tee that was cut above her diamond belly ring, oh Allah. Honestly, I wanted to tell her to go back and put on some proper clothes. But I was standing inside her place and was more grateful toward her than anything else.

She handed me a nicely cut, sturdy cloth shopping bag marked "Takashimaya." I took it and looked inside. There was a huge white box, the kind that something brand-new and expensive would sit inside. Josna smiled at me politely and said, "Your wife's crocodiles." So

I knew they were the 500,000 yen sandals Akemi had instructed Jo to wear to grab and assure my attention.

"If they stay here with me, I'll keep them. They're so tempting, isn't it? But Akemi has the handbag that matches them perfectly," Josna boasted for her best friend. "Chai? Panni, *mizu,* or water?" Josna offered, showing off her command and ease with the English, Hindi, and Japanese languages.

"None" was all I responded.

She seemed surprised and said, *"Honto!"* meaning really in Japanese.

"Hai, arigato," I confirmed.

"Are you going to stand there the entire time?" she asked. "Come in, you can sit down there if you'd like," she offered.

"Do you live alone?" I asked her.

She smiled. "Yes, this is my art palace, where I create. I really need this place. It's three minutes away from my college. Akemi loves it in here also because she can also do her art work here peacefully and it's far enough away from her home. It's like our getaway place. You know that she likes to paint in the nude and stays up late into the night till early morning like me. When she's in her art world, she doesn't want to be interrupted."

My mind was swirling now with exotic images of my naked wife drawing and painting passionate pictures with her erotic Nepali girlfriend in a peculiar art palace. I took some steps further inside. "Would you mind if I looked around your place?"

"I don't mind if you don't mind if I do some work while you're here waiting. I have so much homework and not enough time, and a big art show coming up." She shifted from her peaceful posture into a reflective panic.

"I stayed up all night speaking with Akemi and couldn't resist helping her to meet with you. Now I'm a bit behind my work schedule. Look around. Akemi's drawings and paintings are over there, and my sculptures and such are right here. Are you sure you didn't want tea or water?" she asked again.

"I'm good," I assured her.

Barefooted, Josna evolved from being a gracious host and best friend into a "mud princess." Clutching a fistful of clay, she wiggled toward her art throne, a hand-crafted stool with legs wrapped in thick purple yarn and a carefully cushioned colorful cloth seat. She sat softly, spread her legs around her potter's wheel, stared into the center of the wheel, and tossed the clay right in the middle. Her turquoise, gold-tipped toes tapped a button and the wheel began to turn between her thighs. She leaned over the wheel a bit and placed both hands lightly around the clay, guiding it into a shape. I walked to the other side of the room, where my wife's work was displayed over a serene salmon-colored wall.

I questioned myself. My footsteps became heavy. My heart became heavy. My mind became heavy. As a Muslim man, I was out of balance and I knew it for certain. Even if it were not Ramadan, the images that my eyes had been concentrating on, and the desires that were flooding my physical and the thoughts that were tempting my mind, were not right. In the Holy Quran, in a *sura* titled Al Nur, meaning, "The Light," there is an *ayat* which says

> Say to the believing men that they lower their gaze
> and restrain their sexual passions. That is purer for
> them surely Allah is aware of what they do.

I had not been reading my Quran in Japan, although Ramadan is a holy month when Muslims read the Quran even more than on an average day. Instead I had been flipping my Japanese vocabulary cards in my attempt to learn and memorize and communicate. I had been reading history books on my wife's father and family. I had been focused on getting my wife back. Yet the spiritual cost was high.

Facing the first drawing on the salmon-colored wall, I saw the sort of image that had been flooding my sight and mind all day. It was a detailed drawing of a naked teenaged girl with her legs spread open. Her bush of pussy hairs brushed against the cushion where she was seated on a stool with head hanging low and her three feet of hair hiding her face. The way her legs were drawn so shapely and perfectly, the way both her feet were raised a bit as she balanced on her toes was an incredible display of Akemi's talented fingers and eyes. Yet as I looked even more closely at the drawing, I felt a heat rising up within me. It wasn't passion. It was anger. The stunning girl in the drawing could easily be my wife.

Murder moved to the middle of my mind again. Who really drew the pictures as Akemi posed? Then I was questioning: how could she draw a perfect picture of herself, down to the shape of her vagina and the lengthiness of her clitoris? She is a great artist, I know. Others had told me confidently that in her art world, she is in fact a genius, but what I was seeing was impossible, right?

Each drawing mounted beside the first drawing pictured the same alluring, nude, beautiful teenaged girl, in an array of intensely sexual and seductive positions. So engrossed, Josna stood behind me now. I had not heard her shut off the wheel or her approaching bare footsteps. She tapped me. I didn't turn toward her.

"It's not what it seems," she said softly. "It looks just like Akemi, I know. But it's not her. This exhibit is the winning exhibit that earned your wife a first-prize scholarship to study art in the United States. I guess you could say that if Akemi had not drawn these pictures so passionately, you would never have met her in New York. Because she would never have gotten there for any other reason," Josna confided.

"Look." She pointed at the carefully formed letters around the perimeter of each drawing. "These letters are hangul. It's the Korean language. They are not kanji. I am sure that you noticed that the Korean style of writing is much neater, tighter, and more precise." She dragged one finger across the letters. "This one says, *One Womb.*"

I kept my back to Josna as she narrated. Her voice helped to soothe the fire in me. When the smoke in my mind finally cleared, I realized that I was seeing Joo Eun Lee, Akemi's mother. They were redrawings of the covers of the underground political pamphlets that Akemi's mom and best friend had produced and distributed anonymously. Once I came to understand their meaning, hearing once again the titles—*One Womb, Virgin Oil, Revolutionary Passion*—the drawings shifted from pornography to purpose. But they were still provocative and powerful. Although I understood, such representations would not be acceptable to me if they were of my mother or wife. I wondered what drove Akemi to draw these intimate pictures of her then-teenaged mother, and to place them in the public eye? I turned my face to Josna, calm now. I wondered if she knew the details of Akemi's mother's life. My temper was checked.

"Oh, I see now," she said.

"You see what?" I asked.

"I see now what Akemi was saying about you—about your eyes,"

Josna said slowly. I looked away from her. She laughed a short, light laugh. "Akemi told me not to even look into those eyes of yours for more than three seconds." She emphasized every other word musically and then laughed again.

"What's happening now? Where is Akemi?" I asked solemnly.

"She should've been here already. She said she would be. She always does what she says." Josna walked over to the phone. She lifted the receiver and got clay on the buttons as she pressed them. She held the phone and waited. Seconds later, she had not spoken even one word before hanging up.

"Of course she's not at home," Josna said aloud to herself. "Akemi told me she would come here straightaway from her doctor's office. I don't know what could've kept her."

"Did she say that she was feeling sick?" I asked.

"No, she's fine actually. She simply pretended to be ill so that her father would allow her to remain at her house in Roppongi. Mr. Nakamura wanted her to return to Kyoto to begin school right after Golden Week ended. But she said that she was sure that you would show up there in Tokyo."

Even as I was becoming more concerned, it felt good to hear that my wife was completely certain that I would come to Japan to get her. Even as I had doubted her, she was one hundred percent. She had given me that Roppongi address to write a letter to her father before we were married. She remembered, of course. She knew I would show up there. And as certain as she was about Tokyo, she would be just as certain about my arriving in Kyoto, I now knew. I had given Iwa Ikeda and everyone who was against our love too much credit and consideration. I felt a little more at ease. Further, I figured that right at this moment, even though Akemi wasn't here yet, it was the best place to gather the most information.

"When was the last time that you saw Akemi?" I began.

"Last night was both the first and the last time I've seen Akemi in almost a year. Of course you know she was studying in New York. I was still here in Japan. She was sending me letters every week since she was away. I feel like I saw you at the same time that she first saw you." Josna smiled.

"I have a stack of letters from her at my cottage and even some over there," she said, gesturing to show me how tall the stack was.

Akemi was so cute when she had this crush on you. She watched you closely for three months without ever saying one word to you. It was her first time becoming excited about possibly learning English, and her first time becoming frustrated because she found the language difficult and displeasing. We sat on the phone chatting for more than an hour once. She wanted me to teach her the one perfect English sentence to say to you. It was so funny. She was shy and wanted you to approach her but admitted she was hiding from you. I'd give her something to say and she would think it was too much or too bold or not enough. Akemi said the English words did not sound like they matched her "true feelings."

I was surprised to hear that Akemi had true feelings for me, before we had ever met face-to-face or even exchanged any words. But I didn't express that to Josna.

"Well, anyway, I went home to Nepal for Golden Week. I didn't even know that Akemi had returned to Japan. The last time we spoke before I went to Nepal, the two of you were married and inseparable and so in love . . . I wish!" she said.

"Did Akemi go to the doctor's alone?" I asked.

"No, actually, she can't go anywhere alone these days. Her father won't allow it. He hired Shota to be Akemi's driver. We've known him since forever. Akemi can't go anywhere without him. She was so annoyed about losing her freedom that last night she made Shota stay in the car outside the whole time she was here talking with me—from evening until about two in the morning. At first she had told him to go back home and that she'd call him when she wanted to be picked up, but he refused. So I had Shota sitting outside my front door for eight hours and Makoto guarding outside my side door for eight hours.

Josna took a deep breath and exhaled slowly, bending over and resting both of her hands on her knees. As she stood back up, I asked, "Makoto?"

"Oh, he's one of Nakamura's men. He usually secures Mr. Nakamura. Now he's assigned to Akemi around the clock. I can tell she hates it." Josna tried to soothe me. My jaw tightened.

"Mr. Nakamura is a really great guy if he's on your side. I certainly would never want to be his enemy."

"So why did the 'great guy' give his permission for our marriage and then snatch it back?" I asked her, hoping to hear one reasonable answer to the question that had been irking me for so long.

"You really don't know why?" Josna asked.

"Tell me," I responded.

"Mr. Nakamura never wanted to give Akemi his approval. The father and daughter were having *hankouki* months before she left to study in New York. *Hankouki* is something that I and probably you will never understand. Japanese teenagers—sometimes they go through this thing where they don't speak to their parents at all. They ignore them completely. Both the parents and the child stop talking with one another until they are buried in complete silence. *Hankouki* can go on for months or even longer. Japanese teenagers are much closer to their friends than to their parents anyway."

"You're right, I don't understand," I admitted.

"I knew you wouldn't. I love my parents so much. I would do absolutely anything for either of them. And if there was ever a misunderstanding between us, even if I thought I was right, I would drop on my knees down to the floor and beg their forgiveness." I was watching Josna's painful expression at imagining any type of disagreement with her parents.

"The split between Akemi and her father is a great secret between them. All I can say is it has something to do with her mom. She and her mom were extremely close, like twin sisters instead of mother and daughter. Shiori-san, Akemi's mom, was an amazing mother. She was a mother to me also. Their family seemed happy together. A great sadness came only after she passed away, brain cancer. I am sure you already knew.

"When Akemi entered *these drawings* into the competition, everyone was shocked. But no one seemed more shocked than Mr. Nakamura. The skill of her art was so great; Nakamura-san felt he would lose face with his young daughter drawing such revealing artwork. Besides, the first prize was an all-expense-paid trip to New York and scholarship to that New York art school. Mr. Nakamura hates America and American culture. So of course he was against his daughter going there. I mean, he hates it so much that he says, 'English is not a language.' He told us that he refused to speak it when he was in college even though it was required, and he refused for Akemi to learn or speak it as well. When Akemi won the exhibition competition and was selected to represent not only Japan but the entire artistic Asian continent, she was featured in several newspapers. Mr. Nakamura never admitted to the press that he and his daughter were having *hankouki*. Instead, when the press wanted his comments, he accepted interviews and spoke only on how proud he was of his daughter and how high his expectations were of her. He denied any suggestion that the nude drawings resembled his daughter. Akemi also never publicly explained who the model was in her drawings or the motivation or meaning behind them. When her artwork received more and more exposure, she simply announced that she wanted to address through art 'the controversial issue of the presence of seven hundred thousand Koreans living in Japan, many of them born in Japan, but still not accepted and treated as fairly as Japanese.' That silenced everyone and confused a lot of people as well. Although they wanted to understand her, they were afraid to ask. No one in Japan wants to discuss these kinds of topics, not the elders or the youth. Japan is unlike anyplace in the world!" Josna said, inhaling and exhaling exasperation.

"I have been living here since I was six. I grew up here with Akemi. Really, I should be angry with you for taking her away from me. But I can't be. Akemi loves you. So I love you too," she said warmly but without flirtation. Her words "I love you" made my heart shift some, as those words always do.

Josna looked at the ceramic clock on the wall. Then she dashed across the room and through the velvet curtain to the triangular rear of the house. I followed her, walking slowly. An Indian statue of a shapely woman stood guard on the side of the curtain entrance. Her hands were slim and pretty and she held her fingers in a peculiar position. Pausing, I wondered if Josna had sculpted her. My thought was interrupted by the sound of running water.

"Can I come through?" I asked calmly, before sweeping aside the high-quality, heavy curtain.

"Come, I'm in the water closet," Josna said without hesitation. I expected to enter a kitchen area. Of course I knew that it might also be her bedroom. The Muslim in me knew that I should stay out. The man in me wanted to rush in before she could rearrange anything. I wanted to check to see if there were any traces of another man in her and Akemi's art studio. If there were beer bottles or cigar or cigarette butts, or even a man's house shoes or robe, a jacket, briefcase, or coat, or anything that might cause me to distrust Josna or my wife. It would be bad, but better for me to know than to be played like a puppet.

I pulled back the curtain. The scent of eucalyptus rushed up my nostrils. It was a clean, fresh, welcoming, and soothing scent. When I entered and let the velvet curtain drop behind me, I could feel the difference in the atmosphere. As the sun shone through each of the four-foot-wide stained-glass windows, it cast a kaleidoscope of colors onto the pink satin bedspread and sheets and piles of pillows. Purple curtain, pink bedding, and every variation of purple pouring through. I was beginning to form a picture in my mind.

The floors were made from bamboo, which gave the room a peaceful, clean feeling. Her queen-sized mattress was raised up a foot from the floor and mounted across a wooden frame seated on six sturdy wooden feet, nicely carved. There was no back board and her entire bed was surrounded by a light-colored lace net. I was unsure whether the net was there to stop mosquitos and pests or to seduce men with the exotic lure of its intricate stitching.

Josna was standing with her back toward me facing a strange statue. It was a man with four arms who some sculptor had caught in the midst of a wicked dance move. In one of his four hands, he held a flame of fire. She lit some incense as she stood there. She was more silent than she had been before. I thought maybe she was in some unusual ritual. We Muslims do not believe in religious symbols or idols or worshipping anything or anyone other than Allah.

I took the opportunity to search with only my eyes. There were no men's cologne bottles or men's robes or shoes or an ashtray containing cigarettes or cigar butts, no men's clothes draped over a chair. Nor were both sides of the bed turned down or the blankets or the sheets ruffled or disturbed. There were no condoms or ripped condom plastics or photos of a man or men at her bedside on either of the two short end tables. There were no men's hats or weights or even a piece of sports equipment.

In fact, there was only what was completely familiar in a feminine place. Perfumes, sweet scents, fresh-cut flowers, calming colors, silk, satin and lace, velvet, and a pile of pretty panties in a wicker basket at the foot of her bed.

"This is my room. Come sit down," Josna said, as she spread the lace net open and sat on her bed. I opted to remain standing.

"Sometimes Akemi sleeps in here, but mostly if we do an over-night, she sleeps in her hammock upstairs. You probably already know though, she prefers the swing. She has one in her bedroom here in Kyoto. She likes to rock herself to sleep."

I didn't respond either way. I had swung my wife back and forth without a swing and rocked her until she moaned, cried, and slept. Akemi, so excited and relieved once, she even peed.

"Akemi's bedroom is like another world. Before you leave Japan, you have to see it. Look at it one time. You'll never forget," she said, speaking slowly as if she was imagining it. "That's how we met, Akemi and I. Mr. Nakamura commissioned my father to make the ceiling for Akemi's bedroom."

"The ceiling?" I repeated.

"Yes, my father designs stained-glass windows like these two here, but these are really nothing compared to what he has done in temples and churches and buildings and even restaurants."

"Just these two are dope enough," I said staring at them.

"Huh?" she asked.

"I said your windows right here are no joke. But how do you see outside?" I asked.

"There is not much to see outside on this street. You must have noticed. This was just a great location because my college is three minutes away. My father gifted me these two windows and they're best when the sun is pouring through in a million colors, like now. Akemi prefers when the rainwater from Japan's famous typhoons are beating against the glass. She says it looks like the colors are leaking one onto the other."

I pictured my wife lying down beside Josna on that bed, behind the net, the two of them watching the rain race down the glass.

"Mr. Nakamura summoned Babaji from Nepal with his special order. Babaji says that four-year-old Akemi described exactly what she wanted. It seemed as if she was fascinated with the sky. She only wanted the glass to have colors that she could see in the sky. She even drew the design of the sky, saying that it was how the sky looked on her favorite day."

I listened while keeping my eyes moving around the room on all the trinkets and objects instead of on Josna, who was now holding her legs up and leaning her face on her knees, her bare toes and polished nails burrowing into the satin as she spoke. I was also recalling that in Akemi's mother's poem, there was a line like that. "My first love was the sky." Then I wondered if it was Akemi or her mother who was in love with the sky, or perhaps both of them? Then I nixed that thought and decided it was Akemi who was in love with the sky, and her mother had written these lines while thinking of her only daughter.

"When Mr. Nakamura learned that Babaji had four children—"

"Babaji?" I interrupted.

"That's 'father' in Hindi, sorry," she clarified. "Babaji in this case is my father. Back then, when Mr. Nakamura realized that Babaji had four children and one of them was a six-year-old girl, he asked my father to bring me along with him once he began the work of designing and installing their stained-glass ceiling. Mr. Nakamura said that Akemi was his only child and that she would enjoy the company.

'I couldn't do that,' Babaji, I mean my father replied to Mr. Nakamura. Then, the way Babaji tells the story, Mr. Nakamura told him something that I have heard Mr. Nakamura say at least fifty times over the past twelve years. 'There is nothing that can't be done.'

"And here I am! Mr. Nakamura sponsored our entire family in Japan. My father went through the awesome process of redrawing the design, matching and merging all the colors, and cutting the glass in odd shapes to make them exactly like what Akemi remembered clearly. Then there was the cooking of the glass at incredible temperatures. After the long process of creating the perfect glass picture, my father even supervised the careful installation of the stained-glass ceiling into Akemi's bedroom. When everything was completed, almost two years later, the rest of my family returned to Nepal. Akemi and I were like sisters by then. My father allowed me to remain. After all, Mr. Nakamura's job heightened my father's professional profile in so many ways. So I practically grew up here in Kyoto."

"Don't you miss your family?" I asked her.

"My parents now have a total of ten children. I'm number four. Of course I miss every one of them, but Mr. Nakamura sends me home for every holiday. Once he even sent Akemi along with me."

Instinctively, I checked my watch.

"I know . . ." was all Josna said after observing me checking the time. "She should've definitely come by now."

"Can you hear if someone is at the door when you're all the way back here?" I asked her.

She pointed to a metal rack in the corner where the two walls intersected. It appeared to be a traffic light with three bulbs, one lime green, one yellow, one red.

"Akemi has the key," she said. "Besides, if anyone comes through our front door, the lime light will come on right up there. If someone comes through the side door, the yellow light will come on. If someone comes through the back, well obviously the red light will come on." She clapped her hands together once, proud of her little light system. I thought it was clever.

"You see, sometimes I am listening to music and would not be able to hear my doorbell. Other times I have my pieces in the kiln in that oven you saw out there. It can be quite noisy. Or if I'm at the potter's wheel or whatever. It works well for Akemi too because once she begins drawing and painting and all that she does, who can reach her there in that world? So she also pays attention to the lights."

My eyes landed on her weird statue and burning incense that had become sticks of leaning ash.

"It's Lord Shiva," Josna said. I didn't acknowledge her idol. She noticed my feeling. "I know that you are Muslim," Josna said suddenly. "And Hindus and Muslims have a long history of war and a lot of blood spilled between them. But I am a Hindu girl from Nepal and you are Muslim man from the Sudan. Akemi is my best friend. Akemi loves you, so I love you too, *dosti*," she said, clapping her pretty, unpainted hands together lightly as if to say the subject was closed.

"*Dosti?*" I asked.

"*Ha!*" she said, meaning yes. I was learning.

"*Dosti* means 'friendship,'" she explained.

"In the Hindi language?" I checked.

"*Ha!* Hindi language." She smiled. "But in any language, this is the meaning of friendship. Yes?" she asked. I agreed with her. "So it is only right for me to love you too," Josna said matter-of-factly, agreeing with herself.

I didn't think I could describe in details and words or in feelings the adventures of my life to anyone, male or female. But each day was moving me into a space where I had never stood before. As a youth, I kept on top of knowing when and if I grew taller or was running faster than before or becoming more accurate at hoops, or the current count on my push-ups, pull-ups, sit-ups, and squats. But growing in my thoughts and understanding and feelings as a man was becoming harder to track and even harder to explain. When I turned to ease myself out of this intimate setting and warming mood, I walked instead to her clothing closet, where the sliding doors were already half-opened. I rifled through her belongings. Finally, I found something long and light yet concealing and tossed it at her. It landed on her lap.

"Since you know that I am Muslim, put some more clothes on and come out." She looked at me, lowered her eyes, and didn't say nothing.

As I exited, I saw for the first time the metal dragon swooping down from her bedroom ceiling. Its body was made curiously from metal forks and spoons and its angry face was made more pronounced by two bulging red rubies for eyes.

She emerged into the rectangle wearing her beautiful long dress, a Nepali version of the Sudanese *thobe*, I imagined. Now she was completely covered except for her bare feet. I wondered why some women could not know that *this is better.* Her other clothes just raised a fire in a man, an untamed feeling and wild thoughts attack that are completely physical and not about love. These images and thoughts misled many men and could also slip into disrespect at best or, at worst, violence. For a woman to cover was more respectful and calming. It was better that she be mysterious, a subtle suggestion, rather than a desperate scream. Of course the Islamic *hijab* and *niqab* did much more. It is a protective covering and an announcement from a woman that she doesn't want to be viewed wrongly, misunderstood, harassed, or even approached without respectful purpose.

"Listen," I told Josna. "I gotta go. I'll be back tonight. Is that alright with you?"

She smiled. *"Mi casa es su casa,"* she said, using Spanish.

Every New Yorker knew what that meant, so I did too.

"Here, write down Akemi's home address here in Kyoto and write down her telephone number." I pulled out my notepad. She wrote in it.

"May I use your phone?" I asked her.

"Sure," she agreed. I called the number she had written down and given me for Akemi. I knew now that I had to double- and triple-check each person dealing with my wife, friend or no friend.

The phone rang four times before a voice mail come on. When I heard my wife's sweet voice offering Japanese greetings over the recording, I purposely said nothing. I wouldn't leave any message that might alarm any listener or cause Akemi and me to be traced or trailed. I didn't want to do anything to trigger Nakamura before his trip. I wanted him to leave Japan. With him out of our way, Akemi and I would find each other and be gone from here. I hung up certain I had been given the correct info this time around. It gave me more reason to trust Josna.

"What exactly did Akemi say to you about what she plans to do now?"

"She plans to escape with you. But she has to do something first. It has to do with her mother. She wants to tell you about it. *She wants you to know.* But her father is really tough, really smart, and really rich. He plans to keep Akemi here in Japan. He is using the matter of her mother to force her to obey him."

"Her mother?" I questioned.

"I know you're thinking that since her mother has already passed away many years ago, what could be happening with her now? But her death almost destroyed Akemi. And the anniversary of her mother's death just passed. It was on May third, the same day as her debut and big art show at the MOMA in New York."

I recalled the early morning of May 3. My wife was more emotional on that day than usual. She clung to me even though we were outside. She was looking into my eyes with a lingering look of longing, even though we had been together every day and night leading up to that morning. I gave her a strong hug around her feminine frame. I squeezed her so hard that I lifted her off her feet. The moment I released her, she began holding hands with Umma in the middle of Rockefeller Center. I was remembering that it was before most of the shops had even opened for the day.

How was I to know that she was of mixed emotions—love for her husband, love for Umma, and the memory of love and loss of her own mother? Maybe Akemi also felt the weight of not being home in Kyoto where her mother's body lay—especially on the anniversary. Maybe Akemi felt guilty for choosing to marry and live in New York, seven thousand miles away from the land where her mother must be buried in the soil.

Josna interrupted my thoughts. "Akemi told me that she felt so nervous at the MOMA. Mr. Nakamura was there backstage with her. She said that he served her some tea to calm her. She said that after the tea, she felt drowsy as she made her presentation before the audience but that she pushed and fought to remain upbeat. She remembered the audience applauding her. She remembered posing in her kimono for the press. But as she walked off the stage, she felt faint. When she awakened, she was on a flight in a private jet beside her father, Ichiro, and Makoto."

Josna's words painted a clear picture in my mind. In a few thoughtful sentences she had removed much of my confusion.

"Akemi said she cried all the way home and every day afterward until you showed up."

"Josna, thank you . . . I gotta go."

"Here, you must take my phone number." She wrote it down. "Mr. Nakamura loves Akemi so much, and as I said he's tough, but please don't hurt him. Akemi doesn't agree with what her father's doing. Yet she still loves him as a daughter. Surely you can understand."

"Did Akemi ask you to tell me that?"

"No, she didn't. It's just that you have a certain look in your eyes."

I started moving toward the door to leave. Josna followed me into the ceramic-tiled cave.

"Akemi said you would show up, and you did, all the way from New York. I'm impressed. When the two of you return to New York together, do me a favor?" she said softly. I was listening. She was so helpful to me, I was prepared to do her almost any favor. "When you two reach there, close your eyes and count to one hundred. When you open them, I will be right there beside the two of you. Akemi is my best friend. I can't live without her," Josna said sincerely.

"When Akemi comes here," I told her, "or even if she phones you, tell her I said for her to come over to the studio, to stay here, to wait for me. Tell her I said don't worry about nothing, not money or about her driver or the security or tickets or anything. Tell her to just come. I'll take care of the rest. Got it?" I stared into Josna.

"Got it," she agreed.

As I strolled down the strange block past the warehouse and then

the factory toward the train station, I watched the sun as it began its
final bow of the day. What could Nakamura be thinking? Was it better for his young daughter to be left in the presence of his men in his
employ, rather than in the presence of her husband? And what about
this Shota, Ichiro, and Makoto? How loyal were they to Nakamura?
Would they be willing to give their lives in defense of Nakamura's
plan?

And what of Josna's suggesting that she would move in with
Akemi and me in New York? Why did it appear that I was destined
to be surrounded by a handful of extraordinarily beautiful women? In
my house full of females, it seemed there would only be them and me
and my feet and fist and my guns . . .

* * *

My mind shifted, like a Rubik's trying to get back into its original position. Unknowingly, I had jumped on the local and not the express.
The ride was long and slow. As the windows darkened, I was working
my way back to Chiasa, who I knew would not break her fast without
me. Chiasa, my comrade. The meaning I discovered for the word *comrade* in my dictionary was *"one of two or more soldiers bound together by
a same or similar mission; one who shares and works together with a close
friend toward a mutual goal."*

I thought about Islam, my religion. I believe there is no space
for comrades between men and women in Islam. Of course, two or
more Muslim men could be comrades. Two or more Muslim women
could be comrades with one another. Yet the type of interaction that
was taking place in order for Chiasa and me to work together toward a goal—I had not seen any allowance for that in my reading
of the Quran. There is no free mixing between men and women in
my Islamic culture. Still I had the feeling that although I had no real
understanding of it, Allah had provided Chiasa for me.

Sitting on a bicycle in front of the wall leading to the Hyatt,
Chiasa was a silhouette. As soon as she saw me climbing upward
toward her, she came speeding down toward me.

"Ryoshi!" She called me the strange name that she had chosen for
me the day after we first met.

"What are you calling me?" I asked her, as she squeezed her brakes
and almost flipped her bike.

"Ryoshi, listen first, please. There is a Japanese girl looking for you in the hotel lobby. I overheard her describing you when I was about to return the bike to the front desk. She said 'Mayonaka,' and the hotel clerk checked and said that there was no one registered under that name. She began describing you to the clerk." Chiasa continued, but by that time I was racing up the hill to catch my wife before she jumped into a car and left. Chiasa crashed into me with her bike, pushing me forward before I was able to break my fall. "I said listen first," Chiasa said through clenched teeth. "She is not your wife," Chiasa chided.

"How do you know?" I asked, putting myself in order and walking uphill as she rode beside me explaining.

"I just know," Chiasa said. "I told her to wait there, I was out here looking for you. I even rode up to the college."

"Is she still there?" I asked doubtful and angry.

"Last time I looked. Just her and her dog, twins," Chiasa said. I paused. Now I knew it was Himawari.

"She doesn't speak English," I told Chiasa.

"I'll translate, but you and I gotta get our stories straight first. I told her that I don't know you but I've seen you around the hotel. I told her that I was taking a course at the Red Cross next door."

"Why say all that?" I checked.

"Because I read Akemi's diary and I know what kind of girl she is and all about their friendship. I don't want it to seem like you and I are staying together and then she mixes up the meaning of everything and misleads Akemi." I looked at Chiasa. I understood. I appreciated her. I felt bad for making her feel like she had to run me down and crash her bike into me to make me hear her.

"You go in first. I'll show up less than two minutes later. And the hotel clerk warned me that I should have you bring your passport down to the front desk since you are staying here under my name. I told him that you are not staying in my hotel room, that you were just studying at a local college and we were both studying for the Red Cross course."

I laughed. Chiasa had quite a mind.

The Hyatt valet parkers watched closely as I approached Himawari. Obviously she had raised suspicion about me by asking around. As I heard the growl of her wolf, I motioned for her to come to me. She began walking over. I walked back toward the street curb outside the Hyatt so she would follow. She did. As she arrived, Chiasa rolled up and went into action, speaking Japanese. When Chiasa stopped talking, Himawari's wolflike wild eyes moved around as though she was uncertain. Maybe she wasn't buying whatever Chiasa had said. Her wolf wasn't buying it either. He growled at me. With her curved nails she yanked his chain one swift time and he yielded. She wrapped the leash more tightly around her right palm and he sat.

"Mayonaka," she said, and motioned me to follow her and the wolf. When she saw Chiasa flinch, she put her left hand up as if to say stop. *"Sayonara"* was all that came out of her cold lips.

Because Chiasa wanted us to pretend not to know each other, I followed Himawari, hoping that she would lead me to Akemi somehow.

Her wolf was wearing crocheted boots with a strip of brown leather inlaid on each. Now that I was walking behind her, I could see that Himawari was also wearing crocheted sandals with a hard sole and a brown leather strip running up the back of her calves. It was cooler now that the sun had set, yet I never understood dressing up a dog. Her wolf was well groomed. His coat of hair was fluffed and white and clean. It looked like they both had just come from the hairdresser.

In a dark alley we met up with her invisible crew, which had swelled from three to six. I was tight about it. This situation was growing too well known for ninja warfare.

The six girls bowed to me all at once.

"Konbanwa," I offered the evening greeting. They giggled some. Himawari did not. *"Namae?"* I asked their names.

Lined up like dominoes, they responded one by one; "Kiiro," "Ao," "Midori," "Shiro," "Aka," "Murasaki."

I looked at each of 'em briefly, knowing they were set to make a fool out of a foreigner. I don't speak Japanese, but I had studied my cards and understood clearly that they had given me the names of colors instead of their true selves. Yellow, blue, green, white, red, purple, they had said. But I wouldn't blow their spot. All they knew was Mayonaka, so we were even.

"Mayonaka des," I introduced myself.

Just then Murasaki said, "I speak English to Himawari-san."

"*Hai*," I agreed, but I could hear that she had no real command over English herself. Himawari spoke some Japanese. Murasaki translated.

"We friends Akemi. You know that, right?" she asked me.

"*Hai.*"

"Come please." She turned and they all turned and walked to the nearby front door of a closed and darkened shop. Midori pulled a thin chain from inside her miniskirt and dangled it. She inserted the key into the shop door. When it opened, they all looked at me. Himawari was standing behind me—with her wolf. I didn't know what they wanted. I thought of everything: were they trying to set me up on a B and E? Midori went inside but didn't flip the lights on. The others followed her in and they all stood in a row.

"Please come," Murasaki said. I turned and looked back at Himawari, the unpredictable ice princess, boss of the invisible doll crew. I motioned with my head that she should go inside. I already decided I wouldn't enter if she didn't. Midori came to stand in front of Murasaki. Since Midori held the keys to the place, I figure she was its owner or more likely the real owner's daughter. Midori began speaking to Himawari. Himawari didn't respond. She wrapped her leash around a metal pole planted in the ground beside the shop. She walked in as Midori held the door open. My heart was pounding. Maybe Akemi was inside. I entered. Midori locked the door behind me.

Through the dark I could see racks and racks of clear plastic cases. On closer look, they were each a tiny square filled with beads of every type and color. The line of girls walked to the back of the store. Eight people in a row shook the floor and the beads rattled. Murasaki was the first one to drop down a tight twisted iron spiral staircase into a basement. The seven of us behind her followed.

"Welcome," Murasaki's voice said in English, and the light raised up from dark to dim to bright. I was surrounded now by hundreds of tiny glass figurines carefully placed on three steel racks.

One by one each of them dropped down and sat on wooden cubes like crates, but they weren't crates. The walls that surrounded us were all plastered with pictures of Japanese teens. My eyes searched and scanned. My mind merged. "The all-girls club in a secret location close to the high school" I recalled Chiasa saying.

"Akemi-san," Murasaki said, pointing to a picture of an even younger Akemi arm in arm with a group of girls. I guessed on quick glance that those were the same girls that were sitting right here.

"Hai," I acknowledged. Then she pointed to another photo of Akemi standing alone wearing some short shorts and a summer blouse.

Himawari was the only one still standing up beside me. She was on the bottom step as though she could and would prevent anyone from coming down or leaving the basement. I wanted all seven of them to sit right there where I could watch them all at once and quickly get to the bottom of what they were getting at.

Himawari spoke in Japanese. Murasaki spoke in Japanese. Midori got up and pulled a picture from the wall and handed it over to me. I looked. It was my wife in a mean-ass mink. The hood surrounded her entire face. She wore some bad-ass mink winter boots and amazing mink mittens. Yet it was the guy who was standing beside her leaning on the snowman that I knew they wanted me to see. When they saw my face change, they knew I saw. I looked up and then around the room. They were all silent.

Himawari said something else in Japanese. Shiro plucked a picture from the wall behind where she was seated. Meanwhile, Midori lifted the one I held in my hands and posted it back in its same position. Shiro handed me the next photo. It was a group of girls on a beach with their knees in the sand and some boys standing behind them. Of course I saw my wife in her one-piece yellow bathing suit, also wearing a transparent lace blouse over it.

Ao handed me a third photo. The same guy was in it, and only Akemi. He wore a baseball uniform. She had a stylish outfit and was wearing what I was supposed to assume was his fitted. I had seen enough. I knew I was on stage and these girls were in it for my reactions. So I gave 'em nothing.

"So what's up?" I asked, as they watched closely.

Himawari reached into her handbag and came out with another photo. Kiiro jumped up and retrieved it from her and handed it to me. It was the same guy who was photographed with Akemi. But this photo was Himawari and the guy in a loving embrace.

"Shota Himawari boyfriend is now," Muraski said. I knew she meant Shota and Himawari were hooked up. I thought for some seconds.

Akemi Nakamura, fourteen or fifteen years young, a drawing.

"Shota, the driver," I said to Himawari, motioning my hands holding a make-believe steering wheel.

"*Hai.*" Himawari finally smiled. She said something in Japanese.

"Himawari will help you take Akemi away," Murasaki translated. I figured Himawari thought I wasn't understanding her point, 'cause she broke out of her ice princess stance and spoke these English words:

"Himawari love Shota. Shota love Akemi. Akemi love Mayonaka. Mayonaka love Akemi. Himawari hate Josna. Josna hate Himawari. Ichiro love Josna. Josna love Akemi."

She stared at me with a cold stare, her wild eyes flashing the wolf glare. Her face was back to cold, and suddenly a wicked half smile came across her face like she could tell I finally got it.

"Today, tomorrow, yesterday—" Murasaki said.

Ao interrupted her and said, "Today . . ."

"Today Shota drive away with Akemi and Makoto," Murasaki stated. "Shota not return," she added.

None of this mattered if Akemi was on her way to meet me or if she was already at Josna's. I could dash out and leave these girls to their gossip and girl worries, I thought to myself.

"Phone?" I asked. Midori lifted the phone from the floor behind the cube where she sat. I called Josna.

"*Namaste,*" she greeted anxiously.

"It's Mayonaka. Is she there or on her way?" I asked Josna, speaking discreetly on purpose, with fourteen eyeballs burning a hole in my face.

"No, I'm not going to be able to have the par-tee," Josna said oddly.

"Party?" I asked.

"Play along," she said with a fake-sounding joyfulness. "I am packing now. The tough one sent for me."

"Makoto."

"No," she denied.

"Nakamura."

"*Ha,*" she confirmed.

"Someone is standing over you right now?" I asked her.

"*Ha,*" she confirmed.

"Where is Akemi?"

"Was coming to par-tee but it's all been canceled," she answered strangely. I tried to read between the lines. "I'm packing now."

"Where are you going?" I asked her.

"I am sorry, I didn't mean to cancel," she dodged. Obviously she could not say the name of the location without giving it all way.

"Is Akemi going with you?" I asked hurriedly.

"Already there," she revealed.

"Where?"

"Tough one's parent, I think it might be cold."

"Is it a place here in Japan?" I asked.

"*Ha*," she said, then hurriedly added, "Sure, you can still come here if you please. I won't be here though," she said. Which I took as her asking me to go there, although I didn't know why or what for.

"Where are you going?" I asked Josna.

I heard a speck of her voice and then a click off. She had been talking. Someone else disconnected the call, I believed. I stood thinking. Maybe the man standing over her was a Japanese who didn't speak English. Or maybe he spoke some but not enough to sift through her strange babble. Maybe there was more than one man standing watch over her and listening. She wouldn't and didn't say my name or Akemi's name during the brief exchange. And she wouldn't speak the name of her destination.

Himawari's glare was growing more wolfish. The thought battle had thickened to a degree where I needed to move, think, speak, and step swiftly. Realistically, I didn't have the answers. Yet I was certain of one thing. Himawari would become a problem. She wasn't on my side or Akemi's side. She wasn't a soldier or a ninja like Chiasa. She had now broadened the scenario to a three-front war. She had also entered as a wild card because she knew all the players. She could start running her mouth, sounding alarms, standing witness against everyone, and protecting only her interests. And she brought along her invisible army, six girls who were clearly not on the level of Himawari or Josna and definitely not Akemi. Any one of them trying to come up and gain visibility might easily use this situation to cast themselves in a larger role, I thought.

"Have you spoken to Akemi?" I broke my silence and asked Himawari, after I handed Midori back her phone. Murasaki translated my question to her.

"Just yesterday," Himawari said. Murasaki translated.

"What did Akemi tell you?" I asked. Murasaki translated.

"Akemi say she loves Mayonaka. She marry Mayonaka. She don't love Shota. Shota is always like brother to her," Himawari replied through Murasaki.

"Akemi show me . . ." Himawari gestured, moving one of her hands over the other and making a circle around her marriage finger.

"Her wedding ring?" I asked.

"Hai!" Himawari said. Then she made a circle around her wrist.

"Bangles," I said. The girls showed some confusion.

"Bracelets," I said. Muraski translated.

"Hai," Himawari agreed. Then she moved her hand, with long slim fingers and curved and pretty painted nails across her neck and slid her finger down between her breasts. Then she brought her hands down and rested them between her legs pressing in on the cloth of her already short dress. She stared me dead in the eyes.

"I want," she said.

It was as though she had tapped me in a game of freeze tag. The ice princess had frozen me. I knew she was saying she wanted passion marks pressed on her body, same as I had loved them onto my wife in those exact places. A wave of heat shot through me. Then I was unfrozen.

"Shota-san . . ." is all I answered. Her man needed to take care of that. Her invisible crew was out of the loop and looking around at one another. Himawari spoke Japanese again to Murasaki. Murasaki translated.

"Akemi said she will go to New York in two weeks. She will stay living there. But Himawari don't believe because Akemi left with Shota. Shota says he will be away for ten days."

"Where did Shota go?" I asked.

"Naisho," Himawari said. I knew that word. It meant "secret."

"Shota said it was a secret," Murasaki clarified. "Himawari is angry," she added.

"Why?" I asked, going for as much info as I could get.

"Because Shota say he will not call Himawari before he comes back," Murasaki explained. "And Himawari doesn't know where he's gone."

After a long pause I said, "I'm leaving Kyoto tonight on the Shinkansen. I'll fly back to New York tomorrow morning. In two weeks, Akemi and I will be together." A few of the invisible ones gasped. The others gasped after Murasaki's translation of my words was completed.

"Himawari-san," I said to the ice princess. "My Akemi does not love Shota. You should not worry."

When Murasaki translated my words, Himawari the ice princess began screaming wildly in Japanese. Her pretty face turned anime twisted and evil. She pushed over the metal rack beside her, and all the glass figurines went crashing and smashing into pieces on the floor. Himawari had just proven what I already knew. She was a loose cannon, uncool, a liability. I'm sure Shota didn't know that his girl who loved him, whom he didn't love, was the same one who would easily get his ass set up and clap clap.

Five girls scrambled like servants to clean up the tiny pieces of smashed glass as Midori confronted Himawari. I stepped over the glass and brushed by Himawari up the twisted stairs I walked through the narrow aisle that ran down the fragile and delicate shop of beads and glass toward the door before I remembered it was locked. I turned around and dropped back down halfway.

"Midori, let me out," I said with force. But Midori's arm was twisted behind her back as Himawari held it there. Murasaki unclipped the key chain out of Midori's pocket and walked up to let me out.

As I exited, Murasaki said, "Himawari is good. She loves Shota. Shota loves Akemi. When Akemi was gone, it was good for Himawari and Shota. Please forgive us, and have a safe trip home from Japan." She bowed.

As I moved beyond the shop, I saw Chiasa squatted down beside the wolf, feeding him something and stroking his fur.

"We made friends," Chiasa said, smiling.

"C'mon, change of plans. We gotta go." I talked to her as I walked. *Fucking wolf,* I thought to myself. *He growls at the men and purrs like a pussy for the pretty girls.*

"Where were you all day?" I asked Chiasa.

"I went to Osaka. Why, did you miss me?" she said playfully.

"No, I just plan to make a deduction from your pay. Soldier MIA," I said jokingly. I was trying to soothe my own fury at the same time.

"Soldier on point," she challenged. She reached for her canteen and asked, "Please, can we drink first?"

"Sorry, your throat must be burning," I said, because of the fast.

"I waited," she said, lifting the deep-blue leather pouch from around her shoulder. She unscrewed the top of her water-filled canteen to offer me the first drink.

"Allah," I said, whispering. I drank. She drank. We drank.

"I found the fortress where your hundred-thousand-yen shoe princess lives. It really is a secure location. There are four buildings on the property. I only knew that because I rode above the area in a cable car. When I was on the ground on my bike, the wall that surrounded her place was too high for me to look over or see into. I rode around the perimeter three times and counted five entrances. There are cameras on the main entrance and the rear entrance. Mayu, Akemi's house manager, used a side entrance, slid in a key card and tapped in an additional code. So there are three gated doors that have that system, separate from the main and rear entrance." She inhaled and tried to continue. I interrupted her.

"Good work. Thank you, but it doesn't matter. Things have been changing rapidly all day," I let her know.

It took ten minutes for us to pack and check out of the Hyatt Hotel. We taxied to Kyoto station and threw our belongings into two lockers. We ate light as we moved, jumping on the train toward the Kyoto Seika University. On the the express I filled Chiasa in with every detail that I thought was strategic to our mission.

"If you'd allowed me to read to you from Akemi's diary, I would've warned you about Himawari. She is someone who was friends with Akemi from childhood only because of their fathers' relationship over the years. Even though Himawari is from a rich family also, she envies Akemi-san," Chiasa said softly, as our train raced. "It's not the fact that Akemi is the shoe princess that she envies, or her cars or home or clothes. She envies Akemi's emotions and the effect that Akemi's emotions have on everyone they both know."

I didn't say nothing, although I felt in that moment my like for Chiasa deepen. I appreciated that she seemed to genuinely like my wife without ever having met her or chilled with her. I liked that she tried to understand Akemi through the diary and to protect and defend her. I liked that she put all of that in front of her own feelings. That was dope to me.

Chapter 11
ASHES

At 7:50 p.m. the lights were off on all but two of the factory floors. The warehouse was darkened. We walked on the side of the road with the woods and no sidewalk, in silence. I could see that Josna's studio, half a block down, was also shrouded in darkness. Both Chiasa and I had become part of the night, both blacked out, black T-shirts and black cargo pants, me in my black 1s and her in soft rubber-soled Japanese slip-ons that had a section for three toes and one section for the other two on each foot. Her long, thick hair was pinned tightly in the back. She slid her *zukin* on, the black ninja face mask. If I had not been so tight and if I didn't have to concentrate so hard to deci pher my surroundings and the language and people and to discipline my every movement, I might have noticed and looked very closely at Chiasa and how beautiful and clever and talented a masked martial artist she was. However, when she and I are together, it means there is work that must be done, as it should be.

I led her around the outside of the strangely shaped studio simply to check the perimeter. She kept pace, walking two steps behind me. I could hear each of her steps as the rocks beneath our soles let off a muffled crunchy sound. The left side door was locked. I checked it with my gloved hands.

Around the triangular tip, Chiasa paused at the stained-glass windows. When I turned around to check her, she was trying to see inside. But I already knew that all she would see was an array of darkened colors. At the right side door there was only grass, not rocks like on the driveway. It would not open either. Chiasa stepped up to stand directly beside me.

"There's no one out here," she said. "We'll go in the front door."
She seemed so sure that it would go down just like that. Facing the
front door, Chiasa placed her gloved fingers in the slot below the
keyhole and slid the heavy door open. I checked my watch. It was
8:00 p.m.

Inside of the igloo cave of Josna's art palace, we stood still in the
dark with only the glow of the lime light above our heads. Within a
quarter of a second, Chiasa placed both of her hands on my sides and
pulled me tight toward her body. When my back was pressed against
her front, I turned my head to see what and why. She dropped down
and pulled at my shirt, signaling that she wanted me to duck also. I
ducked.

"There's at least three other people in here with us checking out
the same spot. Do you see them?" she asked, her lips pressed against
my ear with only her *zukin* separating our skin from touching. I stood
up, my smile coming across naturally. I used my left hand to ease up
the light dimmer and extended my right hand to her.

"Get up," I told her. She stood. The lights in the studio were
on now.

"So fucking cool . . . ," she said. Her eyes were rapidly scanning
the sculptures, which had been moved from their original positions
where I saw them this afternoon and placed closer to the igloo cave
entrance. "Can I look?" she asked.

"Ten minutes and we're out," I told her. I wasn't too worried about
being inside Josna's place. She had invited me. It wasn't the same as
breaking in, I told myself. Besides, I knew there would be something
in here that would reveal the truth about what was going on, since she
obviously could not tell me over the telephone.

"There's nobody here. What exactly are we looking for?" Chiasa
asked, still standing stiff.

"Clues, anything she might have left or hidden here for me as she
was rushed out. She probably left it somewhere that Nakamura's men
would not notice. You take the left side. I'll take the right side. Check
the drawers and behind and beneath things. What we really need
most is an address to where they have been taken."

"Taken . . . ," Chiasa repeated softly.

"Yeah, by some of those people who stick their hand in a situation
and try to change the fate of others, like you said," I told her.

Chiasa began moving around with the lightness, precision, and balance of a ballerina. In front of the shapely female sculpture, I saw her strike a playful pose, making her hands, fingers, body, and feet mimic the position and posture of the statue.

"Whatever happened in here, she knows," Chiasa joked, referring to the statue. I knew she was trying to help me to lighten up. Real ninjas know that it is this lightness that makes for a more accurate and successful outcome. Being tight and heavy is a distraction to that deadly focus that is needed to execute and complete the mission.

"These are the same as the drawings in her diary. I mean, they were drawn by the same hand. I recognize the strokes," Chiasa said, as she was paused before the drawings of Akemi's teenaged mom. I didn't respond. I was lifting vases and clay figures, searching for a note.

"Oh, she sure does force you to feel some kind of way, doesn't she?" Chiasa said. "I mean, if you're alive and you see something that this girl draws, or read something that she says or describes, it's impossible not to feel something strong on the inside, right?" Chiasa asked. "That's a really unusual talent, especially here in Japan. We are used to seeing beautiful, orderly, and detailed things, but not so much used to feelings—"

"Move on, Chiasa. Keep looking. Don't get stuck there," I said solemnly.

"I'm gonna go up these stairs," Chiasa said trying to look all the way up into the rectangle.

"Check it out," I agreed.

As I pushed my hands down below the seats of Josna's small couch and searched inside and beneath the cushions, I heard the sound of the rocks in the driveway being crushed under the weight of wheels.

Swiftly, I dashed to the igloo and lowered the dimmer. Now the studio was pitch black except for a glare of light that Chiasa must have switched on upstairs.

"Don't move," I called up to Chiasa, as I carefully walked all the way to the rear of the house and slipped behind the velvet curtain and waited.

The headlights of the vehicle that I could not see briefly lit up some parts of the stained-glass windows. When both the ignition and headlights went off, I could not see anything in the darkened bedroom. I could hear feet moving on the rocks in the driveway. I counted at least two people approaching, maybe three. I couldn't think of any reason that Nakamura's men would return here. And I hoped that no matter what happened here tonight, Chiasa would be safe. I regretted involving her in a situation that could get her knocked. *I should have made her wait outside while I searched the studio* was the thought that now screamed like a siren in my head. That's why I needed to work alone, I defended myself in my thoughts. And why bother working with a woman? Even if she was a comrade, it was impossible for a man not to think of defending a woman first before everything else!

The lime light switched on in the triangular tip where I stood. I knew this meant someone was entering the front door. I waited.

"Dare ka imasuka?" a male voice said. This wasn't the regular greeting that Japanese people seemed to announce when entering a home. Then there were two male voices speaking to one another in Japanese.

I eased my penlight out of my pocket. I pointed it at the bed. It beamed through the net and up and down and across the satin sheets, searching. The bed was still made up neatly. I beamed on the clothing closet. The doors were still opened halfway. I shined it onto the closet floor, searching. I beamed on the door to what Josna had called "the water closet." I could not see inside and did not want to risk moving and creating a sound alarm for whoever was out there in the living room. Yet they were chattering a lot. I heard the ruffling of the thick plastic that was wrapped around a few of the incompleted sculptures. Next I heard things being moved around.

Then suddenly I heard tapping, a light tap coming from the stained-glass window. Frozen in place, I looked through the darkened colors of the glass. I could not see the outline of any human body. Yet I could still hear the light tapping. I knew also that whoever or whatever was creating that sound could also not see inside and discover me either.

The lime traffic light switched on again, meaning the front door had been opened from its previously closed position. I waited.

Seconds later, I heard more Japanese talk outside the stained-glass windows. I also heard the rocks grinding beneath boots. I couldn't hear any more sounds coming from the other side of the velvet curtain. Still I waited, just in case.

The men reentered the studio. The lime light and their constant soft, polite speech made their presence obvious. The plastic ruffled some more. I heard something ripping, and the screeching sound of tape being stripped off its roll. Their speech grew a bit louder and just as constant.

Next I heard the front door close. I waited.

The ignition of what sounded more like a truck than a car started up. I stepped away from the stained glass just in case. After all, their headlights were on now and shining brightly as they began to move out, reverse, and angle their vehicle. The rocks crushed under the grind of their wheels.

After five minutes of standing like one of Josna's sculptures, I pulled the velvet curtain back by just a couple of inches and peered out. The lights were off now and the studio was completely darkened. I watched and watched. Nothing was moving.

The lime light lit. I dropped the curtain closed and stood motionless. I switched even my penlight off. I heard movement but nothing like before and no chatter at all. The velvet curtain was yanked open and Chiasa stood facing me, frozen. She smiled.

"Come out, come out, wherever you are," she sang softly, teasing. "It's clear." I switched on the light, not thinking about nothing except being happy that she was safe and getting out of there before another uninvited guest showed up to Josna's "par-tee."

"What is that behind you?" Chiasa asked, but I didn't turn around, believing that she was trying to fake me out and continue her simulated hide-and-seek game. When her face stayed straight and her eyebrows rose, I went for it and turned.

"Oh, that guy with the four arms. Josna calls him Lord Shiva, the god of destruction," I said matter-of-factly and unimpressed. But then I looked again. Shiva had a flame in one hand, nothing in two of his other hands, and a rolled-up scroll in his fourth hand that wasn't there this afternoon when Josna and I were together in the triangular tip. I had not noticed it when the lights were out. I pulled it from the palm of the statue. As I unrolled it, Chiasa stood beside me like a Siamese twin. We were both staring down at the wrinkled paper.

I am sorry that I could not speak properly to you over the phone. Even now I am scribbling in the water closet. I worry that I will lose

the trust of Mr. Nakamura if I make even one simple mistake.
At the time of your call, his men were here watching me carefully.
Mr. Nakamura sent them to get me, to my great shock, in the form
of an order, not a request. "You are the only one who can console
her," he said to me over the telephone, as the enforcers watched
me receive my orders.

Akemi has been sent far away to her grandmother's house in
the Hidaka Mountains in Hokkaido. She was sent straightaway
from her doctor's visit, also without warning. So this is all very
sudden and strange. We have never been to visit her grandmother's
house before. I hear that it is out in the wilderness. She has no
electricity, only solar power, no telephone or phone service.

Akemi phoned me finally from the airport. She was in quite
a panic, but our call was cut short. She complained that she
was not allowed to go home and collect her belongings and is
very distraught about not having her mother's ashes, which are
in a gold urn in her wing of their estate.

I don't know how far you are willing to go for her. She is gambling
it all. If you choose to go back to NY when you receive this message,
I promise I will make her understand and we will find a way for her to
join you soon in New York. Akemi would kill me for suggesting that,
but I have to be realistic. She is quite a romantic and a dreamer.

Should you choose to come to Hokkaido, we will be there for
at least the next ten days of Mr. Nakamura's Asian tour, which
is not so great for me. I don't know if the security men will remain
there in Hokkaido with us or not. I guess it depends on how
seriously Mr. Nakamura takes your efforts to meet with your
wife. As you can see up to now, like Akemi said, her father is
extremely determined to keep you apart.

I have left the keys and security codes in a container in the
freezer upstairs in the kitchen. It will allow you into my cottage on
the Nakamura estate. You can access Akemi's wing through the
back door of my cottage. From midnight to 4:00 a.m. no one will
be there. If you go earlier than those times, or even ten minutes
later, you will be discovered. If you want to take the risk, please
bring the gold urn. For some reason Akemi is worried about this
urn, but not her own schooling or clothes or shoes or books or art
supplies even.

I pray that Lord Shiva protects you, my Muslim brother. And if this all falls apart, please promise me that you will never reveal my role in helping you.

Love,
Josna

I was fired up, but even my fury was played out and useless. I was still in the battle, but Nakamura was making all the moves and hits. He wasn't bogged down dealing with the girlfriends of Akemi. He was moving the pieces to make all my thoughts and actions obsolete. His daughter Akemi had become his queen in this chess game. He had protected her well enough that she was still in his possession. I had hit him up a few times but nothing worth mentioning at this point. Certainly I had nothing to be proud of.

"Hokkaido, Hidaka Mountains, what do you know about these places?" I asked Chiasa.

"I am so psyched!" she whispered with excited softness. "Let's do it. We can do it!"

She followed me up the stairs to get the keys and codes from the second floor of Josna's studio, where I had never been, the same area where Chiasa had hidden when the men had arrived moments ago. It was an incredible, colorful ceramic-tiled kitchen with a serious ventilation system. Two pots and two pans dangled from the ceiling by the stove. There was a round, glass table with two heavy glass chairs. When I looked at it closely, I saw that the entire set was made of colorful marbles. They were buried in every centimeter of the tabletop and even in the legs and seat and back of the matching chairs.

Her kitchen was spotlessly clean, which led me to believe that Josna wasn't a cook. It was easy to leap to this conclusion because she had grown up in Japan. In a Sudanese or Indian or even Nepali kitchen, where similar spicies are blended and cooked and served, the aroma never leaves, even after careful cleaning. Chiasa pulled open a cabinet and it was stuffed with ramen and other quick-fix junk that I had seen the Japanese throw into their bodies while standing alone or sitting alone inside any one of their numerous convenience stores. They bought and sold and consumed it voraciously like it was delicious and natural and nutritious food.

I opened Josna's refrigerator. There was only a chunk of tofu, floating in some water and wrapped in a clear thin plastic. There was also a jug of some drink, perhaps cold tea. When I opened her freezer, there was a container inside, just as she said there would be. When I peeled back the tight lid, the keys and card and a small piece of folded paper were inside. As I turned to leave, I noticed an open window on the opposite wall in the next room. I went to close it. Chiasa followed.

"Sorry," she said. "I jumped out from there. I didn't get the chance to close it back up."

I looked at her. She was "so fucking cool" to me. I stuck my head by the window and looked down at how far she'd had to leap. I pulled my head back in and shut the window, impressed, but didn't say shit about it.

In the small porchlike room where I stood, I saw Akemi's hammock. It was still and looked and felt lonely.

"Look what I got." Chiasa showed me a paper. Everything on the paper was in Japanese.

"Are you trying to be funny?" I asked her. She knew I couldn't read it.

"No, this is the label from the courier service that just left here. When I saw that they were sending two of the sculptures somewhere, I got curious. They left their truck door standing open, so I lifted this document. Now they have a copy and I have a copy," she confessed.

"But that's different than stealing, right?" I ribbed her.

"Definitely. All is fair in love and war. You heard that before, right? It's an English saying," she said.

"Who said it? Aunt Tasha?" I asked her, as we walked down the iron stairs.

She laughed. "No, not Aunt Tasha! Maybe it was Shakespeare or something I read in school. Whatever, when I first heard it, I thought to myself, that sounds true. A real warrior would do anything when he's at war. And a real lover will do anything when he's in love. Right? Besides, according to Yuka's philosophy, I should blame my African American side for stealing the document. Then what I said about the Japanese people not stealing would still be true." I listened and thought to myself, *Chiasa is clever.*

"What does the paper say?" I asked. "From the courier service."

"Oh this?" she said casually. "This is the exact address where they are sending those two sculptures. It's in Hokkaido."

I was grateful to Allah, but instinctively I hugged Chiasa. Her body stiffened a bit and she dropped her head shyly. I realized and released her.

"I must've done something good?" she asked. "So you shouldn't dock my pay for going to Osaka earlier today . . ." She joked, dodged, and distracted.

"Could you imagine us just roaming around the entire Hidaka Mountains?" She laughed. "We would be two thousand meters in the air, stopping hikers and climbers and asking if they had seen a girl in really expensive, really high heels, walking up this way. Now that would have been crazy!" She laughed and loosened up our serious mission.

We were out, going straight to Josna's cottage.

* * *

"Don't even think about leaving me on watch out here. We both know that no one is home and no one is coming. Nakamura-san has used up all of his soldiers. Let's count," Chiasa said, pulling each of her gloved fingers. "He has men flying out with him to Singapore. He had security that seized Akemi from the doctor. He has men who picked up Josna separate from the ones who dealt with Akemi." She clapped her gloved hands together. "That's it. There is no one left. Of course he could have others. But I'm thinking his most trusted guys are surrounding him, his daughter, and Josna, and he's running out of time. Believe me, you got him scrambling by being here first in Tokyo, then in Kyoto," she said like a military strategist.

"I pay attention," she said solemnly. Her big gray eyes and long black lashes were more pronounced through her *zukin*.

How could Chiasa know that it was not because I feared being captured by security while entering the Nakamura estate that I wanted her to stand outside and wait? It was because I had decided that I would not allow anything bad to happen to her. If anything went wrong, it should happen to me instead. Akemi is my wife, my family. I am the one who should run all the risks gladly. As I turned to walk away, leaving her behind, she followed eagerly.

Josna's cottage revealed the influences and maybe reasons for her loyalty to Nakamura. It was a lovely, tiny place behind a secured wall, accessed from a side entrance behind a locked iron gate. In front of the cottage door there was a stone fountain pouring water continuously. The sound of the water was very calming for our tense circumstances. Surrounded by plants, flowers, and trees, some growing on the bricks and wrapped around the house, it was like a small slice of paradise. We entered. The entire inside of Josna's home was soft and warm and feminine. There was no area designated as a work space, no clay or tools or plastic or incomplete art. Her bed was round and her sheets and spreads were too. Each item seemed hand-crafted and high-quality. She had many framed family photos and hung a beautiful carpet on one wall instead of laying it across her floor.

We breezed through in search of her back door. Outside her cottage was a courtyard. She flew a Nepali and a Japanese flag on a shortened flagpole. The ground had tiny lights that led all the way to her best friend's wing of a separate building on the Nakamura estate. Hurriedly we entered Akemi's code, and automatically the door opened. Chiasa removed her shoes and I did the same.

"I think I'm falling in love with her too," Chiasa said softly. Her expression was funny to me, but when I looked at her face, it revealed nothing but awe. The building, shaped like a crescent moon, was topped with a stained-glass ceiling! Moonbeams poured light through the colors of the glass and gave me the feeling that I was walking not on the ground but up in the sky, close to the stars. The weight of the glass, the design of the glass, and the incredible, unusual curved cut of the glass were a magnificent architectural accomplishment. As Chiasa and I stood still, staring upward, I was imagining an assembly of mathematicians and engineers and architects gathered in a circle, along with Josna's father, calculating the angles, the geometry, and the algebra, to avoid making one incorrect move that could result in the entire crescent-shaped ceiling crashing down.

Born in the land of the pyramids that have never been deciphered or duplicated, despite being raided, I shook myself out of awe.

"Come on, this way . . ." I bumped Chiasa, and as we walked, the light-blue-tinted walls to my left created an underwater feeling. I could not locate a light switch or device anywhere, which led me to believe that the whole wing went on natural light. When the sun shimmered brightly, the wing would light up. When the moonlight ruled the sky, its pieces of blue and white or yellow or purple light would make it nighttime in Akemi's wing of the estate as well.

Her bed was a swing shaped like a clamshell.

"She really lives in a glass house," Chiasa said, still a prisoner of amazement. In Akemi's bedroom, the ceiling was stained glass and the walls were made of thick clear glass behind which two huge yellow and orange sea turtles swam freely. It was designed as though she wanted to live in the infinite sky and on the ocean floor all at once.

"So fucking cool," Chiasa said, her face pressed against the glass, watching the sea turtles maneuver. I found a closet and went inside. It was the size of a small New York boutique stuffed and packed with everything exquisite. Dresses on cloth hangers and boxes piled high in size order and footwear displayed on a foot-high platform. Exotic sandals, high- and low-top Nikes, pretty-colored petite Pumas, necessary Adidas and shoes and boots galore from Gucci to Prada to some exclusive Japanese line. A hat collection of crocheted winter ski caps, and Kangols and berets and a few fitteds. There were leather and suede belts, jeans, shirts, and leather jackets and ski coats. Wow, what the fuck had I gotten myself into?

In another room at the rear, the walls were white. Yet everywhere on the white walls were drawings done in charcoal, pencil, and colored markers. It was like a New York graffiti haven, but better because the artwork was intricate, passionate, and seemed so personal. Where other kids may have been punished for writing on the walls, Akemi was permitted and probably praised. The light from the stained-glass ceilings made the still drawings on the walls appear as though they were moving, like an emotional and complicated animation film.

It was at the tip of the crescent moon where I found the marble mantel that held the solid gold urn with Akemi's mother's ashes. I reminded myself that I didn't have the luxury of time on my side. I wouldn't be able to pause and process the meaning of all of this. I already knew that Muslim burials are not like this, are not cremations. At the same time I know that Muslims respect life whether it is present or deceased. When a Muslim passes away, his body is treated carefully and respectfully. It is washed and shrouded, prayed for and prepared and placed into the earth in a particular way, an Islamic way. I whispered an Islamic prayer over the urn. It is my way and the only way for me. I placed it between my palms and walked out the full length of the crescent, hoping to find no one else but Chiasa along the way.

Chapter 12

THE SKY

We boarded a 6:00 a.m. flight from Osaka International Airport to Sapporo, Hokkaido. I needed rest, but my mind refused to let go. First there was the strategizing. Having to place my mind inside Nakamura's mind and anticipate and then intercept his moves had been difficult. Certain thoughts that had occurred to me while reading *Never Surrender* and *Peculiar People*, the book on Japanese culture, stood out in my mind prominently. Then there were the comments of each person I had spoken to. Piecing the history and culture together with Nakamura's profile and bits and pieces of what Akemi's acquaintances and closest friends had revealed knowingly and unknowingly was complex.

I was realizing and learning the hard way that thinking is a strenuous activity. The same way I could achieve three hundred push-ups, one hundred pull-ups, and an infinite number of sit-ups, thinking took up time, and a massive amount of mental energy. The same way exercising uses muscles and burns fat, thinking is hard work that burned up brain cells and hopefully resulted in eliminating burdens and bringing victory.

I became conscious also that thinking occurs on various levels. There are some thoughts that are too heavy, some thoughts that torture, some thoughts that make the soul shake. My mind maneuvered to shift thoughts into positions that were bearable for me. When packing a grocery bag, you wouldn't put the soft and perishable items on the bottom and the heavy packaged items on the top; I used the same method when storing my thoughts. The heavy, burdensome, torturous, and unbearable thoughts I pushed below and beneath all others. It had to be this way. If I kept my heaviest thoughts on top and directly in my mind's eye, something would crack.

Separate from the strategizing was the financial matter. I was experiencing firsthand a rich opponent who could burn out a rival simply by making the battle so expensive that he couldn't afford to continue the fight. I was more mindful now of my paper. My money stack was still heavy but was slowly dwindling under the weight of Japanese prices, which were five times the average American price and fifteen times the average Sudanese cost of things. And I was learning that some items in Japan that I paid five times more for gave me four times less. I wanted to organize my receipts, but Chiasa's face was lying against my stomach now. If I began moving, I would awaken her. So I collated rough numbers in my mind.

I had paid out $275 American to the Hyatt, which amounted to $75 per night. It was a discounted rate because Chiasa held a Red Cross membership card. Then there were the room taxes and her bike rental. I paid $300 American for Chiasa's round-trip Tokyo to Kyoto Shinkansen train ticket. I paid about $125 total in taxi fees. I paid $1,000 American total for two round-trip Osaka/Hokkaido plane tickets. The binoculars with the other supplies came to about $500. Daily food expenses for us totaled about $200, and Chiasa's fee was rounded at 30,000 yen. I calculated in my head, down $3,000 in one week. There was $7,000 remaining and whatever jewels I carted with me strictly for an extreme and strapped situation.

Of course I knew that I was into an extra week with Chiasa's services. She would issue a new charge. That money I was paying her was minor compared to the mental cost that her presence extracted from me. But then again, her presence had also spared me a lot of confusion, grief, and vulnerability. She had sped up my mission as though I had previously been riding on a donkey and she pulled up in her Porsche or Lamborghini or fuck it, in her jet flashing her pilot's license.

As the plane descended, the mountains came into view. In the midst of spring some of the tops were still capped in snow. I was relieved that we were arriving safely at 8:30 a.m., a half an hour before business officially opened in Japan. By announcing to Himawari that I would leave Kyoto that same night and return to New York the following morning, I believed I had burned my trail. To be certain that

I had burned it, Chiasa and I left separately from the Hyatt and took separate cabs to Kyoto station. If anybody had been lurking, creeping and watching, like the game-faced Japanese seemed to tend to do, they would have been convinced of my departure. I had to assume that Himawari and her six invisibles would run about talking me up. If she ended up speaking with Shota or anyone from the Nakamura family or estate, she would explain that I had bowed out and gone back to Brooklyn. That's what I wanted her to say. By actually leaving Kyoto late at night by cab, riding to nearby Osaka, and boarding the first flight to Hokkaido and arriving before the opening of business, I knew Nakamura, or whoever in his employ he had assigned to keep track of my whereabouts, would be baffled about my movements. I would land in Hokkaido without raising any suspicions. I wanted Nakamura to feel content that his nefarious plans were still working. In fact *nefarious* was a word I had learned while I was reading about him. The author referred to Nakamura this way. I circled the word and looked it up. The more I considered the moves he'd been making against me and my wife and our marriage, the more I agreed that the adjective *nefarious* fit him nicely.

We sat in the corner on the floor at the airport with our belongings and our Hokkaido map unfolded and pulled all the way open. As we both checked out the fine lines, paths and trails, and symbols of the map, Chiasa said, "I've only been to Hokkaido once. It was winter and it was impossibly beautiful and difficult." I thought "impossibly beautiful" was a strange description, so I repeated it. She looked up from our map and said excitedly, "Yes! There was almost fifteen feet of snow up here. I could've stood on top of my own head and stretched and still wouldn't be as tall as the snow pile. My father loved it. He drove me up and down those hills speeding on a superfast snowmobile. It was so much fun, I wished it would be winter all the time and instead of cars, everyone would have traveled that way. Of course my mother just kept warning about avalanches and how we would both be buried alive."

"I think you're telling me indirectly that you don't know your way around out here," I called her out, while moving her to focus on our situation at hand.

She smiled. "I speak Japanese, and also, that's why we have a map!" she said eagerly. "What I can tell you is that this place is the opposite of Tokyo. Here in Hokkaido there's a small population of people spread over a huge amount of land. Of course Tokyo is a small area of land crunched with a gazillion people." She paused and suddenly turned serious, looking more closely at the map.

"The exact address of Akemi's grandmother's house doesn't really show up on the map. But we know it's in the area of the Hidaka Mountains. At least that's what Jo said. But then again she and Akemi have never been there before either."

"Write the address out in English for me, the one from the mailing label," I told her, and handed over my pocket notebook. She wrote first in kanji, then in English. She then spoke out the kanji meanings for Hidaka Mountains. "Sun, High, Mountain, Pulse." And, the name of the place where the sculptures were being delivered was "Serenity Fields." The name made me more curious.

I looked closely at the map. Although it was in Japanese, I could measure the distances between towns and cities and parks and mountain ranges and so on. "It looks like a long trip. We'll be traveling the entire day," I told her, looking up from the map. "We should've flown into Asahikawa Airport, instead of Sapporo," I pointed out to Chiasa. "It's closer to the Hidaka Mountains, and at least there is a town there. The way this map reads, from here in Sapporo, we'll be on a crazy long trek to reach Hidaka. And as we approach the mountains from this side, there're no cities or towns after this point." I showed her exactly where the route veered off into mostly wilderness. She checked it out.

"My fault, I just got my hands on the map of Hokkaido when we got here," she said softly. Then she cheered up instantly and proudly announced, "Japanese people will help us as we go along, you'll see. We tend to be polite in this way."

Chiasa excused herself, grabbed hold of her backpack, and went to the ladies' room. I remained keeping watch over the rest of our stuff and studying the map. When I looked up, she was wearing her high school uniform, the hiked-up mini, tight blouse that lay tightly across her full breasts, bare legs, socks, and penny loafers.

"I know you don't like me to wear this uniform, but, like I said, all over Japan a high school girl in a uniform can get anything she wants. Think of this as my business suit or costume," she said. I wouldn't look at her purposely.

"My sensei taught me that a ninja has to 'subvert her ego,'" Chiasa tried to persuade me.

"Subvert her ego," I repeated.

"Yes, according to Sensei, long-ago ninjas disguised themselves as poor farmers. Or a male ninja might have had to disguise himself as a local woman or a female ninja might disguise herself as a man."

"Oh yeah," I said, and listened halfway.

"And if *you are really handsome* and well dressed and a cool-ass superskilled ninja with killer instincts, *you might think you're too much* to put on a lowly humble costume or to play dumb and stupid or deaf and mute. But *if* your desire for victory outweighs your ego or just the proud way that you view yourself, then you can do whatever it takes," she said solemnly.

She was accurate about one thing. I could never view myself dressed as a woman. Nor could I respect any man who modeled himself after a woman for any reason. For me, man is man, woman is woman, both created from Allah equally but with different purposes and parts and appearances and roles in life. I could on second thought rock a clever costume, something strategic and even inexpensive but definitely made for a man.

Our ride from the airport was ninety minutes long with stops along the way. I caught some sleep; in fact, I slept through the entire journey. The problem was Chiasa did also. Deep in a dream that instantly evaporated, I heard a voice repeating itself. We lifted our own heads to find a four-and-a-half-foot-short bus driver standing over us. He spoke in Japanese. I didn't need a translation. The bus was empty and it was easy to deduce that this was the last stop on his route.

Chiasa jumped up, just missing the metal rack above her, and bowed her head from her inside seat. She began a conversation with him. She opened the map. He said something, which I couldn't understand, then bowed his head and turned to go back down the aisle to his position.

We collected our belongings and exited. Immediately the bus U-turned and sped away.

Standing on a dirt road at 10:30 a.m. surrounded by cornstalks not yet ripened, I looked at Chiasa.

"We'll catch a ride from out here. There are no more buses on this route," she said. I pulled out my compass as I began looking around for directional signs. There were none. "We are headed north, so let's walk this way," I told Chiasa. We began walking, while strapping on our backpacks. Hers was heavier than mine since she couldn't part with a lot of her stuff. I had easily left several items in lockers.

"Give me your backpack," I told her. She looked at me like she wanted to refuse. Then she softened and handed it over. Still she had a pack strapped around her waistline and her canteen strapped across her shoulder and riding nicely on her right hip.

"You see the truck tracks," she said, pointing at the dirt road. "Someone will come along soon."

Forty minutes in, a pink pickup truck appeared. It was approaching us as we both walked backward watching it. Chiasa began waving her hands to slow it down, and bowed her head when it halted three feet in front of her. There were two Japanese men inside a cabin that fit three persons. The driver was old, but the man seated beside him was much older. Riding in the back of the truck was one goat and a stack of caged animals that I could not view closely from where I was standing. Chiasa spoke as I stood still behind her, watching. The Japanese driver stepped out and ran around and opened the passenger door for Chiasa to be seated beside them. I grabbed her hand before she made one move.

"They will take us up forty-five miles. I think we should get in," she advised.

"You sit in the back," I told her as she stared at the elderly man holding the passenger door open.

"They're probably very afraid of you," she said softly.

"We'll both sit in the back," I told her.

Chiasa moved toward the passenger door bowing her head non-stop. She spoke very politely. I recognized her apologizing in between every other sentence. "Sumimasen, Sumimasen . . ." The driver seemed to accept, walked to the back of his truck, and lowered the bed. I helped her into the bed. She got on and I handed her her backpack and then mine and climbed on also. The driver closed the bed and returned to his position. They pulled off.

There were chickens each in an individual cage. There were five rows of five of the birds pushed against the wall behind the front cabin. The bearded and horned goat stared at me shamelessly with his huge dark-brown eyes. The driver was suspicious of me; I was suspicious of the driver. The passenger was suspicious of me. I was suspicious of the passenger. The goat was suspicious of me, and I was suspicious of him too. This is how it goes with the male species. But the goat was roped around the neck and anchored to the truck floor. In many ways I understood that trapped feeling. Yet he was in a much more critical battle than I was, a type of animal heaven or hell. Either he was being taken to mate with the lady goats, or he would end up sliced and sizzling on the grill.

"You see, my school uniform worked," Chiasa announced. "It has neutralizing powers. I don't think you realize how strong you look with your height and those shoulders and that chest and these arms and your eyes . . ." She was using her hands to gesture. "All I know is that without this costume, we would have been *walking forever*," she concluded, exhaling. I didn't speak on it. I thought that she also did not know how powerful her body looked in that tiny uniform. Or maybe she did and that was her point.

It was a rough ride, at about forty-five slow miles per hour for a forty-five-mile distance. The Hokkaido spring air was less warm than in Kyoto and Tokyo but was not cold or uncomfortable. As the breeze soothed me, I watched Chiasa plucking feathers off one of the chickens, her slim fingers working rhythmically right through the cage opening. After she gathered them, she pulled out some napkins and gently laid the feathers inside and carefully placed them right in her waist pack.

When the truck slowed and then pulled to the side of the road, the older guy in the passenger seat got out instead of the driver. He lowered the back door and I jumped off. Chiasa handed me both backpacks and then she jumped off the bed. The elder man began speaking to her, never changing his eye contact from her face. He didn't seem to even acknowledge or notice my presence. However, I was growing accustomed to their brand of ignoring. He had to be about 109 years old with skin like leather and tobacco-stained teeth. Gazing through slightly clouded eyes, he pointed into the forest, speaking slowly and carefully.

When the talking between them ceased, I held out a 10,000 yen note to pay him for his trouble. That caught his eye. Chiasa looked at me and began bowing to the elderly man. Gently, she took the note from my hand and used both her hands to present it to him with her head bowed again. I could see that there was even a ritual that a person needed to perform just to make a payment. I was glad that she was there to do it. I wouldn't. Chiasa was still bowing when the truck pulled off.

"He said that it's through there," Chiasa pointed at the forest. "He said that we should 'walk and walk and walk some more.' Then he said that we should 'climb and climb and climb some more.' After climbing, he said we should 'walk and walk and walk some more until we get there.'"

I was pressing the numbers of his license plates into my mind before writing them down in my notebook for no known reason.

"He's from this area. I believe him," Chiasa said, completely assured.

"Did you ask him if this was the only route?" I questioned.

"Of course. He said that this is the quickest route on foot and that we shouldn't expect anyone to show up out here to offer us a ride. He said that his son had already driven us much further out than they had planned to travel. He said sometimes foreigners come this far out because they're crazy and looking for adventure or because they're just lost."

"We're not lost," I said confidently. "But it's good if he thinks we are."

Chiasa removed her backpack and leaned it against a nearby tree. Then she unzipped her waist pack and pulled out her *zukin*. She shook it like a woman shakes sheets before placing them on a clothesline.

"Here, hold this up just like this," she asked me. I held her two meters of black material.

"Now look the other way until I say *hai*, okay?" she requested.

"Okay," I told her, turning my head from her direction. I heard her moving around feverishly, unzipping her skirt, unbuttoning her blouse, digging through her backpack. I was glad to know she was doing away with the schoolgirl uniform. Then I felt her fingers as she placed them beside mine as I held up her *zukin*.

"*Hai!*" she finally said. "Okay, I said you could look now!"

She was dressed in an olive-green long-sleeved T-shirt and green cargo pants, which she tied at her ankle with a drawstring over her long tube socks. She was wearing beef and broccoli Timberlands and looked like the leaves of the tree that she stood in front of. "Now my backpack is much lighter," she announced as she wrapped her green Champion hoodie by the sleeves around her waist just below her waist pack.

"Seven minutes more, that's all I need," she said, as she spread her *zukin* over some scattered grass like a small picnic blanket and went back into her backpack pockets, removing a pocketknife, a leather tube, some cylinder-shaped film containers, a small, flat rectangular case that could fit in the palm of her hand, and three different types and sizes of string all nicely tied into very loose knots. She also had a three-inch pair of scissors, a few swaths of linen, and her chicken feathers. She laid each of the items on her *zukin* like a surgeon might lay his tools out before performing surgery.

As she unzipped her circular leather tube, I remembered how Akemi used to carry her artwork slung over her shoulder and rolled inside a tube twice the length of the one Chiasa had. But Chiasa didn't have artwork in hers. I watched intently as she pulled out seven thin one-and-a-half-foot-long, sturdy bamboo sticks. As she sliced them slightly at both ends using her pocketknife, she said, "You know there are bears here in Hokkaido. I know I told you that there were bears in Yoyogi Park back in Tokyo. There have been a couple of sightings over the years, but I was mostly joking. *This time I'm not.*"

She opened the small rectangular case. Inside were needles. She removed them one at a time and placed these needles in the top of each of the seven bamboo sticks. With the three-inch pair of scissors, she cut the linen. She opened a film canister and dipped the linen into a liquid it held. She wrapped the linen in a way that now concealed one of the needles and tied some string to hold it on. She repeated the same process for each of the seven sticks. Next she placed one chicken feather on the back end of each of the sticks, into the slot that she had sliced with her pocketknife, and used more thin thread to tie and hold it on. As she removed a sturdy and buffed and glossy mahogany stick from the leather tube, I was certain that she was constructing a bow for her arrows. The bow was small, much smaller than her seven-foot *kyudo* bow that she had cased up in Narita Airport when we first met, and that I later saw standing in her storage shed at her grandfather's home. But as she strung it just right, I knew it was still a deadly weapon. She placed the completed bow onto her *zukin* and placed the arrows back into the leather tube.

"I like bears. This won't kill them, but it will stop them and drop them into an instant hibernation. While that sucker is asleep, we'll make our getaway," she said softly.

Chiasa began removing more items from her backpack, including my wife's diary, which she slid into her back pocket. Some panties, which she folded tightly to keep them out of my eyesight and placed into her front pocket. Some handcuffs, two tight tees, one bra, and her slingshot. She held four rocks like they were coins, then stuffed them in her front pocket. When finally her pack was almost empty, she pulled out a new folded plastic trash bag, dropped her entire backpack inside, and said, "Let's bury it here."

Yo, I was laughing on the inside but I didn't crack a smile. With her portable shovel, I dug her a quick ditch.

She washed the dirt off our hands with water from one of her two canteens. She picked up her bow and leaned it on a tree, grabbed her *zukin* off the grass, shook it out one more time, folded it nicely, and unzipped her waist pack. She removed a small can from her waist pack and put the folded *zukin* back inside, zipping the waist pack closed. She marked the tree where her pack was buried with a wicked-looking kanji in pink fluorescent spray paint.

"What does it say?" I asked.

"Tree," she responded. "It doesn't give away any information, but still we'll know we've marked our trail. It glows in the dark," she said. She picked up her bow and wore it on her back. She slid her knife into a rough leather case and strapped it around her calf. "I'm ready now," she said. She had gone from traveling heavy to traveling light. Now her hands were completely free. I liked that she anticipated a war. Maybe she even craved it, welcomed it, and needed it.

"Do you want to navigate or should I?" She asked me comfortably, like she was good either way and just as happy to follow.

"I'll navigate, you translate," I told her. After all, that was our original arrangement. I opened our map. She had already placed a mark on our destination area.

"It's twenty-three miles away. Eight of them are wilderness, ten are mountains, and five are fields. Come close," I instructed her. "We'll follow this trail." I pointed on the map. I was reading the map by measurements, colors, and symbols. Chiasa of course could decipher the name of each area by reading the kanji. I checked my compass.

As I folded the map back up and put it in my front pocket, Chiasa said, "Did you know that snakes can't close their eyes?"

"Never thought about it," I told her truthfully.

"But they can sleep. So if you see one with his eyes open, he could be asleep or awake."

"True, but the art of the snake is to make sure that you don't see him, and even if you think you can see him, he'll camouflage and bend to fill your head with doubts as he either strikes or slips away."

She had a thoughtful look on her face. Then she smiled and stared at me simultaneously. "I'm wearing indigo; snakes don't like indigo. So they will stay away."

"Oh yeah? It would be best to hope they stay away, while expecting them to appear."

"Snakes don't like people. They'd rather not encounter any of us," she said. Then she asked me, "Did you grow up in the countryside or something?"

"I have a little experience with the wilderness." I was vague while reminiscing on my summers in my Southern Sudanese grandfather's village, the best training a young, young male could receive. We were accustomed to the cobra and the mighty lion, but we did not fear them. Neither did our father or our father's father.

"Me too, comrade," she said. We walked at an even pace.

Previously Chiasa had said that her goal was to be a mercenary soldier. I had looked up the word *mercenary* and found that Chiasa wanted to be a soldier who fights for hire. She wouldn't mind being dropped in the middle of a war. Fully trained and equipped, if the mission paid properly, she was game for it. She felt like more than a mercenary in it for the money to me. She might be a soldier, I thought to myself, but still she is a woman, and women are ruled by their emotions, my father had taught me long ago.

"Comrade, let's move. If we keep a swift pace, we can get through the forest and climb up and then down the other side of the mountain by sunset," I told her.

Our wilderness walk was peaceful and natural. For Chiasa it was home, I imagined. She had experienced this for a while living inside Yoyogi Park. However, the forest we found ourselves in now was not tame. No company or government had rolled through with its team of loggers, mowers, and pruners to make this area into a beautiful picnic place. Every plant, tree, bush, and creature did what Allah set it to do. We did not encounter other humans. We listened to the sound of our own breathing, the songs of the cicadas, and birds of every colorful amazing kind. We heard and caught glimpses of the sneaky swift steps of the squirrels, the shake of the trees when the monkeys played and leaped. The gorgeous eyes of the deer mesmerized us. We were startled by the elk's antlers, as they moved away from the branches that had shaded them. For a while Chiasa watched the path of our feet for sudden streams and water holes. I watched straight ahead and side to side. Then we would switch duties.

"Her father must've really wanted to hide her from you," Chiasa said suddenly, after more than seven miles of silence. "I'm happy that you allowed me to read her diary. If I hadn't by now, I would've believed that you were concealing something from me. I would've doubted you. With her father reacting this way, I would have thought that you had hurt her somehow and were here in Japan trying to make up. But I read her diary. Every word was from a woman's hand and heart. And every woman wants to be loved the way that Akemi writes that you were loving her." Chiasa was speaking as we walked. Our eyes did not meet. I did not respond, but it was sweet to hear her voice and listen to her thoughts being added to nature's chorus in an otherwise silent and unpopulated place.

Eight miles through the wilderness took us three hours to complete. As we approached the clearing at the foot of the mountains, I calculated it would take us five hours to clear the climb, which would be much different from walking an old trail through the untamed but level woods.

"I think you should consider drinking some water," I told Chiasa.

"It's not even hot here in Hokkaido. The breeze is nice," she said.

"That's because we're standing in the shade of all these trees," I explained. "The mountain will be different."

"I'll drink when you drink," she challenged. We both refused and began our climb up the mountains and into the pulse of the sun. As we got higher, the air thinned out. Our pace was slower than when we were in the woods. The climb was more rigorous; our breathing patterns changed. When Chiasa's steps paused, I turned to her. We were hundreds of feet in the air on a narrow path that could only accommodate two people walking side by side. Two droplets of blood fell from Chiasa's nose. She placed her fingers beneath her nostrils and drew them back.

Her eyebrow lifted and both eyes widened at the sight of her own blood, but only for a fraction of a second. Rapidly, she unzipped her waist pack and pulled out a piece of folded brown paper bag. She ripped it into strips. She wet it with water from her canteen and folded it over, wetting each fold. She placed the moist, folded brown paper underneath her top lip and laid over her gums. By this time, I was pressing her nostrils together to stop the slow bleed.

"I'll be fine. Aunt Tasha taught me this way," she murmured through her papered lips. "The bleeding will stop in less than one minute. You'll see."

We were face to face, her big eyes staring into mine with full determination, her long eyelashes nearly grazing my skin. Her mouth was closed now, with the brown paper placed inside. I released her nose.

"Drink water," I scolded her. She refused with a simple blank stare and no attitude. Her nose ceased bleeding a minute and a half later.

"Do you feel dizzy?" I asked her as she soon removed the soaked strip of paper from her mouth.

"No, I'm not dizzy," she answered. Somehow I knew she wouldn't tell me even if she was.

"Let's go," I told her, but I was bent on locating a place for her to rest.

It was the seventh day of Ramadan. Circumstances had taken away my chance to return to my Umma, my opportunity to play in last night's game at the Hustlers League, my scheduled flight home, and perhaps had even caused me to be fired from my job at Cho's, where I had built up a flawless trust. Still, Allah gave us rain on a sundry mountain. Although the sky remained white with sunlight and with barely any visible darkened clouds, the rain began as a mist and turned into a shower, the droplets cooling our skin and moistening Chiasa's lips. As we looked at each other in mutual amazement, we both smiled, then laughed.

Thankfully, I located a ledge. We both squatted beneath it as the shower thickened. We were shielded but she was probably as concerned as I was about what now would be five remaining miles of slippery rocks over steep cliffs in what had evolved into a downpour.

"When I open my company, I'll remember to charge more if the mission involves mountains." She looked at me and smiled. "I'll make a menu, like the ones you get in an expensive restaurant. It will list every possibility: mountains, murder, avalanche, glaciers, kidnapping, and whatever else." She laughed lightly. I laughed too. "Since you are my first customer, *you got the greatest deal.* No one else will get from me what you're getting. In fact, your mission involves everything on the menu, doesn't it?" she asked me. I didn't answer. We just looked at one another.

"My business cards will be so fucking cool," she continued. "I'm not going to have my name printed on them. They will be made of expensive black paper with just a few tiny silver drawings—an airplane, a boat, a motorcycle, and a truck—and a contact number and a motto," she said, as though she was making all these creative decisions right then beneath the mountain ledge in the rain.

"What's the motto?" I asked.

"Fighting!" she said eagerly.

"I think you're gonna confuse your customers."

"How?"

"First of all, a potential customer sees a beautiful girl," I said instinctively. Then I stopped. She was looking directly at me with an emotion in her eyes.

"Nah, I'm saying . . . when a customer sees a woman, he isn't going to think of fighting. When he looks at your card and sees an airplane, he's not gonna put two and two together and know that you're the pilot. A man is not gonna look at you and connect up these things. So you need a better business card," I explained, knowing I wasn't sounding too smooth.

"What will a man think then, when he looks at me?" she asked.

"Here comes the sun. Hopefully the rocks will dry out quickly so we can get moving," I said.

"Hopefully," she said softly.

Half an hour later, we were still squatting there waiting.

"Why 'Chiasa'?" I asked her. I had been curious about her name since I first heard it on the flight from New York. I didn't ask her sooner because I didn't want her to start asking me the same kind of questions. Now I felt much more at ease, so I asked.

"It's a bitter reason," she said.

"Bitter?" I repeated.

"Yes. I wish my name was given to me for a sweeter purpose," she said softly. "It was my grandmother who first spoke this name. When my parents were in love and planned to marry, my Japanese grand-mother was completely against it. She had a way with words. You could say she was like a mean-ass evil poet." Chiasa frowned. "Before I was born, she told my parents, 'Your marriage will never last even one thousand mornings.' Well, one thousand mornings is about—"

"Two years and two hundred and seventy days," I interrupted her. "About two and three-quarters years."

"So Okasan, my mother, decided to name me Chiasa, the kanji meaning 'one thousand mornings.' My mom thought she would prove her mother's words and prediction wrong."

"And your father agreed on that name?" I asked.

"Chiasa came from my grandmother. Hiyoku came from my grandfather—it's his last name—and Brown came from my father. That's his last name . . ." She spoke proudly and then her voice trailed off, I suspected because in her excited recall she had revealed more to me than she had planned to.

"What's the meaning of Chiasa Hiyoku?" I asked, still curious.

"One thousand mornings, wings of fire," she said, as she pretended she was drawing the kanji midair with her finger. "And Brown, of course, is an African-American surname, which we both know has no meaning. Although Aunt Tasha would say that 'it is a reminder that we were slaves, and it is the name of the motherfuckers who were previously our white owners.'"

"Chiasa Hiyoku Brown," I repeated slowly. "It might have started off bitter, but the name is dope. It fits you well," I assured her. She smiled. I wondered if her Japanese grandmother was still alive and if so where she was living. I didn't ask though.

"Me and my grandmother are having *hankouki*. So we don't speak to one another. When I see her, I just bow respectfully, that's it," she said without seeming regretful. "You saw her, you know," Chiasa in-formed me.

"Where?" I asked. "And when?"

"Remember my grandfather's bicycle shop?" she asked me.

"Yeah."

"Well, she owns the candy shop next door. It's so small you could miss it, but I went inside and you waited for me outside the door. She was the old woman in there in that cubicle, surrounded by sweet candy on her left and right and sweets hanging over her head. She's only seventy and she's got a hundred wrinkles already. Japanese elders usually keep smooth skin because we eat well. I think her wrinkles got nothing to do with her age. It's just her wickedness. She doesn't even have a cash register in her store. But kids come in and buy thirty things and her little wrinkled fingers move swifter than a wizard on her abacus, the same one she's been using for sixty years." Chiasa was working herself into an angry memory, so I didn't add to it.

"Imagine, a witch surrounded by sugar and spice and toys, who's so bitter and hates kids!"

"Enough," I said solemnly. She paused. "We should stretch and start climbing again," I told her.

"*Sumimasen*, sorry," she said softly. "But I know you saw her. You put your face to the candy store window and looked in. I saw you," Chiasa said.

"I did," I agreed with her. I wanted to end it for Chiasa, since my questions had begun it in the first place. I could feel the pain easing through her words and pores.

As we descended the mountain, the sun descended as well. "We shouldn't do the fields in the dark," Chiasa warned.

"Are you afraid of the snakes? If they come, I'll catch 'em and kill 'em. Don't worry," I promised her.

"It's not a fear. It's a distrust and dislike. There's a difference you know, between the three."

I looked around. There was nothing but nine and a half miles of mountains behind us and a half mile of mountains in front of us. We faced five miles of fields. I stood thinking.

"Don't think about leaving me," Chiasa said.

I smiled. "Why, soldier? Are you afraid of the dark?" I asked her.

"No. I have no fear of the dark. Since we are here together and we are comrades, we should either stay together or move together for as long as the strategic circumstances allow. Besides, a good soldier does not place herself in unnecessary danger. There could be a deep well in those fields, open water, a septic area in the dark we wouldn't detect properly. In this case sunrise is on our side." She gave me her best military response.

"True, two is better than one," I confirmed. She relaxed a bit. "And sunrise is more manageable than nightfall in this particular case. Here's my plan . . ." I explained it to her.

*   *   *

On the backside of a blue barn with a slanted roof, Chiasa and I began our meal. The moon was far from full and cast a clear but dim light. What the moon did not do, the stars did. They were scattered beautifully and lit brilliantly like sparklers. I had captured this location in the powerful lens of my binoculars, knowing that somewhere in these fields, there had to be a toolshed, dairy barn, chicken coop, or someplace where we could chill and there would be no threat because the owner's day's work had already been completed. We were not beneath any trees or beside any high wall. Out in the distance about a half mile across the field there was a house. Although I had seen it when I first scouted the area, I could not see it anymore. Which meant that they could not see us either, and that was our objective. I didn't have many choices, but I was convinced that this was the place that would make Chiasa feel most comfortable, way up high where the snakes would not slither in search of heated holes to slide in.

When we first entered it the dairy barn did not have a scent. Point-blank, it just stunk. Yet it was a shelter for the night. There were some murmurs and mooing and excitement among the four-legged creatures at first, but Chiasa and I climbed to the second level, where the stacks of hay were stored. With our backpacks off, we lay there resting on the hay for a moment in silence, our muscles sore from the extreme hike. I aimed my penlight and surveyed the ceilling, where I did find an opening. I told Chiasa to climb onto my shoulders. I held still, balancing her five-seven frame. With her arms extended upward, she was able to lift the rectangular wooden cutout that led to the roof. The design was simple, nothing extraordinary like the hydraulic sunroof at Akemi's Roppongi house. Chiasa took the risk without warning, jumped and caught hold of the opening and pulled herself through. I threw her beef and broccolis to her. I tossed my backpack up three times before she caught hold of it. I was laughing some just thinking about how I was going to get up there. About five seconds later I built a makeshift staircase ladder out of six stacks of hay and climbed up.

Chiasa handed me an antiseptic wet napkin sealed in a packet. She cleaned her hands and I cleaned mine. Pouring some water from my canteen into my cleaned palms, I doused my face and cleaned my nose. She sat silently, accustomed by now to my prayer. I bowed down beneath the dimly lit sky. When my prayer was completed, she was there waiting with water.

"Ready, let's drink together." She held up her canteen and I held mine as we both drank our first swallows after a long, tough day.

"Did you kill it?" I asked, as I saw her canteen tilted toward her face.

"I was real thirsty," she said.

"You want some more?" I asked her. "You can get some of mine."

"No, I had enough. I'm gonna wait ten minutes before I eat anything. I'll let my stomach settle. I think I'm losing weight on this mission. I crave the water, but somehow as the days pass, I crave less and less food. But I've never felt better. Let's sleep out here," she added.

"The temperature is gonna drop," I warned her.

"You have your sleeping bag," she pointed out, always wanting to let me know she knew what I had and didn't have and that she watched me closely and was paying attention.

"You're right. You can use it," I told her.

"No, you're the one who has had the least sleep. You sleep first. I'll give you . . ." She touched my hand to check my watch. "It's eight thirty. I'll give you five hours to rest, until one thirty a.m. You sleep and I'll watch; at one thirty I'll sleep and you'll watch," Chiasa proposed.

I thought about it. Sleep was weighing down on me. My body was threatening rebellion if my brain wouldn't agree.

"Aight," I told her. She pulled my sleeping bag out for me and laid it on the slanted roof. I lay down and she zipped it up. I pulled my hoodie over my head, and lying there, I had my eyes on Chiasa still. She pulled her bow to her front, unzipped her case, and lifted out two arrows. She laid them at her feet. She turned, watching me watching her.

"You can't even trust me enough to close your eyes, comrade?" she asked softly. "I'll recite one of Akemi's poems for you. It was so clever, I memorized it in English. Besides you have no choice but to listen to me now. Your eyes are heavy and even you, Ryoshi, must rest."

Facing the stars, Chiasa slowly spoke. "Akemi's father was called to the school for a teacher's conference after Akemi wrote this poem for her Japanese literature class. It's titled, "The Japanese."

We are quiet people,
But our thoughts are very heavy.
Other people are living in the outside world
While we are living inside our own minds.
In our world, for the most part
There is only us, people who live
And look like us and believe and do
The same as us.
Anyone outside of our realm
We call them *gaijin* meaning *foreigner*
We are famous for our eyes, our
Art and our orderliness
We are masters and missus of details
No one can invent rules like we do
And no other people are more loyal to the rules they invent
We obey
While others boast, we whisper
While others strut, we bow
We would rather all of us do the same thing wrong
Than be the only one who does something right all alone.
By Akemi Nakamura

"So fucking true," Chiasa murmured. "Now you know what she was thinking before she left for New York and met Mayonaka," she said, turning to check if I had fallen into a sleep. I was about to, but not yet.

"Still no trust," she whispered. "You have a lot to learn, Ryoshi. *There are girl soldiers!* Female ninjas are called *kunoichi*, and ninjutsu is the art of invisibility. And tomorrow, I'll be your invisible soldier. You'll see," she said softly.

I slept.

* * *

When I awoke, I could not move. It was a temporary paralysis in a very warm place and a comfortable position. I was stuffed inside a skin casing like a beef sausage. Maybe I wasn't really awake. Maybe I was bugging. She was fully dressed and tightly zipped into my sleeping bag beside me, our bodies back to back, me facing east and she facing west, asleep on the side of the bag with the zipper. To turn around would be to reveal myself, or at least my physical reaction. So I didn't. Instead I decided to concentrate on something that would bring my nature down.

Minutes later, I shifted and reached over her, but my weight pressing against her body made her awaken.

"You were right," she said so softly. "The temperature dropped a lot. Don't worry though, this is a strategic position. I needed your body heat." Then she unzipped the bag, and the morning cold air rushed in and all the warm heat escaped as she removed herself. She gathered her few things as I wrapped the sleeping bag and organized my backpack. As she dropped down the hatch through the roof into the hay and moved aside, I handed her my backpack, then did the same.

We were silent with each other. Only the dairy cows spoke. They were discussing the two strangers, their bloated tits, the property owner, and the hired hands. Through the darkness, only their eyes flashed any light. "You better run," one momma cow said to me. "You've got less than ten minutes." We bolted.

"Ryoshi, wake up," Chiasa's soft voice said. "It's four a.m. We gotta move."

I looked around. It was only myself zipped into my sleeping bag. I paused, shook myself, ran my hand over my Caesar cut and then my face.

"Shake it off, comrade," she said. "I gave you eight long hours. You should be brand-new."

She smiled, her gray eyes flashing in the residue of the moonlight. *Pretty as a puma*, I thought to myself. Then I laughed at myself for that crazy-ass dream.

Minutes later we were outside the barn. Chiasa was running in place in the morning dark. I had my penlight on the map as I tried to figure out the directions while shrouded in darkness. I checked my compass.

"Okay, I got it. We'll head this way," I said. She nodded, her bow bouncing on her back as she jogged in place. "You coming?" I asked her.

"I'm doing two things. I'm sending my vibration through the ground. That's how the snakes listen. Since I'm warning them, they'll appreciate it and move out of our path. And I'm raising my body temperature. There's a real chill out here."

As we walked, I used only my penlight. Chiasa had a small flashlight, but the glare it cast would've been too much. So she kept it in her waist pack. The morning dew splashed wet stains on our Tims as we moved through the grass, both bundled in our hoodies. Chiasa had converted her *zukin*, which had been a face mask, a curtain, a blanket, and a pillow so far, into a scarf to warm her neck and throat.

"Did you hear that? Listen . . . ," she said.

"That means there's a road. It's coming from over there," I said.

"We can cut across the cornfield," she suggested. We jogged straight through a mile of organized young cornstalks. Happy to reach the black tar of a road and with the hint of a sun about to rise, we both drank from my water canteen and ate leftover *onigiri* rice triangles with seaweed wraps and cooked fish flakes inside.

"Let's break up," Chiasa said suddenly as we finished up. I looked at her for meaning. "There's only four miles remaining. It would be better from here on if we pretended not to know one another. After you handle your business, we'll meet up at sunset. You can introduce me to everyone, since you're the only one that knows each of us. We can break the fast together, all of us. The sun's up now. I'm good." She smiled.

I looked around. I looked up and down the road. There was no one. Whatever vehicle we had heard before was long gone. Her "break up" suggestion was sinking in. Yet I didn't want to break up and leave her all alone.

Sensing my reluctance, Chiasa said, "Let's go over our scenario for the sake of planning. There's Makoto, the security guy who works for Nakamura; Shota, who I know from her diary is like an older brother to Akemi. You say that there's an Ichiro. I don't know anything about him."

My mind flashed back to his face. Ichiro was Akemi's older cousin who had been sent to get Akemi from me once. I was working the

Ghazzalis' wedding with Umma and our company. Akemi and her young cousin Sachiko, aka Saachi, were there with me. After my work at the wedding finished, as I was putting Umma and Akemi into our car service, Ichiro appeared standing in the dark shade beneath a tree with an unwelcoming glare and stance like he wanted to get at me. I had my hand on my steel but no real-enough reason to use it on him. Akemi wasn't my wife yet and he and she were blood-related, so I let him take her home to her peeps. Ichiro never spoke one word to me, not a greeting or acknowledgment and definitely not a thank-you for caring for both of his girl cousins and cooperating with his efforts. All the while I told myself, *I'll marry her and then no one will be allowed to take her or call her back, blood or no blood.*

"Ichiro is Akemi's cousin," I said solemnly. "He's a disrespectful dude," I added.

"Are there any others who could be at this property? I mean aside from Josna and Akemi's grandmother?" Chiasa was checking and double-checking.

"You don't need to worry about *none of them. I got them,*" I assured her.

"So we agree then?" Chiasa asked me. "From this point on, I'm invisible. You don't see me, don't know me, nothing," she pushed confidently.

"Nah, you stay with me," I told her. "How else will I find you? How will I know if you're alright?"

"Okay then, we can walk separately to the property. The exact point that we split up at is where we'll agree to meet up at three o'clock today. That should give you enough time, right? And at three, the sun will still be blazing, no problem," she pushed.

"You got it," I told her. The sun was up solidly now. I began to move as though I were alone. Chiasa was invisible even though she was a short distance behind me on the opposite side of the road.

Chapter 13
"TWO"

I was feeling funky, unwashed and uncleaned. As the sun heated up, I could feel my underarms beginning to sweat some and tingle. I looked myself over as I moved. If someone who had not seen me yesterday saw me right now, they would probably be fooled into believing I was fresh because my clothes looked crisp. The light wrinkles had fallen out with motion. Even the watermarks on my Tims were dried up. But I knew the real deal.

The call of the crows brought my head up. Three times bigger than Brooklyn birds of the same type, they were deep black, blueberry black, and their voices carried and echoed as they called out over the cornfields.

Soon the green and gold of the cornstalks ceased and I was greeted by fields of open, new green grass sprouting out of rich dark soil. The flight of a white-tailed eagle made my steps stop. The massive bird had remarkable wings. It was the way she worked them that made me pause. It was a slow pump, not a flutter, and the movements were both musical thrusts and menacing in the air. I watched her head turn down and her talons curl, and beautifully she swooped down into the field, grasping a small rabbit before taking a calm flight back into the atmosphere. *That's what I'm doing,* I thought to myself. *I'm grabbing my girl on the first swoop and flying out into the atmosphere. Who's gonna stop me?* I asked myself. "No one . . ." I spoke aloud.

Where the new grass ended there was a fence where I saw a serpent at play. He didn't look frightening to me. His movement was effortless, like water moving in a stream over and under and between smooth rocks. I thought about Chiasa. The serpent won't see her, I joked to myself. She's invisible. Besides, like she said, he didn't want nothing to do with us. His occupation was soaking up the warmth of the sun and what was probably the heated metal of the fence. Should an eagle eye catch him in the sunlight, the serpent would become nothing but a tasty side dish.

Without warning I was walking into a pink storm. I had known the standstorms of my Sudan, and the snowstorms of New York. What surrounded and swirled around me now were pink petals as plentiful as raindrops, being carried by a west wind and blown about beautifully. It was a field of *sakura* trees, the magnificent cherry blossom that my wife loved so much. There were endless rows of them before me. I knew then that I was getting closer to her. Even if she was still three miles away, the beauty of the *sakura* oasis would easily draw her out of her bed and into the fields. I plucked some petals off my shoulders and placed them in my pocket for no known reason other than the fact that they had fallen on me.

Green and gold and then light green and then pink and now brilliant yellow and rich dark brown as a field of sunflowers came into view, lifting five thousand pretty faces facing the sun with the dark brown eye at its center. I realized I felt seduced. *Can a man actually be seduced by nature?* I asked myself. If not, why were the expansive fields of crops, trees, and flowers bringing me into a deeper love of my woman? I felt warm, my blood boiling, my pulse picking up, and love spreading and moving in my chest.

On what I hoped would be my final mile on this journey, a scent so sensational and sensual wafted through the air. Brilliant yellow fields turned purple. It was my last mile, a mile of lavender in every direction. I looked toward the skies and said, *"Alhamdulillah."*

That's when I saw an explosion of colorfully painted kites, one of them white with purple edging and a long streamer painted in English. "Welcome, Mayonaka."

Inside, only on the inside, I cried. My eyes followed the seemingly never-ending strings that extended from the kite's bottom and down a mile to an area of tall grass. I turned to Chiasa, who was forty feet behind me. I pointed toward the sky.

"I see it," she called out, excited for me. She put her palms around her lips to make her light voice carry. "I told you I have perfect vision."

I dropped my backpack from my shoulders and went into it, pulling out my fresh kicks. Hurriedly, I wrapped my Tims inside one of my used T-shirts and dropped them inside my backpack. I checked my pant pockets, felt the shape of my switchblade, zipped my backpack, and put it back on as Chiasa caught up.

"You see that tree over there?" she pointed to the other side of the road. I nodded. "I'm gonna mark it. That will be our meet-up spot only if you don't see me before three o'clock today. And don't forget, when you see me, don't act familiar unless I do," she said, straight-faced. "*Gambatte*," she wished me good luck. "Oh, and hand me that, I'll bury it," she said, referring to my backpack. "You got your passport, wallet, keys, and everything essential on you, right?" she questioned.

"Right," I agreed.

"Right there under that tree, the same place I'm marking for three," she said, very self-assured.

I let go of the pack and set off in the direction of all the kites and their several colorful strings.

"Beware," she said. "Don't let love get you caught up in an ambush." Her words slowed me down, reminded me that I'm not the rabbit. I'm the leopard.

"Let me get my rope," I called Chiasa back. Pockets full, my rope wrapped around my waist loosely and hidden beneath my hoodie, my hands were free. I made my mind shift from longing lover to warmhearted warrior.

Hidden in some tall grass before I could reach the kite strings, I spotted a parked vehicle. I crouched. The ignition was off. I pulled my gloves from my back pockets and put 'em on. I duckwalked closer up on it, but not too close. I pushed the tall grass aside to see if the car wheels were flat. What condition was the car in? Whose was it, or was it simply abandoned?

The wheels were soiled but solid. The car was polished and new, with just a light coat of dust and dew over it. The driver seat was in the reclined position and the others seats were normal. There was moisture on the back window that fogged my ability to view everything clearly. From my front pockets I removed two black bandanas and tied them both together. I duckwalked to the driver's door. The window was lowered by two inches, suggesting that the driver was still inside and probably asleep. Why else would everything be so still and silent and why else would he be parked so far from any residence? I checked the time. It was 6:56 a.m.

In one swift motion, I opened the door and sealed the bandana around the sleeping driver's eyes. Before he could get his eyes fully opened or his words out right, I stuffed a white washcloth in his mouth and tied him to his seat with my rope. Squirming, he kicked his feet but could only hit them against his pedals. I walked around the other side, opened the door, and picked up the keys from underneath ten or so candy wrappers on the front passenger seat. On the floor was a walkie-talkie. I lifted it, then closed the door to stop the low hum of the "door open" buzzer. I turned the knobs to the off position and pushed the walkie-talkie into my hoodie pocket.

He was Shota, same as his photo, I thought to myself. At least two more to go, Ichiro and Makoto. I thought and plotted.

When I arrived at the kite strings, I discovered that there were no human hands holding them and waiting eagerly for me. As I squatted down to inspect, I saw that they were lodged beneath a few scattered boulders.

The grass rustled—not the sound of scattering squirrels, leaping frogs, or bouncing bunnies. It was the pound of men's boots. Still squatting, I did a one-eighty only to see an angry-faced Japanese man spotting me at the same time that I spotted him, his hand gripped tightly round the base of a baseball bat, his clenched fingers turning maroon. Unafraid, he began barreling toward me. Purposely I didn't move. His courage was foolish. I would come up with a kick, relieving him of his weapon, followed by a precise strike that would send his head to an uncomfortable slant and break his fucking neck. I calculated that his next step would bring him right in the target of my kick span. When he lifted his leg to take it, something sped overhead too rapidly for my eyes to detect and lodged in his left shoulder right above his heart. His self-assured grimace turned to shock. His shock turned to paralysis. He fell backward into the dirt. After the thump of his body, there was only silence. I remained squatted for more to come. Minutes passed. No more came.

My eyes surveyed and measured every blade of grass, every rock, every leaf, and every branch. There was only the pretty puma perched behind me.

Makoto

"Don't touch him," she said, her voice as soft and soothing as a mother reading a children's story to a toddler. "He's not dead. He's asleep. He won't move a muscle for six hours or more. Move on with your mission," she ordered me.

Awed, I stood up slowly, a hundred percent certain that what my eyes missed, her eyes would not. I brought the walkie-talkie over to her and turned it over along with the keys. I knew that whoever was holding the other unit or units would be communicating in Japanese. She would handle that. She and I exchanged no words, only a brief stare. Her eyes were powerful and peaceful all at once. She was like a woman after the orgasm. And there was not a trace of the playful person and there was no trace of fear. I respected her.

Beyond the brief gathering of trees and tall grass where Shota had parked, and beyond the dirt where the other guy had fallen, was a field of flowers. With the light wind, I heard the jingling of tiny bells. Nestled in the field, bending over with a basket, between the orchids and the daisies, was the Nepali cheetah. I searched for any movement beside her or behind her, or in the cabins off in the distance, but I saw no one else. So I approached. When she straightened her back, she saw me. Her mouth opened wider than her eyes were then. Her diamond sparkled even from the distance. I picked up my pace. She waited.

When I reached and faced her, she gasped as though she had never seen me even once before, her eyes a mixture of both surprise and fear.

"My lord," she said. "You almost made my heart stop." She stood, holding her hand over her heart. "Akemi is going to be so happy." She shifted her energy, releasing her intitial intimidation and relaxing some.

"Where is she?" I spoke my first words, which came out more urgent and less cool.

"She's in the back of the house making another kite. Did you see—?" she began saying.

"I saw," I interrupted.

"I wrote the English words," she said proudly.

"Point in the direction where my wife is," I requested. I was beyond talking and delaying.

"I can—," she offered.

"Just point," I told her. So she did.

"Where's Makoto and the others?" I asked to know and to see what she knew. "Today is Sunday, so there won't be any field workers."

"Oh, Akemi's grandmother, Hana-san, sent them to a hotel one town over. She said that she didn't like their black suits. She didn't want her son's security people on her peaceful property. So she sent them away. They'll come at ten this morning. But Ichiro is family. So his grandmother kept him close. He slept here last night."

"The grandmother?" I asked. "Where is she?" I asked, but I really needed to pinpoint the location of Ichiro and any and all men. They represented threats that had to be managed swiftly.

"Grandmother and Ichiro walked uphill together to the temple." Josna pointed. "Hana-san wanted to give thanks for finally meeting her eldest son's daughter. Nakamura-san never allowed his mom to meet Akemi. You may not know or believe this, but she is grateful to you. Because of you, she has heard her own son's voice after many, many years and seen her granddaughter's face for the first time. What will you do?" Josna asked me as though I was capable of extremes.

"I'll see Akemi before anything."

* * *

Wearing a dress made from flowers, all flowers, she was on her knees in the grass with bare feet and her paintbrush in her hands. When she turned to look, she dropped the brush and leaped up. She ran and jumped on me. Her legs wrapped around my waist, her flowers shedding onto my clothes. She kissed my dirty neck before leaping down. She took two steps backward to look into me. She put two of her fingers in her mouth and her eyes filled with tears as she wept and laughed and smiled like one of the sunflowers.

"Mayonaka," she whispered.

"Come here." I pulled her close again, stroked her hair and comforted her. When I released her, I put my hand over her belly and asked what I knew she understood. The question that kept me climbing the Hidaka. She smiled and raised two fingers.

"Two," she said in English. She placed one finger over her lips. "*Naisho*, secret, Akemi, Mayonaka, secret."

I knew it wasn't a secret. My talented wife was sensitive and smart

"The flower dress"

in so many ways, yet naïve in others. Of course the doctor had informed Nakamura without Akemi realizing. Of course that is why he forced her to Hokkaido so rapidly and so randomly. Of course that is why he allowed Akemi to finally meet her grandmother, who he had kept her away from for a lifetime, and whom he had avoided for more than half of his own life. Of course he planned to extinguish my seed, my seeds, two, twins, oh Allah, *inshallah*.

"Go put on some shoes," I pointed to her feet. She ran and got her heels from in front of her door and put them on. Then she took them right back off and waved me to come inside the cabin. I followed her, mindful of the time and urgency but remaining calm and cool. In the corner room on the first floor she had a simple room with two single beds intersecting one another. I could see her touches everywhere. She had begun to decorate it, something I think she would do even if she were in a cave in the mountainside.

"Pack," I told Akemi.

"*Okasan . . . ,*" she said softly, her eyes changing from delight to sadness.

"*Wakarimashta,*" I told her, meaning I understood.

"Passport?" I asked her. Her eyes changed again.

"Makoto . . . ," she spilled out softly.

"Makoto what?" I pushed. "Makoto has your passport?"

"*Hai,*" she acknowledged with regret-filled eyes.

"Why?" I asked.

"Otosan . . . ," she spilled out even softer.

But this was a race against time. Allah had made an opening, and no matter what, I needed to take my wife and leave.

When she lifted a blouse from her pillow, I saw a walkie-talkie lying there. I picked it up. She watched me but didn't say a word, didn't instruct, complain, or protest. Josna's face appeared pressed against the bedroom window now. It was half-open, allowing in the morning breeze.

As I purposely raised the volume on the walkie-talkie and pressed the button and held it so that Chiasa could hear and listen in, Josna said, "That one is ours. Shota has one and Makoto has the other."

"They won't be able to use these from their hotel. These are not powerful enough. If they're off this large property, they're completely out of range," I told her.

"You're right! How could you know? We're just using these here on the property. Everyone constantly wants to know where Akemi is. Like yesterday with her kite making and kite flying, these walkie-talkies turned out to be very handy. When Shota and Makoto reach here, at least one of them will tune in to locate us," she explained. Then she began speaking to Akemi through the screen in Japanese. Akemi spoke back to her in their language, walking over toward me, pressing herself against my back. I think this gesture was more of an answer to whatever Josna was asking than Akemi's words. It sure felt good to me.

Also, now I knew that both Josna and Akemi did not know that Shota was here on the property.

"What's next?" Josna asked, still from the outside looking in.

"I need to get my backpack. I have Akemi's urn."

Josna gasped. Immediately, she translated to Akemi, who, still pressed against me, hugged me more tightly. Josna seemed shocked that I had actually brought the urn along, but Akemi seemed confident about me one hundred percent. "Then I want to take Akemi to the next town over so we can have some time to ourselves while we figure out what to do. You will help us, *dosti*, right?" I leaned on her, as I stalled to give Chiasa enough time to get my backpack and also prepare herself to leave here immediately.

"Of course, I'll do all that I can. We really must hurry. Shota and Makoto will arrive at ten, in a bit less than two hours."

It was confirmed in my mind now. The grandmother had sent Shota the driver away to the hotel along with at least Makoto and whoever else was on security. Shota drove the men to the hotel. Then because he was sweating my wife so heavy, he doubled back and hid his car in the bluff by where Akemi had flown the welcome kites. He knew I would show up to get my diamond, because he understood her value. The problem for him was that *it is my diamond*. If he touches it, or ever touched it, he'd pay with his life. So far I had gone mad easy on him because of his relationship to Akemi's family.

It worked out better for me that Josna had no idea that Shota and at least one other man had secretly returned to the property.

"Josna, do you have a driver's license?" I asked her.

"*Ha*," she swiftly confirmed. "But very little driving experience," she confessed.

"Whose station wagon did I see parked by the big house over there?"

"Hana-san's. It's grandmother's." She clarified. "And it turns out that big house does have electricity. It's these old cabins that don't. Oh, and there's a working telephone there in the big house also, thank goodness." She was talking out of a little nervousness, I believed.

"Let's write a note to Grandmother and to Makoto and Ichiro and Shota, letting them know that just you and Akemi went out to shop and take a look around, and that you'll both return by sunset," I told her.

"Ha," she said swiftly. "But where are we actually going?"

"What's the name of the nearby hotel that the security fellas are staying in?" I asked.

"Ana Hotel," she responded.

"What town is that in?"

"They said it's thirty miles from here in Kushiro."

"Then I want to go some place different so that Akemi can feel relaxed. How about Asahikawa?" I asked knowing, that it was where the closest airport was located.

"Ha!" That's the airport we flew into," Josna said happily, and then her eyes switched knowingly. "Akemi doesn't have her passport."

"Do you have yours?" I asked her.

"Yes," she said.

"Okay, come inside. You and Akemi change your clothes; we're going into town," I told her, as though we were headed out for a leisurely day. I knew I had to go easy with Josna. *Akemi is her first priority, but her loyalties are entangled with the whole family,* I thought to myself.

As I excused myself to allow Josna to come in and get dressed also, I walked out of hearing distance and spoke to Chiasa by walkie-talkie. As soon as she heard the sound of my voice, she said, "I got it. Give me ten more minutes. Don't worry about him. We are about to make friends and Sleeping Beauty is hibernating. I'll meet you in Asahikawa at the biggest hotel by ten. The Grand Hotel," she said and signed off.

With Josna's handwritten note nailed to grandmother's front door and my backpack in the trunk, Akemi's mother's urn in her hands, me, Akemi, and Josna left in grandmother's station wagon at

8:45 a.m. It must've been meant to be. The keys had been left in the ignition.

* * *

Nervously, Josna drove like the two old men who had brought Chiasa and me part of the way, doing only about forty-five miles per hour.

On the almost hour-long ride, I heard the story of Akemi's mother's ashes. I heard it twice, once in Japanese as my wife spoke it, and once in English as Josna translated. It started off:

"When my mother was dying, she said she felt more powerful than she had been while she was healthy. She said that in living and being greedy for life, there are many more burdens. Preparing to transcend relieves the soul of all its luggage and hefty, hefty secrets.

My mom relayed to me first her true identity. She was never Shiori Nakamura, and pretending to be so had heaped a great pain in her heart. 'Joo Eun Lee,' my mom introduced herself to me, her twelve-year-old daughter with whom she had spent virtually every available moment of her life." Akemi inhaled, her eyes getting glossy, as she continued.

"Second, she told me the lessons of a mother's love. My mother said she loved me from when I was only an idea in her imagination. She loved me more when I was an egg in her womb. She loved me more when her egg was being fertilized, as she secretly lay in the tall grass surrounding her home, bursting with passion and writhing with pleasure. My mother said she loved me more each day that I became more than an idea, and that this intense love is what led her to do whatever it took to bring me into this world properly, to raise me well and keep me safe. A mother's love is like this, she said. A mother will sacrifice all that she has for her gift from God, including her freedom, her dignity, her possessions, and even the food from her mouth." Akemi's tears formed. I could also see through the rearview that Josna's eyes were flooded. She tried to look only straight ahead at the road.

"Third, my mother told me that just as she loves me and I love her, she loved her own mother, from whom she was separated at thirteen years old. She described a great canyon in her heart and a deep craving in her soul for her mother's embrace, her mother's voice, or even just her mother's scent. She said that only becoming a mother herself could fill a quarter of the canyon in her heart. She said that now that she was dying, her dream was to have her body handed to her mom, who was living in South Korea but in an unknown place. She requested to be cremated because she forbid her body to be placed into the ground anywhere in Japan, which she said was an indescribably beautiful and charming country whose heart was way too cold. She said she would be cold here, even in death, and that anyplace in Korea would be warm for her. But the best place would be to be placed in the palms of her mother's hands.

"Four is the number of death on this side of the world. And because my mother was dying and feeling more powerful than ever before, she told me her fourth secret. She said, 'Akemi, love is better and stronger and more real than all else. Marry the man whom you love, and the man who loves you. If he has only one grain of rice, marry him for love and that will feed you. No one can remain married today because they are not married to the one they love, they are married to their sacrifice, and pretending to love is too damned painful. Love and build, love and work, love and fight. Always love first. Anything placed before love will fail,' Omahnee[1] said.

We rode in silence for a while, the three of us. The weight of Akemi's words and revelations, which seemed to have never been spoken before also helped Josna to see and understand.

Akemi's words helped Josna to continue to help us without swinging back and forth between fear, doubt, and resistance.

My mind was still shifting all the jigsaw pieces around and fitting things together. I wondered if Akemi could read between the lines of her mothers "secrets." Even if she could not understand the implications when she was twelve years young, maybe she could understand them now that she was sixteen and a half. It must be difficult, I thought, to discover that you lived your entire life with an identity that is not true. Akemi, my Japanese wife, was obviously Korean. My math was leading up to that conclusion back when I was reading the Nakamura book on my first trip from Tokyo to Kyoto, and now I was almost one hundred percent certain that it was a Korean man making Akemi's fifteen-year-old mom sweat and burst with passion, perhaps only days or weeks before Naoko Nakamura kidnapped her. When I

---

[1] Omahnee means mother in Korean.

read Joo Eun Lee's poems, I felt that she was a young woman who had been loved and made love to in an unforgettable way but not nearly enough. Her words were laced with a longing for something she had known but had somehow lost along the way.

* * *

I triple-checked that the Asahi Grand Hotel was the largest hotel in Asahikawa. I handed Josna 25,000 yen up front to check us in for one night, although I had not one intention to stay. She did. She and Akemi rode up in one elavator. Josna was purposely wearing my backpack, as I rode up in a separate elevator.

In the one-bedroom suite, I told Josna and Akemi to make themselves comfortable as I dug in my backpack to get fresh everything. Akemi's eyes followed my every move. I handed Josna the television remote. I understood what Akemi must have been going through these past few years and these most recent highly emotional days. I knew that after losing the people and things that she believed in the most, she was left believing in me. I felt and I knew what she wanted to do. And now I knew where a lot of her heat and passion and swing was coming from. I knew how come she could draw such emotional creations and pull out such intensity and cause anyone looking too close to feel something strong. As I looked back into her eyes, I wanted to do the same thing she did, but this time I would complete the mission first.

In the hot shower I had nothing but exit routes running through my mind, ticket exchanges and purchases and costs and of course the sound of the clock ticking in my ear.

Fresh clothes, fresh cut, I walked out through the bedroom door into the sitting room. I picked up my watch from the desk and clamped it on.

It was 9:50 a.m.

"Josna, you know that we need to fly out of here immediately, right?" I was looking straight into her eyes with all the honesty I had. She lowered her eyes and placed both of her hands between her legs and raised her feet up on her toes.

"*Ha*," she said. "But I can't leave yet. My sculptures have just arrived here, and I promised Mr. Nakamura . . . ," she said softly.

"I know," I told her solidly.

"You can't leave right now, but Akemi and I must. If we work together, we can go. You can stay until your promise to Mr. Nakamura
is cleared and everybody can be safe." I was speaking in a peaceful,
even tone.

"What do you want me to do?" she asked.

"Lend Akemi your passport. When she and I are safe, we'll mail
it back to you immediately."

"But how?" she asked, thinking of the difference in their skin and
hair, I'm certain.

"Two phenomenal artists, a sculptor and a painter. I'll leave that
up to your imagination."

"But Akemi's New York travel visa is on her passport. I don't have
a New York visa in my passport," Josna said. "If we go back to Grandmother's, I could figure out a way to get her passport back from Makoto somehow. Maybe I can convince Ichiro to listen to what I say. He
likes me, but it will take some time. No one wants Akemi to leave."

Akemi began speaking softly to Josna. Their dialogue went back
and forth as I agonized over the passport visa scenario. I thought I
had it beat with the Akemi-Josna switch I came up with.

"Akemi says that she will definitely leave here with you now, but
that she wants you to take her to Busan," Josna said.

"Busan?" I asked.

"Busan, South Korea. It's a less than two hours' flight from Tokyo,
and she wouldn't need a visa and neither would you. Akemi said that
she wants to return her mother's ashes to *her* mother before she goes
to New York with you. She says that once she goes to New York with
you, she will stay there with you for good," Josna explained.

"How will she find her Korean grandmother after all these years?"
I asked, feeling suddenly heavy with the thought of another odyssey
in another country where I knew no one and could not speak even
one word of the language.

"That was the trade," Josna said. "Discovering the name and address of her Korean grandmother with the telephone number so she
could meet her was the promise that kept Akemi cooperating with
her father. It was the only thing that he had left that Akemi wanted
so desperately. It was the reason she remained silent and rode quietly
all the way to the airport and on to Hokkaido. She could have called

the police or run for help, but she didn't because her father promised to give her the information if she just followed his orders."

"And did he?" I asked with disbelief.

"He did. She has it now. But then her father had Makoto confiscate Akemi's passport so that she could not leave Japan with you while he was away on his Asian tour. Nor could she leave for the Korea trip without him. Also her credit and bank cards are canceled and she has almost no money or clothing and she's stuck all the way out here, of course. I told you he is quite clever and extremely determined."

"How do you know if she was given the right information and address?" I asked, now that I was wiser at this game.

"She has already called. We also called from here while you were in the shower. They are all waiting to meet Akemi over there. They are not waiting for Nakamura-san. It seems that they hate him. You know there are problems between the Koreans and Japanese," Josna said, not realizing that by now, I knew more than everyone else in this room about what was really going on with my wife and her family and their history and culture.

"Of course, I will take her. She's my wife and I'll take her wherever she needs to go," I said, and I meant it. It was heavy but it made sense to me. Let me allow her to fulfill her mother's final request. Let me put Akemi's heart and soul at ease, so that all that was left was for her to continue to love me and love our seeds.

When I thought of my two babies, I said, "Josna, you are the key to make sure no one on either side, in any family, gets hurt. All I want is my wife and nothing else," I reminded her calmly and carefully.

"With your passport, we can get out of Japan. Once we are in Korea, we can send you your passport, and you can send us Akemi's passport as soon as you get Makoto to give it up. Are you with me?" I asked her solemnly. There was a pause. Moments later, she handed me her passport. I opened it, looked, and then glanced at my wife a few times, comparing.

"I have cosmetics here in my purse. I'll need scissors," Josna said looking straight into me as though she were uncertain if I really wanted her to go through with this. Her eyes were asking me, "Exactly how far will you go?"

"Akemi, I will be right back," I said to my wife. "Stay inside, okay?" I slid Josna's passport into my pocket to be certain she wouldn't change her mind. Then I looked at Josna, "My clippers are in the water closet." I knew she understood.

In the elevator, I pulled out her passport to take a look at her photo. Josna had short hair in the picture, but not as short as her hair is now. At this point, I'd take my wife even without her long beautiful dark hair.

In the lobby I exited the elevator as Chiasa was revolving through the revolving doors. She and I were telepathic now, as she had suggested the second day we met. She stared at me to signal that we should meet discreetly. I veered off toward the washroom. She stalled a bit and did the same. In the Japanese Toto toilet, each toilet has a separate closed-in room. I opened the door and Chiasa stepped in. I checked to see if anyone saw, and then I entered also. It was she and I in the tight Toto closet.

"What's all this?" I asked her, referring to "our breakup," and our pretending not to know one another.

"It's better this way," she said, knowing I was listening for more of an answer. "Shota drove me here. We're friends."

"Friends?" I repeated.

"He believes that I saved him. I removed his blindfold and pulled your washcloth out of his mouth and untied him, so I guess I did," she said coyly.

"He went for that?" I asked.

"Easily. You should've seen him guzzling that water I offered him." She smiled. "And I handed him the keys, telling him that I found them right outside the vehicle."

"What else did you tell him?"

"I told him I was there to buy some lavender from Serenity Fields when I saw him in distress. So I stopped to help him." She was looking straight into me.

"So where is he now?" I asked.

"He left to go get Makoto from his hotel."

"So you are flying back to Osaka with us." I told her.

"How will you two leave Japan once you get to Osaka International without Akemi's passport?" Chiasa questioned my question.

Then she answered it. "Don't tell me . . ." She gasped. "Cool fucking idea," she said with subdued excitement.

"What a costume! Lucky you, you won't need it." Then from out of her waist pack came Akemi's passport. She handed it to me.

"Sleeping Beauty is Makoto," she said. "I searched his pockets. I had my gloves on, of course. It was easy. Usually when they tranquilize a wild bear with that stuff I used, the trappers pull his lips up and check his gums and gawk at his teeth and take a blood sample and really invade his whole seven-foot body while it lays there lifeless. Sometimes they tag him. When he wakes up, he doesn't even realize he's been raided and is wearing a tracking device that won't come off no matter what he does," she told me in excited whispers.

"So why is Shota headed to Makoto's hotel?"

"He's just a neighborhood boy, not a ninja, not Nakamura's security, not too smart. I mixed him up a little. I was stalling for you."

"Will he call the police?"

"I don't think he'll call. He'll want to save face with Makoto, Makoto will want to save face with Nakamura. Nakamura will want to save face with the media and everyone else who knew him. Besides, Makoto won't know what hit him. He saw you and he knows it wasn't you that shot him. He has no witnesses. It was just you and me and him. We two are definitely not telling," she said without a shred of doubt.

"So you'll come to the airport and leave with us?" I said to her.

"I'm invisible today. That won't be possible," she said with a pleasant but serious smile, her white teeth glistening. "I'll take the longer route. I catch a bus from here to Sapporo. I'll use my same return ticket to Osaka. I'll get our stuff from the lockers. Oh yeah, that's right, give me your key for the Kyoto lockers." She held her hand out. "You're not going to Kyoto, right? You'll get to Osaka International Airport and then to New York?" Chiasa asked.

"Nah, I'll go to Osaka and then to Korea," I told her.

"Korea!" she exclaimed.

"Long story, but I have to go there first. Keep it between me and you," I said.

"I have an idea," she said. "Let's fly to Osaka and then we can take the boat from the port in Osaka to Busan, Korea. It's better. When

Nakamura looks for you and he checks all the airports, there will be nothing. Once you get to another country, he loses his pull. He can't do anything to you two over there. I know there's a boat. I rode it over one time when I had a four-day break from ninja camp," she said, remembering. "We went to Busan for shopping. The boat, um, the ferry to Busan is called the Pan Star Line."

When she stopped reminiscing, she found me looking at her. I was still stuck on "Let's take a boat to Korea." I could feel her feeling attached to me. I could feel myself feeling attached to her also. But it was complicated and impossible for now. She knew it also. Maybe that's why she was invisible for the day, to stay away. So our feelings would not grow. And for the first time in my life as a young man, I understood something about my father, which I had never understood up until this second. I used to question, How could he have a woman as beautiful and wise and complete and sweet as Umma and still have space for a second wife to love and share with? Now, standing still in a tight toilet room about to part permanently with my lucky charm, my pretty puma, I had to ask myself, *How could I not love her?*

"I'm just joking," Chiasa said softly, about coming along with me and Akemi to Korea.

"I have to pay you your money for the extra days that you worked," I told her.

"Instead of money, maybe you can give me something else?" she said.

"Something like what?" I asked.

"I gotta think about it. Something like one wish, whatever I ask you for."

"How could I agree to that?" I asked her. "It could be something that conflicts with my beliefs. Then I couldn't do it."

"I wouldn't ask you for something that conflicts with your beliefs. Give me a little trust, can't you?" she said, exasperated.

"Aight then, if it doesn't conflict with my beliefs and it doesn't bankrupt me, I'll do it for you," I made the rare promise to her. She smiled hugely.

"Okay, so I'll see you in Korea. How long are you staying there?" she asked me. "And what city are you going to?" she asked.

"Busan. I'm headed to Busan, but I don't know for how long," I told her. "I have your number and I know where you live." Then

Chiasa looked uncertain. "Why? Can't you just trust me a little?" I asked her.

"I can!" She powered up. "Besides, I have your movie camera and some more of your stuff, so I know you'll call me," she joked. I looked at her without a smile to let her know that my stuff wasn't the reason I would call.

"Leave out of this hotel when I leave out," I told her. "If you want to remain invisible, okay. Come to the airport. I'll buy your ticket. Fly back to Osaka on the same flight so I can know you're safe. At Osaka International Airport, we go our separate ways until I call you," I said. "When we meet, we'll even up and exchange everything that needs to be exchanged."

She agreed.

Chapter 14
AKEMI

Although we ticketed and boarded the flight from Asahikawa Airport in Hokkaido separately, we were all seated in the same coach section, in the same row. Our flight to Osaka International Airport was full. I figured maybe we had gotten these last-minute three open seats because of some cancelation by some other passengers. I was grateful.

Both Chiasa and I had aisle seats. Akemi sat beside me in the middle seat to my right. Of course I felt the impulse to introduce the two of them, but there were some strong points keeping me still. First, Chiasa had made it clear that she wanted to remain invisible. Thinking now ninja to ninja, I decided and understood that this was her strategic position. She wanted to burn her involvement with this mission just in case anything went wrong in the remaining hours or days. It was sharp of her, and I understood. So I stopped considering whether she had personal reasons for wanting us to appear anonymous to one another. With the network of thoughts about what had already taken place so far, what was happening now, and the plans for my and Akemi's future, there was no more space left for me to decipher or confirm or pinpoint anything else.

I also thought that introducing two women, my wife and the woman who had made it possible for me to find my wife, on a plane surrounded by strangers would be an unnecessary security problem. Their talking to one another might reveal too much. Who knows who's listening? Besides, both of them would be speaking Japanese across and over me in a plane packed with primarily Japanese people. Only I would be left out of the language loop. Of course I chose the way that would lead to the well-being of my wife.

Chiasa was a superb ninja. She did not make eye contact with me even once since she'd hopped in her taxi driving behind Josna, Akemi, and me, or when she adjusted her airline ticket as we stood in the same line. Even during our flight she turned her body leftward and laid her face away from me. She slept throughout the entire flight. Or at least she appeared to be sleeping, as I observed her breathing by the subtle and slow rise and fall of her breast. *She must be exhausted*, I thought to myself. The night before, she had sacrificed her sleep to allow me to get mine.

Akemi was warm. She took my right hand and studied the lines that Allah had drawn in my palm. I didn't know what she might be thinking. I did know that after one good look she might make a great drawing of just the inside of my hand—done so well that the viewer would feel that she knew my entire life story through Akemi's passionate pencil strokes. She was like this, my wife. After looking closely, she began caressing my hand, moving her fingers lightly from my fingertips into my palms and up the insides of my wrists. She was feeling each of my veins with her fingertips, slowly and lightly. She is and was a continuous arousal to me. When she released my hand, she placed her hand onto the side of my face, stroking my skin. Then she slid one of her pretty, slim fingers to the inside of my ear. She was touching so lightly that it sent a strong sensation through my body. She swirled her finger out and down onto my jaw. Slowly, she began tracing my jawline. She paused one finger in the corner of my mouth. She traced the outline of my lips. I turned toward her and smiled. "What are you trying to do in here?" I asked her in English. She withdrew her hand and smiled also, her eyes flooded with feelings. She wrapped both of her hands around my arm and pressed her face against my body and steadied there.

I knew I had to lead her and not the other way around. I had a real task to clearly explain Ramadan to her all and the specific beliefs and ways of my life, our new lives, without common words or familiar tongues. I had to be careful with a wife so warm and sweet and lodged so strong up in my heart that instead of focusing on my faith, I found my mind wandering and wanting to pull her up into my lap, facing me. Of course I knew the difference between faith and fantasy. After an intense morning that wasn't truly over yet, the fantasy was very appealing.

My sensual thoughts turned to loving thoughts. My loving thoughts turned to protective thoughts. I didn't know which details Akemi knew and didn't know. But I figured it had to be stressful for Akemi to be the daughter of Joo Eun Lee, who had been kidnapped, and then to be kidnapped herself by the same person, her father, or at least the man she obviously still believed was her father. My mind began juggling images of all the incredible material things that Akemi's father had provided her and her mother with, and all the luxury and opportunities. Did he think his estate and his mountain and the clothes and the travels and the elite status that they enjoyed made it okay—canceled out that he had kidnapped a fifteen-year-young girl, hauled her overseas from her country by force, and married her? Did he believe that it was justifiable to drug my wife and fly her seven thousand miles away from me? Could he reason to himself that killing my twins, or even allowing them to live but hiding them away from their father for a lifetime was right? I was struggling in my narrow airline seat, my thoughts and mind and body in a battle.

I had gone against my own ways and beliefs. I had killed lesser men for lesser violations than the ones Nakamura had committed. I had allowed Chiasa to shoot Makoto. Tranquilizing him was the same as leaving him "half dead," which is something I don't do or haven't done in my young life. If I make the decision that a man because of his evil actions or his evil threat has to go, I don't give that man a chance at a get-back. He doesn't deserve one. Was it okay for Nakamura to be left alone and alive? Would he regroup and try to strike again? Of course he would. He was "the man who never surrenders."

Let him come, I thought to myself. *What makes a man powerful?* I thought further. *His God, his land, his culture, his language, his business, his ability to protect and defend*, I answered back. Then I experienced another first, seated beside my wife, whom I had experienced a bunch of meaningful firsts with. For the first time since Umma and I had landed in the United States of America, my mind shifted from my responsibility and strategy of protecting Umma while we were living there, and building a business with her while we were living there, and buying a house for her while we were there, to a consideration to take Umma and my wife and sister and to return to the Sudan no matter how complicated that might become.

If I had learned one lesson from traveling to Japan, it was that if a man could survive and build on his own land, surrounded by his own like-minded people, speaking his own language, following his own beliefs, he could control the outcome of his circumstances much better.

I had seen that Americans didn't believe what I believed. Japanese didn't believe what I believed, and the environment that they had created made it impossible for a man to secure his wife and raise his children properly. There was no consensus among the men of America or the men of Japan about how to live properly, how to relate to their women, how to raise their sons and secure their daughters. How could there be a belief when the women in America and in Japan were nearly naked out of doors daily? To truly love and protect a woman in these surroundings would be to have to fight constantly. A man would spend most of his seconds and minutes and hours fighting. The only alternative would be to not love the women. If a man did not love women, he wouldn't have any concern over them. He wouldn't protect them. He wouldn't marry them. He would only ignore or use and abuse them. Love makes a man protect his women. Anything else is not love. I was certain of this.

It is not as though I had not witnessed these truths through my own father. I had witnessed them as a child, daily. I had even thought about them. I had remembered and cherished the memories also. Now I was seeing these truths as a man. Now I was deciding. If I had to constantly fight no matter where I lived and stood, why not fight in the land of my father, for the land of my father, and the faith and beliefs of my father? At least there the way of life was worth guarding, maintaining, and enjoying. There was a basic agreement between men over the simple things, like the definition of man, the definition of woman, the sacredness of family, what should be done in our homes versus what shouldn't be done in our homes, and so on. Spilling blood or having my own blood spilled was easy for me to accept if it had a deeper meaning and a meaningful purpose and outcome. In fact, only now after all of this did I realize that, more than land and money and power, men around the globe were fighting over the meaning of life, the meaning of love, and the way we each should be living from day to day. The money and the power was just a method to control the meaning. *Could that be true?* I asked myself.

In a flow of passengers moving at a careful pace toward the luggage carousel, Chiasa walked in front of us. In one sudden movement, she stopped, breaking the rhythm of the crowd, and searched the floor for four rocks that had somehow spilled from her pockets. Naturally I bent to help her pick them up. Quickly she grabbed two and so did I. Inside of the two seconds that we were both bent to the floor she whispered, "Check three o'clock, it's Mayu from the Nakamura estate."

As I stood up looking in the three o'clock direction, Akemi was already seeing Mayu and waving her way. I pulled Akemi back and held her hand as Chiasa eased onward. Turning her focus toward me, Akemi said, "Josna." There weren't enough seconds available for me to think fast or switch plans or even to measure the threat. I was clear that my spot had been blown up now that Mayu saw me walking with Akemi as we exited the flight from Hokkaido and approached the luggage carousel. Mayu was standing among others in clear view on the opposite side of the divide. I recalled that Chiasa had described Mayu as the manager of the Nakamura estate who was secretly "on Akemi's side." I held Akemi with me until my backpack rolled around. I picked it up and we walked together through the luggage area and exited directly where Mayu stood waiting.

Both Akemi and Mayu went into a series of bows. Then Akemi turned herself on an angle toward both Mayu and me and introduced me. I could only catch and understand a few of the Japanese words my wife used. But her tone and gestures held great affection and she went on as though she were presenting Mayu to a royal emissary or an important diplomat and not the hated nemesis of her father— Mayu's longtime and current employer. Mayu bowed to me politely using only her head and not bending to the degrees that I had seen many Japanese people bow.

"*Konichiwa, hajime mashite, bokuwa Mayonaka desu.*" I spoke the standard Japanese self-introduction. In a way that revealed so much about their culture, the woman Mayu barely looked at me. She didn't smile or frown or display any emotion. She placed all her attention on Akemi and stepped to the side and rested one hand on the Louis Vuitton luggage stacked in size order on a cart beside her. Mayu spoke some more to Akemi, softly and calmly.

As my eyes scanned the pile of red Epi leather luggage—a trunk, a suitcase, and a soft Cruiser sack, all matching—I took a deep breath. Either this conservative, crispy clean, and quality, well-dressed woman was a two-faced clever aid to Nakamura who wanted to saddle me with expensive and heavy *red* luggage that made me stand out and slow down so that I could be identified and caught, or she was just a concerned stand-in mother to Akemi who overdid it as mothers do when their love and concern are pushed to an extreme. Further, I guessed that she must think that Akemi was on her way to America. Why else would she pack so many items when Korea was a short jump across the sea? She must've also believed that Akemi would not return anytime soon.

Akemi watched me from the corners of her pretty eyes, while showing respect toward Mayu at the same time. I could hear Mayu using familiar Japanese names, vocabulary words and phrases which I had memorized and learned by now, such as *Nihon*, which means "Japan," *otosan*, which means "father," ai, which means "love," *beikoku*, which means America, *kiotsukete*, which means "be careful." Then Mayu paused her speech for some seconds and asked Akemi in Japanese with a blank face but steady stare, "Are you sure?"

"*Hai!*" Akemi responded. It was the eighth "*Hai!*" I had counted in their conversation filled, I imagined, with instructions, questions, and concerns.

Mayu bowed a deep bow to Akemi and turned and left. Akemi watched me as I watched Mayu walking away. I was looking to see if Mayu joined anyone else. Was she at the airport alone for the sake of helping Akemi to leave the country undetected? Exactly who had unloaded and carried the heavy luggage for her? Was it one of Nakamura's men or just a skycap or airport worker or taxi driver whom she had randomly selected? As she disappeared from my view, walking solemnly in small steps, wearing an expensive skirt suit and sturdy, quality elder-lady pumps, I thought to myself, *Either she is doing a good job of acting, or she is actually all alone.*

What had she been told about Akemi's travel and future plans? I wondered. I figured Josna had called ahead to Mayu—thinking with her heart and not her brain—and had had Mayu prepare Akemi's clothing and essentials. As my wife's best friend, Josna, I'm sure, felt that she knew exactly what Akemi needed and wanted and was accustomed to having.

Earlier in Hokkaido Josna had lent Akemi her olive-green Adidas sweatpants and a tiny olive-green jacket to wear. Akemi had had no luggage or change of clothes since she had no idea that she was going to be sent up there to Hokkaido from her doctor's visit. It was too much of a rush for me to judge or complain about the borrowed outfit. It was better than traveling with a dark-haired beauty dressed in a mini made up only of flowers. Thinking further, although Josna had caused Mayu to become the only person from the Nakamura estate to have actually seen me, other than Nakamura's man Makoto, who lay tranquilized still in the tall Hokkaido grass that shielded him, I told myself not to harden my heart in judgment against Josna. She, after all, had agreed to give up her own passport to Akemi knowing full well that not having her documents in hand while living as a Nepali foreigner in Japan placed herself at legal risk.

Josna had even agreed in the event that Akemi didn't have her own passport, to shave her best friend's head of her long, flowing, soft black locks, and transform her into a brown-skinned Nepali by brushing cosmetics over Akemi's face, neck, hands, feet, and arms, as carefully as she would have prepared and handled one of her treasured sculptures. Josna was willing to do anything to make it possible for Akemi to ease beyond customs and passport inspection with her husband and then out of Japan, even though she really didn't want her best friend and herself to be separated. Josna had moved beyond her fears and doubts and supported our love and marriage even though she probably thought we might be reckless. But her calling and informing Mayu had placed me in an even greater race against time and at a serious risk. What Chiasa had planned out and executed so perfectly had now been compromised by Josna.

I knew that even though Josna and Akemi believed that Mayu was on Akemi's side, we had no true way of knowing if Mayu had also tipped off Nakamura. If she told him, I was certain that even though he was away on his Asian tour, he would send his hired dogs out to descend on the airport or make some influential phone calls to Japanese authorities to intercept and interrupt—and to seize his daughter and stop me, perhaps permanently.

Once again Chiasa had been ahead in her thinking and her strategy—and 100 percent on point.

Now Akemi and I were packed into an immaculate cab exiting

from a random airport exit on purpose. I had decided we would travel to South Korea by sea. Her father Nakamura, I believed, would underestimate me and never consider that I would use the sea route. Akemi and Josna did not know that it was an option either. In fact only Chiasa and I knew. We were both trained to keep our mouths shut—and to swallow our secrets until death. And now I knew the difference between a woman who is a man's friend, and a woman whom a man loves, and a woman who is a man's comrade.

A comrade is like-minded, trained in a similar skill, going for the same goal, loyal to the same rules. She is an asset to the mission.

A woman whom a man loves is most likely untrained. She is moving with her heart as her leader. She is liable to step directly into a minefield—or even to help the opposition by coincidence or by mistake.

A woman who is a man's friend is loyal but not only to one person and not necessarily because she is trained to be loyal or even working toward the same goal. A friend's multiple loyalties could end up sinking the mission and getting everyone including herself hurt or captured or killed.

On the other hand, a comrade places the mission in the first position. She places the mission before her heart and before her personal needs and wants. She is more loyal to the mission than to any one person or thing. She will even cut her own throat before placing her comrade at risk—or before making foolish mistakes consciously or subconsciously. A comrade would never destroy the team's chances of achieving the mission goal.

I understood now that a woman who is a friend, like Josna, or a woman who is a man's true love, like my wife Akemi, is untrained and unskilled in this way and without understanding. Neither a friend nor a love could ever be considered my comrade. Yet a female who is well trained and sharply skilled, who is loyal and thorough could be considered all three: my comrade, my friend, and my love.

* * *

Akemi sat with her luggage while wearing my sunglasses as I walked over to the information counter at the station on the pier in Osaka, where the ships docked. The station was stuffed and buzzing with passengers. Like everyplace I had gone in Japan, it was extremely clean, well lit, and tightly organized. It was a full-scale operation, not a matter of pressing some notes into the palm of a captain of a tiny or midsized boat or yacht even. There were customs forms to be completed and embarkment papers. As I glanced the length of the station, I could see the entrance to the security checkpoint that all passengers had to pass through to board the ships. A random boarding call announcement made first in Japanese, then in Korean, Chinese, and then in English caught my attention late. Hurrying, I picked up the customer checklist printed in four different languages. Number 6 on the checklist read, "Ticket buyers under the age of 20 must have their tickets purchased by an adult, parent, or guardian. Guardian/adult must present his or her passport or a valid form of identification." I paused in disbelief and then read it over again. My jaw tightened and my thoughts raced through my options. Me, Akemi, Chiasa—we're all teenagers. Even Josna, still in Hokkaido, was only eighteen.

Akemi was watching me through the crowds of people rushing through. She seemed to sense that there was some holdup. I picked up a checklist card for her printed in Japanese. I approached the ticket counter to double-check. I already knew that the Japanese were tight with their rules and laws, but for me traveling from America and throughout Japan, I had zero problems purchasing absolutely anything that I could afford: plane tickets, train tickets, hostel and hotel rooms. The Americans and the Japanese made moves once money changed hands, no matter whose hands it came from.

"One ticket to Busan, South Korea," I said to the attendant on the English-only line.

"Passport please," she said immediately. As I presented it and she slid her hand beneath the curved glass to accept it, she asked, "First class, private room, double, single, or group economy?" Before I even answered, she said, "Oh, sorry, you'll need someone twenty or over to purchase your ticket, sir."

I reached in and pulled back my passport. "What time does the ship leave?" I asked.

"It leaves from here at two forty-five p.m.," she answered.

"And what time does the next one leave?" I asked.

"There's one Busan, Korea, trip a day at two forty-five in the afternoon every day. Can I help you with anything else?" she asked, seeming anxious to serve the next person on line.

"Yes, do you have a price list for the tickets?" I asked her.

"It's on the other side of the information card in your hand," she said with a polite half smile.

"Thank you, but uh, why can't I buy a ticket for myself?" I pushed. "I'm a traveling foreign student. My parents are not here traveling with me."

"Pan Star Line is a Korean-owned shipping line. I'd love to sell you a ticket, but these are the rules handed down from the Korean side." She pressed her lips together tightly. "Some students bring a signed and notarized letter of permission from their parents. That can work. We can accept that," she said, offering what was a useless alternative for me and especially for Akemi. "Good luck, sir. Next," she called out.

I stepped to the side, thinking, *Stupid rule! I couldn't purchase the ticket myself, but they would allow me to travel on my own if a parent or guardian or adult purchased it for me.* Also, I now knew that either the Japanese or the Koreans considered the legal age for adulthood to be twenty, not eighteen like the Americans. I checked my watch. The only ship of the day cruising to Busan, Korea, was leaving shortly. Or we could taxi back to Osaka International Airport and book a flight leaving today without a problem. I wanted to close my eyes and think deeply for a minute. I needed to confer with myself, or my father, or with the supreme option, Allah. But I couldn't, so I relied on my own instincts. My gut told me the sea route was the right choice. The airline looked and sounded like the easier and faster option, but shit that's too easy, too open, too available is sometimes the deadliest. Taking one more full glance at the busy station, I saw tens and hundreds of Japanese, many Koreans and Chinese, some Scandinavians and other Europeans, and zero Africans or obviously Muslim persons. I knew that I could approach some adult to buy the tickets on my behalf. Yet I didn't trust asking anyone Japanese. I had no way to gauge how they would react, or which one of them would grow suspicious of the Nakamura name on my wife's passport—or worse, be familiar with her because they saw her picture in the newspaper for her many art achievements.

As it goes in Japan, there were no bums or beggars to whom I could slide a 10,000 yen note in exchange for purchasing our tickets. Matter of fact, everyone was so neatly dressed, quiet, and professional in appearance that I could not detect a single needy person of low status who might cooperate.

I handed the information card to Akemi. She read it following behind me as I pushed her luggage out of the station and into the trunk of a cab. I needed to think it through first. I didn't want to highlight my wife or myself. I had almost twenty-four hours left to solve this ticket-buying problem and to board tomorrow's ship, and I refused to lose. As for now, I would hide my diamond Akemi in a place where I believed Nakamura would not look or would never be able to locate in time.

In the back seat of the cab her eyes questioned me. The driver's eyes were beaming in reverse through his rearview mirror.

"Hotel?" she asked in English.

"*Hai!*" I agreed while pulling out my English-to-Japanese word and phrase dictionary. "A very small and quiet hotel around here by the sea," I wanted to say.

"small"–*chisai*

"quiet hotel"–*shizukana hoteru*

"here,"–*koko*

"sea,"–*kaiyou*

I said.

Akemi laughed and said, "*Hai!*" She began speaking in Japanese to the driver. They spoke for so long, I got vexed, not knowing what he was asking my wife or saying to her. Looking through the windows and onto the streets instead, I checked out the businesses as the taxi weaved in and out of a series of side streets.

It didn't take me long to figure out that Akemi was directing the driver as she searched each block for a suitable place for us to be discreet. "Akemi does not speak English but she is not stupid," Josna had told me firmly in Hokkaido. "In fact she's quite a genius." Josna added.

The area was a tourist haven of all types of eateries and cafés and shops and, of course, bookstores. Everything was labeled in kanji without translation. They had whatever a foreigner could afford, but it was written in the Japanese language so that you would never forget where you are and who's running it. Certain establishments made their presence known by flying their national flags. How else would I have been able to locate the Islamic presence, unless I saw the majes-

tic flag of Saudi Arabia, a rich emerald green cloth with the curve and
precision of the black-inked Arabic letters and the sword accentuat-
ing it? I made a note of the block I was on. I couldn't read the kanji
street signs, but I would use the all-karaoke building on the left and
the Toyota dealer on my right as my landmarks.

"*Tomare!*" Akemi said softly but with enthusiasm. The driver
pressed the brakes. Both the door and the trunk opened automatically.

It was impossible not to be shocked at the weird side street spot
my sweet wife selected. When I hauled in her last piece of luggage, no
attendant had appeared to assist us. The lobby was vacant aside from
some velvet throwback couches and a long wooden table. I looked for
the bell. There was none. Akemi began walking around. When she
reached the opposite side of the room, she waved me over. "*Mayonaka
isoide!*" she said.

I joined her in front of a set of vending machines. We looked
in. Behind the glass were the room keys. They were each attached
to a number and a knob and there was also a set of buttons and a
slot to feed the machine cash bills and coins. Akemi pressed a kanji-
labeled button and the keys spun from our view. Now there were
postcard-sized photos of what I believe were their hotel rooms. Each
room had its own strangeness and its own theme. I couldn't read the
kanji explanations and options. Akemi stood at my side reading them
and reacting and pointing. One room was filled with stuffed animals
that looked like aliens, one room had everything Mickey Mouse, one
room was Japanese traditional with no bed but a thin mat and a hard-
looking pillow. There were twenty-four rooms pictured in total. Ten
of them were marked sold or in use. Akemi faced me and said in English, "Mayonaka choose." I smiled naturally. I knew I had taught her
the English word *choose*, and I knew the Japanese translation, *erabete*.

"Akemi choose," I joked.

"Okay! Akemi choose," she said playfully. Then she pressed a rectangular glass button beneath the picture of a room with sheer black
linen curtains, an American-style mattress with black sheets, a black
desk, a black chair, and a bamboo floor. The pictures disappeared and
the keys to the room Akemi had selected appeared lit up by a thin,
rectangular, neon-green light.

"Five thousand yen," Akemi announced. I pulled out my money

stack. At the same time she went into her pocketbook and pulled out her Epi leather wallet.

"Put it back," I told her. I was sure she understood my tone if not my words, though instead of putting her wallet back, she pulled out 30,000 yen, which when converted to American dollars was less than $300. She flicked it between her fingers as though to show me, "That's all the money I got." Then she pushed it back into the space in her wallet and pulled out her bank card. She bent it in half to let me know she couldn't use it anymore.

"Don't worry about it," I said calmly as I searched my mind for the right words in her language. She pulled out her student ID and flashed it just to show me. Then she took out her Pratt College student ID from New York, where she had taken the art courses as her prize for winning an art competition. She held her face close to the Pace ID card and tried to duplicate her smile in the photo when she was a bit younger and not in so much trouble, before she had married me.

I fed the machine five 1,000 yen notes. The room keys dropped down, and a ticket was spit out with the room number and time printed on it. Impressed, I grabbed the ticket and the keys.

The next vending machine was selling everything a customer might need at a hotel, including condoms. On a business level I was hooked on the whole vending machine concept but I didn't buy none of it. At a big-time overseas hotel like the Hilton or Hyatt everything this place was selling separately in its vending machine would've been provided for free. But I was glad we were here in this low-key weird place whose name I did not know. There was no registration card or anyone to check our passports or anything Nakamura could trace. I figured there was actually someone from this little hotel watching the two of us from somewhere. The Japanese were notorious for secrets, hideouts, trapdoors, and sneak attacks and the art of invisibility. But to whoever was watching, my wife and me, we were simply customers who had already fed the machine and paid the required fee. So they wouldn't have any reason to interfere.

The craftsmanship on our second-floor door was outstanding. Made from heavy metal, each hotel room had a meter on it with a digital clock. Ours was counting down from five hours from the moment I inserted the key.

Once we were inside, the heavy door slammed closed so securely I was certain it was fool proof. There was a much smaller meter on the other side of the door as well. The Japanese had thought of it all and planned it out perfectly. I said to myself, *Be careful, Mayonaka. Their culture has prepared them well for the "thought battles" of life.*

We removed our shoes. I carried in her luggage. Akemi crawled over the mattress and curled up in the corner, her black hair spreading across the black sheets, her petite green leather jacket creeping up and revealing her belly button. Her borrowed Adidas sweats a bit too big, I could see the divide that led to her private places. I removed my backpack and stood it in a corner of the room. From my knapsack I pulled out the urn that contained Akemi's mother's ashes. I placed it on the desk as she watched me intently.

In the bathroom, I washed my hands and face, removing the soil from the flight and travel. When I stepped back into the room, Akemi was looking through her clothes that were professionally packed and wrapped—some tied with ribbons and others with thick string like each item was brand-new.

"I'll be right back," I told her before the heavy door clicked locked.

When I returned from a nearby convenience store, I placed eight bottles of spring water, one lemon, one cup of fresh-sqeezed orange juice, and two *onigiri* rice triangles on the desk. I left a new bar of soap, two toothbrushes, and toothpaste. From my backpack I pulled out Akemi's body oil and a small shampoo. I sat everything beside the rice cooker and the tea set.

I picked up her passport and said, "Akemi, I'm going back out. Dinner at seven, Akemi and Mayonaka." She opened the bathroom door slightly, one pretty eye watching me through the slight opening. *"Hai,"* she said softly. I eased out, looking quickly past her little lavender lace panties and bra laid out on the bed.

* * *

There were three hours remaining on this day of my Ramadan fast. I remembered in the Sudan my father and the men on our estate staying in the mosque throughout the entire Ramadan days, separated from their wives and children. I could feel now why men must separate themselves from their women at times to guard their faith and serve their Maker. Women are so quietly powerful that their presence can separate a man from his beliefs before he even realizes he has done *harom*, the forbidden.

The clock was winding down on our strange hotel room and on my chances of securing an adult broker to buy our Pan Star Line tickets. My mind had been shifting ideas back and forth. I was certain of one thing: there had to be someone out here in this international hub for boats, barges, cargo, and ships who was willing to earn ten or twenty or thirty thousand yen just for showing his identification and purchasing two one-way tickets to Busan.

Outside the spot where the Saudi Arabian flag flew high, I sensed that my idea was a long shot. Up close, I could now see clearly that it was a carpet store called Jeddah Carpets. This was not just any collection of carpets. They were from Saudi Arabia, which ranks among the top three carpet makers in the world. I'm sure business was bringing them bundles. My offer of what amounted to about two or three hundred dollars for the ticket-buying errand would be considered minimal or nothing at all. Determined not to defeat my plan with doubt, I went inside the place anyway.

"Asalaam alaikum, Ramadan Kareem." I greeted the elderly Arab man in Arabic and reminded him of our mutual sacred holiday at the same time.

"Alaikum salaam, Allah hafiz. How can we accommodate you?" he asked. "Our samples have been displayed for your comfort," he added before taking a breath.

"I'm not here to order your fine carpets. I saw your flag and thought you might have information about the closest *masjid* in this area."

"Alhamdulillah! You are trying to locate a mosque in Osaka?" The man said and then smiled doubtfully. "It is easier to find a fish in the desert." He laughed two short grunts. "But the mosque is in the heart, is it not?" he asked me. Suddenly, a younger Saudi man, about forty years old or so, came bursting through the back curtain.

"What is it?" he asked. "We are not hiring."

"I'm not looking for work," I stated. "I have a business of my own."

"Well, then you are here for buying carpet?" He smiled and opened his hands, a gesture to welcome a potential customer.

"He is looking for a mosque," the elder man said.

"What for?" the younger one asked.

"For today's Maghrib prayer," I responded, tolerating him.

"We are not fasting. My father has diabetes and I am traveling," the younger one said.

"I'm also traveling." I showed him his excuse, as we were both foreigners living comfortably, it seemed, and definitely *not* traveling through a hot desert on a camel's back like men were in the old days of Muhammad, peace be upon him.

"So are you better than us?" he asked with his face reddening and tightening some.

"*Salaam,*" I said and turned to leave. It was a brief exchange, but I was clear from the vibe that I wasn't gonna get anything moving from either of these two.

I was not disappointed, just determined. I already knew that just because a man is an Arab does not mean that he is a Muslim, and just because he says he's Muslim does not mean that he's true.

"*Sura* two, *ayat* one eighty-four," the elder Arab man said as he stepped outside his carpet business and onto the sidewalk where I stood.

He was quoting from chapter two of the Holy Quran, the 184th line. I knew it well. It commanded all Muslims to observe the Ramadan fast except if they were sick or traveling. It also said that Muslims who could not fast because of travel or illness should make up the fasting days before the beginning of the next Ramadan fast. Or if a believer could not fast due to illness, he should feed one Muslim a charitable meal each day of Ramadan instead. He then handed me a flyer written in Arabic. I read it. It advertised a free meal to Muslims fasting during Ramadan at sunset each day, and posted the location. "Sponsored by Jeddah Carpets," it read.

"We have set this table at a nice halal restaurant as a form of *zakat* since my son and I are unable to fast during Ramadan. This is what is required from us as believers."

"*Sura* two, *ayat* two sixty-four," I responded. From the change in his facial expression, I could tell that he understood. "I'm not searching for charity. I was looking for like-minded men from our faith, but thank you." I left with a distaste for men who try and pay their way out of Ramadan.

In a phone booth I used my phone card and called Haki, the Kenyan college student who lived in the Harajuku hostel where I once stayed. His hospitality was the opposite feeling of the father and son of Jeddah Carpets. His face had not popped into my thoughts when I reviewed the short list of adults I knew here in Japan. However, it did when I was in the carpet store. Haki had said to me a few times, "If you need anything at all, just ask me."

"*Habari gani,*" Haki picked up my call.

"*Salaam,*" I said. "It's Mayonaka who stayed there at the hostel a few weeks ago."

There was a pause. "Oh yes, brother. How is it? You are still here in Japan, yes?"

"I'm still here—," I said, and he interrupted.

"I mentioned to you once before that it's a difficult place to leave. What can I do for you?"

"Haki, listen carefully, I got a situation," I said.

"As the Englishman says, 'I am all ears.' Strange saying, isn't it?" he joked.

"I'm in Osaka right now. I don't know who you may know out here, but I need to buy a ticket to board the ferryboat from Osaka to Busan, Korea," I explained.

"The loan department is the only department I cannot help you with, my brother. Remember college students have all had our accounts emptied out by our universities."

"Haki, I can help you with that. I have money. I can pay out thirty thousand yen over the cost of the tickets to the person who buys the tickets for me. They won't sell them to me directly because I'm underage."

"Is there something that the Japanese will not sell?" he asked, sounding seriously surprised.

"It's not the Japanese. It's a Korean-owned cruise line."

"Hmm . . . I know at least three students in Osaka. I'll have to try and reach them. It's exam time for me. Man, I wish I was there, even I could use the thirty thousand yen. When do you plan to travel?"

"Tomorrow afternoon. The payment is for the person who can put a rush on it, show up with his passport or any official form of identification. He has to be twenty years or older."

"Twenty or over," he repeated. "Isn't it strange, the clash of culture?"

"What?" I didn't know what he was talking about.

"Back home in Kenya, a boy becomes a man at age fourteen. At fourteen, I am no longer allowed to remain in a house under the same roof with my own mother. My father would forbid it. My people would look down on it. At fourteen my older brother, who already had his own house and me, built a house for me on the property that my parents own. My father gave me a plot of land there. I could have married at that instant and taken my new bride into the house that I built. As you can see, I didn't. I opted to focus on my studies. But it was my choice as a man."

"Word up, a big difference," I acknowledged. At that moment I appreciated Haki's like-mindedness.

"When I first arrived in Japan, everything was crazy for me. It took some getting used to. Japanese men were still dressing in short pants."

"Short pants?" I repeated.

"In my country, only young boys wear short pants outside or as a school uniform. Once you are a man, you wear proper pants and shirts. Isn't it? Yet the Japanese have what they refer to as teenagers! What is that? Neither child nor man, I suppose. Yet they are still dressed as little boys. The Japanese men at twenty, thirty, forty are still reading comic books and playing with their toys and ignoring their women. One Japanese fella I know, a grad student, was always talking about his girlfriend. As it turns out, she was some popular animated character who he fell in love with somehow. But he stupidly believed they were in a real-life relationship."

"Haki, thanks for taking my call, but I'm running low on time," I said with an even tone. "Do you think you can arrange this for me?" I pressed.

"I'm gonna make three calls. Call me back in one hour just in case I gotta track 'em down."

"Aight, thanks," I told him. But he was still talking as I was in motion to hang up. I pulled the phone back to my ear.

"Speaking of women, is it one ticket or two tickets that you need? First you said ticket. Then you said tickets. Which is it?" Haki asked.

"It's two tickets," I confirmed.

"I see . . . I had been meaning to ask you. I hope that it is okay to ask." He spoke hesitantly for some reason.

"What?" I pushed him to get right to it.

"There was a beautiful African girl I saw you with. She was African and Japanese. Forgive me if she is your woman, but if she is not, how about arranging an introduction for me? She seems like the best of both worlds. It's been lonely here for me. I mean, the rigorous studies and the differences in culture and beliefs and things. Brother, I'm not looking for a bargirl. You know that I know exactly where to find them! I'm looking for a good girl, a wife. Is she yours?"

"She is my woman." I told him, and hung up.

I felt confident about Haki's ability to complete the ticket transaction. If he was smart, he would locate a broker and offer him 15,000 or 20,000 yen and keep the rest as a finder's fee. He had led me to find halal foods and Billy's and the Senegalese. I should've thought of him before I ever considered the Saudi Arabians. Many of them are known for their riches and sometimes for their arrogance. Better yet, I should've searched out the neediest, most genuine Muslim man. That way I would be performing *zakat* to help him, while helping myself as well. I wouldn't use the *zakat* as an excuse either. I would do it in addition to maintaining the fast, which is required of all able Muslims.

Then that thought triggered a new idea. I pulled the flyer from my pocket and opened it a second time. I jumped in a cab and headed over to the free meal sponsored by Jeddah Carpets. I scolded myself for the whole ride. Allah had placed the answer directly into the palm of my hands. But I had allowed the messenger to distract me from the gift of the message. Of course there would be at least one willing Muslim adult at the Maghrib prayer, and the free meal for breaking our fast, who could also use the extra pocket money.

* * *

In the back room of a Lebanese restaurant, situated side by side with a Saudi hookah bar, twelve men, including myself, plus five women who stood behind us, made the Maghrib prayer. The small room was much warmer than the air outside. The thick and plush carpet was welcoming to both our bended knees and our lowered foreheads.

When our prayers were completed, some moved through the curtain and into the empty restaurant, where a long table was set and marked with a placard that read in Arabic "Courtesy of Jeddah Carpets." Still in the back with six other Muslim men who remained there also, I peered into faces, but discreetly. There were African Muslims in the mix, I could tell, but none of them black-skinned like me. I was looking not for a common race but for a common faith and mind-set. I knew a Muslim, a true believer, would support and respect a young marriage like mine. It would not pour into their ears as poison. It would be familiar and, for many, expected. It was for these reasons that I sought out a Muslim in particular.

I chose a brother named Ali. He was young but older than me, I could tell. He was wearing an Osaka University T-shirt and jeans. More important, he had arrived accompanying a visibly pregnant wife, which I believed might work in my favor.

"May I talk with you for a moment?" I asked him. He nodded and stepped out of the circle of men he was quietly conversing with.

"I am a student traveling with my young wife. We are trying to purchase tickets here at the pier for the ferry to South Korea. They tell me that I need someone twenty years or older to purchase the tickets for me; someone who has a valid passport or official identification. I need to travel tomorrow. If you are willing, I can pay thirty thousand yen for you to be the broker to buy the tickets on my behalf."

He stood staring at me, a powerful stare without blinking. "Which university do you attend?" he asked me.

"I'm a high school student," I said.

He stood silently for a few seconds and then hummed. "A married high school student?"

"Yes," I responded. *"Alhamdulillah,"* I added.

"Where are you coming from?" He asked.

"Africa," I said, purposely vague.

"A huge place," he commented, letting me know he was too smart for this kind of broad response.

"I have an American passport, my wife has a Japanese passport," I added, still dodging my origin.

"Oh, so there is the trouble," he said knowingly. "Her father and family have forbidden your union?" He asked.

"Her father gave written permission for our union before our marriage and tried to withdraw it after our *agid* was completed and our marriage was performed and consummated," I said. I had a feeling that this information, which I would normally have concealed, would move Ali into my corner.

"*La kadar Allah,*" Ali said quietly, meaning "God forbid." "Now you are running away?"

"I am taking my wife to visit with her grandmother," I said, and then added swiftly, "The ticket office will close today in one hour. It will reopen at nine a.m. tomorrow morning." I pressed.

As he paused for more than sixty seconds of thought, his wife gently pushed the curtain to the side, looking for him. She looked into his eyes and he into hers. She was holding a small plate with two dates and a few slices of fruit. He put his hand up, to signal her to remain where she was. When she released the curtain, he asked me to wait. Now I stood alone, as only three other men remained still talking among themselves.

After five minutes I walked into the restaurant area not knowing if he had secretly diverted. He was there seated with his wife, who wore a *hijab* and long shirt properly concealing her neck and arms and breasts and hips—over her loose-fitting jeans. She looked my way with judging eyes. Soon they both stood up. Ali walked over.

"My wife said that you are good. Somehow she feels certain. But she is a woman. So I must have some confirmation. How do I know that you are not a criminal? Maybe you have killed someone."

"If we all did our jobs as Muslims, everything would go as it should," I assured him.

"Meaning?" he questioned.

"I am a Muslim man following my *deen.* I am married and securing my wife. You are a Muslim man, a husband, a student, right? Allah is the best knower of all things and Allah will hand out the punishment and the rewards, not you or me, right?" I told him. "So Allah will do his work and the police will do theirs, and you and I . . ."

He turned away from me, and he and his wife shifted from the Arabic language that we had been speaking into Persian, which I did not speak. Silently I waited.

"Show me your passport, and where is your wife?" he asked, turning back to me. As I pulled out my passport and Akemi's, I said, "You will have to present these passports to purchase our tickets." He looked at them quickly. "I also have our marriage documents on me," I offered. His wife smiled approvingly.

* * *

Five minutes before the ticket window closed, Ali purchased a ticket for me. His wife, Samira, purchased a ticket for Akemi. They were Shia Muslims, originally from Iran. Both of them were graduate students at Osaka University. Ali was in engineering and Samira was studying medicine.

Samira was captivated by my "love story." She was also curious about "the Japanese girl," as she seemed to have formed an opinion about them as a group.

"Is she Muslim?" she asked.

"Soon, *inshallah*," I answered, "but not yet. She is reading and learning from our Holy Quran."

"She is willing?"

"Akemi thinks Islam is beautiful," I added truthfully.

"*Alhamdulillah!*" Samira said, excited. "Will you both continue your studies?"

"I see that your love hasn't stopped the two of you from your studies." I smiled. Then they both smiled. Just when I thought I had satisfied her curiosity, she asked me more questions.

"Does your wife speak Arabic? Why Korea?" She asked questions one after the other, softly and politely as Muslim women tend to do. Ali did not seem to mind her questioning me, or my responding. So I fed her a few harmless general facts about myself. I kept rephrasing the same information in different ways but thought it was important to keep her smiling and calm. It was clear that Ali trusted her, not me.

"Akemi doesn't speak Arabic! And she doesn't speak English either! And you don't speak Japanese! *E wallah!*" she exclaimed. "So the two of you are communicating through your eyes, your thoughts, and your gestures? How beautiful!" Samira said softly. "Praise Allah! He has given both of you something special."

"And our hearts," I said. "We are communicating through our hearts." And those were my last words before they each purchased our tickets.

Afterward, I paid Ali the 30,000 yen. He embraced me: "There is an Islamic center in South Korea. Be sure and visit there in Itaewon. It's a section of Seoul. There are many halal places and a mosque as well. There are good Muslims there, not many, but enough for a community."

"Thanks, good looking out," I told him.

"And you are right. Allah is the best knower of all things," he said. Then we parted ways.

*   *   *

A well-suited, elderly Japanese man whose breath filled the entrance to my hotel with the stale of alcohol was being held up by a young Japanese female teen. She wasn't robbing him. She was simply keeping him from stumbling while drunk. I moved past them before noticing my wife standing in front of the vending machine across the lobby. I walked up behind her and pressed my body against her back. She was wearing a sleeveless dress. She looked up and over her shoulder at me, with her mischievous smile.

"What are you doing now?" I asked her. She placed her finger on the glass, pointing out some kanji letters. Softly she said, "Five thousand yen." She didn't reach for her purse, and I liked that she didn't make the same mistake twice. I fed the machine the money and walked behind her up the stairs, enjoying the way the expensive black silk dress danced on her subtle curves. I was loving her pretty toes, the nails freshly painted black, and her bare legs in her expensive high heels. She could seduce me, but when we reached upstairs, I would have her change her clothes. From here on in, she would not seduce any other man, which I believe women do when they are uncovered outside of home. As my wife, she would conceal her magnetism. And she had so much of it.

The hotel room door meter was just about to eat up the last two minutes of our payment. I pushed in the new key and it reset until the following morning.

The scent of nail polish rushed up my nose when the door closed behind us. We both took our shoes off. Akemi's clothes were in neat, high stacks piled up in the corner. I had to smile as I glanced around the room. Finally relaxed enough to really notice every detail, the sheer black curtains, revealing the blackened sky, and the clean black sheets pulled taut across the mattress. My wife had beautiful black eyelined eyes and wore an exquisite black silk dress and her petite feet and pretty black toenails were alluring against the tan bamboo floor. *She is art,* I thought to myself as I saw how she blended and decorated herself and everything that surrounded her.

I noticed the one missing bottle of water and the uneaten onigiris.

Right beside them and on the desk lay several crisp brand-new 10,000 yen notes, which were perfectly spaced and arranged like a circular Asian fan. I stepped over.

With my eyes, I counted. There were thirty-five 10,000 yen notes, close to $3,500 US. I didn't say a word, just turned and looked at my wife, who was leaning up against the wall looking back at me. We stared.

"Come close," I said to her. She walked over slowly and came up very close. She looked up into my eyes. I hugged her. "Where did you get all that money?" I asked, feeling her soft hair against my face.

As I looked over and past her, I realized that I did not see her trunk or suitcase. The LV Cruiser bag was there though. I dropped my arms, put my hands on each side of her waist. I pushed her back a step gently. "What did you do?" I asked her.

She pulled my study cards out from my pocket and flipped through them quickly. Then she eased my Japanese-English dictionary out of my pocket. She sat down on the floor in one of her yoga-style sitting ways, her minidress unable to cover her pretty bare legs. She arranged a few of my study cards on the floor with the Japanese side flipped up. I couldn't read that side, so when she finished I squatted down and turned each of them over.

"Akemi suitcase sell," were the words she'd combined. I looked at her.

She pulled up each card and placed down a new sentence. I flipped 'em. "Japan Akemi country." I smiled. Picking up the cards, I asked her, "Where sold?" I placed two word cards down so she would understand.

She answered, "go," which she always said when she meant come. I knew she was offering to take me to whatever location or person she had sold her luggage to.

"*Chotte Matte*," I told her in Japanese, asking her to wait.

"*Hai*," she said softly, watching me stand up. I held out my hand to her. She placed her hand in mine and I pulled her up to her feet.

"This dress," I said. "It's for Mayonaka." I touched the cloth of her dress and gently pulled it some. When I released the material, it lay back down over her now raised-up nipples. I took everything out of my pockets and laid it out on the desk.

"This face"—I touched her skin—"is for Mayonaka." I squeezed her lips until they puckered. "These lips are for Mayonaka." Gently, I kissed her. She exhaled. Her lips parted and our warm tongues welcomed each other, our kissing and licking and sucking expressing our deepest emotions.

Soon I ran my hands down the length of her body until I was squatted with my hands wrapped around each of her ankles. I loosened my grip and stroked her feet with my fingers, then moved my touch over her ankles, then calves, and brushed her knees and pulled up into the inside of her thighs. "These legs are *only* for Mayonaka." My fingertips could now feel the moisture spreading and soaking the lace of her petite panties. Her eyes turned into pools of boiling oil and her breathing picked up and our hearts raced.

When I removed the soft silk dress with the costume jewelry that flooded her neckline and ran down her back, I could see that her breasts were swollen. When I touched them lightly with my tongue, she bit her lip and stepped up and walked backward onto the mattress. She walked backward until she hit the wall. Then she eased her body down to a sitting position. She held her legs with her hands and laid her chin on top of her knees, watching intensely and waiting. I came out of my clothes and she studied my erection. I took two steps and picked up the oil elixir. I sat on the bed facing her. I began massaging the oil onto her body, beginning with her pretty toes. She eased one hand down and began stroking my erection with a light touch, creating an urge that was multiplying rapidly. The scent of Sudanese oils perfumed the air. Akemi released her hands, and her legs cocked open revealing her pretty pussy. I liked her pussy hairs, didn't want her to shave them away. I pulled her closer, then lifted her. I positioned her there and she wiggled until her opening gave way and grabbed me like a tight surgeon's glove. With only the tip at the entrance, pushing against her clitoris, she threw her head back and let out a sound that could only be released this way. I helped her bounce softly until I eased all in.

We rocked slowly at first, in a rhythm that was as natural as the soaring movement of the wings of the white-tailed eagle I saw in the fields of Hokkaido. Her pussy felt fatter and more juicy. As her walls massaged me, and my muscle moved in it, my mind left and only feelings and sensations remained. When her walls began to flutter and she turned into a waterfall, she fell against me, holding me as tight as she could. I eased my back against the sheets. Her body was pressed against me, sealed by her syrup.

I began licking her outer ear. I was not finished. She began wiggling again. I gripped her hips and we were back to grinding. Only the sound of our breathing and the mixing of moisture could be heard. It felt good to her, I knew. She was digging her nails into my flesh. When I flipped her so that she now lay on the bottom, and I eased one of her legs over her head and began thrusting inside her from a side angle, she began purring and moaning all over again. With my eyes closed and my feelings stirring and escalating, and my heart pounding, I saw scenes of myself climbing the Hidaka to find her and suddenly my emotions shifted from longing and desire and pure pleasure to insult and anger that we had ever been separated. Soon I realized that I was fucking her hard. I began sucking her neck and passion-marking her body, same as an animal marks his territory. I could hear her heavy breathing and light voice in my ear. As she cried out repeatedly, "Uuhh, uuhh, uuhn . . . ," I remembered that she was my wife, the mother to my twins, and I spilled all my seeds and swinging emotions inside her until my body weight crushed her.

I rolled to my side, both of us breathing like we had climbed one thousand stairs. Her face was flushed and her eyes filled with tears. Then a smile eased across her lips and she said, *"Aishiteru."*

I grabbed her up and we remained in an embrace. My feelings were still furious. "I fucking love you, girl. I fucking love you like crazy. You belong to me and I belong to you." I knew she didn't know what I said. But I knew she understood.

* * *

At 9:15 p.m. a new hunger aroused me. I showered and put on fresh wears. As I looked through Akemi's clothes, I called out her name.

"Pekko pekko da," I told her in Japanese, meaning "I'm hungry." She smiled and stretched her limbs like a cat. Her movements were slow as though *she* had only needed to satisfy one hunger.

"Come on," I rushed her as I laid out what I wanted her to wear. She saw. There was no resistance in her. She showered. When she emerged in her *yukata*, a beautiful, long, colorful Japanese dress with amazing sleeves, a kind of summer kimono, I was moved in a real big way by how incredible she looked. Now she was covered—arms, legs, shoulders, hips, thighs, and calves. But she seemed even *more* seductive to me.

She went through her LV Cruiser bag and pulled out some Japanese socks with slots to divide her toes. She slid into a pair of wooden shoes with the socks on. She took small steps toward me. I slipknotted her hair. When she glanced down at the desk, I lifted the passports and Pan Star ship tickets and said, "*Ashita* Busan, Korea," letting her know we would travel tomorrow. She smiled brightly and clapped her hands together twice. She swept up the 350,000 yen with her fingertips and then embraced me. I felt her ease the folded stack of bills into my back pocket. She kept holding on to me as though she never wanted to let go.

"Akemi, should I eat you for dinner?" I asked her. She released her hands and smiled a smile that made me wonder if she understood what I had just said. I grabbed her hand and said, "Come on. No more for you."

"*Chotto matte,*" she said softly. She walked over to her handbag and opened it. She pulled out a small box and lifted the top. She began speaking in Japanese to me while walking my way with something concealed inside her small hand. As I leaned against the wall, she touched my hand and placed a band of gold on my married finger. She scolded me. I imagined she was asking, *Where is your wedding ring? Have you lost it or is it off for some other reason?* But I couldn't be sure. Besides, I didn't mind the way she went about loving and claiming me. I checked out the ring. It was engraved in kanji. When I kissed her on her cheek and acknowledged, *"Arigato gozaimasu,"* she smiled.

"And where are your bangles?" I asked her. She looked puzzled. I gestured, holding her wrist in my hand. She rushed back to her bag and dived in and placed the two diamond bracelets that I gifted her for our wedding over her fingers. I grabbed my Jansport and pulled the two gold bangles out that she had given to her friend to attract my attention. I slid them over her fingers and onto her wrist.

"We good now?" I asked her. She leaned against my body. The silk of her *yukata* aroused me, but I told myself to move. A man gotta eat, and if I gave in to her seduction every time it moved me, I would be living inside and between her thighs unable to do anything else.

* * *

Purposely, I avoided returning to the Lebanese restaurant where I had made prayer and broken my fast with a cup of water and two dates. My curious wife and I strolled down the side streets of Osaka, her dressed in her beautiful *yukata*, no head covering, yet concealed behind an exotic umbrella, in the cloudless, rainless night. I enjoyed the silence this time because of our mutual mood. We were in a kind of war, but we were at peace.

Easily, as we walked by, my wife pointed out her red Epi leather LV trunk and suitcase. They were positioned front and center in the window in a now closed and darkened shop that featured used expensive designer goods, from the tiniest purses to the heaviest handbags and even luggage. She didn't have to show me. I trusted her. But it was good that she did. I needed my wife and me to become closer and even tighter than we were so far. This was the only real way for us to protect our marriage. She had to really know me, my thoughts and all. She had to follow what I told her to do, without even a slight change here and there. She had to get in a perfect rhythm with me. If she couldn't, I knew that any outsider could exploit the weakness and attack our love.

Cooks from Kashmir prepared our extra-spicy meal. It was a small dinner place that gave off the feeling that we were eating in a good friend's brick-oven kitchen. There were four other female customers who were also wrapped up in their traditional clothing and eating alongside their husbands. Kashmir is an Islamic country also. The restaurant owner had a unique style of wallpaper plastered across one wall of his intimate setting. It was actual photography of revealing scenes of the beautiful mountain lands of Kashmir. As Akemi and I observed it, the waiter said to me, "You are looking at a piece of heaven, my country."

The dark-skinned Kashmiri waiter, while pouring water into my wife's glass, also became distracted as he glanced at my pretty wife. Apparently he was looking at a piece of heaven also. Even with her body well covered, she needed her long dark hair wrapped. I knew that. I told myself, one step at a time, *inshallah*.

In between dinner and dessert, I slid Akemi the green study cards with the kanji explanation of Ramadan, so that she would understand why I would only be sharing meals with her after sunset each evening. She laid each card out and read it, following the kanji with her pretty painted black fingernails. She looked up at me.

"Hai! Wakarimashta," she said, meaning that she understood.

The waiter brought over some honey-laced fruits.

"Who?" Akemi said in English.

"What?" I asked her.

She pointed to the kanji on the cards. "Who?" she repeated and held out her hand. I gave her the other cards, knowing she wanted to ask me something.

"Who Japanese write?" she spelled out with my study cards.

"Tsuwakeshya," I told her in Japanese, meaning translator.

"Woman?" she asked.

"Hai!" I told her. "Chiasa."

"Chiasa," she repeated softly.

On the way back to our hotel, I copped a duffel bag at a uniform store. Japan was so big on hard work that worker's clothes and accessories could be purchased at all hours of the night. Akemi wanted the pink duffel. But I knew that I would be the one carrying it, of course. So I chose brown.

* * *

Seated on the floor back at our hotel room late night, both Akemi and I listened to some music on her antique handheld battery-operated radio. We sat it in the corner as we read the books that we had purchased from an impressive bookstore that took up an entire building and was packed with books from all around the world and plenty of curious customers, night readers. She was reading a book on pregnancy and childbirth. I was reading a travel guide about Korea.

It seemed she liked my study cards. She positioned her version of an English sentence on the bamboo floor using them. "Two boy, two girl," were the words on the cards she laid down. I smiled. She was asking about our twins, inshallah.

I answered with the cards: "Son good, daughter good also." She laid down her promise, "Akemi, Mayonaka, one daughter, one son."

Around midnight, she and I were stuffed inside a phone booth together. She leaned her body against mine as I followed up with Haki and let him know I had secured the tickets. He wished me a safe trip, apologized for earlier, and then said, "I am here until I achieve my PhD. So remember, brother, you have a friend in Japan."

"Chiasa, are you good?" I asked Chiasa when she picked up.

"So good. You called!" she said with soft-spoken excitement.

"I told you I would."

"I know," she said even softer.

"Is everything okay with your grandfather?"

"Perfect."

"What did he say?"

"He asked me how was ninja camp," she said. "I had told him that I would visit my sensei in Osaka. That's why I left Kyoto that afternoon. I had to make sure I did it, since I told grandfather that I would."

"I want you to introduce yourself to my wife. Say anything that you would like to say."

"Anything?" she repeated.

"Anything," I assured her, and handed Akemi the phone.

Umma answered the phone excited. "Say *salaam alaikum*." I pronounced the Arabic greeting for my wife slowly as I held the phone to her ear. "*Salaam alaikum*," she said softly. "Akemi, Umma love!" she added with great joy.

Holding my wife from behind while talking to my *umi* on the phone was a simple but high moment for me. I am most at ease when I am pleasing the women I love. If I have come up short, or disappointed or failed them, I say nothing. I just keep on pushing and working and fighting until I get it right and a smile spreads across their faces the way I was certain it was on Umma's pretty face, and the way it was on my wife's pretty face right then.

BOOK 3

A KOREAN
DRAMA

Chapter 1
ANYONGHASEYO

A yolk-yellow sun, a white sky; the bluest sea, mounds of gold sand, and an aggressive, warm, and moist wind: it's Busan, Korea. More fishing boats and barges, ships, cruisers, and yachts than you could imagine. Cargo containers were carrying everything from every corner of the world. The scenery made more unusual by the green mountains, the buildings and homes were unevenly stacked and woven around the boats and the water, not vice versa.

Crooked and curved alleys flossed privately owned small businesses, hundreds of them, with thousands of outdoor vendors. Every Korean was at work, it seemed—the grandfather, the grandmother, the mother, the father along with running toddlers and babies clinging on breasts, backs, and butts. It felt like they all knew one another well. Maybe block by block they were all related. What's for sale? Everything! A nation of hustlers, not even an insect or snail was safe.

As Akemi and me moved around on foot, our eyes were equally filled with curiosity and amazement at these new images. Even the feeling here was different and special. Korean people were staring, not ignoring. Some seemed in awe of Akemi separately, and of me individually as well. They seemed even more stunned by the two of us together.

Maybe it was the colorful explosion on her *yukata*, the third beautiful one she had worn and I had seen. Maybe it was because she walked slowly as they hurried. She was dressed for leisure and luxury. They were dressed for labor. Or maybe it was because she was with an African man in the narrow streets ram-packed only by Koreans. Or maybe it wasn't none of that. Perhaps it was the pressure of sixty vendors positioned in a row, all selling the same products. All of them were trying to capture the attention of the same customers to secure a sale. I was puzzled over how exactly that could ever be profitable. I even wondered how one man explained to his business neighbor. "Yes, I am opening my spot right next door to yours and selling the exact same things!" The only way for one vendor to gain an edge on his competitor was with his display style.

This is a place that looked and felt fully lived in. They were unable to keep it clean, neat, and tightly organized as every street was in Japan. In fact, here in Busan I saw a grandmother out in the street dressed in lime-green gauchos and a pink and purple blouse, sporting a mean black afro while squatting on her couch, which she had parked on the curb. Her legs were cocked open as she was cutting and cleaning fish as swiftly as me and Cho. She rocked an orange visor and had a baby strapped to her lower back. She brought a smile to my face naturally.

On the next block, the product changed, but the number of dealers didn't. I finally figured out there were entire alleys dedicated to only one category of goods. For example, all seafood and meats, or thirty noodle stores in a row, or exclusively fruits and vegetables and nuts. There was even a block dedicated to the red pepper and other powerful spices.

The Korean everyday greeting was a long leap from a simple American "hi." Instead they called out *"Anyonghaseyo"* to one another. There were no blank faces here, no lack of emotion, and no strange silences. Everyone was expressing something and voices were both raised and lowered and the language filled with musical melodies.

We lined up for the bus, stood there for five minutes before we realized they didn't believe in lining up. Casually people cut in front of us or jumped in the line behind us but in front of some other people who had been there first. I wasn't stressed about it, more in observation mode than anything else.

When the bus swung into the curb, the people piled up and the problem was the bus driver never stopped the line even after every space was stuffed, every step in use, every seat filled, three squeezed in two spaces. I switched places with Akemi so that she was pressed against a teenaged girl instead of a male. I held her close but everybody was holding somebody even if they didn't arrive together and were complete strangers. It was different than Tokyo, where buses and trains and places could be and usually were packed with people, but there was no touching, or in New York, where if you accidentally touched or bumped somebody, you might get forcefully shoved back by a stranger yelling, "Get the fuck off of me."

The bus driver pulled out. Better yet, he yanked out. As soon as he caught up with the traffic, he slammed on the brakes, causing everyone to fall forward. Except there was nowhere to fall, so we just mashed onto one another. When the traffic advanced, the driver yanked again.

He swept around the corner, bogarting the oncoming traffic's lane. We all leaned leftward, my hand on the window to my left held us in place, my arm extended over the heads of the three guys seated there. When four got off, five got on. The driver drove like he had a vendetta against his passengers. Someone dropped a bag of fruit. Oranges rolled down the narrow aisle. Some got picked up and passed to the back like batons handed off during a relay race. Two tangerines got crushed beneath scuffling feet. For many minutes we got swung and smacked around. A bag fell from a luggage rack and tagged six heads before someone stopped it and tossed it back to its place like in a volleyball match.

When the bus reached our stop, the vehicle jerked so hard, we might've flown through the front windshield. We climbed down, and before my foot cleared the last step, the bus yanked away, leaving a puff of black smoke as its trail. I looked down at Akemi. She looked up at me. She wiped her face and smiled and then began laughing. So did I. We laughed at that bus ride harder than at anything else since we first met. After traveling through a few African countries, as well as the US and Japan, I now knew Korea had the livest, craziest, wildest bus ride, and there weren't even any chicken or goats on board.

We looked up. Our laughter had slowed down and we stood facing the steepest hills I had ever seen in a residential area of any town. They nearly went straight up into the sky, but a bit less. There was a school built on a slant on that steep hill. I wondered how the students kept from flying out of their seats and falling through the windows onto the slanted dirt soccer field. Unable to stand up straight, even the pine trees that lined the block were leaning.

I pulled out the map with the route I had drawn to Akemi's

grandmother's address. Her tall building sat at the top of the highest and steepest hill. I looked at my wife and thought to myself, *Loving you is hard work.* If she wasn't so sweet to me, and if she wasn't so talented, and if she wasn't so pretty, and if she didn't feel so good . . .

We began climbing, feeling like if we would have stopped for even one moment, we would've fallen backward. I got reassured as I saw a clique of grandmothers gliding up the hill like it was an every-day thing, talking expressively to one another and growing louder and louder as they moved along.

Twenty minutes later, our calf muscles pulsating, we arrived at the building marked Hanshin in the Sajikdong section in Busan. No frontin', it could have been mistaken for my projects. One thing I always said about my Brooklyn block was that there's nothing wrong with the building or the sky above: it's about the motherfuckers living inside there.

Inside the elevator, three grandmothers and four toddlers leaned against one wall and Akemi and I stood silently in the middle. One of the kids looked up and said "Hi" to me. I nodded my head and said *"Anyonghaseyo"* back to him. Then the kids all smiled. The grandmoth-ers stood staring at Akemi. Meanwhile all four toddlers and Akemi were staring at me. They got off on six.

On the eighth floor we got off. Surprisingly, there were only two apartments on each floor. They must be large places, I thought to my-self. We knocked. Purposely, I stood out of the range of the peephole. After all, Akemi's grandmother had never seen Akemi before, so I wanted her to see her granddaughter first.

The door opened part way. Akemi said, *"Anyonghaseyo,"* and bowed all the way down. The woman who held the door stood in silence looking at my wife. When Akemi raised up, she gasped at seeing the woman's face. The woman gasped at seeing Akemi's face. Both of their eyes filled with tears. Then I knew. We were definitely at the right place. The woman was obviously not a grandmother, but she had to be a relative. Her tears came too suddenly and flooded and spilled so freely, and I had only known my wife to cry that way, so sincerely, so instantly, so seductively.

The woman took a closer step outside her door and placed both her hands on Akemi's face. She stood staring at her for some seconds before sobbing, a soft and painful sound crept up from her gut. Akemi embraced her.

The door to the apartment facing the woman's opened. An old man looked out, not at the woman but at me. *"Gongpay,"* he uttered. I didn't know what it meant. I said nothing.

The woman in my wife's embrace, at hearing her neighbor's utterance, stepped back from Akemi and glanced at me for an eighth of a second. As she wiped away her tears, she spoke in fluent, rapid Korean to Akemi, her voice rising and falling like a melody to a tricky song. Akemi listened without interruption. When the woman ceased, Akemi said *"nampyeon,"* which I knew meant husband. The woman made a sound of only one syllable slipping out but not a complete word. Soon she managed to mumble a full sentence. Akemi answered, *"Yeolyeosut."* The woman paused for eight seconds and then collapsed onto the floor. Akemi bent to help her.

People from the other apartment came pouring out past the nosy grandfather into the hallway as though they had all been listening all along. Akemi looked at me, panicked. She wanted help picking the woman up. I could've helped easily, but I didn't want to touch the woman. This seemed like a scene that could blow in any direction. I gestured for Akemi to open the top of the woman's shirt. Her blouse was buttoned all the way up. I motioned Akemi to tilt the woman's head back and pull open her mouth. I placed one hand over my other hand and gestured a pressuring motion so Akemi would do compression on the woman's chest. As the woman's eyes had not opened and she was not responding to Akemi's touch, I ripped open a gift-wrapped bottle of Umma's oil and passed it below the woman's nose. She came through. Her eyes opened.

As Akemi and I were now both kneeling and the woman was on the ground and the small crowd was huddled around speaking words I couldn't hear or understand, I stood back up. Akemi extended her hand to the woman, and I reached out my hand to Akemi. We got the woman to ease back onto her feet and walked her inside of her apartment. The door closed behind us, leaving the small chattering gathering in the hallway.

We removed our shoes. The woman had already been wearing house slippers. She walked slowly over to her couch. As she sat down, she pointed. Akemi stood up and walked over to a glass pitcher of some type of drink that looked like iced tea. She poured some into a glass and brought it over to the woman.

"*Daijobu?*" I asked Akemi. Which meant "Are you okay?" in Japanese. "*Hai, daijobu!*" Akemi assured me softly. She sat down on the floor and motioned for me to do the same. We sat in silence for a minute.

The inside of the apartment was a great surprise. Unlike the projects, it was well designed with quality wooden floors and solid walls. Glass doors led to an enclosed glass terrace filled with greenery and revealing an incredible view down over the entire neighborhood. The place was spotless, as though a meal could be eaten from the floor. A low wooden table displayed a Korean ceramic tea set, all the teacups and dishes sparkling clean with no tea in the pot.

The woman began speaking softly in Korean to Akemi. As my eyes continued to move up the wall over her head where she was seated, I saw the cross. It was the same as the Christian cross I had seen in Reverend Broadman's church and in Chris's house. Observing and half listening, all I could decipher at first was the woman asking Akemi if I was Japanese.

"*Aniyo,*" Akemi answered musically, the way the Koreans drag out their syllables. Then my wife laughed a little and explained that I was "Aprican."

The woman continued speaking to Akemi until there was a knock at the door. That knock was the same all around the world. It was the police. My father trained me to be thoughtful. Sensei trained me to remain calm. Brooklyn trained me to stay still when confronted and cornered by the police. A flick of a finger gets a black man executed by Brooklyn blue boys in the ghetto.

The two officers stepped inside. Their eyes moved slowly, carefully scanning the apartment and landing on me as they spoke to the woman.

"Military?" The officer said that one word to me.

"No," I answered one word back.

"Passport," he demanded. I wondered if these were the few English words he knew.

I kept my eyes on him as I now reached in my pocket. I handed him my passport. He opened it and pulled out a flashlight and shined it on my documents even though it was pure daylight with sunshine pouring in through the wide terrace window. Both the woman and Akemi talked nonstop but softly, with respectful tones, to one officer as the other stood over me, examining my passport. He handed it back to me.

"What you in Korea?" the officer asked.

"Visit family," I responded.

The officer looked back at me, looked at Akemi, and looked next at the woman. Then he looked at his partner. The woman stood up from her couch. The two cops spoke in Korean to one another, then turned to leave. Akemi rushed and opened the door for them to leave while the woman apologized, over and over. Three seconds after the door closed, they knocked again. Akemi eased it back open. The officer looked at the woman. The woman walked out into the hallway and pulled the door shut behind her as she spoke with the two officers once again. I guessed that they had to be reassured that this was not a hostage situation. They wanted to question her outside my presence. I didn't give a fuck. They were more curious and suspicious than they were hostile or vicious. They didn't seem like they needed to kill me and call it an accident. Nor would they toss a gun on me and say that I had aimed it at them and that's why they had shot me up thirty-three times. They didn't even seem like the types to lay low in the cut downstairs and chase me down the steepest hills ever, accidentally striking me with their cop cruiser.

No, they only wanted and needed enough information to satisfy the neighbors about "the Japanese girl, the Korean woman, and the *gongpay*." Meanwhile I'm knowing it was the grandpa next door who had sounded the alarm and fingered me. He had slipped away and phoned the police. "*Gongpay*," he had called me. I was going to find out before the end of the day if that word meant "nigger."

Welcome to Korea, I thought to myself. They kept it real here, singled out a black man, confronted him, demanded ID, and questioned him. That's what I was used to. There were no ninjas, trapdoors, or sneaky, deadly silences like with the Japanese.

Chapter 2

BY THE SEA

"*Yimo* and *omahnee*, face same," Akemi said. She meant that her aunt, the woman we had both just met, and her mother, Joo Eun Lee, both had the same-looking face.

"*Omahnee* young," Akemi said. I took that to mean that her mother was younger than the aunt.

We were vibing in our own way while riding on the topside of a convertible double-decker bus. The bus tour would take us around the whole of Busan, including: Haeundae, Kwonganli, Seomyeon, Nampodong, Gwanbokro, and Jungongdong, helping us to become more familiar with the city, which was the second-largest city in Korea and had more than three million people. It would stop at all their major sections, areas, and sights, giving us and the other passengers a chance to look around before loading up and visiting the next site.

Akemi chose to continue writing in kanji in her new hardcover diary. As she began sketching a picture of the woman who I now knew was her aunt, I thought to myself, maybe Akemi's mom was the younger sister. Or maybe because her mom died young, Akemi had a permanent picture in her mind of her mother as a young woman.

I could feel my wife's mounting emotions. While I was glad that she unexpectedly met her aunt, and I could tell that they felt connected to one another instantly and immediately, I was feeling unsettled about how time was slipping away and then spinning out of control. Akemi had still not met her grandmother, who was the true reason for our arrival here in Busan. Her grandmother's hands were where the urn containing Akemi's mother's ashes needed to be delivered in order for the two of us to head back to New York. Now we had agreed to return to her grandmother's apartment tomorrow night at seven for dinner. I needed it all to run swiftly and smoothly even though I was prepared to handle this matter with full respect and consideration to Akemi's mother and to Akemi's feelings.

* * *

When our citywide bus tour finished, we returned to our motel, Bada Ga. Just like its name, which meant On the Sea, we were close to Korea's South Sea; only the sand was closer. The rooms were reasonably priced, at 55,000 won per night, and we registered separately. Akemi went in first and I entered afterward. We each had our own rooms. Since Akemi spoke Korean, her registration was swift. Mine required my passport, before any other words could be exchanged. Then the question, "Military?" and my explanation, "No, I am not in the military. I'm a traveling student, pay as I stay," before the registration card was slid across the desk for my signature.

Secretly we each gave the other copies of our room keys. This was the best way to raise the fewest suspicions in Korea, where everyone was interested in knowing what's going on, and where people's reactions showed up clearly on their faces.

After today's fainting episode with Akemi's aunt, I was suspecting that it was not only race being considered here in Busan, but our ages. Before collapsing in the hallway, the aunt had uttered *"Yeolyeo-sut,"* which I now knew meant "sixteen."

With the urn locked in the safe in my room, I unloaded all our new purchases. Of course I got a Korean-English dictionary and a Korean phrase dictionary also from a huge bookstore named Kyobu Books. I must admit that even though I planned to learn some more Korean words than I already had from my travel book, after listening carefully all around town and in Akemi's grandmother's home, I was certain that it didn't matter if a foreigner saw a Korean-language word printed out in the English alphabet. This language was distinct from Japanese and every other language I had ever heard or paid close attention to. Even if you knew the Korean vocabulary words, you needed to know how to sing each of them, seriously. It was the same as if you had the printed lyrics to some hot-ass song but didn't know the melody or the rhythm. I flipped open to the *G* page in my new dictionary. It didn't list the word *gongpay*.

In the fabric districts of Busan, I had chosen and purchased the most elegant textiles for Umma and our company, Umma Designs. I thought the different textures and patterned cloths would open up a whole new arena of design for my mother.

On that tour through Seomyeon, I observed that Korea was try'na come up. Youth was rocking Guess Jeans, but their fitted and kicks was all bootleg. I saw an opportunity. My mind started thinking *international trade, international styling*. I got stopped on those streets more than a few times because of my style. One older sneaker store owner who spoke some English called me over and questioned me about my style. As he looked me over from head to toe, he had nothing but dollar signs in his eyes. I took his business card. It was the first in a series of business cards I had copped. Shit, I could show them how to rock it right, where to get it wholesale, and what to avoid. I could become that middleman from Brooklyn to Busan. While they tried to catch up with the New York and hood fashions and get it right, I would be steady stacking my paper. That way, when they got too cocky and figured they needed to cut me out of the moneymaking deals, I'd already be paid, laced and chillin'.

I had picked up a few patches from underground vendors lined up against the subway walls. I was pushing around some ideas of re-designing some already dope jeans. I would lay it out for Umma, and she would make it happen.

I had also selected seven silk scarves for my wife so that she could wrap up her beautiful hair. Now that she was back to wearing her bad-ass diamond and gold bangles and her diamond studs in her ears, I would make sure that everything else was concealed. While we were out walking, Akemi wanted to buy a diamond for her belly button, but I told her no in English, *anyo* in Korean, and *iie* in Japanese. She was carrying our babies. Her belly button belonged to us, and if she wanted to pierce it for my pleasure, she could, after she delivered my sons, *inshallah*.

The sun was beginning to set. I jumped out of my day clothes and into my black Nike sweat suit and kicks. I put my wallet and my valuables in the safe and locked it. I grabbed my wool hat and a white washcloth and hit the beach outside my motel door.

Running in the sand is more work than on stable, flat ground. The traction requires more effort. It felt good though. The serene scenes of Busan offered a bunch of blessings that Brooklyn did not.

The sky faded from lavender to deep blue. The scent of the ocean was refreshing, the opposite of the smell of the ghetto. In fact, as I ran faster than a jog but slower than a sprint, I said to myself, *The ocean has a scent and a soul.* As the waves rushed into the shore slowly and without force, pulling back very little as it left, I could feel the ocean was alive and breathing. It even had a natural voice that filled the air and bounced and echoed between their greened mountains and silhouettes of mountains. The ocean was peaceful yet powerful. Unlike an emcee, the ocean didn't need no mic. Unlike a deejay, the ocean didn't need a sound system. Still, everyone from a great distance could hear its voice, and when they did, it caused them to pause.

The ocean made me *feel* something too. The great and deep moving body of water lay on my left side as I was running by, fasting and feeling thirsty.

Miles away from my starting point, from Haeundae Beach to Kwong An Li, I had reached an incredible Ferris wheel. It swung from the sky to the earth and around again. It made me think of my wife.

My tongue felt like sandpaper now. And my intestines felt dry like jerky. I bought four bottles of water from a beach vendor, along with two bananas. I stuffed my wool hat in my back pocket, dumped water over my head, cleaned my nose and my hands and my feet and praised Allah.

Slowly, I drank the three remaining bottles, my chest still heaving from the run. The sky was black now, jet black, and the unending line of lampposts lit up the gold sand. And the Ferris wheel tossed around green light and the boats set globs of yellow into the distance and over the blackened sea, and hundreds of red lights sparkled and outlined the far-off Haeundae Beach pier.

I followed the red lights home to my wife.

Akemi was seated on the boardwalk under a lamppost on the steps that led to the sand that led to the water. Oddly, she was wearing an all-black Nike sweat suit and black Chanel flip-flops, with her hair wrapped in a black silk scarf. Of course she had drawn a crowd who formed a semicircle around her as she sketched an elderly

Korean woman who held her pose still as she sat on a small wooden
stool. I was surprised. I knew Akemi didn't like poses. She normally
liked to see and experience and feel something and then create from
the images in her amazing memory. Glancing over shoulders, I saw
my wife's pencil can was stuffed with pencils of every color and a
thick stack of Korean won. Less than seventy-two hours from dock-
ing on these shores and Akemi was already making money. Random
youths in the crowd spoke to her. She answered back softly in what
sounded like perfectly spoken, musical Korean. She aroused me.

In my room, I showered, dressed, prayed, and headed out. By
then my wife was seated downstairs in the small Bada Ga lobby. As
she saw me approaching, she stood and left. Outside the motel door,
dressed now in a minidress over pants, with her hair wrapped nicely
and her 100,000 yen heels, she looked up at me and smiled. "Time for
eat," she said in English.

We walked outdoors feeling familiar with our seaside surroundings. We mingled into the laidback evening beach crowd both relaxed
and excited. I had a bunch of necessary Korean vocabulary words
marching around my mind, mostly concerning foods. Even though
Akemi is fluent, there were some things I had to know for myself. I
was working overtime to separate the new Korean words from the
recently learned Japanese words, from the well-known English and
native Arabic words.

I knew I had to avoid pork completely and ask questions about
noodles and soups that seemed vegetarian being stewed in pork fat or
meats. The Koreans called pork *"dwaejigogi,"* which bugged me out to
remember and was even crazier to recite. Chicken was *"dakgogi."* The
food I was most likely to eat was fish. They called that *"saengseonyori."*
I had to memorize these words since I hadn't come up on a Halal
food place yet.

Stick to the sea, I told myself. We ate grilled fish and *"heukmi joo-
meokbap,"* which was black rice made with dates, walnuts, and chestnuts. We shared a salad and both bit off of the long red hot chili
pepper they laid in a dish on each table, which made our already hot
blood boil, and our young hearts catch more feelings.

Chapter 3
FOREIGN FAMILY

We were smarter today than the day before. We took a train most of the way, and a taxi from the train station to Akemi's grandmother's apartment. We were both dressed sharply for Akemi's homecoming, and there was no sense in making her hike hills in her heels, bringing on a sweat. I left the urn in the safe. Akemi had gestured for me not to bring it. I was not certain why, or what she had in mind specifically, but I cooperated.

I was carrying a nicely threaded cloth shopping bag marked *"Shinsegae."* In it were gifts from Umma and me as well as gifts Akemi had wrapped for her family. It was from both of our cultures to present gifts this way when visiting new homes or friends and family.

There were many families outdoors sitting, talking, children playing in front of the building. It was night, but the place was well lit. As we eased out of the taxi, everyone noticed. In the lobby, teens were speaking joyfully. As we walked through the doors, they stopped talking. This was nothing, I thought. I had entered buildings in East New York and Harlem and Bed-Stuy and Castle Hill and Soundview and Queensbridge, where people were armed with way more than curiosity. As we got off on the eighth floor, there were already two ladies standing in the hallway. Akemi nodded to the two of them and they responded the same way. We rang the bell. I looked behind me; the peephole on the opposite door was blackened. I was sure that Grandpa had his eye glued there, observing.

When Akemi's grandmother's apartment door opened, there were several people seated on the floor. A quick count. Three older men, in around their thirties or forties, another male around maybe twenty, two male teens, two older women in their early thirties, one teen female, and one girl toddler. The aunt was standing, holding the door and welcoming us in. We exchanged greetings in their language as we removed our shoes. Their low-to-the-floor table, much like the Sudanese table, was set with a feast. Each kind of food was set in its own dish. There were twenty-four separate dishes filled with an array of foods including steaming soups and fruits and rice with chestnuts and hot, spicy cabbage, which I had learned that they call kimchee, and sliced radishes, cucumbers, and carrots, boiled eggs, and grilled beef. There was a teapot, teacups, and bottled drinks, as well as a serving dish piled high with fried chicken. There were two big fresh green watermelons. Each place setting had a silver steel pair of chopsticks and a long-handled steel spoon. They all exchanged greetings, Akemi bowing often, except to the two teen boys, who must've been younger and who, when introduced, bowed to her. We sat down on the floor and joined them. Akemi was seated beside me and I was seated beside our shopping bag filled with gifts.

As my eyes moved around the room, sizing up the situation but not aggressively, I wondered who all these people were and I was certain that none of them was Akemi's Korean grandmother. There was no real elderly woman present. More important, however, were the men in the room, who were therefore in the presence of my wife. The silence was only punctured by the ramblings of the two-year-old girl, yet everyone's eyes were filled with both curiosity and emotion.

Akemi's aunt, who was still standing, began speaking in Korean to everyone gathered and seated there. She began slowly, yet her voice was full and very expressive. As it rose and fell, she began to use her hands. Then her eyes and her hands and her mouth were all talking at the same time. Her talk created a strange feeling in me. I could not understand or translate even one of her words, yet my soul was stirring. It was only eighty or so seconds before tears began to well up in the aunt's eyes. I had been so focused on her that only then did I realize that even the men's eyes were coated with moisture. Then the females were all spilling tears, while the males were able to hold their tears back. My wife was weeping and intensely gazing toward her aunt, who I was certain reminded her too much of her mother. Looking more closely at my wife's eyes, I believed that she somehow was seeing two women standing there, her aunt and her mother.

Meanwhile, the two-year-old was rocking side to side humming lightly, a kind of background singer-musician to the aunt's moving storytelling. One of the men stood and went to the aunt's side, laying his hands on her shoulders and caressing them even as she continued to speak. Then I knew. He was her husband. He wore a crisp, clean, pressed white business shirt, no tie, and quality blue slacks with a rough leather belt and dress socks. His presence must've soothed her. As the aunt's voice wound down, he began speaking.

His voice was deep and expressive. The manner in which the Korean men maneuvered the musical melodies of their language was different than their women's yet still captured my ear. His tones revealed a change in the topic, I thought. He began walking his wife to her sitting place at the table. Akemi, her hair covered in a yellow silk scarf, began wiping away her tears with her pretty fingers and newly polished nails. Her gold bangles jingled some. She was the only woman wearing jewelry.

When the husband sat, he said some more words to all and then was the first to pick up his chopsticks and pull from one of the food dishes. Once he began, everyone began eating. Each woman, including my wife, began skillfully using the chopsticks to choose and pick up bits of food from the serving dishes and place them into a dish for a male. The aunt did for her husband; another woman did for the man seated next to her. Akemi began preparing my dish as well. Yet one older man and the twenty-year-old didn't have women. They and the two male teens served themselves. The two-year-young girl ran and tumbled and then pushed herself between the aunt and her husband. I assumed then that she was their daughter.

It was after the food was finished that the seals on the green bottles were opened. The liquid being poured into the glasses was clear, but I believed that it was alcohol. What had been soft talking between sets of people gathered became a much louder group conversation. During the drinks, we handed our gifts to Akemi's aunt. The two-year-old and two of the teen boys were moving around the apartment doing their own things now, while the adults watched. The aunt unwrapped the gifts as though the paper and even the tape that it was wrapped with were precious. She folded the gift paper nicely into an odd shape and placed it aside before removing the box top and discovering a set of hair combs that Akemi had gifted her. She lifted them from the cotton they lay on, and Akemi began to speak to her aunt softly. The aunt's tears began to form once again. Then I had doubts about the gift that I had handed her, but it was already lying there on the table for opening. As she opened the second gift, she removed the box top and lifted one of the three books that I had given. She raised one up and looked at it carefully, examining the front cover and then the back. When she opened the inside flap and saw the photo of the author, Shiori Nakamura, her sister who was known to her as Joo Eun Lee, she cried out in a painful sound. I had thought she would be pleased to have something of her sister's memory that perhaps she had not discovered or possessed here in Korea, but I was surely wrong. Her husband removed the book from her hands, which held on tightly. He peered into it. Then one of the other men removed it from his hands and he flipped to the photo also. He laid the book down on the table, dropped his head for some seconds, then stood up. The husband stood up and the aunt continued to weep.

Akemi looked surprised and unknowing. She looked at me and then she stood also. I got up, uncertain of the mounting situation. Akemi helped her aunt to her feet. Suddenly, the man who still held the book stepped over to my wife and placed his hands on her shoulders and began to caress her. I pushed him hard, and he was propelled backward and fell to the floor, causing everyone else to gasp. Silence fell. I looked down on him. "Keep your hands off of my wife," I told him in English as he lay there. He got back to his feet and faced me. Immediately, the husband of the aunt stepped between us. The husband said firmly, *jamgganmanyo*. The other man began speaking in Korean boldly, his angry voice escalating. The two teenage boys emerged from the back room and froze in place when they saw and sensed the conflict. I pulled Akemi behind me.

"Say whatever you want, but keep your hands in your pockets," I told him in English. The twenty-year-old stepped to the angry man's side. Now the husband, the angry man, the twenty-year-old, and the two male teens were all on one side facing off with me. It wouldn't be nothing for me to break all of them, I knew. And the man who had touched my wife was still mouthing off. The husband said to me in English, "Let's go outside."

"No problem, *all* men outside," I said, and that was my one condition. Either me and Akemi would leave from here together right then, which would cut their ties from her, which I knew they didn't want to happen, or all the men had to exit the apartment together. This was my Sudanese way. I would not leave my wife in a room unattended in the presence of these men, whose role and relationship I did not know.

The husband began speaking to the Korean males gathered. Only the angered man argued back, but in muted tones. He stormed out the apartment door suddenly, and all the men stepped into their shoes, picked up his and then followed him. I turned to Akemi and said calmly, "Stay here." I went out last behind them; they were piled up right outside the apartment door waiting impatiently. As we began to move, I heard the door locks turn in the apartment across from theirs, and then the door was pulled opened enough for someone to see out, but not enough for me to see in.

The angry man mumbled in his language all the way down on the elevator.

As we moved through the lobby, everyone watched us. Outside the building, they watched some more. I walked behind them, following purposely and aside from the fact that I didn't know where they were headed. As we stood at the top of the steep hill facing down, the husband stepped down first and each of us followed. I suspected that the husband was trying to lessen the fire in the other guy, with a slow walk downhill with a welcomed breeze blowing in our faces underneath a beautiful, deep blue-black sky lit up with stars and constellations. *He needs to cool the fuck down*, I thought to myself. *It would be in his interest to do so.*

Standing on level ground after walking down three steep hills, we were facing a parked police car with its headlights off and two officers seated inside. One officer called out some words to the husband.

I checked to see if he was the same cop from yesterday, but he was not. The husband stopped and answered him, his responses sounding upbeat and calm. The cops seemed satisfied at whatever he was telling and didn't make no moves. This made me get a speck of respect for the husband. He didn't start squealing to the police about there being a problem. He didn't play his trump card of me being the only foreigner and the only black man in their streets. Instead he kept it moving and led us on a sharp turn down a curved side street. In the face of the police, even the angry man was silent. Maybe he had something to hide, or some reason to distrust or fear the police, I thought to myself.

In the middle of the block the husband stopped and ducked into a plastic tent where other men were gathered, some standing, some seated. As I eased in, I saw it was an outdoor bar with no walls—a drinking spot. The husband said some words to the two male teens and sent them back out. I could see them waiting on the outside of the thick, clear plastic tent. From their interaction I decided he was their father. So in my mind I put together that Akemi's aunt had a husband, two teen sons, and one two-years-young daughter.

"Ahjumma!" the husband called out. A woman rushed out, listened to his order, and returned with more green bottles of drink and a set of tiny glasses.

"Anya!" he said to the men. They sat, but the angry man wouldn't. I was watching his hands. They were heavy and rough, his skin thick on both sides. The hands of a worker, I thought. His chest was broad and his clothes were common, unlike those of the husband, who was definitely a professional, behind-the-desk type.

"Chonin Mayonaka midah," I introduced myself, and then held my hand out to the husband to remind him that they had all introduced themselves to my wife in Korean but not to me.

"Sorry, I'm Kim Dong Hwa, your wife's uncle by marriage. He is my brother Che Hwa, but he doesn't speak English. He is my friend Jang Jung Oh, no English," he said introducing the angry guy. I extended my hand to him. He knocked it away with his right and grabbed a bottle from the table behind him and took a swipe at my head. I leaned left and punched with my right and broke either his nose or his blood vessels. He ignored his blood, didn't wipe it or chase it, and took the punch like his head was made from steel and had been slammed with force many times before. He lunged at me. I was quick, dodged, and pushed the flimsy table toward him. Everyone seated behind where I was standing scattered instantly. I grabbed a set of steel chopsticks from the table and held them like *shuriken.* When he came at me again, I would poke them in his lungs or kidneys or just gouge out his eyes. But he didn't charge again. He picked up a wooden crate and hurled it at my head instead. As the *ahjumma* woman yelled and complained, I blocked it with my right arm and a piece of wood broke off as the crate crashed to the floor. The twenty-year-old and Dong Hwa and Che Hwa tried to subdue the angry guy, but he slung them off and they fell to the floor. That caused the two teens, who had been posted outside the tent, to rush in toward the angry guy. I knew they were about to be tossed through the air. They were lightweight and obviously untrained, with hands that looked like they had been served their entire lives and had never labored for nothing.

Instead of them attacking the man who had just tossed their father and uncle, they got down on their knees before him and in begging tones asked him to stop. The twenty-year-old came over to me and held his hand out to relieve me of the chopsticks. I kept my eyes on the angry guy, who was giving way to the two begging teen boys. Just then the angry guy bent over to help Dong Hwa and Che Hwa stand back up. When Dong Hwa accepted his hand, I laid the chopsticks down on the table.

Akemi's uncle Dong Hwa began cleaning off his formerly white shirt and standing up the crates and setting the lady's bar back in order. She stood off in the distance, watching as though she had seen this type of thing more than a few times. Dong Hwa pulled out his wallet and walked over some won and handed it to the woman, which seemed to satisfy her. She handed him some napkins for his friend's bloody face. I could see that in personality Dong Hwa was like my best friend Chris, the type to smooth out conflicts and work hard to avert a crisis or a murder. He set his guys up with drinks and pointed his sons back outside. I wasn't sure if they were keeping watch or being thrown out because of their ages.

Then Dong Hwa walked my way and said in English, "You have some things in common with Jung Oh and Jung Oh has some things in common with you." I heard him but it didn't mean nothing to me. I still had my eye on Jung Oh, who sat throwing back drinks from a glass so tiny I wondered why he didn't just drink straight from the bottle or dump it all in one mug. I knew that the more he drank, the better it was for me. He was already strong and slow; once he became drunk, he would lose his balance, and no matter how much confidence he had, he would be defeated.

"Anya," Dong Hwa said, pointing toward the chair. I pulled the chair around so my view was toward Jung Oh in case he made any more sudden moves. I sat.

"Even though we have gotten off to a bad start, we all have reasons to be friends," Dong Hwa said.

"I'm not here to make friends, but I want to keep it respectful. Akemi is my wife. I'm here in Busan to meet Akemi's grandmother and to return Ms. Joo Eun Lee's ashes to her. The sooner the better. My wife's grandmother is your mother-in-law, is that right?" I asked him.

"Yes, she is," he said solemnly.

"Then if you can arrange for us to meet her, Akemi and I can be on our way back to the United States," I said, observing Jung Oh's boiling energy, as he turned back to look my way.

"Help me out here," Dong Hwa said to me quietly, with pleading eyes. "My friend there does not know that Akemi's mother is dead."

I listened and weighed the man's words. "Is he related to her?" I asked.

"He is Akemi's father," Dong Hwa said.

I felt like I had been hit with a bomb and parts of myself were scattered throughout the bar. "He is Akemi's father" replayed in my mind.

"It's true. He is really a friend of my wife's family from North Korea. He made it over here to South Korea, and my wife made it over safely also *only* because of Akemi's grandmother. But my wife's younger sister, Joo Eun Lee, *she never made it.* She disappeared from their North Korean home when she was fifteen, while her mother was here in South Korea arranging for both her daughters to escape from the North Korean government. Joo Eun was never seen again by any of them. So you can imagine when they saw her as an adult in that book that you gave to my wife, how shocking it was for each of them. All these years, we prayed that Joo Eun hadn't been killed by the North Korean government. We never received *any* information on her until we received the call from Japan a few months ago.

"The Japanese guy who contacted us was typical Japanese, annoyingly polite yet controlling, deceitful, and heartless. He wouldn't give us any information about Joo Eun but wanted to arrange for us to meet Akemi, who he said was Joo Eun's daughter. When we asked why we could not also see Akemi's mother, Joo Eun, he offered us only one option to meet Akemi for one day, for only a few hours here in Korea, but only in his presence. We wanted to refuse, but my wife has been in therapy for many years because of losing her country, being separated from her mother for some time, and then losing her sister, forever."

I leaned over and hung my head, my face facing the floor. I needed to think.

"What was the name of the caller?" I raised my head asking. "The Japanese guy," I explained.

"You are asking the right questions, I see," he said thoughtfully. Then he sighed. "It's a long story. When my mother-in-law, who is Akemi's grandmother, was first contacted, it was in the form of a business inquiry. She receives those kinds of calls often, people wanting her to come and lecture on the topic of North Korea. The caller was a Japanese woman who asked many questions about my mother-in-law, her services and fees. That was normal. However, being invited by a Japanese host or a Japanese college or university was not typical. In fact it was rare. Then more than a month passed by. The woman called us again and said she had some important information that should be shared in private. She wanted to arrange a meeting with us here in Busan. Well, we Koreans are accustomed to the process where, when we're doing business with the Japanese, they want to be invited into a series of preliminary meetings and entertained and it all can become quite a burden. But if the deal is good, their money is strong, their yen. So normally we endure the process.

"We met with her. Then, strangely, she wanted to speak only with my mother-in-law. We tried to convince her otherwise, but she wouldn't compromise. We allowed the woman to meet separately with our mother. After they met, my mother-in-law was upset but refused to discuss with any of us what had been said between the two women.

"Another month passed. We received a call from the same woman. When my mother-in-law picked up, the caller gave the phone to the Japanese man, a Mr. Nakamura. My mother-in-law wrote his name down while she was still on the phone. Again, she was affected by these calls, became sad and quiet but would not discuss.

"Finally, Akemi called our apartment, said she was Akemi Nakamura, Joo Eun Lee's daughter, and that she would be pleased to meet her grandmother. The problem was, Akemi was speaking to my wife over the phone. It was the first that my wife was hearing anything about it, but she collapsed after that call. In the hospital, at my wife's side, was when my mother-in-law finally confided what had been happening. My mother-in-law admitted that she was angry and suspicious of both the Japanese woman whom she met with and the Mr. Nakamura whom she spoke to. She didn't believe a word that they had to say. She didn't want to disturb any of us with this kind of situation, feeling that if it was a hoax, the disappointment would be too great. But once my wife, Sun Eun, got involved, that was it. There was no way for any of us to ignore the situation any further."

"My wife," I said, "Akemi, does not know anything about this man being her father?"

"No, not unless her mother, Joo Eun, told her. Only her mother would have known, of course, and any person who Joo Eun might have confided in."

"I need to be sure, scientifically. We need to get one of those paternity tests done. The Americans do that type of test all of the time," I told him.

He sat thoughtfully.

"Just in case Jung Oh's wrong and he isn't actually my wife's father, we won't tell Akemi. I don't want to upset her," I said.

"I don't know you, but I can see that you love her. I can feel that. This is the same emotion I feel for my wife, to protect her from every tear," he said. "We can arrange for that test."

"Immediately," I said. "Akemi and I are not gonna be here in Korea for long. I have to return also to my mother and family. But it will be better for all of us to know the truth." He offered.

"We'll make the appointment tomorrow. I'll bring her father, Jung Oh, to the hospital. You bring Akemi." I said.

"I need a favor," he added. "I know that you will be taking your Akemi home with you. But for my wife, Sun Eun, for her health, could you allow her to spend some time with Akemi, just those two? Maybe for two or three days? This way my wife will not have to go through such a painful blow when Akemi leaves Korea. If they make some memories together, have some time together, when you take Akemi home, hopefully you will allow them to stay in touch."

Dong Hwa and I were two men in the same position. We both had beautiful wives. We both loved them a lot. We both wanted to remove a type of obstacle from their lives, so that we could go on receiving sweeter love and attention from them and give them our love as well. We were both suspicious of one another and from two separate parts of the world, and of different generations as well, but we were smart enough to tolerate one another. We both were sensible enough to know we had to.

"Okay, two days. But you need to lead us to her grandmother. Where is she?"

"Seoul," he said.

"Does she live there?" I asked, feeling misled.

"No, we all live together in the same apartment, here in Busan. She is a very important woman. She travels around giving presentations about her former life in North Korea. She lectures at colleges and at government and corporate gatherings. This week is special for her. She went to address a group of North Koreans who have recently escaped and safely arrived here. She is part of the training course that allows the incoming North Koreans to adjust to a completely new way of life living here in South Korea. She is quite a smart woman, strong and very powerful."

"When will she return here to Busan?" I asked.

"Next weekend sometime," he said.

"Does she know that Akemi is here in Busan to meet her?"

He hesitated, and then admitted that Akemi's grandmother did not know.

"It is better if they meet face to face, especially now that you have informed us about Joo Eun's ashes," he said. I understood.

* * *

Dong Hwa and I spoke together for two and a half hours. Piece by piece, I was pushing the puzzle into a complete picture and weighing every advantage and disadvantage I had. As specific thoughts came to me, I outlined what I needed him to do. He did the same. Before leaving the spot, he gave me his business card. He was a professor of history at Busan University. We agreed that I would contact him tomorrow and he would let me know when the hospital appointment was set up. At the conclusion of the tests, Akemi would spend the weekend with his wife. I had no objections to Akemi and her aunt remaining in contact for the rest of their lives.

We put a drunken Jang Jung Oh in the taxi to his home address.

Che Hwa and his twenty-year-old son rode in the same cab as well. Dong Hwa and his two sons, who I now knew were twelve and thirteen, and me walked the steep hills back to their building.

"How did you meet your wife?" I asked him.

"I volunteered at the training center where she was received and held by our South Korean government. They hold all of the ones coming from the North for some months. I saw her my first day working there," he said, smiling and seeming as though he was remembering.

"The war between North and South Korea is quite bitter. I don't know what you may know about it, probably nothing at all? You know, when we were young we were told crazy things about the North Koreans by our schoolteachers and even on the television. We were taught that they were stupid, illiterate monsters who wanted to kill every South Korean. We were told that the North Korean women were like men and not soft and beautiful like our South Korean mothers and sisters. We were told never to talk about the northerners with one another. In fact, if any South Korean even mentioned North Korea, he would become a suspected enemy of our South Korean government and our people. If we encountered North Koreans even in our travels out of the country, we were told not to even walk on the same side of the street with them. Most importantly, we were taught never to talk directly *with any North Korean person*. Some South Korean college students had even been accused of being traitors and spies for simply raising the idea that students ought to be allowed to discuss 'the North Korean problem.'" He inhaled and sighed.

"When I first saw North Korean Sun Eun, for me, she was the truth, and from then on, everything else I had learned and been told about North Koreans had turned into a lie. She was the irrefutable evidence. I found out that when you're in love is the only time that you are willing to risk it all. If I had never seen and experienced Sun Eun, maybe I would be just like most South Koreans, unaware and afraid of my own people because we are separated by a border our governments drew between us," he said, placing his hand on top of his younger son's head as we walked.

"I was determined to marry her. I had to work so hard to change my family's idea about North Koreans. It was strange trying to prove that we should be friends with our own people." His face looked pained for some seconds.

He was right, I did not know anything about the battle between the north and south of Korea. I preferred to ignore or maneuver around politics. My father dealt in politics and he is an honorable man in a business that had no honor. Yet even in the Sudan, I did know that there were bitter battles between the north and south, the same as it was for the Koreans. But I was like Dong Hwa in this way, I guess, or maybe more like his sons. My father was born in the south of Sudan, my mother was born in Northern Sudan, and according to Umma, theirs was a forbidden love, a Sudanese epic.

"Your Japanese name will not be popular here in South Korea," Dong Hwa said to me, suddenly interrupting my thoughts. "Your true name would be better. If you knew the history between the Japanese and our Koreans, you would understand why."

"Oh yeah?" was all I responded.

"Even Akemi should have a Korean name. That would be better," he said, not looking toward me and not seeming to be looking for a real response.

"Her mother, Joo Eun Lee, named her Akemi," I said.

"Joo Eun had no choice. I know that without ever having met her. Korean mothers will sacrifice everything for their children. Joo Eun accepted the Japanese way, I'm sure, because she was carrying Akemi in her womb."

"All mothers will sacrifice everything for their children," I corrected him, thinking of my Umma.

"Ask me one day before you leave about *jeong*," he said.

"Jeong?" I repeated. "Is that a person?" I asked him.

"No, some other time," he said. "You are here in Korea now. Keep your heart open. When you and I speak about *jeong*, you will know then that Korean love is unlike any other, because we have *jeong*."

"Are you the only one in your family speaking English?" I asked him.

"All Korean students are learning English. Most don't use it, or have the confidence to speak it with foreigners. I speak Korean because it is my mother tongue. I speak fluent Japanese because it is my enemy's tongue. I speak fluent English because it is my money tongue." We both laughed as his sons stared, searching for our meaning.

Chapter 4
ROMANTIC CALL

She wanted to run on the beach with me, had on her kicks and sweats and pretty smile.

"Nah," I told her. "Not happening!" But she followed me out of Bada Ga and into the sand. It was late night. I gestured to her, making the shape of a pregnant belly. She laughed and held up two fingers to show me that the twins were tiny.

"How many months?" I asked in Japanese. "*Ni*," she answered, meaning "two."

"Do yoga!" I told her. When I turned to start my run, she walked behind me. I sped up to see what she would do next. She just kept walking my way but she did not run, because I told her not to. This was something simple that I loved about her. I ran back to her, which made her smile widen and then burst. Instead of jogging, I worked out on the beach. She did yoga sitting in the sand beside me under the moonlight.

We were underwater for sunrise, swimming with warm waves that were cold just minutes ago. Her body moved smoothly like a sea creature and I liked that she was unafraid of the fish and the depth of the sea. We came up for air wiping water from our faces and both gasping at the pink sky. She dived back under and I followed her of course.

On the shore she collected shells. When the sky pink turned yellow and then slowly became white, I wrapped her in a huge towel and carried her back to the motel. It was Ramadan and this was the most that I could do. It was enough. Our nights had each been passionate.

No one could have peeled us apart. In fact each night was better than the night before and we were completely happy.

In my room I showered and slept.

When I woke, I decided to read Quran and remain in my room for the daylight hours. Reading Quran was good for me. To do so, I had to clear my mind of the maze it had created around my wife's family situation.

Two hours into the sacred pages, I eased the book closed. Thoughts began to emerge: I wondered why even with a book of guidance as meaningful and clear as the Quran, everywhere in the world there seemed to be so much confusion. The simplest everyday matters of man and woman were spelled out in these pages. Yet it seemed clear that most men did not want guidance, and definitely not instructions. Each man wanted to live life his own way as though his way could ever be superior to the path Allah created for all. And the world was divided into separate empires, it seemed, without global translation to lead us all to any one consensus.

When I called Akemi's room, her line was busy. That brought my mind back to maze mode. Who was she talking with? She had agreed not to phone Josna until we arrived in the US. Of course she would never call Nakamura and tip him off that the two of us were here in Korea. Maybe she was speaking to her aunt Sun Eun, I persuaded myself, no problem.

The clock read 4:30 p.m. I remembered I had to contact Professor Dong Hwa. I phoned him.

"*Yumahseyo*," he answered his phone.

"It's Akemi's husband," I said. He chuckled.

"*Agahsimidah*," he said, and then continued. "Oh yes, I understand, sorry. You caught me right between classes, excellent timing. Uh, we're all set for tomorrow. I spoke to my *sunbae*. He's a doctor at Busan University Hospital. It seems that there is no reason for her father and her to be tested at the same time. So Jung Oh is up there right now submitting his sample. Akemi can go tomorrow morning, if you agree. My wife, Sun Eun, will meet you two there. And she and Akemi can spend the weekend together."

"Sounds aight," I said, agreeing but already missing my wife, and she hadn't even gone anywhere yet.

"I'd like to invite you to come up to visit the university tomorrow. Fridays are slow on campus. I'll show you around," he offered. Automatically I thought that he was inviting me up there to make sure our wives would be alone. I didn't sweat it. In a short time, he would find out that I'm a man of my word. After writing down all the info for the hospital and doctor and the college, I hung up. I called my wife's room. Her phone was still busy. I grabbed my keys, shot out and down to her.

When I walked through the door, she was lying down talking, in Japanese. She was relaxed and smiling.

"Who are you talking to?" I gestured and asked her.

"Take," she said, handing me the phone.

"Yeah, whassup?" I said calmly. "Who's this?"

"Ryoshi," the raspy sweet voice responded softly.

"Chiasa," I said, slowly and stupidly, smiling naturally. But then I found myself not saying nothing at all.

"Akemi called me. She seems to like me," Chiasa said.

"How about you?" I said.

"How about me what?" she asked.

"Do you like her too? Or is she bothering you?" I asked.

"She's very easy to love. And I have her diary, remember? So it feels like we are close."

"Did you tell Akemi that you have it?" I asked Chiasa.

"No, my client didn't authorize me to do that," she offered a clever reply.

"Your client told you to introduce yourself to my wife. Say anything that you want to say. Remember?"

"True." She paused. "Sometimes waiting for a guy to make the first move is like waiting for spring to come again, in the summer season," she said softly.

It was her indirect challenge to me. I understood, and I felt it. Of course I felt it, but could I give myself permission to think about Chiasa and care for her or to bring her to me in the middle of the storm where me and my first wife now stood? Could I love Chiasa while loving my wife so intensely and to an extreme? Could I have Chiasa? Should I have her? Or was I like a man who, after the greatest five-course meal, still requests the pecan pie for dessert? And she was Chiasa, a whole woman, not a half. She could not be rightly compared to dessert. *She is a separate five-course meal, or maybe even seven,* I thought to myself.

"It must be hard for you to speak, Ryoshi. Let's talk after sunset when our fast is finished for the day," she said, and my heart moved. Was Chiasa actually still fasting?

"Are you fasting still, Chiasa?" I asked her.

"You said one month. It hasn't been one month yet. I always do what I say," she answered softly. Her words rocked me inside.

"Let me speak to your wife," she said.

"I'll talk to you tonight. Can I call you late, around eleven?" I asked.

"Sure," she said. I handed Akemi the phone.

Akemi began speaking to Chiasa while her eyes were analyzing my every gesture and penetrating through my thoughts too, perhaps. They were big, pretty, curious eyes, not filled with accusations.

*   *   *

I took the run alone from the Haeundae to Kwong An Li as the sun began to set. I knew it was an opportunity I had to grab. I wouldn't be jogging on my Brooklyn blocks or in my new neighborhood in Queens either. Even if I did, I would never get in New York City what I had this moment in Busan, Korea—the blue sea, the gold sand, the scent and sound of the ocean, or especially, the peace.

The banana vendor greeted me warmly. It was only his third time seeing me, but now it seemed like he expected me to appear at sunset each evening. After breaking fast with fruit and water, I decided to walk back. I had to get my mind right before I spoke to Chiasa. She had taken me by surprise earlier. I wouldn't let it happen again.

*   *   *

Akemi had a sweet tooth. She stood, wide eyed all green and blue tonight, a blue silk scarf covering her hair, which she had wrapped in a thick bun in the back. It poked out like she was a Rasta girl. She wore blue jeans and a minidress. The army-green dress covered her arms and hips. Her toenails were blue stars covered with a heavy coat of clear polish. They glistened in her sandals.

She wanted a scoop of everything. I knew she couldn't eat it all, so I didn't order none for myself. We sat in the corner. Playfully she dipped a caramel candy square into her cream and smeared it on my lips. When I smiled, she said, *"hansamu."* I ate one of her caramel candies and fed her creams too. The way she sucked on the spoon and the soft candy squares, she was steady seducing me, although I didn't know why in the ice cream parlor. I wondered if eating ice cream for dinner could be considered one of those cravings I read about in the pregnancy book I'd perused in the bookstore, or if it was just regular for her.

On the way out she bought colorful candy sticks and a bag of M&M's. I was smart enough to know that for Akemi those could be snacks or hair ornaments or part of a sweet art project.

Walking wrapped in the warm wind, once we got back to the beach, we watched a woman making a massive sand sculpture under the glare of the night lights. Akemi intently watched the artist at work, fascinated by her sand sea turtle. I thought about Akemi's live sea turtles in her Japanese bedroom. Maybe she was thinking the same.

Around ten minutes before eleven I eased back to Bada Ga with my wife close behind me. In Akemi's room I removed my kicks before I put down our few bags containing her candies and other items that we had purchased. I looked at the new curtain she had hung in the motel window. Studying it, I saw that she had taken a few yards of some white linen that she had purchased just the other day, and drawn beautiful pictures inside of measured squares. On closer look, I was amazed at this curtain, where each square revealed pieces of our journey from Japan to Korea in intricate drawings. I stood stuck there for some seconds before I turned to jump back into my kicks and head to my room to make the call.

Akemi stepped in front of her door, leaned against it, and smiled. She began to speak to me in soft-spoken Korean, which could only be to keep me spellbound by the music of her language because I couldn't know the meaning of even one of her words.

"Move, girl," I told her. "I'm leaving. I'll be back."

She bowed her head to me. I unwrapped her silk scarf, and her black hair fell over her shoulders. She knew how much I liked when she wrapped up and how much I enjoyed unwrapping her. She leaned up and rocked back and forth, teasing me some. I understood what was happening, and I planned to control the action with both women this time, Akemi and Chiasa.

She unsnapped her jeans and began to remove them, first with her hands and then with her feet. It was two minutes to eleven. I turned and walked over to the phone on her desk.

"Call Chiasa," I told her. She stared into me before she walked over and began pressing the buttons.

"Take," she said, extending her arm, the phone dangling on her fingertips. I took it and sat in the rolling chair behind her desk with my back to Akemi's seductions.

"Ryoshi," Chiasa answered.

"Chiasa," I responded. *"Konbanwa,"* I gave her the greeting.

"I just walked into my house," she said, sounding as though she may have flown up the stairs to receive my call.

"Oh yeah, where were you?" I asked her calmly.

"Everywhere, I had to buy some supplies for flight school. I was thinking about going to the stables in Nagano this weekend to ride Koinichi."

"Koinichi?" I repeated.

"My pretty Arabian mare, remember?" she asked.

She knew I could not forget her beautiful creature, with the mysterious eyes and long jet-black tail and white socks. I also was learning that different women have different ways of seducing. Chiasa seduced me with the adventures of her fearless and fire-filled life. As I sat, memories of her were easing out of storage and into my mind's eyes like a slide show.

"Yeah, of course I remember," I said sincerely.

"Listen ..." As I said that one word, Akemi came behind me and slipped her hands through the neck of my white tee and began caressing my bare skin lightly.

"Hai," Chiasa said, urging me on.

"There's a few things we gotta take care of," I told her. "I'll speak on the business first because I don't want to mix things up."

"Okay, I won't ... ," Chiasa said.

"Won't what?" Now my wife was licking my ear, her hair flowing down onto my chest.

"I won't mix it up," Chiasa said softly.

Chiasa, in real life.

"Good. Buy a small duffel and put all of my things inside," I told her.

Akemi tossed her legs over the chair and was now sitting in my lap facing me. She pressed her face against my skin, the other side from where I held the phone to my ear.

"Remember I mentioned to you about the vending machines?"

"*Hai*," Chiasa said.

"I need you to go and get that information for me. I want to know the names of the top five vending companies, but especially the ones that are vending unusual items like sneakers. I need all the contact information. Call them up and see if they do business overseas, especially in the US or in any country in northern Africa. Also see if they have any execs that speak English."

"I got it," Chiasa said. "Ryoshi, why are you breathing so hard? Are you working out while we're on the phone?"

"Something like that," I said, as I eased my hand onto the outside of my wife's panties and began to stroke back and forth over the area that I was most familiar with, her clitoris. Now Akemi was breathing hard. I eased my finger underneath the panty and into her pretty pussy. She began to bounce.

"Chiasa, hold on a minute," I told her. "Oh, I'll call you back." Now the phone was lying on the floor. I bit my wife's left nipple to punish her. But she liked it a lot. I felt her pussy contracting and she gushed on my hand and her panties. I stood up with her in my arms and carried her to the bed. Gently I laid her down and stood over her.

"Bad girl. You're a bad girl," I scolded her. She cocked her legs open so slightly and I found myself thrusting and thrashing up inside of her. Oh, Allah, what a feeling. The whole time I'm fucking her, she was speaking Korean to me, saying only Allah knows what, but driving me out of my mind. We were biting each other in selected places.

When I rolled off still holding her by her petite waist, her skin was covered with sexy sweat. I looked at her. She smiled. I grabbed her up again and hugged her tight. A feeling so good, this good, had to be a problem and could cause many men to lose their lives. Never fuck with another man's wife. That's my advice to all men, in every empire.

Chapter 5
TEST

Sun Eun is tall and slim and quietly attractive. Her eyes are filled with vulnerability and she seemed like she should have a Fragile sticker posted somewhere on her body. Professor Dong Hwa showed up to the hospital stitched to her side as though he were there to hold her up. Dressed in pale pink linen and sling-back leather shoes, Sun Eun wore a tight, petite white sweater with small pearls on it and carried a Christian Dior purse.

Her eyes livened up when she saw Akemi and me approaching down the hospital hallway. The closer we got to her and her husband, the more her eyes began to dance and her posture strengthened. She must've been filled with doubt about whether or not we'd show up, but I suspected her doubt was mainly because she couldn't understand Akemi's relationship to me. From all that I had learned this week in South Korea, I was sure that her own people couldn't understand her relationship with her husband either. So I called it even.

"*Anyonghaseyo*," Akemi and I both said. Akemi bowed.

"You came," the professor said, smiling.

"Of course," I answered.

The women spoke softly to one another as Professor Dong Hwa spoke with me. "The doctor will be out in a moment. The whole procedure takes less than three minutes."

"Is it a male or female?"

"Eh?"

"The doctor?" I asked.

"Oh, he's a good friend of mine, my senior from undergraduate," Dong Hwa said.

"It would be better for my wife to have a female doctor," I told him.

"Don't misunderstand. It's a simple test. There is no undressing or internal examination. It involves a Q-tip and maybe they'll draw blood from her arm," he assured me.

"How long before we get the results?" I asked.

"I don't know what the standard turnaround time is on this kind of thing. But I've already asked my *sunbae* to place a special rush on it for me. He will."

"Thank you, and that's good. Akemi and I won't be able to stay in Korea for long just waiting on the results. You understand that, right?"

"I understand, but since we are planning to keep this relationship, you and Akemi will know the results as soon as we do, and we will know how to contact you, yes?"

"That's the agreement," I said, smiling slightly at his need to repeat things we'd already confirmed.

It was finished swiftly. Akemi stood in the hallway in her thin beige cotton Benetton dress and leather-heeled sandals, holding her LV Cruiser bag, which lay lightly on her shoulder because she was only carrying two days' worth of clothing. Her hair was wrapped in a beige silk scarf and her eyes were lingering on me as I said, "Take care, I'll call you." She spoke something to her aunt and uncle. Dong Hwa answered her. She spoke again. I didn't know what words they were exchanging.

"Akemi wants to come back to you tonight. She doesn't want to sleep over." Dong Hwa sounded disappointed.

I looked at Akemi. "Come here," I told her. She came and we turned for privacy. "I'll come to you tonight. Don't worry," I promised.

"*Yakusoku,*" she asked, whispering in Japanese.

"*Hai.*" I smiled.

"It's okay, she'll stay over," I told the professor.

Akemi smiled and apologized to her aunt three times before they left together.

"Akemi doesn't know what the lab test was for, does she?" the professor asked as we were heading to his car in the parking garage of the hospital.

"No," I answered.

"Do you mind if I ask you what you told her about coming to the hospital?" he said, opening his car door.

"I told her, tomorrow, me and you, hospital, take test.' "

"That's it?" he asked.

"Yeah," I said.

"What did she say?" the professor asked.

"Hai," I told him.

*   *   *

"I only have one lecture today. We are making it just on time," the professor said as his small black Hyundai powered up to pull up seven steep winding hills onto the Busan University campus. On the low, universities are always amazing to me. My own father, a PhD, graduated from three universities—the University of Khartoum in Sudan, the Sorbonne University in Paris, France, and Columbia University in Harlem, New York. On my first date with Akemi, we went to Columbia University and chilled there at night on the lit-up campus. Maybe it was the architecture, the design and layout of the place, or maybe it was because it seemed like a city of youth who were all vying to learn something powerful and do something great. Or maybe it was as simple as all of the athletic fields, gyms, and stadiums. Colleges are the opposite of public schools and high schools, I think, at least as far as New York goes. It seemed like everybody going to public school was going by force and for no other reason. College flipped the script. You had to want to go there and had to prove it by paying a heap of paper. And even if you really wanted it and were poised to pay for it, you might still get rejected. I like that, earning my way in, working to stay in, and ending up with something useful in the end, hopefully . . .

"Let's go," Professor Dong Hwa said.

There were about fifty-seven students in his class and they were all seated before we rolled in. He pointed to a seat up front with his head. I opted to push all the way up top to the last row. As I climbed the few wide steps, all heads turned to stare. I faced the direction I was moving in, used to it by now: Japanese ignore, Koreans stare. I sat. Notebooks and pens were out, and Professor Dong Hwa started speaking like there was not one second to waste. His deep Korean melody filled up the small lecture hall and bounced off the walls.

I pulled out my small notebook and my mind drifted around the globe into the Ghazzalis' basement, then out to the streets of Brooklyn, then into my sensei's Brooklyn dojo, and out to home court for the Hustlers League. I thought of Ameer and Chris and even Marty Bookbinder. I thought Marty would be in awe of both the Japanese and Korean bookstores I had visited, and more in awe of their inventory. Over a game of chess when I got back, *inshallah*, and when I wasn't stressed, I would tell him how you could buy and read books all night in Japan, and how in Korea the entire family and neighborhood, babies and all, pile up in bookstores and stay there for hours doing everything, including having a full meal in the bookstore restaurants. I would share with him how nobody had to beg the Asians to visit the bookstore, to buy books, to think and learn; it was part of their lifestyle.

Then my mind moved to Sun Eun's apartment, my wife, and how she was feeling and what she was eating and drinking, and what was she thinking about right then when I was thinking about her? I thought about what she was observing when she saw Sun Eun. Did she see gestures similar to what she had seen in her mother, or hear Sun Eun use similar words and phrases? Umma doesn't have a sister. It would be bugged-out, I think, to see two Ummas seated side by side. Then I smiled and said to myself, *Impossible!*

Then I thought of my Southern Sudanese grandfather, his life, thoughts, words, and criticisms. Would he think that a university was a good place? He had never been to one, never studied under any professors or professionals, yet he was the wisest man I knew. And it was his sperm that gave rise to my own father. I thought about whether my Southern Sudanese grandfather would say that a university is the exact place that changes a man's thinking under the guise of making him strong and knowledgeable while actually making him a weak, dependent servant to a deceitful and lesser master. *Yes, that's exactly what he would say.* I smiled. I appreciated the way both my father and grandfather allowed me to "visit" them these days, to go inside their thoughts and feelings and emerge with their expressions.

My mind switched to the streets of Tokyo and down the narrow streets of crazy-ass Harajuku and through those blocks that led to Yoyogi Park, a forest filled with secrets. A stone path led me to the doorstep of Chiasa, the shoes lined up outside.

Could I climb into her heart and mind and search her feelings and thoughts the way I did with my father and grandfather? What about *my* heart and thoughts? The truth was, Chiasa was the only person in this world who made me feel truly guilty. Before her, guilt was mostly unknown to me. *Why?* I asked myself. I felt guilty first for seeing Chiasa on the plane. I felt guilty for being with her, guilty for allowing her to use up all her time on me, guilty for feeling close to her too fast, guilty for loving her, guilty for not loving her, and guilty for arousing her and knowing it, and leaving her alone with a boiling heart and fire in her bones. I felt guilty for wanting her for myself and guilty for feeling like fighting to keep her from any other man, and guilty for coveting her virginity and for feeling a love that led to an urge for me to push up inside of her. Fuck it, when it came to Chiasa, I was just *guilty*, period. *Now I'm clear. I was clear before. Then I got lost. Now I'm clear again.*

If I wanted to keep Chiasa close, I had to first speak with my wife clearly and honestly. I had to introduce them face to face. I knew I could never allow any woman to rock my first love, Akemi, who I still love sincerely, deeply, and strongly and who I would love and secure forever, as long as Allah allowed me life. My wife would have to agree. If not, I would let it burn, and let Chiasa go.

If we two, then three were in harmony, I'd have to contact and confront Chiasa's father. If he agreed, I'd simply marry Chiasa. She would become my second wife. I smiled. Yes, I would marry her easily, love her, work hard for her, fight for her, kill for her, cherish her, and give her babies, *inshallah.*

Oh, but I had messed up already, I knew. I had done something stupid, a mistake that my father would not have made, because his father also didn't. I should've known to keep my intimacies with each of my women separate. I should not have asked Akemi to call Chiasa for me, even though Akemi enjoyed calling Chiasa on her own and for herself. I should not have tried to have an intimate conversation with Chiasa while finger-fucking my wife and becoming overwhelmed by a powerful desire. This incredible urge could also be brought on by Chiasa. What if I was in the midst of and the thick of that urge toward Chiasa? Would I make the same mistake and hurt and disappoint Akemi? A real man had a duty to make his women feel good all over. But it should be done in a private space, one wife receiving all of my attention and desires at a time. A man who disturbs the peace in his home is a fool. Only a fool would disturb his women's peace, because their peace is his own.

If I had the urge without the love, it would be nothing to me. It would be easy to avoid, resist, and forget. While ignoring the sexual urges I definitely have toward Chiasa, the love and feelings that I had for her were mounting instead of lessening. By not seeing Chiasa or calling her up repeatedly, I was avoiding the fact that when and if I saw her again I would definitely make her mine.

I got up from my student seat to ease out to the phone booth. I would use my phone card to call Chiasa and apologize and set things right. I wanted to listen first and hear from her what she wanted. Maybe I was bugging. Maybe she would say, "Yeah, I felt a little something for you, but I gotta go fly my planes, ride my horses, and fight. I'm a solider for hire, remember? I'm not leaving Japan, what for?"

"Yes, very good, class. I want to introduce you to someone. We have a guest today," Professor Dong Hwa announced. All fifty-seven students turned to look back my way.

"Tell them your name, please, my young friend from America. Don't worry, they all speak at least basic English and will enjoy the opportunity to practice the language with a fluent speaker."

On the spot, off guard, and under close observation, I ran my hand over my Caesar.

"Step down to the front, please," the professor asked me in the form of an announcement.

I stepped down to the front.

"Your name?"

"Midnight," I answered. The students began to murmur.

"Where are you coming from?" he asked.

"I came to Korea from Japan," I answered.

"Are you Japanese?" he asked sarcastically. The entire class burst into laughter and a more relaxed feeling began swirling in the air.

"Nah," I said, and cut the professor a mean look.

"Well then?" he said, enjoying his position.

"Before Japan I came from Brooklyn, New York," I said.

"Do you mind answering some questions?" the professor asked.

"It's too late to ask me that," I said, and the students laughed again. "So go ahead," I told him.

"I mean for my students to feel free to ask some questions," he said in English and then spoke some Korean. "Okay," he said, and pointed to a female student. She stood up.

"Do you know Whitney Houston?" she asked me. The class laughed. One male student scolded her in Korean.

"Not personally," I responded.

"What about Eddie Murphy?" another student asked me. Then the same male student who scolded the other girl said, "No, you idiots. Midnight is not an entertainer. He is an athlete. What sport do you play?" he asked me.

"Basketball," I answered.

"Are you any good?" another male asked me.

"I can take on any of you, no problem," I said. It was true but I was really joking with them, since they were joking with me. Oohs and ahs and two guys jumped up. "Challenge!" one of 'em called out.

The professor interrupted sternly. "This is *university*-level history! I meant for my students to ask you smarter questions. I am sorry to you, my friend," he said sincerely.

"It's no problem," I told him, eager to ease out of the spotlight. But the professor began scolding his students in Korean first, and then he switched to speaking in English.

"What about the *Challenger*, which blew up at the beginning of this year? This had a deep effect on America and American science. Isn't anyone interested in hearing comments about that? What about the Chernobyl nuclear power plant explosion that leaked active radiation into the environment? How do South Korean students feel about the nuclear threat and the nuclear arms race coming from even as close as North Korea? And what does our guest Midnight, think?"

His class became completely silent. "We could've seized the opportunity to have meaningful conversation," the professor said in English first, and then swiftly switched to Korean, I assume to translate the same thing.

"Every Korean male will have to perform his military service. South Korean men will serve a mandatory three years. North Korean men will serve a mandatory ten years. These are the issues that will affect all of you, that we discuss each time that we meet here for classes. What about the very recent bombing of the North African country Libya?"

But the professor had no takers. Upset, he dismissed his class. A line formed before him of bowing, apologizing students. One by one they stepped up in a display of respect for their teacher. Meanwhile, a small crowd of students formed around me.

"Do you have Nintendo?"

"Which is better, Super Mario or Zelda?"

"Not Nintendo, Sega Genesis. It's American-made. Nintendo is from Japan," one student said.

"What's your favorite movie?"

"What's your favorite song?"

"Do you have a girlfriend?" one bare-legged, pretty Korean girl in a short skirt with killa eyes asked me aloud. Then everyone stopped talking to listen for my answer, even the professor.

"I have a wife. I'm married," I said. They all began to clap.

"Is she American?" another girl asked.

"No, she's Korean," I answered, surprising myself. There was a chorus of oohs and low murmurs.

"She's Professor Dong Hwa's niece," I added, purposely to show him not to put me on the spot unless he wanted to be exposed and placed on the spot himself. I'm not one of his students so the professor should stop testing me.

The students all looked toward their professor for confirmation. *"Songsehneem!"* they all shouted. He was looking back at them, and for the first time he was without words, basic ones or fancy ones.

"And I love her a lot. She's beautiful," I told them, then turned to the professor and said, "Uncle Dong Hwa, I'm stepping out to find a phone booth. I'll be back."

"I'll walk you," the pretty girl offered me, and began to move my way. Then two males escorted her, escorting me. Now, I knew where the phone booth was located. However, the students never left my side, and three turned into six and six turned into nine. Not one of them asked me any of those current events, history or science questions that Professor Dong Hwa had urged them to ask. Instead they asked about Run DMC.

In the back of a building ten male students eagerly showed me their break-dancing moves. They battled one another, pumping "Apache" and "Dance to the Drummer's Beat," and got more lively on a track that I've never heard before called "Hot Potato." They were nice with their skills. I checked one kid so nice it seemed like he had defeated gravity as he held his pose midair. I thought of the boys on my Brooklyn block and in all the boroughs of New York. I thought about DeQuan and his brothers too. Could they ever know how their style and art was moving across the globe so strong that these kids were at least as good as any hood cats?

The leader of the break-dancing crew named himself Black Sea. After they rocked, he shot straight over to me and introduced himself. He said, "Midnight, great name!" After he ran a style check on me, he followed me around. Rather, he showed me around as he followed me. I asked him what he was studying. He answered, "Physics, third year," and made me lean back some. "It goes together, physics and break dancing. You see what I mean?" he said.

In the huge, spotless gym we got a game up. The dancers broke out and the ballers stepped up. They were eager and unafraid. I liked that.

After game time, they offered me food and water in their immaculate cafeteria. When I refused, they gasped. I sat down with them. It seemed like they thought it was the thing for me to do. They ate and talked a lot, to me and among themselves. When their questions led to me telling them "I'm Muslim," a silence fell on the table. When I explained about Ramadan, they gasped and moaned and one girl said, "You must be really hungry!" Then one girl stupidly added that she heard that all Africans were starving like that.

"He's not African," one male student called out. "He's American!"

Then someone else shouted those two down. "He's African-American."

Certain things caught my eyes and ears. How the students cliqued up according to their year—freshman, sophomore, junior, senior. Also, how the Korean males interacted and got along. When I was chilling with a handful of seniors, about fifteen freshmen flew by, stopped in their tracks, and bowed down to their seniors. There was no joking or laughing on those matters for them. There were levels that everyone respected. Joke among their same-age peers, but bow down to their elders, even if they were only one year older.

They asked my age. I didn't tell them, made them guess instead, and refused to confirm either way.

We ended up in the weight room with Black Sea and nine other guys who weren't around when we first started out. We had a push-up competition and it was hilarious watching their arms, legs, and chests collapse, no competition whatsoever.

When Black Sea showed me the way to Professor Dong Hwa's office, there was a small crowd of female students standing outside. That same girl, the pretty one with the miniskirt and tight tee and heels and the killa eyes, was among them. She approached me and Black Sea. I moved past her and went in to check with the professor.

"Long day," he said.

"Yeah, are you working late?" I asked him. It was 5:00 p.m.

"I'll be wrapping up soon. We can share some dinner together?"

Black Sea and the pretty girl knocked and entered. "Dinner and karaoke?" Black Sea offered.

"Listen, let's set that up for tomorrow night, same time. Hope you don't mind, that would be better for me. I have to take care of a few things," I told them.

"Do you know your way back?" the professor asked me.

"I'm good. I'll stop by to check my wife later. Is that alright with you?"

"Okay, see you then. Be sure to eat something. This is Korea. We don't eat alone!"

Black Sea showed me to the shuttle. I was out.

I wanted to get back to Bada Ga to clean myself up for the Maghrib prayer after this afternoon's unexpected workout. I was looking forward to arriving back just at the right time for breaking my fast properly and alone, and of course taking my run on the beach.

Chapter 6
NOT A DREAM

I ran my regular route even closer to the sea. The Friday night crowd was out, many of them stargazing. Some were lovers, or after-workers breaking open a bucket of chicken while gulping beers. The party boats were on the sea, all lit up in the distance. The daily ferries were carrying people from the pier to the other side of the deep waters. Certain boats were returning from one of the many small Korean islands out there. All I knew was it just felt good to me.

Another runner was coming up from the rear. I could hear his kicks on the damp sand. I was used to being the only runner out here during the tourists' dinner hour. He pulled up on my right side. I glanced at him and nodded. We were both blacked out—black sweats, black kicks, black T-shirts, and black wool hats. I picked up my pace, not wanting to feel like I had a running partner.

Another runner pulled up on my left, keeping pace with me, and the one I left behind pulled back up on my right. Maybe it was some ego shit, but I decided to race ahead of them both, leaving them behind in my dust. So I did.

Two people up ahead were shaking out a blanket in the blackened sky. I swerved to run around them. They tried to move out of my way at the same time, so we clashed. When I stepped back to run around them, they advanced, forcefully bagging me inside their blanket like a shark entangled in a net.

What the fuck? I was pushing against the blanket, angry that these two were so clumsy. The second man was already behind me. Instead of unraveling the damn thing, he was wrapping me in it. I caught on. Now I'm swinging and pushing. The blanket became more taut around my body. The men held it firmly in their grip. Ropes were being strung around my ankles, which were already unable to move. When my feet became immobile, the rope was wrapped swiftly and professionally around my calves and thighs. As I fell to the right, like a tree that had received its last whack of the axe, another rope kept me from hitting the sand. They pulled me back up and tied it around my chest. They pushed me over. I heard some clips snapped shut. I was lifted sideways. Now I was being carried like cargo on the backs of three runners. I began shifting my body to at least put enough pressure to cause my attackers to lose their balance. But I knew it was futile. A rope tied properly can bind its victim even further if he tries to maneuver his way out.

My neck and head were covered by the blanket but not roped. However, there was not even a centimeter of space between my face and the heavy, abrasive material that was scraping against my face with each movement, mine and theirs. The air was coming in only through the tiniest invisible openings in the fiber of the cloth as well as the opening they left above my head. Since they made it possible for me to still continue breathing, I knew that they weren't trying to kill me. Or they at least had a temporary reason to keep me alive.

Killing comes easy to a killer. If that's what they truly wanted to do, it would've been done in seconds, I knew.

Use the time against them, I told myself. The more merciful they were to me, the more they laid the path to their own destruction. But how would I accomplish it?

I heard the clips again before I was tossed like a load of laundry into some type of metal container. I knew it was metal because of the way I hit the floor and the vibration it sent through my bones. Then I heard the door close. It sounded like the closing of the metal security gates that Brooklyn business owners use to make sure their goods are still in the store in the morning. I heard and felt the engine turn on. It began rumbling. So I knew it was a truck, not a storage bin. There was no talking between the drivers up front, at least I couldn't hear anything but the engine and the vibration of the metal and the roll of the tires.

As I searched out the origin of each sound, I sensed that there was a man posted in the back where I was, holding watch over me. Even through the blanket and ropes I felt his presence.

While my options were none, I thought about my enemies. Number one, Naoko Nakamura, of course, a man I'd easily pushed into the recess of my mind over the past week. Why not? I had evaded him, captured his daughter, my wife, and eased out of *his* country and into Korea, where he had natural enemies just because he was Japanese.

My mind raced ahead. Wait a minute. Maybe Dong Hwa the professor had pretended to be Nakamura's enemy and I had naïvely bought in to his act. The professor had set me up, planned for my wife to sleep over at his place for the weekend while he and Nakamura conspired to kidnap me. I tossed the thought around.

Nah, Dong Hwa wouldn't, not because of any love for me, but because of his disgust for the Japanese and for the years of emotional stress that his wife had suffered, not to mention his sister-in-law Joo Eun, who he had never met. Besides, Nakamura was wicked enough to conjure up this whole thing on his own. His pockets were deep enough to buy up as many hands, bodies, and souls as he needed to use.

Then Akemi's Korean father came to mind. Heavy-handed Jung Oh. He was mad vexed the other night and never got no relief from it. He was definitely capable and strong enough to carry me on his back, but I watched him move so slow last time and get faked and dodged out so easily that I was one hundred that he wasn't one of the runners out there on the beach. I thought further. He wasn't rich either, or he didn't look it. So I ruled him out and settled on the obvious choice, Nakamura and his underground army, Omote Tora and them.

The truck, which was riding more like a Jeep, began pulling up steep hills. That didn't mean nothing, I thought to myself. It didn't reveal any significant geographic location. Busan is a beast of a thousand steep hills engulfed in green mountains and sitting on pretty waters. How could I tell one from the other, bound and blind?

A forty-minute rough ride, then I felt the truck stop. The driver turned off the engine and there was silence. Instead of yelling to attract attention after I heard both front doors open and slam shut, or struggling to move around, I lay limp. If these men were ordered by Nakamura to bring me somewhere alive, I would use a ninja technique of slowing down my heart and playing dead to give the one riding back here with me the impression that he had fucked up and allowed me to lose consciousness or worse.

A heavy boot kicked me. I controlled my reflexes. He had confirmed his presence. The problem was, these men must have been ordered not to speak. The fact that no one was speaking threw me off. I had no way of knowing how many of them were guarding me or what language they were using. Were they hired Korean hands or Japanese Yakuza operating on Korean soil? Could any of them speak English? Or were they all gonna communicate with me with only their hands and feet, knives and guns?

I felt the heat from a high-powered flashlight. It appeared as a very dull beam through the thick blanket covering my face. Purposely I peed to give my guard the impression that I had even lost control over my bodily functions. Then the heat was gone. I could no longer see the beam of light. He must have switched it off or laid it aside. Then he yanked the tight rope that was tied around my chest and confining my arms. I remained motionless. When he released the rope, my body slammed back down to the floor. He must've panicked. I felt him grab the chest rope again without lifting me. I felt the ropes loosen. I knew he had cut them. Still I didn't move.

He put his whole hand over my face like a football player palms a football. The only thing between my skin and his hand was the blanket. Rushing, which for me meant he was afraid that I was no longer breathing, he grabbed the top of the blanket material with both hands and began cutting it open from the top down. When the material fell off on either side of my face, I had my eyes opened in a dead man's stare. But it was pitch-black dark. He pushed his face close to mine and I head-butted him hard. He fell over to my right.

Swiftly I pulled my arms and hands out from the blanket. I sat up and felt around for the flashlight. I switched it on and grabbed the knife from the floor. He was out cold. I traced a line down the center of my body with the knifepoint. The blanket fell off to the left and the right, leaving only the ropes around my ankles. I cut them off and got up.

Standing, I flashed the light quickly across his face. It was covered with black paint except for his eyes. I found some gloves on him. I put them on. I grabbed a patch of his hair with my left hand, pulled and held his head forward, then punched him in the face with a heavy right to make sure he was knocked out cold. I rolled him over onto the blanket, wrapped and tied him with the pieces of rope.

My mind switched. Why wasn't anyone coming? If they weren't coming in, they must've expected him to bring me out. I moved the beam of light over the truck floor area slowly, searching for anything else I could use. I saw a plastic crate in the corner and an object on the floor. I took one step closer. It was a pair of goggles.

I dragged his body to the crate that he must have been sitting on and propped him up in sitting position on the crate, his body weight leaning against the wall.

When I picked the goggles up and held them to my eyes, he was a blob of blue light, a target. I switched the flashlight off. He showed up even brighter blue through the goggles. They had some type of night vision capability. They were like a second set of eyes in the black of the night. When I looked away from him and at my own hands, the gloves I was wearing showed up blue. I looked down at my black Nike sweat suit, and it appeared to be covered with blue dust. I took the goggles off. I switched the flashlight back on and looked at him, the gloves, and my sweats with only the flashlight on. There was no blue. Everything was uniformly black. I put the goggles back on.

I took off my sneakers and all my clothes, even my pissy boxers, which were also showing up blue. That's when I heard someone approaching the truck from outside. I went and stood on the opposite side from the propped-up blue man. The truck door was lifted from the bottom. As the number two man stood looking at the number one blue man in the left corner, I kicked him in the back of his neck and he fell forward. I leaped on him and wrestled him down and took his gun. A shot was fired from a distance, and when I looked up, the blue man was covered with fluorescent pink-purple fluid, a paint. Now man one and two were both down.

With the goggles on, I could see into a wooded area. The entire forest appeared through the goggles as a very pale green. When I looked down, however, man number two's shirt showed up fluorescent yellow. So now I knew. I was their target. I was supposed to light up blue. The blanket they had wrapped me in must have been treated with the blue chemical. That's why both me and man number one, who had been guarding me, had both been blue. The attackers were marked with yellow on the chest and over both kneecaps. Shots that are fired and hit explode pink. I got it. I was not supposed to have access to any goggles, or even to know the rules of the war. The enemy would light up yellow to prevent themselves from shooting one another. Aim only at the blue guy. But I was changing the game. I wasn't blue or yellow. I'm black and my bare skin wouldn't light up on their goggles. I took off man number two's boots and put 'em on. They were two sizes too big for me. I tightened the laces. I crawled beneath the truck, using the strength of my right arm to pull myself. My left hand was over my jewels. I waited.

It was twenty-eight minutes before I peeped or heard anyone coming. He came to check out blue man number one, who they thought was me. Number three was a yellow shirt. I let him approach slowly, in case he was not alone. Then I saw a man six feet behind him, another yellow shirt. I took aim and fired four shots. Both men splattered pink and went down. I hadn't moved anything but my trigger finger.

I crawled out the driver's side of the truck and duckwalked to the driver's door. I looked around but saw no one. I opened the door and removed the keys. I crawled to a nearby tree, buried the keys below a big rock. I looked at the position of the truck and the location of the rock. I constructed a grid in my mind and marked it in my memory in case I needed to get the keys back. But for now, I knew I couldn't drive a truck. *Since I can't, no one will*, I thought to myself. *At least not with this set of keys*.

I wouldn't give them the chance to abandon me in an unknown forest. If I could eventually overpower one of them, I could force him to drive me out of here at the threat of losing his life.

As I crept through the wilderness, my eyes established a rhythm—down, up, left, right, side to side, down, up, left, right, side to side. I spotted a yellow target sitting in a tree. I stopped, took aim, caught him. He pinked and dropped. Someone returned fire in my direction, must've heard my shot. He missed. I wasn't wearing a marker. Instead, his pink splattered on a bush. I dropped down and lay there as more shots were fired into my area. *Five men down, how many more are there?* I asked myself.

I crawled fifty feet before squatting behind a wide-trunked tree. I saw a dirt trail leading up to a cabin. Then five yellow targets were scattered like stars in the sky, except they were on earth. I drew a pattern in my mind, measuring their distances. I leaped out running, letting off rapid fire in the pattern I had just locked into my mind.

Some shots were fired by them. Four yellow men went pink, one remained, and my gun was now out of ammo. I scanned the forest as far as I could see, in every direction. I couldn't spot no more yellow shirts. Maybe the missing yellow-shirt man had taken cover inside the cabin or maybe like me, he had also removed his clothes. I approached carefully, using the trees and the bushes as shields. I traveled on a curve to come up behind the cabin.

There behind the trash squatted the yellow shirt. I crept up as close as I could without exposing myself. At the clearing, I threw the gun like a spear. When it landed, he looked in the wrong direction. I ran up on him. Quickly he spun around and let off one shot. He missed. I grabbed his weapon, hit him with the butt, and shot him when he hit the ground.

I looked in the window like he seemed to have been trying to do. There was a woman wearing a see-through nightgown and slippers, moving around in her bedroom. Then she left her bedroom and went into another room where I could not see in.

I looked at man down number ten. I took off his shirt and pants, turned his pants inside out, then put them on. I wore the pants unbuttoned and unzipped and the shirt untucked, of course. I took his gun and moved around the perimeter of the cabin, checking for yellow shirts outdoors and in the windows. There was no more yellow in view. She was alone. I knocked.

"Annyonghaseyo, konbanwa," I said, first Korean, then Japanese. But I could see now she was European. She laughed.

"You made it, come in," she said casually, as though I were her invited dinner guest. "You must be hungry." Hers was the first voice I'd heard in the past two hours.

"Who are you?" I asked.

"You came to my cabin, knocked on my door, and now you're asking *me* who am *I*?" she said, smiling.

"Where are we?" I asked her.

"Anywhere and nowhere both at the same time," she replied strangely. "But the worst part is over and you won," she added.

"Won?" I questioned.

"Since you're here, it means you captured our truck and eliminated ten of our best recruits. The general will be here in the morning.

He told me if you made it here to treat you nice, serve you, and make sure you get a good rest because you have a big match tomorrow."

"Match?"

"Yep" was all she said.

I moved around the cabin, pulling open the closets, checking beneath and below the furniture. She had walked off into the kitchen, ignoring me while checking on some food she had cooking. In her bedroom I pulled some clothes out of her closet. I walked back into the kitchen still holding the weapon.

"Get dressed." I tossed the clothes at her.

She caught the pants and bent down to pick up the shirt. "Why? It's bedtime. After I serve you some dinner, I'm going to sleep and I suggest that you do the same."

I pointed the weapon at her. "Get dressed." She saw my seriousness and began putting herself into the pants right in my face. I turned away. She tried to hit me with the soup ladle. I intercepted it midair, pulled it away from her, and said, "Get dressed."

When she was dressed, I tied her to her chair using bedsheets.

"Where's the phone?" I asked her.

"No phone calls. The general said no phone calls."

"Who's the general?" I asked her.

"He's going to be angry that you treated me bad."

I didn't respond. I walked toward the door.

"It's safer in here," she said casually. "There are cliffs, sharp cliffs, sudden and steep falls and deep waters out there, and you don't know where you are. If he wanted to kill you, he could've killed you already. Untie me, let's just eat and relax and rest." She said.

I turned and walked to the kitchen instead. I pulled a plate and a bowl from a cabinet. I set the food on the table in front of the tied woman.

"It's you who's hungry. I'll feed you." I put some soup in the spoon and brought the spoon to her lips. She opened them and I pushed the spoon in gently. She swallowed. "Umm, so good," she said. Now she seemed more satisfied and easygoing. She thought I was nice now, I could tell. Actually, I was just checking to see if her food was poisoned. If her face would turn blue and if she would begin vomiting and pass out.

When I first saw her, I had thought to myself, she's a decoy, a setup. She's meant to seduce me with her nightgown and poison me with her soups. I didn't find this nineteen- or twenty-years-young, blond-headed woman attractive at all. She talked too much, seemed sleazy and easy. She had to be. What was she doing nearly naked out here in the wilderness with all these men?

An hour later she was knocked out. I didn't know if she was asleep because there was poison or medication in her food, or because she was ready to rest, her "bedtime," as she had said.

I ran water from her faucet. After a minute and a half, I began drinking it. I was thirsty. But I would not eat. She had a bowl of fruit, but I didn't trust it. I had spun an apple around in my hand, inspecting it for needle holes. After a while I put it down, said to myself, *I'll pass.*

I built an obstacle course using her three remaining wooden chairs, and bakery string from some goods she had on her counter for dessert. I opened and emptied her soup cans and bean cans. I rinsed them out. I opened her six-pack and emptied them out. I made alarms out of the cans and bottles. There were alarms for all the windows, and I also strung a few up behind the door. I shook a large box of cornflakes all over the cabin floor.

I slept in the center of the floor underneath the bed with man down number ten's gun. I had the bed blocked off by the two wooden chairs. The third chair was beneath the doorknob, securing the front door from being entered. I had a short pile of raw potatoes lying on my right side, and a short pile of red apples on my left.

If there was a match for me to fight in the morning, then I needed the rest. Her clock read 11:11 p.m. I closed my eyes. I slept.

* * *

I heard the chair pressing up against the knob. Someone was trying to enter. My sleepy eyes opened. It was morning. I pulled close to the edge of the floor at the bottom of the bed, holding the weapon. The clock read 7:07. I saw a head at the window. Then it moved away as quickly as it had appeared. Suddenly the front door got kicked in and I rolled out the potatoes as I fired on two men in fatigues. The impact pushed them back and the pink spread across their chests as they slipped and fell on the hard potato bombs.

No one moved, not me or them. Less than a minute later, I heard a vehicle roll up.

A woman stuck her head in the door and gasped. "Holy shit!" she said. I heard her calling over a handheld radio or walkie-talkie. "Sergeant, two down. We need backup." She entered looking around cautiously.

"This place is a mess. Irene!" She ran into the cabin and began untying the still-asleep woman, whose head fell to the side. She ran to the sink and began throwing water on "Irene," as I watched from beneath the bed. Irene came through.

Chapter 7
THE MATCH AND THE DEAL

Wearing a new black *dogi* that was delivered to me wrapped in plastic and perfectly folded, a perfect fit, I was facing my opponent. He was young, Japanese, maybe my age, maybe eighteen. I was confused, and still had not seen the man they called "the general." Yet I was surrounded by young-faced observers, about twenty on each side of me, eighty in total, representing many different races.

As the battle began, it was as though none of the observers were there. I couldn't see them. I couldn't hear them. I could only see my opponent.

He bowed, his first mistake. I kicked him back upright, had no time for courtesies. It angered him, his second mistake: anger is a weakness to a warrior. I struck him. He was in awe of my disrespect and audacity. It was his third mistake, unaware of the element of surprise. I struck him with the left, he blocked. I kneed him with my right. He buckled. Doubt, his fourth mistake. He doubted my ability. I flipped him. Now he was flat on the floor with my foot on his chest, victory.

A new opponent appeared. He looked like a white American. I welcomed this match, made his face represent all that I had to battle against back in the US.

A quick learner, he didn't bow. He ran up in a flying kick. I remained calm and ready, caught his foot, and used it to twist his body midair. He fell facedown, dragged back two steps, and began standing. He wasn't quick enough. I kicked him in his face before he could get up. He hit the floor again, seemed humiliated. I approached. He tried to trip me up in my steps. I kicked his leg at the joint where the knee and calf connect and broke it. They carried him off reddened. His face was locked in the scream position, but no sound came out.

I waited. They took too long. I began running around the inside perimeter of the fighting space. I chose my target, ran past him, and then stopped. He didn't know I chose him. He wasn't my designated opponent. I did a flying kick backward and kicked him in his face. He fell onto the crowd. Surprised, they pushed him off at first. Then they tried to help him up. He stood up. "Take me to your general" was all I said to him. I had chosen him because he was standing while everyone else was seated. In my mind, that meant that he was higher-ranked. At least that was my guess. Now he wanted to fight me back, no problem.

I knew they had all observed that my legs and feet were dangerous weapons. I switched my style, went octopus and became two hands and fists moving so rapidly it felt like I had eight arms. Now I held his head in a hand lock. One swift movement left, right, backward, or forward and he would be dead.

"Stop, you haven't killed anyone yet. I'll take you to the general." It was Irene. "Let's go, follow me," she said.

As we left, one set of hands began clapping. I cut them a disrespectful look to finalize the most disrespectful matches I had ever fought. Then many others began clapping. It didn't ease my feeling. I had been disrespected. Now I'm disrespectful. Did they think this was a show?

* * *

Irene drove an uncovered convertible Jeep. I rode in the back. We moved swiftly beyond trees. In the clearing the beautiful Busan sky was revealed. I could hear the water below and the water rushing down the rocks.

The general sat beside a desk lined with six hand grenades. They were each within his long-armed reach. He was a man as black as me and about four inches taller. He had an M16 leaning against the wall in the corner behind him. There were several mounted weapons as well.

"Have a seat," he said to me. "Thank you, Irene," he said, dismissing her.

Another woman entered immediately after Irene exited. She was carrying bottled water and hot tea.

"Put it down next to him," the general said. She was a blonde wearing a tight short dress and heels. I watched his eyes and could see that was his taste.

"It's okay, have something to drink," he said calmly.

"No, thank you. What's this all about?" I asked him.

He reached for one of his grenades but moved beyond it and picked something else up instead. He laid it in his lap.

"Listen, and don't move," he said.

He picked up the phone beside him. It was a business phone with a bunch of buttons. He pressed another button. Speakerphone—I could hear the buzzing sound coming through. The volume was up. Swiftly, I looked over my left shoulder and then my right. There were two speakers mounted in both corners of the wall behind me, projecting the sound of the ringing phone.

Someone picked up the call. A male voice answered. *"Mushi, Mushi,"* so I knew he was Japanese. Then the general began speaking smooth and comfortable Japanese to the voice on the other end. When the general stopped talking, the voice on the other end said, *"Chotto matte."* We both sat waiting patiently.

"Ohayou gozaimasu, Daddy," the soft voice said. Then I knew.

It was Chiasa and the general was her father. I felt suddenly like a man who had all of the wind kicked out of him. The general gestured for me to remain silent. He picked up the object that he had placed in his lap and stood it up on his desk facing me. It was a picture of Chiasa, pretty as a puma, seated joyfully on her park bench.

"Good morning, baby. What were you doing?"

"Riding, Daddy, you know I went riding first thing at sunrise. Ooh, you should've seen me. I was riding so fast. Soon I'll be quicker than you."

"You're right, you will! Until then, just keep practicing. Did you have something to eat and drink?" the general asked her.

"Come on, Daddy. We already talked about this. I thought you understood."

"How are you gonna race in the heat of Japan's sunlight without falling out? You'll get dehydrated," he warned with a real-sounding concern.

"No, I won't. This is the fourteenth day. I'm used to it. Besides, I rode at sunrise. I had eight bottles of water before then and some fruit and fish. I take good care of myself," Chiasa said.

"Enough of that," the general said, his tone changing some. "So, when will you go to Korea?" he asked.

"I don't know if I'm going. He didn't ask me," Chiasa said.

"And what's his name again, honey?"

"I never told you! Don't try and trick me, Daddy. You don't need to know him unless he asks me, and then if he does, he'll face you. He's not afraid of anything," she said. "He's like you," she added, and laughed a little.

"I gotta go," the general said.

"No, Daddy, wait. Don't hang up so fast. What are you doing today and where are you?" Chiasa asked him.

"I'm working hard for you, baby!" he said.

"Okay, I see, you don't want to tell me. Well, if you're anywhere on the continent, fly your helicopter over and stop by and see me. We'll ride horses together. Okay?" she asked him.

"Okay," he said in a way that made it easy to see he tries to give her mostly everything. I knew then that his daughter was this strong man's only recognizable weakness.

"I love you, Daddy," Chiasa said, sending a chill through me.

"I love you too." The general pushed the button and the phone cleared. He looked at me. I understood. I looked straight back at him.

"I love her," I said.

"You're married."

"I'm Muslim."

"I know," he said. "I've been stationed in Afghanistan, Iraq, Yemen, Saudi Arabia. I've known men with four wives, eight wives, twelve wives. I've seen their women wearing *hijab, niqab, burkas, abayas*, you name it. For all the years I've wondered, *How do these men get these women to sit beside one another?* Wife number one beside wife number two beside wife number three all seated quietly in one family. I said to myself, *These women do it because they've been beaten. They have been forced. They do it at gunpoint.* But experience taught me—and you might understand this now—to hold a man captive, or to hold anybody captive, takes a whole lot of money, a whole lot of weapons, an army, and a whole lot of time. I knew it was impossible that whole countries of women were doing these things, living this way by force. So I concluded they do it because they're stupid. They're uneducated and unaware. They're just mothers and housewives, local women. They don't know any better." He leaned back in his chair. I didn't say anything. Yet I was listening, carefully.

"I raised Chiasa to be different. I sent my daughter to all the top schools. She skipped two grades and graduated high school at fifteen. She's an expertly trained martial artist in five separate disciplines. She speaks English, Japanese, and French. She's an expert at horseback racing and archery and is about to become a pilot." Leaning forward and easing his chair closer to mine, he was now seated directly before me.

"Now my baby says, 'Daddy, I love him, he's amazing. If he asks me, I'll agree to be his second wife.' She's reading a Quran, fasting for Ramadan. Now Chiasa is not the type to sit idle in the house for anyone. She'll never stop moving or learning or growing, but she's anxious, waiting on you. She said she plans to wait for you for three years and that the two of you will marry in New York when she's nineteen.

"Are you beginning to understand my anger and disappointment?" he asked, now holding one of the grenades in his hand. But I knew he wouldn't blow us up. He enjoyed his position too much and was a man who wouldn't settle for less.

"In the United States Army, we have an unofficial policy called 'Don't ask, Don't tell.' This policy has nothing to do with you except I want you to not ask my daughter to marry you; to not tell my daughter that you and I have ever met; to not ask any questions about this operation; to not tell anyone that it ever happened. Do you understand me?" He shifted closer to intimidate me.

"I understand, but—"

He interrupted me. "I'm not asking for something for nothing. You survived an orchestrated attack by the United States Army. You outperformed my top recruits here on this base. In the war game you defeated ten men last night, two men this morning, and won three matches in our martial arts competition. The actual hits, the accuracy of your shooting, your marksmanship is not what impressed me the most, although it was an incredible achievement for a civilian. *It was your mental endurance that made you a champion.*" He leaned back again.

"Let me tell you what makes the average solider fail. It's mental weakness. He gets captured, he panics. His terror traps him. He can only think of what has happened before he was captured and what will happen to him ultimately. He can't think his way through his present captivity. He can't develop a plan rapidly enough and execute it. He can't fight to win. He's paralyzed! His fear of losing and his fear of death defeat him. In what he believes are his final moments, he thinks only of his loved ones. Dwelling on the emotion of love sinks him." The general smiled, seeming satisfied with his analysis and watching to see if his words were moving me. He leaned forward again, with a fixed stare.

"The naked thing was brilliant!" He smiled as though he was being forced to give me the credit, then laughed. Then he clapped. "You didn't get stuck on stupid morals." He said each word slowly, with extra emphasis. "You focused instead on survival. You made quick analyses and quick plans. You took risks, but not too many. You calculated your risks. You knew you couldn't drive that truck. Smartly, you left it alone. You took the keys though, clever. Some recruits slash the tires and cost the army a fortune."

"I like you!" He stood up. "You are any general's dream soldier. Do you know how many recruits never make it to the cabin during that war exercise? Over the years, the star recruit that makes it to the cabin, the one or two who pull it off, *still fail* once they get inside." He turned toward me.

"You didn't fuck Irene! You didn't even try! You didn't eat her soup. You tied her up and fed her the sedative instead," he said with pride. "I know some Muslim men who are real pricks! They could do anything except *not* fuck the blonde!" He laughed. Then his laughter evaporated. "You are young enough that with the right training you could be one mean-ass weapon. You would have a lifetime career in the military. How about it?"

"Don't ask, don't tell," I repeated, slowly and thoughtfully.

"I can do that. I won't ask you how you know who I am, how you found me, or why you think it was okay to abduct me and drop me into your war game exercise. You have my word. I won't ask you or anybody else," I said solemnly.

"Don't tell . . ." I repeated. "Don't tell your daughter that I love her. I won't. She already knows. Don't ask her to marry me. There's only one way that could happen. That is *if I don't ever see her again.* I can stay away from her, although I don't want to. But I doubt you can keep her away from me," I said. The general's face swelled with insult. Then he absorbed it and wore restraint instead.

"No disrespect, sir, but a woman who is loved by a true Muslim man will love, cover, sit, wait, work beside wife number two or three or four because of the quality of the love that she is receiving, because of our passion, our loyalty, our submission to one God and the boundaries that we are required to respect. Any woman being loved and protected and provided for by a true Muslim man, who may have more than one wife, *gets more* than she can get from a nonbeliever that she has all to herself. That's the big secret, the answer to the question that's been rocking you for all these years." I stood up also.

"So, since we are striking deals, let's agree. Let me walk out of here and back into my life. I won't say a word about this abduction to anyone. I won't ask any questions about it. I won't contact Chiasa or ask her to be my wife. And you guarantee me that I won't see Chiasa Hiyoku Brown ever again. And I'll guarantee you, *if* I don't see her, she's yours. If I do see her, she's mine."

We shook on it.

Chapter 8
SON

"Put this around your eyes," the general said. I looked at the blindfold as he held it in his extended hand. I didn't say nothing.

"Come on. It's almost finished. If I have agreed to be your driver, you should comply and put this on not for yourself but for me," I took the blindfold and put it on and tied it tight.

"Good, son. You're a civilian, so I'll talk civilized to you. If you were my soldier, things would be different," he said.

I was seated in the back of a covered army jeep. He was driving me. He had taken the jeep keys from the driver who was behind the wheel just as I was about to jump inside. When the first driver asked me, "Where should I let you off?" I answered, "Right where you picked me up." He must've taken me for a fool; I could tell he was one of the runners who had snatched me just the night before. Then the general appeared, ordered him out of his seat, and took his place. Now only the general and I were in the vehicle and he had just called me "son."

"Son," I repeated.

"Just a slip," he said dryly. He turned the key and we pulled off.

Blindfolded, I pulled out a piece of paper from the pocket of my black sweats. The running clothes I had worn last night were all returned to me cleaned and laundered and folded and without any evidence of our "evening together" in heated war games.

I had also lifted a half pencil with no eraser out of the office where they had held me after their morning raid on the cabin. In that office I washed in the bathroom and got into the *dogi* for the match. After the match and meeting with the general, I was returned to that same office to change from the *dogi* to my sweats. In that room I had hatched a plan regarding returning to Haeundae Beach. The paper and pencil were necessary to the plan.

As we rode, I wrote down only letters and numbers. *L* was for left. *S50* or *S10* was for straight fifty feet or ten feet or however many feet I had calculated we had gone. *R* was for right. *DH* was for down-hill. *CL* was for curved left. And it went like that. It was a simple map made by a blindfolded civilian, me. Getting it right didn't run as smoothly as I would've liked. The general would interrupt my count and rhythm with his random remarks. Yet I believed that what I was writing was accurate.

"Why are you driving me back?" I asked him.

"To make sure you get home safe. You're not too popular with my recruits after your attack last night. I wouldn't want them to avenge themselves once you were out of my line of vision. Military types can play pretty rough," he said.

He was clever, I thought. Every word he spoke was loaded. He had converted his kidnapping of me into my "attack" on his recruits. He had turned himself into the hero who was getting me "home safe." He had propped up that his recruits were a threat to me and could "play pretty rough," when in fact I had defeated them at their game when all the circumstances had been completely in their favor.

"Thanks for the ride." I played it off, purposely. I knew I was walking a fine line. In my gut, I understood that he could become my father-in-law. On the other hand, I knew he would work hard to make it impossible. He resembled my true father in his appearance but not in his manner, thoughts, and ways. He had called me "son," because he felt it. Then he characterized it as a "slip," since his world is war. I figured he couldn't help but look at himself as America and me as the Sudan.

He said he liked me and praised my marksmanship, yet it was my Holy Quran that made him my enemy in his war. Many men base their opinion of my faith on corrupt Muslim men they've met. But not many military men have taken the time to examine the Quran itself. To read Quran is to learn respect for the faith of Islam whether you embrace it or not. The general didn't know that this is the reason "smart girls" like Chiasa could learn and then accept the faith. She read Quran and slowly it was creating a respect inside her for the truth of something good—a meaningful way of life.

"What do you see yourself doing with your life?" he asked me.

"Family and business," I responded. "That's what all men are supposed to do, right?" I put the question back on him.

"The business is easy," he said vaguely.

"The business is for the family. Without the family, there's no reason for business," I responded. Then there was a long pause between us two for some distance.

"You're a young man, you'll learn," he broke our silence. I didn't respond. I was writing my map notes.

"With the military and with business you get a manual. You get instructions. You get orders. You carry out the orders, simple," he said, as though he were thinking aloud. I didn't say nothing back.

"With women, you get mood swings, attitude, insubordination. I couldn't get my wife to follow one order. My soldiers listen to me." He laughed two times and then turned back to his thoughts.

I felt sorry for him. He was like most African-American men I had seen so far. He thought that life did not come with a manual, even though it does. He thought only soldiers are supposed to "follow orders," even though Allah has set rules and boundaries and limits for every man and woman. He wanted to be respected and admired by his women but never would be, because he didn't recognize his God, himself, or his limits.

"How do you do it?" he asked. But I was focused on the scent and sound of the beach. I knew I had arrived now.

"Do what?" I asked. The army jeep pulled over and stopped. I waited.

"I'll take it off now," I said before removing the blindfold. He didn't respond, so I untied it. He sat looking at me through his rearview with a probing stare. My eyes were adjusting.

"Do what?" I asked again. He sighed, turned to face me, and said, "Forget it."

"Okay, Father," I said purposely.

"Father?" he responded.

"Just a slip." I used his words. We both smiled.

"I hope I never see you again unless you're wearing one of my uniforms," he said sternly.

"You won't see me in uniform," I said. "But you might see me." As I climbed out, my map was already folded inside my pocket.

"Never say never, son," he said, and pulled away.

Chapter 9
BODY SEARCH

I called Umma and spoke briefly. We conversed like nothing special was happening in my life. I wasn't sure if she was feeling any sense of danger because of my abduction. To be sure, I spoke calmly and carefully and joyfully to place her heart at ease.

"Akemi," I called her at her uncle's apartment at 5:30 p.m.

"*Hai!*" she said softly.

"I'm coming." I hung up.

Seoul was a three- to four-hour car ride, depending on the route and the speed. I checked it on the map inside my room at Bada Ga after a shower and a cut. I decided to make arrangements for us to go together. My wife and her grandmother should be introduced as soon as possible. It would take time for her to see and react and adjust to Akemi. Then it would take time for her to learn of Joo Eun's life, death, and ashes. I didn't want to be cold, yet I knew we had to get it all started up right away.

Akemi was excited when she saw me, but acting calm and cool in her aunt and uncle's presence. As usual, it was her eyes that gave her heart away. When I arrived, everyone was ready—Dong Hwa, Sun Eun, their two sons, and the two-year-old daughter. I didn't get the chance to see Akemi separately from them.

Chicken *galbi* was my big outside Korean food experience. In a well-lit restaurant with long and wide wooden family-sized tables, we all sat. Dong Hwa's family, Akemi, and I and Black Sea and the girl with the killa eyes from Busan University were all there as promised. It wasn't as though we were too unusual compared to the other customers, except that I wasn't Korean. Our party of nine was ordinary.

The entire restaurant was packed with families and couples and babies, babies, babies.

The grill was at the center of each table, heating up. The Korean waitress arrived and greeted all of us nicely and set down a large metal ring. She set the table with a long metal spoon and a set of chopsticks for each person. When she returned, she carried a rectangular bucket of raw, thinly sliced chicken breast. It was seasoned, marinated, and drowning in a thick red spicy sauce that resembled Sudanese *shotta*. The waitress placed the chicken, several pounds of it, in the center of the metal ring. When a fillet was too long or thick, she cut it with a huge pair of scissors, which could be found on each table.

When the chicken began to sizzle and cook, she left and returned with two more waitresses who served us each a series of small bowls containing different sides: soup, salad, radish, kimchee, and bean sprouts. I observed that the Koreans liked to have a bunch of small dishes on every table where people gathered to eat and enjoy. They'd rather sip thirty times from tiny glasses than drink all that they could out of one big glass. They'd rather eat small portions out of twenty-four tiny dishes than give each person their own plate and pile the foods up on two or three big serving dishes. I figured it must be a visual arts thing for them.

I'll admit I watched the food process intensely. I had not eaten since before sunrise yesterday, although I did have some water last night in the cabin. The waitress kept appearing and reappearing, moving the chicken around with two thick and long wooden paddles to make sure it was well cooked. The feeling and the energy was good.

Dong Hwa seemed content to have the attention of his wife back on himself. Akemi was feeding me with her chopsticks, while teaching me to hold and maneuver mine properly. I ate more chicken than everyone else at the table, which seemed to fascinate all of them. At moments I would catch each of them separately or in pairs or sets staring at me. "You must be really hungry," Black Sea said. When I had seen him yesterday, he had hair. Tonight he had a Caesar just like mine and rocked a white washcloth in the back pocket of his jeans same as me.

"His body is big, so he has to eat," the girl with the killa eyes said, gesturing and flashing her newly manicured nails. Akemi's eyes moved on her. Akemi said something to the girl in Korean. The girl answered back and then they were talking.

"What about after this? You wanna come check out the music scene, and check out a few parties, right?" Black Sea said.

"I got my wife," I told him.

"You can bring her," he urged.

"Nah, why would I bring her to a party?" I asked him.

"Then come alone, take a look around."

"You got shorty right there. What you gonna do with her?" I pointed out.

He smiled. "She's thinking about you."

"She shouldn't. I'm married. I'm happy. I got more than enough." Black Sea looked like he was thinking.

"Is she a good girl?" I asked him, referring to the girl with the eyes.

"Korean girls are a whole lot of work. But they're good girls," he said.

"Then get to work, my man," I said. We laughed.

"Tell me where the party's at, I'll take my wife home and come through late just to check out the music," I told him. "But if I don't come through, you'll understand. Don't hold it against me," I said.

"You got it," he said.

* * *

At Dong Hwa's apartment, he and I sat alone in the living room.

"Is your wife enjoying my wife?" I asked him.

"Thank you, I meant to thank you. My wife is so happy. She is treating Akemi as a *dong-seng*, not like a niece." I understood Sun Eun and Akemi were like sisters, not aunt and niece.

"Good. I'll be here to get her back tomorrow evening. Oh, and I'll need you to set up the meeting with her grandmother. I decided I'll take Akemi up to Seoul. I can't plan to stay in Busan too much longer," I said.

"Oh, I see. *Jamgganmanyo*," the professor said, getting up. *Jamgganmanyo* means "wait a minute." It's the same phrase as the Japanese *chotto matte*.

He went into the back of his apartment and Akemi came out front. She sat down next to me and leaned against my body.

"Mayonaka," she said.

"Yes," I answered.

"Akemi Mayonaka miss," she said, always putting her English verb at the end of the sentence and out of order. I don't know if she was upset that I didn't show up the night before to check her, but I hope she knew for sure that I'd wanted to and wasn't playing around. I hugged her. One of the sons showed up in the living room.

"What's your name?" I asked him.

"Chonin Kim Jun Hwa Midah," he answered.

"Kim Jun Hwa, do you speak English?" I asked him.

"Very little," he said shyly, seeming much younger and softer than any Brooklyn male at thirteen.

"How do I say in Korean, 'I love you'?" He looked around the room and everywhere except at me. Then he said "*sarang hamida.*" I repeated his words, trying to get the pronunciation right, to Akemi. She smiled so much. Then I asked Jun Hwa, "How do I say, 'Akemi, I'll love you forever'?" He said "*Akemi dangshin sarang hamnida youngwonhi!*" I repeated it. We all began laughing. "Now say in Korean, 'Don't worry. I will never leave you. If I go anywhere, I will always come back to you.'" He said, "*Nanun hangsang dongsingeote dola olgeoya.*" I repeated it. Akemi slid her arms around me.

Dong Hwa and Sun Eun came out together. The professor looked oddly at his son, as though he thought he had missed out on something. They both sat down. Akemi eased her arms and body off of leaning on mine. Now we were five on the floor.

"We contacted Akemi's grandmother. We can all go to Seoul tomorrow night. We'll meet her Monday afternoon, but my wife and I will have to return to Busan immediately after the meeting." He was checking for my reactions. I could tell there was probably more to it, so I didn't say anything. "We decided that we all need to be there when she first sees Akemi and hears the news. It's better this way. We have to be sure." The professor sounded worried.

"What time tomorrow night?" I asked.

"If we leave at eight, we'll get there before midnight," he said, and then laughed at his use of my name in another manner.

"Alright then, in Seoul I'll buy our airline tickets to the US. Akemi and I will fly out from there," I said.

"We'll see," the professor said. "We don't have a way of knowing what will happen in Seoul." He said it in a way that didn't sound like he thought I needed his permission to get the tickets to leave, but like he was expecting or feeling that something big or unusual might happen.

As I started to leave, Akemi said, "Please stay," her eyes pleading. I knew she wanted to be with Sun Eun in the days but definitely wanted to be with me in the nights. I looked at Dong Hwa. This was his apartment, his space.

"You and I can sleep here in the living room, and Akemi and my wife in the back," Dong Hwa said.

I smiled. "We're married, Akemi and me," I reminded him. Why would I want to stay with him, when I could stay with her?

* * *

Late night, the apartment lights were all off, Dong Hwa was asleep on the living room floor, as he wanted it, and I was sitting on the couch in the living room, thinking.

Suddenly I saw Akemi crawling by from behind the couch and out onto their enclosed glass terrace. Now she was seated on her knees behind a plant, waving me over. I smiled and walked over. She placed her pretty palms on the terrace floor, asking me to sit beside her. She was wearing unsexy pajamas, a big shirt and drawstring pants that were too big also, with huge red strawberries all over.

I knew what she was thinking. When the sun rises again, there would be no touching. She wanted to touch me. I wanted to touch her too. Off in the corner of the terrace shielded by the plants, with the terrace door shut, we sat down together. She crawled into my lap, put both her hands on my face and just stroked my skin. I pulled her close and stroked her hair and then her neck. I put my hands underneath her big pajama shirt and felt her goose bumps leading all the way up to her nipples. I stroked the bare skin of her back down to the top of the separation in her butt. Her body heated up. I wasn't gonna make love to her while Dong Hwa was lying down asleep on the other side of the glass, even though we were shielded by the plants. She was breathing in my ear, which raised up my temperature and sped up my pulse. I started tonguing her and that felt good. She came closer, wrapped her legs around my back, and hugged my neck so tight. She pulled back and put her hands beneath my shirt. Her traveling fingers felt the welts and abrasions on my chest from dragging my body underneath the truck the night before. Soon I was under a full body search by her fingertips. Now I was lying on my back being licked.

It wasn't difficult fucking face to face, my back up against the wall, her moving her hips so smoothly and continuously as though she wanted to heal me with her pussy. Our sex life was furious, more turbulence than any flight to anywhere in the world. Meanwhile, she had a love for me that no language could describe.

Chapter 10
REFLECTING

In the cool breeze before sunrise I ran Haeundae Beach, my same route. When I arrived in Kwong An Li, the banana and fruit and water vendor was just setting up. Probably he was surprised that I popped up in the early morning and that I wasn't buying my usual after-sunset order. I simply said *"Anyonghaseyo"* and kept it moving.

I searched out a cab with the sign in the window that read We Speak English or International Taxi. There were many because Busan was designed to absorb the tourist treasure.

I hopped in. "Can you drive as directed?" I asked the cabby.

"Bo?" he said, which means "what" in Korean.

"I'll tell you left, right, straight, whatever. Understand?"

"Agahsimidah," he said, which means "I understand."

I had my homemade map in my hand. I called out "left, right, straight, up, down," and he followed.

We arrived at a place called Taejongdae Park. My cab driver said that he couldn't drive his vehicle any further than that. I paid him and got out. There weren't many more directions remaining on my mapped-out trip. Since no vehicle could move beyond the location where I was now standing, I walked the route following my map as I had written it.

Do Not Enter was written in every language, and every other sign said Unauthorized Area, in every language. Then I knew.

The military hideout that I was abducted to was somewhere right beyond the borders of Taejongdae Park. I didn't have any intention of running up in there like a kamikaze or a one-man army bent on revenge. Instead I only wanted to know where I had been taken. I wanted to see it in the daylight, the route going and coming, neither of which I could see Friday night when I was captured or when I was blindfolded and driven back Saturday afternoon.

I didn't say shit to anyone but I was astounded by the nerve of the general, as well as his range and power. The idea that someone could use military monies for personal reasons, and to smash or intimidate one young man on foreign soil was mind-blowing to me.

When I read the book about Naoko Nakamura and his complaints about American military bases on his Japanese land, I didn't fully understand the insult of them. But now that I had been held on some kind of base, populated by American soldiers, or recent recruits, it was becoming more clear.

Chiasa said those bases were like little Americas inside a foreign country. She said they had their own separate world in there, and she was right. It was a mini America with Campbell's soup, Rice Krispies, Corn Flakes, and Duncan Hines cakes. There was no chicken *galbi* or kimchee or *samgyetang* in there. As far as authority, the American military could kidnap a person, play with him and his life, torture him, and then erase the incident as though it had never happened. If I ever broke my word and brought it up, which I would not, they would probably plaster pictures of my face in the press, portraying me as an insane guerilla terrorist, someone who had attacked them.

Standing on an observation deck inside Taejongdae Park, the part that's open to the public, I felt close to the sky. I was the only one up there at this high altitude early Sunday morning. Reaching here had been another awesome climb up steep and some winding hills on paths built only for the fit and toned. Now I was here. As I glanced down at my sneakers, I saw the incredibly steep drop down into the sea. It was a drop riddled with the jagged edges of massive rocks. Even a professional diver would die here. He'd die because the drop down was too far. He'd die because the rocks were so sharp and random that one of them would detach his head before he even hit the water.

Billions of gallons of water moving: these waters caused my soul to move also. Akemi's mother, Joo Eun, wrote it right. Everyone was nothing compared to Allah, who created the sky, the thunder and lightning, the oceans and mountains, the waterfalls and the sun and the moon and stars. No president or prime minister or king or diplomat or general or army could compare. None of them could bring into existence what Allah created. Allah was and is completely overwhelming and above comprehension.

But man was also created by Allah. It seems that man has always wanted to control it all. But who controls man when he becomes too corrupt? Is that the job of the believers?

There was a heavy wind way up high where I stood. Although it was too early for tourists, boats and ships from China and Russia were crossing the waters right before my eyes, their holds filled with cargo. I guess the world could be a sad place for any man who didn't understand the hustle and how to hustle, or how to get involved and get a piece of the action. A man like that would be the same as a roach—no, an ant, uh-uh, a tick.

Then my personal thoughts came to the surface. What would Chiasa say if she knew that her father was someone who would stick his hands in and try and rearrange someone else's fate?

I wasn't as vexed with the general as I was with Nakamura, though. I believe in fathers and fatherhood. If a man can't or won't protect his women and daughters, his existence is pointless. At least the general was making himself clear before the marriage, before inking his approval and applying his stamp, before the *agid* and the *nikah*, and before I had gone into his virgin daughter. Because of course once all of that had taken place, there would be absolutely no turning back.

I thought about Akemi, my wife. She was certainly enough. Having Chiasa had nothing to do with Akemi not being enough. It had to do with a separate bond that was created by a circumstance beyond my immediate control. The same way that Chiasa had been given to me in the first place, I was sure that she was mine whether or not my eyes would ever see her again.

Chapter 11

BLACK SEA

Black Sea and me met up. "I got something I want to show you. Maybe I can get your opinion," he said.

"No problem," I told him. We hopped on one of those crazy city buses and played the back.

"I want to come to the US," he said.

"For what reason?" I asked him.

"To make money, hook up with some real movers in hip-hop, dance in some videos."

"So you're gonna work in some laboratory during the day and rock your Kangol and Cazals and Adidas at night?"

"De!" he said, hyped up, which means "yes" in Korean. He pulled a flyer out of his pocket. "I'm throwing a party on this Friday night. Run through?" he invited me.

"I don't know if I'll still be around on Friday. I gotta get back to New York."

"So if I make it out there to New York City, will you show me around to, like, the real spots? Not like the Statue of Liberty and shit like that?"

"I'll show you around. You decide what's real and not real for yourself," I told him.

"Maybe you could be my manager. That would be great. You hook up all my business. Keep ten percent for yourself," he offered. I just laughed at the thought.

We got off in Seomyeon, which was a section of Busan that was like Shinjuku, where I first stayed in Japan. We moved past a bunch of busy businesses, beer spots, sneaker joints, vendors, and curious cats playing go on a card table set up on a curb. Eight minutes in, we came up on a record shop. He stopped before heading in.

"Look through the glass," he told me. I looked.

"What am I looking for?" I asked him.

"A shorty," he said, imitating my talk from last night at the chicken *galbi* spot. I looked again. There was a shapely eighteen- or nineteen-years-young African girl in there. She was dark like chocolate with almond eyes, rocking one pretty afro puff at the top of her head. Her jeans were tight enough to stop traffic. She was playing a record. She tapped her fingers on the counter, then tapped her foot, and soon her body bounced. She smiled wide and threw her head back and then threw her shoulders into her dance right behind the cash register where she was working.

"That's you?" I asked him.

"I want. I wish," he said.

"So what's stopping you?" I asked him. "Are you afraid of girls like them Japanese boys?" I knew that would get him tight.

"I'm not afraid of her. It's my father, my mother, my whole family. They would kill me. Worse than that, they would disown me."

"So what are you gonna do?" I asked him.

"That's why I'm asking for your opinion."

"Have you said anything to her?" I asked him.

"Anyo!" he denied it strongly, like a man accused of some crime. "I just go in there every couple of days and buy records from her. If she's not here, I leave and don't buy until she comes back."

"How serious are you about her?" I asked.

"I brought you all the way over here to see her," he said. "I haven't brought none of my boys over here to see her. Not once."

"That's a bus trip, that's nothing," I told him. "Would you fight for her?"

"Fight?" he said, like he didn't know that for men, fighting was automatic.

"I'm a dancer, not a fighter. *You* look like a fighter!" he said.

"Yeah, I was your manager. Now I'm your security," I joked. "Would you marry her?"

"Marry her!" he said, like he never heard of that concept before. "I just want to . . ."

"Play with her?" I asked him.

"I didn't say that," he said.

"If you want to find out your true feeling for a girl, just ask yourself, *What am I willing to do for her? Would I fight for her? Would I work hard for her? Would I kill for her? Would I marry her?* If you think about it, and the answer to all those questions that you asked yourself is no, she ain't the right one," I explained. He fell silent.

"If you couldn't even imagine her as your wife, that means you're setting up to disrespect her," I said. He listened as though he was really considering my words.

"It's not like that," he said. "In Korea, nobody marries so young. We have to go to school forever, and then the military. Then we have to get a great job. Then when we are like twenty-seven or twenty-eight, our families start pushing us to marry someone who they think is best."

"So what are we doing over here then? If you can't imagine yourself marrying her?"

"If I did, we would have to move to China or something. No one around here would accept us," he said. "There's nothing more important to Koreans than blood."

"Blood?" I repeated.

"Yeah, blood, don't ask. What you and your wife did—that was bold. I want to be strong like that, but I would never want to lose my family."

"Forget her then," I told him, testing him.

"I don't want to forget her. She's the real one I like."

"If you don't fight with your fists, and you're afraid of telling your family your true heart, and you're scared of standing alone while doing something that you think is right, why should this girl even want you?" I tried to be real with him. I liked him but hated cowards. "Come back after you man up and after your feelings grow strong enough for you to confront your parents. Until then, just come and stare at her through the window."

"What if I let my feelings grow and I get stronger and when I come back, she already has someone else? I should just at least find out if she already has a man, right?" he asked me.

"Yeah, find out," I told him. "Wait, why this girl?" I asked him. I was hoping it wasn't just how nice her butt fit into those jeans. I thought that wouldn't be a good fight or trade-off for any man. It wasn't enough.

"Look at her. I love her personality. All of her feelings just show up. It's like she is enjoying life more than everyone," he said, and it sounded true.

"Does she speak Korean?"

"She speaks English and Korean. Her mother is Korean," he said.

"And her father?" I asked.

"I don't know, probably a military man. They got a bad reputation. They never stay around for their family. That's why this girl who I like would be considered low status in Korea. You're probably thinking it's only because she's black. But it's more than that. In Korea, if you don't have a mother and father married into a hardworking family, you are the same as trash."

"Do you think she's trash?" I checked.

"Anyo!" he denied it.

"Okay, let's go in," I told him. "Here, wear this." I gave him my fitted. He smiled like it was a magic hat. "Never wear this bootleg shit. I pointed out the shape of his hat and the string running across it. "Get New Era fitted hats. Gimmie that." I took his and trashed it. "That's the same as trash!" I told him.

We went in. I played the back and watched while frontin' like I was checking out the music selection. It didn't take too long for me to notice that Black Sea was frozen by the counter fidgeting with the hat, wearing it straight, then moving it around on different angles. I didn't have a lot of time. I went up front.

"Have you see him in here before?" I asked her.

She looked up and smiled. "Many times," she said.

"He wants to hang a flyer up on your wall. He's having a party on Friday night. You must've heard about it?"

"A flyer, a party, where?" she asked. "Let me see it." Black Sea pulled the flyer out and opened it. He said he wasn't afraid of this girl, but I could see clearly how nervous he was. He handed it to her without pushing out one word.

"He's a break dancer. Let me introduce you. His name is Black Sea."

"Black Sea," she repeated soft and suspiciously. "And you are?" she asked.

"I'm his manager. How about the flyer?" I asked.

"I have to ask my supervisor, but he's not in right now."

"My man can't wait too long. He'll be moving to the United States to perform," I said.

"Oh really." She smiled, impressed.

"If you can give him your name and number, he can call you and check on the flyer situation tomorrow," I told her and handed her a pen from my pocket.

She looked at me suspiciously. Then she wrote her name and number on a piece of paper, and just as she got ready to slide it across the counter, I said "Black Sea, this is Sarang."

"Love," he said. She smiled. I was confused. But I walked away and left him to work the rest out on his own.

I waited outside with my back on the window. When I checked, they were in there talking. She was still smiling, so that was a good sign. Three minutes in and she was changing the record, he was showing her one of his moves, and she was dancing while watching him dance. She tried to learn his move and show him something too, until some customers lined up.

"Her name means 'Love,'" Black Sea said when he came out, beaming like a bum in the bakery. "She's studying at Busan University of Foreign Studies. She plans to be a lawyer. I got her number. Man, you are my *chingoo*. You know what that means?" he asked me.

"Nah."

"You are my friend. I don't know what that means in America. But in Korea, a *chingoo* is a friend and friendship is for life. You and me got *jeong*," he added.

"What is that, *jeong*?" I asked, remembering that the professor had brought that word up the other night.

"It's an unbreakable bond. It's a loyalty and a trust that you can expect and depend on for life. It means no matter where you may go in the world, and no matter where I am or what distance or troubles might be separating us for the moment or even for a very long time, we remain friends for life. Koreans have *jeong* with our friends, our brothers and sisters, our parents, and our wives and children." He was speaking on it passionately. As we walked through the streets, I could tell from his tone that he meant it. I thought about Chris and Ameer. They are my true friends. Still, we never had a talk between us openly the way that Black Sea was relating to me after knowing me for only two or three days.

For the rest of the afternoon I hung with him while he shopped for some kicks and jeans and shirts. He wanted to buy the exact ones that I had on. Before we each went our own way, we exchanged addresses and all of our information. Since he had opened up to me, I felt obligated to let him know he probably wouldn't be seeing me until either he came to the States or I returned to Busan. He was the only person I had ever written out my Queens address for besides my lawyer.

"Yo, hold up," I called him back. "What does *gongpay* mean?"

He frowned. "Who told you that? Did someone call you that?"

I didn't explain. I just wanted him to answer.

"It means 'gangster,'" he told me.

Chapter 12
THE CURTAIN

"We'll go get gas while Akemi collects her things," Dong Hwa said when I met him behind Bada Ga where he pulled up.

I opened the door and extended my hand to help my wife step out of the van. She was wearing a new dress, at least it was one that I had never seen. It was soft like taffeta, a deep, rich green, with tiny pleats and wide sleeves shaped like the calla lily flower. The pleats ran all the way down the dress, which was cut at her calf. She was wearing comfortable, casual espadrilles on her pretty feet. Her hair was wrapped in a sea-green silk scarf. Her diamonds still threw light, even in the dark.

Inside her room, she smiled to see that I had already packed her stuff. None of it was professional or gift-wrapped and ribboned like when Mayu, her Japanese house manager, had packed it, but it was folded as neatly as clothes and shirts are folded and stacked at the Polo store, the way I handled my clothes.

I had fantasized about her as I packed her belongings. It wasn't the predictable items like her little panties and bras or nightwear that I had made love to her in. It was her high heels, shoes, sandals, and boots.

"Mayonaka Chiasa talk?" Akemi asked out of the blue.

"No," I answered her truthfully.

She was searching me with her eyes.

"Come here," I told her. She came. I held her in my arms. The fabric of her dress felt nice against my skin. She laid her head against my chest.

Then I asked her. "Akemi likes Chiasa, yes or no?"

She pulled back only enough for us to face one another. "*Hai*, Akemi like," she said. "Akemi, Chiasa see," she added after a pause.

"Akemi wants to see Chiasa?" I asked, gesturing "to see" with my finger pointing at her eyes.

"*Hai*," she said softly, without a smile.

"Akemi, Mayonaka fly home." I motioned a plane flying through air. "To New York this week."

She smiled and jumped on the bed. She stood up on the mattress to pull down her curtain. I stepped up to help her. When my hands were in the air bringing the rod down so she could reach the cloth, she turned and faced me and asked, "Mayonaka Chiasa likes?" She pulled the curtain off the rod and held it. I put the rod down and laid it on the mattress so we could put the Bada Ga's curtain back on it.

"Mayonaka"—I put my hand on her heart—"loves Akemi." "Mayonaka"—I put my hand on my heart—"loves Chiasa," I showed and told her.

Without three seconds passing, three tears spilled out from Akemi's left eye.

"Mayonaka loves Akemi. Akemi *ichiban* in Mayonaka's heart." Then I said what Dong Hwa's son had taught me the night before in Korean, "Mayonaka loves Akemi forever. Mayonaka will never leave Akemi alone. If Mayonaka goes anywhere, he will always come home to you." I kissed her face beneath the eye where her three tears fell. I did not ever want to hurt her. I wanted the two of us to always talk truth to one another. War and business were separate. I would conceal those things from her, for her. In matters of the mind or heart, however, I wanted the two of us to always be true.

I said that I would always be in love with Akemi, and I meant it. I also believed that I had shown it. I had traveled seven thousand miles to get her, climbed five miles of mountain and walked five miles of forest and three miles of field. I had risked my life and my freedom for Akemi Nakamura, and I always would.

The thing was, Chiasa had risked her life and freedom for Akemi too, and that moved me. Chiasa had come up with Akemi's grandmother's address in the Hidaka Mountains. Chiasa had saved Akemi's passport and made it possible for us to be here in Korea as well as to move on to the United States without legal risk. Without Chiasa, Akemi and I may not have ever gotten back to one another safely.

I knew that without saying it aloud. That mattered a lot. Although these were surely not the only reasons that I also loved Chiasa, they were reasons that gave my connection to Chiasa much more weight than a crush on a bad-ass pretty girl. Chiasa, I believed, was not offensive to Akemi and my love. Chiasa was an asset that made all of us strong, and having more than one wife was my culture and was within the boundaries that Allah has drawn for all believers in our faith, Islam.

Chapter 13
THE CAUTIOUS PROFESSOR

"It would have been nice to drive to Seoul in the daylight, but I had to finish some work in order to prepare my assistant for tomorrow's class that I will be missing," Professor Dong Hwa said.

"It's no problem," I told him. We were riding in his wife's minivan, but the professor was driving.

"You only *think* that it's no problem because you have never seen the beauty of the historic Nakdong River or our rice fields or our bridges."

"I saw the beautiful bridges over Busan, and I saw many rice fields in Japan," I added just to throw him off, the way he tried to do me at times.

"That's not the same thing," he said at a lower volume than everything else he had announced proudly.

The professor booked two rooms at the Hyundai Suites located in Seoul. He warned me that it wasn't a tourist area, but he chose it because it was large enough for his family even though they were only planning on an overnight stay, it had the kitchen, washer and dryer, and other items a normal family needs to be organized. I gave him $150 up front. I assured him whatever Akemi and I needed, I would pay for. We had arrived around midnight, so everyone was preparing to rest.

"Can we talk downstairs in the lobby?" the professor asked me.

"Akemi, I'll be right back." I told her.

She was figuring out the television remote. "*Hai,*" she said, turning and looking into me as she always would.

"About tomorrow," he said cautiously, when we were alone, seated in the hotel lobby.

"What about it?" I asked.

"I'd like to take things one step at a time. I'd like for Sun Eun and I to see Akemi's grandmother alone first. We think it'd be better if Sun Eun tells her mother about Joo Eun and her ashes."

The professor was being careful and considerate to me. I think he was also wary of my reactions, after the situation between me and the guy who claimed to be Akemi's father. I liked that he was cautious. He needed to respect my marriage the same way I respected his.

"No problem," I told him gently.

"What time do you want me and Akemi to come?" I asked him.

"Okay, so now we're on step two," he said, sounding like the professor he was.

"I'd like Akemi's grandmother to meet Akemi alone."

"You mean for her grandmother to meet with her first before meeting me, Akemi's husband? I must be step three?"

"Yes, and I do want her to meet you of course. You and Akemi are married. Here in Korea marriage is sacred and serious," he said, trying to calm me. I had noticed though that he didn't mention when I would actually be introduced to the grandmother.

"When?" I asked.

"Let's check her schedule and see how it goes tomorrow. We really don't know what's gonna happen." He said that thing again, about not knowing what's gonna happen. Meanwhile, I was reflecting on what Black Sea had told me about Koreans and blood. If Sun Eun had fainted when she saw me, could the grandmother go some steps further and catch a heart attack?

"No problem. I have some things I want to check out in Seoul," I told him.

"Really, what?" he asked. He was so eager to know everything, but no one can know everything!

"Itaewon," I said, remembering that the brother named Ali from Iran had told me that I could find an Islamic community in Itaewon that included an Islamic center and halal foods, a mosque, and related products.

"Itaewon," the professor repeated, like he knew something I should know. "Watch your wallet carefully when you're over there."

"Are you still planning to leave late tonight to return to Busan?" I asked him.

"We'll see what happens," he said again.

I was feeling worried for my wife and for his mother-in-law. It seemed like Dong Hwa and his wife were bracing themselves, like people waiting on a storm that may or may not come at all.

Akemi and I went walking in Seoul, into the late night. Our nights were precious to us, especially since I knew now that I would not see her tomorrow once her family matters got rolling. We ate at a fried chicken joint, and there were many to choose from. They rocked until 2 a.m. after other food places were closed. Fried chicken and beer and watermelon—Koreans had that in common with Africans. There were slight differences. Their fried chicken came with sides of cubes of white radishes. On second thought, fried chicken, beer, and watermelon, break dancing, hip-hop, haircuts, and the urge to chill in the right fashions—young Koreans had all these things in common with American blacks.

In the shower and steam together, kissing Akemi felt warm and moist. She had her eyes closed and her hair was soaked through. Her fingers were still exploring my cuts. I didn't stop her from licking each one. I wanted to thank her, for her love and her passion. I moved her back up against the hot wet wall and ran my fingers down the front of her body. In the squatting position with water sprinkling over my head and flowing over her body, I spread her pussy lips and sucked her clitoris. It had been a while since I made her cum this way. It always drove her crazy. As I swirled my tongue around the most sensitive area, her legs collapsed and she gushed all over.

Later I dried her hair for her and even gave her a braid. "*Naisho,*" I told her, meaning "secret" in Japanese. She should never tell anyone that Mayonaka, the black leopard, braided her hair.

We went to sleep the same way we did in my Brooklyn projects, and in Osaka and in Busan by the sea—naked, her breast against my back, her arm beneath my arm and her pretty fingers wrapped around my balls.

* * *

Right before sunrise I peeled myself from my wife. I had to shower away our syrups and prepare to be clean and focused for the prayer.

After Fajr prayer, I was exhausted. I went back to sleep in a separate bed thanks to Professor Dong Hwa, who registered me and Akemi for double beds instead of a king-size. I respected the cat, but from time to time I had to laugh at him. I considered that some people think for whatever strange reason that sex is dirty. The Quran encourages that a man should go into his wife. The boundary in our Quran is not around how a man and woman make love and babies and pleasure for one another. The boundaries are that a woman and a man must be married. Once the *nikah* is performed, enjoy one another.

"*Sayonara*," Akemi said before she left to go next door to join Sun Eun. Why didn't she know I hated that word whenever it came from her lips?

Chapter 14

PANIC

At 11:00 a.m. Korea time I called Umma. Naja picked up. "Oh boy, who is this? I don't even know you anymore," she said.

"Don't say that. What are you doing in Umma's room this late?" I asked her.

"She let me sleep in here with her for three nights already," Naja said, as though she was winning some points.

"What's been happening?" I asked her.

"Panic died," she said, as though I should already know and she was mad that I didn't.

"Who?"

"Panic, my frog," she said, sounding frustrated with me.

"Oh, what happened to him?" I asked, trying to sympathize with her.

"Well, there are a few theories," she said, sounding like a little scientist. Our father is a scientist, so it wasn't too out of reach.

"Tell me, I'm listening," I said.

"Oh, I don't want to talk about it right now."

"How's Umma?" I asked the most important question.

"Well, she's getting prettier every day. That's what everyone around here says."

My chest tightened. "Everybody like who?" I asked my sister.

"Like Basima and Sudana, they just love her," she said, as though the Ghazzali women were competing with her for her mother's love.

"Oh." The sudden tension in my chest was released.

"So stop asking about people and come home already," she said.

"I will." But I didn't want to let on that it would be this week, just in case anything happened as the professor had said. "I'll be home soon, Naja. *inshallah*."

"There is one problem around here though," Naja began whispering.

"Tell me."

"It's Basima," she said, referring to Mr. Ghazzali's eldest daughter. "I think she is in love or something."

"Are the Ghazzalis planning a wedding?" I asked.

"Nope, there's not going to be any wedding around here," she said quietly.

"Come on, Naja. Get to the point. What happened?"

"Basima loves a boy who goes to her college. He's going to be a doctor just like her," Naja explained slowly.

"So what's the problem?" I pushed.

"He's from south Sudan and Mr. and Mrs. Ghazzali are from the north of Sudan. So Mrs. Ghazzali doesn't approve of their love." I didn't say nothing. Then Naja asked, "Our father is from the south, right?"

"You *already* know," I told her firmly, aggravated by the ongoing senseless conflict between the north and south of fucking everywhere.

"Umma says, 'People in southern Sudan are just as good as the people of northern Sudan and that some of the southerners are even better!' So Basima loves Umma a lot. The boy Basima loves—"

"The *man* Basima loves, Naja. He is a man, not a boy," I told her.

"Does Mrs. Ghazzali know what Umma thinks?" I asked, gathering all the information I could from Naja's perspective.

"Nope. Umma told me that me and her should stay quiet and not tell anyone our thoughts."

"So how does Basima know what Umma thinks?" I asked her.

"Because one day Basima was down here crying over the boy, I mean the man, and I guess umi just got feelings because of Basima's tears and she said those good things about the north and the south and Basima's man. I guess umi just wanted Basima to be okay."

"I see. Where's Umma now?"

"She's in the shower. Should I go get her?" Naja asked.

"No, tell Umma don't worry. I'll call her back tomorrow before she leaves for work, early morning." I hung up.

Uneasy, I called the lawyer who has the keys and paperwork for our new house in Queens. I knew it was late in New York and that no one would pick up. I just wanted to leave a voice message. I told our lawyer that I would pick up the keys to our new house on Saturday. I would buy the tickets home for Akemi and me this week.

People who didn't come from countries where it is normal for people to talk about politics every day, to care about it and have a definite opinion about it, will never understand how these kinds of situations escalate and then fall apart. Between men they are sometimes even fatal. I didn't want Umma to be uncomfortable reliving something that she had already lived, survived, and won, the north versus south of Sudan conflict. Umma had told me in great and specific and clear details about her and my father's love story. Because of this, I knew that one day soon, her thoughts and emotions about Basima's dilemma would mix with her own feelings and burst into the Ghazzali home. Then Umma would potentially become an unwelcome guest or worse, an intruder in their personal passionate matters.

I would settle and secure my Umma in a place of her own, the one we had both worked so hard for, the one that was now vacant, paid for, and ours.

At the travel agency I researched and reserved two tickets for Akemi and me, leaving Seoul in three days, the evening flight. The agency gave me twenty-four hours to pay for them. Since Akemi had her passport on her, I would pick the tickets up the following day. By tonight my wife and I would know what happened with her grandmother.

Chapter 15

WAR

I caught a cab to Itaewon. I told the driver to pull over on a long, tree-lined block with well-kept lawns. There was a Howitzer rocket launcher sitting out there on the grass, besides a huge tank as well as American-made fighter jets. The scene reminded me of a talk my father had with me when I was young, introducing me to all types of guns and weapons of war. My father was breaking down for me which countries were manufacturing and selling these weapons. He wanted me to know that in war there is always a handful of businessmen sitting at the top hoping that at least two groups of people, sometimes more, would destroy one another. These businessmen, my father explained, would come walking into someone else's land after the north and south had burned, raped, and crippled one another. Then they would use their poor condition against them both and seize power over their land, government, banks, and schools and women. I wanted to see what this display was all about. I paid the driver and jumped out.

Homemade meals were being eaten on benches and picnic blankets while young children climbed in and out of tanks and were allowed to enter the cockpit of real planes parked in the grass. As I walked by checking it all out, I quickly learned that this place was a "war museum." It was an entire complex dedicated to commemorating the Korean War.

If there was any way to kill somebody, this place had the weapons on display. After checking out the heavy machinery, I climbed the stairs into an outdoor courtyard lined with huge slabs of black marble with perfectly precise rows of Korean hangul letters. Out of habit, I counted. As my eyes moved down from the top to the bottom, I realized these were the names of men killed in the Korean War, the north versus the south. There were 1,500 names of war dead on each marble slab. Where I was standing there were fourteen slabs. *That's 21,000 dead*, I said to myself. But as I left that area, I entered a new area and there were fourteen more slabs times 1,500 war dead. The slabs of the dead continued all the way around and up to the second floor. On the third floor, I stopped counting. Mixed in with their dead were slabs listing American soldiers whose lives were lost in the war fought in Korea. There were 34,000 men listed here, but who knows the real number? I thought about the cats from my Brooklyn block who got gone at age eighteen, deployed around the globe to fight. Was having your name printed on marble at a museum better than having an RIP graffiti mural on the wall on your block? I thought about what felt better to a young man like me—merking someone who disrespected your mother, or killing a whole bunch of people across the globe who you don't know shit about?

As I examined the surface-to-air missiles and rocket launchers, submarines, and even war robots, I thought about what a man or a nation had to do wrong in order for it to be justifiable to drop a two-ton bomb on them. My thoughts raced and intersected. Did the Koreans and the almost two million men sent to fight in Korea, as it said on the wall I was standing there reading, all believe the words of the Quran that imply that a murder is justifiable when a man is spreading corruption, vice, or mischief in the world?

What about the innocents? How many innocent people could be murdered in pursuit of the actual guilty parties? When America was flying over Hiroshima and Nagasaki, Japan, was it to punish a small crew of wicked men, the Naoko Nakamura type? Or his father, Hasashi, the ammunitions dealer? If these men deserved punishment because of their corruption and excesses, did that mean that everyone else living in their country deserved the same?

Heavy thoughts were marching through my mind. I questioned who exactly was responsible for all this stress and destruction. More importantly, I wondered why the wicked had been so successful all over the globe.

As I walked down the cool corridors, that brought up a nice breeze and break from the warmth outdoors, the gun room caught my eye. I had to squat low to look up close on a gun developed by the Koreans called the Corner Shot. This bad-ass weapon was designed for a soldier of urban warfare. It was curved so that the shooter could assassinate someone hiding around the corner. It could clap you as far as fifty meters away and weighed 4.4 kg, according to the label. My eyes damn near pressed up against the glass as my mind wandered into how this weapon would impact my hood, where somebody was always hiding around the corner. I saw a set of lips on the other side of the Corner Shot. I'm not a lip-reader, but I could see the formation of the words "so fucking cool." My body jolted. I stood up and looked over and down. It was Chiasa. Those were her lips and her words. Standing tall behind her while she was still squatting was her father, the general.

Mine and the general's eyes locked. Chiasa stood, saying, "Daddy . . ." It must've been the look in his eyes that caused her to turn swiftly. She saw me.

"Ryoshi," she called me, like she was suddenly out of breath. Her eyes revealed her genuine surprise. She put one hand over her lips and held it there. She let it drop and turned to her father and said, "Daddy . . . he is the one who . . . ," and then she paused and tried to readjust her true emotion, maybe because of her father, or maybe it was because she felt bad that I had not contacted her even though she had waited so patiently, for so long.

Meanwhile, the general was checkmated into silence. He was probably unfamiliar with the words "You win" and was calculating how to cheat me.

"How are you, sir? It's good to meet you," I said, stepping from my side and extending my hand to him. Chiasa's eyes were watching her father for a reaction.

"I'm good, son. Just enjoying my day with my daughter."

"She's so beautiful, sir. I wish she were mine," I said, looking into Chiasa.

"Ryo . . . ," Chiasa said softly, and her eyes lost the barrier of defense she had thrown up and her emotions seeped through.

"Chiasa is a daddy's girl," her father said proudly.

"You're right, I'm sure, sir. Until the right man comes for her, she's a daddy's girl," I said solemnly.

"Let's go, baby," her father said.

Swiftly, I interrupted. "Chiasa, where are you staying?"

"Oh, at the—"

Her father cleared his throat.

"Tell me where you are, Ryoshi," she asked me.

"Hyundai Suites, here in Seoul," I told her. "Akemi said she wants to meet you." Chiasa searched my eyes. I knew what she wanted to know: *What about you, Ryoshi?* But of course she didn't say that out loud.

"How long will you stay in Seoul?" she asked.

"Not long, maybe two days. Then we'll go back to New York," I said. Her father smiled at the news.

"Oh, I . . . see," she said.

"Let's go, Chiasa," her father said with his heavy hand on her shoulder. She left with him, but I knew she didn't want to. I watched as they walked away. She turned and looked back at me.

Chapter 16
OASIS

It was on the walk out of the war museum, less than a mile down, that I saw it, another American military base. Tossed behind a wall that spanned three or four blocks. That explained it.

The walk through Itaewon was nice. There were all cultures and races of foreigners. When I saw the Arabic letters looming large above my head in the corner spot of an elevated winding road, I felt good. It was only 4:30 p.m. There were two more hours to sunset.

In a row of jewelry stores I sifted through the junk. My eyes were keen for the real thing and I would know it the moment I saw it. If it wasn't there, I wouldn't buy anything.

"You are looking for diamonds, yes?" A short man from Namibia offered to show me a private collection, since I had "a good eye for gems," as he put it. I guess he based the observation on the fact that I hadn't bought anything so far and I had been searching for more than half an hour.

At 5:30 p.m. I phoned Umma. I would catch her before she left for work in Mr. Ghazzali's taxi. She picked up on the first ring, expecting me.

"Umma!"

"Are you okay?" she asked me in Arabic, concerned over me when I was concerned over her.

"How about you? I'm coming home," I rushed to say before she could answer my first question.

"But how is our Akemi? Have you visited nicely with her grandmother?" Umma asked, knowing only that we were visiting Akemi's

grandmother but not the whole reason why or any of the details, purposely.

"Almost," I said, being vague.

"Almost?" she repeated in Arabic. "I know Naja has spoken to
you about Basima. If this is the reason that you are hurrying, then
don't. People have had these bad ideas about one another for so many
years. If you come in three or four days, or even two weeks later, their
thinking will be the same. Even fifty years from now, they will be the
same," Umma said.

"I'm not thinking about them. I am thinking about you, Umma.
Our house is ready for us now. I mean it is vacant. I still have to prepare it for you," I said.

"How do you know that I have not already prepared it for you?"
she asked coyly.

I was quiet now on my end. After thinking, I answered her. "Because you are working so hard that you haven't had time to prepare
it for me. Because I know that you wouldn't have gone to the lawyer alone or to Queens alone. And I know that you wouldn't have
given anyone else our address or showed them our place. Since I
know my mother so well, I know that you are only now thinking
that you will rush over there and prepare it for me, so that I won't
rush back to you before Akemi is feeling comfortable with her grandmother."

Now she was quiet on her end.

"Umma, no one is better than you," I said, feeling moved in my
heart suddenly. "How are you really feeling these days? How are the
Ghazzalis treating you? Tell me honestly," I said.

"I have no other way to tell you except honestly, my son. I am be
ing treated very well every day. I am being taken care of in the exact
way that my son had provided that I should be taken care of. I am
content almost every day and grateful to Allah every second.

"Sometimes there is a sadness that comes over me. But it is not
a sadness that anyone can cure. Sometimes I am missing the Sudan.
All the time I am missing your father. Sometimes I want to pack
everything and return there, no matter the troubles. What can they
do? They can only do what Allah will allow to be done. And whatever
Allah will allow must be done. I have decided that finally, after all

these years," she spoke softly and thoughtfully, filling me with emotion.

"I can take you home to the Sudan, Umma. Now I'm a man. I can
do that for you."

"Even when you were a boy, you were a man! I knew that you
would take me to Sudan when you grew up. I used to worry over that.
I knew that you would grow to be the same as your father. This is
what worries me most."

"Why?" I asked, not understanding.

"Because in your father's heart, and in yours also, is a special thing,
an abundance of love. Neither of you can be happy unless you are sharing and expressing your love abundantly. Yet you are both surrounded
by people who are not the same as you in their hearts. You two are the
givers. The others are the takers. You two cannot stop giving. The others will not stop taking. After a while, it wears you down." She paused.

"That is why I worry over you, because of the love that lives in
your soul. Because of the love that does not live in the other souls.
Because of what they might do. People envy people who love. People
who love like you and your father expose the people who do not love
much or at all, just by your being alive. Then those people say, 'We
have to destroy him because of what he *can do* and what we *cannot
do.* If we destroy him, no one will ever know that we cannot love. No
one will ever know what's missing.'" Umma was going in deeper and
deeper in her words and thoughts. I wanted to change the direction
of our talk before it caused her tears to fall.

"I'll bring you home an abundance of love, Umma. I'll bring you
so much love you will be swimming in it. I have a lot of surprises for
you, Umma. And when I return to you, I'll work very hard. In one
year, I promise, we will visit Sudan. We will feel it out. If you want to
stay there, then that's what we will all do. So don't feel sad, my beautiful *umi*, please." I could feel her smiling. I could hear the difference
even in her breathing.

"*Alhamdulillah*, son. Please be well and let Akemi be well. And
don't trouble yourself to rush. You have already paid for the month
and you really do have almost two weeks remaining. I'm fine, and
again, nothing will happen that Allah does not allow to happen."

When I hung up, I weighed her tone and words carefully and

compared them to what Naja had described. Then I separated both of them from my own thoughts. I wasn't one hundred that "nothing will happen that Allah doesn't allow to happen." Maybe that was a woman's mind, I considered.

Men have to make things happen. When men make moves, something happens, good or bad, right or wrong. Somewhere along the line, some man is responsible for whatever went down. I wondered if Allah actually weighed in on every single detail of each life and soul anywhere and everywhere in the world. Or if Allah ruled in general and gave man free will as his test, the Holy Quran as his guide, his soul as his score card, and heaven or hell as his verdict?

What about those wars and bombings? Had Allah granted permission for all that? Or had the men responsible just hidden their trail and hands and faces so well that they escaped responsibility?

Shockingly, as I began to walk, I could hear the calling of the *adhan* off in the distance. For seven years living in New York, I had not heard the call out of doors and in the open atmosphere drifting through the breeze. Now Seoul had moved my soul and allowed me to hear it and feel it also. I picked up my pace and began moving in the direction of the call. As I rounded the corner, there was a hill, of course. It was not nearly as steep as any of the hills I had climbed and traveled up so far in Korea. It was a simple hill. I moved past a Salaam Bakery: just the name of the place made me feel good. I walked through a row of halal restaurants. I turned another corner; another hill appeared, not so steep, and at the top of the simple hill sat the mosque. I moved uphill with a wave of people.

At the mosque entrance was a wall of cubicles for shoes, which must be removed immediately. I removed my shoes. Quickly I moved past others who were obviously already prepared and washed myself—face, hands, nose, feet. Walking through the rows of believers, the women in the rear, the men in the front, I enjoyed even the feeling of the carpet beneath my feet. Standing shoulder to shoulder with many men, we prayed.

A welcome calm came over me. I found my place at a table in an adjoining room where believers were enjoying breaking the fast together. My eyes moved over the faces of Muslims gathering from many different nations. I expected to see men from Arab nations and African nations, and I did. I was real surprised to see tables of Muslims who were Korean, and two who were obviously Chinese. I smiled.

"Brother, where are you coming from?" the voice of a young man seated next to me asked in Arabic.

"Sudan," I said naturally, which I normally would not reveal. However, because the question was asked in Arabic, it was instinctive to answer it truthfully. Normally I speak Arabic only with Umma and Naja.

"I knew it," he said. He stood back up from the table. When I took a look at him, I knew it too. He was from the Sudan as well. I stood and we embraced.

"Where in Sudan?" He asked me immediately.

"Sudan is Sudan," I replied calmly, still fresh from the thoughts of my conversation with Umma. He smiled. We both sat. As I sat, I suddenly saw my Puma walking by from the food table, away from the men and toward where the women were seated. What was she doing here in the mosque? She didn't see me? She has perfect vision.

"What brings you here to Korea?" the Sudanese asked me. But my eyes followed her.

"I'm visiting with family," I answered him, knowing that a fellow Sudanese would ask this many questions and so many more. Because we are from the same place, it would be considered perfectly okay to ask and normal to answer, no matter how many inquiries stacked up.

Now my Puma was saying some words to an older woman who was seated alongside of her young ones. The woman got up from the table and joined her. They both walked away and out of the dining room.

"I'm studying here at the University of Korea," the Sudanese said. "I'm planning to graduate in only two more years, and return to Omdurman." I knew he was finding a way to raise the topic of where he was from again, hoping to cause me to do the same. Of course I knew his city well enough. It was located next door to the city of my birth, Khartoum.

"What are you studying?" he asked me, although I never told him I was studying anything.

"Excuse me brother," I said to him. "I have to run." He seemed taken aback by my exit. I left my fruit uneaten in the dish on the table.

Unfamiliar with the interior of the mosque, but moving around observing, I checked the various rooms.

"Brother," another male voice interrupted me. I turned.

"Imam Jabril Park," he introduced himself. We exchanged greetings.

"I interrupted you for a few reasons my brother. First to welcome you. I see that you are a newcomer to the mosque. Second, to assist you. You are moving into an area reserved for the sisters and their children." He smiled politely. "Let me invite you to break bread with the other believers." He touched my elbow to move me back into the right direction, the area of the gathered men.

"Shukran Imam Park," I thanked him. "If you don't mind, can I ask you some important questions?"

"Of course," he said. The Imam was willing. He led me into his office. Grateful, I put my mind to focusing on the information that I needed most to hear a knowledgeable Muslim man speak on. I figured that was more important in the order of things than chasing the Puma.

Chapter 17
NIGHT OF POWER

Moving away from the mosque and down the hill and into the now darkened sky lit up by the lights of Itaewon, I was comfortable. The narrow alleys reminded me of both the Sudan and Egypt, Khartoum and Cairo. I came up on an international grocer displaying shelves of the spices and ingredients that Umma used most often, as well as coffees, teas, and candies, including packages of henna, an array of incense being sold along with the foods.

An Islamic travel agency that was closed as I sped to the prayer was open now and doing business with four or more customers. I could smell the aroma of fresh foods being prepared. Previously darkened restaurants were now packed, some without air conditioning the way my father preferred it. Their doors were swung open. I was tempted but I passed on sitting down to eat a full meal. I planned to do that with with Akemi.

There were so many small businesses with Arabic awnings and lettering, I had to remind myself I was in Seoul, South Korea.

I turned into the Islamic Center for Books, impressed by just them being located here, as well as by the bright lights and stacked shelves of meaningful reading from all over the world. It was good to see men wearing their turbans, or kufis or fezes. They were engaged in conversations about real things. I could tell by their expressions.

One man dressed in his jelabiya, either a worker or the owner, was talking intensely and confidently to Chiasa who was listening and focused. With her back to me, she was wearing jeans and sandals and a pretty Chinese gold satin blouse that was tapered and fitted to her body and rode down over her hips. Her long, thick wild hair was only one third covered with a gold scarf, which she rocked like a headband. Her golden skin set off by the blouse and headband looked beautiful. She always looked graceful in her stance because of her long ballerina legs and perfect posture.

I stepped up behind her and said some words in Arabic over her shoulder to the man who was talking with her. His eyes were filled with a passionate plea to influence Chiasa in one direction or another concerning Islam. I imagine he did this for all of his customers. But I was feeling tight at him for conversing with her. After my words to him, he stopped.

"Ryoshi!" She looked over her shoulder and then spun all the way to face me.

"What is this name you've been calling me?" I asked her. She smiled. She looked back at the man that she had been listening to and he turned his eyes away from her and his attention shifted onto a customer who was holding and flipping pages of a book he had pulled from the shelf.

"What did you say to him?" Chiasa asked me.

I grabbed her hand and said, "Let's go."

Her palm felt warm. The breeze outside was warm. I was warm. She was completely quiet. We walked and walked. *"Chiasa, one thousand mornings, wings of fire,"* I thought to myself. Now her tongue is quiet and the fire is in her body.

"It's after sunset," I said to her.

"I can see that," she said.

"But you didn't see me in the mosque?" I asked.

"Oh, were you in the mosque?" she asked nonchalantly.

"What were *you* doing in the mosque?" I asked.

"Two things; learning how to make the prayer, and learning how to wrap my hair properly. I think mine is too much. It's thick. It's been a problem the whole time I was growing up in Japan. No one knew what to do with it, especially not my mother."

"It's pretty," I told her truthfully.

"Thank you," she said quietly.

I turned down an alley that incidentally led to a makeshift mini city park. It was the opposite of Chiasa's Yoyogi, which was a wonderful forest of treasures and also her home in Japan. I stopped walking when I reached an available old bench. We both sat down.

"Give me your right hand," I told her. She held it out. I went inside of my pocket and pulled out the tissue paper. I opened the soft paper and slid seven gold bangles over her pretty fingers and onto her wrist. As she looked down on the dark 24-carat gold, she twisted her wrist to make them jingle, but kept her eyes cast down.

"Give me your left hand," I told her. She held it out. I slid a ring onto her finger. It was a simple 24k gold band with a setting that lifted one pear shaped, one karat diamond. She stared at it, then lifted her face.

Her eyes were filled with amazement.

I leaned in toward her. "If I see you again, and you and I are alone, the way that we were for all of those days, I'll go in you. I know it and you know it." The pretty Puma lowered her eyes.

"You have your Quran on you. The only relationship that you and I can have is through marriage. It's written in there. You understand it." I said calmly, then got up.

Standing over her I asked her, "Where are you staying?"

"At the Shilla with my father," she said softly.

"How long before you return to Japan?" I asked her.

"Until Thursday morning. My father has a big banquet to attend here in Seoul on Wednesday night. He invited me here. I'm his date.

"I'd like for you to meet with him, my father. If it's okay, I'll check with him tonight to ask him if he will and when he can," she said sweetly, sounding as though she was mistaking her ferocious father for a toothless tiger.

"No problem, I'll meet him wherever I need to meet him," I said, as her eyes were staring into mine in a concentrated way.

"Akemi . . ." I said.

"I called her . . ." Chiasa said swiftly. "She wants to meet. I wanted to meet also. So we agreed on tomorrow night at eight p.m., me and Akemi at your hotel."

"Chiasa quick like lightning," I said in a lowered voice.

"Ryoshi . . ."

"What?" I said then asked. "Who is that, Ryoshi?" I asked her for the tenth time.

"It means, 'the hunter'. That's my name for you," she said softly.

"The hunter?" I thought about it and smiled.

"Yes, the hunter, and you got me." She pointed at her heart with one slim pretty finger. It brought my eyes to her chest. Her nipples were raised up and making an impression in her gold satin blouse. I moved my eyes away. I was at the breaking point with her. A slight push is all it would take.

"Let me take you back to your hotel." I grabbed her hand. I knew I shouldn't, but I wanted to feel her.

In the taxi, she laid her hand on my leg. We were seated close together.

"I want you to," she whispered. I looked at her.

"I want you to 'go in me,'" she said. Then we were quiet the rest of the way, only my right and her left hand caressing.

The Shilla hotel was some exclusive five-star place. Riding the route that led to it, introduced me to some new night images of Seoul. Like any major city, it had its places of great wealth all the way down to low living. It had places of industry or offices or fashion. It had temples and throw back alleys that gave the feeling that we had traveled back in time and been dropped into their traditions.

I hadn't thought about it. Yet there was no reason to expect the general to stay anywhere else besides in this luxury. I let the general's daughter out in front and continued on with the same driver. I rode for some seconds with my eyes closed. I thought to myself, *She got me. She's very smart and very quick and very, very, clever. She's the real hunter.*

Chapter 18
TEARDROPS

Patiently I waited outside on the steps that led into Hyundai Suites. Akemi and her aunt, uncle, and cousins were not back yet. It was 10:00 p.m. Something must've happened, I thought, as Professor Dong Hwa had suspected that it would.

By 11:00 I was still downstairs sitting, then standing, then pacing.

I shot across the narrow lane and into the impromptu city park which faced the hotel. Seoul had a few of these I'd seen. They were small sitting places with cement grounds, two to four benches, monkey bars, and a couple of swings, that's it. But I checked a place to bust out some pull-ups. I wanted to burn off some energy, beat back my hunger while waiting for my wife. When she arrived, *inshallah*, I would go walking with her and we would eat wherever she wanted to eat. I had waited the whole evening to eat with her.

The park was closed and the lamps were off. I didn't mind the dark or even working out in a Seoul city park. Yet it was clear that it was the opposite of my Busan beach.

One hundred pull-ups, two hundred fifty sit-ups, one hundred fifty-seven push-ups later, Dong Hwa's van appeared and everyone began stepping out of the vehicle beside him. She didn't see me sitting on the chain facing the hotel but in the shadows of the closed park.

"Akemi," I called her.

She turned around and looked in the direction of my voice first, before our eyes met, her standing, me sitting and rocking on the chain. She said some Korean words to her aunt and her cousins. Then she walked my way.

Professor Dong Hwa didn't pull off immediately. Instead he watched my wife until he saw me stand and pull her close into my arms. She was wearing a red silk mini so mean it could only be worn over jeans. Her hair was wrapped. On her pretty fingernails she had painted on black hangul lettering flawless, she brushed over the letters with a clear gloss that glistened. Stray strands of her hair had eased out of her scarf. I moved her hair from her sleepy eyes. She looked up at me. She was still herself, all feelings and seductions. I squeezed her some and carried her down the lane on my back.

In a pasta place she said and gestured that she had already eaten, but she kept pushing her fingers in my sauce and licking it, or offering her saucy finger to me instead.

In her one scoop of vanilla with the caramel drizzled on it, she spilled two tears. I called the waiter the way they do in Korea, *"Yogio!"* I paid him and grabbed her hand and left most of the ice cream and caramel melting on the dish.

In a mostly empty theater we sat a while. A film that was completely foreign to me played on the screen. We didn't need them, the actors. We kissed softly and touched instead, seated in the last row in the corner. One hour in, she fell asleep on my arm. I held her, thought about how she must feel. Eventually my thoughts settled on whether she spilled two tears because of her emotions from meeting her grandmother. After all, today was the first day Akemi had spent with her in her entire lifetime.

Or was my wife crying because she had received a call from Chiasa at some point earlier today? I sincerely hoped it was because of the grandmother.

When I woke her up to leave the theater, she threw both her arms around my neck. Minutes later I carried her back to our suite.

Lying in one bed, with no lights, beneath the sheets, she moved her hands all over my body slowly before climbing on top of me and easing herself onto her favorite place. We had a slow, silent grind with only the sound of moisture mixing. Both my hands were gripping her hips and moving them around. She was so sleepy but still she wanted that feeling. My entire face was covered with her heavy hair and my skin was wet from her hot and continuous tears.

She slept now. I held her tight for a while listening to her breathe and feeling her heart beating against my bare chest. As I drifted off, I thought to myself, *If Chiasa is all fire, and she is, then Akemi is pure sugar, the sweetest feeling I've ever known, the sweetest emotion, the sweetest taste, the sweetest woman.*

Before sunrise, I eased her over onto three pillows and covered her with the bedsheets. I showered, made prayer, and afterward fell into a needed rest lying in the other bed.

When I woke she was gone. She had pasted a piece of paper to my headboard with a strip of lotion on the back to hold it up there. I pulled it down. It was written entirely in Korean hangul.

Not the type to panic, I panicked. I threw on my clothes, the ones I'd worn the night before, and took the stairs down to the front desk. The last letter that I had gotten from my wife led to her disappearance. This second letter had me shook.

"Excuse me, please tell me in English what this says," I asked the desk attendant. She looked at the note curiously, and then she began to blush. Looking at her face, and without hearing her interpretation yet, I felt relieved.

"She says she loves you. She has gone with her grandmother to Wolgyedong and afterward they will visit a school named Yeo-myung, and she will meet you back here tonight. She writes, 'Hopefully at seven p.m.' That's it." The attendant smiled partway and then snatched her smile back.

"*Comsahmidah,*" I said, meaning "thank you" in Korean.

"Oh, you are in room seven-oh-seven, yes?" she asked me. "You have a message." She turned and pulled an envelope from the mail slot.

The flap of the envelope was not glued shut. The note was written in English on Hyundai Suites stationery.

Thank you for being so good to Akemi and us. We have gone back to Busan. I have already extended your reservation until Thursday. If Akemi could please remain in Seoul visiting with her grandmother for today and tomorrow, we would really be so grateful to you. The two of you may travel back to Busan on Thursday with her. Grandmother has decided that we will have a ceremony for Akemi's mother, Joo Eun, on Saturday in Busan. She has decided that Busan is the place that Joo Eun would've preferred. We will scatter her ashes over the South

*Sea on an island not far from North Korea. It will bring peace
to everyone and give Sun Eun and me a chance to make all
of the arrangements. The elder has decided this. In Korean
culture, we follow the elder's way in these matters. Please
understand us.*

Professor Dong Hwa

When I told the desk clerk that I would make the payment for
our room extension, she said, "It has already been taken care of."

Back in our room, I changed into clean clothes. Afterward I made
telephone calls to handle and rearrange all of my business to fit the
new schedule, which was only possible because of Umma's assurance.
I didn't mind making the changes, although I thought that Dong
Hwa should've faced me instead of writing the letter. I knew how
important the ceremony for Akemi's mom's ashes was to her and also
for her newly discovered family. For me, this situation was, as Haki
had once mentioned, "a clash of cultures."

In Sudan men handle the business of burials and funerals. Our
women do not even attend such events. Instead, they gather indoors
and mourn and comfort one another, cook and share and converse.
Men carry the body, which has already been washed and cleaned and
prepared according to our faith and culture.

When I reached downstairs, just as I walked across the hotel
lobby, the same front desk clerk approached me hurrying from behind.

"There's a call for you," she said. "We tried to put it through once
before but your phone line was occupied." I followed her to the front
desk.

Chapter 19
ONE SOUL

"Ryoshi, can you talk for a minute?" Chiasa asked.

"Where are you?" I asked her.

"At my hotel. I just finished speaking to my father. He's gone out now to attend some meetings," she said.

"Let's meet up," I told her, and gave her the address to the travel agency where I was headed.

* * *

Her hair wasn't wild today, but her eyes were. She wore two thick, long cornrows and had more of a glow than before. She was wearing the love she was feeling, it seemed, and the jewels I had gifted her as well. The Seoul sun on a Ramadan day had straightened us up some, both of us. The nighttime has a sensual power that can make passions feel even more urgent. I had planned to give her those jewels after she and Akemi met and spoke specifically about our situation, but after seeing Chiasa in the mosque and then in the bookstore, I felt pushed to mark my territory, and that urgency led me to place one bangle at a time on her wrist and one diamond ring on her finger. All mosques are filled with Muslim men. They are serious men who welcome marriage, wives, and family.

"What time are you leaving tomorrow?" was the first thing she asked me. Her left hand was raised up and shielding her eyes from the sun rays. Now drops of sunlight were dancing on her diamond.

"Change of plans, I'm not leaving tomorrow," I said calmly.

She smiled. "I'm so happy. Now you can meet daddy. I had so

many things I wanted to tell you and so many things I felt we needed to talk about before you left for the States."

I just looked at her. I didn't say any response. I was thinking that she must not know that I was planning to take her home with me. If Akemi agreed, it would be the three of us flying to New York. If not, Chiasa could keep the jewels. They were valuable enough. I had sold my watch to get that pear-shaped diamond. No sweat, Chiasa had given me more. She had given me Akemi.

"Let's talk," I told her. We walked, her messenger bag riding on her hips.

"My father can't meet today. His schedule is so crazy. He can meet tomorrow though. I hope you won't mind. He said if you were still in Seoul we could all meet at the Shilla because that's where the banquet is. He can squeeze us in at seven right before the event. I'll be dressed up, but you don't have to. It's just because I have to attend the banquet with Daddy." She took a breath.

I smiled. I knew the general had selected a time to meet me when he thought I would already be in flight to New York, out of his life and Chiasa's also. "I'll be there, seven sharp," I said calmly.

"Oh, good." She threw both arms up in a touchdown pose, same as when she first came creeping into my Shinjuku hostel.

"Okay, so about the vending machines, I found a connect," she said, shifting into her business mind. "I spoke with one who offered all kinds of options that I thought might work good for you."

I realized right then that one reason I felt so attached to this girl was her energy. The range of her personality was wide. When she wasn't around, I missed the way she made me feel. Her mind was so swift and she was always poised and positioned and moving rapidly toward victory in whatever she was dealing with. She was a problem solver, not a problem. She was stress-free; she was peace to me.

"So what do you want to do about it?" she asked.

"Let's call him."

"Right now?"

"These are business hours," I said.

It was warm inside the phone booth with the door closed all the way so that we could hear the call properly. We were facing one another. We were standing close but not touching. She was speaking to the connect in Japanese, and back and forth to me in English. Then her eyes switched and she said to me in English, "So give me your New York address," while holding the phone to her ear. I gave her my Queens address. Now she was the second person to know what I normally wouldn't allow anyone to know.

She was speaking in a soft, polite Japanese, bowing while speaking as though the caller could see her. It was a part of her, I told myself. It was automatic. It was her Japanese culture.

"It's done. The machine will be sent to your New York address. The purchase order will be sent to me. You give me the money and I'll pay it," Chiasa announced. There was a pause between us.

"What?" she asked me, her eyes widened. I just smiled. I had nothing to say.

"Do you have your passport on you?" I asked Chiasa as we sat inside the travel agency.

"Yes," she said, curious. "Why?" She swung her bag around to her lap and opened it. "It's here." She handed it to me.

"I want to reserve three tickets from Busan International Airport to JFK Airport in New York, leaving Busan on Sunday, May . . ." Chiasa's eyebrows both lifted up. She didn't speak or interrupt or contradict me. She remained silent. Half an hour later, outside the door of the agency, she said, "Ryoshi?"

Avoiding offering her any of the details until after her meeting with Akemi, I changed the topic. "Do you always carry a slingshot?" I asked her.

"Of course." She smiled. "Even if I didn't have one on me, I could make one in less than three minutes out of two pencils and rubber bands. "She was all excited again, speaking about her weapons of choice.

In Itaewon I bought her a scarf to wrap her hair in. In the back of a musical instrument shop, I watched as she showed me that she knew how to wear it. When she got it all wrong, I wrapped it for her. As my hands moved over her head, her eyelashes grazed my skin. I could feel her breathing. When I leaned in a bit more, she gasped. I looked straight into her.

"It's not sunset," I told her.

"I can see that," she said so quietly.

"Why are you doing this?" I asked her. "Why are you fasting and reading Quran and wrapping your hair?" I really wanted to listen and hear her reasoning.

"At first I was doing it out of pure admiration for Ryoshi, really. Then I started reading the Quran for myself. Certain things in there gave me a feeling," she said.

"What kind of feeling?" I asked as we left the music store and walked through the Seoul springtime framed by all of nature blossoming.

"At first when I opened the Quran, I looked at the table of contents. I chose to read Al Nisa, the chapter on the women, before anything else. It said in there that 'Allah created man and woman from one soul.' I thought that was beautiful. I read the entire chapter, but that one line kept repeating in my mind. I thought that if everyone everywhere in the world believed that one line, things would be so much better between men and women and families. All of this time it seemed like everybody everywhere thought that women were less than men, lower and okay to mistreat." She looked at me, smiling.

I thought about how each time I pushed to see if she was bullshitting me about something, she would prove that she wasn't. Like earlier on when she gave her true reasons for following me to Kyoto. Chiasa was thoughtful, like my father raised me to be.

"What about in that same *sura*, Al Nisa, where it says on the thirty-fourth *ayat* that 'Men are the maintainers of women' and that 'Good women are obedient.'" I smiled.

"I'd like a good man to be my maintainer." She smiled. "And it says, 'Good women are obedient to Allah and guard the unseen,'" she corrected me. "That means don't walk around naked and uncovered." She smiled.

We both laughed without a real joke or reason.

"About the two, or three, or four wives situation, I don't know. I'll admit, I wanted it to be true because I want and my heart wants and my body wants to be with you, and you are already married. But it seems like men are given permission to have up to four wives only in certain situations. And it says also 'only if you can do justice with them.' Do you think a man could really treat more than one wife equally and justly?" She looked at me sideways.

I was thinking and silent for some time. Then I told her what was truest to me. "I don't think one man can give two women the exact same things. I don't think that a man has to give his two women the exact same things to do them justice. Each woman is different; probably they wouldn't even want the exact same things because of those differences between them. But I could give two women the same things in general: a true love, a lifetime of loyalty, a hardworking man and provider, a passionate lover, and a man who would risk his life to protect you and give up his life so that you can keep yours, if necessary."

Then I reminded her, "While you are bowing your head and praying to Allah, I am humbling myself and obeying and praying to Allah also."

Chapter 20

INSHALLAH

Akemi was seated on the stairs outside Hyundai Suites. Chiasa saw her first, all the way from the bottom of the block.

"Should I walk up there alone? Would that be better?" she asked me.

"No, we are already walking together so we shouldn't pretend that we are not," I said.

Akemi had her face lying on her knee tops. Her hair was uncovered and hanging down almost to the floor. She was watching as we approached. Her eyes were soft as they always were—soft, mysterious, and a little bit vulnerable. She was wearing a white *yukata* with a long stemmed black rose stitched on it in a wicked design. She wore wooden-heeled flip-flops. All of her fingernails had the kanji for Mayonaka. On her toenails were drawn half moons. She was so subtle in her extreme elegance.

"Akemi." I came in close and reached my hand out to help her up. As she stood up, Chiasa bowed down, then came up speaking in Japanese. Akemi placed her hand in my hand and kept it there. We were now three standing still on the stairs, staring. I saw Akemi's eyes seeing Chiasa's diamond ring and bangles.

Akemi said something to Chiasa. Chiasa turned to me and said, "Akemi is asking me if I am your translator. I told her I was."

"I'll head upstairs so you two can talk," I said to Chiasa and gestured to Akemi at the same time. Akemi wouldn't loosen her hand from mine. She tightened it to halt me.

"Akemi said to me, if I am your translator, then I should translate." Chiasa informed me.

I looked at Akemi. Her eyes told me she wanted the three of us to remain together.

"Then let's all go upstairs," I said. "For privacy," I added.

In the elevator, I stood in the middle. They were on opposite sides, leaning on the wall as though it was the only thing holding them up.

Upstairs in our suite, we all removed our shoes. I sat on the bed and leaned against the headboard. Chiasa sat at the small wooden eating table. Akemi moved around in the tiny kitchenette, preparing tea and rice and soup.

She spoke some Japanese to Chiasa. Chiasa translated to me that Akemi said:

"For the first time, I feel so frustrated at myself for failing to learn to speak the English language. This was never a problem between Mayonaka and me before."

Akemi was looking at me to let me feel and know that her words were for me. Then she said, "Now I feel myself splitting slowly like a glacier that has a tiny crack that threatens to break it into two pieces and send both sides drifting over icy water."

Chiasa looked at me. "You see, this is why I love her words. They are like poetry," Chiasa said softly in English without a trace of humor.

Akemi then turned to Chiasa and expressed the following feelings to her in Japanese, which Chiasa put into English so that I would also hear and understand.

Chapter 21
WHOLE WOMEN

AKEMI'S VOICE

I know why you love my husband. You love him for the same reasons that I love him. Any woman who comes to know Mayonaka will love him just the same. I am not angry that you love him. I have seen many women with either lust or love for my husband in their eyes.

I am angry because *he loves you*. He is loving you while he is loving me. I am also angry at myself, because you would never have come to know him if I had been in his life fully and at his side where I belong.

I am angry because his love is strong, and his love adds, but it never subtracts. So I know that no matter what I do or say, you have become an addition to me and him, a *permanent* part of us.

I am so angry at my father because he caused all of this. He divided a great love, mine and Mayonaka's, and for shallow and stupid reasons. He has kept me away from so many people, family members who love me or who would have loved me and I might have also loved. If I had only known them.

The love between Mayonaka and me is so intense, but now our love will never be as it was, just he and I. Now it is he and I and you and all of our children to come. I feel many children will come, because I know him.

I'm not going to be mean to you, because I already know that would be useless. It would cause distance between me and my man, and I want to hold him close, so close, so close. I know that you will never leave him, because I would never leave him for the same reasons. So here we are, wedded together somehow.

Chiasa, I saw you at Hokkaido. You were impossible for my eyes to miss. I am an artist who appreciates so deeply each beautiful thing in deep detail. I see it. I appreciate it. I remember it. I saw you on the plane, a very beautiful, quiet girl, pretty even while sleeping. I did not know that the girl who I often spoke to over the phone, was the one who rode on the plane beside me and Mayonaka.

I am crying now because even when my husband was coming for me, he was with you. What exactly happened between the two of you? I will never know. Whatever it was, it has created a powerful energy, and a strong bond and a deep feeling between you two. These facts can never be denied. I saw the passion in your writing on the study cards that you made for him. I saw the love in his eyes as he spoke to you over the phone. I feel his body jerk at the mention of your name.

Mayonaka has already told me that he loves me, he tells me that I am number one in his heart, his first love, and that he will love me forever. Mayonaka has already told me that he will never leave me, no matter what. Mayonaka has already told me that if he has gone away from me, he will always return to me. He is my husband. I am his wife.

I cannot ever separate from his words, from his love, from his body.

So if it is okay for you to be number two, then I accept you. Between you and me, woman to woman, and wife to wife, we should never have as our goal to destroy one another. It is impossible for me to destroy you without destroying him. It is impossible for you to destroy me without destroying him. We'll share.

Honestly though, and hopefully *only* in the beginning, while he is loving you, I'll be burning. I'll be burning because I know how good it feels. While he is loving you, I'll be burning because I know how good it feels to him and at that time it will be *you* making him feel that good, not me. But when he returns to me and holds me, I will heal each time. For that healing from him, I would do anything.

Chiasa, if knowing all of this, my true feelings, the lives I carry from him in my womb, you still want to join us, and I know you will, I accept you. We should become great friends. You and I should become close, but we will never become as close as each of us is to him.

CHIASA'S VOICE

I love your husband. You are right in almost everything that you've said. True, I can only love him because of you, but *not* because you were separated from him. During the time that he was looking for you and I was helping him to find you, our tongues never touched.

He was true to you, more perfect than you could imagine and more perfect than I ever wanted or expected any man to be. I am embarrassed to say that even though I was a virgin then, and I am still a virgin even tonight, if he would've attempted in one of those nights that he was searching for you, I would've allowed him. But he did not.

We used your diary to locate you. Only I could read your kanji, and I was his translator. It was you, then, who brought my heart to him. It was your words, your feelings, your impressions, descriptions, and experiences with him. I fell in love with you first. Then I fell in love with him. It all happened in that order. So yes, that makes me second, when I am used to winning first place and being number one.

But what will I have if I pretend to be what I am not? In this love, I am number two. I love and admire you, Akemi, as a woman. I don't hate women, although I know that many women hate every other woman automatically. I also love and admire him as a woman loves a man, in the deepest and most intimate of ways.

Number two is not less. You are right, it is addition, not subtraction. One is first and two is the next number over, but two is more than one. It makes one stronger. So here we are with no shame and no sin committed. I am so grateful you have accepted me. *Inshallah* over time, you will enjoy me genuinely.

MIDNIGHT'S VOICE

I know that if Akemi and Chiasa were American girls, they would've attacked each other. They would have tried to rip each other's hearts out and bloodied as many body parts as possible. They would've burnt down houses and slashed tires and raised up girl armies. They might have even tried to castrate.

They would have labeled me a motherfucker, a dog, an animal, a nigga, or worse. They would've said that I was crazy or full of myself or full of shit. Both of them would've told me to go to hell. The illest thing, however, that I know for sure from seven years in America—if they were American girls, they would've both made a scene, fought, and talked a bunch of shit and refused to marry me and refused to share. Still they both would've continued to allow me to fuck them repeatedly, impregnate them, and abandon them while swearing they were both right and both hadn't done anything wrong. I was proud of Akemi and Chiasa. Them being able to stay cool, talk it out, and be reasonable made me love them even more.

* * *

"Call me in the morning," I said, after walking Chiasa downstairs in front of the hotel. I hailed a cab. It pulled over.

"I want to spend time alone with Akemi, to make friends," Chiasa said as I opened the back door for her. "Maybe I can come by early tomorrow," she said, leaning her face out the window.

I knew from experiencing Chiasa during our search for my wife that she was great at making friends and winning over hearts. Chiasa has a purity in her smile and a gentleness in her talk that soothes and brings out the best in people despite her soul of fire and brave heart.

"Akemi won't be here tomorrow. She has to go with her grand-mother. How about you?" I asked her.

"I'm good until about four. Then I'll have to get ready for the banquet. And will you still come at seven to meet Daddy?" she asked, as though something in me might've changed.

"Definitely, seven sharp," I said. She smiled.

"Meet me at the mosque tomorrow at ten a.m.," I told her as she was looking up at me with those long lashes and pretty eyes.

She seemed unsure. But she said, "Okay, ten a.m. the mosque, and seven p.m. the Shilla."

I tapped the top of the cab and said, "The Shilla." His meter was already running. He pulled off.

Chapter 22

STRUCK BY LIGHTNING

Umma told me to take my Armani suit with me. I should've listened to her, as usual. But I was fresh dressed and more than chilling for the thriller at the Shilla. I was feeling good, extremely calm and peaceful. Meeting the general at his five-star hotel, squeezed in between his last pressing appointment and his banquet of dignitaries, was just a formality for me. I had already married his daughter Chiasa, the sixteen-year-old pretty puma of the legal marrying age. I had affixed Umma's signature on my documents, with her permission, of course.

Chiasa was swirling with emotions, her entire body pulsating like a heartbeat as she eagerly became my second wife. We wed at the mosque in Itaewon under the supervision of Imam Jabril Park and the witnesses he organized on short notice. As far as I was concerned, the general had already given his permission when he and I shook hands at the military property where he had abducted and held me, in Busan.

"Word is bond." That's what I believe and that's what my father and grandfather believe as well. The documents were for the authorities. The ceremony was for the faith. The spiritual permission was all I was truly concerned about. If it was right in Allah's eyes, then it was right for me, period.

Chiasa and my heart were probably married before all of that or perhaps before any words were exchanged between us. Maybe it was when I first saw her sleeping on the plane, or maybe it was much later when it came to me, a thought deposited into my mind: *Chiasa, a gift from Allah.*

I had not gone into her. I would. When our feelings were at their highest height and we were free to express them, just she and I, I would go in. I was excited to give her the deepest feeling that could be given to a woman probably other than childbirth, which I am sure is completely different. I was honored to be the first and only man to break through the skin that separated her from everyone else and brought her closest to me.

"We'll tell Daddy together, but wait for me to wink," she said, speaking of our marriage. "Please promise."

She probably didn't know that I felt so high from having her and Akemi as my own that I would've agreed to almost anything inside of those seconds when she made the request.

There was a long line of limos gliding up the long path to the Shilla, and Benzes and Lexuses and of course Hyundais. The trees were crowded on both sides, like a huge audience gathered for a holiday parade. Slowly my driver eased past the traditional Korean buildings and beneath the arches that lined the winding road. Each arch was made from intricately designed and painted wood. Turquoise was the dominant color. The tops were curled on the edges, the wicked way old-style Asian roofs were uniquely crafted.

When we reached the Hermès shop, I paid the driver and got out. The ride for the next seventy feet to reach the hotel door could take a half hour or more with all the vehicles waiting. I could walk up in less than a minute.

Through the revolving door and into an elegant lobby that was a festival of lights, my eyes were moving rapidly, taking it all in. The Korean designers had the eyes for the fine lighting. Everywhere I had gone in Korea so far was expertly lit, not with typical lamps or bulky bulbs.

At the Shilla the lights were a series of crystals carefully draped and dangling on an eighteen-foot wire slimmer than kite string. Each delicate crystal glistened from the high ceilings down. Each string hung at different lengths and on different angles.

As I stood still admiring it all, I was mixed in a crowd of tuxedos and fine wear. Women were in elegant gowns as well as sleek dresses and skirts of every length from pussy to ankles. In a small opening, I saw Chiasa staring down at me from the balcony. They were waiting for the elevator, I guessed. I was standing exactly at the agreed location. I wasn't worried about locating the general or him locating me.

I was the lone black face in a sea of Asian faces. When he arrived, he would be the second black man in a sea of Asian faces.

As one set of elevator doors opened, he came easing out, a muscular and massive man. He was wearing a well-tailored suit, not a uniform adorned with medals. Even that day that he'd sat on the side of his desk, not behind it, beside six hand grenades, he was not wearing a military uniform. He shook hands as he moved forward through the crowd. He would stop and exchange a few words with various people who sought his attention. His smile was swift and unnatural but seemed very useful to him. Chiasa was shielded behind him.

"Daddy, here is . . ." Chiasa introduced us excitedly yet softly. In his presence she was like a little girl. She was dressed how American men dress their daughters, in a sleeveless chiffon cocktail dress that delivered the contour of her body and featured her golden skin, full breasts, tiny waist, and long legs. She was the opposite of how she'd been at the mosque today. I wanted to take off my jacket and throw it over her head. I didn't. I told myself to be easy. This was her last concession to him, I was sure.

"Baby, go to my room and get my silver cuff links. I want to change these," he interrupted her introduction. She looked at him, knowing she was being sent away for a calculated reason. *Who shifts from wearing gold to wearing silver and not the other way around?* I thought to myself.

"Daddy," she gave a one-word protest.

"It's okay. I'll have a man-to-man talk with him," he told her. I didn't say one word, just watched her make her way through the crowd, saw her finger press the elevator button, saw a small crowd exit the elevator and her walk inside just as the doors began to close. Before it shut completely, her eyes locked into mine.

"Son," the general called me. Or maybe he was not a general. Maybe that was just a code name, a cover for something else that he was doing. I took his use of the word *son* as his acknowledgment of Chiasa's and my relationship. I believed that it would be the only acknowledgment from a man like him, who probably specialized in not acknowledging things.

"It's amazing, the power of a party, isn't it?" he began again. I didn't react. I didn't plan on doing too much talking. I showed up for Chiasa, my wife.

Just then, an immaculately dressed Korean man stepped up to where the general and I were standing. Quickly the general greeted him and they exchanged a few words, all spoken in Korean. I noted that I had now heard the general speak Japanese, Korean, and English of course. I suspected that this was just the small portion of himself that I had been allowed to see, hear, and know.

"Throw a big party where people get to pull up in their limousines and show off their tuxes, shoes, and cuff links, and the slimiest scum come crawling out of their holes voluntarily. They walk right up in the plain view of their enemy. It works every time. It always has, as far back as the days of Napoleon and even before his time." The general's eyes kept moving around the room, never landing on me. Yet he was talking to me strangely.

"That's the thing about a formula, son. If it works one good time, you keep it. Don't change even one ingredient. The party is a formula. It works everywhere on the globe—north, south, east, and west. Only the menus and the venues and costumes change. But that's not a change in the formula. It's a change in the bait," he said.

"You and I are both here at this party, sir." I was reminding him and questioning him at the same time: did he consider the two of us to be men who had swallowed the bait? Or maybe he was only referring to me as the sucker.

He laughed. "Always remember, son, the party throwers and the party goers are two separate sets of people. One set is the power. The other set is the meal." Then I knew, he was one of the party throwers. He waved at another set of men across the room. It was a one-hand wave.

I thought about Chiasa. What was taking her so long? Or did she plan to stay away to allow her father and me to "get to know one another"?

"What if your opponent didn't show up to your party? What then?" I asked him. I was intrigued by how he was not discussing anything personal about what had transpired between him and me and his daughter. Since he was not asking any questions, I assumed he either did not know anything about our new marriage or he knew everything and realized that because of the deal he made, he had no control over us.

"When you are a superpower, it doesn't matter if one of our enemies doesn't show. Enough of them will and we also make some allies by laying out the bait. If we are searching for anyone, no matter who he is, no matter how stubborn or smart, and even if he is the one guy in the world who doesn't like to party, we'll still find him. That kind of enemy is simply delaying his capture. He's eating up the military budget. He just doesn't realize that there actually is no 'military budget.' No matter how much we spend, there will always be more where that came from. Even the smallest countries spend on the military when they don't have even one grain of rice or one bean for their own people. War is endless." He smiled and finally turned toward me.

"So you see, I picked the right industry." He was looking me straight in my eyes.

"Look at these assholes!" he said, suddenly shifting his stance and angle. I shifted also. Through the doors moved a line of Asian men all uniformly dressed in black suits and white dress shirts and hard black shoes. It seemed like they were forming a blockade. They were definitely blocking some of the hotel entrances.

"Can you read faces, son?" he asked me. "I always know a man is a fool when he says, 'They all look the same.' A superior military man has to be able to read faces swiftly. I'm standing here on this side of the world tonight. I'll be standing in the midst of another party on the other side of the world tomorrow night. Wherever I am, I have to be able to read the faces. One slipup, I could lose my life."

His words were moving me now. I was watching the lineup at the entrance.

"Those are some Japanese crashing the party. Sometimes even when you don't invite a certain enemy they show up. Look at their faces and check the differences between them and the Koreans and the Chinese and the Vietnamese . . . To a civilian, there is no difference. To the trained eye, it's obvious. The Japanese always want to form a line. It's an obsessive-compulsive disorder. They'll bow all the way down to the floor," he said, pointing out exactly what both of us were seeing: fifteen men in a row bowing simultaneously with great precision.

"They always reveal their rank," the general said, as one more Japanese man came through the door, obviously the same man the others were all bowing down to. I looked at him, and then I looked at the man coming up immediately behind him. It was Naoko Nakamura.

I stood still. Why should I move? Then I checked the face of the man standing guard in front of Naoko, and it was Makoto. His eyes scanned the room rapidly, like a trained chief of security. When his gaze landed on me, his look shifted from a simple security check and head count to a knowing glare. Less than one second later, his eyeball had been shot out of its socket and his blood was splattering on his clean white dress shirt. The crowded reception area moved like a wave. Teams of security began revealing themselves and scrambling about. The people didn't scream or shout. It was a low murmur and curious facial expressions.

"Don't move, son. Stand right there. You are in the best seat in the house," he said, but we were standing. "Even though thousands of African-American military gave their lives to secure a free South Korea, if you are in the room among them and something goes wrong you will be the first accused. So stand still. We have over two hundred witnesses to the fact that we had nothing to do with this mess."

As everyone else entered into a state of confusion and Nakamura was rushed out the door, and thirteen of his fifteen-man security team followed behind him, while one picked up Makoto and the other, his eyeball, and wrapped it in a handkerchief, I knew.

Maintenance appeared before the ambulance to clean up the blood. One of them picked up the rock that I knew had to be Chiasa's and put it in his pocket as the police arrived at the hotel entrance too late to stop the destruction of the evidence of the crime scene. An argument broke out between the police and the hotel manager, who suddenly appeared in defense of his cleanup crew. An announcement was made that the banquet hall doors were opened and all guests should move inside.

"Come with me," the general said. I followed him into the banquet hall. Chiasa was seated inside, quick like lightning. Pretty as a puma, she was calm and smiling and her hands were steady.

"Take great care with my daughter, or I'll find you and kill you. It won't be a war game but the real thing," the general said. Those were his last words to me after the banquet and before we parted.

Chapter 23
IDENTITY

We left Seoul, South Korea with Akemi's grandmother riding in the car on Thursday, the day after Chiasa shot Makoto in the eye— the second time she had shot him, by the way. We were four people together, yet we were strangers to one another, all outsiders, all foreigners.

The North Korean grandmother was slim but sturdy with a face that had a pronounced bone structure, making her appear serious, like she was, and revealing the struggles and victories that made up the story of her living. Her hair was jet black, soft, and styled with a precise short cut that made her look and feel feminine even with her strong bone structure. She wore expensive gold-rimmed glasses with no tint. Her eyes were dark, big, and observant. When I looked into them I saw softness. *There had to be softness inside of her,* I thought to myself. After all, she had given birth to Joo Eun, who had given birth to my wife Akemi. Her daughter and her granddaughter were both stunning by anyone's standard.

She was a cool older woman who didn't let on her true feelings about riding in a car with her Japanese-Korean granddaughter Akemi, who she had just met this week, or Akemi's half-Japanese, half-black co-wife, or her Sudanese husband, me. Halmonee, which means grandmother in Korea, didn't speak much during the three-and-a-half-hour drive. When she spoke it was only in Korean and there were no gestures or explanations to clarify her to me or Chiasa.

We reached Busan on Thursday afternoon. For security purposes, Halmonee's driver/bodyguard checked us into a new hotel before returning to her apartment. It was on the beach where Akemi and I preferred to stay, and which I paid for.

Chiasa's face was filled with wonder. She was checking out our temporary home on the water where we would remain, we thought, for a few days.

I moved all the luggage into our rooms as Chiasa walked off with Akemi, heading toward the water. She was "making friends," which made me feel good.

We had two rooms. Chiasa and Akemi decided to stay together and allow me to stay in the second room. I smiled, no problem. I had both keys.

I took my run on my familiar route down Haeundae Beach right before sunset. My body celebrated the return of the scent and sound of the ocean and the moist sand beneath my kicks as I moved rapidly, faster than a jogger, slower than a sprinter.

My water and banana vendor was surprised at my arrival. Then his face switched and he welcomed me back. I made *wudu* and my prayer on the water before running back through the black sky, on the gold sand with the colorful globs of light leading the way.

Back in my room, I showered and dressed. I was surprised at the knock on my door. I walked over and opened it. It was Akemi showered and changed. She was all blue, her headscarf and her dress, were both a deep rich blue. The dark colors set off her dark eyes, which were outlined in a heavy black eyeliner. Those eyes looked mischievous and mysterious at the same time.

"Akemi is ready for dinner," she said in soft perfect English, which made me smile. I knew Chiasa had taught her that one line. The verb was in the right position. I pulled her inside and into me. I hugged her tightly and kissed her face and then her mouth. Her tongue welcomed me first. Then, she bit me. After a swift sharp pain I could taste some blood in my mouth. I looked at her and she smiled. The look on her face was half guilt, half self-satisfaction. Playfully, I snatched her up and turned her upside down holding both of her ankles. Her scarf fell to the floor and her hair was dangling. She giggled. Then I remembered that I had to be gentle with her. So carefully I laid her down on the floor.

I sat on the floor beside her. She was lying on her back. "Are you angry, Akemi?" I asked her. She responded in Japanese whispers while staring into my eyes with an intensity and no humor. I laid down beside her, facing her. She turned away from me.

"No love for Mayonaka?" I asked her in English. She didn't turn to face me and wouldn't respond. I began to rub her hair gently and caress the back of her neck. She wouldn't turn, but I was listening carefully for her breathing to change. I moved my hand beneath her dress and began to caress her body. She must've been angry. She still wouldn't face me, so I tiptoed with my fingers under her panties. I pushed my hand pass her butt and around to her long clitoris and pushed my middle finger inside of her. She was really trying to control herself. However, I knew it felt good to her. I know her body well. Then I decided the only way to get a reaction was for me to make her feel good and to suddenly stop. So I did. I stopped stroking her most sensitive spot and withdrew my finger. I reached around to her breast and felt her nipple. It was hard as a marble. Her body was giving her true emotion away. I put my hand beneath her petite body and turned her toward me. As soon as our faces met, she accepted my tongue into her mouth. Now, we were tonguing passionately. She kept reaching for my hands. I knew she wanted my finger back inside of her. I kept moving them away from her. I would only give her my tongue. She went wild, crawled on top of me, and bit my nose and my ear and my chin. We tussled.

When she felt all of me inside of her, she cried out passionately. I kept her crushed beneath the weight of my hard body and thrusted her good until she was breathless and moist and smiling and grateful and calm. I wiped her few tears with my fingers. I knew this was part of it all. She would be fine soon. She and Chiasa would become friends and helpers to one another. I would do whatever it took to make Akemi feel and know for sure that she wasn't losing anything. She definitely was not losing me.

I knocked on their hotel room door. Chiasa opened it. She looked left and then right. "Where is Akemi?" she asked.

"She's in my room. She needs a new dress. Can you grab one for me?" I asked. Chiasa looked at me for some seconds. I looked straight back into her. She went to the closet and picked out something for Akemi. She handed it to me.

"*Pekko pekko,*" she whispered with her hand over her belly.

"Me too, give Akemi twenty minutes more. Then we'll eat together."

"I'm so happy," Chiasa said. "You don't know how much I missed eating meals with you. Sometimes I was so lonely, I cried. My tears fell into my soup. My miso turned sour." She laughed. "Then I wouldn't eat any more of it." She was searching me with her gray eyes.

She was different, completely unique. She was so excited to have a meal with me. She still had not been kissed, caressed, or gone into. I knew her feelings had to be spreading out inside her. I knew she was making sacrifices for Akemi. Akemi, of course, had made a huge sacrifice for her also. Or perhaps it was all for me.

Watching them laugh in a dim Japanese restaurant where we all three sat on the floor, our legs folded beneath a low Japanese table, was really something. They both looked so beautiful to me. They were both covered, smiling, eating, and enjoying. I of course had no idea what either of them was saying. That was bugged out. I didn't care, as long as they were both mine. I needed the time to eat three Japanese dinners so the portions could add up to one normal-sized meal. I thought about Billy, the Senegalese, and laughed. Both Chiasa and Akemi stopped talking to each other and wanted to know what I was laughing about.

"Mind your business," I told them solemnly. Their faces showed the insult, then they broke back into their own laughter.

* * *

Friday morning I got the call. Dong Hwa and I exchanged greetings before he said, "The results are in my hand. Jung Oh is Akemi's father. Akemi is Korean, one hundred percent Korean blood." He was solemn, yet he had a trace of real excitement in his voice.

"I understand," I said. "I'll explain it to my wife. Please don't contact her about none of this. I'll handle it."

"We would like to come and pick her up from you. We'd like her to meet her father, Jung Oh properly."

"Not today," I said. "I'm gonna have a talk with my wife today. Of course we'll be ready for the ceremony tomorrow for Akemi's mother."

"How about tonight then? It would be good if you and Jung Oh could make peace before the ceremony."

"I'll think about it. I'll call you later," I said.

"Contact me at the university. It's Friday all over again. So you know my schedule and exactly how to find me."

"I got it," I told him. We both hung up.

I called their room. Chiasa picked up. "I need to talk to you," I told her.

"I need to talk to you too. I have something to show you," Chiasa said.

"Where's Akemi?" I asked.

"She's eating some leftovers from last night. She said she would go on the beach and do a drawing for hire since you and I are both fasting and she is not. She feels guilty about it," Chiasa revealed.

"She shouldn't. She should be in good health to have babies. She is already going through enough emotional changes."

I wouldn't force Islam on her. It wouldn't be right. With her mind so cloudy and her emotions so scrambled, it wouldn't be sincere, and wouldn't matter.

"Did something happen?" perceptive Chiasa asked.

"Every day something is happening. I'll come over."

After Akemi was situated on the boardwalk, the last strip of cement before the sand, Chiasa and I sat down on the steps nearby, where we could all see each other comfortably. Akemi had already begun drawing, although she had no customer. I figured she was creating something to show her skill to a potential customer who might come along. She was at ease with Chiasa in the daytime. It was the nights that she wanted to belong to her.

Wearing my shades that Sudana had gifted me, I told Chiasa, whose eyes were shielded by a floppy hat that couldn't fit properly over all her thick hair, the story of Akemi's family. In detail, I gave her all the missing parts that she had not known or discovered along the way. I even told her the truth about Naoko Nakamura, his background and how I had suspected ever since I read the unauthorized biography that he might not be Akemi's biological father. When I told her about the paternity test results, and that it had all been confirmed this morning, her mouth dropped open. "So fucking crazy," she said.

"I'll need you to tell Akemi the entire story."

"No way. It's so personal, too touchy. Do you know how the Japanese feel about issues of purity and origin and status?" she asked.

"Believe me, they have reminded me enough times that because I am what they call 'half,' I am less, and 'not Japanese.'"

"Fuck them," I said instinctively. "I only care about Akemi. She has to know because it's the truth and I don't lie to her. I need you to tell her, explain it in detail. I'll be right there with you. If I could say it myself, I would."

"You only care about Akemi, Ryoshi?" Chiasa said, lifting my shades from my eyes.

"That's not what I meant. I meant if it is a situation of being concerned about how the Japanese think about purity, or how the Koreans feel about blood, I don't care about their prejudices. I care about how all of this affects Akemi," I clarified.

"I thought—" Chiasa began, and then I interrupted her.

"Sometimes don't think. Sometimes only feel.

"Sorry, Ryoshi, I'll do it. I understand. I'll do whatever you want me to do, really. That's how I feel," she said softly. She sounded true.

"That part about her mother being Korean and pretending to be Japanese just to save Akemi—explosive." Chiasa exhaled.

"My mind is already beginning to assemble the right words to say it all the best way, the softest way, in Japanese. You know, for Akemi to be able to save face."

"What did you want to show me?" I reminded her.

"Oh, it's in my pocket. I won't pull it out right now," she said, evading.

"What is it? Tell me," I pushed.

"It's a newspaper article about the attack on Nakamura's top security chief at the Shilla."

I smiled. "What do they say?" I asked.

"No suspects," she said. "They just have a bunch of theories. It seems Nakamura has enough enemies that it's become too confusing for them."

"Why did you have a slingshot and a rock on you at a banquet?"

"I told you I always carry one," she said.

"Even when you're wearing a cocktail dress?"

"Hai!" she said instinctively.

"Where did you stash it?" I asked her.

She touched her breasts and smiled coyly.

"Then I won't ask where you hid the ammunition," I said. She was giving me forbidden urges in the daylight hours in the presence of my first wife.

"Did you know that Nakamura would show up there?" I asked.

"No way," she said. "I was on the balcony watching you and daddy. I was watching to see if you two were making friends. I was so overwhelmed, seeing you two talking and so excited that you actually married me. Then I saw Makoto. You know I have perfect vision." Chiasa said. I wanted to hug her. I didn't.

*   *   *

At 3:00 we three went back to the hotel. I called them both into my room.

"Anyaseyo," I told them to sit. I had learned that Korean phrase from Professor Dong Hwa. Akemi sat first, Chiasa followed. I sat behind Akemi and pulled her close inside my legs. Her back was to me. Her face was toward Chiasa. I pulled her shoulders back, so that she would relax on my chest. I gave Chiasa the signal, and slowly and softly in raspy Japanese she told Akemi the long story, a story that took just as long as it took Umma to tell me the story of her and my father's marriage.

Chiasa was beautiful and gentle, a problem solver, not a problem. She used her eyes and her voice and some sheets of paper with random kanji that she wrote while revealing it all. It was a tragic story, but Chiasa's voice still soothed and aroused me. Perhaps because I did not know the meaning of the words.

When Chiasa finished, she asked me, "Ryoshi, can we make the prayer and have some water?" Of course I agreed. Chiasa said something to Akemi in Japanese. Akemi was still in a sad daze.

The sun had set. I washed my nose, mouth, and face, hands, and feet first. Chiasa followed. We said the prayer together, as Akemi lay on the bed.

I phoned Dong Hwa and told him that we should meet tomorrow at the ceremony. He gave me all the information. I wrote it down in my pocket-sized notebook.

I left and got takeout and carried it back to my room for the three of us.

Later that same night I grabbed Akemi up and took her to my

bed. Chiasa had already gone back to their room. After the crazy night of being kidnapped and dropped into a "war game," Akemi had licked my wounds. Now I would lick hers, and rock her into a deep and comfortable sleep.

* * *

At 11:00 p.m. I went out. "Where are you going?" Chiasa asked me when I knocked on her room door and asked her to stay with Akemi while I headed out.

"I'll be back," I told her.

Chapter 24
CHINGOO

"I took a taxi to Busan University to the address printed on the flyer. When I had picked up the takeout, I had hit up Black Sea. I told him I would come through, for him to be on point and to make sure that I didn't have any trouble with the campus police, or any police for that matter.

When my taxi pulled up, someone was there to greet me.

"Anyong!" he said. "For Black Sea, right?" He took me straight into the building where the party was happening.

The lights were dimmed but not off like in a Brooklyn party. The place was packed and the sound system was right. They were booming music. It was "Licensed to Ill" by the Beastie Boys. Although a few girls were dancing with girls, nobody had to tell these Korean cats to dance with the girls. They were on the floor and most of the couples had rhythm. They didn't ride the female bodies like Brooklyn, but they came up close enough to feel the attraction and spit their game, whatever it was. Across the room I could see Black Sea in the DJ booth politicking like he wanted to influence the DJ to spin the records he chose. His man was behind him holding a crate of vinyl.

I walked past Sarang, the black Korean girl from the record shop. She was leaning on the wall alone. She saw me and called out, "Manager." I kept it moving. I don't talk to other men's women. They wouldn't have a chance to talk to mine.

In the booth I gave Black Sea a pound; we embraced. It was strange to see how happy my showing up at his jam made him appear to be.

"You showed up," he said, smiling. "Man, I appreciate that," he said, before introducing me as his *"chingoo"* to all of his friends I hadn't met yet. I smiled to myself, wondering if in translation that was the same thing as Ameer calling me "my nigga" or Chris calling me "Brother!"

The DJ reached back in time and threw on some break beats. Black Sea gathered up his crew as different ones of them started stepping out from the crowds where they had been camouflaged. All the regular partygoers cleared out to make room for Black Sea and his boys to perform. I could tell they had made a name for themselves as the dance floor was now theirs and the crowd around them began to swell. The DJ threw on some electric funk, Hashim's "Al Naafyish." Black Sea's crew went to work transforming into dancers dressed like homeboys but whose bodies had five times more joints than the average human. He was dancing for his girl. I understood.

She let him rock for a while before the beat lifted her feet from the floor and teleported her over to her man. She struck a pose and her powerful body started moving in ways it didn't seem like her tight jeans would allow. Her whole body pulsating, now, she wowed the whole room easily. She was the only African-Korean female, wasn't shy, and had more rhythm than the whole place combined. She spun on her black Converses with the silver laces, twisting her body. When she stopped spinning, her legs were interlocked like a New York pretzel. When she released them she went into a move that finished with a headstand more daring than Yoga with ten times the hype. She was all smiles. The fellas all bigged her up, which led them to bigging Black Sea up. The Korean girls whispered in each other's ears and watched with no option to do anything else besides to be amazed.

Kurtis Blow's "Super Sperm" and the Fat Boys, Grand Master Flash, Spoonie Gee, and the Sugarhill Gang all got some burn before I got ready to break out.

"You're not playing with her are you?" I asked Black Sea when it was just me and him standing there.

"Nah," he said borrowing from my way of talking. I'm not! *Yakusoku!"* he said, like " I swear."

I only stayed for an hour and a half. I didn't mess with any girlies, not even the one or two trying to mess with me. Black Sea accompanied me out of the party, which wasn't over yet. His girl followed him into the light. When we got outside the door, I saw his bruises.

"What happened?" I asked him.

"Oh, nothing," he said.

"It looks like something," I said.

"You said I would have to fight for love. This right here is from *Abojee*," he said, meaning he got pounded on by his father.

"You introduced her to your parents?"

"Yes." He smiled.

"What about that black eye?" I asked him. He turned and pointed to his girl. "Her little brother did that," he confessed.

"I guess I got to teach you how to fight," I told him. "How else will you make it in New York?" He smiled. "You don't look like a scientist no more!" I joked. "Good for you!" I said. His girl was smiling also.

I got a cab and went back to my wives.

Chapter 25
REST IN PEACE

The ceremony was emotional. It was the same as if Joo Eun, who had died years ago, had died just yesterday. It was not only heavy on my wife Akemi, but each person in attendance seemed weighed down with sorrow. I thought about the love that must be inside these people. Even the ones who had not seen Joo Eun since she was fifteen years young, which was sixteen years ago, seemed shocked and overwhelmed. I thought about how I knew more about Joo Eun than many of the people gathered on the ferry where the ashes were scattered in the sea. I thought about how uneasy a person would feel in their soul without knowing the missing pieces to a complicated story about someone they truly loved. I felt for the grandmother, whose posture was solid like a wall but who still shed so many silent tears. She was Joo Eun's mother. How much had she gone through?

I thought about war. I thought about love. I thought about how the general had said there is no budget for the military. "War is endless."

Dong Hwa stepped away from the side of his grieving wife and over toward me. His steps were steady but the boat was rocking on the current of the sea. "This is *jeong* you are seeing and hopefully also feeling right now. When we Koreans love, we love forever, no matter what. Our country has been warred on for thousands of years. Our people have been attacked, colonized, ruled by dictators. Our families have been under pressure. There have been many circumstances that have separated one Korean from another. Even though we are separated by space and time, we are still loving that person, and waiting or fighting or praying for their return. Whenever we are reunited, our love is as though they never left. They are welcomed back into the family and we continue on."

He thought he was describing a love so thick and intense that it was exclusive to Korean people. Yet I had heard these words from my own father in the past. I had felt that kind of love from him and Umma and my entire family. I walk with that same kind of strong love myself. I didn't express that to him. I didn't think this was the time. But I understood what he was saying, the position he was in, the love he had for his own wife as well as his effort to welcome me, while still defending his family from me, just in case I matched a bad image that he may have held in his mind.

The atmosphere moved me to shake hands with Akemi's Korean father. I even spoke the word *mianhapnida,* an apology for knocking him down to the floor and punching him in his face. I didn't feel like I lost anything as a man by apologizing to him. It was the difference between having the information and not having the information. If I had known he was her father, I would not have put my hands on him. But since I didn't know, I did. He wasn't focused on me. He accepted my apology. His hardened face revealed that he was a man with many worries, the least of them the fight that we had.

Akemi's young sensuous eyes had seen so much. I knew her feelings and her experiences being born and raised in Japan as a Japanese girl and living and believing it, was an incredible story that only she herself could ever tell precisely and properly, and in her own soft voice and manner. Perhaps she would never tell it opting to put it into a series of detailed drawings instead.

I knew my wife's heart well. She was standing there on the boat as it rocked on the deep waters still sorting out her love and anger for the only father she had ever known, Naoko Nakamura. I knew that she was surrounded by new faces of blood relatives who love her, yet despite it all, she still loved Naoko. Meanwhile, her eyes were surveying and capturing the image and perhaps even the soul of her true blood father, Jung OH. As I watched my first love, first wife's emotions churning, I knew I would be here in Busan for days longer than I had ever planned.

* * *

A couple days later Chiasa and Akemi had made their peace. Perhaps Akemi felt connected to her now because of the way that Chiasa took the time to explain so well the missing pieces of Akemi's life. Maybe it was because Chiasa held her hand and stayed by her side and slept in her bed beside her. Maybe it was because Chiasa and Akemi shared a common native language. Or because Chiasa was doing what Josna might've done if she were here. Or maybe it was because Akemi could now see what I already saw in Chiasa.

When Akemi asked to go and stay with Sun Eun and her grandmother for the remaining days before our flight back to the United States, I knew that was her gift to Chiasa. She would allow the inevitable to happen, while surrounding herself with her grandmother's and aunt's love.

Chapter 26
WINGS OF FIRE

"For the next three days think only of Chiasa," Chiasa said. "Can you do that for me?"

"It's Ramadan, you and I have to think of Allah."

"Okay, after sunset can you think only of me, as my wedding gift?"

"That's easy."

"Is it?" she asked.

"I think about you all the time anyway, and I did from when we first met."

"You did?"

"When I saw you asleep on the plane, I thought to myself, *She is like a blue diamond.*"

Chiasa was smiling. "A blue diamond," she repeated softly.

"Yeah, if someone ran up on a blue diamond, they'd stare at it for a while. Then somehow, even if their eyes moved away for a second, they would look right back at it again and again."

"Is it just about how I look?" she asked me.

"Nah, but that's a part of it, no doubt. If I looked over in that plane seat and saw a female who couldn't fit in the chair, with a face of a monster and feet like a kangaroo, I doubt we'd be standing here together like this."

She laughed at my joke and then said, "But what if she was a really nice girl?" We both laughed.

She had to know that I loved her mind and the way she expressed her thoughts. She had to know that I loved her courage, her heart and her soul.

"I liked that you were so pretty but that it seemed like you had no idea that you were."

"Oh, I see," she said, thinking. "In Japan, people don't treat me as though I'm pretty or special in any way. At least, not in a good way," she said.

"That's good. I like that. They made it better for me. When I take you back to Brooklyn, there won't be a cloth that could cover and conceal you enough to hide your beauty from the hood niggas. Maybe I'll get you one of those joints from Afghanistan," I said with a serious face, but I was joking.

"You mean . . . ," she said slowly.

"Yeah, like dat. It goes over your entire body and there is a small screen for you to see out and for no one to see in." I gestured.

"You don't scare me, Ryoshi." She smiled. "I love my *zukin*. If I can wear the face garment of a ninja, I can wear an *abaya* or *hijab* easily."

"Who taught you those words?" I asked her, smiling.

"The woman in the mosque who helped me learn how to wrap my hair said the proper name for the head covering was *hijab*. I liked the sound of that word, so I remembered it. My father showed me once how women in Afghanistan dress. He said I should never be like them," she said softly.

"Are you like them now?" I asked her.

"Even back then, I thought those women were beautiful and special. I didn't say it to Daddy." She paused. "My father means well."

"We're not talking about him. We are thinking only of Chiasa," I reminded her.

"Aunt Tasha said something like what you said a moment ago."

"Here we go, what did the infamous Aunt Tasha say now?" I played.

"She said that I wouldn't survive a second in Harlem without the street hustlers eating me up." Chiasa was looking into me, for my reaction.

"Hmm . . . that might be the first thing Aunt Tasha said that was true," I joked.

"That's not *the only thing*, Ryoshi! Aunt Tasha is so good," Chiasa defended and pleaded.

"What does Aunt Tasha know about some street hustlers?" I asked.

"She lives on Strivers' Row!" Chiasa said, as though that should tell me something.

"Strivers' Row?" I repeated.

"In Harlem! You know it, don't you?"

"Nah," I said truthfully.

"What kind of New Yorker wouldn't know Strivers' Row? Aunt Tasha talks about the history of it all the time."

"So when you visit Aunt Tasha, what happens?" I asked. My chest felt tight.

"What do you mean, what happens? Nothing! She just loves, loves, loves me. She has four sons and no daughter. She's my father's sister! So, she treats me as her daughter."

"What happens about the street hustlers who she said would eat you if they saw you?" I pushed.

"I don't get to visit Aunt Tasha often. When I do, I can't stay there for long. I always have a really busy schedule with martial arts, ninja camp, tutors, school, and work . . ." she said.

"What about when you do visit Aunt Tasha?"

"Oh, that can't happen. That's why she never lets me out. She keeps me in the house with her and we have our own world in there. When we go out, she takes me to really cool places and teaches me things. She never lets me sit on the stoop, like you New Yorkers call it," Chiasa explained.

"I like Aunt Tasha," I told her. "Am I gonna have to beat down all four of her sons?" I tested.

Chiasa laughed. "I already thought of that," Chiasa quick like lightning said. "Aunt Tasha is a church lady and she is gonna absolutely flip or faint or both when she sees the changes in me and listens to my new words and thoughts and beliefs. But I decided, once they all see how serious I am, and how I am studying the Quran first before taking a *shahada* and how much I love you, really really a lot, they will accept you and me and respect our way."

I looked at my woman, my wife, so beautiful all the way through the skin and flesh and bone and into her soul.

"How come you never kissed me?" she asked softly. Her mood changing.

I smiled. "You really want to know?"

"Hai!" she said.

"I knew that if I started kissing you, I wouldn't be able to stop myself. I might even lose my mind while I'm inside of you. So when I do kiss you, I gotta take you someplace where it's good and safe and alright for me to lose my mind and to give you my whole self. 'Cause you're Chiasa, a whole woman, not a half, right?" I said quoting her. Her eyes widened, then melted.

"Besides, a smart man has to think carefully before he touches you. You're a little dangerous." I teased her.

"Dangerous?" She asked.

"Yeah you like to play with knives and your father plays with guns. A man has to ask himself, 'Is Chiasa worth my life?' Then a man might decide that some other girl is much easier to deal with."

"But you're not that kind of man, Ryoshi." She said swiftly and at the same time seemed to just be realizing that I was actually saying that she is worth my life and any confrontation that loving her might bring to me.

"My father, that night when he saw my ring and the gold bangles that you placed on my wrist, he just stared. I waited for him to say something, but he didn't. Later that night he called my grandfather. They had a long talk. Grandfather told my father that he had already known that the 'tall, dark, and handsome boy' had 'captured Chiasa's heart.' Grandfather assured daddy that 'the boy has a fearless soul and would take our Chiasa away.'"

"Your father told you about his conversation with your grandfather?" I asked Chiasa.

"No, my grandfather told me about their conversation. I called him right after he and daddy talked. Daddy left out and I called grandfather." Quick and clever Chiasa admitted.

"Early the next morning, my father called my mother. I knew what that meant." She said in a serious but soft tone.

"What did it mean?" I followed.

"Well, the two of them never speak to one another, sadly. If they do speak on occasions it's usually to blame one another concerning who was responsible for something Chiasa had done. 'That happened on your watch,' sometimes my father would say to *okasan*. Or, my mom would blame daddy for, 'Not seeing your daughter as often as you should, then spoiling her terribly when you do.'" Chiasa gave a quick nervous laugh.

"So whose fault is it?" I asked Chiasa. "Me and you, whose to blame that we are together?" I asked her.

"It's not a fault. It's fate and it's a fact." She said solidly.

"I'd like to thank your mother. I want to meet her and thank her." I said calmly.

"For what?!" Chiasa said pushing me playfully.

"First I want to thank her because she brought you into the world. I want to thank her for forcing you to do ballet."

"Ballet!" Chiasa raised her voice.

"Of course, ballet made your legs so pretty." I said calmly. She lowered her eyes.

"I want to thank her for your eyes and those long lashes, for your small waist, and for her not knowing how to comb you hair." I said. Chiasa fell over with laughter.

"Seriously, your hair is wild and you're wild. But you're pure and I like all of it."

We sailed in a hired yacht cruiser with two white sails and one wide wicked red sail in between, to an almost-deserted island called Somaemuldo. "The Lady in Red," was the name of the pretty vessel. It wasn't expensive. It was a short trip across the South Sea from Haeundae Beach in Busan. Korea has hundreds of tiny islands. I knew they must all have something unique going on. There had to be something attracting and pulling people to them. Whenever I went running on the beach, I saw the boats flowing back and forth.

I had asked a fisherman on the pier, "Where can I take my girl to make her love me more?"

He smiled. "*Sarang?*" he said, meaning, "Love?" Then he pointed out over the waters.

"Somaemuldo."

That same morning, I negotiated a small fee with a captain whose yacht I always saw docked more than moving. Eagerly, he agreed to take us over. He welcomed us nicely, made us comfortable, and promised to return for us at the agreed-upon time, three and a half days later.

"How come places are more beautiful when humans haven't rearranged them?" Chiasa asked me. We were both staring at the reddest jagged-edged rocks, the bluest sky, the greenest grass, and into the forest as we climbed out of the transparent waters swarming with colorful sea life.

"Come on, we have to find a hotel," I told her.

"We don't have a reservation?" she asked.

"No, everything that happens here will be whatever you and me make happen," I said.

"So fucking cool," she said.

"Hotel," a little Korean lady said, shaking her head back and forth to say no, and placing her hands across one another to say "none."

"*Sarang?*" she said. She was asking if Chiasa and I were in love. Chiasa held out her hands, showing the woman her wedding ring and bangles.

"Honeymoon," Chiasa said with a soft pride. The lady smiled; she had a tanned face, a black afro, and tilted teeth. She touched Chiasa's hand, then held it to lead the way. Chiasa looked back at me and said, "See, I'm already making friends."

In a bungalow in the woods was where we laid our luggage, surrounded by forest and the sound of the sea. It was not a hotel or condo or motel or rental. It was the home of the woman who waited by the waters for the boats to come in, hoping she could make a few won if she could convince someone to stay.

There was no bed and no kitchen. The cooking area was an outdoor oven and grill. There was no bathroom; the toilet was a short walk to an outdoor structure. The shower was also on the side of the bungalow in the yard. The yard was not a real yard. It was the forest.

"We can leave and go somewhere else. I'm sure they have a hotel somewhere," I told my wife.

"This is perfect," Chiasa said. I paid the woman her full asking fee. She bowed using only her head, more than a few times, which sent Chiasa into bowing.

The woman pointed out the pillows, blankets, and mosquito nets, pots and pans, hot plate for indoors, rice cooker, and chopsticks. She led us outside and showed us the water well and the showerhead, the woodpile and the toolshed, and the lanterns to light up the yard at night. Then she immediately made herself disappear.

We organized and settled.

Exploring, I followed Chiasa through the woods, I knew she didn't like snakes. I didn't tell her, but when we first arrived, on the walk over, I spotted one. It was medium length and green and blended in like a leaf.

When we left the forest and faced a field of camellia flowers, Chiasa bolted. She started running at top speed. I chased her. She was quick and swerving to out maneuver and out distance me. I picked up my speed. I wanted to catch her and I didn't want to catch her. She was burning off some energy that she probably had bottled up from being unusually still over her past days visiting Korea. I was getting closer to her heels and was excited by her ways.

I caught her, snatched her back by her waist and tossed her into the flowers. She laid there breathing hard. I stood over her.

"There are snakes in the grass," was all I said. She jumped right up and chased me back to the bungalow, talking the whole time she was running about how she's not afraid of snakes.

"I feel free," she said. We were back inside our bungalow. "There is no one, just Chiasa and her husband."

I sat on the floor, dry and laid out from our run. I watched her sort through her clothes that were folded inside her duffel. She chose a short dress, grabbed the soap and a washcloth, and left.

From the bungalow window, I watched her unwrap her scarf and unravel her two pretty braids and shake her hair into a wild, thick, and long mane. With her hands crisscrossed, she tucked her pretty fingers below her tee and eased it over her head and tossed it to the side.

She unclipped her bra from the front, and her breasts, the size of mangoes, seemed to leap out. They were firm and soft, nicely shaped and golden with deep-dark-brown nipples. Her waist was small and tight. Her shoulders were the most beautiful I had ever seen. They were slim and toned and cut and feminine and outlined perfectly from years of arching back and firing off her bows.

Her pants were open now, and with both hands she peeled them away from her hips. They dropped down to her ankles; She bent over to step out of them one leg at a time. Her panties were tiny, stretched over her smooth and round backside. The delicate lace stitching was slipping and began hiding in the crease of those soft cheeks. She didn't see me watching her from the bungalow window, the same as she didn't see me that first time in the mosque. Yet she sees everything, "perfect vision." She turned on the shower water.

I spun her around. She was all wet. She cleaned the water from her face like a swimmer coming up for air. I pulled the lace and rolled her panties over her hips and yanked them down to her ankles. She lifted one pretty foot and then the other. I tossed them. I looked up at her and into her eyes. They were flooded with a mixture of love, curiosity, and desire.

"Ryoshi," she said when I stood facing her at full length and thickness. I pushed her back against the bungalow, held one hand on her waist and the other on the back of her neck. My joint was now pressed against her thigh. I leaned in closer. Her lips parted and her breath escaped. I slid in and tongued her gently. The inside of her mouth was warm. Her tongue wasn't in a rhythm with mine at first, so I slowed mine and maneuvered hers until it flowed and felt right. Then I could feel her body relaxing. Her mouth started moving with a hunger. We sucked one another's tongues. When I pulled back some, she moved forward and her tongue was bringing me back inside her. I could feel her mangoes pressed against my bare chest. I sucked her neck. Her breathing picked up and aroused me more. The warm water continued showering over our bare bodies.

"Oh my God, Ryoshi," she whispered in my ear. I slid my hand down the center of her body and paused at a pile of black bush. I just stroked the outside lightly, separating hairs to get to touch the opening. She began breathing faster. I could feel the fire from within her rising and heating up her skin. Gently I pushed my finger in but only slightly. I stroked her clitoris and she screamed out loud.

I stepped back and looked at her. She covered both her eyes with her pretty hands. She held them there and suddenly squeezed her pretty thighs together.

"Oh my God, that feels so good," she said dramatically, as though she could not believe it was happening to her. I turned off the shower. I moved in close to Chiasa and squatted down, petted her pussy, and her thighs relaxed again. I parted the hairs and divided her pussy lips and sucked on her clitoris.

She was on the ground now, my tongue licking and lips locking around her clitoris until she let loose the gushy. When I looked up, her whole body was trembling. Her pretty titties were shaking. Her deep-brown nipples were raised up high. Her eyes were closed and she was sucking her bottom lip.

I pulled up beside her. I began caressing her left titty and sucking the nipple gently. She spread her legs open. I got on top and over her.

Positioning the head, I pushed in and pulled back and pushed in and pulled back, and when it felt too good to me to control the rhythm that way, I thrust inside her. She moaned, "uh," and breathed in, she exhaled. I pulled back and thrust inside her again. She whined, "uh" again, breathed in and then exhaled. Pushing in and out and going in deeper each time, I could feel her tight walls parting and pulsating, massaging me and allowing me all the way in. I could feel her walls go from narrow, tight, and resistant, to eased and welcoming, to hungry and greedy. Now I could hear only sounds of pleasure escaping from her lips. I had one hand on the ground and the other in her hair. I didn't realize I was pulling it, yanking it. Her hips were moving beneath me now. She was feeling it, and grooving with it now. We were grinding in the grass. She eased her ballerina legs around my back. I could no longer think, narrate, control, direct, or resist. Her pussy was bliss and I had lost my mind.

When I showered my seeds into Chiasa, my wife, I eased off. There was a stream of blood running and smeared over her left thigh. I reached for her tiny white tee and used it to wipe up her blood. I planned to keep the bloody shirt just like that without ever rinsing her blood away.

I lay flat on my back facing the sky now. She threw one ballerina leg over and rolled right on top of me, she began kissing my face with her thick and pretty lips as though she was thanking me without out words. She threw her arms around my neck. She screamed one Japanese word, "*subarashi!*" and then whispered with her lips pressed to my ear and said, "Ryoshi, I fucking love you. You make me feel so good." She licked my ear.

I don't know what we both imagined we would do on that island. Whatever it was, all we did was love one another. Of course we did little things like eat, after Chiasa shot a chicken with her arrow and I plucked it, cut and cleaned it, and grilled it.

We played in the forest, ran together and raced to nowhere.

"Run!" she told me, as she took aim at me with her arrow.

"Woman, don't be crazy," I told her. But she was serious.

"I like a live target best," she said, and let off her arrow over my head. I liked the adrenaline rush and started running. I just pretended I was back in my Brooklyn hood running from the police after a block party got shut down. I was dodging and zig-zagging. She was firing off those arrows repeatedly, just missing my head each time till they were all gone. Then she chased each arrow down and I began chasing her.

"I know you could've hit me if you tried," I exposed her.

"Then who would make love to me?" she said, switching from assasin to temptress.

In the middle of the late night, I spread out my sleeping bag.

"Get in," I told her.

"There are blankets," she said softly.

"Get in," I said again. I zipped us inside.

"Ryoshi, you really do love me, don't you?" I just hugged her up. Having her naked inside my sleeping bag was a fantasy, a dream I had had on the rooftop in Hokkaido. Now we were in a warm, darkened hut on an island where only fifty people lived. As my hands rode her curves, and as she kissed me everywhere in an explosion of emotion, it had become real. We were just touching not speaking, not grinding. We were winding down into a sleep, I thought.

"Ryoshi, when did we fall in love? I tried to pinpoint the exact moment in my mind," Chiasa said to me.

"Probably we both fell in love at different times," I said sincerely. "Also, I think a man could fall in love at one time but not acknowl-cdgc it to himself until later on."

"Tell me," she asked.

I was stroking her skin while thinking. My hand paused on her lower back right before the curve of her behind. The moonlight was streaking through the window, cutting through the darkness in our bungalow, but revealing only Chiasa's incredible eyes. "I fell in love with you at the Senegalese restaurant in Tokyo," I told her.

"Really?" she asked. "Why there?"

"Because you were so beautiful and completely quiet. You were surrounded by men but weren't flirting. They all knew you were a precious gem but that they could not have you, because you were mine." She moved her hand to the inside of my leg and left it there. "Besides, you killed them all by throwing those darts into the bull's-eye like it was nothing to you."

She laughed a bit. "Ryoshi, you killed them. You had already beaten them at their own game on their board!" she said with soft excitement. "So when did you acknowledge it, your love for me? You said it was at a separate time." She asked me again. She was very curious. But now she was playing in my pubic hairs. Aroused, I slid my middle finger inside of her, touching her clitoris. Her accelerated breathing was background music to my true response to her.

"When I was in Busan and you were on the telephone speaking to me. When I couldn't even get my words right. When I asked if you were still fasting and you said yes. That sealed it for me. I couldn't ignore it anymore."

I swelled up to a full thickness and full length then. She knew it. Her hand touched it and she moved her fingers away. I eased my finger out before she could explode. I guess she didn't want to seem greedy. She didn't crawl on top of me but her heart was beating in her pussy. I was greedy for her. I moved in the tight space of the sleeping bag that was designed for one body. When I was on top, the pretty puma said, "Yes, please fuck me."

"Dirty-mouth girl," I called her. We were grinding. My sleeping bag was puffing up like a hot-air balloon with our body heat and heavy breathing.

We awakened sticky and glued together. Sunrise came without notice. We showered separately and then made the prayer. We had no early morning meal or water.

*   *   *

In the daylight, we prayed and read Quran together but separately. Chiasa's mind was so sharp. She read slowly and thoughtfully. She would explain her interpretations clearly and ask me about my understanding. It seems she compared each line to her own life and experiences or what she thought she might face in the future. I am a Muslim man and I loved her independent thinking. It was both respectful and beautiful to me. It revealed that she was not simply acting or going through the motions for my sake. She was searching for meaning and she was sincere.

Later, she showed me how to drive a motorcycle on a broke down half-rented, half-borrowed motorbike. After an hour of training, I was riding her. She was on the back with her face pressed against me as we toured the tiny island.

We stopped here and there and bought some rice and vegetables and a few small items for her to cook after sunset. I would not eat from her hands before, but I would eat from hers tonight, eagerly.

Right before sunset we stood on the pier facing the towering lighthouse, but more fascinated by the trail of pinks and oranges that the sun was painting as it prepared to set. We both had handmade fishing rods. The fishes acted in my favor and got hooked on my line and not hers. Chiasa cheered for me. The sound of her voice pierced our silence and drove the fishes away. It wasn't a problem. We'd share my medium-sized catch.

"I can eat it raw or fry it up nice how you New Yorkers like it," she said, squatting down and looking up toward me, her eyes sparkling and her smile so pure that her soul was shining.

After our prayer we lit the lanterns. She cooked the fish after I cleaned them up nice. She wore shorts so short she would never wear them any place again, except on a nearly deserted island in the woods in the presence of only her husband.

She crushed a dry chili pepper, added chopped onions and garlic, salt, and a splash of vinegar and made me some hot sauce. The strong scent drifted on the night breeze. She coughed.

"We Japanese don't need this sauce, but you Africans do!" She joked.

"Yeah, us Africans do!" I told her.

She set everything out nicely. We ate on a short wooden table. Her meal tasted super-fresh and was more delicious to me because she made it, because we were outdoors, because we were alone, because the fire of the lantern was blazing, and because my feelings for her were growing and spreading.

In the bungalow with two buckets of water and her sponge, we washed each other's bodies. Afterward she pulled a small bottle of olive oil out of her duffel. I watched.

She saw me watching and said "You'll see." She began dripping it onto my chest and rubbing it onto my shoulders and spreading it over my arms. I lay back and she oiled my stomach and legs and feet. The soles of my feet feeling her feminine finger sent a sensation throughout my body. She lay on me and began sliding her body back and forth.

"You want some more?" I asked her.

"Oil is expensive. I'm trying to get some oil for me off you," she said coyly. I sat up. We were facing one another now.

"Come here," I told her. I began spreading the oil on her incredible pretty shoulders and arms. I spread the oil over her breasts and her lips parted and began breathing seductively. I squeezed each breast with a slight roughness and she pulled in even closer to me. Still facing her, I was now moving the oil over her back and down to her buttocks. Aroused, she raised her hips and grabbed my joint and pushed it inside her and began to move her hips around. It was a soothing and sensual grind in a silent place, other than the sounds of nature and of our own moaning. She had me moaning! She really got me. I was completely open.

I liked the way she kept kissing me all over even after she had cum, and shaken, and settled. We were hugged up, our naked bodies facing one another and pressed together. Her slim arms were wrapped around my neck as though she never wanted to let go.

"Do you want to know when I fell in love with you?" Chiasa asked me. I didn't speak. I was too caught up in the feeling. So she continued . . .

"My eyes were closed. I was on the plane and you were standing over me. I could feel your eyes moving over my skin. I fell in love with that feeling, of you looking me over as I pretended to sleep. I was listening to the sound of your voice. Anytime anyone asked you a question, you would turn the question around on them and ask about me instead. I liked that feeling." She paused. Then she pulled away a bit and said:

"Then '*you know who*' asked you for something and you said, 'Everything I have, I'm planning to keep.'"

"That was it for me. I think that is the greatest thing a man can say and really do with a woman—for him to really plan to keep her for a lifetime and love her well. No divorce, or abuse or any of that, just love."

"So when you came to my hostel, *Shinjuku Uchi*, and sat down on my bed, you already loved me?" I checked her. "Well, no. I didn't acknowledge it then," she said. She was quite clever.

"When did you acknowledge it?" I followed up.

"When I was riding my horse at full speed. I used to think that is the greatest feeling in the world. But I was riding and my tears were spilling all over and blurring my vision. I missed you so much, I realized nothing would ever feel good anymore if you didn't come for me."

"Sometimes when it comes to women, a man needs a push. You came to Korea. That was the push," I confided.

"I waited for you to invite me. When you didn't, my father invited me, to cheer me up. What if daddy hadn't flown me over? What if I didn't come?" she asked.

"You came," I said. I kissed her lips softly. We were tonguing and touching all over again. I know she wanted me to say something strong and deep and true to her. I would, when I was ready, and could speak it out loud naturally. For now, I was just loving her and she was loving me back.

At sunrise we were up and cleaned and in prayer. We hadn't overslept or missed *suhoor,* our breakfast meal.

After the noon sun reached it's hottest point and then declined some, we climbed mountains together. It seemed that nature had become a huge part of our love naturally. I didn't want to think about Brooklyn or cement or buildings or guns when I was with Chiasa. It was so easy to push those thoughts away. She was always surrounded in the most natural beautiful scenery and I was there with her. She even made her weapons from nature.

When we reached the top of the mountain, she sat down and placed her pretty palms against the rocks. "Hmm they're hot. I wonder how that would feel?," she said curiously. Then she turned her head to the sky. I was watching her. It was impossible but it seemed as though I could see the sun browning her golden face right at that exact moment. Her eyes were closed and she was so silent for a while.

"What are you thinking?" I asked her.

"I was thinking that if anyone ever tried to harm Ryoshi, I will sever his head from his neck with my katana, my longest, sharpest blade."

Her eyes were still closed and her words were spoken without humor. They were swirling in my mind and stirring in my chest.

"It's my job to protect you, Chiasa." I told her solemnly.

Staring at the sky I could see only her pretty profile. "We will protect each other and Chiasa Hiyoku Brown will never betray you in love, in life, or in war." She said the heaviest words with the lightest tongue and softest sound.

* * *

We prayed together and broke our fast for the day with water and sweet tropical fruits that made her lips pucker.

In the back yard between two lanterns, I washed her hair with some shampoo that smelled like strawberries.

Later we washed our clothes outdoors behind the bungalow in a huge round bucket filled with water. We did it Korean style. We washed our clothes with our feet.

Wearing a thin silk dress and no panties, she began hanging our clothes on the clothing line that I ran across our bungalow. I came up on her from behind. I began to move the soft cloth of her short dress and use it to caress her. I moved both hands around front and squeezed her breasts. She pulled her hands down from the clothing line gracefully like the ballerina she is. She turned to me and pressed her body against mine. "Ryoshi, how come we can't stop fucking?" she asked me softly. We both smiled.

"Because we don't want to," I told her.

"Oh my God," she was whispering. We were on the floor now, beneath the dripping wet clothing. I held her long leg over her head and pushed in her.

"Oh my God."

Late night in our bungalow, I could feel in her emotion and in her body that this was our third and last night together on "our island." It was a warm night, without the familiar relief of a night breeze. I was working out. She was reading. She looked up from her book. "It's a powerful thing, this love. It can make your whole world shift. How will I go back to Japan?," she asked suddenly. It shot a shock through my body even though I already knew that she was scheduled to begin flight school next week. I didn't tell her straight out that I wanted her to come to New York with me, that she is my wife now, and belonged at my side with me. I knew that was the only right way, but even when I repeated it to myself it sounded unreasonable because of all of the loose ends she had left behind without knowing that she would see me in Seoul and that I would step up, be honest, and bold, and true enough to make her my wife.

Now I felt panic. I felt so close to her. I was not worried even one bit about her loyalty to me. I felt certain she would never allow any other man to go in her. I was sure. Still, I couldn't "break up," as she once called it. I couldn't have her on one side of the world and me on the other because I love her and had loved her from the moment I first saw her and loved her every second afterward, and loved her even more right now, this second.

"Ryoshi," was all she said. I was sitting on the floor thinking deeply after pulling up out of a sit up. She had come behind me and was now seated there, her lips against the back of my neck. Her legs were opened. My body was seated between them. She pressed her breasts against my back. She linked her fingers together on my stomach, holding me from behind. She would kiss my neck, wait some seconds, and kiss my neck again.

I turned to face her. Throwing my legs over hers.

The inside of Chiasa's mouth was warm and soft and clean and fresh. Her kisses had somehow become as passionate as her pussy. The feeling of love and motion and the pull of her tongue, her sucking and breathing, and the sincerity of her intent blew my mind and moved my soul. The intensity frightened me.

As I began sucking her neck and moved my kisses across her beautiful collarbone, she said, "suck them for me." Her left hand was holding her left nipple between her pretty fingers. She pulled her dress up, I pulled it over her head, and tossed it. I began sucking each nipple, softly at first, then pulling more. She began to moan. Her words, "suck them for me" repeated in my mind rising up the heat in me so strong.

I flipped her over and kissed the back of her neck moving my kisses down over her spine. The back of her body was cut and curved so crazy, her butt round, and raised up just enough. I entered her pussy from behind. Rubbing up against her clitoris from the opposite side made her feel more good. I could feel her pussy walls throbbing rapidly, wildly. I rode her this way smoothly. Then I wanted more to see her pretty face, the expression in her eyes. I pulled out and gently flipped her over. As soon as her back hit the floor she spread her legs some to let me know she was waiting. I slid my tongue into her mouth and my joint rushed back in her pushing deep and hard and repeatedly.

Me and my ballerina danced like that until tears streamed down from her eyes. Her tears moved me. "Comrade," was all I said. Her pussy walls contracted musically, like percussion. As she came, I spilled more sperm in her than stars in the sky and my body collapsed on top of her.

Speaking from my soul I said to her out loud so she could hear it and know it for sure.

"Chiasa, I love you. I love you more than I love myself." I said it. I meant it.

"Don't go. Stay with me. Let's stay together."

I was feeling something stronger than I had ever felt. It was something divine, stronger, and more influential than sex. It was something beautiful, perfect, and extremely dangerous.

BOOK 4

A BROOKLYN FINISH

I ticketed Akemi and Chiasa together and sat myself separated from them by a few rows and aisles, purposely. I knew I couldn't shift continents without shifting my posture, getting my mind right, and restoring my instincts and edge. What was necessary in Asia was different from what surviving the United States of America required. The USA, New York, in particular, Brooklyn specifically was much more stressful. My reactions would have to be as precise and sharp as they had been when I originally flew out from JFK. My eyes had to be more carefully focused to each detail, not for the sake of art, but for the sake of staying alive.

Also, a man has the luxury of emotions in Asia. In the US he would not, especially if he is a young black African like myself. Emotions would have to be processed and packaged and sometimes even stored or frozen until it was safe to use them, let them out, embrace them.

More of a man, I would say that I am. The elders say experience brings wisdom. I'd say I'm wiser now, stronger now. My standards for myself are even higher now. My strength is stronger, my responsibilities are greater. My business mind is sharper. My faith is solid. I left New York as a son and have returned as a father, *inshallah.*

Before, I was a husband searching for my wife. Now I am a husband traveling with wives, whose lives are in my hands. I had to secure them properly and separately, with enough space for them to remain the women they are, but close to me, for me, to watch and love and enjoy.

It would be expensive, this love. I knew. I was preparing to rearrange everything for the better, to make myself better, to allow my wives to grow and become even better. Akemi would have to be set up in a space where it was comfortable for her to create. Chiasa, I knew for certain as her father said, would not sit still and stay home. I didn't need her to do that, as long as we stayed together and true in our bond. I had sent her home to Japan while Akemi and I remained in Korea. I had loved her up well the night before. Both of us so reluctant to part for even only a few days. Both of us glued together even at the airport. I sent her traveling with passion marks between her thighs. She waved wildly with the purest smile, the last image in my eyes before she disappeared. She would tie up her loose ends then transfer to a New York school to get her pilot's license. She would pay for the vending machine with some of the money I had easily provided to her and use the rest for whatever was necessary. She promised me she would sit with her mother and talk nicely. Most important, she promised me to return in a few days. I knew she would, although I missed her every second that she was gone.

I was loving Akemi. Akemi was loving me. Soft, sweet, and sensual, she is my exotic Egyptian house cat, even though she is Korean. Quiet, her silence was soothing. Her emotions were tumultuous and deep, an undercurrent. Her expression of them came out through her body and in beautiful drawings, paintings, and colors. She loved and created, continuously.

The extra time in Busan brought peace to Dong Hwa and his family. "We had made some memories," as he said. He was right. The Professor had let me know in his manner that he was aware that Akemi was going to become a mother. Cautiously, he congratulated me. Then he handed me the name and information for a Korean obstetrician and gynecologist in New York for my wife to receive "excellent medical care." When he handed me the information, he smiled. "This doctor is a woman," he said knowingly. I knew from observing Dong Hwa's ways that the woman doctor he was recommending had most likely gone to the same university as him. The slick professor would attempt to stay closely connected to my wife and her progress through the doctor he recommended. Of course he was doing this for his own wife's comfort. Of course he believed that I wouldn't catch on to his tactic. Of course he was wrong about me, but I understood.

It's something how small the huge world had become for me. Now I could think with ease about returning to Korea or Japan with my wives in the future. I could even imagine returning to Asia flying in from North Africa, the Sudan to be exact. I had promised Dong Hwa that my wife would remain in touch with her Korean family. In time he would learn that I was a man of my word. He should have known that by now.

Nakamura had hung himself. He had brought about his own finish, through his own actions. Although I knew he would not surrender, he also would not win. For him to come after me now would be for him to reveal his past crimes. I was confident that he didn't want to do that. I would allow Akemi to decide how she would relate with him in the future. However, she and I would be side by side. Nakamura had lost his privilege and rights over my wife. He, after all, is not her blood father. I would deal with him now, the same way as I would deal with any man trying to approach my woman.

I met up a few times and chilled with Black Sea. Love had made him cool. He was cooler than he would have ever been.

I am more determined now. A man has to step off of his block, out of his hood to be able to see the whole picture properly and put it in perspective. Stress, misery and hatred, anger, frustration, and fear were no way for a man to live, and none of it had anything to do with love or family. At least, it shouldn't. If it does, a man has to make moves, big moves, wise moves. A man has to grind until he sets it right. A man has to set things right in the right setting with the right community. It has to be a community that is working with him, not against him all the time, all day every day.

*   *   *

The Eid ul Fitr is the Islamic celebration that occurs after the month of the Ramadan fast. On the Eid, which lasts three days, everyone gathers and celebrates the spiritual sacrifice that was made by all believers around the globe. We pray together. We eat together. We exchange gifts.

Mr. Ghazzahli was wearing his *jelabiyah* when he opened his gate on June 9th, the morning of the Eid. His sons emerged from behind him in Islamic wear as well and immediately went to work helping me to move the packages from the taxi. The men spoke only to me, as Chiasa and Akemi stood to the side in the entrance of the gate. Akemi was wearing *hanbok*, a beautiful traditional Korean dress. The skirt was royal red with delicate embroideries around its perimeter. It flared out because of the layers of cloth underneath her skirt. The top blouse was white with a V-neck and long sleeves. The ends of each sleeve were stitched with five inches of embroidered cloth. The white silk V-neck blouse, which was connected to the skirt, was outlined in a thick beautiful black ribbon that draped down the front of her dress. She looked like an empress and was intriguing to anyone who had never seen how the Korean females, still living in Korea, really rock it during their festivals and weddings and celebrations. Chiasa had combed then brushed and pinned Akemi's hair up into four royal buns. She had complimented the beauty of the dress by giving Akemi that hairstyle.

No words had to be exchanged as my elegant wives stood still and waited quietly. I could feel Mr.Ghazalhi searching and waiting for an explanation from me.

"Ramadan Mubarak Amm. You remember my wife, Akemi." I said in Arabic. He smiled and welcomed Akemi.

"This is Chiasa, my second wife," I said in Arabic. The three men, father and two sons, stood stuck for some seconds. I saw Chiasa thinking really hard to remind herself not to instinctively bow before these men, her elders.

In English I said to Chiasa, "This is Mr. Salim Ahmed Amin Ghazzahli."

"*Asalaam alaikum,*" Chiasa said.

Sudana and Naja came running out as her father and brothers were moving our packages inside. Sudana went immediately to hugging Akemi.

Naja said to me "Finally! You came home." I put some bags down and hugged my little sister, lifting her up off her feet. When I brought her up to my shoulder level she said, "Hi Akemi!" with big excitement. "You look so pretty!" Naja said. Akemi smiled a bright genuine smile.

"Who's she?," Naja said as I placed her little feet down onto the grass.

"She's my wife also. Her name is Chiasa. Treat her well," I ordered staring authoritatively into my sister's eyes. Naja's young eyes widened.

"Bring Akemi to Umma," I told Naja.

"Umma's downstairs," Naja said. Now she was holding Akemi's hand and walking her around to the side door, the apartment below.

"Welcome home," Sudana said to me. "Ramadan Mubarak."

"Chiasa, she is Sudana, Mr. Ghazzalhi's daughter." Sudana stared at her. There were two hazel eyes staring into two silver gray eyes. Sudana was wearing a creamy-colored orange thobe. Chiasa was wearing a marigold yukata with a wicked black sash that Akemi had wrapped around her waist. Chiasa's mother had gifted the yukata to her when Chiasa went to Japan to talk nicely with her. Her mother had told her to always remember, "You are a Japanese woman, feminine and regal and polite." She looked so beautiful to me. Her hair was wrapped and it was nice to see what the heels did to my pretty puma.

"*Salaam alaikum*," Chiasa said softly.

"*Alaikum salaam*," Sudana responded.

"Chiasa is my wife also." I said solemnly. "I love her a lot, so please be good to her." I told Sudana.

"Are you Muslim?" I heard Sudana ask her as I was walking inside. I left it to Chiasa. I knew she could handle it no matter which direction it all moved in. Akemi was all right with it, how could anything else matter?

* * *

At the meal of meals there was Mr. Ghazzahli and his wife Temira, their four daughters, Basima, Sudana, Darakhshan, and Faliha and two sons Mustapha and Talil, also Umma, Naja, Akemi, Chiasa, and myself. I wouldn't want to forget my twins. *Inshallah*, and whatever surprises Allah would send through Chiasa, *inshallah*.

Everyone was eating, smiling, talking, and asking and answering questions. It was incredible to hear Japanese, Arabic, and English all at one dinner table. Akemi, of course, could have added Korean, Thai, and Mandarin Chinese. Chiasa could've added French.

Umma was smiling. She was probably smiling because I had made it home safely. She greeted me with happy tears. Tears and women, I had plenty. Perhaps she was smiling, and crying while smiling, because I gifted her two daughters-in-law and three babies in their wombs, *inshallah*. Perhaps she was smiling because the one month had made me more of a man.

Umma Designs would be very successful this year, I believed. Especially with the fabrics I had imported from Asia and the influence of both Chiasa's ninja-style presence and Akemi's incredible art merged with Umma's talented eyes and fingers. I had also expanded my business plans to include a vending machine empire built off of my first machine, which I purchased with my money and the translation assistance of my second wife.

Akemi would always be a moneymaker. She made more money in Asia than the entire trip to Asia had cost me, minus, of course, the price that I willingly spent on jewels, gifts, and money given to Chiasa.

I also said a prayer of thanks to my father. It was his diamonds that saved me. "Three wishes," he had named the three diamonds that he once dropped into the palm of my hand; "three wishes when everything and everyone else around you fails or when you feel trapped." I had only used one of the wishes and spent less than half the money that the one diamond had cashed in at.

If anything were to happen to me now, I knew for sure that I had given my Umma, who is my heart and my purpose, all that one son could offer, a house filled with love and life and a successful small business. I had chosen the right wives, one who was the sweetest and most sensitive woman, an incredible and bankable artist, just like Umma, and another, who would defend Umma with her life and perhaps even pilot the plane that would land Umma back in the land of our people, Sudan.

"There's only one dilemma," Umma said that day of the Eid when the meal was finished and all of the gifts given out. She and I were alone for some moments. Akemi was in Umma's bedroom speaking over the phone. It was a long conversation, long distance to Josna. Chiasa was talking to Naja and trying to "make friends" with Sudana.

Umma said to me, "First, I didn't know that you would choose a second wife so early, so young, and so swiftly. But, you are your father's son and I see both of them, Akemi and Chiasa, in your eyes. Yet you have done something that your father did not do. Your father placed me higher, his first wife, first love. You have not selected a second wife. You have brought home two number ones. That Chiasa is very powerful. Her soul and her presence is very strong. She has agreed to be number two. You and I both know she's a number one. Even she is certain of that. Akemi is certain as well. You are so fortunate to have Akemi. She loves you so tremendously that she would not keep you away from another woman with whom she now has to share. You will have to work twice as hard. Chiasa will need another house or apartment. They are friends now and that is so good. It says a lot about you as a man. Yet, two great loves will need their own space. Even two beautiful plants need their own soil and own flowerpots or the roots would tangle and they would both die."

"Do you like Chiasa, Umma? Could you love her as your daughter?"

"I love her already because you love her so deeply. Her smile is pure. Her heart is light. Her soul is good. She wants to be a good Muslim woman. I can tell. She does not know it, but her soul is Muslim already." I listened and thought carefully about what Umma was saying.

"Do you see her speaking so nicely to Sudana?" Umma asked me about Chiasa.

"Yes," I answered Umma as we were speaking Arabic, which Chiasa could not decipher.

"Chiasa knows that Sudana loves you. She will be nice to Sudana. But she will never allow Sudana to become wife number three." Umma laughed. I smiled.

"I don't want number three. I am completely happy," I admitted. I didn't say more, but I felt an aggressive, powerful love stirring in me as I observed Chiasa. Umma was still watching my second wife closely. "Chiasa will continue to grow and learn and venture out. She will make Akemi stronger. She is not a problem. Chiasa is a blessing," Umma said sincerely.

I was relieved. I already knew that nothing and no one could come between me and each of my wives. Yet it was peace now that Umma approved.

Chiasa turned and looked at me. It was a look that I had seen before. It was a look that I welcomed. She stood up from the couch where she was sitting and went into the bathroom. I followed.

She was there standing in the darkness, silent. I pulled her close. She wrapped her arms around my neck. We kissed slowly, passionately, silently.

She moved my hand to her breast. "Look what you did." She whispered. I moved her hand down. We both smiled.

"Ryoshi, you have overpowered me." I didn't say nothing, just loved her. She had overpowered me also.

It's lights out in the place where I currently find myself. It's a long story that happened very quickly in the borough of Brooklyn. Of course, what would never happen any place else in the world could happen easily in Brooklyn. It is a story that involves my honor and my nine millimeter. It is a story that I won't reveal, at least not tonight, and maybe not ever.

Acknowledgments

All praise is due to OUR CREATOR first, last, and forever. Thank YOU for life, love, mercy, and protection. Thank YOU for your magnificent expressions including the sun and the moon and the stars, the sky, the oceans, and the waterfalls, for our souls, minds, memories, and imagination, and of course for the breath of life!!!!!

Thank YOU for all of the people and cultures and languages that YOU have uniquely created, so beautifully.

Thank YOU for every single word on every single page of every single book and story that YOU have gifted to me. ONE LOVE. Amen.

Home

Thank you to my husband and son for allowing me to live inside of my wild imagination. Love y'all. Thank you to both of you for leading and following me around the globe.

Big up to Brooklyn, Harlem, da Bronx, Queens, Staten Island, NEW YORK, and every single hood in America! Big up to every barrio and favela, quarter, prefecture, section, and area worldwide where the youth swarm, swell, and dwell thirsty for love, guidance, direction, survival, and profits!

Thank you to Jada Pinkett Smith for your conversation and

consideration and for being good to my family and for loving my words and stories. Remember, whatever is meant to happen will and the rest will not! I've been at peace with that forever. Thank you to Will Smith for being smart, funny, and kind. Thank y'all for welcoming my family in Beijing, China, and for "putting us up!" May God protect and keep your family safe and blessed! Big up to Fawn always.

Thank you Kishana for typing thousands of pages! Thank you to Dejah, the last real "GHN." Imani Rain, please believe in love. Your name, Imani means faith! Thank you to Nekyzsa for helping out even though you believe work is for jerks! Thank you Patty, the reader, who came in at the ninth inning. Thank you Bebon, the courier.

Also nomaste to Divyanok and Manjari, thank you for inviting us to the celebration of the new life that the two of you brought into the world. Thank you for sharing your culture and traditions and faith openly.

Shukran to the Joeyness family.

Thank you to Martinique for being so cool and pretty. It was nice to meet you on the streets of Ginza. My family loves and welcomes you always.

Thank you Gabber and Tasha! Thank you Mustapha El Amin and Wafaa Abdalla for the "Sudanese vibration."

Dr. Monica Martin and Dr. Barbara Justice, the medical geniuses, healers, sisters, and friends, thank you.

Thank you Uncle Bobby for your big heart and love for family.

Rest in peace Daddy. You finally brought me home from Tokyo.

A warm and heartfelt thank you to all the women, men, and juveniles who are imprisoned and captured, reading and discussing the pages of my books searching for truth and self-improvement.

My Korean Family

Camsamidah to Ms. Jae Kyung Lee, my "everything lady," thank you for sharing your culture, historical knowledge, translations and insights, and for being open and without prejudice. Comoptah to the entire Lee family: Sam Kyung, Che Wee, and Jo-50. It was a great experience to live with your family. Thank you for traveling with us and welcoming us to South Korea.

Pansa Yun Sun Kim, thank you for your gracious interview and research. Professor Sango Kim, thank you for hosting my family at your university.

"My Professor," comopsimidah for eleven months of laughter and friendship and meaningful conversation. Respect to you and your wife and family. I miss you!

To Ms. Joy Kim, thank you for hosting me and making it possible for me to meet Jung Ji-Hoon. Thank you for concert tickets to the Saitama Super Arena. It was amazing to see 20,000 Asian faces enjoying Rain's music. Hope to work together in the future. Words are powerful and bring communities together.

To Hyejin Kim and Seo Sun Hwa, I love you ladies. Thank you for your friendship. You two will forever be my "chingoo."

To Master Jo and the entire Jo Family. Respect to Hong Moo Kwan.

Thank you to KBS. It's good to see y'all have your own thing! Big up to Seoul for having so much soul. Big up to beautiful Busan.

My Japanese Family

Arigato gozaimashta to Yuki Morita and the entire Morita Family! Big up to Suiko the "Prima Ballerina!" Thank you to Miho Tominari for working extra hard navigating and translating and for making us laugh a lot! And the entire Tominari family, thank you. Thank you to Rezzy for your art and your style. Big up to Japorican. Thank you to Reiko, Sayaka, Jennifer, Yuka, Mr. Masutani.

Special thanks to Moses, Joe Hassan, Mamdou, and Kayoko.

Thank you to Kazuho the lovely one! Thank you for being smart and sweet and cooperative! I appreciate you. Thank you for NOT being a diva, they take up too much time and have so little to offer!

Thank you to Japan, an incredible and unique empire. Thank you to Shinjuku, Roppongi, Harajuku, Kichojoji, Shin Okubu, Takadanobaba, Yokohama, and all of Tokyo. Respect to Kyoto, "The Pretty Place" and Arashiyama. Much love to Osaka for the coolest people and hip-hop and lively youth.

Japan, thank you for being a peaceful place, a healthy place, a polite place, a beautiful place, an exciting place, and for having a nation of calm and orderly people!

Special thanks to Mariko Sensei, a patient and knowledgeable teacher.

My China Girls!

Liu Ying, Pan Ting, and Vivian—my Chinese opera singing, smart, quick, and happy translator.

My Thai Family

To Moo and Penny and Bell, and the entire Pimaan Thai Crew!

To Way and Nana, shout out to Bangkok.

Professional Services

Thank you to my editor, Emily Bestler, for throwing your hard work and continuous presence and heart into my project.

Thank you to Judith Curr, "the publishing boss."

Thank you to Jeanne Lee, Dana Sloan, and Alysha Bullock.

Thank you to production, the unseen workers who toil over every letter.

Thank you to Steve Wasserman and Bob Scheer for getting it all started from *No Disrespect*.

Thank you Mark Edwards, Kazuho Fujiwara, Martinique Brown, Wafaa Abdallah, Monique DiPasalegne, Miho Tominari, Yuki Morita, Jae Kyung Lee, Rezzy, and Danielle Priestor.

YOU CAN GET IN TOUCH WITH SISTER SOULJAH:

E-mail: souljahworkshard@gmail.com

Mailing address: Sister Souljah
Souljah Story Inc.
208 East 51st Street, Suite 2270
New York, New York 10022

Turn the page
to enjoy an excerpt from Sister
Souljah's novel
LIFE AFTER DEATH:
Winter Santiaga is back.

After a nasty breakup of any couple, the war begins. I knew bitches who keyed their ex's ride, or punctured his tires, or banged in his rims with a hammer. I knew bitches who beat the new bitch's ass who their man had replaced them with. Or even choked her, stabbed her, shot her, or mercked her. I knew even live-er bitches who, instead of killing his new bitch, killed him. I knew bitches who ran up his credit cards, crashed his car, cut up his clothes, pawned his jewels, and even burnt down his house. But when a man and woman used to be lovers, living together, working together, eating together, showering and fucking together, and one betrays the other, betrayal makes the matter more meaner than murder. 'Cause you can just kill someone if you want to, no matter who you are. No matter where they hide. They bound to resurface eventually. Let down their guard eventually, and that's precisely when they can get got. But ex-lovers, where one betrayed the other, sold him or her out, flipped on 'em, or was way-worser, like working as an undercover police, spying and telling on her or his lover, murder ain't good enough get back. A betrayed nigga or bitch wants to be the one who delivers the hurt, witnesses the pain and the torture and the downfall of the lover who is the traitor.

I know. Bullet was the main one who betrayed me. He's at the top of my payback list. He was my nigga for many months before I got arrested. Yeah, he was a hustler. I fucking loved that. His fuck game was strong. I loved that too. Once he and I first hooked up, I never fucked around with no other nigga but him. I'm a loyal bitch. Loyalty runs through the Santiaga blood. But he never fully acknowledged my loyalty to him. He never gave his loyalty to me. It wasn't about me thinking, expecting, or believing that he was out fucking some random bitches while we was together. He didn't cause me to feel or think that he was. It was that he . . . I don't know. He loved me with his mind and body but never gave me his heart. He treated me like a suspect who was bound to turn on him or turn him in. I wasn't. I'm the one bitch that wouldn't . . . ever. Santiagas are born snitch-free.

Bullet put our Manhattan condo in my name, and he made every purchase for both of us in my name. Back then, at the time, I thought that meant he loved me. Of course I did, he provided. In turn, I covered for him. Held his coke, concealed his weapons, and carried his cash here and there quietly whenever he told me to. I was trying to earn my way up and also into his heart. I thought we should be on some Bonnie-and-Clyde shit. But fuck Bonnie and Clyde. We should have been on some Winter-and-Bullet shit, handling our business, styling while stacking our chips, eating and fucking, chilling and staying together.

Turned out he put everything in my name not for love or for providing for a top bitch and daughter of legendary hustler and entrepreneur Ricky Santiaga. Instead Bullet was on some Brooklyn scheming. He made it so that if everything or anything went wrong, he could drop all the legalities and blame onto me without losing any street credibility because it wasn't like he actually snitched on me. He simply left a paper trail and documentation all in my name that told the fictitious story of me being the hustler and him being blameless, unarrestable, and scot-free. On the day of my arrest that led to my conviction as a drug dealer sentenced to serve fifteen years on a mandatory minimum, which at the time I had never even heard of, my nigga Bullet had a car rented in my name. In the rental car was me and the product. I was 'bout to ride round trip to Virginia on a run with him, a big and necessary business move.

Simone, who for some reason can't get the fuck out of my mind or life or death story, saw me sitting there on our Brooklyn block in the rental waiting on Bullet. I didn't see her, though. Simone had bullshit beef with me that she swore was real. So soon as she saw me that day, it was on. Bitch threw a brick through the rental window. Bitch dragged me out the car swinging. We thumped. My nigga Bullet saw the rah-rah from a distance. He started rushing over. He fired one shot in the air to cause the commotion to break. Seeing him boosted my confidence, but the gunshot distracted me from keeping my eyes on her. Simone took advantage and sliced my face. Bullet held my bleeding face in his hands. He sat me back in the rental car. He tossed the gun beneath the seat. He walked around to the driver's side. I was relieved that he had rescued me.

But the furious fight and the gunshot drew out the cops. They cops swooped in, and Bullet, instead of jumping into the rental car and speeding away, walked off calmly as though he never intended to get in the car with me at all. I was arrested in the rental car that was in my name, with the weight stuffed inside teddy bears, and the weapon tossed beneath the seat. They cuffed and jailed and grilled and investigated me. They asked me for names or just one big name. I gave them nothing. I rejected their bullshit tricks and game. The name is Santiaga, royalty not snitches. I wasn't mad at Bullet for being a hustler, obviously. I wasn't mad at him for renting me the condo or even for taking me on his big business run to Virginia. I was down for him. I wanted to go. I didn't like being left out of the business or the action. It's that that nigga Bullet didn't come for me. He didn't add a dime to my legal defense. He didn't send one of his men to make sure I had all that I needed. He didn't put one cent on my commissary. He didn't write me one letter, slip me one kite from his peoples on lock. He didn't check for me, and to me, that meant he never loved me. That's why he's on my payback list. He betrayed me. I never betrayed him, not even once.

So I understand this little sixteen-year-young-looking one, oddly named Ubs, who is tight and at war with her ex. He seemed more my age than hers. But I know that once a bitch blossoms, gets curves and titties and hungry between the thighs, whether she's twelve, thirteen, or sixteen, whether or not the law says she's a minor, she is bound to hunt and chase down a man she chooses for herself. A young sexy bitch, I know, can make it impossible for even an older guy to resist her powers, no matter who he is. He could be handsome or ugly, paid or broke, married or single, hustler or preacher, politician or teacher, doctor or lawyer, or even a goddamn judge. I accept that. As long as it's not the other way around, some old guy hunting, chasing, and cornering her young ass. Fucking and raping are never ever the same thing. He says she betrayed him. He says she's the police. She seemed too young to be anybody's police. And in the I guess seconds I had seen her, she didn't seem like a cop. But I ain't from down here. I don't know how shit goes 'round here. Everything is unexpected. It's like I'm stuck in the world of the unseen and unknown and can't control or predict the action.

But now I am not alone down here. Of course I choose him. He chose me in the first place. He was the greatest sex I ever had. The wildest feeling I ever felt. He was the only man who ever caused me to let go of Midnight, who *never fucked me at all*. I like a man who *gives a bitch what she wants*. A man who *doesn't make a bitch feel lonely*. Wife number five! Oh hell no. That would never, ever be me.

My new nigga is my forever nigga, from now until the real

lights-out. Even though he only fucked me once on the same night we met, I was able to exist inside of that fucking memory. And unlike Bullet, who left me because I was cut and bleeding and would obviously wear a scar, and who set me up to take the fall, or didn't set me up but reacted only to secure himself, my forever nigga is different.